OXFORD WORLD'S CLASSICS

THE AMERICAN SENATOR

ANTHONY TROLLOPE (1815–82), the son of a failing London barrister, was brought up an awkward and unhappy youth amidst debt and privation. His mother maintained the family by writing, but Anthony's own first novel did not appear until 1847, when he had at length established a successful Civil Service career in the Post Office, from which he retired in 1867. After a slow start, he achieved fame, with 47 novels and some 16 other books, and sales sometimes topping 100,000. He was acclaimed an unsurpassed portraitist of the lives of the professional and landed classes, especially in his perennially popular *Chronicles of Barsetshire* (1855–67), and his six brilliant Palliser novels (1864–80). His fascinating *Autobiography* (1883) recounts his successes with an enthusiasm which stems from memories of a miserable youth. Throughout the 1870s he developed new styles of fiction, but was losing critical favour by the time of his death.

JOHN HALPERIN is Centennial Professor of English at Vanderbilt University. His publications include *Trollope and Politics*, *Gissing: A Life in Books*, *C. P. Snow: An Oral Biography*, *The Life of Jane Austen*, *Jane Austen's Lovers*, *Novelists in Their Youth*, and *Eminent Georgians*. He is a Fellow of the Royal Society of Literature and has twice been a Guggenheim Fellow.

T0084108

OXFORD WORLD'S CLASSICS

For over 100 years Oxford World's Classics have brought readers closer to the world's great literature. Now with over 700 titles—from the 4,000-year-old myths of Mesopotamia to the twentieth century's greatest novels—the series makes available lesser-known as well as celebrated writing.

The pocket-sized hardbacks of the early years contained introductions by Virginia Woolf, T. S. Eliot, Graham Greene, and other literary figures which enriched the experience of reading. Today the series is recognized for its fine scholarship and reliability in texts that span world literature, drama and poetry, religion, philosophy and politics. Each edition includes perceptive commentary and essential background information to meet the changing needs of readers.

OXFORD WORLD'S CLASSICS

ANTHONY TROLLOPE

The American Senator

Edited with an Introduction and Notes by
JOHN HALPERIN

OXFORD
UNIVERSITY PRESS

OXFORD

UNIVERSITY PRESS

Great Clarendon Street, Oxford OX2 6DP

Oxford University Press is a department of the University of Oxford.
It furthers the University's objective of excellence in research, scholarship,
and education by publishing worldwide in

Oxford New York

Athens Auckland Bangkok Bogotá Buenos Aires Calcutta
Cape Town Chennai Dar es Salaam Delhi Florence Hong Kong Istanbul
Karachi Kuala Lumpur Madrid Melbourne Mexico City Mumbai
Nairobi Paris São Paulo Singapore Taipei Tokyo Toronto Warsaw

with associated companies in Berlin Ibadan

Oxford is a registered trade mark of Oxford University Press
in the UK and in certain other countries

Published in the United States
by Oxford University Press Inc., New York

Introduction, Note on the Text, Notes, and Select Bibliography
© John Halperin 1986
Chronology © N. John Hall 1991

The moral rights of the author have been asserted

Database right Oxford University Press (maker)

First published as a World's Classics paperback 1986
Reissued as an Oxford World's Classics paperback 1999
Reissued 2008

British Library Cataloguing in Publication Data

Data available

Library of Congress Cataloging in Publication Data

Trollope, Anthony, 1815–1882.
The American senator
(Oxford world's classics)
Bibliography: p.
I. Halperin, John, 1941– . II. Title.
PR5684.A8 1986 823'.8 85–25981

ISBN 978–0–19–953763–1

13

Printed and bound in Great Britain by Clays Ltd, Elcograf S.p.A.

CONTENTS

ACKNOWLEDGEMENTS

I AM grateful to Donald Greene, N. John Hall, Laurence Lerner, Gillian Tindall, Robert Tracy, and H. L. Weatherby for their generous help and advice during preparation of the present volume for publication.

J.H.

INTRODUCTION

> In this spirit we Americans and Englishmen go on
> writing books about each other, sometimes with
> bitterness enough, but generally with good final
> results.
>
> *The American Senator*

IN his *Autobiography* (1883) Trollope notes that *The American Senator* (1876–7) was given its title 'very much in opposition to my publisher'. Bentley feared it was misleading, and in most of his advertisements inserted immediately after the title the disclaimer, 'The Scene of which Story is laid in England'. Trollope began the concluding chapter by remarking that the novel 'might perhaps have been better called "The Chronicle of a Winter at Dillsborough"' (p. 552). But he had written to Bentley on 7 December 1875: 'I find that I cannot change the name,—which indeed, (The American Senator) I feel to be in itself a good name. I am sure that nobody can give a name to a novel but its author.' (See *The Letters of Anthony Trollope*, 2 vols., ed. N. John Hall [Stanford, CA: Stanford University Press, 1983], II:673.)

The *Autobiography* also expresses Trollope's astonishment that the reviewers should have preferred *The American Senator* and *Is He Popenjoy?* (1877–8) to *The Prime Minister* (1875–6); he declares here that both novels 'are very inferior to *The Prime Minister*'. In fact reviewers of *The American Senator* were far from pleased with it—though Trollope was right in thinking that *The Prime Minister* was treated more harshly, and with less reason, in the Press.

The novelist says a good deal more in a letter to his indefatigable correspondent Mary Holmes (27 December 1876; see *Letters*, II:701–2). He characterizes 'the Senator from Mickewa' as 'a thoroughly honest man wishing to do good, and . . . not himself half so absurd as things which he criticizes'. Having forgotten, fourteen months after completing the book, the name of his parson Mainwaring, Trollope refers to him here as 'parson Mauleverer'—and to his anti-heroine Arabella Trefoil as 'the odious female'. He adds:

it is the part of the satirist to be heavy on the classes he satirises;—not to deal out impartial justice to the world; but to pick out the evil things. With the parson my idea was not to hold an individual up to scorn but to ridicule the modes of patronage in our church. Lord [Rufford] is what he is, merely as an appendage to the odious female,—in whose character I wished to express the depth of my scorn for women who run down [i.e., hunt] husbands,—an offence which I do fear is gaining ground in this country ... [Lawrence Twentyman's] early schooldays at Cheltenham with his subsequent somewhat illiterate language were the result of a long-ago-entertained dislike of Dean Close & Cheltenham School.

Trollope's reference is to Francis Close (1797–1882), an evangelical divine, rector of Cheltenham and later Dean of Carlisle.

To another correspondent (see *Letters*, II:710–11), he wrote on 17 February 1877:

I have been, and still am very much afraid of Arabella Trefoil. The critics ... will tell me that she is unwomanly, unnatural, turgid,—the creation of a morbid imagination, striving after effect by laboured abominations. But I swear I have known the woman,—not one special woman ... but all the traits, all the cleverness, all the patience, all the courage, all the self-abnegation,—and all the failure ... Will such a one as Arabella Trefoil be damned, and if so why? Think of her virtues; how she works, how true she is to her vocation [husband-hunting], how little there is of self indulgence, or of idleness. I think that she will go to a kind of third class heaven in which she will always be getting third class husbands.

In the event, the reviewers' chief complaints concerned the senator, who was several times pronounced irrelevant to the novel which bore his name. There was some commentary on Trollope's growing misanthropy, but the critics had the good sense to leave Arabella Trefoil alone.

And quite right. Not only is she the best thing in the book: she is one of Trollope's greatest creations. His account of her suggests that he regarded her with some awe, and wondered what others would make of her. Like most great characters in literature she is a mixture of many things, but above all she is vividly believable. Indeed, Arabella Trefoil bears testimony down to the present day of Trollope's mimetic genius.

One may see this, however, without having to disparage the senator as a character, or to assume that Trollope's title was a mistake. He saw *The American Senator* as a wide-ranging satire on contemporary English values. And in order to expose those values, he introduced a visitor from another country into whose mouth he could put sentiments he may not, for fear of alienating his audience, have wished to express in his own voice. As a conduit of Trollope's social commentary the senator, or someone like him, was essential. Mr Gotobed is ridiculous at times—but not so absurd as the things he criticizes, as the novelist told Mary Holmes. The history and the character of Arabella Trefoil represent a substantial portion of what Trollope thought had gone wrong with English society—the reduction of all social intercourse to the level of stock-jobbing, of pecuniary transactions, of 'business'. The book's title makes sense if we see *The American Senator* as a 'condition-of-England' novel and Arabella Trefoil as the chief manifestation of that sorry condition.

Thus the presence of the three awful old ladies—the Honourable Mrs Morton, Lady Augustus Trefoil, and Mrs Masters, so heartless, so materialistic, so cynical in matrimonial matters; thus the assertion, surely ironic, that the book's true hero is the hapless, virtually inarticulate Lawrence Twentyman (p. 556). In Trollope's later novels heroism is frequently a problematic matter, for the age he depicts in them is essentially unheroic. One recognizes the traditional Trollope touch in the story of Mary Masters and Reginald Morton—the romantic element, perfunctory here, which the novelist believed every story of his should contain, largely for the enjoyment of his female readers; and in the various fox-hunting sequences, a feature of so many of his novels. But there is a hard bitterness in *The American Senator* typical only of the later Trollope. Few of his love stories end so oddly as that of Reginald and Mary; on the last page of the novel (p. 557) we see her 'looking up into [her husband's] eyes, and [fooling] him for a while into the most perfect happiness that a man ever knows in this world'. And few of Trollope's many harsh parents are treated as harshly in their turn as he treats Mrs Masters, whose violent absurdity may remind some readers of Mrs Bennet's in *Pride and Prejudice*. At the end of *The American Senator* Mrs Masters, like Mrs Bennet at the end of Jane Austen's novel, having similarly nagged an uncooperative daughter, is 'quite overpowered' by the fact that her 'girl was engaged to marry the richest gentleman in the neighbourhood!' (p. 495).

Once Trollope gets through the impenetrable family matters with which the book begins—reminiscent, perhaps, of the pedigrees which open *Sense and Sensibility*, but far less comprehensible—he moves quickly to the two major matters at hand: the state of the nation, as perceived by an outsider—what in a novel by Henry James we might call the international theme; and the character of Arabella Trefoil, who most vividly personifies that state. While the senator snuffles his way from what he perceives as one disgraceful public policy to another, Arabella gives us at first hand an unforgettable private demonstration of what is wrong with the country. The senator speaks in generalities and platitudes, often choosing poor examples to illustrate sound opinions; Arabella's conduct is precise, specific, and unequivocal. The senator has come to England to see what it is like; it is like Arabella. The novel had to be named after one or the other, and Trollope's choice, underlining as it does the international theme and the subject of comparative culture, is perhaps not such a bad one.

One result of his own visit to America in 1862 was the composition, soon afterwards, of two stories about the American Civil War. Sections of *He Knew He Was Right* (1868–9), *The Duke's Children* (1879–80; written in 1876), and *Mr Scarborough's Family* (1882–3) deal with the same sort of cultural issues Trollope takes up in *The American Senator*. The international theme absorbed him in later years—as it absorbed some of his contemporaries. A series of spectacular intercontinental marriages took place in the 1870s, as the British aristocracy, suffering severe financial losses in the agricultural failures of that decade, attempted to shore up its position by marrying money wherever it was to be found. The union in 1874 of Lord Randolph Churchill, third son of the seventh Duke of Marlborough, and Miss Jennie Jerome of New York, was one such instance. The Duchess of Manchester, of an earlier generation but no more removed from the social limelight, was an American, and there were soon to be other international marriages of this sort, culminating some years later in that of Lord Randolph's nephew, the eighth duke, to Consuela Vanderbilt.

It may be worth pointing out that James's *Daisy Miller* appeared in the *Cornhill Magazine* in June–July 1878, his *An International Episode* in the same journal in December 1878–January 1879, and *The Portrait of A Lady* from October 1880–November 1881 in *Macmillan's Magazine*. All, of course, focused on the international theme. We tend to think of this theme as belonging almost exclusively to James; it also belonged to Trollope, during the same period and earlier. In fact he had devoted a two-volume work, *North America*, to the international question in 1862. The subject clearly interested him. So *The American Senator*, in this respect at least, is no anomaly among his works, especially those composed during the last two decades of his writing life.

Trollope, we should remember, said that in *The American Senator* he wished 'to pick out the evil things' in contemporary England, while in Arabella Trefoil he 'wished to express the depth of my scorn for women who run down husbands'. The evil, both the particular and the general evil, is greedy materialism, as it is in many of the novels Trollope wrote in the 1870s. The genius of Arabella's portrait is that, cold, clever, and conniving as she is, we see too 'all the patience, all the courage, all the self-abnegation,—and all the failure,' as Trollope puts it, of a woman defeated by a society which will not open its doors to her because she has been so open and so long about finding a rich husband. Why should she be specially deprived? In part, perhaps, because she lacks the insight to see that a little tenderness and a little humility might go farther towards opening those doors than aggression and noise.

At times she achieves a stature almost tragic. Whatever her successes or failures, nothing can make her truly happy; she is not the sort to be made happy by anything, even success. 'Sick of the dust of the battle and conscious of fading strength' (p. 134), unable to speak the unvarnished truth to anybody—'But then such ladies as Miss Trefoil can never afford to tell the truth' (p. 212)—she must none the less live through some sort of perceived future. Like all great literary rogues, she commands a certain respect by being single-minded in her purpose and refusing to fool herself; she always knows who and what she is. Unwilling to 'own that she had been conquered in the fight and beaten to death' (p. 518), like Milton's Lucifer she would rather reign in Hell than serve in Heaven (p. 519). There is grandeur here, even if there is no sympathy. But Trollope's point is that the world she inhabits forces her to be dishonest and ruthless, if she wishes to achieve a certain kind of success—or, rather, that it expects dishonesty and ruthlessness in the arena in which she has chosen to compete. If she is redeemed at all, it is, like Shakespeare's Richard III and Thackeray's Becky Sharp, through self-knowledge, through unflinching self-scrutiny. Thus: 'She knew that she was heartless . . . and that she belonged to a heartless world;—but she knew also that there was a world of women who were not heartless' (p. 517). In aspiring to that second world, Arabella, like her great literary predecessors in villainy, earns, if not our forgiveness, at least our understanding. At the end of the novel, we are as relieved as she is when she finds that she can stop acting roles, and relax. Trollope comments that Arabella 'might perhaps have made a better use of the gifts which Providence had put in her way' (p. 467); we must agree with him, even as we see the tragedy of her perversely misused talents unfold.

One word is linked with Arabella's name throughout the novel, and that word is *work*. She 'works' terribly hard at her vocation, which is to make a good match; it is desperate work because she is nearly thirty. Indeed, she works harder than any of the men in the novel, none of whom, except John Morton (who is killed by moderate exertion) and the senator, seems to be doing much of anything. Lord Rufford, perhaps, works as hard at being extravagant and idle as Arabella works at becoming a wife. Because she does work so hard, Trollope is willing, as he says, to admit her 'to a kind of third class heaven' and to give her, at the end, a 'third class husband' as a reward for her labours, ignoble though they may be. She, at least, is *doing* something; she lives, she breathes, she suffers. It is hard to say the same of anyone else in this novel.

It is precisely this national inertia of which Senator Gotobed complains—sometimes, evidently, without the novelist's blessing (no man loved to ride to hounds more than Trollope), and sometimes, clearly, with Trollope's own voice. When the senator observes that so much in England is done for show and so little for substance, we may be certain that he speaks for Trollope; Arabella, meanwhile, acts out the charade for us. 'The habits of one country [may be] incomprehensible to another' (p. 69), as John Morton remarks, but certain habits are always recognizable, anywhere. We know from the novelist's letter to Mary Holmes that in the disagreement between Morton and the senator, after the latter's discussion of church sinecures at parson Mainwaring's table, Trollope takes the senator's side, though as the scene is written Mr Gotobed appears to be in the wrong. Despite his (largely undeserved) reputation for blunt and tactless honesty, Trollope could be skilful at obfuscation when his own beliefs were at issue.

The novelist's indictment of contemporary values, as in such other books of this period as *The Prime Minister* and *The Way We Live Now* (1874–5), is general and all-embracing. 'The spirit of conservatism in this country is so strong that you cannot bear to part with a shred of the

barbarism of the Middle Ages' (p. 79), the senator tells
John Morton, and Trollope, who hated the age of Disraeli,
makes no effort to detach himself from such sentiments as
these. Contemporary English 'principles', the senator
observes, 'are . . . very bad, utterly antagonistic to all
progress, unconscious altogether of the demand for
progressive equality' (p. 195); the latter 'principle' was
one very dear to Trollope's heart. 'But here the greatest
fool that you meet will shine, and will be admitted to be
brilliant; simply because he has possessions' (p. 196). At
the end of the novel the senator delivers his lecture on 'The
Irrationality of Englishmen.' Trollope speaks in his own
voice in such senatorial utterances as these: 'you do not
know how little prone you are to admit the light of reason
into either your public or private life, and how generally
you allow yourselves to be guided by traditions, prejudices, and customs which should be obsolete . . . every
improvement which is made is received by those whom it
most concerns with a horror which amounts almost to
madness' (pp. 535, 542).

Madness, indeed. Most of the people in this book have
been driven mad by the desire for money, for possessions,
for *things*. No wonder the rich, unmarried Lord Rufford
'sometimes feels . . . like a carcase in the midst of vultures'
(p. 313). For that is what he is.

JOHN HALPERIN

NOTE ON THE TEXT

TROLLOPE began writing *The American Senator* on 4 June 1875 and completed it on 24 September 1875. Much of it was composed while he was visiting his son Frederick in Australia and returning home to England via New Zealand, Hawaii, and the United States.

Trollope sold the serial rights to Bentley for £600, and *The American Senator* appeared in *Temple Bar* from May 1876 to July 1877. Chapman and Hall bought the book rights for £1,200 and published the novel in three volumes in June 1877. Harper & Brothers brought out the authorized American edition, also in 1877.

The present edition is a reproduction of the Oxford World's Classics text first published in 1931 and reprinted in 1951 and 1962. The manuscript of *The American Senator* is in the Robert H. Taylor Collection of the Princeton University Library (Princeton, New Jersey).

SELECT BIBLIOGRAPHY

THERE is no collected edition of the works. A facsimile edition of thirty-six titles (62 vols.), *Selected Works of Anthony Trollope*, has been published by the Arno Press (1981; General Editor, N. John Hall). Works by Trollope are also available in the Oxford World's Classics series; in the Harting Grange Library Series (mostly the shorter works), published by the Caledonia Press; and in *Anthony Trollope: The Complete Short Stories* (forty-two stories in 5 vols.), ed. Betty Jane Slemp Breyer (1979–83). Some of Trollope's essays have been collected in *The New Zealander*, ed. N. John Hall (1972). The standard bibliography of the works is Michael Sadleir, *Trollope: A Bibliography* (1928; reprinted 1977). *The Letters of Anthony Trollope*, 2 vols., ed. N. John Hall (1983), is now the standard edition.

There is no definitive life. Among the more useful biographical volumes are Bradford A. Booth, *Anthony Trollope: Aspects of His Life and Work* (1958); James Pope Hennessy, *Anthony Trollope* (1971); Michael Sadleir, *Trollope: A Commentary* (1927); C. P. Snow, *Trollope* (1975); and L. P. and R. P. Stebbins, *The Trollopes: The Chronicle of A Writing Family* (1945). The best sources of information about Trollope's life remain T. H. S. Escott's memoir, *Anthony Trollope: His Public Services, Private Friends and Literary Originals* (1913; reprinted 1967), and the novelist's *Autobiography* (1883). Other useful tools are W. and J. Gerould, *A Guide to Trollope* (1948), and N. John Hall, *Trollope and His Illustrators* (1980).

The best bibliographies of criticism are Rafael Holling, *A Century of Trollope Criticism* (1956), and *The Reputation of Trollope: An Annotated Bibliography 1925–1975*, ed. John Charles Olmsted and Jeffrey Welch (1978). A selection of contemporary criticism may be found in *Trollope: The Critical Heritage*, ed. Donald Smalley (1969). David Skilton, *Anthony Trollope and His Contemporaries* (1972), also discusses early critical responses. Three useful collections of essays: *The Trollope Critics*, ed. N. John Hall (1980); *Anthony Trollope*, ed. T. E. Bareham (1980); and *Trollope Centenary Essays*, ed. John Halperin (1982).

On Trollope's politics and political novels, see John Halperin, *Trollope and Politics* (1977), and Juliet McMaster, *Trollope's Palliser Novels: Theme and Pattern* (1979). Recommended critical studies: Ruth apRoberts, *Trollope: Artist and Moralist (The Moral Trollope in US)* (1971); A. O. J. Cockshut, *Anthony Trollope:*

A Critical Study (1955); James R. Kincaid, *The Novels of Anthony Trollope* (1977); Shirley R. Letwin, *The Gentleman in Trollope: Individuality and Moral Conduct* (1982); Robert M. Polhemus, *The Changing World of Anthony Trollope* (1968); Arthur Pollard, *Anthony Trollope* (1978); Robert Tracy, *Trollope's Later Novels* (1978); and Andrew Wright, *Anthony Trollope: Dream and Art* (1983).

More general studies with helpful sections on Trollope: Robin Gilmour, *The Idea of the Gentleman in the Victorian Novel* (1981); J. Hillis Miller, *The Form of Victorian Fiction* (1968); Robert M. Polhemus, *Comic Faith: The Great Tradition from Austen to Joyce* (1980); and J. A. Sutherland, *Victorian Novelists and Publishers* (1976); and J. Don Vann, *Victorian Novels in Serial* (1985).

A CHRONOLOGY OF ANTHONY TROLLOPE

Virtually all Trollope's fiction after *Framley Parsonage* (1860–1) appeared first in serial form, with book publication usually coming just prior to the final instalment of the serial.

1815   (24 Apr.) Born at 16 Keppel Street, Bloomsbury, the fourth son of Thomas and Frances Trollope.
(Summer ?) Family moves to Harrow-on-the-Hill.

1823   To Harrow School as a day-boy.

1825   To a private school at Sunbury.

1827   To school at Winchester College.

1830   Removed from Winchester and returned to Harrow.

1834   (Apr.) The family flees to Bruges to escape creditors.
(Nov.) Accepts a junior clerkship in the General Post Office, London.

1841   (Sept.) Made Postal Surveyor's Clerk at Banagher, King's County, Ireland.

1843   (mid-Sept.) Begins work on his first novel, *The Macdermots of Ballycloran*.

1844   (11 June) Marries Rose Heseltine.
(Aug.) Transferred to Clonmel, County Tipperary.

1846   (13 Mar.) Son, Henry Merivale Trollope, born.

1847   *The Macdermots of Ballycloran*, published in 3 vols. (Newby).
(27 Sept.) Son, Frederic James Anthony Trollope, born.

1848   *The Kellys and the O'Kellys; or Landlords and Tenants* 3 vols. (Colburn).
(Autumn) Moves to Mallow, County Cork.

1850   *La Vendée; An Historical Romance* 3 vols. (Colburn).
Writes *The Noble Jilt* (A play, published 1923).

1851   (1 Aug.) Sent to south-west of England on special postal mission.

1853   (29 July) Begins *The Warden* (the first of the Barsetshire novels).
(29 Aug.) Moves to Belfast as Acting Surveyor.

1854 (9 Oct.) Appointed Surveyor of Northern District of Ireland.

1855 *The Warden* 1 vol. (Longman).
Writes *The New Zealander*.
(June) Moves to Donnybrook, Dublin.

1857 *Barchester Towers* 3 vols. (Longman).

1858 *The Three Clerks* 3 vols. (Bentley).
Doctor Thorne 3 vols. (Chapman & Hall).
(Jan.) Departs for Egypt on Post Office business.
(Mar.) Visits Holy Land.
(Apr.–May) Returns via Malta, Gibraltar and Spain.
(May–Sept.) Visits Scotland and north of England on postal business.
(16 Nov.) Leaves for the West Indies on postal mission.

1859 *The Bertrams* 3 vols. (Chapman & Hall).
The West Indies and the Spanish Main 1 vol. (Chapman & Hall).
(3 July) Arrives home.
(Nov.) Leaves Ireland; settles at Waltham Cross, Hertfordshire, after being appointed Surveyor of the Euston District of England.

1860 *Castle Richmond* 3 vols. (Chapman & Hall).
First serialized fiction, *Framley Parsonage*, published in the *Cornhill Magazine*.
(Oct.) Visits, with his wife, his mother and brother in Florence; makes the acquaintance of Kate Field, a 22-year-old American for whom he forms a romantic attachment.

1861 *Framley Parsonage* 3 vols. (Smith, Elder).
Tales of All Countries 1 vol. (Chapman & Hall).
(24 Aug.) Leaves for America to write a travel book.

1862 *Orley Farm* 2 vols. (Chapman & Hall).
North America 2 vols. (Chapman & Hall).
The Struggles of Brown, Jones and Robinson: By One of the Firm 1 vol. (New York, Harper—an American piracy; first English edition 1870, Smith, Elder).
(25 Mar.) Arrives home from America.
(5 Apr.) Elected to the Garrick Club.

1863　*Tales of All Countries*, Second Series, 1 vol. (Chapman & Hall).
Rachel Ray 2 vols. (Chapman & Hall).
(6 Oct.) Death of his mother, Mrs Frances Trollope.

1864　*The Small House at Allington* 2 vols. (Smith, Elder).
(12 Apr.) Elected a member of the Athenaeum Club.

1865　*Can You Forgive Her?* 2 vols. (Chapman & Hall).
Miss Mackenzie 1 vol. (Chapman & Hall).
Hunting Sketches 1 vol. (Chapman & Hall).

1866　*The Belton Estate* 3 vols. (Chapman & Hall).
Travelling Sketches 1 vol. (Chapman & Hall).
Clergymen of the Church of England 1 vol. (Chapman & Hall).

1867　*Nina Balatka* 2 vols. (Blackwood).
The Claverings 2 vols. (Smith, Elder).
The Last Chronicle of Barset 2 vols. (Smith, Elder).
Lotta Schmidt and Other Stories 1 vol. (Strahan).
(1 Sept.) Resigns from the Post Office.
Assumes editorship of *Saint Pauls Magazine*.

1868　*Linda Tressel* 2 vols. (Blackwood).
(11 Apr.) Leaves London for the United States on postal mission.
(26 July) Returns from America.
(Nov.) Stands unsuccessfully as Liberal candidate for Beverley, Yorkshire.

1869　*Phineas Finn; the Irish Member* 2 vols. (Virtue & Co).
He Knew He Was Right 2 vols. (Strahan).
Did He Steal It? A Comedy in Three Acts (a version of *The Last Chronicle of Barset*, privately printed by Virtue & Co).

1870　*The Vicar of Bullhampton* 1 vol. (Bradbury, Evans).
An Editor's Tales 1 vol. (Strahan).
The Commentaries of Caesar 1 vol. (Blackwood).
(Jan.–July) Eased out of *Saint Pauls Magazine*.

1871　*Sir Harry Hotspur of Humblethwaite* 1 vol. (Hurst & Blackett).
Ralph the Heir 3 vols. (Hurst & Blackett).
(Apr.) Gives up house at Waltham Cross.
(24 May) Sails to Australia to visit his son.
(27 July) Arrives at Melbourne.

1872 *The Golden Lion of Granpere* 1 vol. (Tinsley).
(Jan.–Oct.) Travelling in Australia and New Zealand.
(Dec.) Returns via the United States.

1873 *The Eustace Diamonds* 3 vols. (Chapman & Hall).
Australia and New Zealand 2 vols. (Chapman & Hall).
(Apr.) Settles in Montagu Square, London.

1874 *Phineas Redux* 2 vols. (Chapman & Hall).
Lady Anna 2 vols. (Chapman & Hall).
Harry Heathcote of Gangoil. A Tale of Australian Bush Life
1 vol. (Sampson Low).

1875 *The Way We Live Now* 2 vols. (Chapman & Hall).
(1 Mar.) Leaves for Australia via Brindisi, the Suez Canal,
and Ceylon.
(4 May) Arrives in Australia.
(Aug.–Oct.) Sailing homewards.
(Oct.) Begins *An Autobiography.*

1876 *The Prime Minister* 4 vols. (Chapman & Hall).

1877 *The American Senator* 3 vols. (Chapman & Hall).
(29 June) Leaves for South Africa.
(11 Dec.) Sails for home.

1878 *South Africa* 2 vols. (Chapman & Hall).
Is He Popenjoy? 3 vols. (Chapman & Hall).
(June–July) Travels to Iceland in the yacht 'Mastiff'
How the 'Mastiffs' Went to Iceland 1 vol. (privately printed,
Virtue & Co).

1879 *An Eye for an Eye* 2 vols. (Chapman & Hall).
Thackeray 1 vol. (Macmillan).
John Candigate 3 vols. (Chapman & Hall).
Cousin Henry 2 vols. (Chapman & Hall).

1880 *The Duke's Children* 3 vols. (Chapman & Hall).
The Life of Cicero 2 vols. (Chapman & Hall).
(July) Settles at South Harting, Sussex, near Petersfield.

1881 *Dr Wortle's School* 2 vols. (Chapman & Hall).
Ayala's Angel 3 vols. (Chapman & Hall).

1882 *Why Frau Frohmann Raised Her Prices; and Other Stories* 1 vol.
(Isbister).
The Fixed Period 2 vols. (Blackwood).
Marion Fay 3 vols. (Chapman & Hall).

Lord Palmerston 1 vol. (Isbister).
Kept in the Dark 2 vols. (Chatto & Windus).
(May) Visits Ireland to collect material for a new Irish novel.
(Aug.) Returns to Ireland a second time.
(2 Oct.) Takes rooms for the winter at Garlant's Hotel, Suffolk St., London.
(3 Nov.) Suffers paralytic stroke.
(6 Dec.) Dies in nursing home, 34 Welbeck St., London.

1883 *Mr. Scarborough's Family* 3 vols. (Chatto & Windus).
      The Landleaguers (unfinished) 3 vols. (Chatto & Windus).
      An Autobiography 2 vols. (Blackwood).

1884 *An Old Man's Love* 2 vols. (Blackwood).

1923 *The Noble Jilt* 1 vol. (Constable).

1927 *London Tradesmen* 1 vol. (Elkin Mathews and Marrat).

1972 *The New Zealander* 1 vol. (Oxford University Press).

The American Senator

CONTENTS

CONTENTS

CHAPTER I

DILLSBOROUGH

I NEVER could understand why anybody should ever have begun to live at Dillsborough, or why the population there should have been at any time recruited by new comers. That a man with a family should cling to a house in which he has once established himself is intelligible. The butcher who supplied Dillsborough, or the baker, or the ironmonger, though he might not drive what is called a roaring trade, nevertheless found himself probably able to live, and might well hesitate before he would encounter the dangers of a more energetic locality. But how it came to pass that he first got himself to Dillsborough, or his father, or his grandfather before him, has always been a mystery to me. The town has no attractions, and never had any. It does not stand on a bed of coal, and has no connection whatever with iron. It has no water peculiarly adapted for beer, or for dyeing, or for the cure of maladies. It is not surrounded by beauty of scenery strong enough to bring tourists and holiday travellers. There is no cathedral there to form, with its bishop, prebendaries, and minor canons, the nucleus of a clerical circle. It manufactures nothing specially. It has no great horse fair, or cattle fair, or even pig market of special notoriety. Every Saturday farmers and graziers and buyers of corn and sheep do congregate in a sleepy fashion about the streets, but Dillsborough has no character of its own, even as a market town. Its chief glory is its parish church, which is ancient and inconvenient, having not as yet received any of those modern improvements which have of late become common throughout England;* but its parish church, though remarkable, is hardly celebrated. The town consists chiefly of one street which is over a mile long, with a square or market-place in the middle, round which a few lanes with queer old names are congregated, and a second small open space among these lanes, in which the church stands. As you pass along the street north-west, away from the railway station and from London, there is a stout hill, beginning to rise just beyond the market-place. Up to that point it is the High Street, thence it is called Bullock's Hill. Beyond that you come to Norrington Road—Norrington being the next town, distant from Dillsborough about twelve miles. Dillsborough, however, stands in the county of Rufford, whereas at the top of Bullock's Hill you enter the county of Ufford, of which Norrington is the assize town. The Dillsborough people are therefore divided, some two thousand five hundred of them belonging to Rufford, and the remaining five hundred to the neighbouring county. This accident has given rise to not a few feuds, Ufford being a large county, with pottery, and ribbons, and watches going on in the farther confines; whereas Rufford is small and thoroughly agricultural. The men at the top of Bullock's Hill are therefore disposed to think themselves better than their fellow-townsfolks, though they are small in number and not specially thriving in their circumstances.

At every interval of ten years, when the census is taken, the population of Dillsborough is always found to have fallen off in some slight degree. For a few months after the publication of the figures a slight tinge of melancholy comes upon the town. The landlord of the Bush Inn, who is really an enterprising man in his way, and who has looked about in every direction for new sources of business, becomes taciturn for a while and forgets to smile upon comers; Mr. Ribbs, the butcher, tells his wife that it is out of the question that she and the children should take that long-talked-of journey to the sea-coast; and Mr. Gregory Masters, the well-known old-established attorney of Dillsborough, whispers to some confidential friend that he might as well take down his plate and shut up his house. But in a month or two all that is forgotten, and new hopes spring up even in Dillsborough. Mr. Runciman at the Bush is putting up new stables for hunting-horses, that being the special trade for which he now finds that there is an opening. Mrs. Ribbs is again allowed to suggest Mare-Slocumb; and Mr. Masters goes on as he has done for the last forty years, making the best he can of a decreasing business.

Dillsborough is built chiefly of brick, and is, in its own way, solid enough. The Bush, which in the time of the present landlord's father was one of the best posting inns* on the road, is not only substantial, but almost handsome. A broad coach way, cut through the middle of the house, leads into a spacious, well-kept, clean yard, and on each side of the coach way there are bay windows looking into the street,—the one belonging to the commercial parlour, and the other to the so-called coffee-room. But the coffee-room has in truth fallen away from its former purposes, and is now used for a farmers' ordinary* on market days, and other similar purposes. Travellers who require the use of a public sitting-room must all congregate in the commercial parlour at the Bush. So far the interior of the house has fallen from its past greatness. But the exterior is maintained with much care. The brick-work up to the eaves is well pointed, fresh and comfortable to look at. In front of the carriage-way swings on two massive supports the old sign of the Bush, as to which it may be doubted whether even Mr. Runciman himself knows that it has swung there, or been displayed in some fashion, since it was the custom for the landlord to beat up wine* to freshen it before it was given to the customers to drink. The church, too, is of brick—though the tower and chancel* are of stone. The attorney's house is of brick —which shall not be more particularly described now as many of the scenes which these pages will have to describe were acted there; and almost the entire High Street in the centre of the town was brick also.

But the most remarkable house in Dillsborough was one standing in a short thoroughfare called Hobbs Gate, leading down by the side of the Bush Inn from the market-place to Church Square, as it is called. As you pass down towards the church this house is on the right hand, and it occupies with its garden the whole space between the market-place and Church Square. But though the house enjoys the privilege of a large garden,—so large that the land being in the middle of a town would be of great

value were it not that Dillsborough is in its decadence,—
still it stands flush up to the street upon which the front
door opens. It has an imposing flight of stone steps
guarded by iron rails leading up to it, and on each side of
the door there is a row of three windows, and on the two
upper stories rows of seven windows. Over the door there
is a covering, on which there are grotesquely-formed,
carved wooden faces; and over the centre of each window,
let into the brickwork, is a carved stone. There are also
numerous underground windows, sunk below the earth
and protected by iron railings. Altogether the house is
one which cannot fail to attract attention; and in the
brickwork is clearly marked the date 1701,—not the very
best period for English architecture as regards beauty,
but one in which the walls and roofs, ceilings and but-
tresses, were built more substantially than they are to-day.
This was the only house in Dillsborough which had a
name of its own, and it was called Hoppet Hall, the Dillsborough chronicles telling that it had been originally
built for and inhabited by the Hoppet family. The only
Hoppet now left in Dillsborough is old Joe Hoppet, the
ostler at the Bush; and the house, as was well known, had
belonged to some member of the Morton family for the
last hundred years at least. The garden and ground it
stands upon comprise three acres, all of which are surrounded by a high brick wall, which is supposed to be
coeval with the house. The best Ribston pippins,*—some
people say the only real Ribston pippins,—in all Rufford
are to be found here, and its Burgundy pears and walnuts
are almost equally celebrated. There are rumours also
that its roses beat everything in the way of roses for ten
miles round. But in these days very few strangers are
admitted to see the Hoppet Hall roses. The pears and
apples do make their way out, and are distributed either
by Mrs. Masters, the attorney's wife, or Mr. Runciman,
the innkeeper. The present occupier of the house is a
certain Mrs. Reginald Morton, with whom we shall also
be much concerned in these pages, but whose introduction to the reader shall be postponed for awhile.

The land around Dillsborough is chiefly owned by two

landlords, of whom the greatest and richest is Lord Rufford. He, however, does not live near the town, but away at the other side of the county, and is not much seen in these parts unless when the hounds bring him here, or when, with two or three friends, he will sometimes stay for a few days at the Bush Inn for the sake of shooting the coverts. He is much liked by all sporting men, but is not otherwise very popular with the people round Dillsborough. A landlord if he wishes to be popular should be seen frequently. If he lives among his farmers they will swear by him, even though he raises his rental every ten or twelve years and never puts a new roof to a barn for them. Lord Rufford is a rich man who thinks of nothing but sport in all its various shapes, from pigeon-shooting at Hurlingham* to the slaughter of elephants in Africa; and though he is lenient in all his dealings, is not much thought of in the Dillsborough side of the county, except by those who go out with the hounds. At Rufford, where he generally has a full house for three months in the year and spends a vast amount of money, he is more highly considered.

The other extensive landlord is Mr. John Morton, a young man, who, in spite of his position as squire of Bragton, owner of Bragton Park, and landlord of the entire parishes of Bragton and Mallingham,—the latter of which comes close up to the confines of Dillsborough,— was at the time of which our story begins, Secretary of Legation at Washington. As he had been an absentee since he came of age,—soon after which time he inherited the property,—he had been almost less liked in the neighbourhood than the lord. Indeed, no one in Dillsborough knew much about him, although Bragton Hall was but four miles from the town, and the Mortons had possessed the property and lived on it for the last three centuries. But there had been extravagance, as will hereafter have to be told, and there had been no continuous residence at Bragton since the death of old Reginald Morton, who had been the best known and the best loved of all the squires in Rufford, and had for many years been master of the Rufford hounds. He had lived to a very great age, and, though the great-grandfather of the present man, had not been dead above twenty years. He was the man of whom the older inhabitants of Dillsborough and the neighbourhood still thought and still spoke when they gave vent to their feelings in favour of gentlemen. And yet the old squire in his latter days had been able to do little or nothing for them,—being sometimes backward as to the payment of money he owed among them. But he had lived all his days at Bragton Park, and his figure had been familiar to all eyes in the High Street of Dillsborough and at the front entrance of the Bush. People still spoke of old Mr. Reginald Morton as though his death had been a sore loss to the neighbourhood.

And there were in the country round sundry yeomen, as they ought to be called,—gentlemen-farmers as they now like to style themselves,—men who owned some acres of land, and farmed these acres themselves. Of these we may specially mention Mr. Lawrence Twentyman, who was quite the gentleman-farmer. He possessed over three hundred acres of land, on which his father had built an excellent house. The present Mr. Twentyman— Lawrence Twentyman, Esquire, as he was called by everybody—was by no means unpopular in the neighbourhood. He not only rode well to hounds but paid twenty-five pounds annually to the hunt, which entitled him to feel quite at home in his red coat. He generally owned a racing colt or two, and attended meetings; but was supposed to know what he was about, and to have kept safely the five or six thousand pounds which his father had left him. And his farming was well done; for though he was, out-and-out, a gentleman-farmer, he knew how to get the full worth in work done for the fourteen shillings a week which he paid to his labourers,—a deficiency in which knowledge is the cause why gentlemen in general find farming so very expensive an amusement. He was a handsome, good-looking man of about thirty, and would have been a happy man had he not been too ambitious in his aspirations after gentry. He had been at school for three years at Cheltenham College, which,

together with his money and appearance and undoubted
freehold property, should, he thought, have made his
position quite secure to him; but, though he sometimes
called young Hampton of Hampton 'Dick Hampton,'
and the son of the rector of Dillsborough 'Mainwaring,'
and always called the rich young brewers from Norrington 'Botsey,'—partners in the well-known firm of Bill-
brook & Botsey; and though they in return called him
'Larry' and admitted the intimacy, still he did not get
into their houses. And Lord Rufford, when he came into
the neighbourhood, never asked him to dine at the Bush.
And—worst of all—some of the sporting men and others
in the neighbourhood, who decidedly were not gentlemen, also called him 'Larry.' Mr. Runciman always did
so. Twenty or twenty-five years ago Runciman had been
his father's special friend,—before the house had been
built and before the days at Cheltenham College.
Remembering this, Lawrence was too good a fellow to
rebuke Runciman; but to younger men of that class he
would sometimes make himself objectionable. There was
another keeper of hunting stables, a younger man, named
Stubbings, living at Stanton Corner, a great hunting
rendezvous about four miles from Dillsborough; and not
long since Twentyman had threatened to lay his whip
across Stubbings' shoulders if Stubbings ever called him
'Larry' again. Stubbings, who was a little man and rode
races, only laughed at Mr. Twentyman who was six feet
high, and told the story round to all the hunt. Mr.
Twentyman was more laughed at than perhaps he
deserved. A man should not have his Christian name
used by every Tom and Dick without his sanction. But
the difficulty is one to which men in the position of
Mr. Lawrence Twentyman are very subject.

Those whom I have named, together with Mr. Mainwaring the rector, and Mr. Surtees his curate, made up
the very sparse aristocracy of Dillsborough. The Hamp-
tons of Hampton West were Ufford men, and belonged
rather to Norrington than Dillsborough. The Botseys,
also from Norrington, were members of the U.R.U., or
Ufford and Rufford United Hunt Club; but they did not

much affect Dillsborough as a town. Mr. Mainwaring, who has been mentioned, lived in another brick house behind the church—the old parsonage of St. John's. There was also a Mrs. Mainwaring, but she was an invalid. Their family consisted of one son, who was at Brasenose* at this time. He always had a horse during the Christmas vacation, and, if rumour did not belie him, kept two or three up at Oxford. Mr. Surtees, the curate, lived in lodgings in the town. He was a painstaking, eager, clever young man, with aspirations in church matters, which were always being checked by his rector. *Quieta non movere* was the motto by which the rector governed his life, and he certainly was not at all the man to allow his curate to drive him into activity.

Such, at the time of our story, was the little town of Dillsborough.

CHAPTER II

THE MORTON FAMILY

I CAN hardly describe accurately the exact position of the Masters family without first telling all that I know about the Morton family; and it is absolutely essential that the reader should know all the Masters family intimately. Mr. Masters, as I have said in the last chapter, was the attorney in Dillsborough, and the Mortons had been for centuries past the squires of Bragton.

I need not take the reader back farther than old Reginald Morton. He had come to the throne of his family as a young man, and had sat upon it for more than half a century. He had been a squire of the old times, having no inclination for London seasons, never wishing to keep up a second house, quite content with his position as squire of Bragton, but with considerable pride about him as to that position. He had always liked to have his house full, and hated petty œconomies. He had for many years hunted the country at his own expense,—the amusement at first not having been so expensive as it afterwards became. When he began the work, it had been

considered sufficient to hunt twice a week. Now the
Rufford and Ufford hounds have four days, and sometimes a bye.* It went much against Mr. Reginald
Morton's pride when he was first driven to take a subscription.

But the temporary distress into which the family fell
was caused not so much by his own extravagance as by
that of two sons, and by his indulgence in regard to them.
He had three children, none of whom were very fortunate
in life. The eldest, John, married the daughter of a peer,
stood for Parliament, had one son, and died before he was
thirty, owing something over £20,000. The estate was
then worth £7,000 a year. Certain lands not lying either
in Bragton or Mallingham were sold, and that difficulty
was surmounted, not without a considerable diminution
of income. In process of time the grandson, who was
a second John Morton, grew up and married, and became
the father of a third John Morton, the young man who
afterwards became owner of the property and Secretary
of Legation at Washington. But the old squire outlived
his son and his grandson, and when he died had three or
four great-grandchildren playing about the lawns of
Bragton Park. The peer's daughter had lived, and had
for many years drawn a dower from the Bragton property,
and had been altogether a very heavy incumbrance.

But the great trial of the old man's life, as also the
great romance, had arisen from the career of his second
son, Reginald. Of all his children, Reginald had been the
dearest to him. He went to Oxford, and had there spent
much money; not as young men now spend money, but
still to an extent that had been grievous to the old squire.
But everything was always paid for Reginald. It was
necessary, of course, that he should have a profession, and
he took a commission in the army. As a young man he
went to Canada. This was in 1829, when all the world was
at peace, and his only achievement in Canada was to
marry a young woman who is reported to have been
pretty and good, but who had no advantages either of
fortune or birth. She was, indeed, the daughter of
a bankrupt innkeeper in Montreal. Soon after this, he

sold out and brought his wife home to Bragton. It was at this period of the squire's life that the romance spoken of occurred. John Morton, the brother with the aristocratic wife, was ten or twelve years older than Reginald, and at this time lived chiefly at Bragton when he was not in town. He was, perhaps, justified in regarding Bragton as almost belonging to him, knowing as he did that it must belong to him after his father's lifetime, and to his son after him. His anger against his brother was hot, and that of his wife still hotter. He himself had squandered thousands, but then he was the heir. Reginald, who was only a younger brother, had sold his commission. And then he had done so much more than this. He had married a woman who was not a lady! John was clearly of opinion that at any rate the wife should not be admitted into Bragton House. The old squire in those days was not a happy man; he had never been very strong-minded, but now he was strong enough to declare that his house-door should not be shut against a son of his,—or a son's wife, as long as she was honest. Hereupon the Honourable Mrs. Morton took her departure, and was never seen at Bragton again in the old squire's time. Reginald Morton came to the house, and soon afterwards another little Reginald was born at Bragton Park. This happened as long ago as 1835, twenty years before the death of the old squire.

But there had been another child, a daughter, who had come between the two sons, still living in those days, who will become known to any reader who will have patience to follow these pages to the end. She married, not very early in life, a certain Sir William Ushant, who was employed by his country for many years in India and elsewhere, but who found, soon after his marriage, that the service of his country required that he should generally leave his wife at Bragton. As her father had been for many years a widower, Lady Ushant became the mistress of the house.

But death was very busy with the Mortons. Almost every one died, except the squire himself and his daughter, and that honourable dowager, with her income and her pride, who could certainly very well have been spared. When at last, in 1855, the old squire went, full of years, full of respect, but laden also with debts and money troubles, not only had his son John, and his grandson John, gone before him, but Reginald and his wife were both lying in Bragton churchyard.

The elder branch of the family, John the great-grandson, and his little sisters, were at once taken away from Bragton by the honourable grandmother. John, who was then about seven years old, was of course the young squire, and was the owner of the property. The dowager, therefore, did not undertake an altogether unprofitable burden. Lady Ushant was left at the house, and with Lady Ushant, or rather immediately subject to her care, young Reginald Morton, who was then nineteen years of age, and who was about to go to Oxford. But there immediately sprang up family lawsuits, instigated by the honourable lady on behalf of her grandchildren, of which Reginald Morton was the object. The old man had left certain outlying properties to his grandson Reginald, of which Hoppet Hall was a part. For eight or ten years the lawsuit was continued, and much money was expended. Reginald was at last successful, and became the undoubted owner of Hoppet Hall; but in the meantime he went to Germany for his education, instead of to Oxford, and remained abroad even after the matter was decided,—living, no one but Lady Ushant knew where, or after what fashion.

When the old squire died, the children were taken away, and Bragton was nearly deserted. The young heir was brought up with every caution, and, under the auspices of his grandmother and her family, behaved himself very unlike the old Mortons. He was educated at Eton, after leaving which he was at once examined for Foreign Office employment, and commenced his career with great *éclat*.* He had been made to understand clearly that he could not enter upon his squirearchy early in life. The estate when he came of age had already had some years to recover itself, and as he went from capital to capital, he was quite content to draw from it an income

which enabled him to shine with peculiar brilliance
among his brethren. He had visited Bragton once since
the old squire's death, and had found the place very dull
and uninviting. He had no ambition whatever to be
master of the U.R.U.; but did look forward to a time
when he might be Minister Plenipotentiary at some
foreign court.

For many years after the old man's death, Lady Ushant,
who was then a widow, was allowed to live at Bragton.
She was herself childless, and, being now robbed of her
great-nephews and nieces, took a little girl to live with
her, named Mary Masters. It was a very desolate house
in those days, but the old lady was careful as to the
education of the child, and did her best to make the home
happy for her. Some two or three years before the com-
mencement of this story there arose a difference between
the manager of the property and Lady Ushant, and she
was made to understand, after some half-courteous
manner, that Bragton House and Park would do better
without her. There would be no longer any cows kept,
and painters must come into the house, and there were
difficulties about fuel. She was not turned out exactly;
but she went and established herself in lonely lodgings at
Cheltenham. Then Mary Masters, who had lived for
more than a dozen years at Bragton, went back to her
father's house in Dillsborough.

Any reader with an aptitude for family pedigrees will
now understand that Reginald, Master of Hoppet Hall,
was first cousin to the father of the Foreign Office paragon,
and that he is therefore the paragon's first cousin once
removed. The relationship is not very distant, but the
two men, one of whom was a dozen years older than the
other, had not seen each other for more than twenty
years,—at a time when one of them was a big boy, and
the other a very little one; and during the greater part of
that time a lawsuit had been carried on between them in
a very rigorous manner. It had done much to injure both,
and had created such a feeling of hostility that no intercourse of any kind now existed between them.

It does not much concern us to know how far back

should be dated the beginning of the connection between
the Morton family and that of Mr. Masters, the attorney;
but it is certain that the first attorney of that name in
Dillsborough became learned in the law through the
patronage of some former Morton. The father of the
present Gregory Masters, and the grandfather, had been
thoroughly trusted and employed by old Reginald
Morton, and the former of the two had made his will.
Very much of the stewardship and management of the
property had been in their hands, and they had throven
as honest men, but as men with a tolerably sharp eye to
their own interests. The late Mr. Masters had died a few
years before the squire, and the present attorney had
seemed to succeed to these family blessings. But the
whole order of things became changed. Within a few
weeks of the squire's death Mr. Masters found that he was
to be entrusted no further with the affairs of the property,
but that, in lieu of such care, was thrown upon him the
task of defending the will which he had made against the
owner of the estate. His father and grandfather had contrived between them to establish a fairly good business,
independently of Bragton, which business, of course, was
now his. As far as instruction went, and knowledge, he
was probably a better lawyer than either of them; but he
lacked their enterprise and special genius, and the thing
had dwindled with him. It seemed to him, perhaps not
unnaturally, that he had been robbed of an inheritance.
He had no title deeds, as had the owners of the property;
but his ancestors before him, from generation to generation, had lived by managing the Bragton property. They
had drawn the leases, and made the wills, and collected
the rents, and had taught themselves to believe that a
Morton could not live on his land without a Masters.
Now there was a Morton who did not live on his land,
but spent his rents elsewhere without the aid of any
Masters, and it seemed to the old lawyer that all the good
things of the world had passed away. He had married
twice, his first wife having, before her marriage, been well
known at Bragton Park. When she had died, and Mr.
Masters had brought a second wife home, Lady Ushant

took the only child of the mother, whom she had known
as a girl, into her own keeping, till she also had been
compelled to leave Bragton. Then Mary Masters had
returned to her father and stepmother.

The Bragton Park residence is a large, old-fashioned,
comfortable house, but by no means a magnificent mansion. The greater part of it was built one hundred and
fifty years ago, and the rooms are small and low. In the
palmy*days of his reign, which is now more than half
a century since, the old squire made alterations, and built
new stables and kennels, and put up a conservatory; but
what he did then has already become almost old-
fashioned now. What he added he added in stone, but
the old house was brick. He was much abused at the
time for his want of taste, and heard a good deal about
putting new cloth as patches on old rents; but, as the
shrubs and ivy have grown up, a certain picturesqueness
has come upon the place, which is greatly due to the
difference of material. The place is somewhat sombre,
as there is no garden close to the house. There is a lawn,
at the back, with gravel walks round it; but it is only
a small lawn; and then divided from the lawn by a ha-ha
fence; is the park. The place, too, has that sad look which
always comes to a house from the want of a tenant. Poor
Lady Ushant, when she was there, could do little or
nothing. A gardener was kept, but there should have
been three or four gardeners. The man grew cabbages
and onions, which he sold, but cared nothing for the
walks or borders. Whatever it may have been in the old
time, Bragton Park was certainly not a cheerful place
when Lady Ushant lived there. In the squire's time the
park itself had always been occupied by deer. Even when
distress came he would not allow the deer to be sold. But
after his death they went very soon, and from that day to
the time of which I am writing, the park has been leased
to some butchers or graziers from Dillsborough.

The ground hereabouts is nearly level, but it falls away
a little and becomes broken and pretty where the river
Dill runs through the park, about half a mile from the
house. There is a walk called the Pleasance, passing down

through shrubs to the river, and then crossing the stream by a foot-bridge, and leading across the fields towards Dillsborough. This bridge is, perhaps, the prettiest spot in Bragton, or, for that matter, anywhere in the county round; but even here there is not much of beauty to be praised. It is here, on the side of the river away from the house, that the home meet of the hounds used to be held; and still the meet at Bragton Bridge is popular in this county.

CHAPTER III

THE MASTERS FAMILY

AT six o'clock one November evening, Mr. Masters the attorney was sitting at home with his family in the large parlour of his house, his office being on the other side of the passage which cut the house in two and was formally called the hall. Upstairs, over the parlour, was a drawing-room; but this chamber, which was supposed to be elegantly furnished, was very rarely used. Mr. and Mrs. Masters did not see much company, and for family purposes the elegance of the drawing-room made it unfit. It added, however, not a little to the glory of Mr. Master's life. The house itself was a low brick building in the High Street, at the corner where the High Street runs into the market-place, and therefore, nearly opposite to the Bush. It had none of the elaborate grandeur of the inn nor of the simple stateliness of Hoppet Hall, but, nevertheless, it maintained the character of the town and was old, substantial, respectable, and dark.

'I think it a very spirited thing of him to do, then,' said Mrs. Masters.

'I don't know, my dear. Perhaps it is only revenge.'

'What have you to do with that? What can it matter to a lawyer whether it's revenge or anything else? He's got the means, I suppose?'

'I don't know, my dear.'

'What does Nickem say?'

'I suppose he has the means,' said Mr. Masters, who was aware that if he told his wife a fib on the matter, she would learn the truth from his senior clerk, Mr. Samuel Nickem. Among the professional gifts which Mr. Masters possessed, had not been that great gift of being able to keep his office and his family distinct from each other. His wife always knew what was going on, and was very free with her advice; generally tendering it on that side on which money was to be made, and doing so with much feminine darkness as to right or wrong. His clerk, Nickem, who was afflicted with no such darkness, but who ridiculed the idea of scruple in an attorney, often took part against him. It was the wish of his heart to get rid of Nickem; but Nickem would have carried business with him, and gone over to some enemy, or, perhaps have set up in some irregular manner on his own bottom; and his wife would have given him no peace had he done so, for she regarded Nickem as the mainstay of the house.

'What is Lord Rufford to you?' asked Mrs. Masters.

'He has always been very friendly.'

'I don't see it at all. You have never had any of his money. I don't know that you are a pound richer by him.'

'I have always gone with the gentry of the county.'

'Fiddlesticks! Gentry! Gentry are very well as long as you can make a living out of them. You could afford to stick up for gentry till you lost the Bragton property.' This was a subject that was always sore between Mr. Masters and his wife. The former Mrs. Masters had been a lady—the daughter of a neighbouring clergyman; and had been much considered by the family at Bragton. The present Mrs. Masters was the daughter of an ironmonger at Norrington, who had brought a thousand pounds with her, which had been very useful. No doubt Mr. Masters' practice had been considerably affected by the lowliness of his second marriage. People who used to know the first Mrs. Masters, such as Mrs. Mainwaring, and the doctor's wife, and old Mrs. Cooper, the wife of the vicar of Mallingham, would not call on the second Mrs. Masters. As Mrs. Masters was too high-spirited to run after people who did not want her, she took to hating gentry instead.

'We have always been on the other side,' said the old attorney,—'I and my father and grandfather before me.'

'They lived on it and you can't. If you are going to say that you won't have any client that isn't a gentleman, you might as well put up your shutters at once.'

'I haven't said so. Isn't Runciman my client?'

'He always goes with the gentry. He a'most thinks he's one of them himself.'

'And old Nobbs, the greengrocer. But it's all nonsense. Any man is my client, or any woman, who can come and pay me for business that is fit for me to do.'

'Why isn't this fit to be done? If the man's been damaged, why shouldn't he be paid?'

'He's had money offered him.'

'If he thinks it ain't enough, who's to say that it is,— unless a jury?' said Mrs. Masters, becoming quite eloquent. 'And how's a poor man to get a jury to say that, unless he comes to a lawyer? Of course, if you won't have it, he'll go to Bearside. Bearside won't turn him away.' Bearside was another attorney, an interloper of about ten years' standing, whose name was odious to Mr. Masters.

'You don't know anything about it, my dear,' said he, aroused at last to anger.

'I know you are letting anybody who likes take the bread out of the children's mouths.' The children, so called, were sitting round the table and could not but take an interest in the matter. The eldest was that Mary Masters, the daughter of the former wife, whom Lady Ushant had befriended, a tall girl, with dark brown hair, so dark as almost to be black, and large, soft, thoughtful grey eyes. We shall have much to say of Mary Masters, and can hardly stop to give an adequate description of her here. The others were Dolly and Kate, two girls aged sixteen and fifteen. The two younger 'children' were eating bread and butter and jam in a very healthy manner, but still had their ears wide open to the conversation that was being held. The two younger girls sympathized strongly with their mother. Mary, who had

known much about the Mortons, and was old enough to
understand the position which her grandfather had held
in reference to the family, of course leaned in her heart
to her father's side. But she was wiser than her father,
and knew that in such discussions her mother often
showed a worldly wisdom which, in their present circumstances, they could hardly afford to disregard, unpalat-
able though it might be.

Mr. Masters disliked these discussions altogether, but
he disliked them most of all in presence of his children.
He looked round upon them in a deprecatory manner,
making a slight motion with his hand and bringing his
head down on one side, and then he gave a long sigh. If
it was his intention to convey some subtle warning to his
wife, some caution that she alone should understand, he
was deceived. The 'children' all knew what he meant
quite as well as did their mother.

'Shall we go out, mamma?' asked Dolly.

'Finish your teas, my dears,' said Mr. Masters, who
wished to stop the discussion rather than to carry it on
before a more select audience.

'You have got to make up your mind to-night,' said
Mrs. Masters, 'and you'll be going over to the Bush at
eight.'

'No, I needn't. He is to come on Monday. I told
Nickem I wouldn't see him to-night; nor, of course, to-
morrow.'

'Then he'll go to Bearside.'

'He may go to Bearside and be ———! Oh, Lord! I do
wish you'd let me drop the business for a few minutes
when I am in here; you don't know anything about it.
How should you?'

'I know that if I didn't speak you'd let everything slip
through your fingers. There's Mr. Twentyman. Kate,
open the door.'

Kate, who was fond of Mr. Twentyman, rushed up and
opened the front door at once. In saying so much of Kate,
I do not mean it to be understood that any precocious
ideas of love were troubling that young lady's bosom.
Kate Masters was a jolly bouncing schoolgirl of fifteen,

who was not too proud to eat toffy, and thought herself
still a child. But she was very fond of Lawrence Twentyman, who had a pony that she could ride, and who was
always good-natured to her. All the family liked Mr.
Twentyman,—unless it might be Mary, who was the one
that he specially liked himself. And Mary was not
altogether averse to him, knowing him to be good-
natured, manly, and straightforward. But Mr. Twentyman had proposed to her, and she had—certainly not
accepted him. This, however, had broken none of the
family friendship. Every one in the house, unless it
might be Mary herself, hoped that Mr. Twentyman might
prevail at last. The man was worth six or seven hundred
a year, and had a good house, and owed no one a shilling.
He was handsome, and about the best-tempered fellow
known. Of course they all desired that he should prevail
with Mary. 'I wish that I were old enough, Larry, that's
all!' Kate had said to him once, laughing. 'I wouldn't
have you, if you were ever so old,' Larry had replied;
'you'd want to be out hunting every day.' That will
show the sort of terms that Larry was on with his friend
Kate. He called at the house every Saturday with the
declared object of going over to the club that was held
that evening in the parlour at the Bush, whither Mr.
Masters also always went. It was understood at home
that Mr. Masters should attend this club every Saturday
from eight till eleven, but that he was not at any other
time to give way to the fascinations of the Bush. On this
occasion, and we may say on almost every Saturday
night, Mr. Twentyman arrived a full hour before the
appointed time. The reason of his doing so was of course
well understood, and was quite approved by Mrs. Masters.
She was not, at any rate as yet, a cruel stepmother; but
still, if the girl could be transferred to so eligible a home
as that which Mr. Twentyman could give her, it would
be well for all parties.

When he took his seat he did not address himself
specially to the lady of his love. I don't know how a
gentleman is to do so in the presence of her father, and
mother, and sisters. Saturday after Saturday he probably

thought that some occasion would arise; but if his words could have been counted, it would probably have been found that he addressed fewer to her than to any one in the room.

'Larry,' said his special friend Kate, 'am I to have the pony at the Bridge meet?'

'How very free you are, miss!' said her mother.

'I don't know about that,' said Larry. 'When is there to be a meet at the Bridge? I haven't heard.'

'But I have. Tony Tuppett told me that they would be there this day fortnight.' Tony Tuppett was the huntsman of the U.R.U.

'That's more than Tony can know. He may have guessed it.'

'Shall I have the pony if he has guessed right?'

Then the pony was promised; and Kate, trusting in Tony Tuppett's sagacity, was happy.

'Have you heard of all this about Dillsborough Wood?' asked Mrs. Masters. The attorney shrank at the question, and shook himself uneasily in his chair.

'Yes; I've heard about it,' said Larry.

'And what do you think about it? I don't see why Lord Rufford is to ride over everybody because he's a lord.' Mr. Twentyman scratched his head. Though a keen sportsman himself, he did not specially like Lord Rufford,—a fact which had been very well known to Mrs. Masters. But, nevertheless, this threatened action against the nobleman was distasteful to him. It was not a hunting affair, or Mr. Twentyman could not have doubted for a moment. It was a shooting difficulty, and as Mr. Twentyman had never been asked to fire a gun on the Rufford preserves, it was no great sorrow to him that there should be such a difficulty. But the thing threatened was an attack upon the country gentry and their amusements, and Mr. Twentyman was a country gentleman who followed sport. Upon the whole his sympathies were with Lord Rufford.

'The man is an utter blackguard, you know,' said Larry. 'Last year he threatened to shoot the foxes in Dillsborough Wood.'

'No!' said Kate, quite horrified.

'I'm afraid he's a bad sort of fellow all round,' said the attorney.

'I don't see why he shouldn't claim what he thinks due to him,' said Mrs. Masters.

'I'm told that his lordship offered him seven and six an acre for the whole of the two fields,' said the gentleman-farmer.

'Goarly declares,' said Mrs. Masters, 'that the pheasants didn't leave him four bushels of wheat to the acre.'

Goarly was the man who had proposed himself as a client to Mr. Masters, and who was desirous of claiming damages to the amount of forty shillings an acre for injury done to the crops on two fields belonging to himself which lay adjacent to Dillsborough Wood, a covert belonging to Lord Rufford, about four miles from the town, in which both pheasants and foxes were preserved with great care.

'Has Goarly been to you?' asked Twentyman.

Mr. Masters nodded his head. 'That's just it,' said Mrs. Masters. 'I don't see why a man isn't to go to law if he pleases,—that is, if he can afford to pay for it. I have nothing to say against gentlemen's sport; but I do say that they should run the same chance as others. And I say it's a shame if they're to band themselves together and make the county too hot to hold any one as doesn't like to have his things ridden over, and his crops devoured, and his fences knocked to Jericho! I think there's a deal of selfishness in sport and a deal of tyranny.'

'Oh, Mrs. Masters!' exclaimed Larry.

'Well, I do. And if a poor man,—or a man whether he's poor or no,' added Mrs. Masters, correcting herself, as she thought of the money which this man ought to have in order that he might pay for his lawsuit,—'thinks hisself injured, it's nonsense to tell me that nobody should take up his case. It's just as though the butcher wouldn't sell a man a leg of mutton because Lord Rufford had a spite against him. Who's Lord Rufford?'

'Everybody knows that I care very little for his lordship,' said Mr. Twentyman.

'Nor I; and I don't see why Gregory should. If Goarly

isn't entitled to what he wants he won't get it; that's all.
But let it be tried fairly.'

Hereupon Mr. Masters took up his hat and left the
room, and Mr. Twentyman followed him, not having yet
expressed any positive opinion on the delicate matter
submitted to his judgment. Of course, Goarly was a brute.
Had he not threatened to shoot foxes? But, then, an
attorney must live by lawsuits, and it seemed to Mr.
Twentyman that an attorney should not stop to inquire
whether a new client is a brute or not.

CHAPTER IV

THE DILLSBOROUGH CLUB

THE club, so called at Dillsborough, was held every
Saturday evening in a back parlour at the Bush, and
was attended generally by seven or eight members. It
was a very easy club. There was no balloting, and no other
expense attending it other than that of paying for the
liquor which each man chose to drink. Sometimes, about
ten o'clock, there was a little supper, the cost of which was
defrayed by subscription among those who partook of it.
It was one rule of the club, or a habit, rather, which had
grown to be a rule, that Mr. Runciman might introduce
into it any one he pleased. I do not know that a similar
position was denied to any one else; but as Mr. Runciman
had a direct pecuniary advantage in promoting the club,
the new-comers were generally ushered in by him. When
the attorney and Twentyman entered the room Mr.
Runciman was seated as usual in an arm-chair at the
corner of the fire nearest to the door, with the bell at his
right hand. He was a hale, good-looking man, about
fifty, with black hair, now turning grey at the edges, and
a clean-shorn chin. He had a pronounced strong face of
his own, one capable of evincing anger and determination when necessary, but equally apt for smiles or, on
occasion, for genuine laughter. He was a masterful but
a pleasant man, very civil to customers and to his friends
generally while they took him the right way; but one who

could be a Tartar if he were offended, holding an opinion that his position as landlord of an inn was one requiring masterdom. And his wife was like him in everything,—except in this, that she always submitted to him. He was a temperate man in the main; but on Saturday nights he would become jovial, and sometimes a little quarrelsome. When this occurred the club would generally break itself up and go home to bed, not in the least offended. Indeed Mr. Runciman was the tyrant of the club, though it was held at his house expressly with the view of putting money into his pocket. Opposite to his seat was another arm-chair,—not so big as Mr. Runciman's, but still a soft and easy chair,—which was always left for the attorney. For Mr. Masters was a man much respected through all Dillsborough, partly on his own account, but more perhaps for the sake of his father and grandfather. He was a round-faced, clean-shorn man, with straggling grey hair, who always wore black clothes and a white cravat. There was something in his appearance which recommended him among his neighbours, who were disposed to say he 'looked the gentleman;' but a stranger might have thought his cheeks to be flabby and his mouth to be weak.

Making a circle, or the beginning of a circle, round the fire, were Nupper, the doctor,—a sporting old bachelor doctor who had the reputation of riding after the hounds in order that he might be ready for broken bones and minor accidents; next to him, in another arm-chair, facing the fire, was Fred Botsey, the younger of the two brewers from Norrington, who was in the habit during the hunting season of stopping from Saturday to Monday at the Bush, partly because the Rufford hounds hunted on Saturday and Monday and on those days seldom met in the Norrington direction, and partly because he liked the sporting conversation of the Dillsborough Club. He was a little man, very neat in his attire, who liked to be above his company, and fancied that he was so in Mr. Runciman's parlour. Between him and the attorney's chair was Harry Stubbings, from Stanton Corner, the man who let out hunters, and whom Twentyman had threatened to thrash. His introduction to the club had taken place lately, not without some opposition; but Runciman had set his foot upon that, saying that it was 'all d—— nonsense.' He had prevailed, and Twentyman had consented to meet the man; but there was no great friendship between them. Seated back on the sofa was Mr. Ribbs, the butcher, who was allowed into the society as being a specially modest man. His modesty, perhaps, did not hinder him in an affair of sheep or bullocks, nor yet in the collection of his debts; but at the club he understood his position, and rarely opened his mouth to speak. When Twentyman followed the attorney into the room there was a vacant chair between Mr. Botsey and Harry Stubbings; but he would not get into it, preferring to seat himself on the table at Botsey's right hand.

'So Goarly was with you, Mr. Masters?' Mr. Runciman began as soon as the attorney was seated. It was clear that they had all been talking about Goarly and his law-suit, and that Goarly and the law-suit would be talked about very generally in Dillsborough.

'He was over at my place this evening,' said the attorney.

'You are not going to take his case up for him, Mr. Masters?' said young Botsey. 'We expect something better from you than that.'

Now Fred Botsey was rather an impudent young man, and Mr. Masters, though he was mild enough at home, did not like impudence from the world at large. 'I suppose, Mr. Botsey,' said he, 'that if Goarly were to go to you for a barrel of beer you'd sell it to him?'

'I don't know whether I should or not. I dare say my people would. But that's a different thing.'

'I don't see any difference at all. You're not very particular as to your customers, and I don't ask you any questions about them. Ring the bell, Runciman, please.' The bell was rung, and the two newcomers ordered their liquor.

It was quite right that Fred Botsey should be put down. Every one in the room felt that. But there was something in the attorney's tone which made the assembled company feel that he had undertaken Goarly's case; whereas, in the opinion of the company, Goarly was a scoundrel with whom Mr. Masters should have had nothing to do. The attorney had never been a sporting man himself, but he had always been, as it were, on that side.

'Goarly is a great fool for his pains,' said the doctor. 'He has had a very fair offer made him, and, first or last, it'll cost him forty pounds.'

'He has got it into his head,' said the landlord, 'that he can sue Lord Rufford for his fences. Lord Rufford is not answerable for his fences.'

'It's the loss of crop he's going for,' said Twentyman.

'How can there be pheasants to that amount in Dillsborough Wood,' continued the landlord, 'when everybody knows that foxes breed there every year? There isn't a surer find for a fox in the whole county. Everybody knows that Lord Rufford never lets his game stand in the way of foxes.'

Lord Rufford was Mr. Runciman's great friend and patron and best customer, and not a word against Lord Rufford was allowed in that room, though elsewhere in Dillsborough ill-natured things were sometimes said of his lordship. Then there came on that well-worn dispute among sportsmen, whether foxes and pheasants are or are not pleasant companions to each other. Every one was agreed that, if not, then the pheasants should suffer, and that any country gentleman who allowed his game-keeper to entrench on the privileges of foxes in order that pheasants might be more abundant was a 'brute' and a 'beast', and altogether unworthy to live in England. Larry Twentyman and Ned Botsey expressed an opinion that pheasants were predominant in Dillsborough Wood, while Mr. Runciman, the doctor, and Harry Stubbings declared loudly that everything that foxes could desire was done for them in that Elysium*of sport.

'We drew the wood blank last time we were there,' said Larry. 'Don't you remember, Mr. Runciman, about the end of last March?'

'Of course I remember,' said the landlord. 'Just the end of the season, when two vixens had litters in the wood! You don't suppose Bean was going to let that old butcher,

Tony, find a fox in Dillsborough at that time.' Bean was his lordship's head gamekeeper in that part of the country. 'How many foxes had we found there during the season?'

'Two or three,' suggested Botsey.

'Seven!' said the energetic landlord; 'seven, including cub-hunting,—and killed four! If you kill four foxes out of an eighty-acre wood, and have two litters at the end of the season, I don't think you have much to complain of.'

'If they all did as well as Lord Rufford, you'd have more foxes than you'd know what to do with,' said the doctor.

Then this branch of the conversation was ended by a bet of a new hat between Botsey and the landlord as to the finding of a fox in Dillsborough Wood when it should next be drawn; as to which, when the speculation was completed, Harry Stubbings offered Mr. Runciman ten shillings down for his side of the bargain.

But all this did not divert the general attention from the important matter of Goarly's attack. 'Let it be how it will,' said Mr. Runciman, 'a fellow like that should be put down.' He did not address him specially to Mr. Masters, but that gentleman felt that he was being talked at.

'Certainly he ought,' said Dr. Nupper. 'If he didn't feel satisfied with what his lordship offered him, why couldn't he ask his lordship to refer the matter to a couple of farmers who understood it?'

'It's the spirit of the thing,' said Mr. Ribbs, from his place on the sofa. 'It's a hodious spirit.'

'That's just it, Mr. Ribbs,' said Harry Stubbings. 'It's all meant for opposition. Whether it's shooting or whether it's hunting, it's all one. Such a chap oughtn't to be allowed to have land. I'd take it away from him by Act of Parliament. It's such as him as is destroying the country.'

'There ain't many of them hereabouts, thank God!' said the landlord.

'Now, Mr. Twentyman,' said Stubbings, who was anxious to make friends with the gentleman-farmer, 'you know what land can do, and what land has done, as well

as any man. What would you say was the real damage
done to them two wheat-fields by his lordship's game last
autumn? You saw the crops as they were growing, and
you know what came off the land.'

'I wouldn't like to say.'

'But if you were on your oath, Mr. Twentyman? Was
there more than seven-and-sixpence an acre lost?'

'No, nor five shillings,' said Runciman.

'I think Goarly ought to take his lordship's offer—if
you mean that,' said Twentyman.

Then there was a pause, during which more drink was
brought in, and pipes were re-lighted. Everybody wished
that Mr. Masters might be got to say that he would not
take the case, but there was a delicacy about asking him.
'If I remember right he was in Rufford Gaol once,' said
Runciman.

'He was let out on bail and then the matter was hushed
up somehow,' said the attorney.

'It was something about a woman,' continued Runciman. 'I know that on that occasion he came out an
awful scoundrel.'

'Don't you remember,' asked Botsey, 'how he used to
walk up and down the covert-side with a gun, two years
ago, swearing he would shoot the fox if he broke over his
land?'

'I heard him say it, Botsey,' said Twentyman.

'It wouldn't have been the first fox he's murdered,' said
the doctor.

'Not by many,' said the landlord.

'You remember that old woman near my place?' said
Stubbings. 'It was he that put her up to tell all them lies
about her turkeys. I ran it home to him! A blackguard
like that! Nobody ought to take him up.'

'I hope you won't, Mr. Masters?' said the doctor. The
doctor was as old as the attorney, and had known him for
many years. No one else could dare to ask the question.

'I don't suppose I shall, Nupper,' said the attorney
from his chair. It was the first word he had spoken since
he had put down young Botsey. 'It wouldn't just suit me;
but a man has to judge of those things for himself.'

Then there was a general rejoicing, and Mr. Runciman stood broiled bones, and ham and eggs, and bottled stout for the entire club; one unfortunate effect of which unwonted conviviality was that Mr. Masters did not get home till near twelve o'clock. That was sure to cause discomfort; and then he had pledged himself to decline Goarly's business.

CHAPTER V

REGINALD MORTON

WE will now go back to Hoppet Hall and its inhabitants. When the old squire died he left by his will Hoppet Hall and certain other houses in Dillsborough, which was all that he could leave, to his grandson Reginald Morton. Then there arose a question whether this property also was not entailed. The former Mrs. Masters, and our friend of the present day, had been quite certain of the squire's power to do what he liked with it; but others had been equally certain on the other side, and there had been a lawsuit. During that time Reginald Morton had been forced to live on a very small allowance. His aunt, Lady Ushant, had done what little she could for him, but it had been felt to be impossible that he should remain at Bragton, which was the property of the cousin who was at law with him. From the moment of his birth the Honourable Mrs. Morton, who was also his aunt by marriage, had been his bitter enemy. He was the son of an innkeeper's daughter, and, according to her theory of life, should never even have been noticed by the real Mortons. And this Honourable old lady was almost adverse to Lady Ushant, whose husband had simply been a knight, and who had left nothing behind him. Thus Reginald Morton had been almost absolutely friendless since his grandfather died, and had lived in Germany, nobody quite knew how. During the entire period of this lawsuit Hoppet Hall had remained untenanted.

When the property was finally declared to belong to Reginald Morton, the Hall, before it could be used, required considerable repair. But there was other property. The Bush Inn belonged to Mr. Morton, as did the house in which Mr. Masters lived, and sundry other smaller tenements in the vicinity. There was an income from these of about five hundred pounds a year. Reginald, who was then nearly thirty years of age, came over to England, and stayed for a month or two at Bragton with his aunt, to the infinite chagrin of the old dowager. The management of the town property was entrusted to Mr. Masters, and Hoppet Hall was repaired. At this period Mr. Mainwaring had just come to Dillsborough, and having a wife with some money and perhaps quite as much pretension, had found the rectory too small, and had taken the Hall on a lease for seven years. When this was arranged Reginald Morton again went to Germany, and did not return till the lease had run out. By that time Mr. Mainwaring, having spent a little money, found that the rectory would be large enough for his small family. Then the Hall was again untenanted for awhile, till, quite suddenly, Reginald Morton returned to Dills-borough, and took up his permanent residence in his own house.

It soon became known that the new-comer would not add much to the gaiety of the place. The only people whom he knew in Dillsborough were his own tenants, Mr. Runciman and Mr. Masters, and the attorney's eldest daughter. During those months which he had spent with Lady Ushant at Bragton, Mary had been living there, then a child of twelve years old; and, as a child, had become his fast friend. With his aunt he had continually corresponded, and partly at her instigation and partly from feelings of his own, he had at once gone to the attorney's house. This was now two years since, and he had found in his old playmate a beautiful young woman, in his opinion very unlike the people with whom she lived. For the first twelve months he saw her occasion-ally,—though not indeed very often. Once or twice he had drunk tea at the attorney's house, on which occasions the drawing-room upstairs had been almost as grand as it was uncomfortable. Then the attentions of Larry

Twentyman began to make themselves visible, infinitely to Reginald Morton's disgust. Up to that time he had no idea of falling in love with the girl himself. Since he had begun to think on such subjects at all he had made up his mind that he would not marry. He was almost the more proud of his birth by his father's side, because he had been made to hear so much of his mother's low position. He had told himself a hundred times that under no circumstances could he marry any other than a lady of good birth. But his own fortune was small, and he knew himself well enough to be sure that he would not marry for money. He was now nearly forty years of age and had never yet been thrown into the society of any one that had attracted him. He was sure that he would not marry. And yet when he saw that Mr. Twentyman was made much of and flattered by the whole Masters family, apparently because he was regarded as an eligible husband for Mary, Reginald Morton was not only disgusted, but personally offended. Being a most unreasonable man, he conceived a bitter dislike to poor Larry, who, at any rate, was truly in love, and was not looking too high in desiring to marry the portionless daughter of the attorney. But Morton thought that the man ought to be kicked and horsewhipped, or, at any rate, banished into some speechless exile for his presumption.

With Mr. Runciman he had dealings, and in some sort friendship. There were two meadows attached to Hoppet Hall,—fields lying close to the town, which were very suitable for the landlord's purposes. Mr. Mainwaring had held them in his own hands, taking them up from Mr. Runciman, who had occupied them while the house was untenanted, in a manner which induced Mr. Runciman to feel that it was useless to go to church to hear such sermons as those preached by the rector. But Morton had restored the fields, giving them rent free, on condition that he should be supplied with milk and butter. Mr. Runciman, no doubt, had the best of the bargain, as he generally had in all bargains; but he was a man who liked to be generous when generously treated. Consequently he almost overdid his neighbour with butter

and cream, and occasionally sent in quarters of lamb and
sweetbreads to make up the weight. I don't know that
the offerings were particularly valued; but friendship was
engendered. Runciman, too, had his grounds for
quarrelling with those who had taken up the management of the Bragton property after the squire's death, and
had his own antipathy to the Honourable Mrs. Morton
and her grandson, the Secretary of Legation. When the
law-suit was going on he had been altogether on Reginald
Morton's side. It was an affair of sides, and quite natural
that Runciman and the attorney should be friendly with
the new-comer at Hoppet Hall, though there were very
few points of personal sympathy between them.

Reginald Morton was no sportsman, nor was he at all
likely to become a member of the Dillsborough Club. It
was currently reported of him in the town that he had
never sat on a horse or fired off a gun. As he had been
brought up as a boy by the old squire this was probably
an exaggeration, but it is certain that at this period of his
life he had given up any aptitudes in that direction for
which his early training might have suited him. He had
brought back with him to Hoppet Hall many cases of
books which the ignorance of Dillsborough had magnified
into an enormous library, and was certainly a sedentary,
reading man. There was already a report in the town
that he was engaged in some stupendous literary work,
and the men and women generally looked upon him as
a disagreeable marvel of learning. Dillsborough of itself
was not bookish, and would have regarded any one known
to have written an article in a magazine almost as a
phenomenon.

He seldom went to church, much to the sorrow of
Mr. Surtees, who ventured to call at the house and
remonstrate with him. He never called again. And
though it was the habit of Mr. Surtees' life to speak as
little ill as possible of any one, he was not able to say any
good of Mr. Morton. Mr. Mainwaring, who would never
have troubled himself though his parishioner had not
entered a place of worship once in a twelvemonth, did say
many severe things against his former landlord. He

hated people who were unsocial and averse to dining out, and who departed from the ways of living common among English country gentlemen. Mr. Mainwaring was, upon the whole, prepared to take the other side.

Reginald Morton, though he was now nearly forty, was a young-looking, handsome man, with fair hair, cut short, and a light beard, which was always clipped. Though his mother had been an innkeeper's daughter in Montreal, he had the Morton blue eyes, and the handsome well-cut Morton nose. He was nearly six feet high, and strongly made, and was known to be a much finer man than the Secretary of Legation, who was rather small, and supposed to be not very robust.

Our lonely man was a great walker, and had investigated every lane and pathway, and almost every hedge within ten miles of Dillsborough before he had resided there two years; but his favourite rambles were all in the neighbourhood of Bragton. As there was no one living in the house—no one but the old housekeeper who had lived there always—he was able to wander about the place as he pleased. On the Tuesday afternoon, after the meeting of the Dillsborough Club which has been recorded, he was seated, about three o'clock, on the rail of the footbridge over the Dill, with a long German pipe hanging from his mouth. He was noted throughout the whole country for this pipe, or for others like it, such a one usually being in his mouth as he wandered about. The amount of tobacco which he had smoked since his return to these parts, exactly in that spot, was considerable, for there he might have been found at some period of the afternoon at least three times a week. He would sit on this rail for half an hour looking down at the sluggish waters of the little river, rolling the smoke out of his mouth at long intervals, and thinking perhaps of the great book which he was supposed to be writing. As he sat there now, he suddenly heard voices and laughter, and presently three girls came round the corner of the hedge, which, at this spot, hid the Dillsborough path—and he saw the attorney's three daughters.

'It's Mr. Morton,' said Dolly in a whisper.

'He's always walking about Bragton,' said Kate in another whisper. 'Tony Tuppett says that he's the Bragton ghost.'

'Kate,' said Mary, also in a low voice, 'you shouldn't talk so much about what you hear from Tony Tuppett.'

'Bosh!' said Kate, who knew that she could not be scolded in the presence of Mr. Morton.

He came forward and shook hands with them all, and took off his hat to Mary. 'You've walked a long way, Miss Masters,' he said.

'We don't think it far. I like sometimes to come and look at the old place.'

'And so do I. I wonder whether you remember how often I've sat you on this rail and threatened to throw you into the river?'

'I remember very well that you did threaten me once, and that I almost believed that you would throw me in.'

'What had she done that was naughty, Mr. Morton?' asked Kate.

'I don't think she ever did anything naughty in those days. I don't know whether she has changed for the worse since.'

'Mary is never naughty now,' said Dolly. 'Kate and I are naughty, and it's very much better fun than being good.'

'The world has found out that long ago, Miss Dolly; only the world is not quite so candid in owning it as you are. Will you come and walk round the house, Miss Masters? I never go in, but I have no scruples about the paths and park.'

At the end of the bridge leading into the shrubbery there was a stile, high indeed, but made commodiously with steps, almost like a double staircase, so that ladies could pass it without trouble. Mary had given her assent to the proposed walk, and was in the act of putting out her hand to be helped over the stile, when Mr. Twenty-man appeared at the other side of it.

'If here isn't Larry!' said Kate.

Morton's face turned as black as thunder, but he immediately went back across the bridge, leading Mary with him. The other girls, who had followed him on to the bridge, had of course to go back also. Mary was made very unhappy by the meeting. Mr. Morton would of course think that it had been planned, whereas by Mary herself it had been altogether unexpected. Kate, when the bridge was free, rushed over it and whispered something to Larry. The meeting had indeed been planned between her and Dolly and the lover, and this special walk had been taken at the request of the two younger girls.

Morton stood stock still, as though he expected that Twentyman would pass by. Larry hurried over the bridge, feeling sure that the meeting with Morton had been accidental and thinking that he would pass on towards the house.

Larry was not at all ashamed of his purpose, nor was he inclined to give way and pass on. He came up boldly to his love, and shook hands with her with a pleasant smile. 'If you are walking back to Dillsborough,' he said, 'maybe you'll let me go a little way with you?'

'I was going round the house with Mr. Morton,' she said timidly.

'Perhaps I can join you?' said he, bobbing his head at the other man.

'If you intended to walk back with Mr. Twentyman——' began Morton.

'But I didn't,' said the poor girl, who in truth understood more of it all than did either of the two men. 'I didn't expect him, and I didn't expect you. It's a pity I can't go both ways, isn't it?' she added, attempting to appear cheerful.

'Come back, Mary,' said Kate; 'we've had walking enough, and shall be awfully tired before we get home.'

Mary had thought that she would like extremely to go round the house with her old friend and have a hundred incidents of her early life called to her memory. The meeting with Reginald Morton had been altogether pleasant to her. She had often felt how much she would have liked it had the chance of her life enabled her to see more frequently one whom as a girl she had so intimately known. But at the moment she lacked the courage to walk boldly across the bridge, and thus to rid herself of Lawrence Twentyman. She had already perceived that Morton's manner had rendered it impossible that her lover should follow them. 'I am afraid I must go home,' she said. It was the very thing she did not want to do,—this going home with Lawrence Twentyman; and yet she herself said that she must do it—driven to say so by a nervous dread of showing herself to be fond of the other man's company.

'Good afternoon to you,' said Morton very gloomily, waving his hat and stalking across the bridge.

Chapter VI

NOT IN LOVE

REGINALD MORTON, as he walked across the bridge towards the house, was thoroughly disgusted with all the world. He was very angry with himself, feeling that he had altogether made a fool of himself by his manner. He had shown himself to be offended, not only by Mr. Twentyman, but by Miss Masters also, and he was well aware, as he thought of it all, that neither of them had given him any cause of offence. If she chose to make an appointment for a walk with Mr. Lawrence Twentyman and to keep it, what was that to him? His anger was altogether irrational, and he knew that it was so. What right had he to have an opinion about it if Mary Masters should choose to like the society of Mr. Twentyman? It was an affair between him and her father and mother in which he could have no interest; and yet he had not only taken offence, but was well aware that he had shown his feeling.

Nevertheless, as to the girl herself, he could not argue himself out of his anger. It was grievous to him that he should have gone out of his way to ask her to walk with him just at the moment when she was expecting this vulgar 'lover—for that she had expected him he felt no doubt. Yet he had heard her disclaim any intention of walking with the man! But girls are sly, especially when their lovers are concerned. It made him sore at heart to feel that this girl should be sly, and doubly sore to think that she should have been able to love such a one as Lawrence Twentyman.

As he roamed about among the grounds this idea troubled him much. He assured himself that he was not in love with her himself, and that he had no idea of falling in love with her; but it sickened him to think that a girl who had been brought up by his aunt, who had been loved at Bragton, whom he had liked, who looked so like a lady, should put herself on a par with such a wretch as that. In all this he was most unjust to both of them. He was specially unjust to poor Larry, who was by no means a wretch. His costume was not that to which Morton had been accustomed in Germany, nor would it have passed without notice in Bond Street. But it was rational and clean. When he came to the bridge to meet his sweetheart he had on a dark-green shooting coat, a billicock hat, brown breeches, and gaiters nearly up to his knees. I don't know that a young man in the country could wear more suitable attire. And he was a well-made man,—just such a one as, in this dress, would take the eye of a country girl. There was a little bit of dash about him—just a touch of swagger—which better breeding might have prevented. But it was not enough to make him odious to an unprejudiced observer. I could fancy that an old lady from London, with an eye in her head for manly symmetry, would have liked to look at Larry, and would have thought that a girl in Mary's position would be happy in having such a lover, providing that his character was good and his means adequate. But Reginald Morton was not an old woman, and to his eyes the smart young farmer with his billicock hat, not quite straight on his head, was an odious thing to behold. He exaggerated the swagger, and took no notice whatever of the well-made limbs. And then this man had proposed to accompany him, had wanted to join his party, had thought it possible that a flirtation might be carried on in his presence! He sincerely hated the man; but what was he to think of such a girl as Mary Masters when she could bring herself to like the attentions of such a lover?

He was very cross with himself because he knew how unreasonable was his anger. Of one thing only could he assure himself—that he would never again willingly put himself in Mary's company. What was Dillsborough and the ways of its inhabitants to him? Why should he so far leave the old fashions of his life as to fret himself about an attorney's daughter in a little English town? And yet he did fret himself, walking rapidly, and smoking his pipe a great deal quicker than was his custom.

When he was about to return home he passed the front of the house, and there, standing at the open door, he saw Mrs. Hopkins, the housekeeper, who had in truth been waiting for him. He said a good-natured word to her, intending to make his way on without stopping, but she called him back. 'Have you heard the news, Mr. Reginald?' she said.

'I haven't heard any news this twelvemonth,' he replied.

'Laws! that is so like you, Mr. Reginald. The young squire is to be here next week.'

'Who is the young squire? I didn't know there was any squire now.'

'Mr. Reginald!'

'A squire as I take it, Mrs. Hopkins, is a country gentleman who lives on his own property. Since my grandfather's time no such gentleman has lived at Bragton.'

'That's true, too, Mr. Reginald. Any way Mr. Morton is coming down next week.'

'I thought he was in America.'

'He has come home, for a turn like—and is staying up in town with the old lady.' The old lady always meant the Honourable Mrs. Morton.

'And is the old lady coming down with him?'

'I fancy she is, Mr. Reginald. He didn't say as much, but only that there would be three or four—a couple of ladies he said, and perhaps more. So I am getting the east bedroom, with the dressing-room, and the blue room for her ladyship.' People about Bragton had been accustomed to call Mrs. Morton her ladyship. 'That's where she always used to be. Would you come in and see, Mr. Reginald?'

'Certainly not, Mrs. Hopkins. If you were asking me into a house of your own, I would go in and see all the rooms and chat with you for an hour; but I don't suppose I shall ever go into this house again unless things change very much indeed.'

'Then I'm sure I hope they will change, Mr. Reginald.' Mrs. Hopkins had known Reginald Morton as a boy growing up into manhood—had almost been present at his birth, and had renewed her friendship while he was staying with Lady Ushant; but of the present squire, as she called him, she had seen almost nothing, and what she had once remembered of him had now been obliterated by an absence of twenty years. Of course she was on Reginald's side in the family quarrel, although she was the paid servant of the Foreign Office paragon.

'And they are to be here next week? What day next week, Mrs. Hopkins?' Mrs. Hopkins didn't know on what day she was to expect the visitors, nor how long they intended to stay. Mr. John Morton had said in his letter that he would send his own man down two days before his arrival, and that was nearly all that he had said.

Then Morton started on his return walk to Dillsborough, again taking the path across the bridge. 'Ah!' he said to himself with a shudder as he crossed the stile, thinking of his own softened feelings as he had held out his hand to help Mary Masters, and then of his revulsion of feeling when she declared her purpose of walking home with Mr. Twentyman. And he struck the rail of the bridge with his stick as though he were angry with the place altogether. And he thought to himself that he would never come there any more, that he hated the place, and that he would never cross that bridge again.

Then his mind reverted to the tidings he had heard from Mrs. Hopkins. What ought he to do when his cousin arrived? Though there had been a long lawsuit, there had been no actual declared quarrel between him and the heir. He had, indeed, never seen the heir for the last twenty years, nor had they ever interchanged letters.

There had been no communication whatever between them, and therefore there could hardly be a quarrel. He disliked his cousin; nay, almost hated him; he was quite aware of that. And he was sure also that he hated that Honourable old woman worse than any one else in the world, and that he always would do so. He knew that the Honourable old woman had attempted to drive his own mother from Bragton, and of course he hated her. But that was no reason why he should not call on his cousin. He was anxious to do what was right. He was specially anxious that blame should not be attributed to him. What he would like best would be that he might call, might find nobody at home—and that then John Morton should not return the courtesy. He did not want to go to Bragton as a guest; he did not wish to be in the wrong himself; but he was by no means equally anxious that his cousin should keep himself free from reproach.

The bridge path came out on the Dillsborough road just two miles from the town, and Morton, as he got over the last stile, saw Lawrence Twentyman coming towards him on the road. The man, no doubt, had gone all the way into Dillsborough with the girls, and was now returning home. The parish of Bragton lies to the left of the high road as you go into the town from Rufford and the direction of London, whereas Chowton Farm, the property of Mr. Twentyman, is on the right of the road, but in the large parish of St. John's, Dillsborough. Dillsborough Wood lies at the back of Larry Twentyman's land, and joining on to Larry's land and also to the wood is the patch of ground owned by 'that scoundrel Goarly'. Chowton Farm gate opens on to the high road, so that Larry was now on his direct way home. As soon as he saw Morton he made up his mind to speak to him. He was quite sure from what had passed between him and the girls, on the road home, that he had done something wrong. He was convinced that he had interfered in some ill-bred way, though he did not at all know how. Of Reginald Morton he was not in the least jealous. He, too, was of a jealous temperament, but it had never occurred to him to join Reginald Morton and Mary Masters together. He was very much in love with Mary, but had no idea that she was in any way above the position which she might naturally hold as daughter of the Dillsborough attorney. But of Reginald Morton's attributes and scholarship and general standing he had a mystified appreciation which saved him from the pain of thinking that such a man could be in love with his sweetheart. As he certainly did not wish to quarrel with Morton, having always taken Reginald's side in the family disputes, he thought that he would say a civil word in passing, and, if possible, apologise. When Morton came up he raised his hand to his head and did open his mouth, though not pronouncing any word very clearly. Morton looked at him as grim as death, just raised his hand, and then passed on with a quick step. Larry was displeased; but the other was so thoroughly a gentleman—one of the Mortons, and a man of property in the county—that he didn't even yet wish to quarrel with him. 'What the deuce have I done?' said he to himself as he walked on—'I didn't tell her not to go up to the house. If I offered to walk with her, what was that to him?' It must be remembered that Lawrence Twentyman was twelve years younger than Reginald Morton, and that a man of twenty-eight is apt to regard a man of forty as very much too old for falling in love. It is a mistake which it will take him fully ten years to rectify, and then he will make a similar mistake as to men of fifty. With his awe for Morton's combined learning and age, it never occurred to him to be jealous.

Morton passed on rapidly, almost feeling that he had been a brute. But what business had the objectionable man to address him? He tried to excuse himself, but yet he felt that he had been a brute—and had so demeaned himself in reference to the daughter of the Dillsborough attorney! He would teach himself to do all he could to promote the marriage. He would give sage advice to Mary Masters as to the wisdom of establishing herself—having not an hour since made up his mind that he would never see her again! He would congratulate the attorney and Mrs. Masters. He would conquer the absurd feeling which at present was making him wretched. He would cultivate some sort of acquaintance with the man, and make the happy pair a wedding present. But, yet, what 'a beast' the man was, with that billicock hat on one side of his head, and those tight leather gaiters!

As he passed through the town towards his own house, he saw Mr. Runciman standing in front of the hotel. His road took him up Hobbs gate, by the corner of the Bush; but Runciman came a little out of the way to meet him. 'You have heard the news?' said the innkeeper.

'I have heard one piece of news.'

'What's that, sir?'

'Come,—you tell me yours first.'

'The young squire is coming down to Bragton next week.'

'That's my news too. It is not likely that there should be two matters of interest in Dillsborough on the same day.'

'I don't know why Dillsborough should be worse off than any other place, Mr. Morton; but, at any rate, the squire's coming.'

'So Mrs. Hopkins told me. Has he written to you?'

'His coachman or his groom has; or perhaps he keeps what they call an ekkery.* He's much too big a swell to write to the likes of me. Lord bless me!—when I think of it, I wonder how many dozen of orders I've had from Lord Rufford under his own hand. "Dear Runciman, dinner at eight; ten of us; won't wait a moment. Yours R." I suppose Mr. Morton would think that his lordship had let himself down by anything of that sort?'

'What does my cousin want?'

'Two pair of horses,—for a week certain, and perhaps longer, and two carriages. How am I to let any one have two pair of horses for a week certain—and perhaps longer? What are other customers to do? I can supply a gentleman by the month and buy horses to suit; or I can supply him by the job. But I guess Mr. Morton don't well know how things are managed in this country. He'll have to learn.'

'What day does he come?'

'They haven't told me that yet, Mr. Morton.'

CHAPTER VII

THE WALK HOME

MARY MASTERS, when Reginald Morton had turned his back upon her at the bridge, was angry with herself and with him, which was reasonable; and very angry also with Larry Twentyman, which was unreasonable. As she had at once acceded to Morton's proposal that they should walk round the house together, surely he should not have deserted her so soon. It had not been her fault that the other man had come up. She had not wanted him. But she was aware that when the option had in some sort been left to herself, she had elected to walk back with Larry. She knew her own motives and her own feelings, but neither of the men would understand them. Because she preferred the company of Mr. Morton, and had at the moment feared that her sisters would have deserted her had she followed him, therefore she had declared her purpose of going back to Dillsborough, in doing which she knew that Larry and the girls would accompany her. But of course Mr. Morton would think that she had preferred the company of her recognized admirer. It was pretty well known in Dillsborough that Larry was her lover. Her stepmother had spoken of it very freely; and Larry himself was a man who did not keep his lights hidden under a bushel. 'I hope I've not been in the way, Mary,' said Mr. Twentyman, as soon as Morton was out of hearing.

'In the way of what?'

'I didn't think there was any harm in offering to go up to the house with you if you were going.'

'Who has said there was any harm?' The path was only broad enough for one, and she was walking first. Larry was following her, and the girls were behind him.

'I think that Mr. Morton is a very stuck-up fellow,' said Kate, who was the last.

'Hold your tongue, Kate,' said Mary. 'You don't know what you are talking about.'

'I know as well as any one when a person is good-natured. What made him go off in that hoity-toity fashion? Nobody had said anything to him.'

'He always looks as though he were going to eat somebody,' said Dolly.

'He shan't eat me,' said Kate.

Then there was a pause, during which they all went along quickly, Mary leading the way. Larry, of course, felt that he was wasting his opportunity, and yet hardly knew how to use it, feeling that the girl was angry with him.

'I wish you'd say, Mary, whether you think that I did anything wrong?'

'Nothing wrong to me, Mr. Twentyman.'

'Did I do anything wrong to him?'

'I don't know how far you may be acquainted with him. He was proposing to go somewhere, and you offered to go with him.'

'I offered to go with you,' said Larry sturdily. 'I suppose I'm sufficiently acquainted with you.'

'Quite so,' said Mary.

'Why should he be so proud? I never said an uncivil word to him. He's nothing to me. If he can do without me, I'm sure that I can do without him.'

'Very well indeed, I should think.'

'The truth is, Mary——'

'There has been quite enough said about it, Mr. Twentyman.'

'The truth is, Mary, I came on purpose to have a word with you.' Hearing this, Kate rushed on and pulled Larry by the tail of his coat.

'How did you know I was to be there?' demanded Mary sharply.

'I didn't know. I had reason to think you perhaps might be there. The girls, I knew, had been asking you to come as far as the bridge. At any rate, I took my chance. I'd seen him some time before, and then I saw you.'

'If I'm to be watched about in that way,' said Mary angrily, 'I won't go out at all.'

'Of course I want to see you. Why shouldn't I? I'm

all fair and above board;—ain't I? Your father and mother know all about it. It isn't as though I were doing anything clandestine.' He paused for a reply, but Mary walked on in silence. She knew quite well that he was warranted in seeking her, and that nothing but a very positive decision on her part could put an end to his courtship. At the present moment she was inclined to be very positive, but he had hardly as yet given her an opportunity of speaking out. 'I think you know, Mary, what it is that I want.' They were now at a rough stile, which enabled him to come close up to her and help her. She tripped over the stile with a light step, and again walked on rapidly. The field they were in enabled him to get up to her side, and now, if ever, was his opportunity. It was a long straggling meadow, which he knew well, with the Dill running by it all the way,—or rather two meadows, with an open space where there had once been a gate. He had ridden through the gap a score of times, and knew that at the further side of the second meadow they would come upon the high road. The fields were certainly much better for his purpose than the road. 'Don't you think, Mary, you could say a kind word to me?'

'I never said anything unkind.'

'You can't think ill of me for loving you better than all the world.'

'I don't think ill of you at all. I think very well of you.'

'That's kind.'

'So I do. How can I help thinking well of you, when I've never heard anything but good of you?'

'Then why shouldn't you say at once that you'll have me, and make me the happiest man in all the county?'

'Because——'

'Well!'

'I told you before, Mr. Twentyman, and that ought to have been enough. A young woman doesn't fall in love with every man that she thinks well of. I should like you as well as all the rest of the family if you would only marry some other girl.'

'I shall never do that.'

'Yes you will, some day.'

'Never. I've set my heart upon it, and I mean to stick to it. I'm not the fellow to turn about from one girl to another. What I want is the girl I love. I've money enough and all that kind of thing of my own.'

'I'm sure you're disinterested, Mr. Twentyman.'

'Yes, I am. Ever since you've been home from Bragton it has been the same thing, and when I felt that it was so, I spoke up to your father honestly. I haven't been beating about the bush, and I haven't done anything that wasn't honourable.' They were very near the last stile now. 'Come, Mary, if you won't make me a promise, say that you'll think of it.'

'I have thought of it, Mr. Twentyman, and I can't make you any other answer. I dare say I'm very foolish.'

'I wish you were more foolish. Perhaps then you wouldn't be so hard to please.'

'Whether I'm wise or foolish, indeed, indeed, it's no good your going on. Now we're on the road. Pray go back home, Mr. Twentyman.'

'It'll be getting dark in a little time.'

'Not before we're in Dillsborough. If it were ever so dark we could find our way home by ourselves. Come along, Dolly.'

Over the last stile he had stayed a moment to help the younger girl, and as he did so Kate whispered a word in his ear. 'She's angry because she couldn't go up to the house with that stuck-up fellow.' It was a foolish word; but then Kate Masters had not had much experience in the world.

Whether overcome by Mary's resolute mode of speaking, or aware that the high road would not suit his purpose, he did turn back as soon as he had seen them a little way on their return towards the town. He had not gone half a mile before he met Morton, and had been half-minded to make some apology to him. But Morton had denied him the opportunity, and he had walked on to his own house,—low in spirits indeed, but still with none of that sorest of agony which comes to a lover from the feeling that his love loves some one else. Mary had been very decided with him,—more so he feared than before; but still he saw no reason why he should not succeed at last. Mrs. Masters had told him that Mary would certainly give a little trouble in winning, but would be the more worth the winner's trouble when won. And she had certainly shown no preference for any other young man about the town. There had been a moment when he had much dreaded Mr. Surtees. Young clergymen are apt to be formidable rivals, and Mr. Surtees had certainly made some overtures of friendship to Mary Masters. But Larry had thought that he had seen that these overtures had not led to much, and then that fear had gone from him. He did believe that Mary was now angry because she had not been allowed to walk about Bragton with her old friend Mr. Morton. It had been natural that she should like to do so. It was the pride of Mary's life that she had been befriended by the Mortons and Lady Ushant. But it did not occur to him that he ought to be jealous of Mr. Morton,—though it had occurred to Kate Masters.

There was very little said between the sisters on their way back to the town. Mary was pretty sure now that the two girls had made the appointment with Larry, but she was unwilling to question them on the subject. Immediately on their arrival at home they heard the great news. John Morton was coming to Bragton with a party of ladies and gentlemen. Mrs. Hopkins had spoken of four persons. Mrs. Masters told Mary that there were to be a dozen at least, and that four or five pairs of horses and half a dozen carriages had been ordered from Mr. Runciman. 'He means to cut a dash when he does begin,' said Mrs. Masters.

'Is he going to stay, mother?'

'He wouldn't come down in that way if it was only for a few days, I suppose. But what they will do for furniture I don't know.'

'There's plenty of furniture, mother.'

'A thousand years old. Or for wine, or fruit, or plate.'

'The old plate was there when Lady Ushant left.'

'People do things now in a very different way from what they used. A couple of dozen silver forks made quite a show on the old squire's table. Now they change the things so often that ten dozen is nothing. I don't suppose there's a bottle of wine in the cellar.'

'They can get wine from Cobbold, mother.'

'Cobbold's wine won't go down with them, I fancy. I wonder what servants they're bringing.'

When Mr. Masters came in from his office the news was corroborated. Mr. John Morton was certainly coming to Bragton. The attorney had still a small unsettled and disputed claim against the owner of the property, and he had now received by the day mail an answer to a letter which he had written to Mr. Morton, saying that that gentleman would see him in the course of the next fortnight.

CHAPTER VIII

THE PARAGON'S PARTY AT BRAGTON

THERE was certainly a great deal of fuss made about John Morton's return to the home of his ancestors,— made altogether by himself and those about him, and not by those who were to receive him. On the Thursday in the week following that of which we have been speaking, two carriages from the Bush met the party at the railway station and took them to Bragton. Mr. Runciman, after due consideration, put up with the inconsiderate nature of the order given, and supplied the coaches and horses as required,—consoling himself, no doubt, with the reflection that he could charge for the unreasonableness of the demand in the bill. The coachman and butler had come down two days before their master, so that things might be in order. Mrs. Hopkins learned from the butler that though the party would at first consist only of three, two other very august persons were to follow on the Saturday, —no less than Lady Augustus Trefoil and her daughter Arabella. And Mrs. Hopkins was soon led to imagine, though no positive information was given to her on the subject, that Miss Trefoil was engaged to be married to their master. 'Will he live here altogether, Mr. Tankard?' Mrs. Hopkins asked. To this question Mr. Tankard was

able to give a very definite answer. He was quite sure
that Mr. Morton would not live anywhere altogether.
According to Mr. Tankard's ideas, the whole foreign
policy of England depended on Mr. John Morton's presence in some capital, either in Europe, Asia, or America
—upon Mr. Morton's presence, and of course upon his
own also. Mr. Tankard thought it not improbable that
they might soon be wanted at Hong Kong, or some very
distant place,—but in the meantime they were bound to
be back at Washington very shortly. Tankard had himself been at Washington, and also before that at Lisbon,
and could tell Mrs. Hopkins how utterly unimportant
had been the actual ministers at those places, and how
the welfare of England had depended altogether on the
discretion and general omniscience of his young master—
and of himself. He, Tankard, had been the only person
in Washington who had really known in what order
Americans should go out to dinner one after another.
Mr. Elias Gotobed, who was coming, was perhaps the
most distinguished American of the day, and was Senator
for Mikewa.

'Mickey war!' said poor Mrs. Hopkins,—'that's been
one of them terrible American wars we used to hear of.'
Then Tankard explained to her that Mikewa was one of
the Western States and Mr. Elias Gotobed was a great
Republican, who had very advanced opinions of his own
respecting government, liberty, and public institutions in
general. With Mr. Morton and the Senator was coming
the Honourable Mrs. Morton. The lady had her lady's
maid,—and Mr. Morton had his own man; so that there
would be a great influx of persons.

Of course there was very much perturbation of spirit.
Mrs. Hopkins, after that first letter, the contents of which
she had communicated to Reginald Morton, had received
various dispatches and been asked various questions.
Could she find a cook? Could she find two housemaids?
And all these were only wanted for a time. In her distress
she went to Mrs. Runciman, and did get assistance. 'I
suppose he thinks he's to have the cook out of my kitchen?'
Runciman had said. Somebody, however, was found

who said she could cook, and two girls who professed that they knew how to make beds. And in this way an establishment was ready before the arrival of the Secretary of Legation and the great American Senator. Those other questions of wine and plate and vegetables had, no doubt, settled themselves after some fashion.

John Morton had come over to England on leave of absence for four months, and had brought with him the Senator from Mikewa. The Senator had never been in England before and was especially anxious to study the British Constitution and to see the ways of Britons with his own eyes. He had only been a fortnight in London before his journey down to the county had been planned. Mr. Gotobed wished to see English country life, and thought that he could not on his first arrival have a better opportunity. It must be explained also that there was another motive for this English rural sojourn. Lady Augustus Trefoil, who was an adventurous lady, had been travelling in the United States with her daughter, and had there fallen in with Mr. John Morton. Arabella Trefoil was a beauty, and a woman of fashion, and had captivated the Paragon. An engagement had been made, subject to various stipulations; the consent of Lord Augustus in the first place,—as to which John Morton, who only understood foreign affairs, was not aware, as he would have been had he lived in England, that Lord Augustus was nobody. Lady Augustus had spoken freely as to settlements, value of property, life insurance and such matters; and had spoken firmly, as well as freely, expressing doubt as to the expediency of such an engagement;—all of which had surprised Mr. Morton considerably, for the young lady had at first been left in his hands with almost American freedom. And now Lady Augustus and her daughter were coming down on a visit of inspection. They had been told, as had the Senator, that things would be in the rough. The house had not been properly inhabited for nearly a quarter of a century. The Senator had expressed himself quite contented. Lady Augustus had only hoped that everything would be made as comfortable as possible for her daughter. I don't know what

more could have been done at so short a notice than to
order two carriages, two housemaids, and a cook.

A word or two must also be said of the old lady who
made one of the party. The Honourable Mrs. Morton
was now seventy, but no old lady ever showed less signs of
advanced age. It is not to be understood from this that
she was beautiful;—but that she was very strong. What
might be the colour of her hair, or whether she had any,
no man had known for many years. But she wore so
perfect a front that some people were absolutely deluded.
She was very much wrinkled;—but as there are wrinkles
which seem to come from the decay of those muscles
which should uphold the skin, so are there others which
seem to denote that the owner has simply got rid of the
watery weaknesses of juvenility. Mrs. Morton's wrinkles
were strong wrinkles. She was thin, but always carried
herself bolt upright, and would never even lean back in
her chair. She had a great idea of her duty, and hated
everybody who differed from her with her whole heart.
She was the daughter of a Viscount, a fact which she
never forgot for a single moment, and which she thought
gave her positive superiority to all women who were not
the daughters of Dukes or Marquises, or of Earls. Therefore, as she did not live much in the fashionable world,
she rarely met any one above herself. Her own fortune on
her marriage had been small, but now she was a rich
woman. Her husband had been dead nearly half a
century and during the whole of that time she had been
saving money. To two charities she gave annually £5
per annum each. Duty demanded it, and the money was
given. Beyond that she had never been known to spend
a penny in charity. Duty, she had said more than once,
required of her that she do something to repair the
ravages made on the Morton property by the preposterous
extravagance of the old squire in regard to the younger
son, and that son's—child. In her anger she had not
hesitated on different occasions to call the present
Reginald a bastard, though the expression was a wicked
calumny for which there was no excuse. Without any aid
of hers the Morton property had repaired itself. There

had been a minority of thirteen or fourteen years, and since that time the present owner had not spent his income. But John Morton was not himself averse to money, and had always been careful to maintain good relations with his grandmother. She had now been asked down to Bragton in order that she might approve, if possible, of the proposed wife. It was not likely that she should approve absolutely of anything; but to have married without an appeal to her would have been to have sent the money flying into the hands of some of her poor paternal cousins. Arabella Trefoil was the grand-daughter of a duke, and a step had so far been made in the right direction. But Mrs. Morton knew that Lord Augustus was nobody, that there would be no money, and that Lady Augustus had been the daughter of a banker, and that her fortune had been nearly squandered.

The Paragon was not in the least afraid of his American visitor, nor, as far as the comforts of his house were concerned, of his grandmother. Of the beauty and her mother he did stand in awe;—but he had two days in which to look to things before they would come. The train reached Dillsborough Station about half-past three, and the two carriages were there to meet them. 'You will understand, Mr. Gotobed,' said the old lady, 'that my grandson has nothing of his own established here as yet.' This little excuse was produced by certain patches and tears in the cushions and linings of the carriages. Mr. Gotobed smiled and bowed and declared that everything was 'fixed convenient.' Then the Senator followed the old lady into one carriage; Mr. Morton followed alone into the other; and they were driven away to Bragton.

When Mrs. Hopkins had taken the two ladies up to their rooms Mr. Morton asked the Senator to walk round the grounds. Mr. Gotobed, lighting an enormous cigar, of which he put half down his throat for more commodious and quick consumption, walked on to the middle of the drive, and turning back looked up at the house. 'Quite a pile,' he said, observing that the offices and outhouses extended a long way to the left till they almost joined other buildings in which were the stables and coach-house.

'It's a good-sized house,' said the owner; 'nothing very particular, as houses are built nowadays.'

'Damp, I should say?'

'I think not. I have never lived here much myself; but I have not heard that it was considered so.'

'I guess it's damp. Very lonely;—isn't it?'

'We like to have our society inside, among ourselves, in the country.'

'Keep a sort of hotel—like?' suggested Mr. Gotobed. 'Well, I don't dislike hotel life, especially when there are no charges. How many servants do you want to keep up such a house as that?'

Mr. Morton explained that at present he knew very little about it himself, then led him away by the path over the bridge, and turning to the left showed him the building which had once been the kennels of the Rufford hounds. 'All that for dogs!' exclaimed Mr. Gotobed.

'All for dogs,' said Morton. 'Hounds, we generally call them.'

'Hounds are they? Well, I'll remember; though "dogs" seems to me more civil. How many used there to be?'

'About fifty couple, I think.'

'A hundred dogs! No wonder your country gentlemen burst up so often. Wouldn't half a dozen do as well,—except for the show of the thing?'

'Half a dozen hounds couldn't hunt a fox, Mr. Gotobed.'

'I guess half a dozen would do just as well, only for the show. What strikes me, Mr. Morton, on visiting this old country is that so much is done for show.'

'What do you say to New York, Mr. Gotobed?'

'There certainly are a couple of hundred fools in New York, who, having more money than brains, amuse themselves by imitating European follies. But you won't find that through the country, Mr. Morton. You won't find a hundred dogs at an American planter's house when ten or twelve would do as well.'

'Hunting is not one of your amusements.'

'Yes, it is. I've been a hunter myself. I've had nothing to eat but what I killed for a month together. That's

more than any of your hunters can say. A hundred dogs
to kill one fox!'

'Not all at the same time, Mr. Gotobed.'

'And you have got none now?'

'I don't hunt myself.'

'And does nobody hunt the foxes about here at present?'
Then Morton explained that on the Saturday following the U.R.U. hounds, under the mastership of that
celebrated sportsman Captain Glomax, would meet at
eleven o'clock exactly at the spot on which they were
then standing, and that if Mr. Gotobed would walk out
after breakfast he would see the whole paraphernalia,
including about half a hundred 'dogs,' and perhaps a
couple of hundred men on horseback. 'I shall be delighted
to see any institution of this great country,' said Mr.
Gotobed, 'however much opposed it may be to my
opinion either of utility or rational recreation.' Then,
having nearly eaten up one cigar, he lit another preparatory to eating it, and sauntered back to the house.

Before dinner that evening there were a few words
between the Paragon and his grandmother. 'I'm afraid
you won't like my American friend,' he said.

'He is all very well, John. Of course, an American
member of Congress can't be an English gentleman. You,
in your position, have to be civil to such people. I dare
say I shall get on very well with Mr. Gotobed.'

'I must get somebody to meet him.'

'Lady Augustus and her daughter are coming.'

'They knew each other in Washington. And there will
be so many ladies.'

'You could ask the Coopers from Mallingham,' suggested the lady.

'I don't think they would dine out. He's getting very old.'

'And I'm told the Mainwarings at Dillsborough are
very nice people,' said Mrs. Morton, who knew that Mr.
Mainwaring at any rate came from a good family.

'I suppose they ought to call first. I never saw them in
my life. Reginald Morton, you know, is living at Hoppet
Hall in Dillsborough.'

'You don't mean to say you wrote to ask him to this house?'

'I think I ought. Why should I take upon myself to quarrel with a man I have not seen since I was a child, and who certainly is my cousin?'

'I do not know that he is your cousin;—nor do you.'

John Morton passed by the calumny which he had heard before, and which he knew that it was no good for him to attempt to subvert. 'He was received here as one of the family, ma'am.'

'I know he was; and with what result?'

'I don't think that I ought to turn my back upon him because my great grandfather left property away from me to him. It would give me a bad name in the county. It would be against me when I settle down to live here. I think quarrelling is the most foolish thing a man can do, —especially with his own relations.'

'I can only say this, John: let me know if he is coming, so that I may not be called upon to meet him. I will not eat at table with Reginald Morton.' So saying, the old lady, in a stately fashion, stalked out of the room.

CHAPTER IX

THE OLD KENNELS

ON the next morning Mrs. Morton asked her grandson what he meant to do with reference to his suggested invitation to Reginald. 'As you will not meet him, of course I have given up the idea,' he said. The 'of course' had been far from true. He had debated the matter very much with himself. He was an obstinate man, with something of independence in his spirit. He liked money, but he liked having his own way too. The old lady looked as though she might live to be a hundred, —and though she might last only for ten years longer, was it worth his while to be a slave for that time? And he was by no means sure of her money, though he should be a slave. He almost made up his mind that he would ask Reginald Morton. But then the old lady would be in her tantrums, and there would be the disagreeable necessity of making an explanation to that inquisitive gentleman Mr. Elias Gotobed.

'I couldn't have met him, John; I couldn't indeed.
I remember so well all that occurred when your poor,
infatuated, old great-grandfather would have that woman
into the house! I was forced to have my meals in my
bedroom, and to get myself taken away as soon as I could
get a carriage and horses. After all that, I ought not to
be asked to meet the child.'

'I was thinking of asking old Mr. Cooper on Monday.
I know she doesn't go out. And perhaps Mr. Mainwaring
wouldn't take it amiss. Mr. Puttock, I know, isn't at
home; but if he were he couldn't come.' Mr. Puttock was
the rector of Bragton, a very rich living, but was unfortunately afflicted with asthma.

'Poor man! I heard of that; and he's only been here
about six years. I don't see why Mr. Mainwaring should
take it amiss at all. You can explain that you are only
here a few days. I like to meet clergymen. I think that it
is the duty of a country gentleman to ask them to his
house. It shows a proper regard for religion. By the by,
John, I hope that you'll see that they have a fire in the
church on Sunday.' The Honourable Mrs. Morton always
went to church, and had no doubt of her own sincerity
when she reiterated her prayer that as she forgave others
their trespasses, so might she be forgiven hers. As
Reginald Morton had certainly never trespassed against
her perhaps there was no reason why her thoughts should
be carried to the necessity of forgiving him.

The Paragon wrote two very diplomatic notes, explaining his temporary residence and expressing his great
desire to become acquainted with his neighbours. Neither
of the two clergymen was offended, and both of them
promised to eat his dinner on Monday. Mr. Mainwaring
was very fond of dining out, and would have gone almost to
any gentleman's house. Mr. Cooper was old enough in the
neighbourhood to have known the old squire, and wrote an
affectionate note expressing his gratification at the prospect
of renewing his acquaintance with the little boy whom he
remembered. So the party was made up for Monday.
John Morton was very nervous on the matter, feeling that
Lady Augustus would think the land to be barren.

The Friday passed by without much difficulty. The
Senator was driven about, and everything was inquired
into. One or two farmhouses were visited, and the
farmers' wives were much disturbed by the questions
asked them. 'I don't think they'd get a living in the
States,' was the Senator's remark after leaving one of the
homesteads in which neither the farmer nor his wife had
shown much power of conversation. 'Then they're right
to stay where they are,' replied Mr. Morton, who in spite
of his diplomacy could not save himself from being
nettled. 'They seem to get a very good living here, and
they pay their rent punctually.'

On the Saturday morning the hounds met at the 'Old
Kennels,' as the meet was always called, and here was an
excellent opportunity of showing to Mr. Gotobed one
of the great institutions of the country. It was close to
the house and therefore could be reached without any
trouble, and as it was held on Morton's own ground, he
could do more towards making his visitor understand the
thing than might have been possible elsewhere. When
the hounds moved, the carriage would be ready to take
them about the roads, and show them as much as could
be seen on wheels.

Punctually at eleven John Morton and his American
guest were on the bridge, and Tony Tuppett was already
occupying his wonted place, seated on a strong grey mare
that had done a great deal of work, but would live,—as
Tony used to say,—to do a great deal more. Round him
the hounds were clustered,—twenty-three couple in all,—
some seated on their haunches, some standing obediently
still, while a few moved about restlessly, subject to the
voices and on one or two occasions to a gentle administra-
tion of thong from the attendant whips. Four or five
horsemen were clustering round, most of them farmers,
and were talking to Tony. Our friend Mr. Twentyman
was the only man in a red coat who had yet arrived, and
with him, on her brown pony, was Kate Masters, who was
listening with all her ears to every word that Tony said.

'That, I guess, is the Captain you spoke of,' said the
Senator pointing to Tony Tuppett.

'Oh no,—that's the huntsman. Those three men in caps are the servants who do the work.'

'The dogs can't be brought out without servants to mind them! They're what you call gamekeepers.' Morton was explaining that the men were not game-keepers when Captain Glomax himself arrived, driving a tandem: There was no road up to the spot, but on hunt mornings,—or at any rate when the meet was at the old kennels,—the park-gates were open so that vehicles could come up on the green sward.

'That's Captain Glomax, I suppose,' said Morton; 'I don't know him, but from the way he's talking to the huntsmen you may be sure of it.'

'He is the great man, is he? All these dogs belong to him?'

'Either to him or the hunt.'

'And he pays for those servants?'

'Certainly.'

'He is a very rich man, I suppose.' Then Mr. Morton endeavoured to explain the position of Captain Glomax. He was not rich. He was no one in particular except Captain Glomax; and his one attribute was a knowledge of hunting. He didn't keep the 'dogs' out of his own pocket. He received £2000 a year from the gentlemen of the county, and he himself only paid anything which the hounds and horses might cost over that. 'He's a sort of upper servant then?' asked the Senator.

'Not at all. He's the greatest man in the county on hunting days.'

'Does he live out of it?'

'I should think not.'

'It's a deal of trouble, isn't it?'

'Full work for an active man's time, I should say.' A great many more questions were asked and answered, at the end of which the Senator declared that he did not quite understand it, but that as far as he saw he did not think very much of Captain Glomax.

'If he could make a living out of it I should respect him,' said the Senator;—'though it's like knife-grinding or handling arsenic,—an unwholesome sort of profession.'

'I think they look very nice,' said Morton, as one or two well-turned-out young men rode up to the place.

'They seem to me to have thought more about their breeches* than anything else,' said the Senator. 'But if they're going to hunt why don't they hunt? Have they got a fox with them?' Then there was a further explanation.

At this moment there was a murmur as of a great coming arrival, and then an open carriage with four post-horses was brought at a quick trot into the open space. There were four men dressed for hunting inside, and two others on the box. They were all smoking, and all talking. It was easy to see that they did not consider themselves the least among those who were gathered together on this occasion. The carriage was immediately surrounded by grooms and horses, and the ceremony of disencumbering themselves of great coats and aprons, of putting on spurs and fastening hat-strings, was commenced. Then there were whispered communications from the grooms, and long faces under some of the hats. This horse hadn't been fit since last Monday's run, and that man's hack wasn't as it should be. A muttered curse might have been heard from one gentleman as he was told, on jumping from the box, that Harry Stubbings hadn't sent him any second horse to ride. 'I didn't hear nothing about it till yesterday, Captain,' said Harry Stubbings, 'and every foot I had fit to come out was bespoke.' The groom, however, who heard this was quite aware that Mr. Stubbings did not wish to give unlimited credit to the Captain, and he knew also that the second horse was to have carried his master the whole day, as the animal which was brought to the meet had been ridden hard on the previous Wednesday. At all this the Senator looked with curious eyes, thinking that he had never in his life seen brought together a set of more useless human beings.

'That is Lord Rufford,' said Morton, pointing to a stout, ruddy-faced, handsome man of about thirty, who was the owner of the carriage.

'Oh, a lord. Do the lords hunt generally?'

'That's as they like it.'

'Senators with us wouldn't have time for that,' said the Senator.

'But you are paid to do your work.'

'Everybody from whom work is expected should be paid. Then the work will be done, or those who pay will know the reason why.'

'I must speak to Lord Rufford,' said Morton. 'If you'll come with me, I'll introduce you.' The Senator followed willingly enough, and the introduction was made while his lordship was still standing by his horse. The two men had known each other in London, and it was natural that Morton, as owner of the ground, should come out and speak to the only man who knew him. It soon was spread about that the gentleman talking to Lord Rufford was John Morton, and many who lived in the county came up to shake hands with him. To some of these the Senator was introduced, and the conversation for a few minutes seemed to interrupt the business on hand. 'I am sorry you should be on foot, Mr. Gotobed,' said the lord.

'And I am sorry that I cannot mount him,' said Mr. Morton.

'We can soon get over that difficulty if he will allow me to offer him a horse.'

The Senator looked as though he would almost like it, but he didn't quite like it. 'Perhaps your horse might kick me off, my lord?'

'I can't answer for that; but he isn't given to kicking, and there he is, if you'll get on him.' But the Senator felt that the exhibition would suit neither his age nor position, and refused.

'We'd better be moving,' said Captain Glomax. 'I suppose, Lord Rufford, we might as well trot over to Dillsborough Wood at once. I saw Bean as I came along, and he seemed to wish we should draw the wood first.' Then there was a little whispering between his lordship and the Master and Tony Tuppett. His lordship thought that as Mr. Morton was there the hounds might as well be run through the Bragton spinnies. Tony made a wry face and shook his head. He knew that, though the old

kennels might be a very good place for meeting, there was
no chance of finding a fox at Bragton. And Captain
Glomax, who, being an itinerary master, had no respect
whatever for a country gentleman who didn't preserve,
also made a long face and also shook his head. But Lord
Rufford, who knew the wisdom of reconciling a new-
comer in the county to foxhunting, prevailed and the
hounds and men were taken round a part of Bragton
Park. 'What'd t' old squire 've said if he'd 've known
there hadn't been a fox at Bragton for more nor ten year?'
This remark was made by Tuppett to Mr. Runciman,
who was riding by him. Mr. Runciman replied that
there was a great difference in people. 'You may say
that, Mr. Runciman. It's all changes. His lordship's
father couldn't bear the sight of a hound nor a horse and
saddle. Well;—I suppose I needn't gammon any furder.
We'll just trot across to the wood at once.'

'They haven't begun yet as far as I can see,' said Mr.
Gotobed standing up in the carriage.

'They haven't found as yet,' replied Morton.

'They must go on till they find a fox? They never
bring him with them?' Then there was an explanation
as to bagged foxes, Morton not being very conversant with
the subject he had to explain. 'And if they shouldn't find
one all day?'

'Then it'll be a blank.'

'And these hundred gentlemen will go home quite
satisfied with themselves?'

'No;—they'll go home quite dissatisfied.'

'And have paid their money and given their time for
nothing? Do you know it doesn't seem to me the most
heart-stirring thing in the world? Don't they ride faster
than that?' At this moment Tony with the hounds at his
heels was trotting across the park at a huntsman's usual
pace from covert to covert. The Senator was certainly
ungracious. Nothing that he saw produced from him
a single word expressive of satisfaction.

Less than a mile brought them to the gate and road
leading up to Chowton Farm. They passed direct by
Larry Twentyman's door, and not a few, though it was

not yet more than half-past eleven, stopped to have a glass of Larry's beer. When the hounds were in the neighbour-hood Larry's beer was always ready. But Tony and his attendants trotted by with eyes averted, as though no thought of beer was in their minds. Nothing had been done, and a huntsman is not entitled to beer till he has found a fox. Captain Glomax followed with Lord Rufford and a host of others. There was plenty of way here for carriages, and half a dozen vehicles passed through Larry's farmyard. Immediately behind the house was a meadow, and at the bottom of the meadow a stubble field,* next to which was a ditch and bank which formed the bounds of Dillsborough Wood. Just at this side of the gate leading into the stubble-field there was already a concourse of people when Tony arrived near it with the hounds, and immediately there was a halloaing and loud screeching of directions, which was soon understood to mean that the hounds were at once to be taken away. The Captain rode on rapidly, and then sharply gave his orders. Tony was to take the hounds back to Mr. Twentyman's farm-yard as fast as he could, and shut them up in a barn. The whips were put into violent commotion. Tony was eagerly at work. Not a hound was to be allowed near the gate. And then, as the crowd of horsemen and carriages came on, the word 'poison' was passed among them from mouth to mouth.

'What does all this mean?' said the Senator.

'I don't at all know. I'm afraid there's something wrong,' replied Morton.

'I heard that man say "poison". They have taken the dogs back again.' Then the Senator and Morton got out of the carriage and made their way into the crowd. The riders who had grooms on second horses were soon on foot and a circle was made, inside which there was some object of intense interest. In the meantime the hounds had been secured in one of Mr. Twentyman's barns.

What was that object of interest shall be told in the next chapter.

CHAPTER X

GOARLY'S REVENGE

THE Senator and Morton followed close on the steps of Lord Rufford and Captain Glomax, and were thus able to make their way into the centre of the crowd. There, on a clean sward of grass, laid out as carefully as though he were a royal child prepared for burial, was—a dead fox. 'It's p'ison, my lord; it's p'ison to a moral,' said Bean, who as keeper of the wood was bound to vindicate himself, and his master, and the wood. 'Feel of him, how stiff he is.' A good many did feel, but Lord Rufford stood still and looked at the poor victim in silence. 'It's easy knowing how he came by it,' said Bean.

The men around gazed into each other's faces with a sad tragic air, as though the occasion were one which at the first blush was too melancholy for many words. There was whispering here and there, and one young farmer's son gave a deep sigh, like a steam-engine beginning to work, and rubbed his eyes with the back of his hand. 'There ain't nothin' too bad,—nothin',' said another,—leaving his audience to imagine whether he were alluding to the wretchedness of the world in general or to the punishment which was due to the perpetrator of this nefarious act. The dreadful word 'vulpecide'*was heard from various lips with an oath or two before it. 'It makes me sick of my own land, to think it should be done so near,' said Larry Twentyman, who had just come up. Mr. Runciman declared that they must set their wits to work not only to find the criminal but to prove the crime against him, and offered to subscribe a couple of sovereigns on the spot to a common fund to be raised for the purpose. 'I don't know what is to be done with a country like this,' said Captain Glomax, who, as an itinerant, was not averse to cast a slur upon the land of his present sojourn.

'I don't remember anything like it on my property before,' said the lord, standing up for his own estate and the county at large.

'Nor in the hunt,' said young Hampton. 'Of course such a thing may happen anywhere. They had foxes poisoned in the Pytchley last year.'

'It shows a d—— bad feeling somewhere,' said the Master.

'We know very well where the feeling is,' said Bean, who had by this time taken up the fox, determined not to allow it to pass into any hands less careful than his own.

'It's that scoundrel Goarly,' said one of the Botseys. Then there was an indignant murmur heard, first of all from two or three, and then running among the whole crowd. Everybody knew as well as though he had seen it that Goarly had baited meat with strychnine and put it down in the wood. 'Might have p'isoned half the pack!' said Tony Tuppett, who had come up on foot from the barn where the hounds were still imprisoned, and had caught hold in an affectionate manner of a fore pad of the fox, which Bean had clutched by the two hind legs. Poor Tony Tuppett almost shed tears as he looked at the dead animal, and thought what might have been the fate of the pack. 'It's him, my lord,' he said, 'as we run through Littleton gorse Monday after Christmas last, and up to Impington Park, where he got away from us in a hollow tree. He's four year old,' added Tony, looking at the animal's mouth, 'and there warn't a finer dog fox in the county.'

'Do they know all the foxes?' asked the Senator. In answer to this Morton only shook his head, not feeling quite sure himself how far a huntsman's acquaintance in that line might go, and being also too much impressed by the occasion for speculative conversation.

'It's that scoundrel Goarly,' had been repeated again and again; and then on a sudden Goarly himself was seen standing on the further hedge of Larry's field with a gun in his hand. He was not at this time above two hundred yards from them, and was declared by one of the young farmers to be grinning with delight. The next field was Goarly's, but the hedge and ditch belonged to Twenty-man. Larry rushed forward as though determined to thrash the man, and two or three followed him. But

Lord Rufford galloped on and stopped them. 'Don't get into a row with a fellow like that,' he said to Twentyman.

'He's on my land, my lord,' said Larry impatiently.

'I'm on my own now, and let me see who'll dare to touch me,' said Goarly, jumping down.

'You've put poison down in that wood,' said Larry.

'No I didn't, but I knows who did. It ain't I as am afeard for my young turkeys.' Now it was well known that old Mrs. Twentyman, Larry's mother, was fond of young turkeys, and that her poultry-yard had suffered. Larry, in his determination to be a gentleman, had always laughed at his mother's losses. But now to be accused in this way was terrible to his feelings. He made a rush as though to jump over the hedge, but Lord Rufford again intercepted him. 'I didn't think, Mr. Twentyman, that you'd care for what such a fellow as that might say.' By this time Lord Rufford was off his horse, and had taken hold of Larry.

'I'll tell you all what it is,' screamed Goarly, standing just at the edge of his own field; 'if a hound comes out of the wood on to my land, I'll shoot him. I don't know nothing about p'isoning, though I dare say Mr. Twentyman does. But if a hound comes on my land, I'll shoot him,—open before you all.' There was, however, no danger of such a threat being executed on this day, as of course no hound would be allowed to go into Dillsborough Wood.

Twentyman was reluctantly brought back into the meadow where the horses were standing, and then a consultation was held as to what they should do next. There were some who thought that the hounds should be taken home for the day. It was as though some special friend of the U.R.U. had died that morning, and that the spirits of the sportsmen were too dejected for their sport. Others, with prudent foresight, suggested that the hounds might run back from some distant covert to Dillsborough, and that there should be no hunting till the wood had been thoroughly searched. But the strangers, especially those who had hired horses, would not hear of this; and, after considerable delay, it was arranged that the hounds should be trotted off as quickly as possible to Impington Gorse, which was on the other side of Impington Park, and fully five miles distant. And so they started, leaving the dead fox in the hands of Bean, the gamekeeper.

'Is this the sort of thing that occurs every day?' asked the Senator as he got back into the carriage.

'I should fancy not,' answered Morton. 'Somebody has poisoned a fox, and I don't think that that is very often done about here.'

'Why did he poison him?'

'To save his fowls, I suppose.'

'Why shouldn't he poison him if the fox takes his fowls? Fowls are better than foxes.'

'Not in this country,' said Morton.

'Then I'm very glad I don't live here,' said Mr. Gotobed. 'These friends of yours are dressed very nicely and look very well; but a fox is a nasty animal. It was that man standing on the bank, wasn't it?' continued the Senator, who was determined to understand it all to the very bottom, in reference to certain lectures which he intended to give on his return to the States, and perhaps also in the old country before he left it.

'They suspect him.'

'That man with the gun! One man against two hundred! Now, I respect that man; I do with all my heart.'

'You had better not say so here, Mr. Gotobed.'

'I know how full of prejudice you all are, but I do respect him. If I comprehend the matter rightly, he was on his own land when we saw him.'

'Yes; that was his own field.'

'And they meant to ride across it, whether he liked it or no?'

'Everybody rides across everybody's land out hunting.'

'Would they ride across your park, Mr. Morton, if you didn't let them?'

'Certainly they would,—and break down all my gates if I had them locked, and pull down my park pailings to let the hounds through.'

'And you could get no compensation?'

'Practically none. And certainly I should not try. The greatest enemy to hunting in the whole county would not be foolish enough to make the attempt.'

'Why so?'

'He would get no satisfaction, and everybody would hate him.'

'Then I respect that man the more. What is that man's name?' Morton hadn't heard the name, or had forgotten it. 'I shall find that man out, and have some conversation with him, Mr. Morton. I respect that man, Mr. Morton. He's one against two hundred, and he insists upon his rights. Those men standing round and wiping their eyes, and stifled with grief because a fox had been poisoned, as though some great patriot had died among them in the service of his country, formed one of the most remarkable phenomena, sir, that ever I beheld in any country. When I get among my own people in Mikewa and tell them that,—they won't believe me, sir.'

In the meantime the cavalcade was hurrying away to Impington Gorse, and John Morton, feeling that he had not had an opportunity as yet of showing his American friend the best side of hunting, went with them. The five miles were five long miles, and as the pace was not above seven miles an hour, nearly an hour was occupied. There was therefore plenty of opportunity for the Senator to inquire whether the gentlemen around him were as yet enjoying their sport. There was an air of triumph about him as to the misfortunes of the day, joined to a battery of continued raillery, which made it almost impossible for Morton to keep his temper. He asked whether it was not at any rate better than trotting a pair of horses backwards and forwards over the same mile of road for half the day, as is the custom in the States. But the Senator, though he did not quite approve of trotting matches, argued that there was infinitely more of skill and ingenuity in the American pastime. 'Everybody is so gloomy,' said the Senator, lighting his third cigar. 'I've been watching that young man in pink boots for the last half hour, and he hasn't spoken a word to any one.'

'Perhaps he's a stranger,' said Morton.

'And that's the way you treat him!'

It was past two when the hounds were put into the Gorse, and certainly no one was in a very good humour. A trot of five miles is disagreeable, and two o'clock in November is late for finding a first fox; and then poisoning is a vice that may grow into a habit! There was a general feeling that Goarly ought to be extinguished, but an idea that it might be difficult to extinguish him. The whips, nevertheless, cantered to the corner of the covert, and Tony put in his hounds with a cheery voice. The Senator remarked that the Gorse was a very little place,—for as they were on the side of a hill they could not see it all. Lord Rufford, who was standing by the carriage, explained to him that it was a favourite resort of foxes, and difficult to draw, as being very close. 'Perhaps they've poisoned him too,' said the Senator. It was evident from his voice that had such been the case, he would not have been among the mourners. 'The blackguards are not yet thick enough in our country for that,' said Lord Rufford, meaning to be sarcastic.

Then a whimper was heard from a hound,—at first very low, and then growing into a fuller sound. 'There he is,' said young Hampton. 'For Heaven's sake get those fellows away from that side, Glomax!' This was uttered with so much vehemence that the Senator looked up in surprise. Then the Captain galloped round the side of the covert, and, making use of some strong language, stopped the ardour of certain gentlemen who were in a hurry to get away on what they considered good terms. Lord Rufford, Hampton, Larry Twentyman, and others sat stock-still on their horses, watching the Gorse. Fred Botsey urged himself a little forward down the hill, and was creeping on when Captain Glomax asked him whether he would be so ——— obliging kind as to remain where he was for half a minute. Fred took the observation in good part and stopped his horse. 'Does he do all that cursing and swearing for the £2000?' asked the Senator.

The fox traversed the Gorse back from side to side and from corner to corner again and again. There were two sides certainly at which he might break, but though he came out more than once he could not be got to go away.

'They'll kill him now before he breaks,' said the elder Botsey.

'Brute!' exclaimed his brother.

'They're hot on him now,' said Hampton. At this time the whole side of the hill was ringing with the music of the hounds.

'He was out then, but Dick turned him,' said Larry. Dick was one of the whips.

'Will you be so kind, Mr. Morton,' asked the Senator, 'as to tell me whether they're hunting yet? They've been at it for three hours and a half, and I should like to know when they begin to amuse themselves.'

Just as he had spoken there came from Dick a cry that he was away. Tony, who had been down at the side of the Gorse, at once jumped into it, knowing the passage through. Lord Rufford, who for the last five or six minutes had sat perfectly still on his horse, started down the hill as though he had been thrown from a catapult. There was a little hand-gate through which it was expedient to pass, and in a minute a score of men were jostling for the way, among whom were the two Botseys, our friend Runciman, and Larry Twentyman, with Kate Masters on the pony close behind him. Young Hampton jumped a very nasty fence by the side of the wicket, and Lord Rufford followed him. A score of elderly men, with some young men among them too, turned back into a lane behind them, having watched long enough to see that they were to take the lane to the left, and not the lane to the right. After all, there was time enough, for when the men had got through the hand-gate the hounds were hardly free of the covert, and Tony, riding up the side of the hill opposite, was still blowing his horn. But they were off at last, and the bulk of the field got away on good terms with the hounds. 'Now they are hunting,' said Mr. Morton to the Senator.

'They all seemed to be very angry with each other at that narrow gate.'

'They were in a hurry, I suppose.'

'Two of them jumped over the hedge. Why didn't they

all jump? How long will it be now before they catch him?'

'Very probably they may not catch him at all.'

'Not catch him after all that! Then the man was certainly right to poison that other fox in the wood. How long will they go on?'

'Half an hour perhaps.'

'And you call that hunting! Is it worth the while of all those men to expend all that energy for such a result? Upon the whole, Mr. Morton, I should say that it is one of the most incomprehensible things that I have ever seen in the course of a rather long and varied life. Shooting I can understand, for you have your pheasants. Fishing I can understand, as you have your fish. Here you get a fox to begin with, and are all broken-hearted. Then you come across another, after riding about all day, and the chances are you can't catch him!'

'I suppose,' said Mr. Morton angrily, 'the habits of one country are incomprehensible to another. When I see Americans loafing about in the bar-room of an hotel, I am lost in amazement.'

'There is not a man you see who couldn't give a reason for his being there. He has an object in view,—though perhaps it may be no better than to rob his neighbour. But here there seems to be no possible motive.'

CHAPTER XI

FROM IMPINGTON GORSE

THE fox ran straight from the coverts through his well-known haunts to Impington Park, and as the hounds were astray there for two or three minutes there was a general idea that he too had got up into a tree,— which would have amused the Senator very much had the Senator been there. But neither had the country nor the pace been adapted to wheels, and the Senator and the Paragon were now returning along the road to Bragton. The fox had tried his old earths at Impington High Wood, and had then skulked back along the outside of the covert. Had not one of the whips seen him he would have been troubled no further on that day,—a fact, which if it could have been explained to the Senator in all its bearings, would greatly have added to his delight. But Dick viewed him; and with many holloas and much blowing of horns, and prayers from Captain Glomax that gentlemen would only be so good as to hold their tongues, and a full-tongued volley of abuse from half the field against an unfortunate gentleman who rode after the escaping fox before a hound was out of the covert, they settled again to their business. It was pretty to see the quiet ease and apparent nonchalance and almost affected absence of bustle of those who knew their work,—among whom were especially to be named young Hampton, and the elder Botsey, and Lord Rufford, and, above all, a dark-visaged, long-whiskered, sombre, military man who had been in the carriage with Lord Rufford, and who had hardly spoken a word to any one the whole day. This was the celebrated Major Caneback, known to all the world as one of the dullest men and best riders across country that England had ever produced. But he was not so dull but that he knew how to make use of his accomplishment, so as always to be able to get a mount on a friend's horse. If a man wanted to make a horse, or to try a horse, or to sell a horse, or to buy a horse, he delighted to put Major Caneback up. The Major was sympathetic and made his friend's horses, and tried them, and sold them. Then he would take his two bottles of wine,—of course from his friend's cellar,—and when asked about the day's sport would be oracular in two words, 'Rather slow,' 'Quick spurt,' 'Goodish thing,' 'Regularly mulled,'* and such like. Nevertheless, it was a great thing to have Major Caneback with you. To the list of those who rode well and quietly must in justice be added our friend Larry Twentyman, who was in truth a good horseman. And he had three things to do, which it was difficult enough to combine. He had a young horse which he would have liked to sell; he had to coach Kate Masters on his pony; and he desired to ride like Major Caneback.

From Impington Park they went in a straight line to

Littleton Gorse, skirting certain small woods which the
fox disdained to enter. Here the pace was very good, and
the country was all grass. It was the very cream of
U.R.U.; and could the Senator have read the feelings of
the dozen leading men in the run, he would have owned
that they were for the time satisfied with their amusement.
Could he have read Kate Masters' feelings he would have
had to own that she was in an earthly Paradise. When
the pony paused at the big brook, brought his four legs
steadily down on the brink as though he were going to
bathe, then with a bend of his back leaped to the other
side, dropping his hind legs in and instantly recovering
them, and when she saw that Larry had waited just a
moment for her, watching to see what might be her fate,
she was in heaven. 'Wasn't it a big one, Larry?' she asked
in her triumph. 'He did go in behind!' 'Those cats of
things always do it somehow,' Larry replied, darting forward again and keeping the Major well in his eye. The
brook had stopped one or two, and tidings came up that
Fred Botsey had broken his horse's back. The knowledge
of the brook had sent some round by the road,—steady
riding men such as Mr. Runciman and Doctor Nupper.
Captain Glomax had got into it and came up afterwards
wet through, with temper by no means improved. But
the glory of the day had been the way in which Lord
Rufford's young bay mare, who had never seen a brook
before, had flown over it with the Major on her back,
taking it, as Larry afterwards described, 'just in her stride,
without condescending to look at it. I was just behind
the Major, and saw her do it.' Larry understood that
a man should never talk of his own place in a run, but he
didn't quite understand that neither should he talk of
having been close to another man who was supposed to
have had the best of it. Lord Rufford, who didn't talk
much of these things, quite understood that he had
received full value for his billet and mount in the improved
character of his mare.

Then there was a little difficulty at the boundary fence
of Impington Hall Farm. The Major, who didn't know
the ground, tried it at an impracticable place, and

brought his mare down. But she fell at the right side, and he was quick enough in getting away from her, not to fall under her in the ditch. Tony Tuppet, who knew every foot of that double ditch and bank, and every foot in the hedge above, kept well to the left and crept through a spot where one ditch ran into the other, intersecting of the fence. Tony, like a knowing huntsman as he was, rode always for the finish, and not for immediate glory. Both Lord Rufford and Hampton, who in spite of their affected nonchalance were in truth rather riding against one another, took it all in a fly, choosing a lighter spot than that which the Major had encountered. Larry had longed to follow them, or rather to take it alongside of them, but was mindful at last of Kate and hurried down the ditch to the spot which Tony had chosen, and which was now crowded by horsemen. 'He would have done it as well as the best of them,' said Kate, panting for breath.

'We're all right,' said Larry. 'Follow me. Don't let them hustle you out. Now, Mat, can't you make way for a lady half a minute?' Mat growled, quite understanding the use which was being made of Kate Masters; but he did give way and was rewarded with a gracious smile. 'You are going uncommon well, Miss Kate,' said Mat, 'and I won't stop you.' 'I am so much obliged to you, Mr. Ruggles,' said Kate, not scrupling for a moment to take the advantage offered her. The fox had turned a little to the left, which was in Larry's favour, and the Major was now close to him, covered on one side with mud, but still looking as though the mud were all right. There are some men who can crush their hats, have their boots and breeches full of water, and be covered with dirt from their faces downwards, and yet look as though nothing were amiss, while, with others, the marks of a fall are always provocative either of pity or ridicule. 'I hope you're not hurt, Major Caneback,' said Larry, glad of the occasion to speak to so distinguished an individual. The Major grunted as he rode on, finding no necessity here even for his customary two words. Little accidents, such as that, were the price he paid for his day's entertainment.

As they got within view of Littleton Gorse, Hampton,

Lord Rufford, and Tony had the best of it, though two or
three farmers were very close to them. At this moment
Tony's mind was much disturbed, and he looked round
more than once for Captain Glomax, Captain Glomax
had got into the brook, and had then ridden down to the
high road which ran here near to them, and which, as he
knew, ran within one field of the Gorse. He had lost his
place and had got a ducking, and was a little out of
humour with things in general. It had not been his
purpose to go to Impington on this day, and he was still,
in his mind, saying evil things of the U.R.U. respecting
that poisoned fox. Perhaps he was thinking, as itinerant
masters often must think, that it was very hard to have to
bear so many unpleasant things for a poor £2000 a year,
and meditating, as he had done for the last two seasons,
a threat that unless the money was increased, he wouldn't
hunt the country more than three times a week. As Tony
got near to the Gorse and also near to the road, he
managed with infinite skill to get the hounds off the scent,
and to make a fictitious cast to the left as though he
thought the fox had traversed that way. Tony knew well
enough that the fox was at that moment in Littleton
Gorse; but he knew also that the Gorse was only six acres,
that such a fox as he had before him wouldn't stay there
two minutes after the first hound was in it, and that Dillsborough Wood—which to his imagination was full of
poison—would then be only a mile and a half before him.
Tony, whose fault was a tendency to mystery,—as is the
fault of most huntsmen,—having accomplished his object
in stopping the hounds, pretended to cast about with
great diligence. He crossed the road and was down one
side of a field and along another, looking anxiously for
the Captain. 'The fox has gone on to the Gorse,' said the
elder Botsey; 'what a stupid old pig he is!'—meaning
that Tony Tuppet was the pig.

'He was seen going on,' said Larry, who had come
across a man mending a drain.

'It would be his run of course,' said Hampton, who was
generally up to Tony's wiles, but who was now as much
in the dark as others. Then four or five rode up to the

huntsman and told him that the fox had been seen heading for the Gorse. Tony said not a word, but bit his lips and scratched his head and bethought himself what fools men might be, even though they did ride to hounds. One word of explanation would have settled it all, but he would not speak that word till he whispered it to Captain Glomax.

In the meantime there was a crowd in the road waiting to see the result of Tony's manœuvres. And then, as is usual on such occasions, a little mild repartee went about, —what the sportsmen themselves would have called 'chaff'. Fred Botsey came up, not having broken his horse's back as had been rumoured, but having had to drag the brute out of the brook with the help of two countrymen; and the Major was asked about his fall till he was forced to open his mouth. 'Double ditch;—mare fell;—matter of course.' And then he got himself out of the crowd, disgusted with the littleness of mankind. Lord Rufford had been riding a very big chestnut horse, and had watched the anxious struggles of Kate Masters to hold her place. Kate, though fifteen, and quite up to that age in intelligence and impudence, was small and looked almost a child. 'That's a nice pony of yours, my dear,' said the lord. Kate, who didn't quite like being called 'my dear,' but who knew that a lord has privileges, said that it was a very good pony. 'Suppose we change,' said his lordship. 'Could you ride my horse?' 'He's very big,' said Kate. 'You'd look like a tom-tit on a haystack,' said his lordship. 'And if you got on my pony, you'd look like a haystack on a tom-tit,' said Kate. Then it was felt that Kate Masters had had the best of that little encounter. 'Yes;—I got one there,' said Lord Rufford, while his friends were laughing at him.

At length Captain Glomax was seen in the road and Tony was with him at once, whispering in his ear that the hounds if allowed to go on would certainly run into Dillsborough Wood. 'D—— the hounds,' muttered the Captain; but he knew too well what he was about, to face so terrible a danger. 'They're going home,' he said as soon as he had joined Lord Rufford and the crowd.

'Going home!' exclaimed a pink-coated young rider of a hired horse which had been going well with him; and as he said so he looked at his watch.

'Unless you particularly wish me to take the hounds to some covert twenty miles off,' answered the sarcastic master.

'The fox certainly went on to Littleton,' said the elder Botsey.

'My dear fellow,' said the Captain, 'I can tell you where the fox went quite as well as you can tell me. Do allow a man to know what he's about sometimes.'

'It isn't generally the custom here to take the hounds off a running fox,' continued Botsey, who subscribed £50, and did not like being snubbed.

'And it isn't generally the custom to have fox-coverts poisoned,' said the Captain, assuming to himself the credit due to Tony's sagacity. 'If you wish to be master of these hounds I haven't the slightest objection, but while I'm responsible you must allow me to do my work according to my own judgment.' Then the thing was understood, and Captain Glomax was allowed to carry off the hounds and his ill-humour without another word.

But just at that moment, while the hounds and the master, and Lord Rufford and his friends, were turning back in their own direction, John Morton came up with his carriage and the Senator. 'Is it all over?' asked the Senator.

'All over for to-day,' said Lord Rufford.

'Did you catch the animal?'

'No, Mr. Gotobed; we couldn't catch him. To tell the truth, we didn't try; but we had a nice little skurry*for four or five miles.'

'Some of you look very wet.' Captain Glomax and Fred Botsey were standing near the carriage; but the Captain as soon as he heard this, broke into a trot and followed the hounds.

'Some of us are very wet,' said Fred. 'That's part of the fun.'

'Oh,—that's part of the fun. You found one fox dead and you didn't kill another because you didn't try. Well;

Mr. Morton, I don't think I shall take to fox-hunting even though they should introduce it in Mikewa. What's become of the rest of the men?'

'Most of them are in the brook,' said Fred Botsey as he rode on towards Dillsborough.

Mr. Runciman was also there and trotted on homewards with Botsey, Larry, and Kate Masters. 'I think I've won my bet,' said the hotel-keeper.

'I don't see that at all. We didn't find in Dillsborough Wood.'

'I say we did find in Dillsborough Wood. We found a fox, though unfortunately the poor brute was dead.'

'The bet's off, I should say. What do you say, Larry?'

Then Runciman argued his case at great length and with much ability. It had been intended that the bet should be governed by the fact whether Dillsborough Wood did or did not contain a fox on that morning. He himself had backed the wood, and Botsey had been strong in his opinion against the wood. Which of them had been practically right? Had not the presence of the poisoned fox shown that he was right? 'I think you ought to pay,' said Larry.

'All right,' said Botsey riding on, and telling himself that that was what came from making a bet with a man who was not a gentleman.

'He's as unhappy about that hat,' said Runciman, 'as though beer had gone down a penny a gallon.'

CHAPTER XII

ARABELLA TREFOIL

ON the Sunday the party from Bragton went to the parish church—and found it very cold. The duty was done by a young curate who lived in Dillsborough, there being no house in Bragton for him. The rector himself had not been in the church for the last six months, being an invalid. At present he and his wife were away in London, but the vicarage was kept up for his use. The service was certainly not alluring. It was a very wet morning and the curate had ridden over from Dills-borough on a little pony which the rector kept for him in addition to the £100 per annum paid for his services. That he should have got over his service quickly was not a matter of surprise, nor was it wonderful that there should have been no soul-stirring matter in his discourse, as he had two sermons to preach every week and to per-form single-handed all the other clerical duties of a parish lying four miles distant from his lodgings. Perhaps had he expected the presence of so distinguished a critic as the Senator from Mikewa he might have done better. As it was, being nearly wet through and muddy up to his knees, he did not do the work very well. When Morton and his friends left the church and got into the carriage for their half-mile drive home across the park, Mrs. Morton was the first to speak. 'John,' she said, 'that church is enough to give any woman her death. I won't go there any more.'

'They don't understand warming a church in the country,' said John apologetically.

'Is it not a little too large for the congregation?' asked the Senator.

The church was large and straggling and ill-arranged, and on this particular Sunday had been almost empty. There was in it an harmonium, which Mrs. Puttock played when she was at home, but in her absence the attempt made by a few rustics to sing the hymns had not been a musical success. The whole affair had been very sad, and so the Paragon had felt it, who knew,—and was remembering through the whole service,—how these things are done in transatlantic cities.

'The weather kept the people away, I suppose,' said Morton.

'Does that gentleman generally draw large congrega-tions?' asked the persistent Senator.

'We don't go in for drawing congregations here.' Under the cross-examination of his guest, the Secretary of Legation almost lost his diplomatic good temper. 'We have a church in every parish for those who choose to attend it.'

'And very few do choose,' said the Senator. 'I can't say that they're wrong.' There seemed at the moment to be no necessity to carry the disagreeable conversation any further as they had now reached the house. Mrs. Morton immediately went upstairs, and the two gentlemen took themselves to the fire in the so-called library, which room was being used as more commodious than the big drawing-room. Mr. Gotobed placed himself on the rug with his back to the fire and immediately reverted to the church. 'That gentleman is paid by tithes, I suppose.'

'He's not the rector. He's a curate.'

'Ah;—just so. He looked like a curate. Doesn't the rector do anything?' Then Morton, who was by this time heartily sick of explaining, explained the unfortunate state of Mr. Puttock's health, and the conversation was carried on till gradually the Senator learned that Mr. Puttock received £800 a year and a house for doing nothing, and that he paid his deputy £100 a year with the use of a pony. 'And how long will that be allowed to go on, Mr. Morton?' asked the Senator.

To all these inquiries Morton found himself compelled not only to answer, but to answer the truth. Any prevarication or attempt at mystification fell to the ground at once under the Senator's tremendous powers of inquiry. It had been going on for four years and would probably go on now till Mr. Puttock died. 'A man of his age with the asthma may live for twenty years,' said the Senator, who had already learned that Mr. Puttock was only fifty. Then he ascertained that Mr. Puttock had not been presented to, or selected for, the living on account of any peculiar fitness;—but that he had been a fellow of Rufford at Oxford till he was forty-five, when he had thought it well to marry and take a living. 'But he must have been asthmatic then?' said the Senator.

'He may have had all the ailments endured by the human race, for anything I know,' said the unhappy host.

'And for anything the bishop cared, as far as I can see,' said the Senator. 'Well now, I guess, that couldn't occur in our country. A minister may turn out badly with us as well as with you. But we don't appoint a man without inquiry as to his fitness,—and if a man can't do his duty he has to give way to some one who can. If the sick gentleman took the small portion of the stipend and the working man the larger, would not better justice be done, and the people better served?'

'Mr. Puttock has a freehold in the parish.'

'A freehold possession of men's souls! The fact is, Mr. Morton, that the spirit of conservatism in this country is so strong that you cannot bear to part with a shred of the barbarism of the Middle Ages. And when a rag is sent to the winds you shriek with agony at the disruption, and think that the wound will be mortal.' As Mr. Goto-bed said this he extended his right hand and laid his left on his breast, as though he were addressing the Senate from his own chair. Morton, who had offered to enter-tain the gentleman for ten days, sincerely wished that he were doing so.

On the Monday afternoon the Trefoils arrived. Mr. Morton, with his mother and both the carriages, went down to receive them, with a cart also for the luggage, which was fortunate, as Arabella Trefoil's big box was very big indeed, and Lady Augustus, though she was economical in most things, had brought a comfortable amount of clothes. Each of them had her own lady's maid, so that the two carriages were necessary. How it was that these ladies lived so luxuriously was a mystery to their friends, as for some time past they had enjoyed no particular income of their own. Lord Augustus had spent everything that came to his hand, and the family owned no house at all. Nevertheless, Arabella Trefoil was to be seen at all parties magnificently dressed, and never stirred anywhere without her own maid. It would have been as grievous to her to be called on to live without food as to go without this necessary appendage. She was a big, fair girl, whose copious hair was managed after such a fashion that no one could guess what was her own and what was purchased. She certainly had fine eyes, though I could never imagine how any one could look at them and think it possible that she should be in love. They were very large, beautifully blue, but never bright; and the eye-

brows over them were perfect. Her cheeks were somewhat too long and the distance from her well-formed nose
to her upper lip too great. Her mouth was small and her
teeth excellent. But the charm of which men spoke the
most was the brilliance of her complexion. If, as the
ladies said, it was all paint, she, or her maid, must have
been a great artist. It never betrayed itself to be paint.
But the beauty on which she prided herself was the grace
of her motion. Though she was tall and big she never
allowed an awkward movement to escape from her. She
certainly did it very well. No young woman could walk
across an archery ground with a finer step, or manage
a train with more perfect ease, or sit upon her horse with
a more complete look of being at home there. No doubt
she was slow, but though slow she never seemed to drag.
Now she was, after a certain fashion, engaged to marry
John Morton, and perhaps she was one of the most
unhappy young persons in England.

She had long known that it was her duty to marry, and
especially her duty to marry well. Between her and her
mother there had been no reticence on this subject. With
worldly people in general, though the worldliness is
manifest enough, and is taught by plain lessons from
parents to their children, yet there is generally some thin
veil even among themselves, some transparent tissue of
lies, which, though they never quite hope to deceive each
other, does produce among them something of the comfort of deceit. But between Lady Augustus and her
daughter there had for many years been nothing of the
kind. The daughter herself had been too honest for it.
'As for caring about him, mamma,' she had once said,
speaking of a suitor, 'of course I don't. He is nasty and
odious in every way. But I have got to do the best I can,
and what is the use of talking about such trash as that?'
Then there had been no more trash between them.

It was not John Morton whom Arabella Trefoil had
called nasty and odious. She had had many lovers, and
had been engaged to not a few, and perhaps she liked
John Morton as well as any of them—except one. He
was quiet, and looked like a gentleman, and was reputed

for no vices. Nor did she quarrel with her fate in that he himself was not addicted to any pleasures. She herself did not care much for pleasure. But she did care to be a great lady,—one who would be allowed to swim out of rooms before others, one who could snub others, one who could show real diamonds when others wore paste, one who might be sure to be asked everywhere, even by the people who hated her. She rather liked being hated by women, and did not want any man to be in love with her, —except as far as might be sufficient for the purpose of marriage. The real diamonds and the high rank would not be hers with John Morton. She would have to be content with such rank as is accorded to ministers at the courts at which they are employed. The fall would be great from what she had once expected, and therefore she was miserable. There had been a young man, of immense wealth, of great rank, whom at one time she really had fancied that she had loved; but just as she was landing her prey, the prey had been rescued from her by powerful friends, and she had been all but broken-hearted. Mr. Morton's fortune was in her eyes small, and she was beginning to learn that he knew how to take care of his own money. Already there had been difficulties as to settlements, difficulties as to pin-money, difficulties as to residence, Lady Augustus having been very urgent. John Morton, who had really been captivated by the beauty of Arabella, was quite in earnest; but there were subjects on which he would not give way. He was anxious to put his best leg foremost, so that the beauty might be satisfied and might become his own, but there was a limit beyond which he would not go. Lady Augustus had more than once said to her daughter that it would not do;—and then there would be all the weary work to do again!

Nobody seeing the meeting on the platform would have imagined that Mr. Morton and Miss Trefoil were lovers; and as for Lady Augustus, it would have been thought that she was in some special degree offended with the gentleman who had come to meet her. She just gave him the tip of her fingers, and then turned away to her maid, and called for the porters, and made herself particular and disagreeable. Arabella vouchsafed a cold smile; but then her smiles were always cold. After that she stood still and shivered. 'Are you cold?' asked Morton. She shook her head and shivered again. 'Perhaps you are tired?' Then she nodded her head. When her maid came to her in some trouble about the luggage, she begged that she might not be 'bothered,' saying that no doubt her mother knew all about it. 'Can I do anything?' asked Morton. 'Nothing at all, I should think,' said Miss Trefoil. In the meantime old Mrs. Morton was standing by as black as thunder, for the Trefoil ladies had hardly noticed her.

The luggage turned up alright at last, as luggage always does, and was stowed away in the cart. Then came the carriage arrangement. Morton had intended that the two elder ladies should go together with one of the maids, and that he should put his love into the other, which, having a seat behind, could accommodate the second girl without disturbing them in the carriage. But Lady Augustus had made some exception to this, and had begged that her daughter might be seated with herself. It was a point which Morton could not contest out there among the porters and drivers, so that at last he and his grandmother had the phaeton* together, with the two maids in the rumble. 'I never saw such manners in all my life,' said the Honourable Mrs. Morton, almost bursting with passion.

'They are cold and tired, ma'am.'

'No lady should be too cold or too tired to conduct herself with propriety. No real lady is ever so.'

'The place is strange to them, you know.'

'I hope with all my heart that it may never be otherwise than strange to them.'

When they arrived at the house the strangers were carried into the library, and tea was of course brought to them. The American Senator was there, but the greetings were very cold. Mrs. Morton took her place and offered her hospitality in the most frigid manner. There had not been the smallest spark of love's flame shown as yet, nor did the girl as she sat sipping her tea seem to think that any such spark was wanted. Morton did get a seat beside her and managed to take away her muff and one of her shawls, but she gave them to him almost as she might have done to a servant. She smiled indeed,— but she smiled as some women smile at everybody who has any intercourse with them. 'I think perhaps Mrs. Morton will let us go upstairs,' said Lady Augustus. Mrs. Morton immediately rang the bell, and prepared to precede the ladies to their chambers. Let them be as insolent as they would she would do what she conceived to be her duty. Then Lady Augustus stalked out of the room and her daughter swum after her. 'They don't seem to be quite the same as they were in Washington,' said the Senator.

John Morton got up and left the room without making any reply. He was thoroughly unhappy. What was he to do for a week with such a houseful of people? And then, what was he to do for all his life if the presiding spirit of the house was to be such a one as this? She was very beautiful,—certainly. So he told himself; and yet as he walked round the park he almost repented of what he had done. But after twenty minutes' fast walking he was able to convince himself that all the fault on this occasion lay with the mother. Lady Augustus had been fatigued with her journey and had therefore made everybody near her miserable.

CHAPTER XIII

AT BRAGTON

WHEN the ladies went upstairs the afternoon was not half over and they did not dine till half-past seven. As Morton returned to the house in the dusk he thought that perhaps Arabella might make some attempt to throw herself in his way. She had often done so when they were not engaged, and surely she might do so now. There was nothing to prevent her coming down to the library when she had got rid of her travelling clothes, and in this hope he looked into the room. As soon as the door was open, the Senator, who in his mind was preparing his lecture, at once asked whether no one in England had an apparatus for warming rooms such as was to be found in every well-built house in the States. The Paragon hardly vouchsafed him a word of reply, but escaped upstairs, trusting that he might meet Miss Trefoil on the way. He was a bold man, and even ventured to knock at her door; —but there was no reply, and, fearing the Senator, he had to betake himself to his own privacy. Miss Trefoil had migrated to her mother's room, and there, over the fire, was holding a little domestic conversation. 'I never saw such a barrack in my life,' said Lady Augustus.

'Of course, mamma, we knew that we should find the house such as it was left a hundred years ago. He told us that himself.'

'He should have put something in it to make it, at any rate, decent before we came in.'

'What's the use if he's to live always at foreign courts?'

'He intends to come home sometimes, I suppose, and, if he didn't, you would.' Lady Augustus was not going to let her daughter marry a man who could not give her a home for, at any rate, a part of the year. 'Of course he must furnish the place and have an immense deal done before he can marry. I think it is a piece of impudence to bring one to such a place as this.'

'That's nonsense, mamma, because he told us all about it.'

'The more I see of it all, Arabella, the more sure I am that it won't do.'

'It must do, mamma.'

'Twelve hundred a year is all that he offers, and his lawyer says that he will make no stipulation whatever as to an allowance.'

'Really, mamma, you might leave that to me.'

'I like to have everything fixed, my dear,—and certain.'

'Nothing really ever is certain. While there is anything to get you may be sure that I shall have my share. As far as money goes I'm not a bit afraid of having the worst of it,—only there will be so very little between us.'

'That's just it.'

'There's no doubt about the property, mamma.'

'A nasty beggarly place!'

'And from what everybody says he's sure to be a minister or ambassador, or something of that sort.'

'I've no doubt he will. And where'll he have to go to? To Brazil, or the West Indies, or some British Colony,' said her ladyship, showing her ignorance of the Foreign Office service. 'That might be very well. You could stay at home. Only where would you live? He wouldn't keep a house in town for you. Is this the sort of place you'd like?'

'I don't think it makes any difference where one is,' said Arabella disgusted.

'But I do,—a very great difference. It seems to me that he's altogether under the control of that hideous old termagant. Arabella, I think you'd better make up your mind that it won't do.'

'It must do,' said Arabella.

'You're very fond of him, it seems.'

'Mamma, how you do delight to torture me;—as if my life weren't bad enough without your making it worse.'

'I tell you, my dear, what I'm bound to tell you—as your mother. I have my duty to do whether it's painful or not.'

'That's nonsense, mamma. You know it is. That might have been all very well ten years ago.'

'You were almost in your cradle, my dear.'

'Psha! cradle! I'll tell you what it is, mamma. I've been at it till I'm nearly broken down. I must settle somewhere;—or else die;—or else run away. I can't stand this any longer, and I won't. Talk of work,—men's work! What man ever has to work as I do?' I wonder which was the hardest part of the work, the hairdressing and painting and companionship of the lady's maid, or the continual smiling upon unmarried men to whom she had nothing to say and for whom she did not in the least care! 'I can't do it any more, and I won't. As for Mr. Morton, I don't care that for him. You know I don't. I never cared much for anybody, and shall never again care at all.'

'You'll find that will come all right after you are married.'

'Like you and papa, I suppose.'

'My dear, I had no mother to take care of me, or I shouldn't have married your father.'

'I wish you hadn't, because then I shouldn't be going to marry Mr. Morton. But, as I have got so far, for Heaven's sake let it go on! If you break with him I'll tell him everything and throw myself into his hands.' Lady Augustus sighed deeply. 'I will, mamma. It was you spotted this man, and when you said that you thought it would do, I gave way. He was the last man in the world I should have thought of myself.'

'We had heard so much about Bragton!'

'And Bragton is here. The estate is not out of elbows.'

'My dear, my opinion is that we've made a mistake. He's not the sort of man I took him to be. He's as hard as a file.'

'Leave that to me, mamma.'

'You are determined then?'

'I think I am. At any rate let me look about me. Don't give him an opportunity of breaking off till I have made up my mind. I can always break off, if I like it. No one in London has heard of the engagement yet. Just leave me alone for this week to see what I think about it.' Then Lady Augustus threw herself back in her chair and went to sleep, or pretended to do so.

A little after half-past seven she and her daughter, dressed for dinner, went down to the library together. The other guests were assembled there, and Mrs. Morton was already plainly expressing her anger at the tardiness of her son's guests. The Senator had got hold of Mr. Mainwaring and was asking pressing questions as to church patronage,—a subject not very agreeable to the rector of St. John's, as his living had been bought for him with his wife's money during the incumbency of an old gentleman of seventy-eight. Mr. Cooper, who was himself nearly that age and who was vicar of Mallingham, a parish which ran into Dillsborough and comprehended a part of its population, was listening to these queries with awe,—and perhaps with some little gratification, as he had been presented to his living by the bishop after a curacy of many years. 'These kind of things, I believe, can be bought and sold in the market,' said the Senator, speaking every word with absolute distinctness. But as he paused for an answer the two ladies came in and the conversation was changed. Both the clergymen were introduced to Lady Augustus and her daughter, and Mr. Mainwaring at once took refuge under the shadow of the ladies' title.

Arabella did not sit down, so that Morton had an opportunity of standing near to his love. 'I suppose you are very tired,' he said.

'Not in the least.' She smiled her sweetest as she answered him,—but yet it was not very sweet. 'Of course we were tired and cross when we got out of the train. People always are; aren't they?'

'Perhaps ladies are.'

'We were. But all that about the carriages, Mr. Morton, wasn't my doing. Mamma had been talking to me so much that I didn't know whether I was on my head or my heels. It was very good of you to come and meet us, and I ought to have been more gracious.' In this way she made her peace, and as she was quite in earnest,— doing a portion of the hard work of her life,—she continued to smile—as sweetly as she could. Perhaps he liked it;—but any man endowed with that power of appreciation which we call sympathy, would have felt it to be as cold as though it had come from a figure on a glass window.

The dinner was announced. Mr. Morton was honoured with the hand of Lady Augustus. The Senator handed the old lady into the dining-room and Mr. Mainwaring the younger lady,—so that Arabella was sitting next to her lover. It had all been planned by Morton and acceded to by his grandmother. Mr. Gotobed throughout the dinner had the best of the conversation, though Lady Augustus had power enough to snub him on more than one occasion. 'Suppose we were to allow at once,' she said, 'that everything is better in the United States than anywhere else, shouldh't we get along easier?'

'I don't know that getting along easy is what we have particularly got in view,' said Mr. Gotobed, who was certainly in quest of information.

'But it is what I have in view, Mr. Gotobed;—so if you please we'll take the pre-eminence of your country for granted.' Then she turned to Mr. Mainwaring on the other side. Upon this the Senator addressed himself for a while to the table at large and had soon forgotten altogether the expression of the lady's wishes.

'I believe you have a good many churches about here,' said Lady Augustus, trying to make conversation, to her neighbour.

'One in every parish, I fancy,' said Mr. Mainwaring, who preferred all subjects to clerical subjects. 'I suppose London is quite empty now.'

'We came direct from the Duke's,' said Lady Augustus, —'and did not even sleep in town;—but it is empty.' The Duke was the brother of Lord Augustus, and a compromise had been made with Lady Augustus, by which she and her daughter should be allowed a fortnight every year at the Duke's place in the country, and a certain amount of entertainment in town.

'I remember the Duke at Christchurch,' said the parson. 'He and I were of the same par.* He was Lord Mistletoe then. Dear me, that was a long time ago. I wonder whether he remembers being upset out of a trap with me one day after dinner. I suppose we had dined in earnest. He has gone his way, and I have gone mine, and I've never seen him since. Pray remember me to him.' Lady Augustus said she would, and did entertain some little increased respect for the clergyman who could boast that he had been tipsy in company with her worthy brother-in-law.

Poor Mr. Cooper did not get on very well with Mrs. Morton. All his remembrances of the old squire were eulogistic and affectionate. Hers were just the reverse. He had a good word to say for Reginald Morton,—to which she would not even listen. She was willing enough to ask questions about the Mallingham tenants;—but Mr. Cooper would revert back to the old days, and so conversation was at an end.

Morton tried to make himself agreeable to his left-hand neighbour,—trying also very hard to make believe that he was happy in his immediate position. How often in the various amusements of the world is one tempted to pause a moment and ask one's self whether one really likes it! He was conscious that he was working hard, struggling to be happy, painfully anxious to be sure that he was enjoying the luxury of being in love. But he was not at all contented. There she was, and very beautiful she looked; and he thought that he could be proud of her if she sat at the end of his table;—and he knew that she was engaged to be his wife. But he doubted whether she was in love with him; and he almost doubted sometimes whether he was very much in love with her. He asked her in so many words what he should do to amuse her. Would she like to ride with him? as if so he would endeavour to get saddle-horses. Would she like to go out hunting? Would she be taken round to see the neighbouring towns, Rufford and Norrington? 'Lord Rufford lives somewhere near Rufford?' she asked. Yes; —he lived at Rufford Hall, three or four miles from the town. Did Lord Rufford hunt? Morton believed that he was greatly given to hunting. Then he asked Arabella whether she knew the young lord. She had just met him, she said, and had only asked the question because of the name. 'He is one of my neighbours down here,' said Morton;—'but being always away, of course I see nothing of him.' After that Arabella consented to be taken out on horseback to see a meet of the hounds, although she could not hunt. 'We must see what we can do about horses,' he said. She however professed her readiness to go in the carriage if a saddle-horse could not be found.

The dinner party, I fear, was very dull. Mr. Mainwaring perhaps liked it, because he was fond of dining anywhere away from home. Mr. Cooper was glad once more to see his late old friend's old dining-room. Mr. Gotobed perhaps obtained some information. But otherwise the

affair was dull. 'Are we to have a week of this?' said
Lady Augustus when she found herself upstairs.

'You must, mamma, if we are to stay till we go to the
Gores. Lord Rufford is here in the neighbourhood.'

'But they don't know each other.'

'Yes they do;—slightly. I am to go to the meet some
day, and he'll be there.'

'It might be dangerous.'

'Nonsense, mamma! And after all you've been saying
about dropping Mr. Morton!'

'But there is nothing so bad as a useless flirtation.'

'Do I ever flirt? Oh, mamma, that after so many years
you shouldn't know me! Did you ever see me yet making
myself happy in any way? What nonsense you talk!'
Then without waiting for, or making, any apology, she
walked off to her own room.

CHAPTER XIV

THE DILLSBOROUGH FEUD

'IT'S that nasty, beastly, drunken club,' said Mrs.
Masters to her unfortunate husband on the Wednesday
morning. It may perhaps be remembered that the
poisoned fox was found on the Saturday, and it may be
imagined that Mr. Goarly had risen in importance since
that day. On the Saturday, Bean, with a couple of men
employed by Lord Rufford, had searched the wood, and
found four or five red herrings poisoned with strychnine.
There had been no doubt about the magnitude of the
offence. On the Monday a detective policeman, dressed
of course in rustic disguise, but not the less known to
every one in the place, was wandering about between
Dillsborough and Dillsborough Wood and making futile
inquiries as to the purchase of strychnine, and also as to
the purchase of red herrings. But every one knew, and
such leading people as Runciman and Dr. Nupper were
not slow to declare, that Dillsborough was the only place
in England in which one might be sure that those articles
had not been purchased. And on the Tuesday it began to

be understood that Goarly had applied to Bearside, the other attorney, in reference to his claim against Lord Rufford's pheasants. He had contemptuously refused the 7s. 6d. an acre offered him, and put his demand at 40s. As to the poisoned fox, and the herrings and the strychnine, Goarly declared that he didn't care if there were twenty detectives in the place. He stated it to be his opinion that Larry Twentyman had put down the poison. It was all very well, Goarly said, for Larry to be fond of gentlemen and to ride to hounds, and make pretences; but Larry liked his turkeys as well as anybody else, and Larry had put down the poison. In this matter Goarly overreached himself. No one in Dillsborough could be brought to believe that. Even Harry Stubbings was ready to swear that he should suspect himself as soon. But nothing was clearer than this, that Goarly was going to make a stand against the hunt, and especially against Lord Rufford. He had gone to Bearside, and Bearside had taken up the matter in a serious way. Then it became known very quickly that Bearside had already received money, and it was surmised that Goarly had some one at his back. Lord Rufford had lately ejected from a house of his on the other side of the county a discontented, litigious, retired grocer from Rufford, who had made some money and had set himself up in a pretty little residence with a few acres of land. The man had made himself objectionable, and had been dispossessed. The man's name was Scrobby; and hence had come these sorrows. This was the story that had already made itself known in Dillsborough on the Tuesday evening. But up to that time not a tittle of evidence had come to light as to the purchase of the red herrings or the strychnine. All that was known was the fact that had not Tony Tuppet stopped the hounds before they reached the wood, there must have been a terrible mortality. 'It's that nasty, beastly, drunken club,' said Mrs. Masters to her husband. Of course it was at this time known to the lady that her husband had thrown away Goarly's business, and that it had been transferred to Bearside. It was also surmised by her, as it was by the town in general, that Goarly's business would come to considerable dimensions—just the sort of case as would have been sure to bring popularity if carried through, as Nickem, the senior clerk, would have carried it. And as soon as Scrobby's name was heard by Mrs. Masters there was no end to the money in the lady's imagination to which this very case might not have amounted.

'The club had nothing to do with it, my dear.'

'What time did you come home on Saturday night—or Sunday morning, I mean? Do you mean to tell me you didn't settle it there?'

'There was no nastiness, and no beastliness, and no drunkenness about it. I told you before I went that I wouldn't take it.'

'No, you didn't. How on earth are you to go on if you chuck the children's bread out of their mouths in that way?'

'You won't believe me. Do you ask Twentyman what sort of a man Goarly is.' The attorney knew that Larry was in great favour with his wife, as being the favoured suitor for Mary's hand, and had thought that this argument would be very strong.

'I don't want Mr. Twentyman to teach me what is proper for my family, nor yet to teach you your business. Mr. Twentyman has his own way of living. He brought home Kate the other day with hardly a rag of her sister's habit left. She don't go out hunting any more.'

'Very well, my dear.'

'Indeed, for the matter of that, I don't see how any of them are to do anything. What'll Lord Rufford do for you?'

'I don't want Lord Rufford to do anything for me.' The attorney was beginning to have his spirit stirred within him.

'You don't want anybody to do anything, and yet you will do nothing yourself, just because a set of drinking fellows in a tap-room, which you call a club——'

'It isn't a tap-room.'

'It's worse, because nobody can see what you're doing. I know how it was. You hadn't the pluck to hold to your own when Runciman told you not.' There was a spice of truth in this which made it all the more bitter. 'Runciman knows on which side his bread is buttered. He can make his money out of these swearing-tearing fellows. He can send in his bills, and get them paid, too. And it's all very well for Larry Twentyman to be hobbing and nobbing with the likes of them Botseys. But for a father of a family like you to be put off his business by what Mr. Runciman says is a shame.'

'I shall manage my business as I think fit,' said the attorney.

'And when we're all in the poor-house what'll you do then?' said Mrs. Masters, with her handkerchief out at the spur of the moment. Whenever she roused her husband to a state of bellicose ire by her taunts, she could always reduce him again by her tears. Being well aware of this, he would bear the taunts as long as he could, knowing that the tears would be still worse. He was so soft-hearted that, when she affected to be miserable, he could not maintain the sternness of his demeanour and leave her in her misery. 'When everything has gone away from us, what are we to do? My little bit of money has disappeared ever so long.' Then she sat herself down in her chair and had a great cry. It was useless for him to remind her that, hitherto, she had never wanted anything for herself or her children. She was resolved that everything was going to the dogs, because Goarly's case had been refused. 'And what will all those sporting men do for you?' she repeated. 'I hate the very name of a gentleman—so I do. I wish Goarly had killed all the foxes in the county. Nasty vermin! What good are the likes of them'?

Nickem, the senior clerk, was at first made almost as unhappy as Mrs. Masters by the weak decision to which his employer had come, and had in the first flush of his anger resolved to leave the office. He was sure that the case was one which would just have suited him. He would have got up the evidence as to the fertility of the land, the enormous promise of crop, and the ultimate absolute barrenness, to a marvel. He would have proved clouds of pheasants. And then Goarly's humble position,

futile industry, and general poverty, might have been
contrasted beautifully with Lord Rufford's wealth, idleness, and devotion to sport. Anything above the 7s. 6d. an
acre obtained against the lord would have been a triumph,
and he thought that if the thing had been well managed,
they might probably have got 15s. And then, in such
a case, Lord Rufford could hardly have taxed the costs.
It was really suicide for an attorney to throw away business so excellent as this. And now it had gone to Bearside,
whom Nickem remembered as a junior to himself when
they were both young hobbledehoys*at Norrington,—a
dirty, blear-eyed, pimply-faced boy who was suspected of
purloining halfpence out of coat-pockets. The thing was
very trying to Nat Nickem. But suddenly, before that
Wednesday was over, another idea had occurred to him,
and he was almost content. He knew Goarly, and he had
heard of Scrobby, and Scrobby's history in regard to the
tenement at Rufford. As he could not get Goarly's case,
why should he not make something out of the case against
Goarly? That detective was merely eking out his time
and having an idle week among the public-houses. If he
could set himself up as an amateur detective he thought
he might perhaps get to the bottom of it all. It is not a
bad thing to be concerned on the same side with a lord
when the lord is in earnest. Lord Rufford was very angry
about the poison in the covert, and would probably be
ready to pay very handsomely for having the criminal
found and punished. The criminal, of course, was Goarly.
Nickem did not doubt that for a moment, and would not
have doubted it whichever side he might have taken.
Nickem did not suppose that any one for a moment really
doubted Goarly's guilt. But to his eyes such certainty
amounted to nothing if evidence of the crime were not
forthcoming. He probably felt within his own bosom
that the last judgment of all would depend in some way
on terrestrial evidence, and was quite sure that it was by
such that a man's conscience should be affected. If
Goarly had so done the deed as to be beyond the possibility
of detection, Nickem could not have brought himself to
regard Goarly as a sinner. As it was he had considerable

respect for Goarly;—but might it not be possible to drop down upon Scrobby? Bearside with his case against the lord would be nowhere, if Goarly could be got to own that he had been suborned by Scrobby to put down the poison. Or, if in default of this, any close communication could be proved between Goarly and Scrobby,—Scrobby's injury and spirit of revenge being patent,—then too, Bearside would not have much of a case. A jury would look at that question of damages with a very different eye if Scrobby's spirit of revenge could be proved at the trial, and also the poisoning, and also machinations between Scrobby and Goarly.

Nickem was a little red-haired man about forty, who wrote a good flourishing hand, could endure an immense amount of work, and drink a large amount of alcohol without being drunk. His nose and face were all over blotches, and he looked to be dissipated and disreputable. But, as he often boasted, no one could say that 'black was the white of his eye;'—by which he meant to insinuate that he had not been detected in anything dishonest, and that he was never too tipsy to do his work. He was a married man and did not keep his wife and children in absolute comfort; but they lived, and Mr. Nickem in some fashion paid his way.

There was another clerk in the office, a very much younger man, named Sundown, and Nickem could not make his proposition to Mr. Masters till Sundown had left the office. Nickem himself had only matured his plans at dinner time and was obliged to be reticent, till at six o'clock Sundown took himself off. Mr. Masters was, at that moment, locking his own desk, when Nickem winked at him to stay. Mr. Masters did stay, and Sundown did at last leave the office.

'You couldn't let me leave home for three days?' said Nickem. 'There ain't much a-doing.'

'What do you want it for?'

'That Goarly is a great blackguard, Mr. Masters.'

'Very likely. Do you know anything about him?'

Nickem scratched his head and rubbed his chin. 'I think I could manage to know something.'

'In what way?'

'I don't think I'm quite prepared to say, sir. I shouldn't use your name, of course. But they're down upon Lord Rufford, and if you could lend me a trifle of 30s., sir, I think I could get to the bottom of it. His lordship would be awful obliged to any one who could hit it off.'

Mr. Masters did give his clerk leave for three days, and did advance the required money. And when he suggested in a whisper that perhaps the circumstance need not be mentioned to Mrs. Masters, Nickem winked again and put his forefinger to the side of his big carbuncle nose.

That evening Larry Twentyman came in, but was not received with any great favour by Mrs. Masters. There was growing up at this moment in Dillsborough the bitterness of real warfare between the friends and enemies of sport in general, and Mrs. Masters was ranking herself thereby among the enemies. Larry was, of course, one of the friends. But unhappily there was a slight difference of sentiment in Larry's own house, and on this very morning old Mrs. Twentyman had expressed to Mrs. Masters a feeling of wrong which had gradually risen from the annual demolition of her pet broods of turkeys. She declared that for the last three years every turkey poult * had gone, and that at last she was beginning to feel it. 'It's over a hundred of 'em they've had, and it is wearing,' said the old woman. Larry had twenty times begged her to give up rearing turkeys, but her heart had been too high for that. 'I don't know why Lord Rufford's foxes are to be thought of always, and nobody is to think about your poor mother's poultry,' said Mrs. Masters, lugging the subject in neck and heels.

'Has she been talking to you, Mrs. Masters, about her turkeys?'

'Your mother may speak to me I suppose if she likes it, without offence to Lord Rufford.'

'Lord Rufford has got nothing to do with it.'

'The wood belongs to him,' said Mrs. Masters.

'Foxes are much better than turkeys anyway,' said Kate Masters.

'If you don't hold your tongue, miss, you'll be sent to

bed. The wood belongs to his lordship, and the foxes are a nuisance.'

'He keeps the foxes for the county, and where would the county be without them?' began Larry. 'What is it brings money into such a place as this?'

'To Runciman's stables and Harry Stubbings and the like of them! What money does it bring in to steady, honest people?'

'Look at all the grooms,' said Larry.

'The impudentest set of young vipers about the place,' said the lady.

'Look at Grice's business.' Grice was the saddler.

'Grice, indeed! What's Grice?'

'And the price of horses?'

'Yes;—making everything dear that ought to be cheap. I don't see, and I never shall see, and I never will see any good in extravagant idleness. As for Kate she shall never go out hunting again. She has torn Mary's habit to pieces. And shooting is worse. Why is a man to have a flock of voracious cormorants come down upon his corn fields? I'm all in favour of Goarly, and so I tell you, Mr. Twentyman.' After this poor Larry went away, finding that he had no opportunity for saying a word to Mary Masters.

CHAPTER XV

A FIT COMPANION,—FOR ME AND MY SISTERS

ON that same Wednesday, Reginald Morton had called at the attorney's house, had asked for Miss Masters, and had found her alone. Mrs. Masters at the time had been out, picking up intelligence about the great case, and the two younger girls had been at school. Reginald, as he walked home from Bragton all alone on that occasion when Larry had returned with Mary, was quite sure that he would never willingly go into Mary's presence again. Why should he disturb his mind about such a girl,—one who could rush into the arms of such a man as Larry Twentyman? Or, indeed, why disturb his mind about any girl? That was not the manner of life which he planned for himself. After that he shut himself up for a few days and was not much seen by any of the Dillsborough folk. But on this Wednesday he received a letter, and,—as he told himself, merely in consequence of that letter,—he called at the attorney's house and asked for Miss Masters.

He was shown up into the beautiful drawing-room, and in a few minutes Mary came to him. 'I have brought you a letter from my aunt,' he said.

'From Lady Ushant? I am so glad.'

'She was writing to me and she put this under cover. I know what it contains. She wants you to go to her at Cheltenham for a month.'

'Oh, Mr. Morton!'

'Would you like to go?'

'How should I not like to go? Lady Ushant is my dearest, dearest friend. It is so very good of her to think of me.'

'She talks of the first week in December and wants you to be there for Christmas.'

'I don't at all know that I can go, Mr. Morton.'

'Why not go?'

'I'm afraid mamma will not spare me.' There were many reasons. She could hardly go on such a visit without some renewal of her scanty wardrobe, which perhaps the family funds would not permit. And, as she knew very well, Mrs. Masters was not at all favourable to Lady Ushant. If the old lady had altogether kept Mary it might have been very well; but she had not done so, and Mrs. Masters had more than once said that that kind of thing must be all over;—meaning that Mary was to drop her intimacy with high-born people that were of no real use. And then there was Mr. Twentyman and his suit. Mary had for some time felt that her step-mother intended her to understand that her only escape from home would be by becoming Mrs. Twentyman. 'I don't think it will be possible, Mr. Morton.'

'My aunt will be very sorry.'

'Oh,—how sorry shall I be! It is like having another little bit of heaven before me.'

Then he said what he certainly should not have said. 'I thought, Miss Masters, that your heaven was all here.'

'What do you mean by that, Mr. Morton?' she asked, blushing up to her hair. Of course she knew what he meant, and of course she was angry with him. Ever since that walk her mind had been troubled by ideas as to what he would think about her, and now he was telling her what he thought.

'I fancied that you were happy here without going to see an old woman, who, after all, has not much amusement to offer to you.'

'I don't want any amusement.'

'At any rate, you will answer Lady Ushant?'

'Of course I shall answer her.'

'Perhaps you can let me know. She wishes me to take you to Cheltenham. I shall go for a couple of days, but I shall not stay longer. If you are going, perhaps you would allow me to travel with you.'

'Of course it would be very kind; but I don't suppose that I shall go. I am sure Lady Ushant won't believe that I am kept away from her by any pleasure of my own here. I can explain it all to her and she will understand me.' She hardly meant to reproach him. She did not mean to assume an intimacy sufficient for reproach. But he felt that she had reproached him. 'I love Lady Ushant so dearly that I would go anywhere to see her if I could.'

'Then I think it could be managed. Your father——'

'Papa does not attend much to us girls. It is mamma that manages all that. At any rate, I will write to Lady Ushant, and will ask papa to let you know.'

Then it seemed as though there were nothing else for him but to go;—and yet he wanted to say some other word. If he had been cruel in throwing Mr. Twentyman in her teeth, surely he ought to apologize. 'I did not mean to say anything to offend you.'

'You have not offended me at all, Mr. Morton.'

'If I did think that—that——'

'It does not signify in the least. I only want Lady Ushant to understand that if I could possibly go to her I would rather do that than anything else in the world.

Because Lady Ushant is kind to me I needn't expect other people to be so.' Reginald Morton was, of course, the 'other people'.

Then he paused a moment. 'I did so long,' he said, 'to walk round the old place with you the other day before these people came there, and I was so disappointed when you would not come with me.'

'I was coming.'

'But you went back with—that other man.'

'Of course I did when you showed so plainly that you didn't want him to join you. What was I to do? I couldn't send him away. Mr. Twentyman is a very intimate friend of ours, and very kind to Dolly and Kate.'

'I wished so much to talk to you about the old days.'

'And I wish to go to your aunt, Mr. Morton; but we can't all of us have what we wish. Of course I saw that you were very angry, but I couldn't help that. Perhaps it was wrong in Mr. Twentyman to offer to walk with you.'

'I didn't say so at all.'

'You looked it at any rate, Mr. Morton. And as Mr. Twentyman is a friend of ours——'

'You were angry with me.'

'I don't say that. But as you were too grand for our friend, of course you were too grand for us.'

'That is a very unkind way of putting it. I don't think I am grand. A man may wish to have a little conversation with a very old friend without being interrupted, and yet not be grand. I dare say Mr. Twentyman is just as good as I am.'

'You don't think that, Mr. Morton.'

'I believe him to be a great deal better, for he earns his bread, and takes care of his mother, and as far as I know does his duty thoroughly.'

'I know the difference, Mr. Morton, and of course I know how you feel it. I don't suppose that Mr. Twentyman is a fit companion for any of the Mortons, but for all that he may be a fit companion,—for me and my sisters.' Surely she must have said this with the express object of declaring to him that in spite of the advantages of her education she chose to put herself in the ranks of the

Twentymans, Runcimans, and such like. He had come
there ardently wishing that she might be allowed to go to
his aunt, and resolved that he would take her himself if it
were possible. But now he almost thought that she had
better not go. If she had made her election she must be
allowed to abide by it. If she meant to marry Mr.
Twentyman, what good could she get by associating with
his aunt or with him? And had she not as good as told
him that she meant to marry Mr. Twentyman? She had,
at any rate, very plainly declared that she regarded Mr.
Twentyman as her equal in rank. Then he took his leave
without any further explanation. Even if she did go to
Cheltenham he would not take her.

After that he walked straight out to Bragton. He was,
of course, altogether unconscious what grand things his
cousin John had intended to do by him had not the
Honourable old lady interfered; but he made up his
mind that duty required him to call at the house. So he
walked by the path across the bridge, and when he came
out on the gravel road near the front door he found a
gentleman smoking a cigar and looking around him. It
was Mr. Gotobed, who had just returned from a visit
which he had made, the circumstances of which must be
narrated in the next chapter. The Senator lifted his hat
and remarked that it was a very fine afternoon. Reginald
lifted his hat and assented. 'Mr. Morton, sir, I think is out
with the ladies, taking a drive.'

'I will leave a card then.'

'The old lady is at home, sir, if you wish to see her,'
continued the Senator, following Reginald up to the door.

'Oh, Mr. Reginald, is that you?' said old Mrs. Hopkins,
taking the card. 'They are all out,—except herself.' As
he certainly did not wish to see 'herself', he greeted the
old woman and left his card.

'You live in these parts, sir?' asked the Senator.

'In the town yonder.'

'Because Mr. Morton's housekeeper seems to know you.'

'She knows me very well, as I was brought up in this
house. Good morning to you.'

'Good afternoon to you, sir. Perhaps you can tell me

who lives in that country residence,—what you call a farm-house,—on the other side of the road?'

Reginald said that he presumed the gentleman was alluding to Mr. Twentyman's house.

'Ah, yes—I dare say. That was the name I heard up there. You are not Mr. Twentyman, sir?'

'My name is Morton.'

'Morton, is it?—perhaps my friends—ah—ah,—yes.' He didn't like to say uncle, because Reginald didn't look old enough, and he knew he ought not to say brother, because the elder brother in England would certainly have had the property.

'I am Mr. John Morton's cousin.'

'Oh;—Mr. Morton's cousin. I asked whether you were the owner of that farm-house, because I intruded just now by passing through the yards, and I would have apologized. Good afternoon to you, sir.' Then Reginald, having thus done his duty, returned home.

Mary Masters, when she was alone, was again very angry with herself. She knew thoroughly how perverse she had been when she declared that Larry Twentyman was a fit companion for herself, and that she had said it on purpose to punish the man who was talking to her. Not a day passed, or hardly an hour of a day, in which she did not tell herself that the education she had received, and the early associations of her life, had made her unfit for the marriage which her friends were urging upon her. It was the one great sorrow of her life. She even repented of the good things of her early days, because they had given her a distaste for what might have otherwise been happiness and good fortune. There had been moments in which she had told herself that she ought to marry Larry Twentyman, and adapt herself to the surroundings of her life. Since she had seen Reginald Morton frequently she had been less prone to tell herself so than before;— and yet to this very man she had declared her fitness for Larry's companionship!

CHAPTER XVI

MR. GOTOBED'S PHILANTHROPY

MR. GOTOBED, when the persecutions of Goarly were described to him at the scene of the dead fox, had expressed considerable admiration for the man's character as portrayed by what he then heard. The man,—a poor man too and despised in the land,—was standing up for his rights, all alone, against the aristocracy and plutocracy of the county. He had killed the demon whom the aristocracy and plutocracy worshipped, and had appeared there in arms ready to defend his own territory,—one against so many, and so poor a man against men so rich! The Senator had at once said that he would call upon Mr. Goarly, and the Senator was a man who always carried out his purposes. Afterwards, from John Morton, and from others who knew the country better than Morton, he learned further particulars. On the Monday and Tuesday he fathomed,—or nearly fathomed,—that matter of the 7s. 6d. an acre. He learned at any rate that the owner of the wood admitted a damage done by him to the corn, and then had, himself, assessed the damage without consultation with the injured party; and he was informed also that Goarly was going to law with the lord for a fuller compensation. He liked Goarly for killing the fox, and he liked him more for going to law with Lord Rufford.

He declared openly at Bragton his sympathy with the man and his intention of expressing it. Morton was annoyed, and endeavoured to persuade him to leave the man alone, but in vain. No doubt, had he expressed himself decisively, and told his friend that he should be annoyed by a guest from his house taking part in such a matter, the Senator would have abstained, and would merely have made one more note as to English peculiarities and English ideas of justice; but Morton could not bring himself to do this. 'The feeling of the country will be altogether against you,' he had said, hoping to deter the

Senator. The Senator had replied that though the feeling of that little bit of the country might be against him, he did not believe that such would be the case with the feeling of England generally. The ladies had all become a little afraid of Mr. Gotobed, and hardly dared to express an opinion. Lady Augustus did say that she supposed that Goarly was a low, vulgar fellow, which of course strengthened the Senator in his purpose.

The Senator on Wednesday would not wait for lunch, but started a little before one, with a crust of bread in his pocket, to find his way to Goarly's house. There was no difficulty in this, as he could see the wood as soon as he had got upon the high road. He found Twentyman's gate, and followed directly the route which the hunting party had taken, till he came to the spot on which the crowd had been assembled. Close to this there was a hand-gate leading into Dillsborough Wood, and standing in the gateway was a man. The Senator thought that this might not improbably be Goarly himself, and asked the question, 'Might your name be Mr. Goarly, sir?'

'Me Goarly!' said the man in infinite disgust. 'I ain't nothing of the kind,—and you knows it.'

That the man should have been annoyed at being taken for Goarly, that man being Bean the gamekeeper, who would willingly have hung Goarly if he could, and would have thought it quite proper that a law should be now passed for hanging him at once,—was natural enough. But why he should have told the Senator that the Senator knew he was not Goarly, it might be difficult to explain. He probably at once regarded the Senator as an enemy, as a man on the other side, and therefore as a cunning knave who would be sure to come creeping about on false pretences. Bean, who had already heard of Bearside, and had heard of Scrobby in connection with this matter, looked at the Senator very hard. He knew Bearside. The man certainly was not the attorney, and from what he had heard of Scrobby, he didn't think he was Scrobby. The man was not like what in his imagination Scrobby would be. He did not know what to make of Mr. Gotobed, who was a person of an imposing appear-

ance, tall and thin, with a long nose and look of great
acuteness, dressed in black from head to foot, but not yet
looking quite like an English gentleman. He was a man
to whom Bean in an ordinary way would have been civil,
—civil in a cold, guarded way; but how was he to be civil
to anybody who addressed him as Goarly?

'I did not know it,' said the Senator. 'As Goarly lives
near here, I thought you might be Goarly. When I saw
Goarly he had a gun, and you have a gun. Can you tell
me where Goarly lives?'

'T'other side of the wood,' said Bean, pointing back
with his thumb. 'He never had a gun like this in his hand
in all his born days.'

'I dare say not, my friend. I can go through the wood,
I guess?' for Bean had pointed exactly over the gateway.

'I guess you can't, then,' said Bean. The man who,
like other gamekeepers, lived much in the company of
gentlemen, was ordinarily a civil, courteous fellow, who
knew how to smile and make things pleasant. But at this
moment he was very much put out. His covert had been
found full of red herrings and strychnine, and his fox had
been poisoned. He had lost his guinea on the day of the
hunt—the guinea which would have been his perquisite
had they found a live fox in his wood. And all this was
being done by such a fellow as Goarly! And now this
abandoned wretch was bringing an action against his
lordship, and was leagued with such men as Scrobby and
Bearside! It was a dreadful state of things! How was it
likely that he should give a passage through the wood to
anybody coming after Goarly? 'You're on Mr. Twentyman's land now, as I dare say you know.'

'I don't know anything about it.'

'Well, that wood is Lord Rufford's wood.'

'I did not know as much as that, certainly.'

'And you can't go into it.'

'How shall I find Mr. Goarly's house?'

'If you'll get over that there ditch you'll be on Mister
Goarly's land, and that's all about it.' Bean, as he said
this, put a strongly ironical emphasis on the term of
respect, and then turned back into the wood.

The Senator made his way down the fence to the bank on which Goarly had stood with his gun, then over into Goarly's field, and so round the back of the wood till he saw a small red brick house standing perhaps four hundred yards from the covert, just on the elbow of a lane. It was a miserable-looking place, with a pigsty and a dungheap and a small horse-pond or duck-puddle all close around it. The stack of chimneys seemed to threaten to fall, and as he approached from behind, he could see that the two windows opening that way were stuffed with rags. There was a little cabbage garden, which now seemed to be all stalks, and a single goose waddling about the duck-puddle. The Senator went to the door, and, having knocked, was investigated by a woman from behind it. Yes, this was Goarly's house. What did the gentleman want? Goarly was at work in the field. Then she came out, the Senator having signified his friendly intentions, and summoned Goarly to the spot.

'I hope I see you well, sir,' said the Senator, putting out his hand as Goarly came up dragging a dung-fork behind him.

Goarly rubbed his hand on his breeches before he gave it to be shaken, and declared himself to be 'pretty tidy, considering.'

'I was present the other day, Mr. Goarly, when that dead fox was exposed to view.'

'Was you, sir?'

'I was given to understand that you had destroyed the brute.'

'Don't you believe a word on it, then,' said the woman interposing. 'He didn't do nothing of the kind. Who ever seed him a' buying red herrings and p'ison?'

'Hold your jaw,' said Goarly, familiarly. 'Let 'em prove it. I don't know who you are, sir; but let 'em prove it.'

'My name, Mr. Goarly, is Elias Gotobed. I am an American citizen, and Senator for the State of Mikewa.' Mr. and Mrs. Goarly shook their heads at every separate item of information tendered to them. 'I am on a visit to this country, and am at present staying at the house of my friend, Mr. John Morton.'

'He's the gentl'man from Bragton, Dan.'

'Hold your jaw, can't you?' said the husband. Then he touched his hat to the Senator, intending to signify that the Senator might, if he pleased, continue his narrative.

'If you did kill that fox, Mr. Goarly, I think you were quite right to kill him.' Then Goarly winked at him. 'I cannot imagine that even the laws of England could justify a man in perpetuating a breed of wild animals that are destructive to his neighbours' property.'

'I could shoot 'un; not a doubt about that, Mister. I could shoot 'un, and I wull.'

'Have a care, Dan,' whispered Mrs. Goarly.

'Hold your jaw, will ye? I could shoot 'un, Mister. I don't rightly know about p'ison.'

'That fox we saw was poisoned, I suppose?' said the Senator, carelessly.

'Have a care, Dan; have a care!' whispered the wife.

'Allow me to assure both of you,' said the Senator, 'that you need fear nothing from me. I have come quite as a friend.'

'Thank 'ee, sir,' said Goarly, again touching his hat.

'It seems to me,' said the Senator, 'that in this matter a great many men are leagued together against you.'

'You may say that, sir. I didn't just catch your name, sir.'

'My name is Gotobed;—Gotobed; Elias Gotobed, Senator from the State of Mikewa to the United States Congress.' Mrs. Goarly, who understood nothing of all these titles, and who had all along doubted, dropped a suspicious curtsey. Goarly, who understood as little now, took his hat altogether off. He was very much puzzled but inclined to think that if he managed matters rightly, profit might be got out of this very strange meeting. 'In my country, Mr. Goarly, all men are free and equal.'

'That's a fine thing, sir.'

'It is a fine thing, my friend, if properly understood and properly used. Coming from such a country I was shocked to see so many rich men banded together against one who I suppose is not rich.'

'Very far from it,' said the woman.

'It's my own land, you know,' said Goarly, who was proud of his position as a landowner. 'No one can't touch me on it, as long as the rates is paid. I'm as good a man here,'—and he stamped his foot on the ground,—'as his lordship is in that there wood.'

This was the first word spoken by the Goarlys that had pleased the Senator, and this set him off again. 'Just so; —and I admire a man that will stand up for his own rights. I am told that you have found his lordship's pheasants destructive to your corn.'

'Didn't leave him hardly a grain last August,' said Mrs. Goarly.

'Will you hold your jaw, woman, or will you not?' said the man, turning round fiercely at her. 'I'm going to have the law of his lordship, sir. What's seven and six an acre? There's that quantity of pheasants in that wood as'd eat up any mortal thing as ever was growed. Seven and six!'

'Didn't you propose arbitration?'

'I never didn't propose nothin'. I've axed two pound, and my lawyer says as how I'll get it. What I sold come off that other bit of ground down there. Wonderful crop! And this 'd 've been the same. His lordship ain't nothin' to me, Mr. Gotobed.'

'You don't approve of hunting, Mr. Goarly?'

'Oh, I approves if they'd pay a poor man for what harm they does him. Look at that there goose.' Mr. Gotobed did look at the goose. 'There's nine and twenty they've tuk from me, and only left un that.' Now Mrs. Goarly's goose was well known in those parts. It was declared that she was more than a match for any fox in the county, but that Mrs. Goarly for the last two years had never owned any goose but this one.

'The foxes have eaten them all?' asked the Senator.

'Every mortal one.'

'And the gentlemen of the hunt have paid you nothing.'

'I had four half-crowns once,' said the woman.

'If you don't send the heads you don't get it,' said the man, 'and then they'll keep you waiting months and months, just for their pleasures. Who's a-going to put up with that? I ain't.'

'And now you're going to law?'

'I am,—like a man. His lordship ain't nothin' to me. I ain't afeard of his lordship.'

'Will it cost you much?'

'That's just what it will do, sir,' said the woman.

'Didn't I tell you, hold your jaw?'

'The gentl'man was going to offer to help us a little, Dan.'

'I was going to say that I am interested in the case, and that you have all my good wishes. I do not like to offer you pecuniary help.'

'You're very good, sir; very good. This bit of land is mine; not a doubt of it;—but we're poor, sir.'

'Indeed we is,' said the woman. 'What with taxes and rates, and them foxes as won't let me rear a head of poultry, and them brutes of birds as eats up the corn, I often tells him he'd better sell the bit o' land and just set up for a public.'

'It belonged to my feyther and grandfeyther,' said Goarly.

Then the Senator's heart was softened again, and he explained at great length that he would watch the case and, if he saw his way clearly, befriend it with substantial aid. He asked about the attorney and took down Bearside's address. After that he shook hands with both of them, and then made his way back to Bragton through Mr. Twentyman's farm.

Mr. and Mrs. Goarly were left in a state of great perturbation of mind. They could not in the least make out among themselves who the gentleman was, or whether he had come for good or evil. That he called himself Gotobed, Goarly did remember, and also that he had said that he was an American. All that which he had referred to senatorial honours and the State of Mikewa had been lost upon Goarly. The question, of course, arose whether he was not a spy sent out by Lord Rufford's man of business, and Mrs. Goarly was clearly of opinion that such had been the nature of his employment. Had he really been a friend, she suggested, he would have left a sovereign behind him. 'He didn't get no information from me,' said Goarly.

'Only about Mr. Bearside.'

'What's the odds of that? They all knows that. Bearside! Why should I be ashamed of Bearside? I'll do a deal better with Bearside than I would with that old woman, Masters.'

'But he took it down in writing, Dan.'

'What the d——'s the odds in that?'

'I don't like it when they puts it down in writing.'

'Hold your jaw,' said Goarly as he slowly shouldered the dung-fork to take it back to his work. But as they again discussed the matter that night the opinion gained ground upon them that the Senator had been an emissary from the enemy.

Chapter XVII

LORD RUFFORD'S INVITATION

ON that same Wednesday afternoon when Morton returned with the ladies in the carriage he found that a mounted servant had arrived from Rufford Hall with a letter and had been instructed to wait for an answer. The man was now refreshing himself in the servant's hall. Morton, when he had read the letter, found that it required some consideration before he could answer it. It was to the following purport: Lord Rufford had a party of ladies and gentlemen at Rufford Hall, as his sister, Lady Penwether, was staying with him. Would Mr. Morton and his guests come over to Rufford Hall on Monday and stay till Wednesday? On Tuesday there was to be a dance for the people of the neighbourhood. Then he specified, as the guests invited, Lady Augustus and her daughter and Mr. Gotobed,—omitting the Honourable Mrs. Morton, of whose sojourn in the county he might have been ignorant. His lordship went on to say that he

trusted the abruptness of the invitation might be excused
on account of the nearness of their neighbourhood and the
old friendship which had existed between their families.
He had had, he said, the pleasure of being acquainted
with Lady Augustus and her daughter in London and
would be proud to see Mr. Gotobed at his house during his
sojourn in the county. Then he added in a postscript that
the hounds met at Rufford Hall on Tuesday, and that he
had a horse that carried a lady well if Miss Trefoil would
like to ride him. He could also put up a horse for Mr.
Morton.

This was all very civil, but there was something in it
that was almost too civil. There came upon Morton a
suspicion, which he did not even define to himself, that
the invitation was due to Arabella's charms. There were
many reasons why he did not wish to accept it. His
grandmother was left out, and he feared that she would
be angry. He did not feel inclined to take the American
Senator to the lord's house, knowing as he did that the
American Senator was interfering in a ridiculous manner
on behalf of Goarly. And he did not particularly wish
to be present at Rufford Hall with the Trefoil ladies.
Hitherto he had received very little satisfaction from their
visit to Bragton,—so little that he had been more than
once on the verge of asking Arabella whether she wished
to be relieved from her engagement. She had never quite
given him the opportunity. She had always been gracious
to him in a cold, disagreeable, glassy manner,—in a
manner that irked his spirit but still did not justify him in
expressing anger. Lady Augustus was almost uncivil to
him, and from time to time said little things which were
hard to bear; but he was not going to marry Lady
Augustus, and could revenge himself against her by resolving in his own breast that he would have as little as
possible to do with her after his marriage. That was the
condition of his mind towards them, and in that condition
he did not want to take them to Lord Rufford's house.
Their visit to him would be over on Monday, and it
would, he thought, be better for him that they should
then go on their way to the Gores' as they had proposed.

But he did not like to answer the letter by a refusal without saying a word to his guests on the subject. He would not object to ignore the Senator, but he was afraid that if nothing were to be said to Arabella she would hear of it hereafter and would complain of such treatment. He therefore directed that the man might be kept waiting while he consulted the lady of his choice. It was with difficulty that he found himself alone with her,—and then only by sending her maid in quest of her. He did get her at last into his own sitting-room and then, having placed her in a chair near the fire, gave her Lord Rufford's letter to read. 'What can it be,' said she looking up into his face with her great inexpressive eyes, 'that has required all this solemnity?' She still looked at him and did not even open the letter.

'I did not like to answer that without showing it to you. I don't suppose you would care to go.'

'Go where?'

'It is from Lord Rufford,—for Monday.'

'From Lord Rufford!'

'It would break up all your plans and your mother's, and would probably be a great bore.'

Then she did read the letter, very carefully and very slowly, weighing every word of it as she read it. Did it mean more than it said? But though she read it slowly and carefully, and was long before she made him any answer, she had very quickly resolved that the invitation should be accepted. It would suit her very well to know Lady Penwether. It might possibly suit her still better to become intimate with Lord Rufford. She was delighted at the idea of riding Lord Rufford's horse. As her eyes dwelt on the paper she, too, began to think that the invitation had been chiefly given on her account. At any rate, she would go. She had understood perfectly well from the first tone of her lover's voice that he did not wish to subject her to the allurements of Rufford Hall. She was clever enough, and could read it all. But she did not mean to throw away a chance for the sake of pleasing him. She must not at once displease him by declaring her purpose strongly, and therefore, as she slowly continued her reading, she resolved that she would throw the burden upon her mother. 'Had I not better show this to mamma?' she said.

'You can if you please. You are going to the Gores on Monday.'

'We could not go earlier; but we might put it off for a couple of days if we pleased. Would it bore you?'

'I don't mind about myself. I'm not a very great man for dances.'

'You'd sooner write a report,—wouldn't you,—about the products of the country?'

'A great deal sooner,' said the Paragon.

'But, you see, we haven't all of us got products to write about. I don't care very much about it myself;—but if you don't mind I'll ask mamma.' Of course he was obliged to consent, and merely informed her as she went off with the letter that a servant was waiting for an answer.

'To go to Lord Rufford's!' said Lady Augustus.

'From Monday till Wednesday, mamma. Of course we must go.'

'I promised poor Mrs. Gore.'

'Nonsense, mamma! The Gores can do very well without us. That was only to be a week, and we can still stay out our time. Of course this has only been sent because we are here.'

'I should say so. I don't suppose Lord Rufford would care to know Mr. Morton. Lady Penwether goes everywhere; doesn't she?'

'Everywhere. It would suit me to a 't' to get on to Lady Penwether's books. But, mamma, of course it's not that. If Lord Rufford should say a word, it is so much easier to manage down in the country than up in London. He has £40,000 a year, if he has a penny.'

'How many girls have tried the same thing with him! But I don't mind. I've always said that John Morton and Bragton would not do.'

'No, mamma, you haven't. You were the first to say they would do.'

'I only said that if there were nothing else——'

'Oh, mamma, how can you say such things! Nothing else,—as if he were the last man! You said distinctly that Bragton was £7,000 a year, and that it would do very well. You may change your mind if you like; but it's no good trying to back out of your own doings.'

'Then I have changed my mind.'

'Yes,—without thinking what I have to go through. I'm not going to throw myself at Lord Rufford's head so as to lose my chance here;—but we'll go and see how the land lies. Of course you'll go, mamma?'

'If you think it is for your advantage, my dear.'

'My advantage! It's part of the work to be done, and we may as well do it. At any rate, I'll tell him to accept. We shall have this odious American with us, but that can't be helped.'

'And the old woman?'

'Lord Rufford doesn't say anything about her. I don't suppose he's such a muff but what he can leave his grandmother behind for a couple of days.' Then she went back to Morton and told him that her mother was particularly anxious to make the acquaintance of Lady Penwether, and that she had decided upon going to Rufford Hall. 'It will be a very nice opportunity,' said she, 'for you to become acquainted with Lord Rufford.'

Then he was almost angry. 'I can make plenty of such opportunities for myself, when I want them,' he said. 'Of course if you and Lady Augustus like it, we will go. But let it stand on its right bottom.'

'It may stand on any bottom you please.'

'Do you mean to ride the man's horse?'

'Certainly I do. I never refuse a good offer. Why shouldn't I ride the man's horse? Did you never hear before of a young lady borrowing a gentleman's horse?'

'No lady belonging to me will ever do so,—unless the gentleman be a very close friend indeed.'

'The lady in this case does not belong to you, Mr. Morton, and therefore, if you have no other objection, she will ride Lord Rufford's horse. Perhaps you will not think it too much trouble to signify the lady's acceptance of the mount in your letter.' Then she swam out of the room, knowing that she left him in anger. After that he had to find Mr. Gotobed. The going was now decided on as far as he was concerned, and it would make very little difference whether the American went or not,—except that his letter would have been easier to him in accepting the invitation for three persons than for four. But the Senator was of course willing. It was the Senator's object to see England, and Lord Rufford's house was an additional bit of England. The Senator would be delighted to have an opportunity of saying what he thought about Goarly at Lord Rufford's table. After that, before this weary letter could be written, he was compelled to see his grandmother, and explain to her that she had been omitted.

'Of course, ma'am, they did not know that you were at Bragton, as you were not in the carriage at the "meet".'

'That's nonsense, John. Did Lord Rufford suppose that you were entertaining ladies here without some one to be mistress of the house? Of course he knew that I was here. I shouldn't have gone;—you may be sure of that. I'm not in the habit of going to the houses of people I don't know. Indeed I think it's an impertinence in them to ask in that way. I'm surprised that you would go on such an invitation.'

'The Trefoils knew them.'

'If Lady Penwether knew them, why could not Lady Penwether ask them independently of us? I don't believe they ever spoke to Lady Penwether in their lives. Lord Rufford and Miss Trefoil may very likely be London acquaintances. He may admire her and therefore choose to have her at his ball. I know nothing about that. As far as I am concerned he's quite welcome to keep her.'

All this was not very pleasant to John Morton. He knew already that his grandmother and Lady Augustus hated each other, and said spiteful things not only behind each other's backs, but openly to each other's faces. But now he had been told by the girl who was engaged to be his wife that she did not belong to him; and by his grandmother,—who stood to him in the place of his mother,— that she wished that this girl belonged to some one else!

He was not quite sure that he did not wish it himself. But, even were it to be so, and should there be reason for him to be gratified at the escape, still he did not relish the idea of taking the girl himself to the other man's house. He wrote the letter, however, and dispatched it. But even the writing of it was difficult and disagreeable. When various details of hospitality have been offered by a comparative stranger a man hardly likes to accept them all. But in this case he had to do it. He would be delighted, he said, to stay at Rufford Hall from the Monday to the Wednesday;—Lady Augustus and Miss Trefoil would also be delighted;—and so also would Mr. Gotobed be delighted. And Miss Trefoil would be further delighted to accept Lord Rufford's offer of a horse for the Tuesday. As for himself, if he rode at all, a horse would come for him to the meet. Then he wrote another note to Mr. Harry Stubbings, bespeaking a mount for the occasion.

On that evening the party at Bragton was not a very pleasant one. 'No doubt you are intimate with Lady Penwether, Lady Augustus?' said Mrs. Morton. Now Lady Penwether was a very fashionable woman whom to know was considered an honour.

'What makes you ask, ma'am?' said Lady Augustus.

'Only as you were taking your daughter to her brother's house, and as he is a bachelor.'

'My dear Mrs. Morton, really you may leave me to take care of myself and of my daughter too. You have lived so much out of the world for the last thirty years that it is quite amusing.'

'There are some persons' worlds that it is a great deal better for a lady to be out of,' said Mrs. Morton. Then Lady Augustus put up her hands, and turned round, and affected to laugh, of all which things Mr. Gotobed, who was studying English society, made notes in his own mind.

'What sort of a position does that man Goarly occupy here?' the Senator asked immediately after dinner.

'No position at all,' said Morton.

'Every man created holds some position, as I take it. The land is his own.'

'He has, I believe, about fifty acres.'

'And yet he seems to be in the lowest depth of poverty and ignorance.'

'Of course he mismanages his property and probably drinks.'

'I dare say, Mr. Morton. He is proud of his rights, and talked of his father and his grandfather, and yet I doubt whether you would find a man so squalid and so ignorant in all the States. I suppose he is injured by having a lord so near him.'

'Quite the contrary if he would be amenable.'

'You mean if he would be a creature of the lord's. And why was that other man so uncivil to me;—the man who was the lord's game-keeper?'

'Because you went there as a friend of Goarly.'

'And that's his idea of English fair play?' asked the Senator with a jeer.

'The truth is, Mr. Gotobed,' said Morton endeavouring to explain it all, 'you see a part only and not the whole. That man Goarly is a rascal.'

'So everybody says.'

'And why can't you believe everybody?'

'So everybody says on the lord's side. But before I'm done I'll find out what people say on the other side. I can see that he is ignorant and squalid; but that very probably is the lord's fault. It may be that he is a rascal and that the lord is to blame for that too. But if the lord's pheasants have eaten up Goarly's corn, the lord ought to pay for the corn whether Goarly be a rascal or not.' Then John Morton made up his mind that he would never ask another American Senator to his house.

CHAPTER XVIII

THE ATTORNEY'S FAMILY IS DISTURBED

ON that Wednesday evening Mary Masters said nothing to any of her family as to the invitation from Lady Ushant. She very much wished to accept it. Latterly, for the last month or two, her distaste to the

kind of life for which her stepmother was preparing her
had increased upon her greatly. There had been days in
which she had doubted whether it might not be expedient
that she should accept Mr. Twentyman's offer. She
believed no ill of him. She thought him to be a fine,
manly young fellow, with a good heart and high principles. She never asked herself whether he were or were
not a gentleman. She had never even inquired of herself whether she herself were or were not especially a lady.
But with all her efforts to like the man—because she
thought that by doing so she would relieve and please her
father—yet he was distasteful to her; and now, since that
walk home with him from Bragton Bridge, he was more
distasteful than ever. She did not tell herself that a short
visit, say for a month, to Cheltenham would prevent his
further attentions, but she felt that there would be a
temporary escape. I do not think that she dwelt much on
the suggestion that Reginald Morton should be her
companion on the journey, but the idea of such companionship, even for a short time, was pleasant to her.
If he did this, surely then he would forgive her for having
left him at the bridge. She had much to think of before
she could resolve how she should tell her tidings. Should
she show the letter first to her stepmother or to her father?
In the ordinary course of things in that house the former
course would be expected. It was Mrs. Masters who
managed everything affecting the family. It was she who
gave permission or denied permission for every indulgence.
She was generally fair to the three girls, taking special
pride to herself for doing her duty by her stepdaughter;
but on this very account she was the more likely to be
angry if Mary passed her by on such an occasion as this
and went to her father. But should her stepmother have
once refused her permission, then the matter would have
been decided against her. It would be quite useless to
appeal from her stepmother to her father; nor would such
an appeal come within the scope of her own principles.
The Mortons, and especially Lady Ushant, had been her
father's friends in old days, and she thought that perhaps
she might prevail in this case if she could speak to her

father first. She knew well what would be the great, or
rather the real objection. Her mother would not wish
that she should be removed so long from Larry Twentyman. There might be difficulties about her clothes, but
her father, she knew, would be kind to her.

At last she made up her mind that she would ask her
father. He was always at his office desk for half an hour
in the morning, before the clerks had come, and on the
following day, a minute or two after he had taken his seat,
she knocked at the door. He was busy reading a letter
from Lord Rufford's man of business, asking him certain
questions about Goarly, and almost employing him to get
up the case on Lord Rufford's behalf. There was a certain
triumph to him in this. It was not by his means that
tidings had reached Lord Rufford of his refusal to undertake Goarly's case. But Runciman, who was often
allowed by his lordship to say a few words to him in the
hunting-field, had mentioned the circumstance. 'A man
like Mr. Masters is better without such a blackguard as
that,' the lord had said. Then Runciman had replied,
'No doubt, my lord; no doubt. But Dillsborough is a poor
place, and business is business, my lord.' Then Lord
Rufford had remembered it, and the letter which the
attorney was somewhat triumphantly reading had been
the consequence.

'Is that you, Mary? What can I do for you, my love?'

'Papa, I want you to read this.' Then Mr. Masters
read the letter. 'I should so like to go.'

'Should you, my dear?'

'Oh, yes. Lady Ushant has been so kind to me, all my
life. And I do so love her!'

'What does mamma say?'

'I haven't asked mamma?'

'Is there any reason why you shouldn't go?'

Of that one reason—as to Larry Twentyman—of course
she would say nothing. She must leave him to discuss that
with her mother. 'I should want some clothes, papa; a
dress, and some boots, and a new hat, and there would be
money for the journey, and a few other things.' The
attorney winced, but at the same time remembered that

something was due to his eldest child in the way of garments and relaxation. 'I never like to be an expense, papa.'

'You are very good about that, my dear. I don't see why you shouldn't go. It's very kind of Lady Ushant. I'll talk to mamma.' Then Mary went away to get the breakfast, fearing that before long there would be black looks in the house.

Mr. Masters at once went up to his wife, having given himself a minute or two to calculate that he would let Mary have twenty pounds for the occasion, and made his proposition. 'I never heard of such nonsense in my life,' said Mrs. Masters.

'Nonsense, my dear! Why should it be nonsense?'

'Cocking her up with Lady Ushant! What good will Lady Ushant do her? She's not going to live with ladies of quality all her life.'

'Why shouldn't she live with ladies?'

'You know what I mean, Gregory. The Mortons have dropped you, for any use they were to you, long ago, and you may as well make up your mind to drop them. You'll go on hankering after gentlefolks till you've about ruined yourself.'

When he remembered that he had that very morning received a commission from Lord Rufford he thought that this was a little too bad. But he was not now in a humour to make known to her this piece of good news. 'I like to feel that she has got friends,' he said, going back to Mary's proposed visit.

'Of course she has got friends, if she'll only take up with them as she ought to do. Why does she go on shilly-shallying with that young man, instead of closing on it at once? If she did that she wouldn't want such friends as Lady Ushant. Why did the girl come to you with all this instead of asking me?'

'There would be a little money wanted.'

'Money! Yes, I dare say. It's very easy to want money but very hard to get it. If you send clients away out of the office with a flea in their ear I don't see how she's to have all manner of luxuries. She ought to have come to me.'

'I don't see that at all, my dear.'

'If I'm to look after her she shall be said by me;—that's all. I've done for her just as I have for my own, and I'm not going to have her turn up her nose at me directly she wants anything for herself. I know what's fit for Mary, and it ain't fit that she should go trapesing away to Cheltenham, doing nothing in that old woman's parlour, and losing her chances for life. Who is to suppose that Larry Twentyman will go on dangling after her in this way, month after month? The young man wants a wife, and of course he'll get one.'

'You can't make her marry the man if she don't like him.'

'Like him! She ought to be made to like him. A young man well off as he is, and she without a shilling! All that comes from Ushanting.' It never occurred to Mrs. Masters that perhaps the very qualities that had made poor Larry so vehemently in love with Mary had come from her intercourse with Lady Ushant. 'If I'm to have my way she won't go a yard on the way to Cheltenham.'

'I've told her she may go,' said Mr. Masters, whose mind was wandering back to old days,—to his first wife, and to the time when he used to be an occasional guest in the big parlour at Bragton. He was always ready to acknowledge to himself that his present wife was a good and helpful companion to him and a careful mother to his children; but there were moments in which he would remember with soft regret a different phase of his life. Just at present he was somewhat angry, and resolving in his own mind that in this case he would have his own way.

'Then I shall tell her she mayn't,' said Mrs. Masters, with a look of dogged determination.

'I hope you will do nothing of the kind, my dear. I've told her that she shall have a few pounds to get what she wants, and I won't have her disappointed.' After that Mrs. Masters bounced out of the room, and made herself very disagreeable indeed over the tea-things.

The whole household was much disturbed that day. Mrs. Masters said nothing to Mary about Lady Ushant all the morning, but said a great deal about other things. Poor Mary was asked whether she was not ashamed to treat a young man as she was treating Mr. Twentyman. Then again it was demanded of her whether she thought it right that all the house should be knocked about for her. At dinner Mrs. Masters would hardly speak to her husband but addressed herself exclusively to Dolly and Kate. Mr. Masters was not a man who could, usually, stand this kind of thing very long and was accustomed to give up in despair and then take himself off to the solace of his office-chair. But on the present occasion he went on through his meal like a Spartan, and retired from the room without a sign of surrender. In the afternoon about five o'clock Mary watched her opportunity and found him again alone. It was incumbent on her to reply to Lady Ushant. Would it not be better that she should write and say how sorry she was that she could not come? 'But I want you to go,' said he.

'Oh, papa;—I cannot bear to cause trouble.'

'No, my dear, no; and I'm sure I don't like trouble myself. But in this case I think you ought to go. What day has she named?' Then Mary declared that she could not possibly go so soon as Lady Ushant had suggested, but that she could be ready by the 18th of December. 'Then write and tell her so, my dear, and I will let your mother know that it is fixed.' But Mary still hesitated, desiring to know whether she had not better speak to her mother first. 'I think you had better write your letter first,'—and then he absolutely made her write in the office and give it to him to be posted. After that he promised to communicate to Reginald Morton what had been done.

The household was very much disturbed the whole of that evening. Poor Mary never remembered such a state of things, and when there had been any difference of opinion, she had hitherto never been the cause of it. Now it was all owing to her! and things were said so terrible that she hardly knew how to bear them. Her father had promised her the twenty pounds, and it was insinuated that all the comforts of the family must be stopped because of this lavish extravagance. Her father sat still and bore it, almost without a word. Both Dolly and Kate were silent and wretched. Mrs. Masters every now and then gurgled in her throat, and three or four times wiped her eyes. 'I'm better out of the way altogether,' she said at last, jumping up and walking towards the door as though she were going to leave the room,—and the house, for ever.

'Mamma,' said Mary, rising from her seat, 'I won't go. I'll write to Lady Ushant that I can't do it.'

'You're not to mind me,' said Mrs. Masters. 'You're to do what your papa tells you. Everything that I have been striving at is to be thrown away. I'm to be nobody, and it's quite right that your papa should tell you so.'

'Dear mamma, don't talk like that,' said Mary, clinging hold of her stepmother.

'Your papa sits there and won't say a word,' said Mrs. Masters, stamping her foot.

'What's the good of speaking, when you go on like that before the children?' said Mr. Masters, getting up from his chair. 'I say that it's a proper thing that the girl should go to see the old friend who brought her up, and has been always kind to her—and she shall go.' Mrs. Masters seated herself on the nearest chair, and leaning her head against the wall, began to go into hysterics. 'Your letter has already gone, Mary; and I desire you will write no other without letting me know.' Then he left the room and the house, and absolutely went over to the Bush. This latter proceeding was, however, hardly more than a bravado; for he merely took the opportunity of asking Mrs. Runciman a question at the bar, and then walked back to his own house, and shut himself up in the office.

On the next morning he called on Reginald Morton and told him that his daughter had accepted Lady Ushant's invitation, but could not go till the 18th. 'I shall be proud to take charge of her,' said Reginald. 'And as for the change in the day it will suit me all the better.' So that was settled.

On the next day, Friday, Mrs. Masters did not come

down to breakfast, but was waited upon upstairs by her own daughters. This with her was a most unusual circumstance. The two maids were of opinion that such a thing had never occurred before, and that therefore master must have been out half the night at the public-house although they had not known it. To Mary she would hardly speak a word. She appeared at dinner, and called her husband Mr. Masters when she helped him to stew. All the afternoon she averred that her head was splitting, but managed to say many very bitter things about gentlemen in general, and expressed a vehement hope that the poor man Goarly would get at least a hundred pounds. It must be owned, however, that at this time she had heard nothing of Lord Rufford's commission to her husband. In the evening Larry came in and was at once told the terrible news. 'Larry,' said Kate, 'Mary is going away for a month.'

'Where are you going, Mary?' asked the lover eagerly.

'To Lady Ushant's, Mr. Twentyman.'

'For a month!'

'She has asked me for a month,' said Mary.

'It's a regular fool's errand,' said Mrs. Masters. 'It's not done with my consent, Mr. Twentyman. I don't think she ought to stir from home till things are more settled.'

'They can be settled this moment as far as I am concerned,' said Larry standing up.

'There now,' said Mrs. Masters. At this time Mr. Masters was not in the room. 'If you can make it straight with Mr. Twentyman I won't say a word against your going away for a month.'

'Mamma, you shouldn't!' exclaimed Mary.

'I hate such nonsense. Mr. Twentyman is behaving honest and genteel. What more would you have? Give him an answer like a sensible girl.'

'I have given him an answer and I cannot say anything more,' said Mary as she left the room.

Chapter XIX

'WHO VALUED THE GEESE?'

BEFORE the time had come for the visit to Rufford Hall Mr. Gotobed had called upon Bearside the attorney and had learned as much as Mr. Bearside chose to tell him of the facts of the case. This took place on the Saturday morning and the interview was on the whole satisfactory to the Senator. But then having a theory of his own in his head, and being fond of ventilating his own theories, he explained thoroughly to the man the story which he wished to hear before the man was called upon to tell his story. Mr. Bearside of course told it accordingly. Goarly was a very poor man, and very ignorant; was perhaps not altogether so good a member of society as he might have been; but no doubt he had a strong case against the lord. The lord, so said Mr. Bearside, had fallen into a way of paying a certain recompense in certain cases for crops damaged by game;—and having in this way laid down a rule for himself did not choose to have that rule disturbed. 'Just feudalism!' said the indignant Senator. 'No better, nor yet no worse than that, sir,' said the attorney, who did not in the least know what feudalism was. 'The strong hand backed by the strong rank, and the strong purse determined to have its own way!' continued the Senator. 'A most determined man is his lordship,' said the attorney. Then the Senator expressed his hope that Mr. Bearside would be able to see the poor man through it, and Mr. Bearside explained to the Senator that the poor man was a very poor man indeed, who had been so unfortunate with his land that he was hardly able to provide bread for himself and his children. He went so far as to insinuate that he was taking up this matter himself solely on the score of charity, adding that, as he could not of course afford to be money out of pocket for expenses of witnesses, etc., he did not quite see how he was to proceed. Then the Senator made certain promises. He was, he said, going back to London in the course of next week, but he did not mind making himself responsible to the extent of fifty dollars if the thing were carried on, bonâ fide, to a conclusion. Mr. Bearside declared that it would of course be bonâ fide, and asked the Senator for his address. Would Mr. Gotobed object to putting his name to a little docket certifying to the amount promised? Mr. Gotobed gave an address, but thought that in such a matter as that his word might be trusted. If it were not trusted, then the offer might fall to the ground. Mr. Bearside was profuse in his apologies and declared that the gentleman's word was as good as his bond.

Mr. Gotobed made no secret of his doings. Perhaps he had a feeling that he could not justify himself in so strange a proceeding without absolute candour. He saw Mr. Mainwaring in the street as he left Bearside's office and told him all about it. 'I just want, sir, to see what'll come of it.'

'You'll lose your fifty dollars, Mr. Gotobed, and only cause a little vexation to a high-spirited young nobleman.'

'Very likely, sir. But neither the loss of my dollars, nor Lord Rufford's slight vexation, will in the least disturb my rest. I'm not a rich man, sir, but I should like to watch the way in which such a question will be tried and brought to a conclusion in this aristocratic country. I don't quite know what your laws may be, Mr. Mainwaring?'

'Just the same as your own, Mr. Gotobed, I take it.'

'We have no game laws, sir. As I was saying I don't understand your laws, but justice is the same everywhere. If this great lord's game has eaten up the poor man's wheat the great lord ought to pay for it.'

'The owners of game pay for the damage they do three times over,' said the parson, who was very strongly on that side of the question. 'Do you think that such men as Goarly would be better off if the gentry were never to come into the country at all?'

'Perhaps, Mr. Mainwaring, I may think that there would be no Goarlys if there were no Ruffords. That, however, is a great question which cannot be argued on this case. All we can hope here is that one poor man may have an act of justice done him, though in seeking for it he has to struggle against so wealthy a magnate as Lord Rufford.'

'What I hope is that he may be found out,' replied Mr. Mainwaring with equal enthusiasm, 'and then he will be in Rufford gaol before long. That's the justice I look for. Who do you think put down the poison in Dillsborough Wood?'

'How was it that the poor woman lost all her geese?' asked the Senator.

'She was paid for a great many more than she lost, Mr. Gotobed.'

'That doesn't touch upon the injustice of the proceeding. Who assessed the loss, sir? Who valued the geese? Am I to keep a pet tiger in my garden, and give you a couple of dollars when he destroys your pet dog, and think myself justified because dogs as a rule are not worth more than two dollars each? She has a right to her own geese on her own ground.'

'And Lord Rufford, sir, as I take it,' said Runciman, who had been allowed to come up and hear the end of the conversation, 'has a right to his own foxes in his own coverts.'

'Yes,—if he could keep them there, my friend. But as it is the nature of foxes to wander away and to be thieves, he has no such right.'

'Of course, sir, begging your pardon,' said Runciman, 'I was speaking of England.' Runciman had heard of the Senator Gotobed, as indeed had all Dillsborough by this time.

'And I am speaking of justice all the world over,' said the Senator, slapping his hand upon his thigh. 'But I only want to see. It may be that England is a country in which a poor man should not attempt to hold a few acres of land.'

On that night the Dillsborough club met as usual and, as a matter of course, Goarly and the American Senator were the subjects chiefly discussed. Everybody in the room knew,—or thought that he knew,—that Goarly was a cheating, fraudulent knave, and that Lord Rufford was,

at any rate, in this case acting properly. They all understood the old goose, and were aware, nearly to a bushel, of
the amount of wheat which the man had sold off those
two fields. Runciman knew that the interest on the
mortgage had been paid, and could only have been paid
out of the produce; and Larry Twentyman knew that if
Goarly took his 7s. 6d. an acre he would be better off than
if the wood had not been there. But yet among them all
they didn't quite see how they were to confute the
Senator's logic. They could not answer it satisfactorily,
even among themselves; but they felt that if Goarly could
be detected in some offence, that would confute the
Senator. Among themselves it was sufficient to repeat
the well-known fact that Goarly was a rascal; but with
reference to this aggravating, interfering, and most ob-
noxious American it would be necessary to prove it.

'His lordship has put it into Masters's hands, I'm told,'
said the doctor. At this time neither the attorney nor
Larry Twentyman was in the room.

'He couldn't have done better,' said Runciman, speaking from behind a long clay pipe.

'All the same he was nibbling at Goarly,' said Fred
Botsey.

'I don't know that he was nibbling at Goarly at all,
Mr. Botsey,' said the landlord. 'Goarly came to him, and
Goarly was refused. What more would you have?'

'It's all one to me,' said Botsey, 'only I do think that in
a sporting county like this the place ought to be made too
hot to hold a blackguard like that. If he comes out at me
with his gun I'll ride over him. And I wouldn't mind
riding over that American too.'

'That's just what would suit Goarly's book,' said the
doctor.

'Exactly what Goarly would like,' said Harry Stubbings.

Then Mr. Masters and Larry entered the room. On
that evening two things had occurred to the attorney.
Nickem had returned, and had asked for and received an
additional week's leave of absence. He had declined to
explain accurately what he was doing, but gave the
attorney to understand that he thought that he was on

the way to the bottom of the whole thing. Then, after Nickem had left him, Mr. Masters had a letter of instructions from Lord Rufford's steward. When he received it, and found that his paid services had been absolutely employed on behalf of his lordship, he almost regretted the encouragement he had given to Nickem. In the first place he might want Nickem. And then he felt that in his present position he ought not to be a party to anything underhand. But Nickem was gone, and he was obliged to console himself by thinking that Nickem was at any rate employing his intellect on the right side. When he left his house with Larry Twentyman he had told his wife nothing about Lord Rufford. Up to this time he and his wife had not as yet reconciled their difference, and poor Mary was still living in misery. Larry, though he had called for the attorney, had not sat down in the parlour, and had barely spoken to Mary. 'For gracious' sake, Mr. Twentyman, don't let him stay in that place there half the night,' said Mrs. Masters. 'It ain't fit for a father of a family.'

'Father never does stay half the night,' said Kate, who took more liberties in that house than any one else.

'Hold your tongue, miss. I don't know whether it wouldn't be better for you, Mr. Twentyman, if you were not there so often yourself.' Poor Larry felt this to be hard. He was not even engaged as yet, and as far as he could see was not on the way to be engaged. In such condition surely his possible mother-in-law could have no right to interfere with him. He condescended to make no reply, but crossed the passage and carried the attorney off with him.

'You've heard what that American gentleman has been about, Mr. Masters?' asked the landlord.

'I'm told he's been with Bearside.'

'And has offered to pay his bill for him if he'll carry on the business for Goarly. Whoever heard the like of that?'

'What sort of a man is he?' asked the doctor.

'A great man in his own country, everybody says,' answered Runciman. 'I wish he'd stayed there. He comes over here and thinks he understands everything

just as though he had lived here all his life. Did you say
gin cold, Larry;—and rum for you, Mr. Masters?' Then
the landlord gave the orders to the girl who had answered
the bell.

'But they say he's actually going to Lord Rufford's,'
said young Botsey, who would have given one of his
fingers to be asked to the lord's house.

'They are all going from Bragton,' said Runciman.

'The young squire is going to ride one of my horses,'
said Harry Stubbings.

'That'll be an easy three pounds in your pockets, Harry,'
said the doctor. In answer to which Harry remarked
that he took all that as it came, the heavies and lights
together, and that there was not much change to be got
out of three sovereigns when some gentlemen had had
a horse out for the day,—particularly when a gentleman
didn't pay perhaps for twelve months.

'The whole party is going,' continued the landlord.
'How he is to have the cheek to go into his lordship's house
after what he is doing is more than I can understand.'

'What business is it of his?' said Larry angrily. 'That's
what I want to know. What'd he think if we went and
interfered over there? I shouldn't be surprised if he got
a little rough usage before he's out of the county. I'm
told he came across Bean when he was ferreting about
the other day, and that Bean gave him quite as good as
he brought.'

'I say he's a spy,' said Ribbs the butcher, from his seat
on the sofa. 'I hates a spy.'

Soon after that Mr. Masters left the room and Larry
Twentyman followed him. There was something almost
ridiculous in the way the young man would follow the
attorney about on these Saturday evenings,—as though
he could make love to the girl by talking to the father.
But on this occasion he had something special to say.
'So Mary's going to Cheltenham, Mr. Masters?'

'Yes, she is. You don't see any objection to that, I hope.'

'Not in the least, Mr. Masters. I wish she might go
anywhere to enjoy herself. And from all I've heard Lady
Ushant is a very good sort of lady.'

'A very good sort of lady. She won't do Mary any harm, Twentyman.'

'I don't suppose she will. But there's one thing I should like to know. Why shouldn't she tell me before she goes that she'll have me?'

'I wish she would with all my heart.'

'And Mrs. Masters is all on my side.'

'Quite so.'

'And the girls have always been my friends.'

'I think we are all your friends, Twentyman. I'm sure Mary is. But that isn't marrying;—is it?'

'If you would speak to her, Mr. Masters.'

'What would you have me say? I couldn't bid my girl to have one man or another. I could only tell her what I think, and that she knows already.'

'If you were to say that you wished it! She thinks so much about you.'

'I couldn't tell her that I wished it in a manner that would drive her into it. Of course it would be a very good match. But I have only to think of her happiness, and I must leave her to judge what will make her happy.'

'I should like to have it fixed some way before she starts,' said Larry, in an altered tone.

'Of course you are your own master, Twentyman. And you have behaved very well.'

'This is a kind of thing that a man can't stand,' said the young farmer sulkily. 'Good-night, Mr. Masters.' Then he walked off home to Chowton Farm meditating on his own condition, and trying to make up his mind to leave the scornful girl and become a free man. But he couldn't do it. He couldn't even quite make up his mind that he would try to do it. There was a bitterness within as he thought of permanent fixed failure which he could not digest. There was a craving in his heart which he did not himself quite understand, but which made him think that the world would be unfit to be lived in if he were to be altogether separated from Mary Masters. He couldn't separate himself from her. It was all very well thinking of it, talking of it, threatening it; but, in truth, he couldn't do it. There might, of course. be an emergency in which he must do it. She might declare that she loved some one else and she might marry that other person. In that event he saw no other alternative but,—as he expressed it to himself,—'to run a mucker.'* Whether the 'mucker' should be run against Mary, or against the fortunate lover, or against himself, he did not at present resolve.

But he did resolve as he reached his own hall-door that he would make one more passionate appeal to Mary herself before she started for Cheltenham, and that he would not make it out on a public path, or in the Masters' family parlour before all the Masters' family;—but that he would have her secluded, by herself, so that he might speak out all that was in him, to the best of his ability.

CHAPTER XX

THERE ARE CONVENANCES

BEFORE the Monday came the party to Rufford Hall had become quite a settled thing and had been very much discussed. On the Saturday the Senator had been driven to the meet, a distance of about ten miles, on purpose that he might see Lord Rufford and explain his views about Goarly. Lord Rufford had bowed, and stared, and laughed, and had then told the Senator that he thought he would 'find himself in the wrong box.' 'That's quite possible, my lord. I guess, it won't be the first time I've been in the wrong box, my lord. Sometimes I do get right. But I thought I would not enter your lordship's house as a guest without telling you what I was doing.' Then Lord Rufford assured him that this little affair about Goarly would make no difference in that respect. Mr. Gotobed again scrutinised the hounds and Tony Tuppett, laughed in his sleeve because a fox wasn't found in the first quarter of an hour, and after that was driven back to Bragton.

The Sunday was a day of preparation for the Trefoils. Of course they didn't go to church. Arabella, indeed, was never up in time for church, and Lady Augustus only

went when her going would be duly registered among
fashionable people. Mr. Gotobed laughed when he was
invited and asked whether anybody was ever known to
go to church two Sundays running at Bragton. 'People
have been known to refuse with less acrimony,' said
Morton. 'I always speak my mind, sir,' replied the
Senator. Poor John Morton, therefore, went to his parish
church alone.

 There were many things to be considered by the
Trefoils. There was the question of dress. If any good
was to be done by Arabella at Rufford it must be done
with great despatch. There would be the dinner on
Monday, the hunting on Tuesday, the ball, and then the
interesting moment of departure. No girl could make
better use of her time; but then, think of her difficulties!
All that she did would have to be done under the very
eyes of the man to whom she was engaged, and to whom
she wished to remain engaged,—unless, as she said to
herself, she could 'pull off the other event.' A great deal
must depend on appearance. As she and her mother
were out on a lengthened cruise among long-suffering
acquaintances, going to the De Brownes after the Gores,
and the Smijthes after the De Brownes, with as many
holes to run to afterwards as a four-year-old fox,—though
with the same probability of finding them stopped,—of
course she had her wardrobe with her. To see her night
after night one would think that it was supplied with all
that wealth would give. But there were deficiencies and
there were make-shifts, very well known to herself and
well understood by her maid. She could generally supply
herself with gloves by bets, as to which she had never any
scruple in taking either what she did win or did not, and
in dunning any who might chance to be defaulters. On
occasions too, when not afraid of the bystanders, she
would venture on a hat, and though there was difficulty
as to the payment, not being able to give her number as
she did with gloves, so that the tradesmen could send the
article, still she would manage to get the hat,—and the
trimmings. It was said of her that she once offered to lay
an Ulster to a sealskin jacket, but that the young man had

coolly said that a sealskin jacket was beyond a joke and had asked her whether she was ready to 'put down' her Ulster. These were little difficulties from which she usually knew how to extricate herself without embarrassment; but she had not expected to have to marshal her forces against such an enemy as Lord Rufford, or to sit down for the besieging of such a city this campaign. There were little things which required to be done, and the lady's-maid certainly had not time to go to church on Sunday.

But there were other things which troubled her even more than her clothes. She did not much like Bragton, and at Bragton, in his own house, she did not very much like her proposed husband. At Washington he had been somebody. She had met him everywhere then, and had heard him much talked about. At Washington he had been a popular man and had had the reputation of being a rich man also;—but here, in the country of England, he seemed to her to fall off in importance, and he certainly had not made himself pleasant. Whether any man could be pleasant to her in the retirement of a country house,— any man whom she should have no interest in running down, she did not ask herself. An engagement to her must under any circumstances be a humdrum thing,—to be brightened only by wealth. But here she saw no signs of wealth. Nevertheless, she was not prepared to shove away the plank from below her feet, till she was sure that she had a more substantial board on which to step. Her mother, who perhaps did not see in the character of Morton all the charms which she would wish to find in a son-in-law, was anxious to shake off the Bragton alliance; but Arabella, as she said so often both to herself and to her mother, was sick of the dust of the battle and conscious of fading strength. She would make this one more attempt, but must make it with great care. When last in town this young lord had whispered a word or two to her, which then had set her hoping for a couple of days, and now, when chance had brought her into his neighbourhood, he had gone out of his way,—very much out of his way,—to renew his acquaintance with her. She would be mad not to give herself the chance; but yet she could not afford to let the plank go from under her feet.

But the part she had to play was one which even she felt to be almost beyond her powers. She could perceive that Morton was beginning to be jealous,—and that his jealousy was not of that nature which strengthens a tie but which is apt to break it altogether. His jealousy, if fairly aroused, would not be appeased by a final return to himself. She had already given him occasion to declare himself off, and if thoroughly angered he would no doubt use it. Day by day, and almost hour by hour, he was becoming more sombre and hard, and she was well aware that there was reason for it. It did not suit her to walk about alone with him through the shrubberies. It did not suit her to be seen with his arm round her waist. Of course the people of Bragton would talk of the engagement, but she would prefer that they should talk of it with doubt. Even her own maid had declared to Mrs. Hopkins that she did not know whether there was or was not an engagement,—her own maid being at the time almost in her confidence. Very few of the comforts of a lover had been vouchsafed to John Morton during this sojourn at Bragton and very little had been done in accordance with his wishes. Even this visit to Rufford, as she well knew, was being made in opposition to him. She hoped that her lover would not attempt to ride to hounds on the Tuesday, so that she might be near the lord unseen by him,—and that he would leave Rufford on the Wednesday before herself and her mother. At the ball, of course, she could dance with Lord Rufford, and could keep her eye on her lover at the same time.

She hardly saw him on the Sunday afternoon, and she was again closeted on the Monday till lunch. They were to start at four, and there would not be much more than time after lunch for her to put on her travelling gear. Then, as they all felt, there was a difficulty about the carriages. Who was to go with whom? Arabella, after lunch, took the bull by the horns. 'I suppose,' she said as Morton followed her out into the hall, 'mamma and I had better go in the phaeton.'

'I was thinking that Lady Augustus might consent to travel with Mr. Gotobed and that you and I might have the phaeton.'

'Of course it would be very pleasant,' she answered smiling.

'Then why not let it be so?'

'There are convenances.'*

'How would it be if you and I were going without anybody else? Do you mean to say that in that case we might not sit in the same carriage?'

'I mean to say that in that case I should not go at all. It isn't done in England. You have been in the States so long that you forget all our old-fashioned ways.'

'I do think that is nonsense.' She only smiled and shook her head. 'Then the Senator shall go in the phaeton, and I will go with you and your mother.'

'Yes, and quarrel with mamma all the time as you always do. Let me have it my own way this time.'

'Upon my word, I believe you are ashamed of me,' he said, leaning back upon the hall table. He had shut the dining-room door, and she was standing close to him.

'What nonsense!'

'You have only got to say so, Arabella, and let there be an end of it all.'

'If you wish it, Mr. Morton.'

'You know I don't wish it. You know I am ready to marry you to-morrow.'

'You have made ever so many difficulties, as far as I can understand.'

'You have unreasonable people acting for you, Arabella, and of course I don't mean to give way to them.'

'Pray don't talk to me about money. I know nothing about it, and have taken no part in the matter. I suppose there must be settlements.'

'Of course there must.'

'And I can only do what other people tell me. You, at any rate, have something to do with it all, and I have absolutely nothing.'

'That is no reason you shouldn't go in the same carriage with me to Rufford.'

'Are you coming back to that, just like a big child? Do let us consider that as settled. I'm sure you'll let mamma and me have the use of the phaeton?' Of course the little contest was ended in the manner proposed by Arabella.

'I do think,' said Arabella, when she and her mother were seated in the carriage, 'that we have treated him very badly.'

'Quite as well as he deserves. What a house to bring us to; and what people! Did you ever come across such an old woman before? And she has him completely under her thumb. Are you prepared to live with that harridan?'

'You may let me alone, mamma, for all that. She won't be in my way after I'm married, I can tell you.'

'You'll have something to do, then.'

'I ain't a bit afraid of her.'

'And to ask us to meet such people as this American!'

'He's going back to Washington, and it suited him to have him. I don't quarrel with him for that. I wish I were married to him and back in the States.'

'You do?'

'I do.'

'You have given it all up about Lord Rufford, then?'

'No; that's just where it is. I haven't given it up, and I still see trouble upon trouble before me. But I know how it will be. He doesn't mean anything. He's only amusing himself.'

'If he'd once say the word he couldn't get back again. The duke would interfere then.'

'What would he care for the duke? The duke is no more than anybody else nowadays. I shall just fall to the ground between two stools. I know it as well as if it were done already. And then I shall have to begin again! If it comes to that I shall do something terrible, I know I shall.' Then they turned in at Lord Rufford's gates; and as they were driven up beneath the oaks through the gloom, both mother and daughter thought how charming it would be to be the mistress of such a park.

CHAPTER XXI

THE FIRST EVENING AT RUFFORD HALL

THE phaeton arrived the first, the driver having been especially told that he need not delay on the road for the other carriage. She had calculated that she might make her entrance with better effect alone with her mother than in company with Morton and the Senator. It would have been worth the while of any one who had witnessed her troubles on that morning to watch the bland serenity and happy ease with which she entered the room. Her mother was fond of a prominent place, but was quite contented on this occasion to play a second fiddle for her daughter. She had seen at a glance that Rufford Hall was a delightful house. Oh, if it might become the home of her child and her grandchildren, and possibly a retreat for herself! Arabella was certainly very handsome at this moment. Never did she look better than when got up with care for travelling, especially as seen by an evening light. Her slow motions were adapted to heavy wraps, and however she might procure her large sealskin jacket, she graced it well when she got it. Lord Rufford came to the door to meet them, and immediately introduced them to his sister. There were six or seven people in the room, mostly ladies, and tea was offered to the new comers. Lady Penwether was largely made, like her brother; but was a languidly lovely woman, not altogether unlike Arabella herself in her figure and movements, but with a more expressive face, with less colour, and much more positive assurance of high breeding. Lady Penwether was said to be haughty, but it was admitted by all people that when Lady Penwether had said a thing or had done a thing, it might be taken for granted that the way in which she had done or said that thing was the right way. The only other gentleman there was Major Caneback, who had just come in from hunting with some distant pack, and who had been brought into the room by Lord Rufford that he might give some account of the doings of the day. According to Caneback, they had been talking in the Brake country about nothing but Goarly and the enormities which had been perpetrated in the U.R.U. 'By-the-by, Miss Trefoil,' said Lord Rufford, 'What have you done with your Senator?'

'He's on the road, Lord Rufford, examining English institutions as he comes along. He'll be here by midnight.'

'Imagine the man coming to me and telling me that he was a friend of Goarly's. I rather liked him for it. There was a thorough pluck about it. They say he's going to find all the money.'

'I thought Mr. Scrobby was to do that?' said Lady Penwether.

'Mr. Scrobby will not have the slightest objection to have that part of the work done for him. If all we hear is true Miss Trefoil's Senator may have to defend both Scrobby and Goarly.'

'My Senator as you call him will be quite up to the occasion.'

'You knew him in America, Miss Trefoil?' asked Lady Penwether.

'Oh yes. We used to meet him and Mrs. Gotobed everywhere. But we didn't exactly bring him over with us;—though our party down to Bragton was made up in Washington,' she added, feeling that she might in this way account in some degree for her own presence in John Morton's house. 'It was mamma and Mr. Morton arranged it all.'

'Oh, my dear, it was you and the Senator,' said Lady Augustus, ready for the occasion.

'Miss Trefoil,' said the lord, 'let us have it all out at once. Are you taking Goarly's part?'

'Taking Goarly's part!' ejaculated the major.

Arabella affected to give a little start, as though frightened by the major's enthusiasm. 'For Heaven's sake let us know our foes,' continued Lord Rufford. 'You see the effect such an announcement had upon Major Caneback. Have you made an appointment before dawn with Mr. Scrobby under the elms? Now I look at you I believe in my heart you're a Goarlyite—only without the Senator's courage to tell me the truth beforehand.'

'I really am very much obliged to Goarly,' said Arabella, 'because it is so nice to have something to talk about.'

'That's just what I think, Miss Trefoil,' declared a young lady, Miss Penge, who was a friend of Lady Penwether. 'The gentlemen have so much to say about hunting which nobody can understand! But now this delightful man has scattered poison all over the country there is something that comes home to our understanding. I declare myself a Goarlyite at once, Lord Rufford, and shall put myself under the Senator's leading directly he comes.'

During all this time not a word had been said of John Morton, the master of Bragton, the man to whose party these new comers belonged. Lady Augustus and Arabella clearly understood that John Morton was only a peg on which the invitation to them had been hung. The feeling that it was so grew upon them with every word that was spoken,—and also the conviction that he must be treated like a peg at Rufford. The sight of the hangings of the room, so different to the old-fashioned dingy curtains at Bragton, the brilliancy of the mirrors, all the decorations of the place, the very blaze from the big grate, forced upon the girl's feelings a conviction that this was her proper sphere. Here she was, being made much of as a new comer, and here if possible she must remain. Everything smiled on her with gilded dimples, and these were the smiles she valued. As the softness of the cushions sank into her heart, and mellow nothingness from well-trained voices greeted her ears, and the air of wealth and idleness floated about her cheeks, her imagination rose within her and assured her that she could secure something better than Bragton. The cautions with which she had armed herself faded away. This,—this was the kind of thing for which she had been striving. As a girl of spirit was it not worth while to make another effort even though there might be danger? Aut Cæsar aut nihil! She knew nothing about Cæsar, but she declared to herself that she would be Lady Rufford before the tardy wheels which brought the Senator and Mr. Morton had stopped at the door. The fresh party was of course brought into the drawing-room and tea was offered; but Arabella hardly spoke to them, and Lady Augustus did not speak to them at all, and they were shown up to their bedrooms with very little preliminary conversation.

It was very hard to put Mr. Gotobed down; or it might be more correctly said,—as there was no effort to put him down,—that it was not often that he failed in coming to the surface. He took Lady Penwether out to dinner and was soon explaining to her that this little experiment of his in regard to Goarly was being tried simply with the view of examining the institutions of the country. 'We don't mind it from you,' said Lady Penwether, 'because you are in a certain degree a foreigner.' The Senator declared himself flattered by being regarded as a foreigner only 'in a certain degree'. 'You see you speak our language, Mr. Gotobed, and we can't help thinking you are half-English.'

'We are two-thirds English, my lady,' said Mr. Gotobed; 'but we think the other third is an improvement.'

'Very likely.'

'We have nothing so nice as this.' As he spoke he waved his right hand to the different corners of the room. 'Such a dinner-table as I am sitting down to now couldn't be fixed in all the United States, though a man might spend three times as many dollars on it as his lordship does.'

'That is very often done, I should think.'

'But then, as we have nothing so well done as a house like this, so also we have nothing so ill done as the houses of your poor people.'

'Wages are higher with you, Mr. Gotobed.'

'And public spirit, and the philanthropy of the age, and the enlightenment of the people, and the institutions of the country all round. They are all higher.'

'Canvas-back ducks,' said the major, who was sitting two or three off on the other side.

'Yes, sir, we have canvas-back ducks.'

'Make up for a great many faults,' said the major.

'Of course, sir; when a man's stomach rises above his

intelligence, he'll have to argue accordingly,' said the Senator.

'Caneback, what are you going to ride to-morrow?' asked the lord, who saw the necessity of changing the conversation, as far, at least, as the major was concerned.

'Jemima—mare of Purefoy's; have my neck broken, they tell me.'

'It's not improbable,' said Sir John Purefoy, who was sitting at Lady Penwether's left hand. 'Nobody ever could ride her yet.'

'I was thinking of asking you to let Miss Trefoil try her,' said Lord Rufford. Arabella was sitting between Sir John Purefoy and the major.

'Miss Trefoil is quite welcome,' said Sir John. 'It isn't a bad idea. Perhaps she may carry a lady, because she has never been tried. I know that she objects strongly to carry a man.'

'My dear,' said Lady Augustus, 'you shan't do anything of the kind.' And Lady Augustus pretended to be frightened.

'Mamma, you don't suppose Lord Rufford wants to kill me at once.'

'You shall either ride her, Miss Trefoil, or my little horse Jack. But I warn you beforehand that, as Jack is the easiest-ridden horse in the country, and can scramble over anything, and never came down in his life, you won't get any honour and glory; but on Jemima you might make a character that would stick to you till your dying day.'

'But if I ride Jemima, that dying day might be to-morrow. I think I'll take Jack, Lord Rufford, and let Major Caneback have the honour. Is Jack fast?' In this way the anger arising between the Senator and the major was assuaged. The Senator still held his own, and, before the question was settled between Jack and Jemima, had told the company that no Englishman knew how to ride, and that the only seat fit for a man on horseback was that suited for the pacing horses of California and Mexico. Then he assured Sir John Purefoy that eighty miles a day was no great journey for a pacing horse, with a man of fourteen stone and a saddle and accoutrements weighing four more. The major's countenance, when the Senator declared that no Englishman could ride, was a sight worth seeing.

That evening, in the drawing-room, the conversation was chiefly about horses and hunting, and those terrible enemies—Goarly and Scrobby. Lady Penwether and Miss Penge, who didn't hunt, were distantly civil to Lady Augustus, of whom, of course, a woman so much in the world as Lady Penwether knew something. Lady Penwether had shrugged her shoulders when consulted as to these special guests, and had expressed a hope that Rufford 'wasn't going to make a goose of himself.' But she was fond of her brother, and as both Lady Purefoy and Miss Penge were special friends of hers, and as she had also been allowed to invite a couple of Godolphin's girls to whom she wished to be civil, she did as she was asked. The girl, she said to Miss Penge that evening, was handsome, but penniless and a flirt. The mother she declared to be a regular old soldier. As to Lady Augustus she was right; but she had perhaps failed to read Arabella's character correctly. Arabella Trefoil was certainly not a flirt. In all the horsey conversation Arabella joined, and her low, clear, slow voice could be heard now and then as though she were really animated with the subject. At Bragton she had never once spoken as though any matter interested her. During this time Morton fell into conversation first with Lady Purefoy, and then with the two Miss Godolphins, and afterwards for a few minutes with Lady Penwether, who knew that he was a county gentleman and a respectable member of the diplomatic profession. But during the whole evening his ear was intent on the notes of Arabella's voice; and also, during the whole evening, her eye was watching him. She would not lose her chance with Lord Rufford for want of any effort on her part. If aught were required from her in her present task that might be offensive to Mr. Morton—anything that was peremptorily demanded for the effort— she would not scruple to offend the man. But if it might be done without offence, so much the better. Once he

came across the room and said a word to her as she was
talking to Lord Rufford and the Purefoys. 'You are really
in earnest about riding to-morrow?'

'Oh dear, yes. Why shouldn't I be in earnest?'

'You are coming out yourself, I hope,' said the lord.

'I have no horses here of my own, but I have told that
man Stubbings to send me something, and as I haven't
been at Bragton for the last seven years I have nothing
proper to wear. I shan't be called a Goarlyite, I hope, if
I appear in trousers.'

'Not unless you have a basket of red herrings on your
arm,' said Lord Rufford. Then Morton retired back to
the Miss Godolphins finding that he had nothing more to
say to Arabella.

He was very angry,—though he hardly knew why or
with whom. A girl when she is engaged is not supposed
to talk to no one but her recognised lover in a mixed
party of ladies and gentlemen, and she is especially
absolved from such a duty when they chance to meet in
the house of a comparative stranger. In such a house and
amongst such people it was natural that the talk should
be about hunting, and as the girl had accepted the loan
of a horse it was natural that she should join in such conversation. She had never sat for a moment apart with
Lord Rufford. It was impossible to say that she had
flirted with the man,—and yet Morton felt that he was
neglected, and felt also that he was only there because
this pleasure-seeking young lord had liked to have in his
house the handsome girl, whom he, Morton, intended to
marry. He felt thoroughly ashamed of being there as it
were in the train of Miss Trefoil. He was almost disposed
to get up and declare that the girl was engaged to marry
him. He thought that he could put an end to the engagement without breaking his heart; but if the engagement
was an engagement he could not submit to treatment
such as this, either from her or from others. He would see
her for the last time in the country at the ball on the
following evening,—as of course he would not be near
her during the hunting,—and then he would make her
understand that she must be altogether his or altogether

cease to be his. And so resolving he went to bed, refusing to join the gentlemen in the smoking-room.

'Oh, mamma,' Arabella said to her mother that evening, 'I do so wish I could break my arm to-morrow.'

'Break your arm, my dear!'

'Or my leg would be better. I wish I could have the courage to chuck myself off going over some gate. If I could be laid up here now with a broken limb I really think I could do it.'

CHAPTER XXII

JEMIMA

AS the meet on the next morning was in the park the party at Rufford Hall was able to enjoy the luxury of an easy morning together with the pleasures of the field. There was no getting up at eight o'clock, no hurry and scurry to do twenty miles and yet be in time, no necessity for the tardy dressers to swallow their breakfasts while their more energetic companions were raving at them for compromising the chances of the day by their delay. There was a public breakfast down-stairs, at which all the hunting farmers of the country were to be seen, and some who only pretended to be hunting farmers on such occasions. But upstairs there was a private breakfast for the ladies and such of the gentlemen as preferred tea to champagne and cherry brandy. Lord Rufford was in and out of both rooms, making himself generally agreeable. In the public room there was a great deal said about Goarly, to all of which the Senator listened with eager ears,—for the Senator preferred the public breakfast as offering another institution to his notice. 'He'll swing on a gallows afore he's dead,' said one energetic farmer who was sitting next to Mr. Gotobed,—a fat man with a round head, and a bullock's neck, dressed in a black coat with breeches and top-boots. John Runce was not a riding man. He was too heavy and short-winded;—too fond of his beer and port wine; but he was a hunting man all over, one who always had a fox in the springs at the bottom of his big meadows, one to whom it was the very breath of his nostrils to shake hands with the hunting gentry and to be known as a staunch friend to the U.R.U. A man did not live in the county more respected than John Runce, or who was better able to pay his way. To his thinking an animal more injurious than Goarly to the best interests of civilization could not have been produced by all the evil influences of the world combined. 'Do you really think,' said the Senator calmly, 'that a man should be hanged for killing a fox?' John Runce, who was not very ready, turned round and stared at him. 'I haven't heard of any other harm that he has done, and perhaps he had some provocation for that.' Words were wanting to Mr. Runce, but not indignation. He collected together his plate and knife and fork and his two glasses and his lump of bread, and, looking the Senator full in the face, slowly pushed back his chair and, carrying his provisions with him, toddled off to the other end of the room. When he reached a spot where place was made for him he had hardly breath left to speak. 'Well,' he said, 'I never——!' He sat a minute in silence shaking his head, and continued to shake his head and look round upon his neighbours as he devoured his food.

Upstairs there was a very cosy party, who came in by degrees. Lady Penwether was there soon after ten, with Miss Penge and some of the gentlemen, including Morton, who was the only man seen in that room in black. Young Hampton, who was intimate in the house, made his way up there, and Sir John Purefoy joined the party. Sir John was a hunting man, who lived in the county, and was an old friend of the family. Lady Purefoy hunted also, and came in later. Arabella was the last—not from laziness, but aware that in this way the effect might be the best. Lord Rufford was in the room when she entered it, and of course she addressed herself to him. 'Which is it to be, Lord Rufford—Jack or Jemima?'

'Whichever you like.'

'I am quite indifferent. If you put me on the mare I'll ride her—or try.'

'Indeed, you won't,' said Lady Augustus.

'Mamma knows nothing about it, Lord Rufford. I believe I could do just as well as Major Caneback.'

'She never had a lady on her in her life,' said Sir John.

'Then it's time for her to begin. But, at any rate, I must have some breakfast first.' Then Lord Rufford brought her a cup of tea, and Sir John gave her a cutlet, and she felt herself to be happy. She was quite content with her hat, and though her habit was not exactly a hunting habit, it fitted her well. Morton had never before seen her in a riding dress, and acknowledged that it became her. He struggled to think of something special to say to her, but there was nothing. He was not at home on such an occasion. His long trousers weighed him down, and his ordinary morning coat cowed him. He knew in his heart that she thought nothing of him as he was now. But she said a word to him, with that usual smile of hers. 'Of course, Mr. Morton, you are coming with us?'

'A little way, perhaps.'

'You'll find that any horse from Stubbings' can go,' said Lord Rufford. 'I wish I could say as much of all mine.'

'Jack can go, I hope, Lord Rufford?' Lord Rufford nodded his head. 'And I shall expect you to give me a lead.' To this he assented, though it was perhaps more than he intended. But on such an occasion it is almost impossible to refuse such a request.

At half-past eleven they were all out in the park, and Tony was elate as a prince, having been regaled with a tumbler of champagne. But the great interest of the immediate moment were the frantic efforts made by Jemima to get rid of her rider. Once or twice Sir John asked the major to give it up, but the major swore that the mare was a good mare, and only wanted riding. She kicked and squealed and backed, and went round the park with him at a full gallop. In the park there was a rail with a 'ha-ha' ditch, and the major rode her at it in a gallop. She went through the timber, fell in the ditch, and then was brought up again without giving the man a fall. He at once put her back again at the same fence, and she took it, almost in her stride, without touching it. 'Have her like a spaniel before the day's over,' said the major, who thoroughly enjoyed these little encounters.

Among the laurels at the bottom of the park a fox was found, and then there was a great deal of riding about the grounds. All this was much enjoyed by the ladies who were on foot, and by the Senator, who wandered about the place alone. A gentleman's park is not always the happiest place for finding a fox. The animal has usually many resources there, and does not like to leave it. And when he does go away, it is not always easy to get after him. But ladies in a carriage or on foot on such occasions have their turn of the sport. On this occasion it was nearly one before the fox allowed himself to be killed, and then he had hardly been outside the park palings. There was a good deal of sherry drank before the party got away, and hunting men such as Major Caneback began to think that the day was to be thrown away. As they started off for Shugborough Springs, the little covert on John Runce's farm, which was about four miles from Rufford Hall, Sir John asked the major to get on another animal. 'You've had trouble enough for one day, and given her enough to do.' But the major was not of that way of thinking. 'Let her have the day's work,' said the major. 'Do her good. Remember what she's learned.' And so they trotted off to Shugborough.

While they were riding about the park, Morton had kept near to Miss Trefoil. Lord Rufford, being on his own place and among his own trees, had had cares on his hand, and been unable to devote himself to the young lady. She had never for a moment looked up at her lover, or tried to escape from him. She had answered all his questions, saying, however, very little, and had bided her time. The more gracious she was to Morton now, the less ground would he have for complaining of her when she should leave him by-and-by. As they were trotting along the road Lord Rufford came up and apologized. 'I'm afraid I've been very inattentive, Miss Trefoil; but I dare say you've been in better hands.'

'There hasn't been much to do, has there?'

'Very little. I suppose a man isn't responsible for having foxes that won't break. Did you see the Senator? He seemed to think it was all right. Did you hear of John Runce?' Then he told the story of John Runce, which had been told to him.

'What a fine old fellow! I should forgive him his rent.'

'He is much better able to pay me double. Your Senator, Mr. Morton, is a very peculiar man.'

'He is peculiar,' said Morton, 'and I am sorry to say can make himself very disagreeable.'

'We might as well trot on, as Shugborough is a small place, and a fox always goes away from it at once. John Runce knows how to train them better than I do.' Then they made their way on through the straggling horses, and John Morton, not wishing to seem to be afraid of his rival, remained alone. 'I wish Caneback had left that mare behind,' said the lord as they went. 'It isn't the country for her, and she is going very nastily with him. Are you fond of hunting, Miss Trefoil?'

'Very fond of it,' said Arabella, who had been out two or three times in her life.

'I like a girl to ride to hounds,' said his lordship. 'I don't think she ever looks so well.' Then Arabella determined that come what might she would ride to hounds.

At Shugborough Springs a fox was found before half the field was up, and he broke almost as soon as he was found. 'Follow me through the hand-gates,' said the lord, 'and from the third field out it's fair riding. Let him have his head, and remember he hangs a moment as he comes to his fence. You won't be left behind unless there's something out of the way to stop us.' Arabella's heart was in her mouth, but she was quite resolved. Where he went she would follow. As for being left behind she would not care the least for that if he were left behind with her. They got well away, having to pause a moment while the hounds came up to Tony's horn out of the wood. Then there was plain sailing, and there were very few before them. 'He's one of the old sort, my lord,' said Tony as he pressed on, speaking of the fox. 'Not too near me, and you'll go like a bird,' said his lordship. 'He's a nice little horse, isn't he? When I'm going to be married, he'll be the first present I shall make her.'

'He'd tempt almost any girl,' said Arabella.

It was wonderful how well she went, knowing so little about it as she did. The horse was one easily ridden, and on plain ground she knew what she was about in a saddle. At any rate she did not disgrace herself, and when they had already run some three or four miles Lord Rufford had nearly the best of it and she had kept with him. 'You don't know where you are, I suppose,' he said when they came to a check.

'And I don't in the least care, if they'd only go on,' said she eagerly.

'We're back at Rufford Park. We've left the road nearly a mile to our left, but there we are. Those trees are the park.'

'But must we stop there?'

'That's as the fox may choose to behave. We shan't stop unless he does. Then young Hampton came up, declaring that there was the very mischief going on between Major Caneback and Jemima. According to Hampton's account, the major had been down three or four times, but was determined to break either the mare's neck or her spirit. He had been considerably hurt, so Hampton said, in one shoulder, but had insisted on riding on. 'That's the worst of him,' said Lord Rufford. 'He never knows when to give up.'

Then the hounds were again on the scent and were running very fast towards the Park. 'That's a nasty ditch before us,' said the lord. 'Come down a little to the left. The hounds are heading that way, and there's a gate.' Young Hampton in the meantime was going straight for the fence.

'I'm not afraid,' said Arabella.

'Very well. Give him his head and he'll do it.'

Just at that moment there was a noise behind them and the major on Jemima rushed up. She was covered with foam and he with dirt, and her sides were sliced with the spur. His hat was crushed, and he was riding almost altogether with his right hand. He came close to Arabella and she could see the rage in his face as the animal rushed on with her head almost between her knees. 'He'll have another fall there,' said Lord Rufford.

Hampton, who had passed them, was the first over the fence, and the other three all took it abreast. The major was to the right, the lord to the left, and the girl between them. The mare's head was perhaps the first. She rushed at the fence, made no leap at all, and of course went headlong into the ditch. The major still stuck to her, though two or three voices implored him to get off. He afterwards declared that he had not strength to lift himself out of the saddle. The mare lay for a moment;—then blundered out, rolled over him, jumped on to her feet, and lunging out kicked her rider on the head as he was rising. Then she went away and afterwards jumped the palings into Rufford Park. That evening she was shot.

The man when kicked had fallen back close under the feet of Miss Trefoil's horse. She screamed and, half-fainting, fell also;—but fell without hurting herself. Lord Rufford of course stopped, as did also Mr. Hampton and one of the whips,—with several others in the course of a minute or two. The major was senseless,—but they who understood what they were looking at were afraid that the case was very bad. He was picked up and put on a door and within half an hour was on his bed in Rufford Hall. But he did not speak for some hours, and before six o'clock that evening the doctor from Rufford had declared that he had mounted his last horse and ridden his last hunt!

'Oh, Lord Rufford,' said Arabella, 'I shall never recover that. I heard the horse's feet against his head.' Lord Rufford shuddered and put his hand round her waist to support her. At that time they were standing on the ground. 'Don't mind me if you can do any good to him.' But there was nothing that Lord Rufford could do, as four men were carrying the major on a shutter. So he and Arabella returned together, and when she got off her horse she was only able to throw herself into his arms.

Chapter XXIII

POOR CANEBACK

A CLOSER intimacy will occasionally be created by
some accident, some fortuitous circumstance, than
weeks of ordinary intercourse will produce. Walk down
Bond Street in a hailstorm of peculiar severity and you
may make a friend of the first person you meet, whereas
you would be held to have committed an affront were you
to speak to the same person in the same place on a fine
day. You shall travel smoothly to York with a lady and
she will look as though she would call the guard at once
were you so much as to suggest that it were a fine day;
but if you are lucky enough to break a wheel before you
get to Darlington, she will have told you all her history
and shared your sherry by the time you have reached
that town. Arabella was very much shocked by the
dreadful accident she had seen. Her nerves had suffered,
though it may be doubted whether her heart had been
affected much. But she was quite conscious when she
reached her room that the poor major's misfortune,
happening as it had done just beneath her horse's feet,
had been a godsend to her. For a moment the young
lord's arm had been round her waist and her head had
been upon his shoulder. And again when she had slipped
from her saddle she had felt his embrace. His fervour to
her had been simply the uncontrolled expression of his
feeling at the moment,—as one man squeezes another
tightly by the hand in any crisis of sudden impulse. She
knew this;—but she knew also that he would probably
revert to the intimacy which the sudden emotion had
created. The mutual galvanic shock might be continued
at the next meeting,—and so on. They had seen the
tragedy together, and it would not fail to be a bond of
union. As she told the tragedy to her mother, she
delicately laid aside her hat and whip and riding dress,
and then asked whether it was not possible that they
might prolong their stay at Rufford. 'But the Gores, my

dear! I put them off, you know, for two days only.'
Then Arabella declared that she did not care a straw for
the Gores. In such a matter as this what would it signify
though they should quarrel with a whole generation of
Gores? For some time she thought that she would not
come down again that afternoon or even that evening.
It might well be that the sight of the accident should have
made her too ill to appear. She felt conscious that in that
moment and in the subsequent half-hour she had carried
herself well, and that there would be an interest about her
were she to own herself compelled to keep her room.
Were she now to take to her bed they could not turn her
out on the following day. But at last her mother's counsel
put an end to that plan. Time was too precious. 'I think
you might lose more than you'd gain,' said her mother.

Both Lord Rufford and his sister were very much disturbed as to what they should do on the occasion. At
half-past six Lord Rufford was told that the major had
recovered his senses, but that the case was almost hopeless.
Of course he saw his guest. 'I'm all right,' said the major.
The lord sat there by the bedside, holding the man's hand
for a few moments, and then got up to leave him. 'No
nonsense about putting off,' said the major in a faint
voice; 'beastly bosh, all that!'

But what was to be done? The dozen people who were
in the house must of course sit down to dinner. And then
all the neighbourhood for miles round were coming to a
ball. It would be impossible to send messages to everybody. And there was the feeling too that the man was as
yet only ill, and that his recovery was possible. A ball,
with a dead man in one of the bedrooms, would be dreadful. With a dying man it was bad enough;—but then
a dying man is always also a living man! Lord Rufford
had already telegraphed for a first-class surgeon from
London, it having been whispered to him that perhaps
old Nokes from Rufford might be mistaken. The surgeon
could not be there till four o'clock in the morning, by
which time care would have been taken to remove the
signs of the ball; but if there was reason to send for a
London surgeon, then also was there reason for hope;—

and if there was ground for hope, then the desirability of putting off the ball was very much reduced. 'He's at the farthest end of the corridor,' the lord said to his sister, 'and won't hear a sound of the music.'

Though the man were to die, why shouldn't the people dance? Had the major been dying three or four miles off, at the hotel at Rufford, there would only have been a few sad looks, a few shakings of the head, and the people would have danced without any flaw in their gaiety. Had it been known at Rufford Hall that he was lying at that moment in his mortal agony at Aberdeen, an exclamation or two,— 'Poor Caneback;'—'Poor major!'—would have been the extent of the wailing, and not the pressure of a lover's hand would have been lightened, or the note of a fiddle delayed. And nobody in that house really cared much for Caneback. He was not a man worthy of much care. He was possessed of infinite pluck, and now that he was dying could bear it well. But he had loved no one particularly, and had been dear to no one in these latter days of his life, had been of very little use in the world, and had done very little more for society than any other horse-trainer! But, nevertheless, it is a bore when a gentleman dies in your house,—and a worse bore when he dies from an accident than from an illness for which his own body may be supposed to be responsible. Though the gout should fly to a man's stomach in your best bedroom, the idea never strikes you that your Burgundy has done it! But here the mare had done the mischief.

Poor Caneback;—and poor Lord Rufford! The major was quite certain that it was all over with him. He had broken so many of his bones, and had his head so often cracked, that he understood his own anatomy pretty well. There he lay quiet and composed, sipping small modicums of brandy and water, and taking his outlook into such transtygian world as he had fashioned for himself in his dull imagination. If he had misgivings, he showed them to no bystander. If he thought then that he might have done better with his energies than devote them to dangerous horses, he never said so. His voice was

weak, but it never quailed; and the only regret he expressed
was that he had not changed the bit in Jemima's mouth.
Lord Rufford's position was made worse by an expression
from Sir John Purefoy that the party ought to be put off.
Sir John was in a measure responsible for what his mare
had done, and was in a wretched state. 'If it could
possibly affect the poor fellow, I would do it,' said Lord
Rufford. 'But it would create very great inconvenience
and disappointment. I have to think of other people.'
'Then I shall send my wife home,' said Sir John. And
Lady Purefoy was sent home. Sir John himself, of course,
could not leave the house while the man was alive. Before
they all sat down to dinner the major was declared to be
a little stronger. That settled the question, and the ball
was not put off.

The ladies came down to dinner in a melancholy guise.
They were not fully dressed for the evening, and were, of
course, inclined to be silent and sad. Before Lord Rufford
came in, Arabella managed to get herself on to the sofa
next to Lady Penwether, and then to undergo some little
hysterical manifestation. 'Oh, Lady Penwether, if you
had seen it, and heard it!'

'I am very glad that I was spared anything so horrible.'

'And the man's face as he passed me going to the leap!
It will haunt me to my dying day!' Then she shivered
and gurgled in her throat, and, turning suddenly round,
hid her face on the elbow of the sofa.

'I've been afraid all the afternoon that she would be
ill,' whispered Lady Augustus to Miss Penge. 'She is so
susceptible!'

When Lord Rufford came into the room Arabella at
once got up and accosted him with a whisper. Either he
took her or she took him into a distant part of the room,
where they conversed apart for five minutes. And he, as
he told her how things were going and what was being
done, bent over her and whispered also. 'What good
would it do, you know?' she said with affected intimacy
as he spoke of his difficulty about the ball. 'One would
do anything if one could be of service; but that would do

nothing.' She felt completely that her presence at the accident had given her a right to have peculiar conversations, and to be consulted about everything. Of course, she was very sorry for Major Caneback. But as it had been ordained that Major Caneback was to have his head split in two by a kick from a horse, and that Lord Rufford was to be there to see it, how great had been the blessing which had brought her to the spot at the same time!

Everybody there saw the intimacy, and most of them understood the way in which it was being used. 'That girl is very clever, Rufford,' his sister whispered to him before dinner. 'She is very much excited rather than clever just at present,' he answered, upon which Lady Penwether shook her head. Miss Penge whispered to Miss Godolphin that Miss Trefoil was making the most of it; and Mr. Morton, who had come into the room while the conversation apart was going on, had certainly been of the same opinion.

She had seated herself in an armchair away from the others after that conversation was over, and as she sat there, Morton came up to her. He had been so little intimate with the members of the party assembled, and had found himself so much alone, that he had only lately heard the story about Major Caneback, and had now only heard it imperfectly. But he did see that an absolute intimacy had been effected where, two days before, there had only been a slight acquaintance; and he believed that this sudden rush had been in some way due to the accident of which he had been told. 'You know what has happened?' he said.

'Oh, Mr. Morton, do not talk to me about it!'

'Were you not speaking of it to Lord Rufford?'

'Of course I was. We were together.'

'Did you see it?' Then she shuddered, put her handkerchief up to her eyes, and turned her face away. 'And yet the ball is to go on?' he asked.

'Pray, pray do not dwell on it—unless you wish to force me back to my room. When I left it I felt that I was attempting to do too much.' This might have been all very well had she not been so manifestly able to talk to

Lord Rufford on the same subject. If there is any young man to whom a girl should be able to speak when she is in a state of violent emotion, it is the young man to whom she is engaged. So, at least, thought Mr. John Morton.

Then dinner was announced, and the dinner certainly was sombre enough. A dinner before a ball in the country never is very much of a dinner. The ladies know that there is work before them, and keep themselves for the greater occasion. Lady Purefoy had gone, and Lady Penwether was not very happy in the prospects for the evening. Neither Miss Penge nor either of the two Miss Godolphins had entertained personal hopes in regard to Lord Rufford, but nevertheless they took badly the great favour shown to Arabella. Lady Augustus did not get on particularly well with any of the other ladies, and there seemed during the dinner to be an air of unhappiness over them all. They retired as soon as it was possible, and then Arabella at once went up to her bedroom.

'Mr. Nokes says he is a little stronger, my lord,' said the butler, coming into the room. Mr. Nokes had gone home and had returned again.

'He might pull through yet,' said Mr. Hampton. Lord Rufford shook his head. Then Mr. Gotobed told a wonderful story of an American who had had his brains knocked almost out of his head, and had sat in Congress afterwards. 'He was the finest horseman I ever saw on a horse,' said Hampton.

'A little too much temper,' said Captain Battersby, who was a very old friend of the major.

'I'd give a good deal that that mare had never been brought to my stables,' said Lord Rufford. 'Purefoy will never get over it, and I shan't forget it in a hurry.' Sir John at this time was upstairs with the sufferer. Even while drinking their wine they could not keep themselves from the subject, and were convivial in a cadaverous fashion.

CHAPTER XXIV

THE BALL

THE people came of course, but not in such numbers as had been expected. Many of those in Rufford had heard of the accident, and, having been made acquainted with Nokes's report, stayed away. Everybody was told that supper would be on the table at twelve, and that it was generally understood that the house was to be cleared by two. Nokes seemed to think that the sufferer would live at least till the morrow, and it was ascertained to a certainty that the music could not affect him. It was agreed among the party in the house, that the ladies staying there should stand up for the first dance or two, as otherwise the strangers would be discouraged and the whole thing would be a failure. This request was made by Lady Penwether because Miss Penge had said that she thought it impossible for her to dance. Poor Miss Penge, who was generally regarded as a brilliant young woman, had been a good deal eclipsed by Arabella, and had seen the necessity of striking out some line for herself. Then Arabella had whispered a few words to Lord Rufford, and the lord had whispered a few words to his sister, and Lady Penwether had explained what was to be done to the ladies around. Lady Augustus nodded her head and said that it was all right. The other ladies of course agreed, and partners were selected within the house party. Lord Rufford stood up with Arabella, and John Morton with Lady Penwether. Mr. Gotobed selected Miss Penge, and Hampton and Battersby the two Miss Godolphins. They all took their places with a lugubrious but business-like air, as aware that they were sacrificing themselves in the performance of a sad duty. But Morton was not allowed to dance in the same quadrille with the lady of his affections. Lady Penwether explained to him that she and her brother had better divide themselves,—for the good of the company generally,—and therefore he and Arabella were also divided.

A rumour had reached Lady Penwether of the truth in

regard to their guests from Bragton. Mr. Gotobed had whispered to her that he had understood that they certainly were engaged; and even before that the names of the two lovers had been wafted to her ears from the other side of the Atlantic. Both John Morton and Lady Augustus were 'somebodies', and Lady Penwether generally knew what there was to be known of anybody who was anybody. But it was quite clear to her,—more so even than to poor John Morton,—that the lady was conducting herself now as though she were fettered by no bonds, and it seemed to Lady Penwether also that the lady was very anxious to contract other bonds. She knew her brother well. He was always in love with somebody; but as he had hitherto failed of success where marriage was desirable, so had he avoided disaster when it was not. He was one of those men who are generally supposed to be averse to matrimony. Lady Penwether and some other relatives were anxious that he should take a wife; but his sister was by no means anxious that he should take such a one as Arabella Trefoil. Therefore she thought that she might judiciously ask Mr. Morton a few questions. 'I believe you knew the Trefoils in Washington?' she said. Morton acknowledged that he had seen much of them there. 'She is very handsome, certainly.'

'I think so.'

'And rides well, I suppose?'

'I don't know. I never heard much of her riding.'

'Has she been staying long at Bragton?'

'Just a week.'

'Do you know Lord Augustus?' Morton said that he did not know Lord Augustus, and then answered sundry other questions of the same nature in the same uncommunicative way. Though he had once or twice almost fancied that he would like to proclaim aloud that the girl was engaged to him, yet he did not like to have the fact pumped out of him. And if she were such a girl as she now appeared to be, might it not be better for him to let her go? Surely her conduct here at Rufford Hall was opportunity enough. No doubt she was handsome. No doubt he loved her,—after his fashion of loving. But to lose her now would not break his heart, whereas to lose her after he was married to her, would, he knew well, bring him to the very ground. He would ask her a question or two this very night, and then come to some resolution. With such thoughts as these crossing his mind he certainly was not going to proclaim his engagement to Lady Penwether. But Lady Penwether was a determined woman. Her smile, when she condescended to smile, was very sweet,—lighting up her whole face and flattering for the moment the person on whom it shone. It was as though a rose in emitting its perfume could confine itself to the nostrils of its one favoured friend. And now she smiled on Morton as she asked another question. 'I did hear,' she said, 'from one of your Foreign Office young men that you and Miss Trefoil were very intimate.'

'Who was that, Lady Penwether?'

'Of course I shall mention no name. You might call out the poor lad and shoot him, or, worse still, have him put down to the bottom of his class. But I did hear it. And then, when I find her staying with her mother, at your house, of course I believe it to be true.'

'Now she is staying at your brother's house, which is much the same thing.'

'But I am here.'

'And my grandmother is at Bragton.'

'That puts me in mind, Mr. Morton. I am so sorry that we did not know it, so that we might have asked her.'

'She never goes out anywhere, Lady Penwether.'

'And there is nothing, then, in the report I heard?'

Morton paused a moment before he answered, and during that moment collected his diplomatic resources. He was not a weak man, who could be made to tell anything by the wiles of a pretty woman. 'I think,' he said, 'that when people have anything of that kind which they wish to be known, they declare it.'

'I beg your pardon. I did not mean to unravel a secret.'

· 'There are secrets, Lady Penwether, which people do like to unravel, but which the owners of them sometimes won't abandon.' Then there was nothing more said on the subject. Lady Penwether did not smile again, and left him, to go about the room on her business as hostess, as soon as the dance was over. But she was sure that they were engaged.

In the meantime the conversation between Lord Rufford and Arabella was very different in its tone, though on the same subject. He was certainly very much struck with her, not probably ever waiting to declare to himself that she was the most beautiful woman he had ever seen in his life, but still feeling towards her an attraction which for the time was strong. A very clever girl would frighten him; a very horsey girl would disgust him; a very quiet girl would bore him; or a very noisy girl annoy him. With a shy girl he could never be at his ease, not enjoying the labour of overcoming such a barrier; and yet he liked to be able to feel that any female intimacy which he admitted was due to his own choice and not to that of the young woman. Arabella Trefoil was not very clever, but she had given all her mind to this peculiar phase of life, and, to use a common phrase, knew what she was about. She was quite alive to the fact that different men require different manners in a young woman; and as she had adapted herself to Mr. Morton at Washington, so could she at Rufford adapt herself to Lord Rufford. At the present moment the lord was in love with her, as much as he was wont to be in love. 'Doesn't it seem an immense time since we came here yesterday?' she said to him. 'There has been so much done.'

'There has been a great misfortune.'

'I suppose that is it. Only for that how very, very pleasant it would have been!'

'Yes, indeed. It was a nice run, and that little horse carried you charmingly. I wish I could see you ride him again.' She shook her head as she looked up into his face. 'Why do you shake your head?'

'Because I am afraid there is no possible chance of such happiness. We are going to such a dull house to-morrow! And then to so many dull houses afterwards.'

'I don't know why you shouldn't come back and have another day or two—when all this sadness has gone by.'

'Don't talk about it, Lord Rufford.'

'Why not?'

'I never like to talk about any pleasure, because it always vanishes as soon as it has come; and when it has been real pleasure, it never comes back again. I don't think I ever enjoyed anything so much as our ride this morning,—till that tragedy came.'

'Poor Caneback!'

'I suppose there is no hope?' He shook his head. 'And we must go on to those Gores to-morrow without knowing anything about it. I wonder whether you could send me a line?'

'Of course I can, and I will.' Then he asked her a question, looking into her face. 'You are not going back to Bragton.'

'Oh dear, no.'

'Was Bragton dull?'

'Awfully dull; frightfully dull.'

'You know what they say?'

'What who say, Lord Rufford? People say anything—the more ill-natured the better they like it, I think.'

'Have you not heard what they say about you and Mr. Morton?'

'Just because mamma made a promise, when in Washington, to go to Bragton with that Mr. Gotobed. Don't you find they marry you to everybody?'

'They have married me to a good many people. Perhaps they'll marry me to you to-morrow. That would not be so bad.'

'Oh, Lord Rufford! Nobody has ever condemned you to anything so terrible as that.'

'There was no truth in it, then, Miss Trefoil?'

'None at all, Lord Rufford. Only I don't know why you should ask me.'

'Well, I don't know. A man likes sometimes to be sure how the land lies. Mr. Morton looks so cross that I thought that perhaps the very fact of my dancing with you might be an offence.'

'Is he cross?'

'You know him better than I do. Perhaps it's his

nature. Now, I must do one other dance with a native, and then my work will be over.'

'That isn't very civil, Lord Rufford.'

'If you don't know what I meant, you're not the girl I take you to be.' Then, as she walked with him back out of the ball-room into the drawing-room, she assured him that she did know what he meant, and that, therefore, she was the girl he took her to be.

She had determined that she would not dance again and had resolved to herd with the other ladies of the house,—waiting for any opportunity that chance might give her for having a last word with Lord Rufford before they parted for the night,—when Morton came up to her and demanded rather than asked that she would stand up with him for a quadrille. 'We settled it all among ourselves, you know,' she said. 'We were to dance only once, just to set the people off.' He still persisted, but she still refused, alleging that she was bound by the general compact, and though he was very urgent she would not yield. 'I wonder how you can ask me,' she said. 'You don't suppose that after what has occurred I can have any pleasure in dancing.' Upon this he asked her to take a turn with him through the rooms, and to that she found herself compelled to assent. Then he spoke out to her. 'Arabella,' he said, 'I am not quite content with what has been going on since we came to this house.'

'I am sorry for that.'

'Nor, indeed, have I been made very happy by all that has occurred since your mother and you did me the honour of coming to Bragton.'

'I must acknowledge you haven't seemed to be very happy, Mr. Morton.'

'I don't want to distress you; and as far as possible I wish to avoid distressing myself. If it is your wish that our engagement should be over, I will endeavour to bear it. If it is to be continued,—I expect that your manner to me should be altered.'

'What am I to say?'

'Say what you feel.'

'I feel that I can't alter my manner, as you call it.'

'You do wish the engagement to be over, then?'

'I did not say so. The truth is, Mr. Morton, that there is some trouble about the lawyers.'

'Why do you always call me Mr. Morton?'

'Because I am aware how probable it is that all this may come to nothing. I can't walk out of the house and marry you as the cook-maid does the gardener. I've got to wait till I'm told that everything is settled; and at present I'm told that things are not settled because you won't agree.'

'I'll leave it to anybody to say whether I've been unreasonable.'

'I won't go into that. I haven't meddled with it, and I don't know anything about it. But until it is all settled, as a matter of course there must be some little distance between us. It's the commonest thing in the world, I should say.'

'What is to be the end of it?'

'I do not know. If you think yourself injured you can back out of it at once. I've nothing more to say about it.'

'And you think I can like the way you're going on here?'

'If you're jealous, Mr. Morton, there's an end of it. I tell you fairly, once for all, that as long as I'm a single woman I will regulate my conduct as I please. You can do the same, and I shall not say a word to you.' Then she withdrew her arm from him, and, leaving him, walked across the room and joined her mother. He went off at once to his own room, resolving that he would write to her from Bragton. He had made his propositions in regard to money, which he was quite aware were as liberal as was fit. If she would now fix a day for their marriage, he would be a happy man. If she would not bring herself to do this, then he would have no alternative but to regard their engagement as at an end.

At two o'clock the guests were nearly all gone. The major was alive, and likely to live at least for some hours, and the Rufford people were generally glad that they had not put off the ball. Some of them who were staying in the house had already gone to bed, and Lady Penwether, with Miss Penge at her side, was making her last adieux in the drawing-room. The ball-room was reached from the drawing-room, with a vestibule between them, and opening from this was a small chamber, prettily furnished but seldom used, which had no peculiar purpose of its own, but in which during the present evening many sweet words had probably been spoken. Now, at this last moment, Lord Rufford and Arabella Trefoil were there alone together. She had just got up from a sofa, and he had taken her hand in his. She did not attempt to withdraw it, but stood looking down upon the ground. Then he passed his arm round her waist and lifting her face to his held her in a close embrace from which she made no effort to free herself. As soon as she was released she hastened to the door which was all but closed, and as she opened it and passed through to the drawing-room said some ordinary word to him quite aloud in her ordinary voice. If his action had disturbed her she knew very well how to recover her equanimity.

CHAPTER XXV

THE LAST MORNING AT RUFFORD HALL

'WELL, my love?' said Lady Augustus, as soon as her daughter had joined her in her bedroom. On such occasions there was always a quarter of an hour before going to bed in which the mother and daughter discussed their affairs, while the two ladies' maids were discussing their affairs in the other room. The two maids probably did not often quarrel, but the mother and daughter usually did.

'I wish that stupid man hadn't got himself hurt.'

'Of course, my dear; we all wish that. But I really don't see that it has stood much in your way.'

'Yes, it has. After all, there is nothing like dancing, and we shouldn't all have been sent to bed at two o'clock.'

'Then it has come to nothing?'

'I didn't say that at all, mamma. I think I have done uncommonly well. Indeed, I know I have. But then if everything had not been upset, I might have done so much the better.'

'What have you done?' asked Lady Augustus, timidly. She knew perfectly well that her daughter would tell her nothing, and yet she always asked these questions and was always angry when no information was given to her. Any young woman would have found it very hard to give the information needed:—'When we were alone he sat for five minutes with his arm round my waist, and then he kissed me. He didn't say much, but then I knew perfectly well that he would be on his guard not to commit himself by words. But I've got him to promise that he'll write to me, and of course I'll answer in such a way that he must write again. I know he'll want to see me, and I think I can go very near doing it. But he's an old stager and knows what he's about: and, of course, there'll be ever so many people to tell him I'm not the sort of girl he ought to marry. He'll hear about Colonel de B——, and Sir C. D——, and Lord E. F——, and there are ever so many chances against me. But I've made up my mind to try it. It's taking the long odds. I can hardly expect to win, but if I do pull it off I'm made for ever!' A daughter can hardly say all that to her mother. Even Arabella Trefoil could not say it to her mother,—or, at any rate, she would not. 'What a question that is to ask, mamma!' she did say, tossing her head.

'Well, my dear, unless you tell me something, how can I help you?'

'I don't know that I want you to help me,—at any rate not in that way.'

'In what way?'

'Oh, mamma, you are so odd!'

'Has he said anything?'

'Yes, he has. He said he liked dry champagne, and that he never ate supper.'

'If you won't tell me how things are going, you may fight your own battles by yourself.'

'That's just what I must do. Nobody else can fight my battles for me.'

'What are you going to do about Mr. Morton?'

'Nothing.'

'I saw him talking to you, and looking as black as thunder.'

'He always looks as black as thunder.'

'Is that to be all off? I insist upon having an answer to that question.'

'I believe you fancy, mamma, that a lot of men can be played like a parcel of chessmen, and that as soon as a knight is knocked on the head you can take him up and put him into the box, and have done with him.'

'You haven't done with Mr. Morton, then?'

'Poor Mr. Morton! I do feel he is badly used, because he is so honest. I sometimes wish that I could afford to be honest too, and to tell somebody the downright truth. I should like to tell him the truth, and I almost think I will. "My dear fellow, I did for a time think I couldn't do better, and I'm not at all sure now that I can. But then you are so very dull, and I'm not certain that I should care to be Queen of the English society at the Court of the Emperor of Morocco! But if you'll wait for another six months, I shall be able to tell you." That's what I should have to say to him.'

'Who is talking nonsense now, Arabella?'

'I am not. But I shan't say it. And now, mamma, I'll tell you what we must do.'

'You must tell me why also.'

'I can do nothing of the kind. He knows the duke.' The duke with the Trefoils always meant the Duke of Mayfair, who was Arabella's ducal uncle.

'Intimately?'

'Well enough to go there. There is to be a great shooting at Mistletoe' (Mistletoe was the duke's place) 'in January. I got that from him, and he can go if he likes. He won't go as it is; but if I tell him I'm to be there, I think he will.'

'What did you tell him?'

'Well, I told him a tarradiddle,* of course. I made him understand that I could be there if I pleased, and he thinks that I mean to be there if he goes.'

'But I'm sure the duchess won't have me again.'

'She might let me come.'

'And what am I to do?'

'You could go to Brighton with Miss De Groat; or what does it matter for a fortnight? You'll get the advantage when it's done. It's as well to have the truth out at once, mamma. I cannot carry on if I'm always to be stuck close to your apron-strings. There are so many people won't have you.'

'Arabella, I do think you are the most ungrateful, hardhearted creature that ever lived!'

'Very well; I don't know what I've to be grateful about, and I need to be hard-hearted. Of course I am hardhearted. The thing will be to get papa to see his brother.'

'Your papa?'

'Yes; that's what I mean to try. The duke, of course, would like me to marry Lord Rufford. Do you think that, if I were at home here, it wouldn't make Mistletoe a very different sort of place for you? The duke does like papa in a sort of way, and he's civil enough to me when I'm there. He never did like you.'

'Everybody is so fond of you! It was what you did when young Stranorlar was there which made the duchess almost turn us out of the house.'

'What's the good of your saying that, mamma? If you go on like that I'll separate myself from you and throw myself on papa.'

'Your father wouldn't lift his little finger for you.'

'I'll try, at any rate. Will you consent to my going there without you if I can manage it?'

'What did Lord Rufford say?' Arabella here made a grimace. 'You can tell me something. What are the lawyers to say to Mr. Morton's people?'

'Whatever they like.'

'If they come to arrangements, do you mean to marry him?'

'Not for the next two months, certainly, I shan't see him again now Heaven knows when. He'll write, no doubt—one of his awfully sensible letters, and I shall take my time about answering him. I can stretch it out for two months. If I'm to do any good with this man, it will be

all arranged before that time. If the duke could really be
made to believe that Lord Rufford was in earnest, I'm
sure he'd have me there. As to her, she always does what
he tells her.'

'He is going to write to you?'

'I told you that before, mamma. What is the good of
asking a lot of questions? You know now what my plan
is, and if you won't help me I must carry it out alone.
And, remember, I don't want to start to-morrow till after
Morton and that American have gone.' Then, without
a kiss or wishing her mother good-night, she went off to
her own room.

The next morning, at about nine, Arabella heard from
her maid that the major was still alive, but senseless. The
London surgeon had been there, and had declared it to
be possible that the patient should live,—but barely
possible. At ten they were all at breakfast, and the
carriage from Bragton was already at the door to take
back Mr. Morton and his American friend. Lady
Augustus had been clever enough to arrange that she
should have the phaeton to take her to the Rufford Station
a little later on in the day, and had already hinted to one
of the servants that perhaps a cart might be sent with the
luggage. The cart was forthcoming. Lady Augustus was
very clever in arranging her locomotion, and seldom paid
for much more than her railway tickets.

'I had meant to say a few words to you, my lord, about
that man Goarly,' said the Senator, standing before the
fire in the breakfast room, 'but this sad catastrophe has
stopped me.'

'There isn't much to say about him, Mr. Gotobed.'

'Perhaps not; only I would not wish you to think that
I would oppose you without some cause. If the man is in
the wrong according to law, let him be proved to be so.
The cost to you will be nothing; to him it might be of
considerable importance.'

'Just so. Won't you sit down and have some breakfast?
If Goarly ever makes himself nuisance enough, it may be
worth my while to buy him out at three times the value of
his land. But he'll have to be a very great nuisance before

I shall do that. Dillsborough Wood is not the only fox covert in the county.' After that there was no more said about it; but neither did Lord Rufford understand the Senator, nor did the Senator understand Lord Rufford. John Runce had a clearer conviction on his mind than either of them. Goarly ought to be hanged, and no American should, under any circumstances, be allowed to put his foot upon British soil. That was Runce's idea of the matter.

The parting between Morton and the Trefoils was very chill and uncomfortable. 'Good-bye, Mr. Morton; we had such a pleasant time at Bragton!' said Lady Augustus. 'I shall write to you this afternoon,' he whispered to Arabella as he took her hand. She smiled and murmured a word of adieu, but made him no reply. Then they were gone, and as he got into the carriage he told himself that in all probability he would never see her again. It might be that he would curtail his leave of absence, and get back to Washington as quickly as possible.

The Trefoils did not start for an hour after this, during which Arabella could hardly find an opportunity for a word in private. She could not quite appeal to him to walk with her in the grounds, or even to take a turn with her round the empty ball-room. She came down dressed for walking, thinking that so she might have the best chance of getting him for a quarter of an hour to herself, but he was either too wary or else the habits of his life prevented it. And in what she had to do it was so easy to go beyond the proper line. She would wish him to understand that she would like to be alone with him after what had passed between them on the previous evening, but she must be careful not to let him imagine that she was too anxious. And then, whatever she did, she had to do with so many eyes upon her. And when she went, as she would do now in so short a time, so many hostile tongues would attack her. He had everything to protect him, and she had nothing, absolutely nothing, to help her! It was thus that she looked at it, and yet she had courage for the battle. Almost at the last moment she did get a word with him in the hall. 'How is he?'

'Oh, better, decidedly.'

'I am so glad. If I could only think that he could live! Well, my lord, we have to say good-bye.'

'I suppose so.'

'You'll write me a line,—about him.'

'Certainly.'

'I shall be so glad to have a line from Rufford. Maddox Hall, you know; Stafford.'

'I will remember.'

'And dear old Jack! Tell me when you write what Jack has been doing.' Then she put out her hand and he held it. 'I wonder whether you will ever remember——' But she did not quite know what to bid him remember, and therefore turned away her face and wiped away a tear, and then smiled as she turned it back on him. The carriage was at the door, and the ladies flocked into the hall, and then not another word could be said.

'That's what I call a really nice country house,' said Lady Augustus as she was driven away. Arabella sat back in the phaeton lost in thought and said nothing. 'Everything so well done, and yet none of all that fuss that there is at Mistletoe.' She paused but still her daughter did not speak. 'If I were beginning the world again I would not wish for a better establishment than that. Why can't you answer me a word when I speak to you?'

'Of course it's all very nice. What's the good of going on in that way? What a shame it is that a man like that should have so much and that a girl like me should have nothing at all. I know twice as much as he does, and am twice as clever, and yet I've got to treat him as though he were a god. He's all very well, but what would anybody think of him if he were a younger brother with £300 a year.' This was a kind of philosophy which Lady Augustus hated. She threw herself back therefore in the phaeton and pretended to go to sleep.

The wheels were not out of sight of the house before the attack on the Trefoils began. 'I had heard of Lady Augustus before,' said Lady Penwether, 'but I didn't think that any woman could be so disagreeable.'

'So vulgar,' said Miss Penge.

'Wasn't she the daughter of an ironmonger?' asked the elder Miss Godolphin.

'The girl, of course, is handsome,' said Lady Penwether.

'But so self-sufficient,' said Miss Godolphin.

'And almost as vulgar as her mother,' said Miss Penge.

'She may be clever,' said Lady Penwether, 'but I do not think I should ever like her.'

'She is one of those girls whom only gentlemen like,' said Miss Penge.

'And whom they don't like very long,' said Lady Penwether.

'How well I understand all this,' said Lord Rufford turning to the younger Miss Godolphin. 'It is all said for my benefit, and considered to be necessary because I danced with the young lady last night.'

'I hope you are not attributing such a motive to me,' said Miss Penge.

'Or to me,' said Miss Godolphin.

'I look on both of you and Eleanor as all one on the present occasion. I am considered to be falling over a precipice, and she has got hold of my coat tails. Of course you wouldn't be Christians if you didn't both of you seize a foot.'

'Looking at it in that light I certainly wish to be understood as holding on very fast,' said Miss Penge.

CHAPTER XXVI

GIVE ME SIX MONTHS

THERE was a great deal of trouble and some very genuine sorrow in the attorney's house at Dillsborough during the first week in December. Mr. Masters had declared to his wife that Mary should go to Cheltenham, and a letter was written to Lady Ushant accepting the invitation. The £20, too, was forthcoming and the dress and the boots and the hat were bought. But while this was going on, Mrs. Masters took care that there should be no comfort whatever around them and made every meal a separate curse to the unfortunate lawyer. She told him ten times a day that she had been a mother to his daughter, but declared that such a position was no longer possible to her, as the girl had been taken altogether out of her hands. To Mary she hardly spoke at all and made her thoroughly wish that Lady Ushant's kindness had been declined. 'Mamma,' she said one day, 'I had rather write now and tell her that I cannot come.'

'After all the money has been wasted!'

'I have only got things that I must have had very soon.'

'If you have got anything to say you had better talk to your father. I know nothing about it.'

'You break my heart when you say that, mamma.'

'You think nothing about breaking mine;—or that young man's who is behaving so well to you. What makes me mad is to see you shilly-shallying with him.'

'Mamma, I haven't shilly-shallied.'

'That's what I call it. Why can't you speak him fair and tell him you'll have him and settle yourself down properly? You've got some idea into your silly head that what you call a gentleman will come after you.'

'Mamma, that isn't fair.'

'Very well, miss. As your father takes your part, of course you can say what you please to me. I say it is so.' Mary knew very well what her mother meant and was safe at least from any allusion to Reginald Morton. There was an idea prevalent in the house, and not without some cause, that Mr. Surtees the curate had looked with an eye of favour on Mary Masters. Mr. Surtees was certainly a gentleman, but his income was strictly limited to the sum of £120 per annum, which he received from Mr. Mainwaring. Now Mrs. Masters disliked clergymen, disliked gentlemen, and especially disliked poverty; and therefore was not disposed to look upon Mr. Surtees as an eligible suitor for her stepdaughter. But as the curate's courtship had hitherto been of the coldest kind, and as it had received no encouragement from the young lady, Mary was certainly justified in declaring that the allusion was not fair. 'What I want to know is this;—are you prepared to marry Lawrence Twentyman?' To this question, as Mary could not give a favourable answer, she thought it best to make none at all. 'There is a man as has got a house fit for any woman, and means to keep it; who can give a young woman everything that she ought to want;—and a handsome fellow too, with some life in him; one who really dotes on you,—as men don't often do on young women now as far as I can see. I wonder what it is that you would have?'

'I want nothing, mamma.'

'Yes, you do. You have been reading books of poetry till you don't know what it is you do want. You've got your head full of claptraps and tantrums till you haven't a grain of sense belonging to you. I hate such ways. It's a spurning of the gifts of Providence not to have such a man as Lawrence Twentyman when he comes in your way. Who are you I wonder, that you shouldn't be contented with such as him? He'll go and take some one else and then you'll be fit to break your heart, fretting after him, and I shan't pity you a bit. It'll serve you right and you'll die an old maid, and what there will be for you to live upon, God in heaven only knows. You're breaking your father's heart, as it is.' Then she sat down in a rocking-chair and throwing her apron over her eyes gave herself up to a deluge of hysterical tears.

This was very hard upon Mary, for though she did not believe all the horrible things which her stepmother said to her, she did believe some of them. She was not afraid of the fate of an old maid which was threatened, but she did think that her marriage with this man would be for the benefit of the family, and a great relief to her father. And she knew, too, that he was respectable, and believed him to be thoroughly earnest in his love. For such love as that it is impossible that a girl should not be grateful. There was nothing to allure him, nothing to tempt him to such a marriage, but a simple appreciation of her personal merits. And in life he was at any rate her equal. She had told Reginald Morton that Larry Twentyman was a fit companion for her and her sisters, and she owned as much to herself every day. When she acknowledged all this she was tempted to ask herself whether she ought not

to accept the man,—if not for her own sake, at least for
that of the family.

That same evening her father called her into the office
after the clerks were gone and spoke to her thus. 'Your
mamma is very unhappy, my dear,' he said.

'I'm afraid I have made everybody unhappy by wanting to go to Cheltenham.'

'It is not only that. That is reasonable enough, and you
ought to go. Mamma would say nothing more about
that,—if you would make up your mind to one thing.'

'What thing, papa?' Of course she knew very well what
the thing was.

'It is time for you to think of settling in life, Mary.
I never would put it into a girl's head that she ought to
worry herself about getting a husband unless the opportunity seemed to come in her way. Young women should
be quiet and wait till they're sought after. But here is a
young man seeking you, whom we all like and approve.
A good house is a very good thing when it's fairly come by.'

'Yes, papa.'

'And so is a full house. A girl shouldn't run after money,
but plenty is a great comfort in this world, when it can be
had without blushing for.'

'Yes, papa.'

'And so is an honest man's love. I don't like to see any
girl wearying after some fellow to be always fal-lalling
with her. A good girl will be happy and contented without that. But a lone life is a poor life, and a good husband
is about the best blessing that a young woman can have.'
To this proposition Mary perhaps agreed in her own
mind, but she gave no spoken assent. 'Now this young
man that is wanting to marry you has got all these things,
and as far as I can judge with my experience in the world,
is as likely to make a good husband as any one I know.'
He paused for an answer, but Mary could only lean close
upon his arm and be silent. 'Have you anything to say
about it, my dear? You see it has been going on now a
long time, but of course he'll look to have it decided.'
But still she could say nothing. 'Well, now;—he has been
with me to-day.'

'Mr. Twentyman?'

'Yes,—Mr. Twentyman. He knows you're going to Cheltenham, and of course he has nothing to say against that. No young man such as he would be sorry that his sweetheart should be entertained by such a lady as Lady Ushant. But he says that he wants to have an answer before you go.'

'I did answer him, papa.'

'Yes,—you refused him. But he hopes that perhaps you may think better of it. He has been with me, and I have told him that if he will come to-morrow you will see him. He is to be here after dinner, and you had better just take him upstairs and hear what he has to say. If you can make up your mind to like him, you will please all your family. But if you can't,—I won't quarrel with you, my dear.'

'Oh papa, you are always so good.'

'Of course I am anxious that you should have a home of your own;—but let it be how it may I will not quarrel with my child.'

All that evening, and almost all the night, and again on the following morning Mary turned it over in her mind. She was quite sure that she was not in love with Larry Twentyman; but she was by no means sure that it might not be her duty to accept him without being in love with him. Of course he must know the whole truth; but she could tell him the truth and then leave him to decide. What right had she to stand in the way of her friends, or to be a burden to them, when such a mode of life was offered to her? She had nothing of her own, and regarded herself as being a dead weight on the family. And she was conscious, in a certain degree, of isolation in the household,—as being her father's only child by the first marriage. She would hardly know how to look her father in the face and tell him that she had again refused the man. But yet there was something awful to her in the idea of giving herself to a man without loving him,—in becoming a man's wife when she would fain remain away from him! Would it be possible that she should live with him while her feelings were of such a nature? And then she blushed as she lay in the dark, with her cheek on her pillow, when she found herself forced to inquire within her own heart whether she did not love some one else. She would not own it, and yet she blushed, and yet she thought of it. If there might be such a man it was not the young clergyman to whom her mother had alluded.

Through all that morning she was very quiet, very pale, and, in truth, very unhappy. Her father said no further word to her, and her stepmother had been implored to be equally reticent. 'I shan't speak another word,' said Mrs. Masters; 'her fortune is in her own hands, and if she don't choose to take it, I've done with her. One man may lead a horse to water, but a hundred can't make him drink. It's just the same with an obstinate, pig-headed young woman.'

At three o'clock Mr. Twentyman came and was at once desired to go up to Mary, who was waiting for him in the drawing-room. Mrs. Masters smiled and was gracious as she spoke to him, having for the moment wreathed herself in good humour so that he might go to his wooing in better spirit. He had learned his lesson by heart or nearly as he was able, and began to recite it as soon as he had closed the door. 'So you are going to Cheltenham on Thursday?' he said.

'Yes, Mr. Twentyman.'

'I hope you will enjoy your visit there. I remember Lady Ushant myself very well. I don't suppose she will remember me, but you can give her my compliments.'

'I certainly will do that.'

'And now, Mary, what have you got to say to me?' He looked for a moment as though he expected she would say what she had to say at once,—without further questions from him; but he knew that it could not be so, and he had prepared his lesson further than that. 'I think you must believe that I really do love you with all my heart.'

'I know that you are very good to me, Mr. Twentyman.'

'I don't say anything about being good; but I'm true: —that I am. I'd take you for my wife to-morrow if you hadn't a friend in the world, just for downright love. I've got you so in my heart, Mary, that I couldn't get rid of you if I tried ever so. You must know that it's true.'

'I do know that it's true.'

'Well! Don't you think that a fellow like that deserves something from a girl?'

'Indeed, I do.'

'Well!'

'He deserves a great deal too much for any girl to deceive him. You wouldn't like a young woman to marry you without loving you. I think you deserve a great deal too well of me for that.'

He paused a moment before he replied. 'I don't know about that,' he said at last. 'I believe I should be glad to take you just anyhow. I don't think you can hate me.'

'Certainly not. I like you as well, Mr. Twentyman, as one friend can like another,—without loving.'

'I'll be content with that, Mary, and chance it for the rest. I'll be that kind to you that I'll make you love me before twelve months are over. You come and try. You shall be mistress of everything. Mother isn't one that will want to be in the way.'

'It isn't that, Larry,' she said.

She hadn't called him Larry for a long time, and the sound of his own name from her lips gave him infinite hope. 'Come and try. Say you'll try. If ever a man did his best to please a woman, I'll do it to please you.' Then he attempted to take her in his arms, but she glided away from him round the table. 'I won't ask you not to go to Cheltenham, or anything of that. You shall have your own time. By George! you shall have everything your own way.' Still she did not answer him, but stood looking down upon the table. 'Come, say a word to a fellow.'

Then at last she spoke. 'Give me—six months to think of it.'

'Six months! If you'd say six weeks.'

'It is such a serious thing to do.'

'It is serious, of course. I'm serious, I know. I shouldn't hunt above half as often as I do now; and as for the club, I don't suppose I should go near the place once a month. Say six weeks, and then, if you'll let me have one kiss, I'll not trouble you till you're back from Cheltenham.'

Mary at once perceived that he had taken her doubt almost as a complete surrender, and had again to become obdurate. At last she promised to give him a final answer in two months, but declared as she said so that she was afraid she could not bring herself to do as he desired. She declined altogether to comply with that other request which he made, and then left him in the room, declaring that at present she could say nothing further. As she did so, she felt sure that she would not be able to accept him in two months' time, whatever she might bring herself to do when the vast abyss of six months should have passed by.

Larry made his way down into the parlour with hopes considerably raised. There he found Mrs. Masters, and when he told her what had passed, she assured him that the thing was as good as settled. Everybody knew, she said, that when a girl doubted she meant to yield. And what were two months? The time would have nearly gone by the end of her visit to Cheltenham. It was now early in December, and they might be married and settled at home before the end of April. Mrs. Masters, to give him courage, took out a bottle of currant wine and drank his health, and told him that in three months' time she would give him a kiss and call him her son. And she believed what she said. This, she thought, was merely Mary's way of letting herself down without a sudden fall.

Then the attorney came in, and also congratulated him. When the attorney was told that Mary had taken two months for her decision he also felt that the matter was almost as good as settled. This, at any rate, was clear to him,—that the existing misery of his household would for the present cease, and that Mary would be allowed to go upon her visit without further opposition. He at present did not think it wise to say another word to Mary about the young man;—nor would Mrs. Masters condescend to do so. Mary would, of course, now accept her lover like any other girl, and had been such a fool,—so thought Mrs. Masters,—that she had thoroughly deserved to lose him.

Chapter XXVII

'WONDERFUL BIRD!'

THERE were but two days between the scenes described in the last chapter and the day fixed for Mary's departure, and during these two days Larry Twentyman's name was not mentioned in the house. Mrs. Masters did not make herself quite pleasant to her stepdaughter, having still some grudge against her as to the £20. Nor, though she had submitted to the visit to Cheltenham, did she approve of it. It wasn't the way, she said, to make such a girl as Mary like her life at Chowton Farm, going and sitting and doing nothing in old Lady Ushant's drawing-room. It was cocking her up with gimcrack notions about ladies till she'd be ashamed to look at her own hands after she had done a day's work with them. There was no doubt some truth in this. The woman understood the world and was able to measure Larry Twentyman and Lady Ushant and the rest of them. Books and pretty needlework and easy conversation would consume the time at Cheltenham, whereas at Chowton Farm there would be a dairy and a poultry yard,—under difficulties on account of the foxes,—with a prospect of baby linen and children's shoes and stockings. It was all that question of gentlemen and ladies, and of non-gentlemen and non-ladies! They ought, Mrs. Masters thought, to be kept distinct. She had never, she said, wanted to put her finger into a pie that didn't belong to her. She had never tried to be a grand lady. But Mary was perilously near the brink on either side, and as it was to be her lucky fate at last to sit down to a plentiful but work-a-day life at Chowton Farm, she ought to have been kept away from the maundering idleness of Lady Ushant's lodgings at Cheltenham. But Mary heard nothing of this during these two days, Mrs. Masters bestowing the load of her wisdom upon her unfortunate husband.

Reginald Morton had been twice over at Mrs. Masters' house with reference to the proposed journey. Mrs.

Masters was hardly civil to him, as he was supposed to be
among the enemies;—but she had no suspicion that he
himself was the enemy of enemies. Had she entertained
such an idea she might have reconciled herself to it, as the
man was able to support a wife, and by such a marriage
she would have been at once relieved from all further
charge. In her own mind she would have felt very strongly
that Mary had chosen the wrong man, and thrown herself into the inferior mode of life. But her own difficulties
in the matter would have been solved. There was, however, no dream of such a kind entertained by any one of
the family. Reginald Morton was hardly regarded as
a young man, and was supposed to be gloomy, misan-
thropic, and bookish. Mrs. Masters was not at all averse
to the companionship of the journey, and Mr. Masters
was really grateful to one of the old family for being kind
to his girl.

Nor must it be supposed that Mary herself had any
expectations or even any hopes. With juvenile aptness to
make much of the little things which had interested her,
and prone to think more than was reasonable of any
intercourse with a man who seemed to her to be so
superior to others as Reginald Morton, she was anxious
for an opportunity to set herself right with him about that
scene at the bridge. She still thought that he was offended
and that she had given him cause for offence. He had
condescended to make her a request to which she had
acceded,—and she had then not done as she had promised.
She thought she was sure that this was all she had to say
to him, and yet she was aware that she was unnaturally
excited at the idea of spending three or four hours alone
with him. The fly which was to take him to the railway
station called for Mary at the attorney's door at ten
o'clock, and the attorney handed her in. 'It is very good
of you indeed, Mr. Morton, to take so much trouble with
my girl,' said the attorney, really feeling what he said.
'It is very good of you to trust her to me,' said Reginald,
also sincerely. Mary was still to him the girl who had
been brought up by his aunt at Bragton, and not the fit
companion for Larry Twentyman.

Reginald Morton had certainly not made up his mind to ask Mary Masters to be his wife. Thinking of Mary Masters very often as he had done during the last two months, he was quite sure that he did not mean to marry at all. He did acknowledge to himself that were he to allow himself to fall in love with any one, it would be with Mary Masters,—but for not doing so there were many reasons. He had lived so long alone that a married life would not suit him; as a married man he would be a poor man; he himself was averse to company, whereas most women prefer society. And then, as to this special girl, had he not reason for supposing that she preferred another man to him, and a man of such a class that the very preference showed her to be unfit to mate with him? He also cozened himself with an idea that it was well that he should have the opportunity which the journey would give him of apologizing for his previous rudeness to her.

In the carriage they had the compartment to themselves with the exception of an old lady at the further end, who had a parrot in a cage, for which she had taken a first-class ticket. 'I can't offer you this seat,' said the old lady, 'because it has been booked and paid for for my bird.' As neither of the new passengers had shown the slightest wish for the seat, the communication was perhaps unnecessary. Neither of the two had any idea of separating from the other for the sake of the old lady's company.

They had before them a journey of thirty miles on one railway; then a stop of half an hour at the Hinxton Junction; and then another journey of about equal length. In the first hour very little was said that might not have been said in the presence of Lady Ushant,—or even of Mrs. Masters. There might be a question whether, upon the whole, the parrot had not the best of the conversation, as the bird, which the old lady declared to be the wonder of his species, repeated the last word of nearly every sentence spoken either by our friends or by the old lady herself. 'Don't you think you'd be less liable to cold with that window closed?' the old lady said to Mary. 'Cosed, —cosed,—cosed,' said the bird, and Morton was of course constrained to shut the window. 'He is a wonderful bird,' said the old lady. 'Wonderful bird,—wonderful bird,— wonderful bird,' said the parrot, who was quite at home with this expression. 'We shall be able to get some lunch at Hinxton,' said Reginald. 'Inxton,' screamed the bird —'Caw,—caw,—caw.' 'He's worth a deal of money,' said the lady. 'Deal o' money,—deal o' money,' repeated the bird, as he scrambled round the wire cage with a tremendous noise, to the great triumph of the old lady.

No doubt the close attention which the bird paid to everything that passed, and the presence of the old lady as well, did for a time interfere with their conversation. But, after awhile, the old lady was asleep, and the bird, having once or twice attempted to imitate the somnolent sounds which his mistress was making, seemed also to go to sleep himself. Then Reginald, beginning with Lady Ushant and the old Morton family generally, gradually got the conversation round to Bragton and the little bridge. He had been very stern when he had left her there, and he knew also that at that subsequent interview, when he had brought Lady Ushant's note to her at her father's house, he had not been cordially kind to her. Now they were thrown together for an hour or so in the closest companionship, and he wished to make her comfortable and happy. 'I suppose you remember Bragton?' he said.

'Every path and almost every tree about the place.'

'So do I. I called there the other day. Family quarrels are so silly, you know.'

'Did you see Mr. Morton?'

'No;—and he hasn't returned my visit yet. I don't know whether he will,—and I don't much mind whether he does or not. That old woman is there, and she is very bitter against me. I don't care about the people, but I am sorry that I cannot see the place.'

'I ought to have walked with you that day,' she said, in a very low tone. The parrot opened his eyes and looked at them as though he were striving to catch his cue.

'Of course you ought.' But as he said this he smiled, and there was no offence in his voice. 'I dare say you didn't guess how much I thought of it. And then I was a bear to you. I always am a bear when I am not pleased.'

'Peas,—peas,—peas,' said the parrot.

'I shall be a bear to that brute of a bird before long.'

'What a very queer bird he is!'

'He is a public nuisance,—and so is the old lady who brought him here.' This was said quite in a whisper. 'It is very odd, Miss Masters, but you are literally the only person in all Dillsborough in regard to whom I have any genuine feeling of old friendship.'

'You must remember a great many.'

'But I did not know any well enough. I was too young to have seen much of your father. But when I came back at that time, you and I were always together.'

'Gedder,—gedder,—gedder,' said the parrot.

'If that bird goes on like that, I'll speak to the guard,' said Mr. Morton with affected anger.

'Polly mustn't talk,' said the old lady, waking up.

'Tok,—tok,—tok,—tok,' screamed the parrot. Then the old lady threw a shawl over him and again went to sleep.

'If I behaved badly, I beg your pardon,' said Mary.

'That's just what I wanted to say to you, Miss Masters, —only a man never can do those things as well as a lady. I did behave badly, and I do beg your pardon. Of course, I ought to have asked Mr. Twentyman to come with us. I know that he is a very good fellow.'

'Indeed, he is,' said Mary Masters, with all the emphasis in her power. 'Deedy is,—deedy is,—deedy is, —deedy is,' repeated the parrot in a very angry voice about a dozen times under his shawl, and while the old lady was remonstrating with her too talkative companion, their tickets were taken and they ran into the Hinxton station. 'If the old lady is going on to Cheltenham, we'll travel third class before we'll sit in the same carriage again with that bird,' said Morton, laughing, as he took Mary into the refreshment-room. But the old lady did not get into the same compartment as they started, and the last that was heard of the parrot at Hinxton was a quarrel between him and the guard as to certain railway privileges.

When they had got back into the railway carriage, Morton was very anxious to ask whether she was in truth engaged to marry the young man as to whose good fellowship she and the parrot had spoken up so emphatically, but he hardly knew how to put the question. And were she to declare that she was engaged to him, what should he say then? Would he not be bound to congratulate her? And yet it would be impossible that any word of such congratulation should pass his lips. 'You will stay a month at Cheltenham?' he said.

'Your aunt was kind enough to ask me for so long.'

'I shall go back on Saturday. If I were to stay longer I should feel myself to be in her way. And I have come to live a sort of hermit's life. I hardly know how to sit down and eat my dinner in company, and have no idea of seeing a human being before two o'clock.'

'What do you do with yourself?'

'I rush in and out of the garden, and spend my time between my books and my flowers and my tobacco pipes.'

'Do you mean to live always like that?' she asked,—in perfect innocency.

'I think so. Sometimes I doubt whether it is wise.'

'I don't think it wise at all,' said Mary.

'Why not?'

'People should live together, I think.'

'You mean that I ought to have a wife?'

'No;—I didn't mean that. Of course, that must be just as you might come to like anyone well enough. But a person need not shut himself up and be a hermit because he is not married. Lord Rufford is not married, and he goes everywhere.'

'He has money and property, and is a man of pleasure.'

'And your cousin, Mr. John Morton.'

'He is essentially a man of business, which I never could have been. And they say he is going to be married to that Miss Trefoil who has been staying there. Unfortunately, I have never had anything that I need do in all my life, and therefore I have shut myself up, as you call it. I wonder what your life will be.' Mary blushed and said nothing. 'If there were anything to tell I wish I knew it.'

'There is nothing to tell.'

'Nothing?'

She thought a moment before she answered him, and then she said, 'Nothing. What should I have to tell?' she added, trying to laugh.

He remained for a few moments silent, and then put his head out towards her as he spoke. 'I was afraid that you might have to tell that you were engaged to marry Mr. Twentyman.'

'I am not.'

'Oh!—I am so glad to hear it.'

'I don't know why you should be glad. If I had said I was, it would have been very uncivil if you hadn't declared yourself glad to hear that.'

'Then I must have been uncivil, for I couldn't have done it. Knowing how my aunt loves you, knowing what she thinks of you and what she would think of such a match, remembering myself what I do of you, I could not have congratulated you on your engagement to a man whom I think so much inferior to yourself in every respect. Now you know it all—why I was angry at the bridge, why I was hardly civil to you at your father's house; and, to tell the truth, why I have been so anxious to be alone with you for half an hour. If you think it an offence that I should take so much interest in you, I will beg your pardon for that also.'

'Oh, no!'

'I have never spoken to my aunt about it, but I do not think that she would have been contented to hear that you were to become the wife of Mr. Twentyman.'

What answer she was to make to this, or whether she was to make any, she had not decided when they were interrupted by the reappearance of the lady and the bird. She was declaring to the guard at the window, that as she had paid for a first-class seat for her parrot she would get into any carriage she liked in which there were two empty seats. Her bird had been ill-treated by some scurrilous, ill-conditioned travellers and she had therefore returned to the comparative kindness of her former companions.

'They threatened to put him out of the window, sir,' said the old woman to Morton, as she was forcing her way in.

'Windersir,—windersir,' said the parrot.

'I hope he'll behave himself here, ma'am,' said Morton.

'Heremam,—heremam,—heremam,' said the parrot.

'Now go to bed like a good bird,' said the old lady, putting her shawl over the cage,—whereupon the parrot made a more diabolical noise than ever under the curtain.

Mary felt that there was no more to be said about Mr. Twentyman and her hopes and prospects, and for the moment she was glad to be left in peace. The old lady and the parrot continued their conversation till they all arrived in Cheltenham; and Mary as she sat alone thinking of it afterwards might perhaps feel a soft regret that Reginald Morton had been interrupted by the talkative animal.

Chapter XXVIII

MOUNSER GREEN

'SO Peter Boyd is to go to Washington in the Paragon's place, and Jack Slade goes to Vienna, and young Palliser is to get Slade's berth at Lisbon.' This information was given by a handsome young man, known as Mounser Green, about six feet high, wearing a velvet shooting coat—more properly called an office coat from its present uses—who had just entered a spacious, well-carpeted, comfortable room in which three other gentlemen were sitting at their different tables. This was one of the rooms in the Foreign Office, and looked out into St. James's Park. Mounser Green was a distinguished clerk in that department,—and distinguished also in various ways, being one of the fashionable young men about town, a great adept at private theatricals, remarkable as a billiard player at his club, and a contributor to various magazines. At this moment he had a cigar in his mouth, and when he entered the room he stood with his back to the fire ready for conversation, and looking very unlike a clerk who intended to do any work. But there was a general idea that Mounser Green was invaluable to the Foreign Office. He could speak and write two or three foreign languages; he could do a spurt of work—ten hours at a sitting when required; he was ready to go through fire and water for his chief; and was a gentleman all round. Though still nominally a young man,—being perhaps thirty-five years of age—he had entered the service before competitive examination had assumed its present shape, and had therefore the gifts which were required for his special position. Some critics on the Civil Service were no doubt apt to find fault with Mounser Green. When called upon at his office he was never seen to be doing anything, and he always had a cigar in his mouth. These gentlemen found out, too, that he never entered his office till half-past twelve, perhaps not having also learned that he was generally there till nearly seven. No doubt during that time he read a great many newspapers, and wrote a great many private notes,—on official paper! But there may be a question whether even these employments did not help to make Mounser Green the valuable man he was.

'What a lounge for Jack Slade,' said young Hoffmann.

'I'll tell you who it won't be a lounge for, Green,' said Archibald Currie, the clerk who held the second authority among them. 'What will Bell Trefoil think of going to Patagonia?'

'That's all off,' said Mounser Green.

'I don't think so,' said Charley Glossop, one of the numerous younger sons of Lord Glossop. 'She was staying only the other day down at the Paragon's place in Rufford, and they went together to my cousin Rufford's house. His sister,—that's Lady Penwether, told me they were certainly engaged then.'

'That was before the Paragon had been named for Patagonia. To tell you a little bit of my own private mind,—which isn't scandal,' said Mounser Green, 'because it is only given as opinion,—I think it just possible that the Paragon has taken this very uncomfortable mission because it offered him some chance of escape.'

'Then he has more sense about him than I gave him credit for,' said Archibald Currie.

'Why should a man like Morton go to Patagonia?' continued Green. 'He has an independent fortune and doesn't want the money. He'd have been sure to have something comfortable in Europe very soon, if he had waited, and was much better off second at a place like Washington. I was quite surprised when he took it.'

'Patagonia isn't bad at all,' said Currie.

'That depends on whether a man has got money of his own. When I heard about the Paragon and Bell Trefoil at Washington, I knew there had been a mistake made. He didn't know what he was doing. I'm a poor man, but I wouldn't take her with £5000 a year, settled on myself.' Poor Mounser Green!

'I think she's the handsomest girl in London,' said Hoffmann, who was a young man of German parentage and perhaps of German taste.

'That may be,' continued Green:—'but, heaven and earth! what a life she would lead a man like the Paragon! He's found it out, and therefore thought it well to go to South America. She has declined already, I'm told; but he means to stick to the mission.' During all this time Mounser Green was smoking his cigar with his back to the fire, and the other clerks looked as though they had nothing to do but talk about the private affairs of ministers abroad and their friends. Of course, it will be understood that since we last saw John Morton the position of Minister Plenipotentiary*at Patagonia had been offered to him, and that he had accepted the place in spite of Bragton and of Arabella Trefoil.

At that moment a card was handed to Mounser Green by a messenger, who was desired to show the gentleman up. 'It's the Paragon himself,' said Green.

'We'll make him tell us whether he's going out single or double,' said Archibald Currie.

'After what the Rufford people said to me, I'm sure he's going to marry her,' said young Glossop. No doubt Lady Penwether had been anxious to make it understood by every one connected with the family that if any gossip should be heard about Rufford and Arabella Trefoil there was nothing in it.

Then the Paragon was shown into the room, and Mounser Green and the young men were delighted to see him. Colonial governors at their seats of government, and Ministers Plenipotentiary in their ambassadorial residences are very great persons indeed; and when met in society at home, with the stars and ribbons which are common among them now, they are less, indeed, but still something. But at the Colonial and Foreign Offices in London, among the assistant secretaries and clerks, they are hardly more than common men. All the gingerbread is gone there. His Excellency is no more than Jones, and the Representative or Alter Ego of Royalty mildly asks little favours of the junior clerks.

'Lord Drummond only wants to know what you wish and it shall be done,' said Mounser Green. Lord Drummond was the Minister for Foreign Affairs of the day. 'I hope I need hardly say that we were delighted that you accepted the offer.'

'One doesn't like to refuse a step upward,' said Morton; 'otherwise Patagonia isn't exactly the place one would like.'

'Very good climate,' said Currie. 'Ladies I have known who have gone there have enjoyed it very much.'

'A little rough, I suppose?'

'They didn't seem to say so. Young Barttetot took his wife out there,—just married. He liked it. There wasn't much society, but they didn't care about that just at first.'

'Ah;—I'm a single man,' said Morton laughing. He was too good a diplomate to be pumped in that simple way by such a one as Archibald Currie.

'You'll like to see Lord Drummond. He is here and will be glad to shake hands with you. Come into my room.' Then Mounser Green led the way into a small inner sanctum in which it may be presumed that he really did his work. It was here, at any rate, that he wrote the notes on official note paper.

'They haven't settled as yet how they're to be off it,' said Currie in a whisper, as soon as the two men were gone, 'but I'll bet a five-pound note that Bell Trefoil doesn't go out to Patagonia as his wife.'

'We know the Senator here well enough.' This was said in the inner room by Mounser Green to Morton, who had breakfasted with the Senator that morning and had made an appointment to meet him at the Foreign Office. The Senator wanted to secure a seat for himself at the opening of Parliament which was appointed to take place in the course of the next month, and being a member of the Committee on Foreign Affairs in the American Senate, of course thought himself entitled to have things done for him by the Foreign Office clerks. 'Oh yes, I'll see him. Lord Drummond will get him a seat as a matter of course. How is he getting on with your neighbour at Dills-borough?'

'So you've heard of that?'

'Heard of it! who hasn't heard of it?'—At this moment the messenger came in again and the Senator was announced. 'Lord Drummond will manage about the seats in the House of Lords, Mr. Gotobed. Of course he'll see you if you wish it; but I'll take a note of it.'

'If you'll do that, Mr. Green, I shall be fixed up straight. And I'd a great deal sooner see you than his lordship.'

'That's very flattering, Mr. Gotobed, but I'm sure I don't know why.'

'Because Lord Drummond always seems to me to have more on hand than he knows how to get through, and you never seem to have anything to do.'

'That's not quite so flattering,—and would be killing only that I feel that your opinion is founded on error. Mens conscia recti,* Mr. Gotobed.'

'Exactly. I understand English pretty well;—better, as far as I can see, than some of those I meet around me here; but I don't go beyond that, Mr. Green.'

'I merely meant to observe, Mr. Gotobed, that as, within my own breast, I am conscious of my zeal and diligence in Her Majesty's service your shafts of satire pass me by without hurting me. Shall I offer you a cigar? A candle burned at both ends is soon consumed.' It was quite clear that as quickly as the Senator got through one end of his cigar by the usual process of burning, so quickly did he eat the other end. But he took that which Mounser Green offered him without any displeasure at the allusion. 'I'm sorry to say that I haven't a spittoon,' said Mounser Green, 'but the whole fire-place is at your service.' The Senator could hardly have heard this, as it made no difference in his practice.

Morton at this moment was sent for by the Secretary of State, and the Senator expressed his intention of waiting for him in Mr. Green's room. 'How does the great Goarly case get on, Mr. Gotobed?' asked the clerk.

'Well! I don't know that it's getting on very much.'

'You are not growing tired of it, Senator?'

'Not by any means. But it's getting itself complicated, Mr. Green. I mean to see the end of it, and if I'm beat,— why I can take a beating as well as another man.'

'You begin to think you'll be beat?'

'I didn't say so, Mr. Green. It is very hard to understand all the ins and outs of a case like that in a foreign country.'

'Then I shouldn't try it, Senator.'

'There I differ. It is my object to learn all I can.'

'At any rate, I shouldn't pay for the lesson as you are like to do. What'll the bill be? Four hundred dollars?'

'Never mind, Mr. Green. If you'll take the opinion of a good deal older man than yourself and one who has perhaps worked harder, you'll understand that there's no knowledge got so thoroughly as that for which a man pays.' Soon after this Morton came out from the great man's room and went away in company with the Senator.

Chapter XXIX

THE SENATOR'S LETTER

SOON after this Senator Gotobed went down, alone, to Dillsborough and put himself up at the Bush Inn. Although he had by no means the reputation of being a rich man, he did not seem to care much what money he

spent in furthering any object he had taken in hand. He
never knew how near he had been to meeting the direst
of inhospitality at Mr. Runciman's house. That worthy
innkeeper, knowing well the Senator's sympathy with
Goarly, Scrobby, and Bearside, and being heart and
soul devoted to the Rufford interest, had almost refused
the Senator the accommodation he wanted. It was
only when Mrs. Runciman represented to him that
she could charge ten shillings a day for the use of her
sitting-room, and also that Lord Rufford himself had
condescended to entertain the gentleman, that Runciman gave way. Mr. Gotobed would, no doubt, have
delighted in such inhospitality. He would have gone
to the second-rate inn, which was very second-rate
indeed, and have acquired a further insight into British
manners and British prejudices. As it was he made
himself at home in the best upstairs sitting-room at
the Bush, and was quite unaware of the indignity
offered to him when Runciman refused to send him up
the best sherry. Let us hope that this refusal was remembered by the young woman in the bar when she
made out the Senator's bill.

He stayed at Dillsborough for three or four days, during
which he saw Goarly once and Bearside on two or three
occasions,—and moreover handed to that busy attorney
three bank notes for £5 each. Bearside was clever enough
to make him believe that Goarly would certainly obtain
serious damages from the lord. With Bearside he was
fairly satisfied, thinking however that the man was much
more illiterate and ignorant than the general run of
lawyers in the United States; but with Goarly he was
by no means satisfied. Goarly endeavoured to keep out of
his way and could not be induced to come to him at the
Bush. Three times he walked out to the house near Dillsborough Wood, on each of which occasions Mrs. Goarly
pestered him for money, and told him at great length the
history of her forlorn goose. Scrobby, of whom he had
heard, he could not see at all; and he found that Bearside
was very unwilling to say anything about Scrobby.
Scrobby and the red herrings and the strychnine and the

dead fox were, according to Bearside, to be kept quite distinct from the pheasants and the wheat. Bearside declared over and over again that there was no evidence to connect his client with the demise of the fox. When asked whether he did not think that his client had compassed the death of the animal, he assured the Senator that in such matters he never ventured to think. 'Let us go by the evidence, Mr. Gotobed,' he said.

'But I am paying my money for the sake of getting at the facts.'

'Evidence is facts, sir,' said the attorney. 'Any way, let us settle about the pheasants first.'

The condition of the Senator's mind may perhaps be best made known by a letter which he wrote from Dillsborough to his especial and well-trusted friend Josiah Scroome, a member of the House of Representatives from his own state of Mikewa. Since he had been in England he had written constantly to his friend, giving him the result of his British experiences.

> 'Bush Inn, Dillsborough,
> 'Ufford County, England,
> 'December 16, 187–.

'My DEAR SIR,

'Since my last I have enjoyed myself very well, and I am, I trust, beginning to understand something of the mode of thinking of this very peculiar people. That there should be so wide a difference between us Americans and these English, from whom we were divided, so to say, but the other day, is one of the most peculiar physiological phenomena that the history of the world will have afforded. As far as I can hear, a German or even a Frenchman thinks much more as an Englishman thinks than does an American. Nor does this come mainly from the greater prevalence with us of democratic institutions. I do not think that any one can perceive in half an hour's conversation the difference between a Swiss and a German; but I fancy, and I may say I flatter myself, that an American is as easily distinguished from an Englishman, as a sheep from a goat, or a tall man from one who is short.

'And yet there is a pleasure in associating with those here of the highest rank which I find it hard to describe, and which perhaps I ought to regard as a pernicious temptation to useless luxury. There is an ease of manner with them which recalls with unfavourable reminiscences the hard self-consciousness of the better class of our citizens. There is a story of an old hero who with his companions fell among beautiful women and luscious wine, but the hero had been warned in time that they would all be turned into filthy animals should they yield to the allurements around them. The temptation here is perhaps the same. I am not a hero; and, though I too have been warned by the lessons I have learned under our happy Constitution, I feel that I might easily become one of the animals in question.

'And, to give them their due, it is better than merely beautiful women and luscious wine. There is a reality about them, and a desire to live up to their principles, which is very grand. Their principles are no doubt very bad, utterly antagonistic to all progress, unconscious altogether of the demand for progressive equality which is made by the united voices of suffering mankind. The man who is born a lord, and who sees a dozen serfs around him who have been born to be half-starved ploughmen, thinks that God arranged it all, and that he is bound to maintain a state of things so comfortable to himself, as being God's vicegerent here on earth. But they do their work as vicegerents with an easy grace, and with sweet pleasant voices and soft movements, which almost make a man doubt whether the Almighty has not, in truth, intended that such injustice should be permanent. That one man should be rich and another poor is a necessity in the present imperfect state of civilization;—but that one man should be born to be a legislator, born to have every-thing, born to be a tyrant,—and should think it all right, is to me miraculous. But the greatest miracle of all is that they who are not so born,—who have been born to suffer the reverse side,—should also think it to be all right.

'With us it is necessary that a man, to shine in society, should have done something, or should, at any rate, have the capacity of doing something. But here the greatest fool that you meet will shine, and will be admitted to be brilliant, simply because he has possessions. Such a one will take his part in conversation though he knows nothing, and, when inquired into, he will own that he knows nothing. To know anything is not in his line in life. But he can move about, and chatter like a child of ten, and amuse himself from morning to night with various empty playthings,—and be absolutely proud of his life!

'I have lately become acquainted with a certain young lord here of this class, who has treated me with great kindness, although I have taken it into my head to oppose him as to a matter in which he is very keen. I ventured to inquire of him as to the pursuits of his life. He is a lord, and therefore a legislator, but he made no scruple to tell me that he never went near the Chamber in which it is his privilege to have a seat. But his party does not lose his support. Though he never goes near the place he can vote and is enabled to trust his vote to some other more ambitious lord who does go there. It required the absolute evidence of personal information from those who are themselves concerned to make me believe that legislation in Great Britain could be carried on after such a fashion as this! Then he told me what he did do. All the winter he hunts and shoots, going about to other rich men's houses when there is no longer sufficient for him to shoot left on his own estate. That lasts him from the 1st of September to the end of March, and occupies all his time. August he spends in Scotland, also shooting other animals. During the other months he fishes, and plays cricket and tennis, and attends races, and goes about to parties in London. His evenings he spends at a card table when he can get friends to play with him. It is the employment of his life to fit in his amusements so that he may not have a dull day. Wherever he goes he carries his wine with him and his valet and his grooms;—and if he thinks there is anything to fear, his cook also. He very rarely opens a book. He is more ignorant than a boy of fifteen with us, and yet he manages to have something to say about everything. When his ignorance has been made as clear as the sun at noon-day, he is no whit ashamed. One would say that such a life would break the heart of any man, but, upon my word, I doubt whether I ever came across a human being so self-satisfied as this young lord.

'I have come down here to support the case of a poor man who is, I think, being trampled on by this do-nothing legislator. But I am bound to say that the lord in his kind is very much better than the poor man in his. Such a wretched, squalid, lying, cowardly creature I did not think that even England could produce. And yet the man has a property in land on which he ought to be able to live in humble comfort. I feel sure that I have leagued myself with a rascal, whereas I believe the lord, in spite of his ignorance and his idleness, to be honest. But yet the man is being hardly used, and has had the spirit, or rather perhaps has been instigated by others, to rebel. His crops have been eaten up by the lord's pheasants, and the lord, exercising plenary power as though he were subject to no laws, will only pay what compensation he himself chooses to award. The whole country here is in arms against the rebel, thinking it monstrous that a man living in a hovel should contest such a point with the owner of half-a-dozen palaces. I have come forward to help the man for the sake of seeing how the matter will go; and I have to confess that though those under the lord have treated me as though I were a miscreant, the lord himself and his friends have been civil enough.

'I say what I think wherever I go, and I do not find it taken in bad part. In that respect we might learn something from them. When a Britisher over in the States says what he thinks about us, we are apt to be a little rough with him. I have, indeed, known towns in which he couldn't speak out with personal safety. Here there is no danger of that kind. I am getting together the materials for a lecture on British institutions in general, in which I shall certainly speak my mind plainly, and I think I shall venture to deliver it in London before I leave for New York in the course of next spring. I will, however, write to you again before that time comes.

'Believe me to be,
'Dear sir,
'With much sincerity,
'Yours truly,
'ELIAS GOTOBED.'

'The Honble. Josiah Scroome,
'125, Q Street,
'Minnesota Avenue,
'Washington.'

On the morning of the Senator's departure from Dillsborough, Mr. Runciman met him standing under the covered way leading from the inn yard into the street. He was waiting for the omnibus which was being driven about the town, and which was to call for him and take him down to the railway station. Mr. Runciman had not as yet spoken to him since he had been at the inn, and had not even made himself personally known to his guest. 'So, sir, you are going to leave us,' said the landlord, with a smile which was intended probably as a smile of triumph.

'Yes, sir,' said the Senator. 'It's about time, I guess, that I should get back to London.'

'I dare say it is, sir,' said the landlord. 'I dare say you've seen enough of Mr. Goarly by this time.'

'That's as may be. I don't know whom I have the pleasure of speaking to.'

'My name is Runciman, sir. I'm the landlord here.'

'I hope I see you well, Mr. Runciman. I have about come to an end of my business here.'

'I dare say you have, sir. I should say so. Perhaps I might express an opinion that you never came across a greater blackguard than Goarly either in this country or your own.'

'That's a strong opinion, Mr. Runciman.'

'It's the general opinion here, sir. I should have thought you'd found it out before this.'

'I don't know that I am prepared at this moment to declare all that I have found out.'

'I thought you'd have been tired of it by this time, Mr. Gotobed.'

'Tired of what?'

'Tired of the wrong side, sir.'

'I don't know that I'm on the wrong side. A man may be in the right on one point even though his life isn't all that it ought to be.'

'That's true, sir, but if they told you all that they knew up the street,'—and Runciman pointed to the part of the town in which Bearside's office was situated, 'I should have thought you would have understood who was going to win and who was going to lose. Good day, sir; I hope you'll have a pleasant journey. Much obliged to you for your patronage, sir,' and Runciman, still smiling unpleasantly, touched his hat as the Senator got into the omnibus.

The Senator was not very happy as to the Goarly business. He had paid some money and had half promised more, and had found out that he was in a boat with thoroughly disreputable persons. As he had said to the landlord, a man may have the right on his side in an action at law though he be a knave or a rascal; and if a lord be unjust to a poor man, the poor man should have justice done him, even though he be not quite a pattern poor man. But now he was led to believe, by what the landlord had said to him, that he was being kept in the dark, and that there were facts generally known that he did not know. He had learned something of English manners and English institutions by his interference, but there might be a question whether he was not paying too dearly for his whistle. And there was growing upon him a feeling that before he had done he would have to blush for his colleagues.

As the omnibus went away Dr. Nupper joined Mr. Runciman under the archway. 'I'm blessed if I can understand that man,' said Runciman. 'What is it he's after?'

'Notoriety,' said the doctor, with the air of a man who has completely solved a difficult question.

'He'll have to pay for it, and that pretty smart,' said Runciman. 'I never heard of such a foolish thing in all my life. What the dickens is it to him? One can understand Bearside, and Scrobby too. When a fellow has

something to get, one does understand it. But why an old
fellow like that should come down from the moon to pay
ever so much money for such a man as Goarly, is what
I don't understand.'

'Notoriety,' said the doctor.

'He evidently don't know that Nickem has got round
Goarly,' said the landlord.

CHAPTER XXX

AT CHELTENHAM

THE month at Cheltenham was passed very quietly,
and would have been a very happy month with Mary
Masters but that there grew upon her from day to day
increasing fears of what she would have to undergo when
she returned to Dillsborough. At the moment when she
was hesitating with Larry Twentyman, when she begged
him to wait six months, and then at last promised to give
him an answer at the end of two, she had worked herself
up to think that it might possibly be her duty to accept
her lover for the sake of her family. At any rate, she had
at that moment thought that the question of duty ought
to be further considered, and therefore she had vacillated.
When the two months' delay was accorded her, and within that period the privilege of a long absence from Dillsborough, she put the trouble aside for a while with the
common feeling that the chapter of accidents might do
something for her. Before she had reached Cheltenham
the chapter of accidents had done much. When Reginald
Morton told her that he could not have congratulated her
on such prospects, and had explained to her why, in
truth, he had been angry at the bridge,—how he had
been anxious to be alone with her that he might learn
whether she were really engaged to this man,—then she
had known that her answer to Larry Twentyman at the
end of the two months must be a positive refusal.

But as she became aware of this, a new trouble arose
and harassed her very soul. When she had asked for the
six months she had not at the moment been aware, she
had not then felt, that a girl who asks for time is supposed

to have already surrendered. But since she had made that unhappy request the conviction had grown upon her. She read it in every word her stepmother said to her, and in her father's manner. The very winks and hints and little jokes which fell from her younger sisters told her that it was so. She could see around her the satisfaction which had come from the settlement of that difficult question,—a satisfaction which was perhaps more apparent with her father than even with the others. Then she knew what she had done, and remembered to have heard that a girl who expresses a doubt is supposed to have gone beyond doubting. While she was still at Dillsborough there was a feeling that no evil would arise from this if she could at last make up her mind to be Mrs. Twentyman; but when the settled conviction came upon her, after hearing Reginald Morton's words, then she was much troubled.

He stayed only a couple of days at Cheltenham, and during that time said very little to her. He certainly spoke no word which would give her a right to think that he himself was attached to her. He had been interested about her, as was his aunt, Lady Ushant, because she had been known, and her mother had been known, by the old Mortons. But there was nothing of love in all that. She had never supposed that there would be;—and yet there was a vague feeling in her bosom that as he had been strong in expressing his objection to Mr. Twentyman, there might have been something more to stir him than the memory of those old days at Bragton.

'To my thinking there is a sweetness about her which I have never seen equalled in any young woman.' This was said by Lady Ushant to her nephew after Mary had gone to bed on the night before he left.

'One would suppose,' he answered, 'that you wanted me to ask her to be my wife.'

'I never want anything of that kind, Reg. I never make in such matters,—or mar if I can help it.'

'There is a man at Dillsborough wants to marry her.'

'I can easily believe that there should be two or three. Who is the man?'

'Do you remember old Twentyman, of Chowton?'

'He was our nearest neighbour. Of course I remember him. I can remember well when they bought the land.'

'It is his son.'

'Surely, he can hardly be worthy of her, Reg.'

'And yet they say he is worthy. I have asked about him, and he is not a bad fellow. He keeps his money, and has ideas of living decently. He doesn't drink or gamble. But he's not a gentleman nor anything like one. I should think he never opens a book. Of course it would be a degradation.'

'And what does Mary say herself?'

'I fancy she has refused him.' Then he added after a pause, 'Indeed, I know she has.'

'How should you know? Has she told you?' In answer to this he only nodded his head at the old lady. 'There must have been close friendship, Reg, between you two when she told you that. I hope you have not made her give up one suitor by leading her to love another who does not mean to ask her.'

'I certainly have not done that,' said Reg. Men may often do much without knowing that they do anything, and such probably had been the case with Reginald Morton during the journey from Dillsborough to Cheltenham.

'What would her father wish?'

'They all want her to take the man.'

'How can she do better?'

'Would you have her marry a man who is not a gentleman, whose wife will never be visited by other ladies;— in marrying whom she would go altogether down into another and a lower world?'

This was a matter on which Lady Ushant and her nephew had conversed often, and he thought he knew her to be thoroughly wedded to the privileges which she believed to be attached to her birth. With him the same feeling was almost the stronger, because he was so well aware of the blot upon himself caused by the lowness of his own father's marriage. But a man, he held, could raise a woman to his own rank, whereas a woman must accept the level of her husband.

'Bread and meat and chairs and tables are very serious things, Reg.'

'You would then recommend her to take this man, and pass altogether out of your own sphere?'

'What can I do for her? I am an old woman who will be dead probably before the first five years of her married life have passed over her. And as for recommending, I do not know enough to recommend anything. Does she like the man?'

'I am sure she will feel herself degraded by marrying him.'

'I trust she will never live to feel herself degraded. I do not believe that she could do anything that she thought would degrade her. But I think that you and I had better leave her to herself in this matter.' Further on in the same evening, or rather late in the night,—for they had then sat talking together for hours over the fire,—she made a direct statement to him. 'When I die, Reg, I have but £5,000 to leave behind me, and this I have divided between you and her. I shall not tell her because I might do more harm than good. But you may know.'

'That would make no difference to me,' he said.

'Very likely not, but I wish you to know it. What troubles me is that she will have to pay so much out of it for legacy duty. I might leave it all to you and you could give it her.' An honester or more religious or better woman than old Lady Ushant there was not in Cheltenham, but it never crossed her conscience that it would be wrong to cheat the revenue. It may be doubted whether any woman has ever been brought to such honesty as that.

On the next morning Morton went away without saying another word in private to Mary Masters, and she was left to her quiet life with the old lady. To an ordinary visitor nothing could have been less exciting, for Lady Ushant very seldom went out and never entertained company. She was a tall thin old lady with bright eyes and grey hair and a face that was still pretty in spite of sunken eyes and sunken cheeks and wrinkled brow. There was ever present with her an air of melancholy which told a whole tale of the sadness of a long life. Her chief excitement was in her two visits to church on Sunday, and in the letter which she wrote every week to her nephew at Dillsborough. Now she had her young friend with her, and that too was an excitement to her,—and the more so since she had heard of the tidings of Larry Twentyman's courtship.

She made up her mind that she would not speak on the subject to her young friend unless her young friend should speak to her. In the first three weeks nothing was said; but four or five days before Mary's departure there came up a conversation about Dillsborough and Bragton. There had been many conversations about Dillsborough and Bragton, but in all of them the name of Lawrence Twentyman had been scrupulously avoided. Each had longed to name him, and each had determined not to do so. But at length it was avoided no longer. Lady Ushant had spoken of Chowton Farm and the widow. Then Mary had spoken of the place and its inhabitants. 'Mr. Twentyman comes a great deal to our house now,' she said.

'Has he any reason, my dear?'

'He goes with papa once a week to the club; and he sometimes lends my sister Kate a pony. Kate is very fond of riding.'

'There is nothing else?'

'He has got to be intimate and I think mamma likes him.'

'He is a good young man, then?'

'Very good;' said Mary, with an emphasis.

'And Chowton belongs to him?'

'Oh yes;—it belongs to him.'

'Some young men make such ducks and drakes of their property when they get it.'

'They say that he's not like that at all. People say that he understands farming very well, and that he minds everything himself.'

'What an excellent young man! There is no other reason for his coming to your house, Mary?'

Then the sluice-gates were opened and the whole story was told. Sitting there late into the night Mary told it all

as well as she knew how,—all of it except in regard to any
spark of love which might have fallen upon her in respect
to Reginald Morton. Of Reginald Morton in her story of
course she did not speak; but all the rest she declared.
She did not love the man. She was quite sure of that.
Though she thought so well of him there was, she was
quite sure, no feeling in her heart akin to love. She had
promised to take time, because she had thought that she
might perhaps be able to bring herself to marry him without loving him,—to marry him because her father wished
it, and because her going from home would be a relief to
her stepmother and sisters, because it would be well for
them all that she should be settled out of the way. But
since that she had made up her mind,—she thought that she
had quite made up her mind,—that it would be impossible.

'There is nobody else, Mary?' said Lady Ushant,
putting her hand on Mary's lap. Mary protested that
there was nobody else without any consciousness that she
was telling a falsehood. 'And you are quite sure that you
cannot do it?'

'Do you think that I ought, Lady Ushant?'

'I should be very sorry to say that, my dear. A young
woman in such a matter must be governed by her feelings.
Only he seems to be a deserving young man!' Mary
looked askance at her friend, remembering at the moment
Reginald Morton's assurance that his aunt would have
disapproved of such an engagement. 'But I never would
persuade a girl to marry a man she did not love. I think
it would be wicked. I always thought so.'

There was nothing about degradation in all this. It
was quite clear to Mary that had she been able to tell
Lady Ushant that she was head over ears in love with this
young man and that therefore she was going to marry
him, her old friend would have found no reason to
lament such an arrangement. Her old friend would have
congratulated her. Lady Ushant evidently thought
Larry Twentyman to be good enough as soon as she
heard what Mary found herself compelled to say in the
young man's favour. Mary was almost disappointed; but
reconciled herself to it very quickly, telling herself that

there was yet time for her to decide in favour of her lover if she could bring herself to do so.

And she did try that night and all the next day, thinking that if she could so make up her mind she would declare her purpose to Lady Ushant before she left Cheltenham. But she could not do it, and in the struggle with herself at last she learned something of the truth. Lady Ushant saw nothing but what was right and proper in a marriage with Lawrence Twentyman, but Reginald Morton had declared it to be improper, and therefore it was out of her reach. She could not do it. She could not bring herself, after what he had said, to look him in the face and tell him that she was going to become the wife of Larry Twentyman. Then she asked herself the fatal question, was she in love with Reginald Morton? I do not think that she answered herself in the affirmative, but she became more and more sure that she could never marry Larry Twentyman.

Lady Ushant declared herself to be more than satisfied with the visit, and expressed a hope that it might be repeated in the next year. 'I would ask you to come and make your home here while I have a home to offer you, only that you would be so much more buried here than at Dillsborough. And you have duties there which perhaps you ought not to leave. But come again when your papa will spare you.'

On her journey back she certainly was not very happy. There were yet three weeks wanting to the time at which she would be bound to give her answer to Larry Twentyman; but why should she keep the man waiting for three weeks when her answer was ready? Her stepmother, she knew, would soon force her answer from her, and her father would be anxious to know what had been the result of her meditations. The real period of her reprieve had been that of her absence at Cheltenham, and that period was now coming to an end. At each station as she passed them she remembered what Reginald Morton had been saying to her, and how their conversation had been interrupted,—and perhaps occasionally aided,—by the absurdities of the bird. How sweet it had been to be near him and to listen to his whispered voice! How great was the difference between him and that other young man, the smartness of whose apparel was now becoming peculiarly distasteful to her! Certainly it would have been better for her not to have gone to Cheltenham if it was her fate to become Mrs. Twentyman. She was quite sure of that now.

She came up from the Dillsborough Station alone in the Bush omnibus. She had not expected any one to meet her. Why should any one meet her? The porter put up her box, and the omnibus left her at the door. But she remembered well how she had gone down with Reginald Morton, and how delightful had been every little incident of the journey. Even to walk with him up and down the platform while waiting for the train had been a privilege. She thought of it as she got out of the carriage, and remembered that she had felt that the train had come too soon.

At her own door her father met her and took her into the parlour where the tea-things were spread, and where her sisters were already seated. Her stepmother soon came in and kissed her kindly. She was asked how she had enjoyed herself, and no disagreeable questions were put to her that night. No questions, at least, were asked which she felt herself bound to answer. After she was in bed Kate came to her and did say a word. 'Well, Mary, do tell me. I won't tell any one.' But Mary refused to speak a word.

CHAPTER XXXI

THE RUFFORD CORRESPONDENCE

IT might be surmised from the description which Lord Rufford had given of his own position to his sister and his sister's two friends, when he pictured himself as falling over the edge of the precipice while they hung on behind to save him, that he was sufficiently aware of the inexpediency of the proposed intimacy with Miss Trefoil. Any one hearing him would have said that Miss Trefoil's chances in that direction were very poor,—that a man seeing his danger so plainly, and so clearly understanding the nature of it, would certainly avoid it. But what he had said was no more than Miss Trefoil knew that he would say,—or, at any rate, would think. Of course she had against her not only all his friends;—but the man himself also and his own fixed intentions. Lord Rufford was not a marrying man:—which was supposed to signify that he intended to lead a life of pleasure till the necessity of providing an heir should be forced upon him, when he would take to himself a wife out of his own class in life twenty years younger than himself for whom he would not care a straw. The odds against Miss Trefoil were, of course, great;—but girls have won even against such odds as these. She knew her own powers, and was aware that Lord Rufford was fond of feminine beauty and feminine flutter and feminine flattery, though he was not prepared to marry. It was quite possible that she might be able to dig such a pit for him that it would be easier for him to marry her than to get out in any other way. Of course she must trust something to his own folly at first. Nor did she trust in vain. Before her week was over at Mrs. Gore's she received from him a letter, which, with the correspondence to which it immediately led, shall be given in this chapter.

LETTER No. I.

'Rufford, Sunday.

'MY DEAR MISS TREFOIL,

'We have had a sad house since you left us. Poor Caneback got better and then worse and then better,— and at last died yesterday afternoon. And now;—there is to be the funeral! The poor dear old boy seems to have had nobody belonging to him and very little in the way of possessions. I never knew anything of him except that he was, or had been, in the Blues; and that he was about the best man in England to hounds on a bad horse. It now turns out that his father made some money in India, —a sort of Commissary purveyor,—and bought a commission for him twenty-five years ago. Everybody knew

him, but nobody knew anything about him. Poor old
Caneback! I wish he had managed to die anywhere else,
and I don't feel at all obliged to Purefoy for sending that
brute of a mare here. He said something to me about that
wretched ball,—not altogether so wretched! was it? But
I didn't like what he said, and told him a bit of my mind.
Now we're two for a while; and I don't care for how long
unless he comes round.

'I cannot stand a funeral, and I shall get away from
this. I will pay the bill and Purefoy may do the rest. I'm
going for Christmas to Surbiton's, near Melton, with a
string of horses. Surbiton is a bachelor, and as there will
be no young ladies to interfere with me I shall have the
more time to think of you. We shall have a little play
there instead. I don't know whether it isn't the better of
the two, as if one does get sat upon, one doesn't feel so
confoundedly sheep-faced. I have been out with the
hounds two or three times since you went, as I could do
no good staying with that poor fellow, and there was a
time when we thought he would have pulled through.
I rode Jack one day, but he didn't carry me as well as he
did you. I think he's more of a lady's horse. If I go to
Mistletoe I shall have some horses in the neighbourhood
somewhere and I'll make them take Jack, so that you may
have a chance.

'I never know how to sign myself to young ladies.
Suppose I say that I am yours,

'Anything you like best,
'R.'

This was a much nicer letter than Arabella had expected, as there were one or two touches in it, apart from
the dead man and the horses, which she thought might
lead to something,—and there was a tone in the letter
which seemed to show that he was given to correspondence. She took care to answer it so that he should
get her letter on his arrival at Mr. Surbiton's house. She
found out Mr. Surbiton's address, and then gave a great
deal of time to her letter.

LETTER No. 2.

'Murray's Hotel, Green Street,
'Thursday.

'MY DEAR LORD RUFFORD,

'As we are passing through London on our way from
one purgatory with the Gores to another purgatory with
old Lady De Browne, and as mamma is asleep in her
chair opposite, and as I have nothing else on earth to do,
I think I might as well answer your letter. Poor old
major! I am sorry for him, because he rode so bravely.
I shall never forget his face as he passed us, and again as
he rose upon his knee when that horrid blow came!
How very odd that he should have been like that, without any friends! What a terrible nuisance to you! I think
you were quite wise to come away. I am sure I should
have done so. I can't conceive what right Sir John Purefoy can have had to say anything, for, after all, it was his
doing. Do you remember when you talked of my riding
Jemima? When I think of it I can hardly hold myself for
shuddering.

'It is so kind of you to think of me about Jack. I am
never very fond of Mistletoe. Don't you be mischievous
now and go and tell the Duchess I said so. But with Jack
in the neighbourhood I can stand even her Grace. I
think I shall be there about the middle of January, but it
must depend on all those people mamma is going to.
I shall have to make a great fight, for mamma thinks that
ten days in the year at Mistletoe is all that duty requires.
But I always stick up for my uncle, and mean in this
instance to have a little of my own way. What are
parental commands in opposition to Jack and all his
glories? Besides mamma does not mean to go herself.

'I shall leave it to you to say whether the ball was
"altogether wretched". Of course there must have been
infinite vexation to you, and to us, who knew of it all,
there was a feeling of deep sorrow. But perhaps we were
able, some of us, to make it a little lighter for you. At any
rate, I shall never forget Rufford, whether the memory

be more pleasant or more painful. There are moments which one never can forget!

'Don't go and gamble away your money among a lot of men. Though I dare say you have got so much that it doesn't signify whether you lose some of it or not. I do think it is such a shame that a man like you should have such a quantity, and that a poor girl such as I am shouldn't have enough to pay for her hats and gloves. Why shouldn't I send a string of horses about just when I please? I believe I could make as good a use of them as you do, and then I could lend you Jack. I would be so good-natured. You should have Jack every day you wanted him.

'You must write and tell me what day you will be at Mistletoe. It is you that have tempted me and I don't mean to be there without you,—or, I suppose I ought to say, without the horse. But, of course, you will have understood that. No young lady ever is supposed to desire the presence of any young man. It would be very improper of course. But a young man's Jack is quite another thing.'

So far her pen had flown with her, but then there came the necessity for a conclusion which must be worded in some peculiar way, as his had been so peculiar. How far might she dare to be affectionate without putting him on his guard? Or in what way might she be saucy so as best to please him? She tried two or three, and at last she ended her letter as follows:—

'I have not had much experience in signing myself to young gentlemen and am therefore quite in as great a difficulty as you were; but, though I can't swear that I am everything that you like best, I will protest that I am pretty nearly what you ought to like,—as far as young ladies go.

'In the meantime I certainly am,
'Yours truly,
'A. T.'

'P.S. Mind you write—about Jack; and address to Lady Smijth, Greenacres Manor, Hastings.'

There was a great deal in this letter which was not true. But then such ladies as Miss Trefoil can never afford to tell the truth.

The letter was not written from Murray's Hotel, Lady Augustus having insisted on staying at certain lodgings in Orchard Street, because her funds were low. But on previous occasions they had stayed at Murray's. And her mamma, instead of being asleep when the letter was written, was making up her accounts. And every word about Mistletoe had been false. She had not yet secured her invitation. She was hard at work on the attempt, having induced her father absolutely to beg the favour from his brother. But at the present moment she was altogether diffident of success. Should she fail, she must only tell Lord Rufford that her mother's numerous engagements had at the last moment made her happiness impossible. That she was going to Lady Smijth's was true, and at Lady Smijth's house she received the following note from Lord Rufford. It was then January, and the great Mistletoe question was not as yet settled:—

LETTER No. 3.

'December 31.

'MY DEAR MISS TREFOIL,—

'Here I am still at Surbiton's, and we have had such good sport that I'm half inclined to give the duke the slip. What a pity that you can't come here instead! Wouldn't it be nice for you and half a dozen more, without any of the dowagers or duennas?* You might win some of the money which I lose. I have been very unlucky, and, if you had won it all, there would have been plenty of room for hats and gloves, and for sending two or three Jacks about all the winter into the bargain. I never did win yet. I don't care very much about it, but I don't know why I should always be so uncommonly unlucky.

'We had such a day yesterday,—an hour and ten minutes all in the open, and then a kill just as the poor fellow was trying to make a drain under the high road. There were only five of us up. Surbiton broke his horse's back at a bank, and young De Canute came down on to

a road and smashed his collar bone. Three or four of the
hounds were so done that they couldn't be got home. I was
riding Black Harry, and he won't be out again for a fortnight. It was the best thing I've seen these two years.
We never have it quite like that with the U.R.U.

'If I don't go to Mistletoe, I'll send Jack and a groom
if you think the duke would take them in and let you ride
the horse. If so, I shall stay here pretty nearly all
January, unless there should be a frost. In that case I
should go back to Rufford, as I have a deal of shooting to
do. I shall be so sorry not to see you; but there is always
a sort of sin in not sticking to hunting when it's good. It
so seldom is just what it ought to be.

'I rather think that, after all, we shall be down on that
fellow who poisoned our fox, in spite of your friend the
Senator.

'Yours always faithfully,
'R.'

There was a great deal in this letter which was quite
terrible to Miss Trefoil. In the first place, by the time she
received it, she had managed the matter with her uncle.
Her father had altogether refused to mention Lord
Rufford's name, though he had heard the very plain
proposition which his daughter made to him with perfect
serenity. But he had said to the duke that it would be
a great convenience if Bell could be received at Mistletoe
for a few days, and the duke had got the duchess to assent.
Lady Augustus, too, had been disposed of, and two very
handsome new dresses had been acquired. Her habit had
been altered with reckless disregard of the coming spring,
and she was fully prepared for her campaign. But what
would Mistletoe be to her without Lord Rufford? In
spite of all that had been done she would not go there.
Unless she could turn him by her entreaties she would
pack up everything and start for Patagonia, with the
determination to throw herself overboard on the way
there, if she could find the courage.

She had to think very much of her next letter. Should
she write in anger, or should she write in love, or should

she mingle both? There was no need for care now, as there had been at first. She must reach him at once, or everything would be over. She must say something that would bring him to Mistletoe, whatever that something might be. After much thought she determined that mingled anger and love would be the best. So she mingled them as follow:—

LETTER No. 4.

'Greenacre Manor, Monday.

'Your last letter, which I have just got, has killed me. You must know that I have altered my plans, and done it at immense trouble, for the sake of meeting you at Mistletoe. It will be most unkind—I might say worse—if you put me off. I don't think you can do it as a gentleman. I'm sure you would not if you knew what I have gone through with mamma and the whole set of them to arrange it. Of course I shan't go if you don't come. Your talk of sending the horse there is adding an insult to the injury. You must have meant to annoy me, or you wouldn't have pretended to suppose that it was the horse I wanted to see. I didn't think I could have taken so violent a dislike to poor Jack as I did for a moment. Let me tell you that I think you are bound to go to Mistletoe, though the hunting at Melton should be better than was ever known before. When the hunting is good in one place, of course it is good in another. Even I am sportsman enough to know that. I suppose you have been losing a lot of money, and are foolish enough to think you can win it back again.

'Please, please come. It was to be the little cream of the year for me. It wasn't Jack. There! That ought to bring you. And yet, if you come, I will worship Jack. I have not said a word to mamma about altering my plans, nor shall I while there is hope. But to Mistletoe I will not go, unless you are to be there. Pray answer this by return of post. If we have gone your letter will, of course, follow us. Pray come. Yours, if you do come——; what shall I say? Fill it as you please.

'A. T.'

Lord Rufford, when he received the above very ardent epistle, was quite aware that he had better not go to Mistletoe. He understood the matter nearly as well as Arabella did herself. But there was a feeling with him that, up to that stage of the affair, he ought to do what he was asked by a young lady, even though there might be danger. Though there was danger, there would still be amusement. He therefore wrote again as follows:—

LETTER No. 5.

'DEAR MISS TREFOIL,—

'You shan't be disappointed, whether it be Jack or any less useful animal that you wish to see. At any rate, Jack—and the other animal—will be at Mistletoe on the 15th. I have written to the duke by this post. I can only hope that you will be grateful. After all your abuse about my getting back my money, I think you ought to be very grateful. I have got it back again, but I can assure you that has had nothing to do with it.

'Yours ever,
'R.'

'We had two miserably abortive days last week.'

Arabella felt that a great deal of the compliment was taken away by the postscript; but still she was grateful and contented.

CHAPTER XXXII

'IT IS A LONG WAY'

WHILE the correspondence given in the last chapter was going on, Miss Trefoil had other troubles besides those there narrated, and other letters to answer. Soon after her departure from Rufford she received a very serious but still an affectionate epistle from John Morton in which he asked her if it was her intention to become his wife or not. The letter was very long as well as very serious and need not be given here at length. But that was the gist of it; and he went on to say that in regard to

money he had made the most liberal proposition in his
power, that he must decline to have any further communication with lawyers, and that he must ask her to let
him know at once,—quite at once,—whether she did or
did not regard herself as engaged to him. It was a manly
letter, and ended by a declaration that, as far as he himself was concerned, his feelings were not at all altered.
This she received while staying at the Gores', but, in
accordance with her predetermined strategy, did not at
once send any answer to it. Before she heard again from
Morton she had received that pleasant first letter from
Lord Rufford, and was certainly then in no frame of
mind to assure Mr. Morton that she was ready to declare
herself his affianced wife before all the world. Then, after
ten days, he had written to her again and had written
much more severely. It wanted at that time but a few
days to Christmas, and she was waiting for a second letter
from Lord Rufford. Let what might come of it she could
not now give up the Rufford chance. As she sat thinking
of it, giving the very best of her mind to it, she remembered the warmth of that embrace in the little room
behind the drawing-room, and those halcyon minutes in
which her head had been on his shoulder, and his arm
round her waist. Not that they were made halcyon to her
by any of the joys of love. In giving the girl her due it
must be owned that she rarely allowed herself to indulge
in simple pleasures. If Lord Rufford, with the same rank
and property, had been personally disagreeable to her it
would have been the same. Business to her had for many
years been business, and her business had been so very
hard that she had never allowed lighter things to interfere with it. She had had justice on her side when she
rebuked her mother for accusing her of flirtations. But
could such a man as Lord Rufford,—with his hands so
free,—venture to tell himself that such tokens of affection
with such a girl would mean nothing? If she might contrive to meet him again of course they would be repeated,
and then he should be forced to say that they did mean
something. When therefore the severe letter came from
Morton,—severe and pressing, telling her that she was

bound to answer him at once, and that were she still
silent he must, in regard to his own honour, take that as
an indication of her intention to break off the match,—
she felt that she must answer it. The answer must, however, still be ambiguous. She would not if possible throw
away that stool quite as yet, though her mind was intent
on ascending to the throne which it might be within her
power to reach. She wrote to him an ambiguous letter,—
but a letter which certainly was not intended to liberate
him. 'He ought,' she said, 'to understand that a girl
situated as she was could not ultimately dispose of herself
till her friends had told her that she was free to do so. She
herself did not pretend to have any interest in the affairs
as to which her father and his lawyers were making themselves busy. They had never even condescended to tell
her what it was they wanted on her behalf;—nor, for the
matter of that, had he, Morton, ever told her what it was
that he refused to do. Of course she could not throw herself into his arms till these things were settled.'—By that
expression she had meant a metaphorical throwing of herself, and not such a flesh and blood embracing as she had
permitted to the lord in the little room at Rufford. Then
she suggested that he should appeal again to her father.
It need hardly be said that her father knew very little
about it, and that the lawyers had long since written to
Lady Augustus to say that better terms as to settlement
could not be had from Mr. John Morton.

Morton, when he wrote his second letter, had received
the offer of the mission to Patagonia, and had asked for
a few days to think of it. After much consideration he
determined that he would say nothing to Arabella of the
offer. Her treatment of him gave her no right to be consulted. Should she at once write back declaring her
readiness to become his wife, then he would consult her,
—and would not only consult her but would be prepared
to abandon the mission at the expression of her lightest
wish. Indeed, in that case he thought that he would himself advise that it should be abandoned. Why should he
expatriate himself to such a place with such a wife as
Arabella Trefoil? He received her answer and at once

accepted the offer. He accepted it, though he by no means assured himself that the engagement was irrevocably annulled. But now, if she came to him, she must take her chance. She must be told that he, at any rate, was going to Patagonia, and that unless she could make up her mind to do so too, she must remain Arabella Trefoil for him. He would not even tell her of his appointment. He had done all that in him lay, and would prepare himself for his journey as a single man. A minister going out to Patagonia would, of course, have some little leave of absence allowed him, and he arranged with his friend Mounser Green that he should not start till April.

But when Lord Rufford's second letter reached Miss Trefoil down at Greenacre Manor, where she had learned by common report that Mr. Morton was to be the new minister at Patagonia,—when she believed as she then did that the lord was escaping her, that, seeing and feeling his danger he had determined not to jump into the lion's mouth by meeting her at Mistletoe, that her chance there was all over; then she remembered her age, her many seasons, the hard work of her toilet, those tedious, long, and bitter quarrels with her mother, the ever-renewed trouble of her smiles, the hopelessness of her future should she smile in vain to the last, and the countless miseries of her endless visitings; and she remembered, too, the £1,200 a year that Morton had offered to settle on her and the assurance of a home of her own, though that home should be at Bragton. For an hour or two she had almost given up the hope of Rufford, and had meditated some letter to her other lover which might at any rate secure him. But she had collected her courage sufficiently to make that last appeal to the lord, which had been successful. Three weeks now might settle all that and for three weeks it might still be possible so to manage her affairs that she might fall back upon Patagonia as her last resource.

About this time Morton returned to Bragton, waiting however till he was assured that the Senator had completed his visit to Dillsborough. He had been a little ashamed of the Senator in regard to the great Goarly conflict and was not desirous of relieving his solitude by

the presence of the American. On this occasion he went
quite alone and ordered no carriages from the Bush, and
no increased establishment of servants. He certainly was
not happy in his mind. The mission to Patagonia was
well paid, being worth, with house and etceteras, nearly
£3,000 a year; and it was great and quick promotion for
one so young as himself. For one neither a lord nor connected with a Cabinet Minister, Patagonia was a great
place at which to begin his career as Plenipotentiary on
his own bottom;—but it is a long way off and has its
drawbacks. He could not look to be there for less than
four years; and there was hardly reason why a man in his
position should expatriate himself to such a place for so
long a time. He felt that he should not have gone but for
his engagement to Arabella Trefoil, and that neither
would he have gone had his engagement been solid and
permanent. He was going in order that he might be rid
of that trouble, and a man's feelings in such circumstances
cannot be satisfactory to himself. However he had said
that he would go, and he knew enough of himself to be
certain that having said so he would not alter his mind.
But he was very melancholy and Mrs. Hopkins declared
to old Mrs. Twentyman that the young squire was
'hipped,'*—'along of his lady love,' as she thought.

His hands had been so full of his visitors when at Bragton before, and he had been carried off so suddenly to
Rufford, and then had hurried up to London in such
misery, that he had hardly had time to attend to his own
business. Mr. Masters had made a claim upon him since
he had been in England for £127 8s. 4d. in reference to
certain long-gone affairs in which the attorney declared
he had been badly treated by those who had administered
the Morton estate. John Morton had promised to look
into the matter and to see Mr. Masters. He had partially
looked into it and now felt ashamed that he had not fully
kept his promise. The old attorney had not had much
hope of getting his money. It was doubtful to himself
whether he could make good his claim against the squire
at law, and it was his settled purpose to make no such
attempt although he was quite sure that the money was

his due. Indeed, if Mr. Morton would not do anything
further in the matter, neither would he. He was almost
too mild a man to be a successful lawyer, and had a dislike to asking for money. Mr. Morton had promised to
see him, but Mr. Morton had probably—forgotten it.
Some gentlemen seem apt to forget such promises.

Mr. Masters was somewhat surprised, therefore, when
he was told one morning in his office that Mr. Morton
from Bragton wished to see him. He thought that it must
be Reginald Morton, having not heard that the Squire
had returned to the country. But John Morton was
shown into the office, and the old attorney immediately
arose from his arm-chair. Sundown was there, and was
at once sent out of the room. Sundown on such occasions
was accustomed to retire to some settlement seldom
visited by the public, which was called the back office.
Nickem was away intent on unravelling the Goarly
mystery, and the attorney could ask his visitor to take
a confidential seat. Mr. Morton, however, had very little
to say. He was full of apologies and at once handed out
a cheque for the sum demanded. The money was so
much to the attorney that he was flurried by his own
success. 'Perhaps,' said Morton, 'I ought in fairness to
add interest.'

'Not at all;—by no means. Lawyers never expect that.
Really, Mr. Morton, I am very much obliged. It was so
long ago that I thought that perhaps you might think——'

'I do not doubt that it's all right.'

'Yes, Mr. Morton—it's all right. It's quite right. But
your coming in this way is quite a compliment. I am so
proud to see the owner of Bragton once more in this
house. I respect the family as I always did; and as for the
money——'

'I am only sorry that it has been delayed so long.
Good morning, Mr. Masters.'

The attorney's affairs were in such a condition that an
unexpected cheque for £127 8s. 4d. sufficed to exhilarate
him. It was as though the money had come down to him
from the very skies. As it happened, Mary returned from
Cheltenham on that same evening, and the attorney felt

that if she had brought back with her an intention to be Mrs. Twentyman he could still be a happy and contented man.

And there had been another trouble on John Morton's mind. He had received his cousin's card, but had not returned the visit while his grandmother had been at Bragton. Now he walked on to Hoppet Hall and knocked at the door.—Yes; Mr. Morton was at home, and then he was shown into the presence of his cousin whom he had not seen since he was a boy. 'I ought to have come sooner,' said the squire, who was hardly at his ease.

'I heard you had a house full of people at Bragton.'

'Just that,—and then I went off rather suddenly to the other side of the country; and then I had to go up to London. Now I'm going to Patagonia.'

'Patagonia! That's a long way off.'

'We Foreign Office slaves have to be sent a long way off.'

'But we heard, John,' said Reginald, who did not feel it to be his duty to stand on any ceremony with his younger cousin,—'we heard that you were going to be married to Miss Trefoil. Are you going to take a wife out to Patagonia?'

This was a question which he certainly had not expected. 'I don't know how that may be,' he said, frowning.

'We were told here in Dillsborough that it was all settled. I hope I haven't asked an improper question.'

'Of course people will talk.'

'If it's only talk, I beg pardon. Whatever concerns Bragton is interesting to me, and from the way in which I heard this I thought it was a certainty. Patagonia;— well! You don't want an assistant private secretary, I suppose? I should like to see Patagonia.'

'We are not allowed to appoint those gentlemen ourselves.'

'And I suppose I should be too old to get in at the bottom. It seems a long way off for a man who is the owner of Bragton.'

'It is a long way.'

'And what will you do with the old place?'

'There's no one to live there. If you were married you might perhaps take it.' This was of course said in a joke, as old Mrs. Morton would have thought Bragton to be disgraced for ever, even by such a proposition.

'You might let it.'

'Who would take such a place for five years? I suppose old Mrs. Hopkins will remain, and that it will become more and more desolate every year. I mustn't let the old house tumble down;—that's all.' Then the Minister Plenipotentiary to Patagonia took his departure and walked back to Bragton, thinking of the publicity of his engagement. All Dillsborough had heard that he was to be married to Miss Trefoil, and this cousin of his had been so sure of the fact that he had not hesitated to ask a question about it in the first moment of their first interview. Under such circumstances it would be better for him to go to Patagonia than to remain in England.

CHAPTER XXXIII

THE BEGINNING OF PERSECUTION

WHEN Mary Masters got up on the morning after her arrival, she knew that she would have to endure much on that day. Everybody had smiled on her the preceding evening, but the smiles were of a nature which declared themselves to be preparatory to some coming events. The people around her were gracious on the presumption that she was going to do as they wished, and would be quite prepared to withdraw their smiles should she prove to be contumacious. Mary, as she crept down in the morning, understood all this perfectly. She found her mother alone in the parlour, and was at once attacked with the all-important question. 'My dear, I hope you have made up your mind about Mr. Twentyman.'

'There were to be two months, mamma.'

'That's nonsense, Mary. Of course you must know what you mean to tell him.' Mary thought that she did know, but was not at the present moment disposed to make known her knowledge, and therefore remained silent. 'You should remember how much this is to your papa and me, and should speak out at once. Of course you need not tell Mr. Twentyman till the end of the time unless you like it.'

'I thought I was to be left alone for two months.'

'Mary, that is wicked. When your papa has so many things to think of and so much to provide for, you should be more thoughtful of him. Of course he will want to be prepared to give you what things will be necessary.' Mrs. Masters had not as yet heard of Mr. Morton's cheque, and perhaps would not hear of it till her husband's bank book fell into her hands. The attorney had lately found it necessary to keep such matters to himself when it was possible, as otherwise he was asked for explanations which it was not always easy for him to give. 'You know,' continued Mrs. Masters, 'how hard your father finds it to get money as it is wanted.'

'I don't want anything, mamma.'

'You must want things if you are to be married in March or April.'

'But I shan't be married in March or April. Oh, mamma, pray don't.'

'In a week's time or so you must tell Larry. After all that has passed, of course he won't expect to have to wait long; and you can't ask him. Kate, my dear,'—Kate had just entered the room,—'go into the office and tell your father to come in to breakfast in five minutes. You must know, Mary, and I insist on your telling me.'

'When I said two months,—only it was he said two months——'

'What difference does it make, my dear?'

'It was only because he asked me to put it off. I knew it could make no difference.'

'Do you mean to tell me, Mary, that you are going to refuse him after all?'

'I can't help it,' said Mary, bursting out into tears.

'Can't help it! Did anybody ever see such an idiot since girls were first created? Not help it, after having given him as good as a promise! You must help it. You must be made to help it.'

There was an injustice in this which nearly killed poor Mary. She had been persuaded among them to put off her final decision, not because she had any doubt in her own mind, but at their request, and now she was told in granting this delay she had 'given as good as a promise!' And her stepmother also had declared that she 'must be made to help it,'—or in other words, be made to marry Mr. Twentyman in opposition to her own wishes! She was quite sure that no human being could have such right of compulsion over her. Her father would not attempt it, and it was, after all, to her father alone that she was bound by duty. At the moment she could make no reply, and then her father with the two girls came in from the office.

The attorney was still a little radiant with his triumph about the cheque, and was also pleased with his own discernment in the matter of Goarly. He had learned that morning from Nickem that Goarly had consented to take 7s. 6d. an acre from Lord Rufford, and was prepared to act 'quite the honourable part' on behalf of his lordship. Nickem had seemed to think that the triumph would not end here, but had declined to make any very definite statements. Nickem clearly fancied that he had been doing great things himself, and that he might be allowed to have a little mystery. But the attorney took great credit to himself in that he had rejected Goarly's case, and had been employed by Lord Rufford in lieu of Goarly. When he entered the parlour he had for the moment forgotten Larry Twentyman and his love, and was disposed to greet his girl lovingly;—but he found her dissolved in bitter tears. 'Mary, my darling, what is it ails you?' he said.

'Never mind about your darling now, but come to breakfast. She is giving herself airs,—as usual.'

But Mary never did give herself airs, and her father could not endure the accusation. 'She would not be crying,' he said, 'unless she had something to cry for.'

'Pray don't make a fuss about things you don't understand,' said his wife. 'Mary, are you coming to the table? If not you had better go upstairs. I hate such ways, and I won't have them. This comes of Ushanting! I knew

what it would be. The place for girls is to stay at home
and mind their work,—till they have got houses of their
own to look after. That's what I intend my girls to do.
There's nothing on earth so bad for girls as that twiddle-
your-thumbs visiting about when they think they've
nothing to do but to show what sort of ribbons and gloves
they've got. Now, Dolly, if you've got any hands will you
cut the bread for your father? Mary's a deal too fine
a lady to do anything but sit there and rub her eyes.'
After that the breakfast was eaten in silence.

When the meal was over, Mary followed her father
into the office, and said that she wanted to speak to him.
When Sundown had disappeared, she told her tale.
'Papa,' she said, 'I am so sorry, but I can't do what you
want about Mr. Twentyman.'

'Is it so, Mary?'

'Don't be angry with me, papa.'

'Angry! No;—I won't be angry. I should be very
sorry to be angry with my girl. But what you tell me will
make us all very unhappy;—very unhappy indeed. What
will you say to Lawrence Twentyman?'

'What I said before, papa.'

'But he is quite certain now that you mean to take him.
Of course we were all certain when you only wanted
a few more days to think of it.' Mary felt this to be the
cruellest thing of all. 'When he asked me I said I
wouldn't pledge you, but I certainly had no doubt.
What is the matter, Mary?'

She could understand that a girl might be asked why
she wanted to marry a man, and that in such a condition
she ought to be able to give a reason; but it was, she
thought, very hard that she should be asked why she
didn't want to marry a man. 'I suppose, papa,' she said
after a pause, 'I don't like him in that way.'

'Your mamma will be sure to say that it is because you
went to Lady Ushant's.'

And so in part it was,—as Mary herself very well knew;
though Lady Ushant herself had had nothing to do with
it. 'Lady Ushant,' she said, 'would be very pleased,—if
she thought that I liked him well enough.'

'Did you tell Lady Ushant?'

'Yes; I told her all about it,—and how you would all be pleased. And I did try to bring myself to it. Papa,— pray, pray don't want to send me away from you.'

'You would be so near to us all at Chowton Farm!'

'I am nearer here, papa.' Then she embraced him, and he in a manner yielded to her. He yielded to her so far as to part with her at the present moment with soft loving words.

Mrs. Masters had a long conversation with her husband on the subject that same day, and condescended even to say a few words to the two girls. She had her own theory and her own plan in the present emergency. According to her theory girls shouldn't be indulged in any vagaries, and this rejecting of a highly valuable suitor was a most inexcusable vagary. And, if her plan were followed, a considerable amount of wholesome coercion would at once be exercised towards this refractory young woman. There was, in fact, more than a fortnight wanting to the expiration of Larry's two months, and Mrs. Masters was strongly of opinion that if Mary were put into a sort of domestic 'Coventry'*during this period, if she were debarred from friendly intercourse with the family and made to feel that such wickedness as hers, if continued, would make her an outcast, then she would come round and accept Larry Twentyman before the end of the time. But this plan could not be carried out without her husband's co-operation. Were she to attempt it single-handed, Mary would take refuge in her father's softness of heart, and there would simply be two parties in the household. 'If you would leave her to me and not speak to her, it would be all right,' Mrs. Masters said to her husband.

'Not speak to her!'

'Not cosset her and spoil her for the next week or two. Just leave her to herself and let her feel what she's doing. Think what Chowton Farm would be, and you with your business all slipping through your fingers.'

'I don't know that it's slipping through my fingers at all,' said the attorney mindful of his recent successes.

'If you mean to say you don't care about it—!'

'I do care about it very much. You know I do. You ought not to talk to me in that way.'

'Then why won't you be said by me? Of course if you cocker her up, she'll think she's to have her own way like a grand lady. She don't like him because he works for his bread,—that's what it is; and because she's been taught by that old woman to read poetry. I never knew that stuff do any good to anybody. I hate them fandangled lines that are all cut up short to make pretence. If she wants to read why can't she take the cookery book and learn something useful? It just comes to this;—if you want her to marry Larry Twentyman you had better not notice her for the next fortnight. Let her go and come and say nothing to her. She'll think about it, if she's left to herself.'

The attorney did want his daughter to marry the man and was half convinced by his wife. He could not bring himself to be cruel and felt that his heart would bleed every hour of the day that he separated himself from his girl;—but still he thought that he might perhaps best in this way bring about a result which would be so manifestly for her advantage. It might be that the books of poetry and the modes of thought which his wife described as 'Ushanting' were of a nature to pervert his girl's mind from the material necessities of life, and that a little hardship would bring her round to a more rational condition. With a very heavy heart he consented to do his part,—which was to consist mainly of silence. Any words which might be considered expedient were to come from his wife.

Three or four days went on in this way, which were days of absolute misery to Mary. She soon perceived and partly understood her father's silence. She knew at any rate that for the present she was debarred from his confidence. Her mother did not say much, but what she did say was all founded on the theory that Ushanting and softness in general are very bad for young women. Even Dolly and Kate were hard to her,—each having some dim idea that Mary was to be coerced towards Larry

Twentyman and her own good. At the end of that time, when Mary had been at home nearly a week, Larry came as usual on the Saturday evening. She, well knowing his habit, took care to be out of the way. Larry, with a pleasant face, asked after her, and expressed a hope that she had enjoyed herself at Cheltenham.

'A nasty idle place where nobody does anything, as I believe,' said Mrs. Masters. Larry received a shock from the tone of the lady's voice. He had allowed himself to think that all his troubles were now nearly over, but the words and the voice frightened him. He had told himself that he was not to speak of his love again till the two months were over, and, like an honourable man, was prepared to wait the full time. He would not now have come to the attorney's house but that he knew the attorney would wait for him before going over to the club. He had no right to draw deductions till the time should be up. But he could not help his own feelings and was aware that his heart sank within him when he was told that Cheltenham was a nasty idle place. Abuse of Cheltenham at the present moment was, in fact, abuse of Mary;—and the one sin which Mary could commit was persistence in her rejection of his suit. But he determined to be a man as he walked across the street with his old friend, and said not a word about his love. 'They tell me that Goarly has taken his 7s. 6d., Mr. Masters.'

'Of course he has taken it, Larry. The worse luck for me. If he had gone on I might have had a bill against his lordship as long as my arm. Now it won't be worth looking after.'

'I'm sure you're very glad, Mr. Masters.'

'Well, yes; I am glad. I do hate to see a fellow like that who hasn't got a farthing of his own, propped up from behind just to annoy his betters.'

'They say that Bearside got a lot of money out of that American.'

'I suppose he got something.'

'What an idiot that man must be! Can you understand it, Mr. Masters?'

They now entered the club, and Goarly and Nickem

and Scrobby were of course being discussed. 'Is it true, Mr. Masters, that Scrobby is to be arrested?' asked Fred Botsey at once.

'Upon my word I can't say, Mr. Botsey; but if you tell me it is so I shan't cry my eyes out.'

'I thought you would have known.'

'A gentleman may know a thing, Mr. Botsey,' said the landlord, 'and not exactly choose to tell it.'

'I didn't suppose there was any secret,' said the brewer. As Mr. Masters made no further remark it was, of course, conceived that he knew all about it, and he was therefore treated with some increased deference. But there was on that night great triumph in the club as it was known as a fact that Goarly had withdrawn his claim, and that the American Senator had paid his money for nothing. It was moreover very generally believed that Goarly was going to turn evidence against Scrobby in reference to the poison.

CHAPTER XXXIV

MARY'S LETTER

THE silent system in regard to Mary was carried on in the attorney's house for a week, during which her sufferings were very great. From the first she made up her mind to oppose her stepmother's cruelty by sheer obstinacy. She had been told that she must be made to marry Mr. Twentyman, and the injustice of that threat had at once made her rebel against her stepmother's authority. She would never allow her stepmother to make her marry any one. She put herself into a state of general defiance, and said as little as was said to her. But her father's silence to her nearly broke her heart. On one or two occasions, as opportunity offered itself to her, she said little soft words to him in privacy. Then he would partly relent, would kiss her and bid her be a good girl, and would quickly hurry away from her. She could understand that he suffered as well as herself, and she perhaps got some consolation from the conviction. At last, on the following Saturday, she watched her opportunity and brought to him when he was alone in his office a letter which she had written to Larry Twentyman. 'Papa,' she said, 'would you read that?' He took and read the letter, which was as follows:—

'MY DEAR MR. TWENTYMAN,
    'Something was said about two months, which are now nearly over. I think I ought to save you from the trouble of coming to me again by telling you in a letter that it cannot be as you would have it. I have thought of it a great deal, and have, of course, been anxious to do as my friends wish. And I am very grateful to you, and know how good and how kind you are. And I would do anything for you,—except this. But it never can be. I should not write like this unless I were quite certain. I hope you won't be angry with me and think I should have spared you the trouble of doubting so long. I know now that I ought not to have doubted at all; but I was so anxious not to seem to be obstinate, that I became foolish about it when you asked me. What I say now is quite certain.
    'Dear Mr. Twentyman,—I shall always think of you with esteem and regard, because I know how good you are; and I hope you will come to like somebody a great deal better than me, who will always love you with her whole heart.
                              'Yours very truly,
                                   'MARY MASTERS.
    'P.S.—I shall show this letter to papa.'

Mr. Masters read the letter as she stood by him, and then read it again very slowly, rubbing one hand over the other as he did so. He was thinking what he should do— or rather what he should say. The idea of stopping the letter never occurred to him. If she chose to refuse the man, of course she must do so; and perhaps, if she did refuse him, there was no way better than this. 'Must it be so, Mary?' he said at last.
    'Yes, papa.'

'But why?'

'Because I do not love him as I should have to love any man that I wanted to marry. I have tried it, because you wished it, but I cannot do it.'

'What will mamma say?'

'I am thinking more, papa, of you,' she said, putting her arm over his shoulder. 'You have always been so good to me, and so kind.' Here his heart misgave him, for he felt that, during the last week, he had not been kind to her. 'But you would not wish me to give myself to a man and then not care for him?'

'No, my dear.'

'I couldn't do it. I should fall down dead first. I have thought so much about it,—for your sake; and have tried it with myself. I couldn't do it.'

'Is there anybody else, Mary?' As he asked the question he held her hand beneath his own on the desk, but he did not dare to look into her face. He had been told by his wife that there was somebody else; that the girl's mind was running upon Mr. Surtees, because Mr. Surtees was a gentleman. He was thinking of Mr. Surtees, and certainly not of Reginald Morton.

To her the moment was very solemn, and when the question was asked, she felt that she could not tell her father a falsehood. She had gradually grown bold enough to assure herself that her heart was occupied with that man who had travelled with her to Cheltenham; and she felt that that feeling alone must keep her apart from any other love. And yet, as she had no hope, as she had assured herself that her love was a burden to be borne and could never become a source of enjoyment, why should her secret be wrested from her? What good would such a violation do? But she could not tell the falsehood, and therefore she held her tongue.

Gradually he looked up into her face, still keeping her hand pressed on the desk under his. It was his left hand that so guarded her, while she stood by his right shoulder. Then he gently wound his right arm round her waist, and pressed her to him. 'Mary,' he said, 'if it is so, had you not better tell me?' But she was sure that she had better not mention that name, even to him. It was impossible that she should mention it. She would have outraged to herself her own maiden modesty by doing so. 'Is it,' he asked very softly, 'is it—Mr. Surtees?'

'Oh 'no!' she said quickly, almost escaping from the grasp of his arm in her start.

Then he was absolutely at a loss. Beyond Mr. Surtees or Larry Twentyman he did not know what possible lover Dillsborough could have afforded. And yet the very rapidity of her answer when the curate's name had been mentioned had convinced him that there was some other person,—had increased the strength of that conviction which her silence had produced. 'Have you nothing that you can tell me, Mary?'

'No, papa.' Then he gave her back the letter and she left the room without another word. Of course his sanction to the letter had now been given, and it was addressed to Chowton Farm and posted before half an hour was over. She saw him again in the afternoon of the same day, and asked him to tell her stepmother what she had done. 'Mamma ought to know,' she said.

'But you haven't sent it.'

'Yes, papa;—it is in the post.'

Then it occurred to him that his wife would tell him that he should have prevented the sending of the letter, —that he should have destroyed it and altogether taken the matter with a high hand. 'You can't tell her yourself?' he asked.

'I would rather you did. Mamma has been so hard to me since I came home.'

He did tell his wife, and she overwhelmed him by the violence of her reproaches. He could never have been in earnest, or he would not have allowed such a letter as that to pass through his hands. He must be afraid of his own child. He did not know his own duty. He had been deceiving her,—his wife,—from first to last. Then she threw herself into a torrent of tears, declaring that she had been betrayed. There had been a conspiracy between them, and now everything might go to the dogs, and she would not lift up her hands to save them. But before the evening came round she was again on the alert, and again resolved that she would not even yet give way. What was there in a letter more than in a spoken word? She would tell Larry to disregard the letter. But first she made a futile attempt to clutch the letter from the guardianship of the Post Office, and she went to the Postmaster assuring him that there had been a mistake in the family, that a wrong letter had been put into a wrong envelope, and begging that the letter addressed to Mr. Twentyman might be given back to her. The Postmaster, half vacillatory in his desire to oblige a neighbour, produced a letter and Mrs. Masters put out her hand to grasp it; but the servant of the public,—who had been thoroughly grounded in his duties by one of those trusty guardians of our correspondence who inspect and survey our provincial post offices,—remembered himself at the last moment, and expressing the violence of his regret, replaced the letter in the box. Mrs. Masters, in her anger and grief, condescended to say very hard things to her neighbour;—but the man remembered his duty and was firm.

On that evening Larry Twentyman did not attend the Dillsborough Club,—having in the course of the week notified to the attorney that he should be a defaulter. Mr. Masters himself went over earlier than usual, his own house having become very uncomfortable to him. Mrs. Masters for an hour sat expecting that Larry would come, and when the evening passed away without his appearance, she was convinced that the unusual absence was a part of the conspiracy against her.

Larry did not get his letter till the Monday morning. On the last Thursday and Saturday he had consoled himself for his doubts with the U.R.U., and was minded to do so on the Monday also. He had not gone to the club on Saturday and had moped about Chowton all the Sunday in a feverish state because of his doubts. It seemed to him that the two months would never be over. On the Monday he was out early on the farm, and then came down in his boots and breeches, and had his red coat ready at the fire while he sat at breakfast. The meet was fifteen miles off, and he had sent on his hunter intending to travel thither in his dog cart. Just as he was cutting himself a slice of beef the postman came, and of course he read his letter. He read it with the carving knife in his hand, and then he stood gazing at his mother. 'What is it, Larry?' she asked; 'is anything wrong?'

'Wrong,—well; I don't know,' he said. 'I don't know what you call wrong. I shan't hunt; that's all.' Then he threw aside the knife and pushed away his plate and marched out of the room with the open letter in his hands.

Mrs. Twentyman knew very well of his love,—as indeed did nearly all Dillsborough; but she had heard nothing of the two months, and did not connect the letter with Mary Masters. Surely he must have lost a large sum of money. That was her idea till she saw him again late in the afternoon.

He never went near the hounds that day or near his business. He was not then man enough for either. But he walked about the fields, keeping out of sight of everybody. It was all over now. It must be all over when she wrote to him a letter like that. Why had she tempted him to thoughts of happiness and success by that promise of two months' grace? He supposed that he was not good enough;—or that she thought he was not good enough. Then he remembered his acres, and his material comforts, and tried to console himself by reflecting that Mary Masters might very well do worse in the world. But there was no consolation in it. He had tried his best because he had really loved the girl. He had failed, and all the world,—all his world,—would know that he had failed. There was not a man in the club,—hardly a man in the hunt,—who was not aware that he had offered to Mary Masters. During the last two months he had not been so reticent as was prudent, and had almost boasted to Fred Botsey of success. And then how was he to live at Chowton Farm without Mary Masters as his wife? As he returned home he almost made up his mind that he would not continue to live at Chowton Farm.

He came back through Dillsborough Wood; and there, prowling about, he met Goarly. 'Well, Mr. Twentyman,' said the man, 'I am making it all straight now with his lordship.'

'I don't care what you're doing,' said Larry, in his misery. 'You are an infernal blackguard, and that's the best of you.'

CHAPTER XXXV

CHOWTON FARM FOR SALE

JOHN MORTON had returned to town soon after his walk into Dillsborough and had there learned from different sources that both Arabella Trefoil and Lord Rufford had gone or were going to Mistletoe. He had seen Lord Augustus who, though he could tell him nothing else about his daughter, had not been slow to inform him that she was going to the house of her noble uncle. When Morton had spoken to him very seriously about the engagement he declared that he knew nothing about it, except that he had given his consent if the settlements were all right. Lady Augustus managed all that. Morton had then said that under those circumstances he feared he must regard the honour which he had hoped to enjoy as being beyond his reach. Lord Augustus had shrugged his shoulders and had gone back to his whist, this interview having taken place in the strangers' room of his club. That Lord Rufford was also going to Mistletoe he heard from young Glossop at the Foreign Office. It was quite possible that Glossop had been instructed to make this known to Morton by his sister Lady Penwether. Then Morton declared that the thing was over and that he would trouble himself no more about it. But this resolution did not make him at all contented, and in his misery he went again down to his solitude at Bragton.

And now when he might fairly consider himself to be free, and when he should surely have congratulated himself on a most lucky escape from the great danger into which he had fallen, his love and admiration for the girl returned to him in a most wonderful manner. He thought of her beauty and her grace, and the manner in which she would sit at the head of his table when the time should come for him to be promoted to some great capital. To him she had fascinations which the reader, who perhaps knows her better than he ever did, will not share. He could forgive the coldness of her conduct to himself—he himself not being by nature demonstrative or impassioned, —if only she were not more kind to any rival. It was the fact that she should be visiting at the same house with Lord Rufford after what he had seen at Rufford Hall which had angered him. But now in his solitude he thought that he might have been wrong at Rufford Hall. If it were the case that the girl feared that her marriage might be prevented by the operations of lawyers and family friends, of course she would be right not to throw herself into his arms,—even metaphorically. He was a cold, just man, who, when he had loved, could not easily get 'rid of his love, and now he would ask himself whether he was not hard upon the girl. It was natural that she should be at Mistletoe; but, then, why should Lord Rufford be there with her?

His prospects at Patagonia did not console him much. No doubt it was a handsome mission for a man of his age, and there were sundry Patagonian questions of importance at the present moment which would give him a certain weight. Patagonia was repudiating a loan, and it was hoped that he might induce a better feeling in the Patagonian Parliament. There was the Patagonian railway, for joining the Straits to the Cape, the details of which he was now studying with great diligence. And then there was the vital question of boundary between Patagonia and the Argentine Republic, by settling which, should he be happy enough to succeed in doing so, he would prevent the horrors of warfare. He endeavoured to fix his mind with satisfaction on these great objects as he pored over the reports and papers which had been heaped upon him since he had accepted the mission. But there was present to him always a feeling that the men at the Foreign Office had been glad to get any respectable diplomate to go to Patagonia, and that his brethren in the profession had marvelled at his acceptance of such a mission. One never likes to be thanked over much for doing anything. It creates a feeling that one has given more than was expedient. He knew that he must now go to Patagonia, but he repented the alacrity with which he had acceded to the proposition. Whether he did marry Arabella Trefoil or whether he did not, there was no adequate reason for such a banishment. And yet he could not now escape it!

It was on a Monday morning that Larry Twentyman had found himself unable to go hunting. On the Tuesday he gave his workmen about the farm such a routing as they had not received for many a month. There had not been a dungheap or a cowshed which he had not visited, nor a fence about the place with which he had not found fault. He was at it all day, trying thus to console himself, but in vain; and when his mother in the evening said some word of her misery in regard to the turkeys he had told her that as far as he was concerned Goarly might poison every fox in the county. Then the poor woman knew that matters were going badly with her son. On the Wednesday, when the hounds met within two miles of Chowton, he again stayed at home; but in the afternoon he rode into Dillsborough and contrived to see the attorney without being seen by any of the ladies of the family. The interview did not seem to do him any good. On the Thursday morning he walked across to Bragton, and with a firm voice asked to see the squire. Morton who was deep in the boundary question put aside his papers, and welcomed his neighbour.

Now it must be explained that when, in former years, his son's debts had accumulated on old Mr. Reginald Morton, so that he had been obliged to part with some portion of his unentailed property, he had sold that which lay in the parish of St. John's, Dillsborough. The lands in Bragton and Mallingham he could not sell;—but Chowton Farm, which was in St. John's, had been bought by Larry Twentyman's grandfather. For a time there had been some bitterness of feeling; but the Twentymans had been well-to-do respectable people, most anxious to be good neighbours, and had gradually made themselves liked by the owner of Bragton. The present squire had of course known nothing of Chowton as a part of the Morton property, and had no more desire for it than for any of Lord Rufford's acres, which were contiguous to his own. He shook hands cordially with his neighbour, as though this visit were the most natural thing in the world, and asked some questions about Goarly and the hunt.

'I believe that'll all come square, Mr. Morton. I'm not interesting myself much about it now.' Larry was not dressed like himself. He had on a dark brown coat, and dark pantaloons and a chimney-pot hat. He was conspicuous generally for light-coloured close-fitting garments and for a billicock hat. He was very unlike his usual self on the present occasion.

'I thought you were just the man who did interest himself about those things.'

'Well; yes; once it was so, Mr. Morton. What I've got to say now, Mr. Morton, is this. Chowton Farm is in the market! But I wouldn't say a word to any one about it till you had had the offer.'

'You going to sell Chowton?'

'Yes, Mr. Morton, I am.'

'From all I have heard of you I wouldn't have believed it if anybody else had told me.'

'It's a fact, Mr. Morton. There are three hundred and twenty acres. I put the rental at 30s. an acre. You know what you get, Mr. Morton, for the land that lies next to it. And I think twenty-eight years' purchase isn't more than it's worth. Those are my ideas as to price, Mr. Morton. There isn't a halfpenny owing on it—not in the way of mortgage.'

'I dare say it's worth that.'

'Up at auction I might get a turn more, Mr. Morton;— but those are my ideas at present.'

John Morton, who was a man of business, went to work at once with his pencil and in two minutes had made out a total. 'I don't know that I could put my hand on £14,000 even if I were minded to make the purchase.'

'That needn't stand in the way, sir. Any part you please could lie on mortgage at 4½ per cent.' Larry in the midst of his distress had certain clear ideas about business.

'This is a very serious proposition, Mr. Twentyman.'

'Yes, indeed, sir.'

'Have you any other views in life?'

'I can't say as I have any fixed. I shan't be idle, Mr. Morton. I never was idle. I was thinking perhaps of New Zealand.'

'A very fine colony for a young man, no doubt. But, seeing how well you are established here——.'

'I can't stay here, Mr. Morton. I've made up my mind about that. There are things which a man can't bear,— not and live quiet. As for hunting I don't care about it any more than—nothing.'

'I am sorry that anything should have made you so unhappy.'

'Well;—I am unhappy. That's about the truth of it. And I always shall be unhappy here. There's nothing else for it but going away.'

'If it's anything sudden, Mr. Twentyman, allow me to say that you ought not to sell your property without grave consideration.'

'I have considered it,—very grave, Mr. Morton.'

'Ah,—but I mean long consideration. Take a year to think of it. You can't buy such a place back in a year. I don't know you well enough to be justified in inquiring into the circumstances of your trouble;—but unless it be something which makes it altogether inexpedient, or almost impossible that you should remain in the neighbourhood, you should not sell Chowton.'

'I'll tell you, Mr. Morton,' said Larry, almost weeping. Poor Larry whether in his triumph or his sorrow had no gift of reticence and now told his neighbour the whole story of his love. He was certain it had become quite hopeless. He was sure that she would never have written him a letter if there had been the smallest chance left. According to his ideas a girl might say 'No' half-a-dozen times and yet not mean much; but when she had committed herself to a letter she could not go back from it.

'Is there anybody else?' asked Morton.

'Not as I know. I never saw anything like—like lightness with her, with any man. They said something about the curate, but I don't believe a word of it.'

'And the family approve of it?'

'Every one of them,—father and stepmother and sisters and all. My own mother too! There ain't a ha'porth against it. I don't want any one to give me sixpence in money. And she should live just like a lady. I can keep a servant for her to cook and do every mortal thing. But it ain't nothing of all that, Mr. Morton.'

'What is it, then?'

The poor man paused before he made his answer; but when he did, he made it plain enough. 'I ain't good enough for her! No more I ain't, Mr. Morton. She was brought up in this house, Mr. Morton, by your own grand-aunt.'

'So I have heard, Mr. Twentyman.'

'And there's more of Bragton than there is of Dillsborough about her;—that's just where it is. I know what I am, and I know what she is, and I ain't good enough for her. It should be somebody that can talk books to her. I can tell her how to plant a field of wheat, or how to run a foal;—but I can't sit and read poetry, nor yet be read to. There's plenty of 'em would sell themselves because the land's all there, and the house, and the things in it. What makes me mad is that I should love her all the better because she won't. My belief is, Mr. Morton, they're as poor as Job.* That makes no difference to me, because I don't want it;—but it makes no difference to her neither! She's right, Mr. Morton. I'm not good enough, and so I'll just cut it as far as Dillsborough is concerned. You'll think of what I said of taking the land?'

Mr. Morton said much more to him, walking with him to the gate of Chowton Farm. He assured him that the young lady might yet be won. He had only, Morton said, to plead his cause to her as well as he had done up at Bragton and he thought that she would be won. 'I couldn't speak out free to her,—not if it was to save the whole place,' said the unfortunate lover. But Morton still continued his advice. As to leaving Chowton because a young lady refused him, that would be unmanly. 'There isn't a bit of a man left about me,' said Larry, weeping. Morton, nevertheless, went on. Time would cure these wounds; but no time would give him back Chowton should he once part with it. If he must leave the place for a time let him put a care-taker on the farm, even though by doing so the loss might be great. He should do any-thing rather than surrender his house. As to buying the land himself Morton would not talk about it in the pre-sent circumstances. Then they parted at Chowton gate with many expressions of friendship on each side.

John Morton, as he returned home, could not help thinking that the young farmer's condition was after all better than his own. There was an honesty about both the persons concerned of which at any rate they might be proud. There was real love,—and though that love was not at present happy it was of a nature to inspire perfect respect. But in his own case he was sure of nothing.

CHAPTER XXXVI

MISTLETOE

WHEN Arabella Trefoil started from London for Mistletoe, with no companion but her own maid, she had given more serious consideration to her visit than she had probably ever paid to any matter up to that time. She had often been much in earnest, but never so much in earnest as now. Those other men had perhaps been worthy,—worthy as far as her ideas went of worth,—but none of them so worthy as this man. Everything was there, if she could only get it—money, rank, fashion, and an appetite for pleasure. And he was handsome, too, and good-humoured, though these qualities told less with her than the others. And now she was to meet him in the house of her great relations—in a position in which her rank and her fashion would seem to be equal to his own. And she would meet him with the remembrance fresh in his mind, as in her own, of those passages of love at Rufford. It would be impossible that he should even

seem to forget them. The most that she could expect
would be four or five days of his company, and she knew
that she must be upon her mettle. She must do more now
than she had ever attempted before. She must scruple at
nothing that might bind him. She would be in the house
of her uncle, and that uncle a duke, and she thought that
those facts might help to quell him. And she would be
there without her mother, who was so often a heavy
incubus on her shoulders. She thought of it all, and made
her plans carefully and even painfully. She would be, at
any rate, two days in the house before his arrival. During
that time she would curry favour with her uncle by all
her arts, and would, if possible, reconcile herself to her
aunt. She thought once of taking her aunt into her full
confidence, and balanced the matter much in her mind.
The duchess, she knew, was afraid of her, or rather afraid
of the relationship, and would, of course, be pleased to
have all fears set at rest by such an alliance. But her aunt
was a woman who had never suffered hardships, whose
own marriage had been easily arranged, and whose two
daughters had been pleasantly married before they were
twenty years old. She had had no experience of feminine
difficulties, and would have no mercy for such labours as
those to which her less fortunate niece was driven. It
would have been a great thing to have the cordial co-
operation of her aunt, but she could not venture to ask
for it.

She had stretched her means and her credit to the
utmost in regard to her wardrobe, and was aware that she
had never been so well equipped since those early days of
her career in which her father and mother had thought
that her beauty, assisted by a generous expenditure, would
serve to dispose of her without delay. A generous expenditure may be incurred once even by poor people, but cannot possibly be maintained over a dozen years. Now she
had taken the matter into her own hands, and had done
that which would be ruinous if not successful. She was
venturing her all upon the die—with the prospect of
drowning herself on the way out to Patagonia should the
chances of the game go against her. She forgot nothing.

She could hardly hope for more than one day's hunting, and yet that had been provided for as though she were going to ride with the hounds through all the remainder of the season.

When she reached Mistletoe, there were people going and coming every day, so that an arrival was no event. She was kissed by her uncle, and welcomed with characteristic coldness by her aunt, then allowed to settle in among the other guests as though she had been there all the winter. Everybody knew that she was a Trefoil, and her presence, therefore, raised no questions. The Duchess of Omnium was among the guests. The duchess knew all about her, and vouchsafed to her the smallest possible recognition. Lady Chiltern had met her before, and, as Lady Chiltern was always generous, she was gracious to Arabella. She was sorry to see Lady Drummond, because she connected Lady Drummond with the Foreign Office, and feared that the conversation might be led to Patagonia and its new minister. She contrived to squeeze her uncle's hand, and to utter a word of warm thanks, which his grace did not perfectly understand. The girl was his niece, and the duke had an idea that he should be kind to the family of which he was the head. His brother's wife had become objectionable to him, but as to the girl, if she wanted a home for a week or two, he thought it to be his duty to give it to her.

Mistletoe is an enormous house with a frontage nearly a quarter of a mile long, combining as it does all the offices, coach-houses, and stables. There is nothing in England more ugly or perhaps more comfortable. It stands in a huge park which, as it is quite flat, never shows its size, and is altogether unattractive. The duke himself was a hospitable easy man, who was very fond of his dinner and performed his duties well; but could never be touched by any sentiment. He always spent six months in the country, in which he acted as landlord to a great crowd of shooting, hunting, and flirting visitors, and six in London, in which he gave dinners and dined out, and regularly took his place in the House of Lords without ever opening his mouth. He was a grey-haired comely man of sixty, with a large body and a wonderful appetite. By many who understood the subject he was supposed to to be the best amateur judge of wine in England. His son, Lord Mistletoe, was member for the county, and as the duke had no younger sons he was supposed to be happy at all points. Lord Mistletoe, who had a large family of his own, lived twenty miles off,—so that the father and son could meet pleasantly without fear of quarrelling.

During the first evening Arabella did contrive to make herself very agreeable. She was much quieter than had been her wont when at Mistletoe before, and though there were present two or three very well circumstanced young men she took but little notice of them. She went out to dinner with Sir Jeffrey Bunker, and made herself agreeable to that old gentleman in a remarkable manner. After dinner, something having been said of the respectable old game called cat's cradle, she played it to perfection with Sir Jeffrey,—till her aunt thought that she must have been unaware that Sir Jeffrey had a wife and family. She was all smiles and all pleasantness, and seemed to want no other happiness than what the present moment gave her. Nor did she once mention Lord Rufford's name.

On the next morning after breakfast her aunt sent for her to come upstairs. Such a thing had never happened to her before. She could not recollect that, on any of those annual visits which she had made to Mistletoe for more years than she now liked to think of, she had ever had five minute's conversation alone with her aunt. It had always seemed that she was to be allowed to come and go by reason of her relationship, but that she was to receive no special mark of confidence or affection. The message was whispered into her ear by her aunt's own woman as she was listening with great attention to Lady Drummond's troubles in regard to her nursery arrangements. She nodded her head, heard a few more words from Lady Drummond, and then, with a pretty apology and a statement made so that all should hear her, that her aunt wanted her, followed the maid upstairs. 'My dear,' said her aunt, when the door was closed, 'I want to ask

you whether you would like me to ask Mr. Morton to
come here while you are with us?' A thunderbolt at her
feet could hardly have surprised or annoyed her more.
If there was one thing that she wanted less than another
it was the presence of the Paragon at Mistletoe. It would
utterly subvert everything and rob her of every chance.
With a great effort she restrained all emotion, and simply
shook her head. She did it very well, and betrayed
nothing. 'I ask,' said the duchess, 'because I have been
very glad to hear that you are engaged to marry him.
Lord Drummond tells me that he is a most respectable
young man.'

'Mr. Morton will be so much obliged to Lord Drummond.'

'And I thought that if it were so, you would be glad
that he should meet you here. I could manage it very
well, as the Drummonds are here, and Lord Drummond
would be glad to meet him.'

They had not been above a minute or two together,
and Arabella had been called upon to expend her energy
in suppressing any expression of her horror; but still, by
the time that she was called on to speak, she had fabricated
her story. 'Thanks, aunt; it is so good of you; and if
everything was going straight, there would be nothing of
course that I should like so much.'

'You are engaged to him?'

'Well; I was going to tell you. I dare say it is not his
fault; but papa and mamma and the lawyers thinks that
he is not behaving well about money;—settlements and
all that. I suppose it will all come right; but in the meantime perhaps I had better not meet him.'

'But you were engaged to him?'

This had to be answered without a moment's pause.
'Yes,' said Arabella, 'I was engaged to him.'

'And he is going out as minister to Patagonia almost
immediately?'

'He is going, I know.'

'I suppose you will go with him?'

This was very hard. She could not say that she certainly
was not going with him. And yet she had to remember

that her coming campaign with Lord Rufford must be carried on in part beneath her aunt's eyes. When she had come to Mistletoe she had fondly hoped that none of the family there would know anything about Mr. Morton. And now she was called upon to answer these horrid questions without a moment's notice! 'I don't think I shall go with him, aunt; though I am unable to say anything certain just at present. If he behaves badly of course the engagement must be off.'

'I hope not. You should think of it very seriously. As for money, you know, you have none of your own, and I am told that he has a very nice property in Rufford. There is a neighbour of his coming here to-morrow, and perhaps he knows him.'

'Who is the neighbour, aunt?' asked Arabella, innocently.

'Lord Rufford. He is coming to shoot. I will ask him about the property.'

'Pray don't mention my name, aunt. It would be so unpleasant if nothing were to come of it. I know Lord Rufford very well.'

'Know Lord Rufford very well!'

'As one does know men that one meets about.'

'I thought it might settle everything if we had Mr. Morton here.'

'I couldn't meet him, aunt; I couldn't indeed. Mamma doesn't think that he is behaving well.' To the duchess condemnation from Lady Augustus almost amounted to praise. She felt sure that Mr. Morton was a worthy man who would not probably behave badly, and though she could not unravel the mystery, and certainly had no suspicion in regard to Lord Rufford, she was sure that there was something wrong. But there was nothing more to be said at present. After what Arabella had told her, Mr. Morton could not be asked there to meet her niece. But all the slight feelings to the girl which had been created by the tidings of so respectable an engagement were at once obliterated from the duchess's bosom. Arabella, with many expressions of thanks and a good-humoured countenance, left the room, cursing the un-

towardness of her fate which would let nothing run
smooth.

Lord Rufford was to come. That, at any rate, was
now almost certain. Up to the present she had doubted,
knowing the way in which such men will change their
engagements at the least caprice. But the duchess
expected him on the morrow. She had prepared the way
for meeting him as an old friend without causing surprise,
and had gained that step. But should she succeed, as she
hoped, in exacting continued homage from the man,—
homage for the four or five days of his sojourn at Mistletoe,—this must be carried on with the knowledge on the
part of many in the house that she was engaged to that
horrid Patagonian Minister! Was ever a girl called upon
to risk her entire fate under so many disadvantages?

When she went up to dress for dinner on the day of his
expected arrival Lord Rufford had not come. Since the
interview in her aunt's room she had not heard his name
mentioned. When she came into the dining-room, a little
late, he was not there. 'We won't wait, duchess,' said the
duke to his wife at three minutes past eight. The duke's
punctuality at dinner-time was well known, and everybody else was then assembled. Within two minutes after
the duke's word dinner was announced, and a party
numbering about thirty walked away into the dinner-
room. Arabella, when they were all settled, found that
there was a vacant seat next herself. If the man were to
come, fortune would have favoured her in that.

The fish and soup had already disappeared and the
duke was wakening himself to eloquence on the first
entrée when Lord Rufford entered the room. 'There
never were trains so late as yours, duchess,' he said, 'nor
any part of the world in which hired horses travel so
slowly. I beg the duke's pardon, but I suffer the less
because I know his grace never waits for anybody.'

'Certainly not,' said the duke, 'having some regard for
my friends' dinners.'

'And I find myself next to you,' said Lord Rufford, as
he took his seat. 'Well; that is more than I deserve.'

Chapter XXXVII

HOW THINGS WERE ARRANGED

'JACK is here,' said Lord Rufford, as soon as the fuss of his late arrival had worn itself away.

'I shall be proud to renew my acquaintance.'

'Can you come to-morrow?'

'Oh yes,' said Arabella, rapturously.

'There are difficulties, and I ought to have written to you about them. I am going with the Fitzwilliam.'* Now Mistletoe was in Lincolnshire, not very far from Peterborough, not very far from Stamford, not very far from Oakham. A regular hunting man like Lord Rufford knew how to compass the difficulties of distance in all hunting countries. Horses could go by one train or over night, and he could follow by another. And a postchaise* could meet him here or there. But when a lady is added, the difficulty is often increased fivefold.

'Is it very far?' asked Arabella.

'It is a little far. I wonder who are going from here?'

'Heaven only knows. I have passed my time in playing cat's cradle with Sir Jeffrey Bunker for the amusement of the company, and in confidential communications with my aunt and Lady Drummond. I haven't heard hunting mentioned.'

'Have you anything on wheels going across to Holcombe Cross to-morrow, duke?' asked Lord Rufford. The duke said that he did not know of anything on wheels going to Holcombe Cross. Then a hunting man who had heard the question said that he and another intended to travel by train to Oundle. Upon this Lord Rufford turned round and looked at Arabella mournfully.

'Cannot I go by train to Oundle?' she asked.

'Nothing on earth so jolly if your pastors and masters and all that will let you.'

'I haven't got any pastors and masters.'

'The duchess!' suggested Lord Rufford.

'I thought all that kind of nonsense was over,' said Arabella.

'I believe a great deal is over. You can do many things that your mother and grandmother couldn't do; but absolute freedom,—what you may call universal suffrage, —hasn't come yet, I fear. It's twenty miles by road, and the duchess would say something awful if I were to propose to take you in a postchaise.'

'But the railway!'

'I'm afraid that would be worse. We couldn't ride back, you know, as we did at Rufford. At the best it would be rather a rough and tumble kind of arrangement. I'm afraid we must put it off. To tell you the truth I'm the least bit in the world afraid of the duchess.'

'I am not at all,' said Arabella, angrily.

Then Lord Rufford ate his dinner and seemed to think that that matter was settled. Arabella knew that he might have hunted elsewhere,—that the Cottesmore would be out in their own county within twelve miles of them, and that the difficulty of that ride would be very much less. The duke might have been persuaded to send a carriage that distance. But Lord Rufford cared more about the chance of a good run than her company! For a while she was sulky;—for a little while, till she remembered how ill she could afford to indulge in such a feeling. Then she said a demure word or two to the gentleman on the other side of her who happened to be a clergyman, and did not return to the hunting till Lord Rufford had eaten his cheese. 'And is that to be the end of Jack as far as I'm concerned?'

'I have been thinking about it ever since. This is Thursday.'

'Not a doubt about it.'

'To-morrow will be Friday and the duke has his great shooting on Saturday. There's nothing within a hundred miles of us on Saturday. I shall go with the Pytchley if I don't shoot, but I shall have to get up just when other people are going to bed. That wouldn't suit you.'

'I wouldn't mind if I didn't go to bed at all.'

'At any rate, it wouldn't suit the duchess. I had meant to go away on Sunday. I hate being anywhere on Sunday except in a railway carriage. But if I thought the duke would keep me till Tuesday morning, we might manage Peltry on Monday. I meant to have got back to Surbiton's on Sunday, and have gone from there.'

'Where is Peltry?'

'It's a Cottesmore meet, about five miles this side of Melton.'

'We could ride from here.'

'It's rather far for that; but we could talk over the duke to send a carriage. Ladies always like to see a meet, and perhaps we could make a party. If not, we must put a good face on it and go in anything we can get. I shouldn't fear the duchess so much for twelve miles as I should for twenty.'

'I don't mean to let the duchess interfere with me,' said Arabella, in a whisper.

That evening Lord Rufford was very good-natured, and managed to arrange everything. Lady Chiltern and another lady said that they would be glad to go to the meet, and a carriage or carriages were organized. But nothing was said as to Arabella's hunting, because the question would immediately be raised as to her return to Mistletoe in the evening. It was, however, understood that she was to have a place in the carriage.

Arabella had gained two things. She would have her one day's hunting, and she had secured the presence of Lord Rufford at Mistletoe for Sunday. With such a man as his lordship it was almost impossible to find a moment for confidential conversation. He worked so hard at his amusements that he was as bad a lover as a barrister who has to be in court all day,—almost as bad as a sailor who is always going round the world. On this evening it was ten o'clock before the gentleman came into the drawing-room, and then Lord Rufford's time was spent in arranging the party for the meet on Monday. When the ladies went up to bed Arabella had had no other opportunity than what fortune had given her at dinner.

And even then she had been watched. That juxta-position at the dinner-table had come of chance, and had been caused by Lord Rufford's late arrival. Old Sir Jeffrey should have been her neighbour, with the clergy-

man on the other side, an arrangement which her grace
had thought safe with reference to the rights of the
minister to Patagonia. The duchess, though she was at
some distance down the table, had seen that her niece and
Lord Rufford were intimate, and remembered immediately what had been said upstairs. They could not have
talked as they were then talking—sometimes whispering,
as the duchess could perceive very well—unless there had
been considerable former intimacy. She began gradually
to understand various other things;—why Arabella Trefoil had been so anxious to come to Mistletoe just at this
time, why she had behaved so unlike her usual self
before Lord Rufford's arrival, and why she had been so
unwilling to have Mr. Morton invited. The duchess was
in her way a clever woman, and could see many things.
She could see that though her niece might be very anxious
to marry Lord Rufford, Lord Rufford might indulge
himself in a close intimacy with the girl without any such
intention on his part. And, as far as the family was con
cerned, she would have been quite contented with the
Morton alliance. She would have asked Morton now,
only that it would be impossible that he should come in
time to be of service. Had she been consulted in the first
instance, she would have put her veto on that drive to the
meet; but she had heard nothing about it until Lady
Chiltern had said that she would go. The Duchess of
Omnium had since declared that she also would go, and
there were to be two carriages. But still it never occurred
to the duchess that Arabella intended to hunt. Nor did
Arabella intend that she should know it till the morning
came.

The Friday was very dull; the hunting men, of course,
gone before Arabella had come down to breakfast. She
would willingly have got up at seven to pour out Lord
Rufford's tea, had that been possible; but, as it was, she
strolled into the breakfast-room at half-past ten. She
could see by her aunt's eye, and hear in her voice, that
she was in part detected, and that she would do herself
no further service by acting the good girl; and she therefore resolutely determined to listen to no more twaddle.

She read a French novel which she had brought with her, and spent as much of the day as she could in her bedroom. She did not see Lord Rufford before dinner, and at dinner sat between Sir Jeffrey and an old gentleman out of Stamford, who dined at Mistletoe that evening. 'We've had no such luck to-night,' Lord Rufford said to her in the drawing-room.

'The old dragon took care of that,' replied Arabella.

'Why should the old dragon think that I'm dangerous?'

'Because—— I can't very well tell you why, but I dare say you know.'

'And do you think I am dangerous?'

'You're a sort of a five-barred gate,' said Arabella, laughing. 'Of course there is a little danger, but who is going to be stopped by that?'

He could make no reply to this, because the duchess called him away to give some account to Lady Chiltern about Goarly and the U.R.U., Lady Chiltern's husband being a master of hounds and a great authority on all matters relating to hunting. 'Nasty old dragon!' Arabella said to herself when she was thus left alone.

The Saturday was the day of the great shooting, and at two o'clock the ladies went out to lunch with the gentlemen by the side of the wood. Lord Rufford had at last consented to be one of the party. With logs of trees, a few hurdles, and other field appliances, a rustic banqueting hall was prepared, and everything was very nice. Tons of game had been killed, and tons more were to be killed after luncheon. The duchess was not there, and Arabella contrived so to place herself that she could be waited upon by Lord Rufford, or could wait upon him. Of course a great many eyes were upon her, but she knew how to sustain that. Nobody was present who could dare to interfere with her. When the eating and drinking were over, she walked with him to his corner by the next covert, not heeding the other ladies; and she stood with him for some minutes after the slaughter had begun. She had come to feel that the time was slipping between her fingers, and that she must say something effective. The fatal word upon which everything would depend must be spoken at the very latest on their return home on Monday, and she was aware that much must probably be said before that. 'Do we hunt or shoot to-morrow?' she said.

'To-morrow is Sunday.'

'I am quite aware of that, but I didn't know whether you could live a day without sport.'

'The country is so full of prejudice that I am driven to Sabbatical quiescence.'

'Take a walk with me to-morrow,' said Arabella.

'But the duchess?' exclaimed Lord Rufford, in a stage whisper. One of the beaters was so near that he could not but have heard; but what does a beater signify?

'H'm h'm, the duchess! You be at the path behind the great conservatory at half-past three, and we won't mind the duchess.' Lord Rufford was forced to ask for many other particulars as to the locality, and then promised that he would be there at the time named.

CHAPTER XXXVIII

'YOU ARE SO SEVERE'

ON the next morning Arabella went to church, as did of course a great many of the party. By remaining at home she could only have excited suspicion. The church was close to the house, and the family pew consisted of a large room screened off from the rest of the church, with a fire-place of its own,—so that the labour of attending divine service was reduced to a minimum. At two o'clock they lunched, and that amusement lasted nearly an hour. There was an afternoon service at three, in attending which the duchess was very particular. The duke never went at that time, nor was it expected that any of the gentlemen would do so; but ladies are supposed to require more church than men, and the duchess rather made it a point that, at any rate, the young ladies staying in the house should accompany her. Over the other young ladies there her authority could only be that of influence, but such authority generally sufficed. From her niece it might be supposed that she would exact obedience, and

in this instance she tried it. 'We start in five minutes,' she
said to Arabella as that young lady was loitering at the
table.

'Don't wait for me, aunt; I'm not going,' said Arabella
boldly.

'I hope you will come to church with us,' said the
duchess sternly.

'Not this afternoon.'

'Why not, Arabella?'

'I never do go to church twice on Sundays. Some
people do, and some people don't. I suppose that's
about it.'

'I think that all young women ought to go to church on
Sunday afternoon unless there is something particular to
prevent them.' Arabella shrugged her shoulders and the
duchess stalked angrily away.

'That makes me feel so awfully wicked,' said the
Duchess of Omnium, who was the only other lady then
left in the room. Then she got up and went out, and
Arabella of course followed her. Lord Rufford had heard
it all, but had stood at the window and said nothing. He
had not been to church at all, and was quite accustomed
to the idea that as a young nobleman who only lived
for pleasure he was privileged to be wicked. Had the
Duchess of Mayfair been blessed with a third daughter
fit for marriage, she would not have thought of repudiating such a suitor as Lord Rufford because he did not go
to church.

When the house was cleared, Arabella went upstairs
and put on her hat. It was a bright beautiful winter's day,
not painfully cold, because the air was dry, but still a day
that warranted furs and a muff. Having prepared herself she made her way alone to a side door which led from
a branch of the hall on to the garden terrace, and up and
down that she walked two or three times,—so that any of
the household that saw her might perceive that she had
come out simply for exercise. At the end of the third turn
instead of coming back she went on quickly to the conservatory and took the path which led round to the further
side. There was a small lawn here fitted for garden games,

and on the other end of it an iron gate leading to a path into the woods. At the further side of the iron gate and leaning against it, stood Lord Rufford, smoking a cigar. She did not pause a moment, but hurried across the lawn to join him. He opened the gate and she passed through. 'I'm not going to be done by a dragon,' she said, as she took her place alongside of him.

'Upon my word, Miss Trefoil, I don't think I ever knew a human being with so much pluck as you have got.'

'Girls have to have pluck if they don't mean to be sat upon;—a great deal more than men. The idea of telling me that I was to go to church as though I were twelve years old!'

'What would she say if she knew that you were walking here with me?'

'I don't care what she'd say. I dare say she walked with somebody once;—only I should think the somebody must have found it very dull.'

'Does she know that you're to hunt to-morrow?'

'I haven't told her and don't mean. I shall just come down in my habit and hat and say nothing about it. At what time must we start?'

'The carriages are ordered at half-past nine. But I'm afraid you haven't clearly before your eyes all the difficulties which are incidental to hunting.'

'What do you mean?'

'It looks as like a black frost as anything I ever saw in my life.'

'But we should go?'

'The horses won't be there if there is a really hard frost. Nobody would stir. It will be the first question I shall ask the man when he comes to me, and if there have been seven or eight degrees of frost I shan't get up.'

'How am I to know?'

'My man shall tell your maid. But everybody will soon know all about it. It will alter everything.'

'I think I shall go mad.'

'In white satin?'

'No;—in my habit and hat. It will be the hardest thing, after all! I ought to have insisted on going to Holcombe

Cross on Friday. The sun is shining now. Surely it cannot freeze.'

'It will be uncommonly ill-bred if it does.'

But, after all, the hunting was not the main point. The hunting had been only intended as an opportunity; and if that were to be lost,—in which case Lord Rufford would no doubt at once leave Mistletoe,—there was the more need for using the present hour, the more for using even the present minute. Though she had said that the sun was shining, it was the setting sun, and in another half hour the gloom of the evening would be there. Even Lord Rufford would not consent to walk about with her in the dark. 'Oh, Lord Rufford,' she said, 'I did so look forward to your giving me another lead.' Then she put her hand upon his arm, and left it there.

'It would have been nice,' said he, drawing her hand a little on, and remembering as he did so his own picture of himself on the cliff with his sister holding his coat tails.

'If you could possibly know,' she said, 'the condition I am in.'

'What condition?'

'I know that I can trust you. I am sure that I can trust you.'

'Oh dear, yes. If you mean about telling, I never tell anything.'

'That's what I do mean. You remember that man at your place?'

'What man? Poor Caneback?'

'Oh dear no! I wish they could change places because then he could give me no more trouble.'

'That's wishing him to be dead, whoever he is.'

'Yes. Why should he persecute me? I mean that man we were staying with at Bragton.'

'Mr. Morton?'

'Of course I do. Don't you remember your asking me about him, and my telling you that I was not engaged to him?'

'I remember that.'

'Mamma and this horrid old duchess here want me to marry him. They've got an idea that he is going to be

ambassador at Pekin or something very grand, and they're
at me day and night.'

'You needn't take him unless you like him.'

'They do make me so miserable!' And then she leaned
heavily upon his arm. He was a man who could not
stand such pressure as this without returning it. Though
he were on a precipice, and though he must go over, still
he could not stand it. 'You remember that night after
the ball?'

'Indeed I do.'

'And you, too, asked me whether I cared for that
horrid man.'

'I didn't see anything horrid. You had been staying at
his house and people had told me. What was I to think?'

'You ought to have known what to think. There; let
me go,'—for now he had got his arm round her waist.
'You don't care for me a bit. I know you don't. It
would be all the same to you whom I married;—or
whether I died.'

'You don't think that, Bella?' He fancied that he had
heard her mother call her Bella, and that the name was
softer and easier than the full four syllables. It was, at
any rate, something for her to have gained.

'I do think it. When I came here on purpose to have
a skurry over the country with you, you went away to
Holcombe Cross, though you could have hunted here,
close in the neighbourhood. And now you tell me there
will be a frost to-morrow.'

'Can I help that, darling?'

'Darling! I ain't your darling. You don't care a bit for
me. I believe you hope there'll be a frost.' He pressed
her tighter, but laughed as he did so. It was evidently
a joke to him;—a pleasant joke no doubt. 'Leave me
alone, Lord Rufford. I won't let you, for I know you
don't love me.' Very suddenly he did leave his hold of
her and stood erect with his hands in his pockets, for the
rustle of a dress was heard. It was still daylight, but the
light was dim and the last morsel of the grandeur of
the sun had ceased to be visible through the trees. The
church-going people had been released, and the duchess,

having probably heard certain tidings, had herself come to take a walk in the shrubbery behind the conservatory. Arabella had probably been unaware that she and her companion by a turn in the walks were being brought back towards the iron gate. As it was they met the duchess face to face.

Lord Rufford had spoken the truth when he had said that he was a little afraid of the duchess. Such was his fear that at the moment he hardly knew what he was to say. Arabella had boasted when she had declared that she was not at all afraid of her aunt;—but she was steadfastly minded that she would not be cowed by her fears. She had known beforehand that she would have occasion for much presence of mind, and was prepared to exercise it at a moment's notice. She was the first to speak. 'Is that you, aunt? you are out of church very soon.'

'Lord Rufford,' said the duchess, 'I don't think this is a proper time for walking out.'

'Don't you, duchess? The air is very nice.'

'It is becoming dark, and my niece had better return to the house with me. Arabella, you can come this way. It is just as short as the other. If you go on straight, Lord Rufford, it will take you to the house.' Of course Lord Rufford went on straight, and of course Arabella had to turn with her aunt. 'Such conduct as this is shocking,' began the duchess.

'Aunt, let me tell you.'

'What can you tell me?'

'I can tell you a great deal if you will let me. Of course I am quite prepared to own that I did not intend to tell you anything.'

'I can well believe that.'

'Because I could hardly hope for your sympathy. You have never liked me.'

'You have no right to say that.'

'I don't do it in the way of finding fault. I don't know why you should. But I have been too much afraid of you to tell you my secrets. I must do so now, because you have found me walking with Lord Rufford. I could not otherwise excuse myself.'

'Is he engaged to marry you?'

'He has asked me.'

'No!'

'But he has, aunt. You must be a little patient, and let me tell you it all. Mamma did make up an engagement between me and Mr. Morton at Washington.'

'Did you know Lord Rufford then?'

'I knew him, but did not think he was behaving quite well. It is very hard sometimes to know what a man means. I was angry when I went to Washington. He has told me since that he loves me, and has offered.'

'But you are engaged to marry the other man.'

'Nothing on earth shall make me marry Mr. Morton. Mamma did it, and mamma now has very nearly broken it off, because she says he is very shabby about money. Indeed, it is broken off. I had told him so even before Lord Rufford had proposed to me.'

'When did he propose, and where?'

'At Rufford. We were staying there in November.'

'And you asked to come here that you might meet him?'

'Just so. Was that strange? Where could I be better pleased to meet him than in my own uncle's house?'

'Yes; if you had told us all this before.'

'Perhaps I ought; but you are so severe, aunt, that I did not dare. Do not turn against me now. My uncle could not but like that his niece should marry Lord Rufford.'

'How can I turn against you if it is settled? Lord Rufford can do as he pleases. Has he told your father,— or your mother?'

'Mamma knows it.'

'But not from him?' asked the duchess.

Arabella paused a moment, but hardly a moment, before she answered. It was hard upon her that she should have to make up her mind on matters of such importance, with so little time for consideration. 'Yes,' she said, 'mamma knows it from him. Papa is so very indifferent about everything that Lord Rufford has not spoken to him.'

'If so, it will be best that the duke should speak to him.'

There was another pause, but hardly long enough to attract notice. 'Perhaps so,' she said; 'but not quite yet. He is so peculiar, so touchy. The duke is not quite like my father, and he would think himself suspected.'

'I cannot imagine that if he is in earnest.'

'That is because you do not know him as I do. Only think where I should be if I were to lose him!'

'Lose him!'

'Oh, aunt, now that you know it I do hope that you will be my friend. It would kill me if he were to throw me over now.'

'But why should he throw you over if he proposed to you only last month?'

'He might do it if he thought that he were interfered with. Of course I should like my uncle to speak to him, but not quite immediately. If he were to say that he had changed his mind, what could I do, or what could my uncle do?'

'That would be very singular conduct.'

'Men are so different now, aunt. They give themselves so much more latitude. A man has only to say that he has changed his mind and nothing ever comes of it.'

'I have never been used to such men, my dear.'

'At any rate, don't ask the duke to speak to him to-day. I will think about it and perhaps you will let me see you to-morrow, after we all come in.' To this the duchess gravely assented. 'And I hope you won't be angry because you found me walking with him, or because I did not go to church. It is everything to me. I am sure, dear aunt, you will understand that.' To this the duchess made no reply, and they both entered the house together. What became of Lord Rufford neither of them saw.

Arabella when she regained her room thought that upon the whole fortune had favoured her by throwing her aunt in her way. She had, no doubt, been driven to tell a series of barefaced, impudent lies,—lies of such a nature that they almost made her own hair stand on end as she thought of them;—but they would matter nothing if she succeeded; and if she failed in this matter she did not care much what her aunt thought of her. Her aunt

might now give her a good turn; and some lies she must
have told;—such had been the emergencies of her position!
As she thought of it all she was glad that her aunt had met
her; and when Lord Rufford was summoned to take her
out to dinner on that very Sunday,—a matter as to which
her aunt managed everything herself,—she was immediately aware that her lies had done her good service.

'This was more than I expected,' Lord Rufford said
when they were seated.

'She knew that she had overdone it when she sent you
away in that cavalier way,' replied Arabella, 'and now
she wants to show that she didn't mean anything.'

CHAPTER XXXIX

THE DAY AT PELTRY

THE duchess did tell the duke the whole story about
Lord Rufford and Arabella that night,—as to which
it may be said that she also was false. But according to
her conscience there were two ways of telling such a secret.
As a matter of course she told her husband everything.
That idle, placid, dinner-loving man was in truth consulted about each detail of the house and family;—but
the secret was told to him with injunctions that he was to
say nothing about it to any one for twenty-four hours.
After that the duchess was of opinion that he should speak
to Lord Rufford. 'What could I say to him?' asked the
duke, 'I'm not her father.'

'But your brother is so indifferent.'

'No doubt. But that gives me no authority, If he does
mean to marry the girl he must go to her father;—or it is
possible that he might come to me. But if he does not
mean it, what can I do?' He promised, however, that he
would think of it.

It was still dark night, or the morning was still dark as
night, when Arabella got out of bed and opened her
window. The coming of a frost now might ruin her. The
absence of it might give her everything in life that she
wanted. Lord Rufford had promised her a tedious com-

munication through servants as to the state of the weather. She was far too energetic, far too much in earnest, to wait for that. She opened the window and putting out her hand she felt a drizzle of rain. And the air, though the damp from it seemed to chill her all through, was not a frosty air. She stood there a minute so as to be sure and then retreated to her bed.

Fortune was again favouring her;—but then how would it be if it should turn out to rain hard? In that case Lady Chiltern and the other ladies certainly would not go, and how in such case should she get herself conveyed to the meet? She would, at any rate, go down in her hat and habit and trust that somebody would provide for her. There might be much that would be disagreeable and difficult, but hardly anything could be worse than the necessity of telling such lies as those which she had fabricated on the previous afternoon.

She had been much in doubt whether her aunt had or had not believed her. That the belief was not a thorough belief she was almost certain. But then there was the great fact that after the story had been told she had been sent out to dinner leaning on Lord Rufford's arm. Unless her aunt had believed something that would not have taken place. And then so much of it was true. Surely it would be impossible that he should not propose after what had occurred! Her aunt was evidently alive to the advantage of the marriage,—to the advantage which would accrue not to her, Arabella, individually, but to the Trefoils generally. She almost thought that her aunt would not put spokes in her wheel for this day. She wished now that she had told her aunt that she intended to hunt, so that there need not be any surprise.

She slept again, and again looked out of the window. It rained a little, but still there were hours in which the rain might cease. Again she slept, and at eight her maid brought her word that there would be hunting. It did rain a little, but very little. Of course she would dress herself in riding attire.

At nine o'clock she walked into the breakfast parlour, properly equipped for the day's sport. There were four

or five men there in red coats and top boots, among whom
Lord Rufford was conspicuous. They were just seating
themselves at the breakfast table, and her aunt was
already in her place. Lady Chiltern had come into the
room with herself, and at the door had spoken some good-
natured words of surprise. 'I did not know that you were
a sportswoman, Miss Trefoil.' 'I do ride a little when
I am well mounted,' Arabella had said, as she entered
the room. Then she collected herself, and arranged her
countenance, and endeavoured to look as though she
were doing the most ordinary thing in the world. She
went round the room and kissed her aunt's brow. This
she had not done on any other morning; but, then, on
other mornings she had been late. 'Are you going to ride?'
said the duchess.

'I believe so, aunt.'

'Who is giving you a horse?'

'Lord Rufford is lending me one. I don't think even
his good nature will extend to giving away so perfect an
animal. I know him well, for I rode him when I was at
Rufford.' This she said so that all the room should hear
her.

'You need not be afraid, duchess,' said Lord Rufford.
'He is quite safe.'

'And his name is Jack,' said Arabella, laughing, as she
took her place with a little air of triumph. 'Lord Rufford
offered to let me have him all the time I was here, but I
didn't know whether you would take me in so attended.'

There was no one who heard her who did not feel that
she spoke as though Lord Rufford were all her own.
Lord Rufford felt it himself, and almost thought he might
as well turn himself round and bid his sister and Miss
Penge let him go. He must marry some day, and why
should not this girl do as well as any one else? The
duchess did not approve of young ladies hunting. She
certainly would not have had her niece at Mistletoe had
she expected such a performance. But she could not find
fault now. There was a feeling in her bosom that if there
were an engagement, it would be cruel to cause obstruc-
tions. She certainly could not allow a lover in her house

for her husband's niece without having official authenticated knowledge of the respectability of the lover;—but the whole thing had come upon her so suddenly that she was at a loss what to do or what to say. It certainly did not seem to her that Arabella was in the least afraid of being found out in any untruth. If the girl were about to become Lady Rufford, then it would be for Lord Rufford to decide whether or no she should hunt. Soon after this the duke came in, and he also alluded to his niece's costume, and was informed that she was to ride one of Lord Rufford's horses. 'I didn't hear it mentioned before,' said the duke. 'He'll carry Miss Trefoil quite safely,' said Lord Rufford, who was at the moment standing over a game pie on the sideboard. Then the subject was allowed to drop.

At half-past nine there was no rain, and the ladies were so punctual that the carriages absolutely started at ten. Some of the men rode on; one got a seat on the carriage; and Lord Rufford drove himself and a friend in a dogcart, tandem. The tandem was off before the carriages, but Lord Rufford assured them that he would get the master to allow them a quarter of an hour. Arabella contrived to say one word to him. 'If you start without me I'll never speak to you again.' He nodded and smiled; but perhaps thought that if so it might be as well that he should start without waiting for her.

At the last moment, the duchess had taken it into her head that she too would go to the meet. No doubt she was actuated by some feeling in regard to her niece; but it was not till Arabella was absolutely getting on to Jack at the side of the carriage,—under the auspices of Jack's owner,—that the idea occurred to her grace that there would be a great difficulty as to the return home. 'Arabella, how do you mean to get back?' she asked.

'That will be all right, aunt,' said Arabella.

'I will see to that,' said Lord Rufford.

The gracious, but impatient, master of the hounds had absolutely waited full twenty minutes for the duchess's party;—and was not minded to wait a minute longer for conversation. The moment that the carriages were there

the huntsmen had started, so that there was an excuse for
hurry. Lord Rufford, as he was speaking, got on to his
own horse, and before the duchess could expostulate they
were away. There was a feeling of triumph in Arabella's
bosom as she told herself that she had, at any rate,
secured her day's hunting in spite of such heart-breaking
difficulties.

The sport was fairly good. They had twenty minutes
in the morning and a kill. Then they drew a big wood,
during which they ate their lunch and drank their sherry.
In the big wood they found a fox, but could not do anything with him. After that, they came on a third in a
stubble field, and ran him well for half an hour, when he
went to ground. It was then three o'clock; and as the days
were now at the shortest, the master declined to draw
again. They were then about sixteen miles from Mistletoe, and about ten from Stamford, where Lord Rufford's
horses were standing. The distance from Stamford to
Mistletoe was eight. Lord Rufford proposed that they
should ride to Stamford, and then go home in a hired
carriage. There seemed, indeed, to be no other way of
getting home without taking three tired horses fourteen
miles out of their way. Arabella made no objection whatever to the arrangement. Lord Rufford did, in truth,
make a slight effort—the slightest possible—to induce
a third person to join their party. There was still something pulling at his coat-tail, so that there might yet be
a chance of saving him from the precipice. But he failed.
The tired horseman, before whom the suggestion was
casually thrown out, would have been delighted to accept
it, instead of riding all the way to Mistletoe;—but he did
not look upon it as made in earnest. Two, he knew, were
company, and three none.

The hunting-field is by no means a place suited for real
love-making. Very much of preliminary conversation
may be done there in a pleasant way, and intimacies may
be formed. But when lovers have already walked with
arms round each other in a wood, riding together may be
very pleasant, but can hardly be ecstatic. Lord Rufford
might, indeed, have asked her to be Lady R. while they

were breaking up the first fox, or as they loitered about in
the big wood;—but she did not expect that. There was
no moment during the day's sport in which she had a
right to tell herself that he was misbehaving because he
did not so ask her. But in a postchaise it would be different.

At the inn at Stamford the horses were given up, and
Arabella condescended to take a glass of cherry brandy.
She had gone through a long day,—it was then half-past
four, and she was not used to be many hours on horseback.
The fatigue seemed to her to be very much greater than
it had been when she got back to Rufford immediately
after the fatal accident. The ten miles along the road,
which had been done in little more than an hour, had
almost overcome her. She had determined not to cry for
mercy as the hard trot went on. She had passed herself
off as an accustomed horsewoman, and having done so
well across the country, would not break down coming
home. But, as she got into the carriage, she was very
tired. She could almost have cried with fatigue;—and
yet she told herself that now,—now,—must the work be
done. She would perhaps tell him that she was tired.
She might even assist her cause by her languor;—but,
though she should die for it, she would not waste her
precious moments by absolute rest. 'May I light a cigar?'
he said, as he got in.

'You know you may. Wherever I may be with you do
you think that I would interfere with your gratifications?'

'You are the best girl in all the world,' he said as he
took out his case and threw himself back in the corner.

'Do you call that a long day?' she asked, when he had
lit his cigar.

'Not very long.'

'Because I am so tired.'

'We came home pretty sharp. I thought it best not to
shock her grace by too great a stretch into the night. As
it is you will have time to go to bed for an hour or two
before you dress. That's what I do when I am in time.
You'll be right as a trivet*then.'

'Oh; I'm right now,—only tired. It was very nice.'

'Pretty well. We ought to have killed that last fox.

And why on earth we made nothing of that fellow in Gooseberry Grove I couldn't understand. Old Tony would never have left that fox alive above ground. Would you like to go to sleep?'

'Oh dear, no.'

'Afraid of gloves?' said he, drawing nearer to her. They might pull him as they liked by his coat-tails, but as he was in a postchaise with her he must make himself agreeable. She shook her head and laughed as she looked at him through the gloom. Then, of course, he kissed her.

'Lord Rufford, what does this mean?'

'Don't you know what it means?'

'Hardly.'

'It means that I think you the jolliest girl out. I never liked anybody so well as I do you.'

'Perhaps you never liked anybody?' said she.

'Well;—yes, I have; but I am not going to boast of what fortune has done for me in that way. I wonder whether you care for me?'

'Do you want to know?'

'I should like to know. You have never said that you did.'

'Because you have never asked me.'

'Am I not asking you now, Bella?'

'There are different ways of asking,—but there is only one way that you will get an answer from me. No;—no. I will not have it. I have allowed too much to you already. Oh, I am so tired.' Then she sank back almost into his arms,—but recovered herself very quickly. 'Lord Rufford,' she said, 'if you are a man of honour let there be an end of this. I am sure you do not wish to make me wretched.'

'I would do anything to make you happy.'

'Then tell me that you love me honestly, sincerely, with all your heart,—and I shall be happy.'

'You know I do.'

'Do you? Do you?' she said, and then she flung herself on to his shoulder, and for a while she seemed to faint. For a few minutes she lay there, and as she was lying she calculated whether it would be better to try at this moment to drive him to some clearer declaration, or to make use of what he had already said without giving him an opportunity of protesting that he had not meant to make her an offer of marriage. He had declared that he loved her honestly and with his whole heart. Would not that justify her in setting her uncle at him? And might it not be that the duke would carry great weight with him; —that the duke might induce him to utter the fatal word though she, were she to demand it now, might fail? As she thought of it all she affected to swoon, and almost herself believed that she was swooning. She was conscious, but hardly more than conscious, that he was kissing her;—and yet her brain was at work. She felt that he would be startled, repelled, perhaps disgusted, were she absolutely to demand more from him now. 'Oh, Rufford; —oh, my dearest,' she said as she woke up, and with her face close to his, so that he could look into her eyes and see their brightness even through the gloom. Then she extricated herself from his embrace with a shudder and a laugh. 'You would hardly believe how tired I am,' she said putting out her ungloved hand. He took it and drew her to him and there she sat in his arms for the short remainder of the journey.

They were now in the park, and as the lights of the house came in sight he gave her some counsel. 'Go up to your room at once, dearest, and lay down.'

'I will. I don't think I could go in among them. I should fall.'

'I will see the duchess and tell her that you are all right,—but very tired. If she goes up to you you had better see her.'

'Oh, yes. But I had rather not.'

'She'll be sure to come. And, Bella, Jack must be yours now.'

'You are joking.'

'Never more serious in my life. Of course he must remain with me just at present, but he is your horse.' Then, as the carriage was stopping, she took his hand and kissed it.

She got to her room as quickly as possible; and then,

before she had even taken off her hat, she sat down to think of it all,—sending her maid away meanwhile to fetch her a cup of tea. He must have meant it for an offer. There had, at any rate, been enough to justify her in so taking it. The present he had made her of the horse could mean nothing else. Under no other circumstances would it be possible that she should either take the horse or use him. Certainly it was an offer, and as such she would instruct her uncle to use it. Then she allowed her imagination to revel in thoughts of Rufford Hall, of the Rufford house in town, and a final end to all those weary labours which she would thus have brought to so glorious a termination.

CHAPTER XL

LORD RUFFORD WANTS TO SEE A HORSE

LORD RUFFORD had been quite right about the duchess. Arabella had only taken off her hat, and was drinking her tea when the duchess came up to her. 'Lord Rufford says that you were too tired to come in,' said the duchess.

'I am tired, aunt;—very tired. But there is nothing the matter with me. We had to ride ever so far coming home, and it was that knocked me up.'

'It was very bad, your coming home with him in a postchaise, Arabella.'

'Why was it bad, aunt? I thought it very nice.'

'My dear, it shouldn't have been done. You ought to have known that. I certainly wouldn't have had you here had I thought that there would be anything of the kind.'

'It is going to be all right,' said Arabella, laughing.

According to her grace's view of things it was not and could not be made 'all right.' It would not have been all right were the girl to become Lady Rufford to-morrow. The scandal, or loud reproach due to evil doings, may be silenced by subsequent conduct. The merited punishment may not come visibly. But nothing happening after could make it right that a young lady should come home from hunting in a postchaise alone with a young unmarried man. When the duchess first heard it, she thought what would have been her feelings if such a thing had been suggested in reference to one of her own daughters! Lord Rufford had come to her in the drawing-room, and had told her the story in a quiet, pleasant manner,—merely saying that Miss Trefoil was too much fatigued to show herself at the present moment. She had thought from his manner that her niece's story had been true. There was a cordiality and apparent earnestness as to the girl's comfort which seemed to be compatible with the story. But still she could hardly understand that Lord Rufford should wish to have it known that he travelled about the country in such a fashion with the girl he intended to marry. But if it were true, then she must look after her niece. And even if it were not true,—in which case she would never have the girl at Mistletoe again,—yet she could not ignore her presence in the house. It was now the 18th of January. Lord Rufford was to go on the following day, and Arabella on the 20th. The invitation had not been given so as to stretch beyond that. If it could be at once decided,—declared by Lord Rufford to the duke,—that the match was to be a match, then the invitation should be renewed, Arabella should be advised to put off her other friends, and Lord Rufford should be invited to come back early in the next month, and spend a week or two in the proper fashion with his future bride. All that had been settled between the duke and the duchess. So much should be done for the sake of the family. But the duke had not seen his way to asking Lord Rufford any question.

The duchess must now find out the truth if she could,—so that if the story were false she might get rid of the girl, and altogether shake her off from the Mistletoe roof-tree. Arabella's manner was certainly free from any appearance of hesitation or fear. 'I don't know about being all right,' said the duchess. 'It cannot be right that you should have come home with him alone in a hired carriage.'

'Is a hired carriage wickeder than a private one?'

'If a carriage had been sent from here for you, it would have been different; but even then he should not have come with you.'

'But he would, I'm sure;—and I should have asked him. What;—the man I'm engaged to marry! Mayn't he sit in a carriage with me?'

The duchess could not explain herself, and thought that she had better drop that topic. 'What does he mean to do now, Arabella?'

'What does who mean, aunt?'

'Lord Rufford.'

'He means to marry me. And he means to go from here to Mr. Surbiton's to-morrow. I don't quite understand the question.'

'And what do you mean to do?'

'I mean to marry him. And I mean to join mamma in London on Wednesday. I believe we are to go to the Connop Greens' the next day. Mr. Connop Green is a sort of cousin of mamma;—but they are odious people.'

'Who is to see Lord Rufford? However, my dear, if you are very tired, I will leave you now.'

'No, aunt. Stay a moment if you will be so very kind. I am tired; but if I were twice as tired I would find strength to talk about this. If my uncle would speak to Lord Rufford at once, I should take it as the very kindest thing he could do. I could not send him to my uncle; for, after all, one's uncle and one's father are not the same. I could only refer him to papa. But if the duke would speak to him!'

'Did he renew his offer to-day?'

'He has done nothing else but renew it ever since he has been in the carriage with me. That's the plain truth. He made his offer at Rufford. He renewed it in the wood yesterday;—and he repeated it over and over again as we came home to-day. It may have been very wrong, but so it was.' Miss Trefoil must have thought that kissing and proposing were the same thing. Other young ladies have, perhaps, before now made such a mistake. But this young lady had had much experience, and should have known better.

'Lord Rufford had better perhaps speak to your uncle.'

'Will you tell him so, aunt?'

The duchess thought about it for a moment. She certainly could not tell Lord Rufford to speak to the duke without getting the duke's leave to tell him so. And then, if all this were done, and Lord Rufford were to assure the duke that the young lady had made a mistake, how derogatory would all that be to the exalted quiescence of the house of Mayfair! She thoroughly wished that her niece were out of the house; for, though she did believe the story, her belief was not thorough. 'I will speak to your uncle,' she said. 'And now you had better go to sleep.'

'And, dear aunt, pray excuse me at dinner. I have been so excited, so flurried, and so fatigued, that I fear that I should make a fool of myself if I attempted to come down. I should get into a swoon, which would be dreadful. My maid shall bring me a bit of something and a glass of sherry, and you shall find me in the drawing-room when you come out.' Then the duchess went, and Arabella was left alone to take another view of the circumstances of the campaign.

Though there were still infinite dangers, yet she could hardly wish that anything should be altered. Should Lord Rufford disown her, which she knew to be quite possible, there would be a general collapse, and the world would crash over her head. But she had known, when she took this business in hand, that as success would open Elysium to her, so would failure involve her in absolute ruin. She was determined that she would mar nothing now by cowardice, and having so resolved, and having fortified herself with perhaps two glasses of sherry, she went down to the drawing-room a little before nine, and laid herself out upon a sofa till the ladies should come in.

Lord Rufford had gone to bed, as was his wont on such occasions, with orders that he should be called to dress for dinner at half-past seven. But as he laid himself down he made up his mind that, instead of sleeping, he would give himself up to thinking about Arabella Trefoil. The

matter was going beyond a joke, and would require some
thinking. He liked her well enough, but was certainly not
in love with her. I doubt whether men are ever in love
with girls who throw themselves into their arms. A man's
love, till it has been chastened and fastened by the feeling
of duty which marriage brings with it, is instigated
mainly by the difficulty of pursuit. 'It is hardly possible
that anything so sweet as that should ever be mine; and
yet, because I am a man, and because it is so heavenly
sweet, I will try.' That is what men say to themselves, but Lord Rufford had had no opportunity of
saying that to himself in regard to Miss Trefoil. The
thing had been sweet, but not heavenly sweet; and he
had never for a moment doubted the possibility. Now
at any rate he would make up his mind. But, instead
of doing so, he went to sleep, and when he got up
he was ten minutes late, and was forced, as he
dressed himself, to think of the duke's dinner instead of
Arabella Trefoil.

The duchess before dinner submitted herself and all her
troubles at great length to the duke, but the duke could
give her no substantial comfort. Of course it had all been
wrong. He supposed that they ought not to have been
found walking together in the dark on Sunday afternoon.
The hunting should not have been arranged without
sanction; and the return home in the hired carriage had
no doubt been highly improper. But what could he do?
If the marriage came off it would be all well. If not, this
niece must not be invited to Mistletoe again. As to speaking to Lord Rufford, he did not quite see how he was to
set about it. His own girls had been married in so very
different a fashion! He could imagine nothing so disagreeable as to have to ask a gentleman his intentions.
Parental duty might make it necessary when a daughter
had not known how to keep her own position intact;—
but here there was no parental duty. If Lord Rufford
would speak to him, then indeed there would be no
difficulty. At last he told his wife that if she could find
an opportunity of suggesting to the young lord that he
might perhaps say a word to the young lady's uncle with-

out impropriety,—if she could do this in a light easy way, so as to run no peril of a scene,—she might do so.

When the two duchesses and all the other ladies came out into the drawing-room, Arabella was found upon the sofa. Of course she became the centre of a little interest for a few minutes, and the more so as her aunt went up to her and made some inquiries. Had she had any dinner? Was she less fatigued? The fact of the improper return home in the postchaise had become generally known, and there were some there who would have turned a very cold shoulder to Arabella had not her aunt noticed her. Perhaps there were some who had envied her Jack, and Lord Rufford's admiration, and even the postchaise. But as long as her aunt countenanced her it was not likely that any one at Mistletoe would be unkind to her. The Duchess of Omnium did indeed remark to Lady Chiltern that she remembered something of the same kind happening to the same girl soon after her own marriage. As the duchess had now been married a great many years this was unkind;—but it was known that when the Duchess of Omnium did dislike any one, she never scrupled to show it. 'Lord Rufford is about the silliest man of his day,' she said afterwards to the same lady; 'but there is one thing which I do not think even he is silly enough to do.'

It was again nearly ten o'clock when the gentlemen came into the room, and then it was that the duchess,—Arabella's aunt,—must find the opportunity of giving Lord Rufford the hint of which the duke had spoken. He was to leave Mistletoe on the morrow, and might not improbably do so early. Of all women she was the steadiest, the most tranquil, the least abrupt in her movements. She could not pounce upon a man, and nail him down, and say what she had to say, let him be as unwilling as he might to hear it. At last, however, seeing Lord Rufford standing alone—he had then just left the sofa on which Arabella was still lying—without any apparent effort, she made her way up to his side. 'You had rather a long day,' she said.

'Not particularly, duchess.'

'You had to come home so far!'

'About the average distance. Did you think it a hard day, Maurice?' Then he called to his aid a certain Lord Maurice St. John, a hard-riding and hard-talking old friend of the Trefoil family, who gave the duchess a very clear account of all the performance, during which Lord Rufford fell into an interesting conversation with Mrs. Mulready, the wife of the neighbouring bishop.

After that the duchess made another attempt. 'Lord Rufford,' she said, 'we should be so glad if you would come back to us the first week in February. The Prices will be here, and the Mackenzies, and——'

'I am pledged to stay with my sister till the fifth, and on the sixth Surbiton and all his lot come to me. Battersby, is it not the sixth that you and Surbiton come to Rufford?'

'I rather think it is,' said Battersby.

'I wish it were possible. I like Mistletoe so much. It's so central.'

'Very well for hunting, is it not, Lord Rufford?' But that horrid Captain Battersby did not go out of the way.

'I wonder whether Lady Chiltern would do me a favour?' said Lord Rufford, stepping across the room in search of that lady. He might be foolish, but when the Duchess of Omnium declared him to be the silliest man of the day, I think she used a wrong epithet. The duchess was very patient, and intended to try again, but on that evening she got no opportunity.

Captain Battersby was Lord Rufford's particular friend on this occasion, and had come over with him from Mr. Surbiton's house. 'Bat,' he said, as they were sitting close to each other in the smoking-room that night, 'I mean to make an early start to-morrow.'

'What; to get to Surbiton's?'

'I've got something to do on the way. I want to look at a horse at Stamford.'

'I'll be off with you.'

'No; don't do that. I'll go in my own cart. I'll make my man get hold of my groom and manage it somehow.

I can leave my things, and you can bring them. Only say to-morrow that I was obliged to go.'

'I understand.'

'Heard something, you know, and all that kind of thing. Make my apologies to the duchess. In point of fact, I must be in Stamford at ten.'

'I'll manage it all,' said Captain Battersby, who made a very shrewd guess at the cause which drew his friend to such an uncomfortable proceeding. After that Lord Rufford went to his room and gave a good deal of trouble that night to some of the servants in reference to the steps which would be necessary to take him out of harm's way before the duchess would be up on the morrow.

Arabella, when she heard of the man's departure on the following morning, which she luckily did from her own maid, was for some time overwhelmed by it. Of course the man was running away from her. There could be no doubt of it. She had watched him narrowly on the previous evening, and had seen that her aunt had tried in vain to speak to him. But she did not on that account give up the game. At any rate, they had not found her out at Mistletoe. That was something. Of course it would have been infinitely better for her could he have been absolutely caught and nailed down before he left the house; but that was perhaps more than she had a right to expect. She could still pursue him, still write to him; and at last, if necessary, force her father to do so. But she must now trust chiefly to her own correspondence.

'He told me, aunt, the last thing last night, that he was going,' she said.

'Why did you not mention it?'

'I thought he would have told you. I saw him speaking to you. He had received some telegram about a horse. He's the most flighty man in the world about such things. I am to write to him before I leave this to-morrow.' Then the duchess did not believe a word of the engagement. She felt, at any rate, certain that, if there was an engagement, Lord Rufford did not mean to keep it.

Chapter XLI

THE SENATOR IS BADLY TREATED

WHILE these great efforts were being made by
Arabella Trefoil at Mistletoe, John Morton was
vacillating in an unhappy mood between London and
Bragton. It may be remembered that an offer was made
to him as to the purchase of Chowton Farm. At that
time the Mistletoe party was broken up, and Miss Trefoil
was staying with her mother at the Connop Greens'. By
the morning post on the next day he received a note from
the Senator, in which Mr. Gotobed stated that business
required his presence at Dillsborough, and suggested that
he should again become a guest at Bragton for a few days.
Morton was so sick of his own company, and so tired of
thinking of his own affairs, that he was almost glad to
welcome the Senator. At any rate, he had no means of
escaping, and the Senator came. The two men were
alone at the house, and the Senator was full of his own
wrongs, as well as those of Englishmen in general. Mr.
Bearside had written to him very cautiously, but pressing
for an immediate remittance of £25, and explaining that
the great case could not be carried on without that sum of
money. This might have been very well as being open to
the idea that the Senator had the option of either paying
the money or of allowing the great case to be abandoned,
but that the attorney in the last paragraph of his letter
intimated that the Senator would be of course aware that
he was liable for the whole cost of the action, be it what
it might. He had asked a legal friend in London his
opinion, and the legal friend had seemed to think that
perhaps he was liable. What orders he had given to Bearside he had given without any witness, and at any rate
had already paid a certain sum. The legal friend, when
he heard all that Mr. Gotobed was able to tell him about
Goarly, had advised the Senator to settle with Bearside,—
taking a due receipt, and having some person with him
when he did so. The legal friend had thought that a small
sum of money would suffice. 'He went so far as to suggest,'

said the Senator, with indignant energy, 'that if I contested my liability to the man's charges, the matter would go against me, because I had interfered in such a case on the unpopular side. I should think that in this great country I should find justice administered on other terms than that.' Morton attempted to explain to him that his legal friend had not been administering justice, but only giving advice. He had, so Morton told him, undoubtedly taken up the case of one blackguard, and in urging it had paid his money to another. He had done so as a foreigner, loudly proclaiming as his reason for such action that the man he supported would be unfairly treated unless he gave his assistance. Of course he could not expect sympathy. 'I want no sympathy,' said the Senator; 'I only want justice.' Then the two gentlemen had become a little angry with each other. Morton was the last man in the world to have been aggressive on such a matter; but with the Senator it was necessary either to be prostrate or to fight.

But with Mr. Gotobed such fighting never produced ill blood. It was the condition of his life, and it must be supposed that he liked it. On the next morning he did not scruple to ask his host's advice as to what he had better do, and they agreed to walk across to Goarly's house and to ascertain from the man himself what he thought or might have to say about his own case. On their way they passed up the road leading to Chowton Farm, and at the gate leading into the garden they found Larry Twentyman standing. Morton shook hands with the young farmer and introduced the Senator. Larry was still woe-begone, though he endeavoured to shake off his sorrows and to appear to be gay. 'I never see much of the man,' he said, when they told him that they were going across to call upon his neighbour, 'and I don't know that I want to.'

'He doesn't seem to have much friendship among you all,' said the Senator.

'Quite as much as he deserves, Mr. Gotobed,' replied Larry. The Senator's name had lately become familiar as a household word in Dillsborough, and was, to tell the

truth, odious to such men as Larry Twentyman. 'He's
a thundering rascal, and the only place fit for him in the
county is Rufford gaol. He's like to be there soon,
I think.'

'That's what provokes me,' said the Senator. 'You
think he's a rascal, Mister?'

'I do.'

'And, because you take upon yourself to think so, you'd
send him to Rufford gaol! There was one gentleman
somewhere about here told me he ought to be hung, and
because I would not agree with him, he got up and
walked away from me at table, carrying his provisions
with him. Another man in the next field to this insulted
me because I said I was going to see Goarly. The clergyman in Dillsborough and the hotel-keepers were just as
hard upon me. But you see, Mister, that what we want
to find out is, whether Goarly or the lord has the right of it
in this particular case.'

'I know which has the right without any more finding
out,' said Larry. 'The shortest way to his house is by the
ride through the wood, Mr. Morton. It takes you out on
his land on the other side. But I don't think you'll find
him there. One of my men told me that he had made
himself scarce.' Then he added, as the two were going on,
'I should like to have just a word with you, Mr. Morton.
I've been thinking of what you said, and I know it was
kind. I'll take a month over it. I won't talk of selling
Chowton till the end of February; but if I feel about it
then as I do now, I can't stay.'

'That's right, Mr. Twentyman—and work hard, like
a man, through the month. Go out hunting, and don't
allow yourself a moment for moping.'

'I will,' said Larry, as he retreated to the house; and
then he gave directions that his horse might be ready for
the morrow.

They went in through the wood, and the Senator
pointed out the spot at which Bean the gamekeeper had
been so insolent to him. He could not understand, he
said, why he should be treated so roughly, as these men
must be aware that he had nothing to gain himself. 'If

I were to go into Mikewa,' said Morton, 'and interfere
there with the peculiarities of the people as you have done
here, it's my belief that they'd have had the eyes out of
my head long before this.'

'That only shows that you don't know Mikewa,' said
the Senator. 'Its people are the most law-abiding population on the face of the earth.'

They passed through the wood, and a couple of fields
brought them to Goarly's house. As they approached it
by the back, the only live thing they saw was the old
goose which had been so cruelly deprived of her companions and progeny. The goose was waddling round the
dirty pool, and there were to be seen sundry ugly signs of
a poor man's habitation, but it was not till they had
knocked at the window as well as the door that Mrs.
Goarly showed herself. She remembered the Senator at
once, and curtseyed to him; and when Morton introduced
himself, she curtseyed again to the Squire of Bragton.
When Goarly was asked for, she shook her head, and
declared that she knew nothing about him. He had been
gone, she said, for the last week, and had left no word
as to whither he was going;—nor had he told her why.
'Has he given up his action against Lord Rufford?' asked
the Senator.

'Indeed then, sir, I can't tell you a word about it.'

'I've been told that he has taken Lord Rufford's
money.'

'He ain't 'a taken no money as I've seed, sir. I wish he
had, for money's sore wanted here, and if the gen'leman
has a mind to be kind-hearted——' Then she intimated
her own readiness to take any contribution to the good
cause which the Senator might be willing to make at that
moment. But the Senator buttoned up his breeches
pockets with stern resolution. Though he still believed
Lord Rufford to be altogether wrong, he was beginning
to think that the Goarlys were not worthy his benevolence.
As she came to the door with them and accompanied
them a few yards across the field, she again told the tragic
tale of her goose;—but the Senator had not another word
to say to her.

On that same day, Morton drove Mr. Gotobed into Dillsborough, and consented to go with him to Mr. Bearside's office. They found the attorney at home, and before anything was said as to payment they heard his account of the action. If Goarly had consented to take any money from Lord Rufford, he knew nothing about it. As far as he was aware the action was going on. Ever so many witnesses must be brought from a distance who had seen the crop standing, and who would have no bias against the owner,—as would be the case with neighbours, such as Lawrence Twentyman. Of course it was not easy to oppose such a man as Lord Rufford, and a little money must be spent. Indeed, such, he said, was his interest in the case that he had already gone further than he ought to have done out of his own pocket. Of course, they would be successful,—that is, if the matter were carried on with spirit, and then the money would all come back again. But just at present a little money must be spent. 'I don't mean to spend it,' said the Senator.

'I hope you won't stick to that, Mr. Gotobed.'

'But I shall, sir. I understand from your letter that you look to me for funds.'

'Certainly I do, Mr. Gotobed;—because you told me to do so.'

'I told you nothing of the kind, Mr. Bearside.'

'You paid me £15 on account, Mr. Gotobed.'

'I paid you £15 certainly.'

'And told me that more should be coming as it was wanted. Do you think I should have gone on for such a man as Goarly,—a fellow without a shilling,—unless he had some one like you to back him? It isn't likely. Now, Mr. Morton, I appeal to you.'

'I don't suppose that my friend has made himself liable for your bill because he paid you £15 with the view of assisting Goarly,' said Morton.

'But he said he meant to go on, Mr. Morton; he said that plain, and I can swear it. Now, Mr. Gotobed, you just say out like an honest man whether you didn't give me to understand that you meant to go on.'

'I never employed you or made myself responsible for your bill.'

'You authorized me, distinctly,—most distinctly, and I shall stick to it. When a gentleman comes to a lawyer's office and pays his money, and tells that lawyer as how he means to see the case out,—explaining his reasons as you did when you said all that against the landlords and squires and nobility of this here country, why then that lawyer has a right to think that that gentleman is his mark.'

'I thought you were employed by Mr. Scrobby,' said Morton, who had heard much of the story by this time.

'Then, Mr. Morton, I must make bold to say that you have heard wrong. I know nothing of Mr. Scrobby, and don't want. There ain't nothing about the poisoning of that fox in this case of ours. Scrobby and Goarly may have done that, or Scrobby and Goarly may be as innocent as two babes unborn for aught I know or care. Excuse me, Mr. Morton, but I have to be on my p's and q's, I see. This is a case for trespass and damage against Lord Rufford, in which we ask for 40s. an acre. Of course there is expenses. There's my own time. I ain't to be kept here talking to you two gentlemen for nothing, I suppose. Well, this gentleman comes to me and pays me £15 to go on. I couldn't have gone on without something. The gentleman saw that plain enough. And he told me he'd see me through the rest of it.'

'I said nothing of the kind, sir.'

'Very well. Then we must put it to a jury. May I make bold to ask whether you are going out of the country all at once?'

'I shall be here for the next two months, at least.'

'Happy to hear it, sir, and have no doubt it will all be settled before that time,—amiable or otherwise. But as I am money out of pocket, I did hope you would have paid me something on account to-day.'

Then Mr. Gotobed made his offer, informing Mr. Bearside that he had brought his friend, Mr. Morton, with him in order that there might be a witness. 'I could see that, sir, with half an eye,' said the attorney unabashed. He was willing to pay Mr. Bearside a further sum of £10 immediately to be quit of the affair, not because he thought that any such sum was due, but because he wished to free himself from further trouble in the matter. Mr. Bearside hinted, in a very cavalier way, that £20 might be thought of. A further payment of £20 would cover the money he was out of pocket. But this proposition Mr. Gotobed indignantly refused, and then left the office with his friend. 'Wherever there are lawyers there will be rogues,' said the Senator, as soon as he found himself in the street. 'It is a noble profession, that of the law; the finest that perhaps the work of the world affords; but it gives scope and temptation for roguery. I do not think, however, that you would find anything in America so bad as that.'

'Why did you go to him without asking any questions?'

'Of whom was I to ask questions? When I took up Goarly's case he had already put it into this man's hands.'

'I am sorry you should be troubled, Mr. Gotobed; but, upon my word, I cannot say but what it serves you right.'

'That is because you are offended with me. I endeavoured to protect a poor man against a rich man, and that in this country is cause of offence.'

After leaving the attorney's office they called on Mr. Mainwaring, the rector, and found that they knew, or professed to know, a great deal more about Goarly than they had learned from Bearside. According to his story, Nickem, who was clerk to Mr. Masters, had Goarly in safe keeping somewhere. The rector, indeed, was acquainted with all the details. Scrobby had purchased the red herrings and strychnine, and had employed Goarly to walk over by night to Rufford and fetch them. The poison at that time had been duly packed in the herrings. Goarly had done this, and had, at Scrobby's instigation, laid the bait down in Dillsborough Wood. Nickem was now at work trying to learn where Scrobby had purchased the poison, as it was feared that Goarly's evidence alone would not suffice to convict the man. But if the strychnine could be traced, and the herrings, then there would be almost a certainty of punishing Scrobby.

'And what about Goarly?' asked the Senator.

'He would escape, of course,' said the rector. 'He would get a little money, and after such an experience, would probably become a good friend to fox-hunting.' 'And quite a respectable man!' The rector did not guarantee this, but seemed to think that there would, at any rate, be promise of improved conduct. 'The place ought to be too hot to hold him!' exclaimed the Senator indignantly. The rector seemed to think it possible that he might find it uncomfortable at first, in which case he would sell the land at a good price to Lord Rufford, and every one concerned would have been benefited by the transaction,—except Scrobby, for whom no one would feel any pity.

The two gentlemen then promised to come and dine with the rector on the following day. He feared, he said, that he could not make up a party, as there was, he declared, nobody in Dillsborough. 'I never knew such a place,' said the rector. 'Except old Nupper, who is there? Masters is a very decent fellow himself, but he has got out of that kind of thing;—and you can't ask a man without asking his wife. As for clergymen, I'm sick of dining with my own cloth and discussing the troubles of sermons. There never was such a place as Dillsborough!' Then he whispered a word to the squire. Was the squire unwilling to meet his cousin, Reginald Morton? Things were said, and people never knew what was true and what was false. Then John Morton declared that he would be very happy to meet his cousin.

CHAPTER XLII

MR. MAINWARING'S LITTLE DINNER

THE company at the rector's house consisted of the Senator, the two Mortons, Mr. Surtees the curate, and old Doctor Nupper. Mrs. Mainwaring was not well enough to appear, and the rector therefore was able to indulge himself in what he called a bachelor party. As a rule, he disliked clergymen, but at the last had been driven to invite his curate because he thought six a better

number than five for joviality. He began by asking
questions as to the Trefoils, which were not very fortunate.
Of course he had heard that Morton was to marry
Arabella Trefoil, and though he made no direct allusion
to the fact, as Reginald had done, he spoke in that bland,
eulogistic tone which clearly showed his purpose. 'They
went with you to Lord Rufford's, I was told.'

'Yes; they did.'

'And now they have left the neighbourhood. A very
clever young lady, Miss Trefoil; and so is her mother,
a very clever woman.' The Senator, to whom a sort of
appeal was made, nodded his assent. 'Lord Augustus,
I believe, is a brother of the Duke of Mayfair?'

'Yes, he is,' said Morton. 'I am afraid we are going to
have frost again.' Then Reginald Morton was sure that
the marriage would never take place.

'The Trefoils are a very distinguished family,' continued the rector. 'I remember the present duke's father
when he was in the cabinet, and knew this man almost
intimately when we were at Christ Church together.
I don't think this duke ever took a prominent part in
politics?'

'I don't know that he ever did,' said Morton.

'Dear, dear! how tipsy he was once driving back to
Oxford with me in a gig! But he has the reputation of
being one of the best landlords in the country now.'

'I wonder what it is that gives a man the reputation of
being a good landlord. Is it foxes?' asked the Senator.
The rector acknowledged with a smile that foxes helped.
'Or does it mean that he lets his land below the value?
If so, he certainly does more harm than good, though he
may like the popularity which he is rich enough to buy.'

'It means that he does not exact more than his due,'
said the rector, indiscreetly.

'When I hear a man so highly praised for common
honesty I am, of course, led to suppose that dishonesty in
his particular trade is the common rule. The body of
English landlords must be exorbitant tyrants when one
among them is so highly eulogised for taking no more
than his own.' Luckily, at that moment dinner was

announced, and the exceptional character of the Duke of Mayfair was allowed to drop.

Mr. Mainwaring's dinner was very good and his wines were excellent,—a fact of which Mr. Mainwaring himself was much better aware than any of his guests. There is a difficulty in the giving of dinners, of which Mr. Mainwaring and some other hosts have become painfully aware. What service do you do to any one in pouring your best claret down his throat, when he knows no difference between that and a much more humble vintage,—your best claret, which you feel so sure you cannot replace? Why import canvas-back ducks for appetites which would be quite as well satisfied with those out of the next farmyard? Your soup, which has been a care since yesterday, your fish, got down with so much trouble from Bond Street on that very day, your saddle of mutton, in selecting which you have affronted every butcher in the neighbourhood, are all plainly thrown away! And yet the hospitable hero who would fain treat his friends as he would be treated himself can hardly arrange his dinners according to the palates of his different guests; nor will he like, when strangers sit at his board, to put nothing better on his table than that cheaper wine with which needful economy induces him to solace himself when alone. I,—I who write this,—have myself seen an honoured guest deluge with the pump my, ah! so hardly earned, most scarce and most peculiar vintage! There is a pang in such usage which some will not understand, but which cut Mr. Mainwaring to the very soul. There was not one among them there who appreciated the fact that the claret on his dinner table was almost the best that its year had produced. It was impossible not to say a word on such a subject at such a moment;—though our rector was not a man who usually lauded his own viands. 'I think you will find that claret what you like, Mr. Gotobed,' he said. 'It's a '57 Mouton, and judges say that it is good.'

'Very good indeed,' said the Senator. 'In the States we haven't got into the way yet of using dinner clarets.' It was as good as a play to see the rector wince under the ignominious word. 'Your great statesman added much to your national comfort when he took the duty off the lighter kinds of French wines.'

The rector could not stand it. He hated light wines. He hated cheap things in general. And he hated Gladstone in particular. 'Nothing,' said he, 'that the statesman you speak of ever did could make such wine as that any cheaper. I am sorry, sir, that you don't perceive the difference.'

'In the matter of wine,' said the Senator, 'I don't think that I have happened to come across anything so good in this country as our old Madeiras. But then, sir, we have been fortunate in our climate. The English atmosphere is not one in which wine seems to reach its full perfection.' The rector heaved a deep sigh as he looked up to the ceiling with his hands in his trowsers-pockets. He knew, or thought that he knew, that no one could ever get a glass of good wine in the United States. He knew, or thought that he knew, that the best wine in the world was brought to England. He knew, or thought he knew, that in no other country was wine so well understood, so diligently sought for, and so truly enjoyed as in England. And he imagined that it was less understood and less sought for and less enjoyed in the States than in any other country. He did not as yet know the Senator well enough to fight with him at his own table, and could only groan and moan and look up at the ceiling. Doctor Nupper endeavoured to take away the sting by smacking his lips, and Reginald Morton, who did not in truth care a straw what he drank, was moved to pity and declared the claret to be very fine. 'I have nothing to say against it,' said the Senator, who was not in the least abashed.

But when the cloth was drawn,—for the rector clung so lovingly to old habits that he delighted to see his mahogany beneath the wine glasses,—a more serious subject of dispute arose suddenly, though perhaps hardly more disagreeable. 'The thing in England,' said the Senator, 'which I find most difficult to understand, is the matter of what you call Church patronage.'

'If you'll pass half an hour with Mr. Surtees to-morrow

morning, he'll explain it all to you,' said the rector, who did not like that any subject connected with his profession should be mooted after dinner.

'I should be delighted,' said Mr. Surtees.

'Nothing would give me more pleasure,' said the Senator; 'but what I mean is this:—the question is, of course, one of paramount importance.'

'No doubt it is,' said the deluded rector.

'It is very necessary to get good doctors.'

'Well, yes, rather;—considering that all men wish to live.' That observation, of course, came from Doctor Nupper.

'And care is taken in employing a lawyer,—though, after my experience of yesterday, not always, I should say, so much care as is needful. The man who wants such aid looks about him and gets the best doctor he can for his money, or the best lawyer. But here in England he must take the clergyman provided for him.'

'It would be very much better for him if he did,' said the rector.

'A clergyman, at any rate, is supposed to be appointed; and that clergyman he must pay.'

'Not at all,' said the rector. 'The clergy are paid by the wise provision of former ages.'

'We will let that pass for the present,' said the Senator. 'There he is, however he may be paid. How does he get there?' Now it was the fact that Mr. Mainwaring's living had been bought for him with his wife's money,—a fact of which Mr. Gotobed was not aware, but which he would hardly have regarded had he known it. 'How does he get there?'

'In the majority of cases the bishop puts him there,' said Mr. Surtees.

'And how is the bishop governed in his choice? As far as I can learn the stipends are absurdly various, one man getting £100 a year for working like a horse in a big town, and another £1000 for living an idle life in a luxurious country house. But the bishop, of course, gives the bigger plums to the best men. How is it then that the big plums find their way so often to the sons and sons-in-law and nephews of the bishops?'

'Because the bishop has looked after their education and principles,' said the rector.

'And taught them how to choose their wives,' said the Senator, with imperturbable gravity.

'I am not the son of a bishop, sir,' exclaimed the rector.

'I wish you had been, sir, if it would have done you any good. A general can't make his son a colonel at the age of twenty-five, or an admiral his son a first lieutenant, or a judge his a Queen's Counsellor,—nor can the head of an office promote his to be a chief secretary. It is only a bishop can do this;—I suppose because a cure of souls is so much less important than the charge of a ship or the discipline of twenty or thirty clerks.'

'The bishops don't do it,' said the rector fiercely.

'Then the statistics which have been put into my hands belie them. But how is it with those the bishops don't appoint? There seems to me to be such a complication of absurdities as to defy explanation.'

'I think I could explain them all,' said Mr. Surtees mildly.

'If you can do so satisfactorily, I shall be very glad to hear it,' continued the Senator, who seemed, in truth, to be glad to hear no one but himself. 'A lad of one-and-twenty learns his lessons so well that he has to be rewarded at his college, and a part of his reward consists in his having a parish entrusted to him when he is forty years old, to which he can maintain his right whether he be in any way trained for such work or no. Is that true?'

'His collegiate education is the best training he can have,' said the rector.

'I came across a young fellow the other day,' continued the Senator, 'in a very nice house, with £700 a year, and learned that he had inherited the living because he was his father's second son. Some poor clergyman had been keeping it ready for him for the last fifteen years and had to turn out as soon as this young spark could be made a clergyman.'

'It was his father's property,' said the rector, 'and the poor man had had great kindness shown him for those fifteen years.'

'Exactly;—his father's property! And this was what you call a cure of souls! And another man had absolutely had his living bought for him by his uncle,—just as he might have bought him a farm. He couldn't have bought him the command of a regiment or a small judgeship. In those matters you require capacity. It is only when you deal with the Church that you throw to the winds all ideas of fitness. "Sir," or "Madam," or perhaps, "my little dear, you are bound to come to your places in church and hear me expound the word of God, because I paid a heavy sum of money for the privilege of teaching you, at the moderate salary of £600 a year!"'

Mr. Surtees sat aghast with his mouth open, and knew not how to say a word. Doctor Nupper rubbed his red nose. Reginald Morton attempted some suggestion about the wine, which fell wretchedly flat. John Morton ventured to tell his friend that he did not understand the subject. 'I shall be most happy to be instructed,' said the Senator.

'Understand it!' said the rector, almost rising in his chair to rebuke the insolence of his guest—'He understands nothing about it, and yet he ventures to fall foul with unmeasured terms on an establishment which has been brought to its present condition by the fostering care of perhaps the most pious set of divines that ever lived, and which has produced results, with which those of no other Church can compare!'

'Have I represented anything untruly?' asked the Senator.

'A great deal, sir.'

'Only put me right, and no man will recall his words more readily. Is it not the case that livings in the Church of England can be bought and sold?'

'The matter is one, sir,' said the rector, 'which cannot be discussed in this manner. There are two clergymen present to whom such language is distasteful; as it is also, I hope, to the others, who are all members of the Church of England. Perhaps you will allow me to request that the subject may be changed.' After that, conversation flagged, and the evening was by no means joyous. The

rector certainly regretted that his "'57' claret should have
been expended on such a man. 'I don't think,' said he,
when John Morton had taken the Senator away, 'that in
my whole life before I ever met such a brute as that
American Senator.'

Chapter XLIII

PERSECUTION

THERE was great consternation in the attorney's
house after the writing of the letter to Lawrence
Twentyman. For twenty-four hours Mrs. Masters did not
speak to Mary, not at all intending to let her sin pass with
such moderate punishment as that, but thinking during
that period that, as she might perhaps induce Larry to
ignore the letter, and look upon it as though it were not
written, it would be best to say nothing till the time
should come in which the lover might again urge his suit.
But when she found on the evening of the second day
that Larry did not come near the place, she could control
herself no longer, and accused her step-daughter of ruining herself, her father, and the whole family. 'That is very
unfair, mamma,' Mary said. 'I have done nothing. I
have only not done that which nobody had a right to ask
me to do.'

'Right indeed! And who are you with your rights?
A decent, well-behaved young man with five or six hundred
a year has no right to ask you to be his wife! All this
comes of you staying with an old woman with a handle
to her name.'

It was in vain that Mary endeavoured to explain that
she had not alluded to Larry when she declared that no
one had a right to ask her to do it. She had, she said,
always thanked him for his good opinion of her, and had
spoken well of him whenever his name was mentioned.
But it was a matter on which a young woman was entitled
to judge for herself, and no one had a right to scold her
because she could not love him. Mrs. Masters hated such
arguments, despised this rhodomontade*about love, and
would have crushed the girl into obedience could it have

been possible. 'You are an idiot,' she said, 'an ungrateful idiot; and unless you think better of it, you'll repent your folly to your dying day. Who do you think is to come running after a moping slut like you?' Then Mary gathered herself up and left the room, feeling that she could not live in the house if she were to be called a slut.

Soon after this, Larry came to the attorney and got him to come out into the street, and to walk with him round the churchyard. It was the spot in Dillsborough in which they would most certainly be left undisturbed. This took place on the day before his proposition for the sale of Chowton Farm. When he got the attorney into the churchyard, he took out Mary's letter and in speechless agony handed it to the attorney. 'I saw it before it went,' said Masters, putting it back with his hand.

'I suppose she means it?' asked Larry.

'I can't say to you but what she does, Twentyman. As far as I know her, she isn't a girl that would ever say anything that she didn't mean.'

'I was sure of that. When I got it and read it, it was just as though some one had come behind me and hit me over the head with a wheel-spoke. I couldn't have ate a morsel of breakfast if I knew I wasn't to see another bit of food for four and twenty hours.'

'I knew you would feel it, Larry.'

'Feel it! Till it came to this I didn't think of myself but what I had more strength. It has knocked me about till I feel all over like drinking.'

'Don't do that, Larry.'

'I won't answer for myself what I'll do. A man sets his heart on a thing,—just on one thing,—and has grit enough in him to be sure of himself that if he can get that, nothing shall knock him over. When that thoroughbred mare of mine slipped her foal, who can say I ever whimpered? When I got pleuro* among the cattle, I killed a'most the lot of 'em out of hand, and never laid awake a night about it. But I've got it so heavy this time I can't stand it. You don't think I have any chance, Mr. Masters?'

'You can try, of course. You're welcome to the house.'

'But what do you think? You must know her.'

'Girls do change their minds.'

'But she isn't like other girls. Is she now? I come to you because I sometimes think Mrs. Masters is a little hard on her. Mrs. Masters is about the best friend I have. There isn't anybody more on my side than she is. But I feel sure of this;—Mary will never be drove.'

'I don't think she will, Larry.'

'She's got a will of her own as well as another.'

'No man alive ever had a better daughter.'

'I'm sure of that, Mr. Masters; and no man alive'll ever have a better wife. But she won't be drove. I might ask her again, you think?'

'You certainly have my leave.'

'But would it be any good? I'd rather cut my throat, and have done with it, than go about teasing her because her parents let me come to her.' Then there was a pause during which they walked on, the attorney feeling that he had nothing more to say. 'What I want to know,' said Larry, 'is this. Is there anybody else?'

That was just the point on which the attorney himself was perplexed. He had asked Mary that question, and her silence had assured him that it was so. Then he had suggested to her the name of the only probable suitor that occurred to him, and she had repelled the idea in a manner that had convinced him at once. There was some one, but Mr. Surtees was not the man. There was some one, he was sure, but he had not been able to cross-examine her on the subject. He had, since that, cudgelled his brain to think who that some one might be, but had not succeeded in suggesting a name even to himself. That of Reginald Morton, who hardly ever came to the house, and whom he regarded as a silent, severe, unapproachable man, did not come into his mind. Among the young ladies of Dillsborough Reginald Morton was never regarded as even a possible lover. And yet there was assuredly some one. 'If there is any one else, I think you ought to tell me,' continued Larry.

'It is quite possible.'

'Young Surtees, I suppose?'

'I do not say there is anybody; but if there be anybody, I do not think it is Surtees.'

'Who else, then?'

'I cannot say, Larry. I know nothing about it.'

'But there is some one?'

'I do not say so. You ask me, and I tell you all I know.'

Again they walked round the churchyard in silence, and the attorney began to be anxious that the interview might be over. He hardly liked to be interrogated about the state of his daughter's heart, and yet he had felt himself bound to tell what he knew to the man who had in all respects behaved well to him. When they had returned for the third or fourth time to the gate by which they had entered Larry spoke again. 'I suppose I may as well give it up?'

'What can I say?'

'You have been fair enough, Mr. Masters. And so has she. And so has everybody. I shall just get away as quick as I can, and go and hang myself. I feel above bothering her any more. When she sat down to write a letter like that she must have been in earnest.'

'She certainly was in earnest, Larry.'

'What's the use of going on after that? Only it is so hard for a fellow to feel that everything is gone. It is just as though the house was burnt down, and I was to wake in the morning and find that the land didn't belong to me.'

'Not so bad as that, Larry.'

'Not so bad, Mr. Masters! Then you don't know what it is I'm feeling. I'd let his lordship or Squire Morton have it all, and go in upon it as a tenant at 30s. an acre, so that I could take her along with me. I would, and sell the horses and set to and work in my shirt-sleeves. A man could stand that. Nobody wouldn't laugh at me then. But there's an emptiness now here that makes me sick all through, as though I hadn't got stomach left for anything.'

Then poor Larry put his hand upon his heart, and hid his face upon the churchyard wall. The attorney made some attempt to say a kind word to him, and then, leaving him there, slowly made his way back to his office.

We already know what first step Larry took with the intention of running away from his cares. In the house at Dillsborough things were almost as bad as they were with him. Over and over again Mrs. Masters had told her husband that it was all his fault, and that if he had torn the letter when it was showed to him everything would have been right by the end of the two months. This he bore with what equanimity he could, shutting himself up very much in his office, occasionally escaping for a quarter of an hour of ease to his friends at the Bush, and eating his meals in silence. But when he became aware that his girl was being treated with cruelty, that she was never spoken to by her stepmother without harsh words, and that her sisters were encouraged to be disdainful to her, then his heart rose within him and he rebelled. He declared aloud that Mary should not be persecuted, and if this kind of thing were continued, he would defend his girl, let the consequences be what they might.

'What are you going to defend her against?' asked his wife.

'I won't have her ill-used because she refuses to marry at your bidding.'

'Bah! You know as much how to manage a girl as though you were an old maid yourself. Cocker her up and make her think that nothing is good enough for her. Break her spirit, and make her come round, and teach her to know what it is to have an honest man's house offered to her. If she don't take Larry Twentyman's, she's like to have none of her own before long.' But Mr. Masters would not assent to this plan of breaking his girl's spirit, and so there was continual war in the place, and every one there was unhappy.

Mary herself was so unhappy that she convinced herself that it was necessary that some change should be made. Then she remembered Lady Ushant's offer of a home, and not only the offer, but the old lady's assurance that to herself such an arrangement, if possible, would be very comfortable. She did not suggest to herself that she would leave her father's home for ever and always; but it might be that an absence of some months might relieve the absolute misery of their present mode of living. The effect on her father was so sad that she was almost driven to regret that he should have taken her own part. Her stepmother was not a bad woman, nor did Mary even now think her to be bad. She was a hardworking, painstaking wife, with a good general idea of justice. In the division of puddings and pies and other material comforts of the household she would deal evenly between her own children and her stepdaughter. She had not desired to send Mary away to an inadequate home, or with a worthless husband. But when the proper home and the proper man were there she was prepared to use any amount of hardship to secure these good things to the family generally. This hardship Mary could not endure, nor could Mary's father on her behalf, and therefore Mary prepared a letter to Lady Ushant, in which, at great length, she told her old friend the whole story. She spoke as tenderly as was possible of all concerned, but declared that her stepmother's feelings on the subject were so strong that every one in the house was made wretched. Under these circumstances—for her father's sake if only for that—she thought herself bound to leave the house. 'It is quite impossible,' she said, 'that I should do as they wish me. That is a matter on which a young woman must judge for herself. If you could have me for a few months it would, perhaps, all pass by. I should not dare to ask this but for what you said yourself; and, dear Lady Ushant, pray remember that I do not want to be idle. There are a great many things I can do; and though I know that nothing can pay for kindness, I might perhaps be able not to be a burden.' Then she added in a postscript, 'Papa is everything that is kind; but then all this makes him so miserable!'

When she had kept the letter by her for a day she showed it to her father, and by his consent it was sent. After much consultation it was agreed between them that nothing should be said about it to Mrs. Masters till the answer should come; and that, should the answer be favourable, the plan should be carried out in spite of any domestic opposition. In this letter Mary told, as accurately as she could, the whole story of Larry's courtship, and was very clear in declaring that, under no possible circumstances, could she encourage any hope. But, of course, she said not a word as to any other man, or as to any love on her side. 'Have you told her everything?' said her father as he closed the letter.

'Yes, papa; everything that there is to be told.' Then there arose within his own bosom an immense desire to know that secret, so that, if possible, he might do something to relieve her pain; but he could not bring himself to ask further questions.

Lady Ushant, on receiving the letter, much doubted what she ought to do. She acknowledged at once Mary's right to appeal to her, and assured herself that the girl's presence would be a comfort and a happiness to herself. If Mary were quite alone in the world, Lady Ushant would have been at once prepared to give her a home. But she doubted as to the propriety of taking the girl from her own family. She doubted even whether it would not be better that Mary should be left within the influence of Larry Twentyman's charms. A settlement, an income, and mutual comforts for life are very serious things to all people who have reached Lady Ushant's age. And then she had a doubt within her own mind whether Mary might not be debarred from accepting this young man by some unfortunate preference for Reginald Morton. She had seen them together, and had suspected something of the truth before it had glimmered before the eyes of any one in Dillsborough. Had Reginald been so inclined, Lady Ushant would have been very glad to see him marry Mary Masters. For both their sakes she would have preferred such a match to one with the owner of Chowton Farm. But she did not think that Reginald himself was that way minded, and she fancied that poor Mary might be throwing away her prosperity in life were she to wait for Reginald's love. Larry Twentyman was, at any rate, sure; and perhaps it might be unwise to separate the girl from her lover.

In her doubt she determined to refer the case to Reginald himself, and instead of writing to Mary she wrote to him. She did not send him Mary's letter,—which would, she felt, have been a breach of faith; nor did she mention the name of Larry Twentyman. But she told him that Mary had proposed to come to Cheltenham for a long visit because there were disturbances at home,— which disturbances had arisen from her rejection of a certain suitor. Lady Ushant said a great deal as to the inexpediency of fostering family quarrels, and suggested that Mary might perhaps have been a little impetuous. The presence of this lover could hardly do her much injury. These were not days in which young women were forced to marry men. What did he, Reginald Morton, think about it? He was to remember that as far as she herself was concerned, she dearly loved Mary Masters and would be delighted to have her at Cheltenham; and, so remembering, he was to see the attorney, and Mary herself, and if necessary Mrs. Masters;—and then to report his opinion to Cheltenham.

Then, fearing that her nephew might be away for a day or two, or that he might not be able to perform his commission instantly, and thinking that Mary might be unhappy if she received no immediate reply to such a request as hers had been, Lady Ushant by the same post wrote to her young friend as follows:—

'DEAR MARY,
    'Reginald will go over and see your father about your proposition. As far as I myself am concerned, nothing would give me so much pleasure. This is quite sincere. But the matter is in other respects very important. Of course I have kept your letter all to myself, and in writing to Reginald I have mentioned no names.
                        'Your affectionate friend,
                                'MARGARET USHANT.'

Chapter XLIV

'PARTICULARLY PROUD OF YOU'

ARABELLA TREFOIL left her uncle's mansion on the day after her lover's departure, certainly not in triumph, but with somewhat recovered spirits. When she first heard that Lord Rufford was gone,—that he had fled away, as it were, in the middle of the night without saying a word to her, without a syllable to make good the slight assurances of his love that had been given to her in the post carriage, she felt that she was deserted and betrayed. And when she found herself altogether neglected on the following day, and that the slightly valuable impression which she had made on her aunt was apparently gone, she did for half an hour think in earnest of the Paragon and Patagonia. But after a while she called to mind all that she knew of great efforts successfully made in opposition to almost overwhelming difficulties. She had heard of forlorn hopes, and perhaps in her young days had read something of Cæsar still clinging to his Commentaries as he struggled in the waves? This was her forlorn hope, and she would be as brave as any soldier of them all. Lord Rufford's embraces were her Commentaries, and let the winds blow and the waves roll as they might, she would still cling to them. After lunch she spoke to her aunt with great courage,—as the duchess thought, with great effrontery. 'My uncle wouldn't speak to Lord Rufford before he went?'

'How could he speak to a man who ran away from his house in that way?'

'The running away as you call it, aunt, did not take place till two days after I told you all about it. I thought he would have done as much as that for his brother's daughter.'

'I don't believe in it at all,' said the duchess sternly.

'Don't believe in what, aunt? You don't mean to say that you don't believe that Lord Rufford has asked me to be his wife!' Then she paused, but the duchess absolutely lacked the courage to express her conviction again. 'I don't suppose it signifies much,' continued Arabella, 'but of course it would have been something to me that Lord Rufford should have known that the duke was anxious for my welfare. He was quite prepared to have assured my uncle of his intentions.'

'Then why didn't he speak himself?'

'Because the duke is not my father. Really, aunt, when I hear you talk of his running away I do feel it to be unkind. As if we didn't all know that a man like that goes and comes as he pleases. It was just before dinner that he got the message, and was he to run round and wish everybody good-bye like a schoolgirl going to bed?'

The duchess was almost certain that no message had come, and, from various little things which she had observed and from tidings which reached her, very much doubted whether Arabella had known anything of his intended going. She, too, had a maid of her own who on occasions could bring information. But she had nothing further to say on the subject. If Arabella should ever become Lady Rufford she would, of course, among other visitors be occasionally received at Mistletoe. She could never be a favourite, but things would to a certain degree have rectified themselves. But if, as the duchess expected, no such marriage took place, then this ill-conducted niece should never be admitted within the house again.

Later on in the afternoon, some hours after it became dusk, Arabella contrived to meet her aunt in the hall with a letter in her hand, and asked where the letter-box was. She knew where to deposit her letters as well as did the duchess herself; but she desired an opportunity of proclaiming what she had done. 'I am writing to Lord Rufford. Perhaps as I am in your house I ought to tell you what I have done.'

'The letter-box is in the billiard-room, close to the door,' said the duchess, passing on. Then she added as she went, 'The post for to-day has gone already.'

'His lordship will have to wait a day for his letter. I dare say it won't break his heart,' said Arabella, as she turned away to the billiard-room.

All this had been planned; and, moreover, she had so

written her letter that if her magnificent aunt should
condescend to tamper with it all that was in it should
seem to corroborate her own story. The duchess would
have considered herself disgraced if ever she had done
such a thing; but the niece of the duchess did not quite
understand that this would be so. The letter was as
follows:

'Mistletoe, 19th Jany., 1875.
'DEAREST R.,

'Your going off like that was, after all, very horrid.
My aunt thinks that you were running away from me.
I think that you were running away from her. Which
was true? In real earnest I don't for a moment think that
either I or the duchess had anything to do with it, and
that you did go because some horrid man wrote and
asked you. I know you don't like being bound by any of
the conventionalities. I hope there is such a word, and
that if not you'll understand it just the same.

'Oh, Peltry,—and oh, Jack,—and oh, that road back to
Stamford! I am so stiff that I can't sit upright, and everybody is cross to me, and everything is uncomfortable.
What horrible things women are! There isn't one here,
not even old Lady Rumpus, who hasn't an unmarried
daughter left in the world, who isn't jealous of me, because—because——. I must leave you to guess why they
all hate me so! And I'm sure if you had given Jack to any
other woman I should hate her, though you may give
every horse you have to any man that you please. I
wonder whether I shall have another day's hunting before
it is all over. I suppose not. It was almost by a miracle
that we managed yesterday—only fancy—yesterday! It
seems to be an age ago!

'Pray, pray, pray write to me at once,—to the Connop
Greens' so that I may get a nice, soft, pleasant word
directly I get among those nasty, hard, unpleasant people.
They have lots of money, and plenty of furniture, and I
dare say the best things to eat and drink in the world, but
nothing else. There will be no Jack; and if there were,
alas! alas! no one to show me the way to ride him.

'I start to-morrow, and, as far as I understand, shall

have to make my way into Hampshire all by myself, with only such security as my maid can give me. I shall make her go in the same carriage, and shall have the gratification of looking at her all the way. I suppose I ought not to say that I will shut my eyes and try to think that somebody else is there.

'Good-bye, dear, dear R. I shall be dying for a letter from you. Yours ever, with all my heart.—A.

'I shall write you such a serious epistle when I get to the Greens'.'

This was not such a letter as she thought that her aunt would approve; but it was, she fancied, such as the duchess would believe that she would write to her lover. And if it were allowed to go on its way, it would make Lord Rufford feel that she was neither alarmed nor displeased by the suddenness of his departure. But it was not expected to do much good. It might produce some short, joking, half-affectionate reply, but would not draw from him that serious word which was so necessary for the success of her scheme. Therefore, she had told him that she intended to prepare a serious missile. Should this pleasant little message of love miscarry, the serious missile would still be sent, and the miscarriage would occasion no harm.

But then further plans were necessary. It might be that Lord Rufford would take no notice of the serious missile, which she thought very probable. Or it might be that he would send back a serious reply, in which he would calmly explain to her that she had unfortunately mistaken his sentiments, which she believed would be a stretch of manhood beyond his reach. But in either case she would be prepared with the course which she would follow. In the first, she would begin by forcing her father to write him a letter which she herself would dictate. In the second, she would set the whole family at him as far as the family were within her reach. With her cousin, Lord Mistletoe, who was only two years older than herself, she had always held pleasant relations. They had been children together, and as they had grown up the

young lord had liked his pretty cousin. Latterly they had
seen each other but rarely, and therefore the feeling still
remained. She would tell Lord Mistletoe her whole story,
—that is, the story as she would please to tell it,—and
implore his aid. Her father should be driven to demand
from Lord Rufford an execution of his alleged promises.
She herself would write such a letter to the duke as an
uncle should be unable not to notice. She would move
heaven and earth as to her wrongs. She thought that if
her friends would stick to her, Lord Rufford would be
weak as water in their hands. But it must be all done
immediately, so that if everything failed she might be
ready to start to Patagonia some time in April. When she
looked back and remembered that it was hardly more
than two months since she had been taken to Rufford
Hall by Mr. Morton she could not accuse herself of having
lost any time.

In London she met her mother,—as to which meeting
there had been some doubt—and underwent the tortures
of a close examination. She had thought it prudent on
this occasion to tell her mother something, but not to tell
anything quite truly. 'He has proposed to me,' she said.

'He has!' said Lady Augustus, holding up her hands
almost in awe.

'Is there anything so wonderful in that?'

'Then it is all arranged? Does the duke know it?'

'It is not all arranged by any means, and the duke does
know it. Now, mamma, after that I must decline to
answer any more questions. I have done all this myself,
and I mean to continue it in the same way.'

'Did he speak to the duke? You will tell me that?'

'I will tell you nothing.'

'You will drive me mad, Arabella.'

'That will be better than your driving me mad just at
present. You ought to feel that I have a great deal to
think of.'

'And have not I?'

'You can't help me;—not at present.'

'But he did propose,—in absolute words?'

'Mamma, what a goose you are! Do you suppose that

men do it all now just as it is done in books? "Miss
Arabella Trefoil, will you do me the honour to become
my wife?" Do you think that Lord Rufford would ask
the question in that way?"

'It is a very good way.'

'Any way is a good way that answers the purpose. He
has proposed, and I mean to make him stick to it.'

'You doubt, then?'

'Mamma, you are so silly. Do you not know what such
a man is well enough to be sure that he'll change his
mind half a dozen times if he can? I don't mean to let
him; and now, after that, I won't say another word.'

'I have got a letter here from Mr. Short saying that
something must be fixed about Mr. Morton.' Mr. Short
was the lawyer who had been instructed to prepare the
settlements.

'Mr. Short may do whatever he likes,' said Arabella.
There were very hot words between them that night in
London, but the mother could obtain no further informa-
tion from her daughter.

That serious epistle had been commenced even before
Arabella had left Mistletoe; but the composition was one
which required great care, and it was not completed and
copied and re-copied till she had been two days in Hampshire. Not even when it was finished did she say a word
to her mother about it. She had doubted much as to the
phrases which in such an emergency she ought to use, but
she thought it safer to trust to herself than to her mother.
In writing such a letter as that posted at Mistletoe she
believed herself to be happy. She could write it quickly,
and understood that she could convey to her correspondent some sense of her assumed mood. But her
serious letter would, she feared, be stiff and repulsive.
Whether her fears were right the reader shall judge, for
the letter when written was as follows:—

'Marygold Place, Basingstoke,
'Saturday.

'MY DEAR LORD RUFFORD,

'You will, I suppose, have got the letter that I wrote
before I left Mistletoe, and which I directed to Mr.

Surbiton's. There was not much in it, except a word or two as to your going and as to my desolation, and just a reminiscence of the hunting. There was no reproach that you should have left me without any farewell, or that you should have gone so suddenly, after saying so much, without saying more. I wanted you to feel that you had made me very happy, and not to feel that your departure in such a way had robbed me of part of the happiness.

'It was a little bad of you, because it did, of course, leave me to the hardness of my aunt, and because all the other women there would, of course, follow her. She had inquired about our journey home,—that dear journey home,—and I had, of course, told her,——well I had better say it out at once; I told her that we were engaged. You, I am sure, will think that the truth was best. She wanted to know why you did not go to the duke. I told her that the duke was not my father; but that, as far as I was concerned, the duke might speak to you or not as he pleased. I had nothing to conceal. I am very glad he did not, because he is pompous, and you would have been bored. If there is one thing I desire more than another it is that nothing belonging to me shall ever be a bore to you. I hope I may never stand in the way of anything that may gratify you,—as I said when you lit that cigar. You will have forgotten, I dare say. But, dear Rufford,— dearest; I may say that, mayn't I?—say something, or do something, to make me satisfied. You know what I mean, don't you? It isn't that I'm a bit afraid myself. I don't think so little of myself, or so badly of you. But I don't like other women to look at me as though I ought not to be proud of anything. I am proud of everything; particularly proud of you,—and of Jack.

'Now there is my serious epistle, and I am sure that you will answer it like a dear, good, kind-hearted, loving— lover. I won't be afraid of writing the word, nor of saying that I love you with all my heart, and that I am always your own

'ARABELLA.'

She kept the letter till the Sunday, thinking that she

might have an answer to that written from Mistletoe, and that his reply might alter its tone, or induce her to put it aside altogether; but when on Sunday morning none came, her own was sent. The word in it which frightened herself was the word 'engaged'. She tried various other phrases, but declared to herself at last that it was useless to 'beat about the bush'. He must know the light in which she was pleased to regard those passages of love which she had permitted, so that there might be no mistake. Whether the letter would be to his liking or not, it must be of such a nature that it would certainly draw from him an answer on which she could act. She herself did not like the letter; but, considering her difficulties, we may own that it was not much amiss.

CHAPTER XLV

LORD RUFFORD MAKES UP HIS MIND

AS it happened, Lord Rufford got the two letters together, the cause of which was as follows:

When he ran away from Mistletoe, as he certainly did, he had thought much about that journey home in the carriage, and was quite aware that he had made an ass of himself. As he sat at dinner on that day at Mistletoe his neighbour had said some word to him in joke as to his attachment to Miss Trefoil, and after the ladies had left the room another neighbour of the other sex had hoped that he had had a pleasant time on the road. Again, in the drawing-room it had seemed to him that he was observed. He could not refrain from saying a few words to Arabella as she lay on the sofa. Not to do so after what had occurred would have been in itself peculiar. But when he did so, some other man who was near her made way for him, as though she were acknowledged to be altogether his property. And then the duchess had striven to catch him, and lead him into a special conversation. When this attempt was made he decided that he must at once retreat,—or else make up his mind to marry the young lady. And therefore he retreated.

He breakfasted that morning at the inn at Stamford, and as he smoked his cigar afterwards, he positively resolved that he would under no circumstances marry Arabella Trefoil. He was being hunted and run down, and, with the instinct of all animals that are hunted, he prepared himself for escape. It might be said, no doubt would be said, that he behaved badly. That would be said because it would not be open to him to tell the truth. The lady in such a case can always tell her story, with what exaggeration she may please to give, and can complain. The man never can do so. When inquired into, he cannot say that he has been pursued. He cannot tell her friends that she began it, and, in point of fact, did it all. 'She would fall into my arms; she would embrace me; she persisted in asking me whether I loved her!' Though a man have to be shot for it, or kicked for it, or even though he have to endure perpetual scorn for it, he cannot say that let it be ever so true. And yet is a man to be forced into a marriage which he despises? He would not be forced into the marriage,—and the sooner he retreated the less would be the metaphorical shooting and kicking and the real scorn. He must get out of it as best he could;—but that he would get out of it he was quite determined.

That afternoon he reached Mr. Surbiton's house, as did also Captain Battersby, and his horses, grooms, and other belongings. When there he received a lot of letters, and among others one from Mr. Runciman, of the Bush, inquiring as to a certain hiring of rooms and preparation for a dinner or dinners which had been spoken of in reference to a final shooting decreed to take place in the neighbourhood of Dillsborough in the last week of January. Such things were often planned by Lord Rufford, and afterwards forgotten or neglected. When he declared his purpose to Runciman, he had not intended to go to Mistletoe, nor to stay so long with his friend Surbiton. But now he almost thought that it would be better for him to be back at Rufford Hall, where at present his sister was staying with her husband, Sir George Penwether.

In the evening of the second or third day his old friend Tom Surbiton said a few words to him which had the effect of sending him back to Rufford. They had sat out the rest of the men who formed the party and were alone in the smoking-room. 'So you're going to marry Miss Trefoil,' said Tom Surbiton, who perhaps of all his friends was the most intimate.

'Who says so?'

'I am saying so at present.'

'You are not saying it on your own authority. You have never seen me and Miss Trefoil in a room together.'

'Everybody says so. Of course such a thing cannot be arranged without being talked about.'

'It has not been arranged.'

'If you don't mean to have it arranged, you had better look to it. I am speaking in earnest, Rufford. I am not going to give up authorities. Indeed if I did I might give up everybody. The very servants suppose that they know it, and there isn't a groom or horseboy about who isn't in his heart congratulating the young lady on her promotion.'

'I'll tell you what it is, Tom.'

'Well;—what is it?'

'If this had come from any other man than yourself I should quarrel with him. I am not engaged to the young lady, nor have I done anything to warrant anybody in saying so.'

'Then I may contradict it.'

'I don't want you either to contradict it or affirm it. It would be an impertinence to the young lady if I were to instruct any one to contradict such a report. But, as a fact, I am not engaged to marry Miss Trefoil, nor is there the slightest chance that I ever shall be so engaged.' So saying, he took up his candlestick and walked off.

Early on the next morning he saw his friend and made some sort of laughing apology for his heat on the previous evening. 'It is so d—— hard when these kind of things are said because a man has lent a young lady a horse. However, Tom, between you and me the thing is a lie.'

'I am very glad to hear it,' said Tom.

'And now I want you to come over to Rufford on the twenty-eighth.' Then he explained the details of his proposed party, and got his friend to promise that he would come. He also made it understood that he was going home at once. There were a hundred things, he said, which made it necessary. So the horses and grooms and servant and portmanteaus were again made to move, and Lord Rufford left his friend on that day and went up to London on his road to Rufford.

He was certainly disturbed in his mind, foreseeing that there might be much difficulty in his way. He remembered with fair accuracy all that had occurred during the journey from Stamford to Mistletoe. He felt assured that up to that time he had said nothing which could be taken to mean a real declaration of love. All that at Rufford had been nothing. He had never said a word which could justify the girl in a hope. In the carriage she had asked him whether he loved her, and he had said that he did. He had also declared that he would do anything in his power to make her happy. Was a man to be bound to marry a girl because of such a scene as that? There was, however, nothing for him to do except to keep out of the girl's way. If she took any steps, then he must act. But as he thought of it, he swore to himself that nothing should induce him to marry her.

He remained a couple of days in town and reached Rufford Hall on the Monday,—just a week from the day of that fatal meet at Peltry. There he found Sir George and his sister and Miss Penge, and spent his first evening in quiet. On the Tuesday he hunted with the U.R.U., and made his arrangements with Runciman. He invited Hampton to shoot with him. Surbiton and Battersby were coming, and his brother-in-law. Not wishing to have less than six guns, he asked Hampton how he could make up his party. 'Morton doesn't shoot,' he said, 'and is as stiff as a post.' Then he was told that John Morton was supposed to be very ill at Bragton. 'I'm sick of both the Botseys,' continued the lord, thinking more of his party than of Mr. Morton's health. 'Purefoy is still sulky with me because he killed poor old Caneback.' Then

Hampton suggested that if he would ask Lawrence Twentyman it might be the means of saving that unfortunate young man's life. The story of his unrequited love was known to every one at Dillsborough, and it was now told to Lord Rufford. 'He is not half a bad fellow,' said Hampton, 'and quite as much like a gentleman as either of the Botseys.'

'I shall be delighted to save the life of so good a man on such easy terms,' said the lord. Then and there, with a pencil, on the back of an old letter, he wrote a line to Larry asking him to shoot on next Saturday, and dine with him afterwards at the Bush.

That evening on his return home he found both the letters from Arabella. As it happened, he read them in the order in which they had been written, first the laughing letter, and then the one that was declared to be serious. The earlier of the two did not annoy him much. It contained hardly more than those former letters which had induced him to go to Mistletoe. But the second letter opened up her entire strategy. She had told the duchess that she was engaged to him, and the duchess of course would have told the duke. And now she wrote to him asking him to acknowledge the engagement in black and white. The first letter he might have ignored. He might have left it unanswered without gross misconduct. But the second letter, which she herself had declared to be a serious epistle, was one which he could not neglect. Now had come his difficulty. What must he do? How should he answer it? Was it imperative on him to write the words with his own hand? Would it be possible that he should get his sister to undertake the commission? He said nothing about it to any one for four and twenty hours; but he passed those hours in much discomfort. It did seem so hard to him that, because he had been forced to carry a lady home from hunting in a postchaise, he should be driven to such straits as this! The girl was evidently prepared to make a fight of it. There would be the duke and the duchess and that prig Mistletoe, and that idle ass Lord Augustus, and that venomous old woman her mother, all at him. He almost doubted whether a shooting excursion in Central Africa, or a visit to the Pampas, would not be the best thing for him. But still, though he should resolve to pass five years among the Andes, he must answer the lady's letter before he went.

Then he made up his mind that he would tell everything to his brother-in-law, as far as everything can be told in such a matter. Sir George was near fifty, full fifteen years older than his wife, who was again older than her brother. He was a man of moderate wealth, very much respected, and supposed to be possessed of almost infinite wisdom. He was one of those few human beings who seem never to make a mistake. Whatever he put his hand to came out well;—and yet everybody liked him. His brother-in-law was a little afraid of him, but yet was always glad to see him. He kept an excellent house in London, but, having no country house of his own, passed much of his time at Rufford Hall when the owner was not there. In spite of the young peer's numerous faults, Sir George was much attached to him, and always ready to help him in his difficulties. 'Penwether,' said the lord, 'I have got myself into an awful scrape.'

'I am sorry to hear it. A woman, I suppose?'

'Oh, yes. I never gamble, and therefore no other scrape can be awful. A young lady wants to marry me.'

'That is not unnatural.'

'But I am quite determined, let the result be what it may, that I won't marry the young lady.'

'That will be unfortunate for her, and the more so if she has a right to expect it. Is the young lady Miss Trefoil?'

'I did not mean to mention any name,—till I was sure it might be necessary. But it is Miss Trefoil.'

'Eleanor had told me something of it.'

'Eleanor knows nothing about this, and I do not wish you to tell her. The young lady was here with her mother,—and for the matter of that with a gentleman to whom she was certainly engaged;—but nothing particular occurred here. That unfortunate ball was going on when poor Caneback was dying. But I met her since that at Mistletoe.'

'I can hardly advise, you know, unless you tell me everything.'

Then Lord Rufford began. 'These kind of things are sometimes deuced hard upon a man. Of course, if a man were a saint or a philosopher or a Joseph he wouldn't get into such scrapes,—and perhaps every man ought to be something of that sort. But I don't know how a man is to do it, unless it's born with him.'

'A little prudence, I should say.'

'You might as well tell a fellow that it is his duty to be six feet high.'

'But what have you said to the young lady,—or what has she said to you?'

'There has been a great deal more of the latter than the former. I say so to you, but, of course, it is not to be said that I have said so. I cannot go forth to the world complaining of a young lady's conduct to me. It is a matter in which a man must not tell the truth.'

'But what is the truth?'

'She writes me word to say that she has told all her friends that I am engaged to her, and kindly presses me to make good her assurances by becoming so.'

'And what has passed between you?'

'A fainting fit in a carriage and half-a-dozen kisses.'

'Nothing more?'

'Nothing more that is material. Of course, one cannot tell it all down to each mawkish word of humbugging sentiment. There are her letters, and what I want you to remember is that I never asked her to be my wife, and that no consideration on earth shall induce me to become her husband. Though all the duchesses in England were to persecute me to death I mean to stick to that.'

Then Sir George read the letters and handed them back. 'She seems to me,' said he, 'to have more wit about her than any of the family that I have had the honour of meeting.'

'She has wit enough,—and pluck too.'

'You have never said a word to her to encourage these hopes.'

'My dear Penwether, don't you know that if a man

with a large income says to a girl like that that the sun
shines he encourages hope. I understand that well
enough. I am a rich man with a title, and a big house,
and a great command of luxuries. There are so many
young ladies who would also like to be rich, and to have
a title, and a big house, and a command of luxuries! One
sometimes feels oneself like a carcase in the midst of
vultures.'

'Marry after a proper fashion, and you'll get rid of all
that.'

'I'll think about it, but in the meantime what can I say
to this young woman? When I acknowledge that I kissed
her, of course I encouraged hopes.'

'No doubt.'

'But St. Anthony*would have had to kiss this young
woman if she had made her attack upon him as she did
on me;—and, after all, a kiss doesn't go for everything.
These are things, Penwether, that must not be inquired
into too curiously. But I won't marry her, though it were
a score of kisses. And now what must I do?' Sir George
said that he would take till the next morning to think
about it,¹—meaning to make a draft of the reply which he
thought his brother-in-law might best send to the lady.

CHAPTER XLVI

IT CANNOT BE ARRANGED

WHEN Reginald Morton received his aunt's letter he
understood from it more than she had intended.
Of course, the man to whom allusion was made was
Mr. Twentyman; and, of course, the discomfort at home
had come from Mrs. Masters' approval of that suitor's
claim. Reginald, though he had seen but little of the
inside of the attorney's household, thought it very
probable that the step-mother would make the girl's
home very uncomfortable for her. Though he knew well
all the young farmer's qualifications as a husband,—
namely, that he was well to do in the world and bore a
good character for honesty and general conduct,—still he

thoroughly, nay heartily, approved of Mary's rejection of the man's hand. It seemed to him to be sacrilege that such a one should have given to him such a woman. There was, to his thinking, something about Mary Masters that made it altogether unfit that she should pass her life as the mistress of Chowton Farm, and he honoured her for the persistence of her refusal. He took his pipe and went out into the garden in order that he might think of it all as he strolled round his little domain.

But why should he think so much about it? Why should he take so deep an interest in the matter? What was it to him whether Mary Masters married after her kind, or descended into what he felt to be an inferior manner of life? Then he tried to tell himself what were the gifts in the girl's possession which made her what she was, and he pictured her to himself, running over all her attributes. It was not that she specially excelled in beauty. He had seen Miss Trefoil as she was being driven about the neighbourhood, and having heard much of the young lady as the future wife of his own cousin, had acknowledged to himself that she was very handsome. But he had thought at the same time that under no possible circumstances could he have fallen in love with Miss Trefoil. He believed that he did not care much for female beauty, and yet he felt that he could sit and look at Mary Masters by the hour together. There was a quiet, even composure about her, always lightened by the brightness of her modest eyes, which seemed to tell him of some mysterious world within, which was like the unseen loveliness that one fancies to be hidden within the bosom of distant mountains. There was a poem to be read there of surpassing beauty, rhythmical and eloquent as the music of the spheres, if it might only be given to a man to read it. There was an absence, too, of all attempt at feminine self-glorification which he did not analyse but thoroughly appreciated. There was no fussy amplification of hair, no made-up smiles, no affectation either in her good humour or her anger, no attempt at effect in her gait, in her speech, or her looks. She seemed to him to be one who had something within her on which she could feed independently of the grosser details of the world to which it was her duty to lend her hand. And then her colour charmed his eyes. Miss Trefoil was white and red; —white as pearl powder and red as paint. Mary Masters, to tell the truth, was brown. No doubt that was the prevailing colour, if one colour must be named. But there was so rich a tint of young life beneath the surface, so soft but yet so visible an assurance of blood and health and spirit, that no one, could describe her complexion by so ugly a word without falsifying her gifts. In all her movements she was tranquil, as a noble woman should be. Even when she had turned from him with some anger at the bridge, she had walked like a princess. There was a certainty of modesty about her which was like a granite wall or a strong fortress. As he thought of it all he did not understand how such a one as Lawrence Twentyman should have dared to ask her to be his wife,—or should even have wished it.

We know what were her feelings in regard to himself,— how she had come to look almost with worship on the walls within which he lived; but he had guessed nothing of this. Even now, when he knew that she had applied to his aunt in order that she might escape from her lover, it did not occur to him that she could care for himself. He was older than she, nearly twenty years older, and even in his younger years, in the hard struggles of his early life, had never regarded himself as a man likely to find favour with women. There was in his character much of that modesty for which he gave her such infinite credit. Though he thought but little of most of those around him, he thought also but little of himself. It would break his heart to ask and be refused;—but he could, he fancied, live very well without Mary Masters. Such, at any rate, had been his own idea to himself hitherto; and now, though he was driven to think much of her, though on the present occasion he was forced to act on her behalf, he would not tell himself that he wanted to take her for his wife. He constantly assured himself that he wanted no wife, that for him a solitary life would be the best. But yet it made him wretched when he reflected that some man

would assuredly marry Mary Masters. He had heard of
that excellent but empty-headed young man Mr. Surtees.
When the idea occurred to him he found himself reviling
Mr. Surtees as being of all men the most puny, the most
unmanly, and the least worthy of marrying Mary
Masters. Now that Mr. Twentyman was certainly disposed of, he almost became jealous of Mr. Surtees.

It was not till three or four o'clock in the afternoon that
he went out on his commission to the attorney's house,
having made up his mind that he would do everything in
his power to facilitate Mary's proposed return to Cheltenham. He asked first for Mr. Masters and then for Miss
Masters, and learned that they were both out together.
But he had been desired also to see Mrs. Masters, and on
inquiring for her was again shown into the grand
drawing-room. Here he remained a quarter of an hour
while the lady of the house was changing her cap and
apron, which he spent in convincing himself that this
house was altogether an unfit residence for Mary. In the
chamber in which he was standing it was clear enough
that no human being ever lived. Mary's drawing-room
ought to be a bower in which she at least might pass her
time with books and music and pretty things around her.
The squalor of the real living room might be conjectured
from the untouched cleanliness of this useless sanctum.
At last the lady came to him and welcomed him with very
grim courtesy. As a client of her husband he was very
well;—but as a nephew of Lady Ushant he was injurious.
It was he who had carried Mary away to Cheltenham,
where she had been instigated to throw her bread-and-
butter into the fire,—as Mrs. Masters expressed it,—by
that pernicious old woman Lady Ushant. 'Mr. Masters
is out walking,' she said. Reginald clearly understood by
the contempt which she threw almost unconsciously into
her words that she did not approve of her husband going
out walking at such an hour.

'I had a message for him,—and also for you. My aunt,
Lady Ushant, is very anxious that your daughter Mary
should return to her at Cheltenham for a while.' The
proposition, to Mrs. Masters' thinking, was so monstrous,

and was at the same time so unexpected, that it almost took away her breath. At any rate, she stood for a moment speechless. 'My aunt is very fond of your daughter,' he continued, 'and, if she can be spared, would be delighted to have her. Perhaps she has written to Miss Masters, but she has asked me to come over and see if it cannot be arranged.'

'It cannot be arranged,' said Mrs. Masters. 'Nothing of the kind can be arranged.'

'I am sorry for that.'

'It is only disturbing the girl, and upsetting her, and filling her head full of nonsense. What is she to do at Cheltenham? This is her home, and here she had better be.' Though things had hitherto gone very badly, though Larry Twentyman had not shown himself since the receipt of the letter, still Mrs. Masters had not abandoned all hope. She was fixed in opinion that if her husband were joined with her they could still, between them, so break the girl's spirit as to force her into a marriage. 'As for letters,' she continued, 'I don't know anything about them. There may have been letters, but if so they have been kept from me.' She was so angry that she could not even attempt to conceal her wrath.

'Lady Ushant thinks——' began the messenger.

'Oh yes, Lady Ushant is very well, of course. Lady Ushant is your aunt, Mr. Morton, and I haven't anything to say against her. But Lady Ushant can't do any good to that girl. She has got her bread to earn, and if she won't do it one way, then she must do it another. She's obstinate and pig-headed; that's the truth of it. And her father's just as bad. He has taken her out now merely because she likes to be idle, and to go about thinking herself a fine lady. Lady Ushant doesn't do her any good at all by cockering her up.'

'My aunt, you know, saw very much of her when she was young.'

'I know she did, Mr. Morton; and all that has to be undone,—and I have got the undoing of it. Lady Ushant is one thing, and her papa's business is quite another. At any rate, if I have my say she'll not go to Cheltenham any more. I don't mean to be uncivil to you, Mr. Morton, or to say anything as oughtn't to be said of your aunt. But when you can't make people anything but what they are, it's my opinion that it's best to leave them alone. Goodday to you, sir, and I hope you understand what it is that I mean.'

Then Morton retreated and went down the stairs, leaving the lady in possession of her own grandeur. He had not quite understood what she had meant, and was still wondering at the energy of her opposition, when he met Mary herself at the front door. Her father was not with her, but his retreating form was to be seen entering the portal of the Bush. 'Oh, Mr. Morton!' exclaimed Mary, surprised to have the house-door opened for her by him.

'I have come with a message from my aunt.'

'She told me that you would do so.'

'Lady Ushant would, of course, be delighted to have you if it could be arranged.'

'Then Lady Ushant will be disappointed,' said Mrs. Masters, who had descended the stairs. 'There has been something going on behind my back.'

'I wrote to Lady Ushant,' said Mary.

'I call that sly and deceitful;—very sly and very deceitful. If I know it, you won't stir out of this house to go to Cheltenham. I wonder Lady Ushant would go to put you up in that way against those you're bound to obey.'

'I thought Mrs. Masters had been told,' said Reginald.

'Papa did know that I wrote,' said Mary.

'Yes;—and in this way a conspiracy is to be made up in the house! If she goes to Cheltenham I won't stay here. You may tell Lady Ushant that I say that. I'm not going to be made one thing one day and another another, and to be made a tool of all round.' By this time, Dolly and Kate had come down from the upper regions, and were standing behind their mother. 'What do you two do there, standing gaping like fools?' said the angry mother. 'I suppose your father has gone over to the public-house again. That, miss, is what comes from your pig-headedness. Didn't I tell you that you were ruining everybody

belonging to you?' Before all this was over, Reginald
Morton had escaped, feeling that he could do no good to
either side by remaining a witness to such a scene. He
must take some other opportunity of finding the attorney,
and of learning from him whether he intended that his
daughter should be allowed to accept Lady Ushant's
invitation.

Poor Mary, as she shrunk into the house, was nearly
heartbroken. That such things should be at all was very
dreadful, but that the scene should have taken place in
the presence of Reginald Morton was an aggravation of
the misery which nearly overwhelmed her. How could
she make him understand whence had arisen her stepmother's anger, and that she herself had been neither sly
nor deceitful nor pig-headed?

Chapter XLVII

'BUT THERE IS SOME ONE'

WHEN Mr. Masters had gone across to the Bush, his
purpose had certainly been ignoble, but it had had
no reference to brandy and water. And the allusion made
by Mrs. Masters to the probable ruin which was to come
from his tendencies in that direction had been calumnious,
for she knew that the man was not given to excess in
liquor. But as he approached his own house, he bethought
himself that it would not lead to domestic comfort if he
were seen returning from his walk with Mary, and he had
therefore made some excuse as to the expediency of saying
a word to Runciman, whom he espied at his own door.
He said his word to Runciman, and so loitered away
perhaps a quarter of an hour, and then went back to his
office. But his wife had kept her anger at burning heat,
and pounced upon him before he had taken his seat.
Sundown was there copying, sitting with his eyes intent
on the board before him, as though he were quite unaware
of the sudden entrance of his master's wife. She, in her
fury, did not regard Sundown in the least, but at once
commenced her attack. 'What is all this, Mr. Masters,'

she said, 'about Lady Ushant and going to Cheltenham? I won't have any going to Cheltenham, and that's flat.' Now the attorney had altogether made up his mind that his daughter should go to Cheltenham if her friend would receive her. Whatever might be the consequences, they must be borne. But he thought it best to say nothing at the first moment of the attack, and simply turned his sorrowful round face in silence up to the partner of all his cares, and the source of so many of them. 'There have been letters,' continued the lady;—'letters which nobody has told me nothing about. That proud peacock from Hoppet Hall has been here, as though he had nothing to do but carry Mary away about the country just as he pleased. Mary won't go to Cheltenham with him nor yet without him;—not if I am to remain here.'

'Where else should you remain, my dear?' asked the attorney.

'I'd sooner go into the workhouse than have all this turmoil. That's where we are all likely to go if you pass your time between walking about with that minx and the public-house opposite.' Then the attorney was aware that he had been watched, and his spirit began to rise within him. He looked at Sundown, but the man went on copying quicker than ever.

'My dear,' said Mr. Masters, 'you shouldn't talk in that way before the clerk. I wanted to speak to Mr. Runciman, and, as to the workhouse, I don't know that there is any more danger now than there has been for the last twenty years.'

'It's always off and on, as far as I can see. Do you mean to send that girl to Cheltenham?'

'I rather think she had better go—for a time.'

'Then I shall leave this house, and go with my girls to Norrington.' Now this threat, which had been made before, was quite without meaning. Mrs. Masters' parents were both dead, and her brother, who had a large family, certainly would not receive her. 'I won't remain here, Mr. Masters, if I ain't to be mistress of my own house. What is she to go to Cheltenham for, I should like to know?'

Then Sundown was desired by his wretched employer to go into the back settlement, and the poor man prepared himself for the battle as well as he could. 'She is not happy here,' he said.

'Whose fault is that? Why shouldn't she be happy? Of course, you know what it means. She's got round you because she wants to be a fine lady. What means have you to make her a fine lady? If you was to die to-morrow, what would there be for any of 'em? My little bit of money is all gone. Let her stay here and be made to marry Lawrence Twentyman. That's what I say.'

'She will never marry Mr. Twentyman.'

'Not if you go on like this she won't. If you'd done your duty by her like a real father, instead of being afraid of her when she puts on her tantrums, she'd have been at Chowton Farm by this time.'

It was clear to him that now was the time not to be afraid of his wife when she put on her tantrums, or, at any rate, to appear not to be afraid. 'She has been very unhappy of late.'

'Oh, unhappy! She's been made more of than anybody else in this house.'

'And a change will do her good. She has my permission to go; and go she shall!' Then the word had been spoken. 'She shall!'

'It is very much for the best. While she is here the house is made wretched for us all.'

'It'll be wretcheder yet, unless it would make you happy to see me dead on the threshold, which I believe it would. As for her, she's an ungrateful, sly, wicked slut.'

'She has done nothing wicked that I know of.'

'Not writing to that old woman behind my back?'

'She told me what she was doing, and showed me the letter.'

'Yes; of course. The two of you were in it. Does that make it any better? I say it was sly and wicked; and you were sly and wicked as well as she. She has got the better of you, and now you are going to send her away from the only chance she'll ever get of having a decent home of her own over her head.'

'There's nothing more to be said about it, my dear. She'll go to Lady Ushant.' Having thus pronounced his dictum with all the marital authority he could assume, he took his hat and sallied forth. Mrs. Masters, when she was left alone, stamped her foot and hit the desk with a ruler that was lying there. Then she went upstairs and threw herself on her bed in a paroxysm of weeping and wailing.

Mr. Masters, when he closed his door, looked up the street and down the street, and then again went across to the Bush. Mr. Runciman was still there, and was standing with a letter in his hand, while one of the grooms from Rufford Hall was holding a horse beside him. 'Any answer, Mr. Runciman?' said the groom.

'Only to tell his lordship that everything will be ready for him. You'd better go through and give the horse a feed of corn, and get a bit of something to eat and a glass of beer yourself.' The man wasn't slow to do as he was bid; and in this way the Bush had become very popular with the servants of the gentry around the place. 'His lordship is to be here from Friday to Sunday with a party, Mr. Masters.'

'Oh, indeed.'

'For the end of the shooting. And who do you think he has asked to be one of the party?'

'Not Mr. Reginald?'

'I don't think they ever spoke in their lives. Who but Larry Twentyman!'

'No!'

'It'll be the making of Larry. I only hope he won't cock his beaver too high.'*

'Is he coming?'

'I suppose so. He'll be sure to come. His lordship only tells me that there are to be six of 'em on Saturday and five on Friday night. But the lad there knew who they all were. There's Mr. Surbiton and Captain Battersby and Sir George are to come over with his lordship from Rufford. And young Mr. Hampton is to join them here, and Larry Twentyman is to shoot with them on Saturday, and dine afterwards. Won't those two Botseys be jealous; that's all?'

'It only shows what they think of Larry,' said the attorney.

'Larry Twentyman is a very good fellow,' said the landlord. 'I don't know a better fellow round Dillsborough, or one who is more always on the square. But he's weak. You know him as well as I, Mr. Masters.'

'He's not so weak but what he can keep what he's got.'

'This'll be the way to try him. He'd melt away like water into sand if he were to live for a few weeks with such men as his lordship's friends. I suppose there's no chance of his taking a wife home to Chowton with him?' The attorney shook his head. 'That'd be the making of him, Mr. Masters; a good girl like that who'd keep him at home. If he takes it to heart, he'll burst out somewhere and spend a lot of money.'

The attorney declined Mr. Runciman's offer of a glass of beer, and slowly made his way round the corner of the inn by Hobbs's gate to the front door of Hoppet Hall. Then he passed on to the churchyard, still thinking of the misery of his position. When he reached the church he turned back, still going very slowly, and knocked at the door of Hoppet Hall. He was shown at once by Reginald's old house-keeper up to the library, and there in a few minutes he was joined by the master of the house. 'I was over looking for you an hour or two ago,' said Reginald.

'I heard you were there, Mr. Morton, and so I thought I would come to you. You didn't see Mary?'

'I just saw her, but could hardly say much. She had written to my aunt about going to Cheltenham.'

'I saw the letter before she sent it, Mr. Morton.'

'So she told me. My aunt would be delighted to have her, but it seems that Mrs. Masters does not wish her to go.'

'There is some trouble about it, Mr. Morton, but I may as well tell you at once that I wish her to go. She would be better for a while at Cheltenham with such a lady as your aunt than she can be at home. Her stepmother and she cannot agree on a certain point. I dare say you know what it is, Mr. Morton?'

'In regard, I suppose, to Mr. Twentyman?'

'Just that. Mrs. Masters thinks that Mr. Twentyman

would make an excellent husband. And so do I. There's nothing in the world against him, and as compared with me, he's a rich man. I couldn't give the poor girl any fortune, and he wouldn't want any. But money isn't everything.'

'No, indeed.'

'He's an industrious, steady young man, too, and he has had my word with him all through. But I can't compel my girl to marry him if she don't like him. I can't even try to compel her. She's as good a girl as ever stirred about a house.'

'I can well believe that.'

'And nothing would take such a load off me as to know that she was going to be well married. But, as she don't like the young man well enough, I won't have her hardly used.'

'Mrs. Masters perhaps is—hard to her.'

'God forbid that I should say anything against my wife. I never did, and I won't now. But Mary will be better away; and if Lady Ushant will be good enough to take her, she shall go.'

'When will she be ready, Mr. Masters?'

'I must ask her about that. In a week, perhaps, or ten days.'

'She is quite decided against the young man?'

'Quite. At the bidding of all of us she said she'd take two months to think of it. But, before the time was up, she wrote to him to say it could never be. It quite upset my wife; because it would have been such an excellent arrangement.'

Reginald wished to learn more, but hardly knew how to ask the father questions. Yet, as he had been trusted so far, he thought that he might be trusted altogether. 'I must own,' he said, 'that I think that Mr. Twentyman would hardly be a fit husband for your daughter.'

'He is a very good young man.'

'Very likely;—but she is something more than a very good young woman. A young lady with her gifts will be sure to settle well in life some day.' The attorney shook his head. He had lived long enough to see many young ladies with good gifts find it difficult to settle in life; and perhaps that mysterious poem which Reginald found in Mary's eyes was neither visible nor audible to Mary's father. 'I did hear,' said Reginald, 'that Mr. Surtees——'

'There's nothing in that.'

'Oh, indeed, I thought that perhaps as she is so determined not to do as her friends would wish, that there might be something else.' He said this almost as a question, looking close into the attorney's eyes as he spoke.

'It is almost possible,' said Mr. Masters.

'But you don't think there is anybody?'

'It is very hard to say, Mr. Morton.'

'You don't expect anything of that sort?'

Then the attorney broke forth into sudden confidence. 'To tell the truth then, Mr. Morton, I think there is somebody, though who it is I know as little as the baby unborn. She sees nobody here at Dillsborough to be intimate with. She isn't one of those who would write letters or do anything on the sly.'

'But there is some one?'

'She told me as much herself. That is, when I asked her she would not deny it. Then I thought that perhaps it might be somebody at Cheltenham.'

'I think not.'

'She was there so short a time, Mr. Morton; and Lady Ushant would be the last person in the world to let such a thing as that go on without telling her parents.'

'I don't think there was any one at Cheltenham. She was only there a month.'

'I did fancy that perhaps that was one reason why she should want to go back.'

'I don't believe it. I don't in the least believe it,' said Reginald enthusiastically. 'My aunt would have been sure to have seen it. It would have been impossible without her knowledge. But there is somebody?'

'I think so, Mr. Morton;—and if she does go to Cheltenham perhaps Lady Ushant had better know.' To this Reginald agreed, or half agreed. It did not seem to him to be of much consequence what might be done at Cheltenham. He felt certain that the lover was not there.

And yet who was there at Dillsborough? He had seen those young Botseys about. Could it possibly be one of them? And during the Christmas vacation the rector's scamp of a son had been home from Oxford,—to whom Mary Masters had barely spoken. Was it young Mainwaring? or could it be possible that she had turned an eye of favour on Dr. Nupper's elegantly-dressed assistant. There was nothing too monstrous for him to suggest to himself as soon as the attorney had left him.

But there was a young man in Dillsborough,—one man at any rate young enough to be a lover,—of whom Reginald did not think; as to whom, had his name been suggested as that of the young man to whom Mary's heart had been given, he would have repudiated such a suggestion with astonishment and anger. But now, having heard this from the girl's father, he was again vexed, and almost as much disgusted as when he had first become aware that Larry Twentyman was a suitor for her hand. Why should he trouble himself about a girl who was ready to fall in love with the first man that she saw about the place? He tried to pacify himself by such a question as this, but tried in vain.

CHAPTER XLVIII

THE DINNER AT THE BUSH

HERE is the letter which at his brother-in-law's advice Lord Rufford wrote to Arabella:—

'Rufford, 3rd February, 1875.

'MY DEAR MISS TREFOIL,

'It is a great grief to me that I should have to answer your letter in a manner that will I fear not be satisfactory to you. I can only say that you have altogether mistaken me if you think that I have said anything which was intended as an offer of marriage. I cannot but be very much flattered by your good opinion. I have had much pleasure from our acquaintance, and I should have been glad if it could have been continued.

But I have had no thoughts of marriage. If I have said a word which has, unintentionally on my part, given rise to such an idea, I can only beg your pardon heartily. If I were to add more after what I have now said perhaps you would take it as an impertinence.

'Yours most sincerely,
'RUFFORD.'

He had desired to make various additions and suggestions, which, however, had all been disallowed by Sir George Penwether. He had proposed among other things to ask her whether he should keep Jack for her for the remainder of the season, or whether he should send the horse elsewhere, but Sir George would not allow a word in the letter about Jack. 'You did give her the horse, then?' he asked.

'I had hardly any alternative as the things went. She would have been quite welcome to the horse if she would have let me alone afterwards.'

'No doubt; but when young gentlemen give young ladies horses——'

'I know all about it, my dear fellow. Pray don't preach more than you can help. Of course I have been an infernal ass. I know all that. But as the horse is hers——'

'Say nothing about the horse. Were she to ask for it, of course she could have it; but that is not likely.'

'And you think that I had better say nothing else.'

'Not a word. Of course it will be shown to all her friends, and may possibly find its way into print. I don't know what steps such a young lady may be advised to take. Her uncle is a man of honour. Her father is an ass and careless about everything. Mistletoe will not improbably feel himself bound to act as though he were her brother. They will, of course, all think you to be a rascal, —and will say so.'

'If Mistletoe says so, I'll horsewhip him.'

'No, you won't, Rufford. You will remember that this woman is a woman, and that a woman's friends are bound to stand up for her. After all, your hands are not quite clean in the matter.'

'I am heavy enough on myself, Penwether. I have been a fool, and I own it. But I have done nothing unbecoming a gentleman.' He was almost tempted to quarrel with his brother-in-law, but at last he allowed the letter to be sent just as Sir George had written it, and then tried to banish the affair from his mind for the present, so that he might enjoy his life till the next hostile step should be taken by the Trefoil clan.

When Larry Twentyman received the lord's note, which was left at Chowton Farm by Hampton's groom, he was in the lowest depth of desolation. He had intended to hunt that day in compliance with John Morton's advice, but had felt himself quite unable to make the effort. It was not only that he had been thrown over by Mary Masters, but that everybody knew that he had been thrown over. If he had kept the matter a secret, perhaps he might have borne it;—but it is so hard to bear a sorrow of which all one's neighbours are conscious. When a man is reduced by poverty to the drinking of beer instead of wine, it is not the loss of the wine that is so heavy on him, as the consciousness that those around him are aware of the reason. And he is apt to extend his idea of this consciousness to a circle that is altogether indifferent of the fact. That a man should fail in his love seems to him to be of all failures the most contemptible, and Larry thought that there would not be one in the field unaware of his miserable rejection. In spite of his mother's prayers he refused to go, and had hung about the farm all day.

Then there came to him Lord Rufford's note. It had been quite unexpected, and a month or two before, when his hopes had still been high in regard to Mary Masters, would have filled him with delight. It was the foible of his life to be esteemed a gentleman, and his poor ambition to be allowed to live among men of higher social standing than himself. Those dinners of Lord Rufford's at the Bush had been a special grief to him. The young lord had been always courteous to him in the field, and he had been able, as he thought, to requite such courtesy by little attentions in the way of game preserving. If pheasants

from Dillsborough Wood ate Goarly's wheat, so did they
eat Larry Twentyman's barley. He had a sportsman's
heart, above complaint as to such matters, and had
always been neighbourly to the lord. No doubt pheasants
and hares were left at his house whenever there was
shooting in the neighbourhood,—which to his mother
afforded great consolation. But Larry did not care for the
pheasants and hares. Had he so pleased he could have
shot them on his own land; but he did not preserve, and
as a good neighbour he regarded the pheasants and hares
as Lord Rufford's property. He felt that he was behaving
as a gentleman as well as a neighbour, and that he should
be treated as such. Fred Botsey had dined at the Bush
with Lord Rufford, and Larry looked on Fred as in no
way better than himself.

Now at last the invitation had come. He was asked to
a day's shooting and to dine with the lord and his party at
the inn. How pleasant would it be to give a friendly nod
to Runciman as he went into the room, and to assert
afterwards in Botsey's hearing something of the joviality
of the evening! Of course Hampton would be there, as
Hampton's servant had brought the note, and he was
very anxious to be on friendly terms with Mr. Hampton.
Next to the lord himself there was no one in the hunt who
carried his head so high as young Hampton.

But there arose to him the question whether all this had
not arrived too late! Of what good is it to open up the
true delights of life to a man when you have so scotched
and wounded him that he has no capability left of enjoying anything? As he sat lonely with his pipe in his mouth
he thought for a while that he would decline the invitation. The idea of selling Chowton Farm and of establishing himself at some Antipodes in which the name of Mary
Masters should never have been heard, was growing upon
him. Of what use would the friendship of Lord Rufford
be to him at the other side of the globe?

At last, however, the hope of giving that friendly nod to
Runciman overcame him, and he determined to go. He
wrote a note, which caused him no little thought,
presenting his compliments to Lord Rufford and

promising to meet his lordship's party at Dillsborough Wood.

The shooting went off very well, and Larry behaved himself with propriety. He wanted the party to come in and lunch, and had given sundry instructions to his mother on that head. But they did not remain near to his place throughout the day, and his efforts in that direction were not successful. Between five and six he went home, and at half-past seven appeared at the Bush attired in his best. He never yet had sat down with a lord, and his mind misgave him a little; but he had spirit enough to look about for Runciman,—who, however, was not to be seen.

Sir George was not there, but the party had been made up, as regarded the dinner, by the addition of Captain Glomax, who had returned from hunting. Captain Glomax was in high glee, having had,—as he declared,— the run of the season. When a Master has been deserted on any day by the choice spirits of his hunt he is always apt to boast to them that he had on that occasion the run of the season. He had taken a fox from Impington right across to Hogsborough, which, as every one knows, is just on the borders of the U.R.U., had then run him for five miles into Lord Chiltern's country, and had killed him in the centre of the Brake Hunt, after an hour and a half, almost without a check. 'It was one of those straight things that one doesn't often see nowadays,' said Glomax.

'Any pace?' asked Lord Rufford.

'Very good indeed for the first forty minutes. I wish you had all been there. It was better fun I take it than shooting rabbits.'

Then Hampton put the Captain through his facings as to time and distance and exact places that had been passed, and ended by expressing an opinion that he could have kicked his hat as fast on foot. Whereupon the Captain begged him to try, and hinted that he did not know the country. In answer to which Hampton offered to bet a five-pound note that young Jack Runce would say that the pace had been slow. Jack was the son of the old farmer whom the Senator had so disgusted, and was supposed to know what he was about on a horse. But Glomax declined the bet, saying that he did not care a —— for Jack Runce. He knew as much about pace as any farmer, or for the matter of that any gentleman, in Ufford or Rufford, and the pace for forty minutes had been very good. Nevertheless, all the party were convinced that the 'thing' had been so slow that it had not been worth riding to;—a conviction which is not uncommon with gentlemen when they have missed a run. In all this discussion poor Larry took no great part, though he knew the country as well as any one. Larry had not as yet got over the awe inspired by the lord in his black coat.

Perhaps Larry's happiest moment in the evening was when Runciman himself brought in the soup, for at that moment Lord Rufford put his hand on his shoulder and desired him to sit down,—and Runciman both heard and saw it. And at dinner, when the champagne had been twice round, he became more comfortable. The conversation got upon Goarly, and in reference to that matter he was quite at home. 'It's not my doing,' said Lord Rufford. 'I have instructed no one to keep him locked up.'

'It's a very good job from all that I can hear,' said Tom Surbiton.

'All I did was to get Mr. Masters here to take up the case for me, and I learned from him to-day that the rascal had already agreed to take the money I offered. He only bargains that it shall be paid into his own hands,—no doubt desiring to sell the attorney he has employed.'

'Bearside has got his money from the American Senator, my lord,' said Larry.

'They may fight it out among them. I don't care who gets the money or who pays it as long as I'm not imposed upon.'

'We must proceed against that man Scrobby,' said Glomax, with all the authority of a Master.

'You'll never convict him on Goarly's evidence,' said the lord.

Then Larry could give them further information.

Nickem had positively traced the purchase of the red herrings. An old woman in Rufford was ready to swear that she herself had sold them to Mrs. Scrobby. Tom Surbiton suggested that the possession of red herrings was not of itself a crime. Hampton thought that it was corroborative. Captain Battersby wanted to know whether any of the herrings were still in existence, so that they could be sworn to. Glomax was of opinion that villainy of so deep a dye could not have taken place in any other hunting country in England.

'There's been strychnine put down in the Brake, too,' said Hampton.

'But not in cartloads,' said the Master.

'I rather think,' said Larry, 'that Nickem knows where the strychnine was bought. That'll make a clear case of it. Hanging would be too good for such a scoundrel.' This was said after the third glass of champagne, but the opinion was one which was well received by the whole company. After that the Senator's conduct was discussed, and they all agreed that in the whole affair that was the most marvellous circumstance. 'They must be queer people over there,' said Larry.

'Brutes!' said Glomax. 'They once tried a pack of hounds somewhere in one of the States, but they never could run a yard.'

There was a good deal of wine drank, which was not unusual at Lord Rufford's dinners. Most of the company were seasoned vessels, and none of them were much the worse for what they drank. But the generous wine got to Larry's heart, and perhaps made his brain a little soft. Lord Rufford, remembering what had been said about the young man's misery, tried to console him by attention; and as the evening wore on, and when the second cigars had been lit all round, the two were seated together in confidential conversation at a corner of the table. 'Yes, my lord; I think I shall hook it,' said Larry. 'Something has occurred that has made the place not quite so comfortable to me; and as it is all my own I think I shall sell it.'

'We shall miss you immensely in the hunt,' said Lord

Rufford, who, of course, knew what the something was.

'It's very kind of you to say so, my lord. But there are things which may make a man go.'

'Nothing serious, I hope.'

'Just a young woman, my lord. I don't want it talked about, but I don't mind mentioning it to you.'

'You should never let those troubles touch you so closely,' said his lordship, whose own withers at this moment were by no means unwrung.

'I dare say not. But if you feel it, how are you to help it? I shall do very well when I get away. Chowton Farm is not the only spot in the world.'

'But a man so fond of hunting as you are!'

'Well;—yes. I shall miss the hunting, my lord,—shan't I? If Mr. Morton don't buy the place I should like it to go to your lordship. I offered it to him first because it came from them.'

'Quite right. By-the-bye, I hear that Mr. Morton is very ill.'

'So I heard,' said Larry. 'Nupper has been with him, I know, and I fancy they have sent for somebody from London. I don't know that he cares much about the land. He thinks more of the foreign parts he's always in. I don't believe we shall fall out about the price, my lord.' Then Lord Rufford explained that he would not go into that matter just at present, but that if the place were in the market he would certainly like to buy it. He, however, did as John Morton had done before, and endeavoured to persuade the poor fellow that he should not alter the whole tenor of his life because a young lady would not look at him.

'Good-night, Mr. Runciman,' said Larry as he made his way down-stairs to the yard. 'We've had an uncommon pleasant evening.'

'I'm glad you've enjoyed yourself, Larry.' Larry thought that his Christian name from the hotel-keeper's lips had never sounded so offensively as on the present occasion.

Chapter XLIX

MISS TREFOIL'S DECISION

LORD RUFFORD'S letter reached Arabella at her cousin's house, in due course, and was handed to her in the morning as she came down to breakfast. The envelope bore his crest and coronet, and she was sure that more than one pair of eyes had already seen it. Her mother had been in the room some time before her, and would, of course, know that the letter was from Lord Rufford. An indiscreet word or two had been said in the hearing of Mrs. Connop Green,—as to which Arabella had already scolded her mother most vehemently, and Mrs. Connop Green, too, would probably have seen the letter, and would know that it had come from the lover of whom boasts had been made. The Connop Greens would be ready to worship Arabella down to the very soles of her feet if she were certainly,—without a vestige of doubt, —engaged to be the wife of Lord Rufford. But there had been so many previous mistakes! And they, too, had heard of Mr. John Morton. They, too, were a little afraid of Arabella, though she was undoubtedly the niece of a duke.

She was aware now,—as always,—how much depended on her personal bearing; but this was a moment of moments! She would fain have kept the letter, and have opened it in the retirement of her own room. She knew its terrible importance, and was afraid of her own countenance when she should read it. All the hopes of her life were contained in that letter. But were she to put it in her pocket she would betray her anxiety by doing so. She found herself bound to open it and read it at once,— and she did open it and read it.

After all, it was what she had expected. It was very decided, very short, very cold, and carrying with it no sign of weakness. But it was of such a letter that she had thought when she resolved that she would apply to Lord Mistletoe, and endeavour to put the whole family of Trefoil in arms. She had been,—so she had assured her-

self,—quite sure that that kind, loving response which she
had solicited, would not be given to her. But yet the stern
fact, now that it was absolutely in her hands, almost overwhelmed her. She could not restrain the dull, dead look
of heart-breaking sorrow which for a few moments clouded
her face,—a look which took away all her beauty,
lengthening her cheeks, and robbing her eyes of that
vivacity which it was the task of her life to assume. 'Is
anything the matter, my dear?' asked Mrs. Connop
Green.

Then she made a final effort,—an heroic effort. 'What
do you think, mamma?' she said, paying no attention to
her cousin's inquiry.

'What is it, Arabella?'

'Jack got some injury that day at Peltry, and is so lame
that they don't know whether he'll ever put his foot to the
ground again.'

'Poor fellow!' said Mr. Green. 'Who is Jack?'

'Jack is a horse, Mr. Green;—and such a horse that one
cannot but be sorry for him. Poor Jack! I don't know
any Christian whose lameness would be such a nuisance.'

'Does Lord Rufford write about his horses?' asked
Mrs. Connop Green, thus betraying that knowledge as to
the letter which she had obtained from the envelope.

'If you must know all the truth about it,' said Arabella,
'the horse is my horse, and not Lord Rufford's. And as
he is the only horse I have got, and as he's the dearest
horse in all the world, you must excuse my being a little
sorry about him. Poor Jack!' After that the breakfast
was eaten and everybody in the room believed the story
of the horse's lameness—except Lady Augustus.

When breakfast and the loitering after breakfast were
well over, so that she could escape without exciting any
notice, she made her way up to her bed-room. In a few
minutes,—so that again there should be nothing notice-
able,—her mother followed her. But her door was locked.
'It is I, Arabella,' said her mother.

'You can't come in at present, mamma. I am busy.'

'But, Arabella!'

'You can't come in at present, mamma.' Then Lady

Augustus slowly glided away to her own room and there waited for tidings.

The whole form of the girl's face was altered when she was alone. Her features in themselves were not lovely. Her cheeks and chin were heavy. Her brow was too low, and her upper lip too long. Her nose and teeth were good, and would have been very handsome had they belonged to a man. Her complexion had always been good till it had been injured by being improved,—and so was the carriage of her head and the outside lines of her bust and figure, and her large eyes, though never soft, could be bright and sparkle. Skill had done much for her and continued effort almost more. But now the effort was dropped and that which skill had done turned against her. She was haggard, lumpy, and almost hideous in her bewildered grief.

Had there been a word of weakness in the short letter she might have founded upon it some hope. It did not occur to her that he had had the letter written for him, and she was astonished at its curt strength. How could he dare to say that she had mistaken him? Had she not lain in his arms while he embraced her? How could he have found the courage to say that he had had no thought of marriage when he had declared to her that he loved her? She must have known that she had hunted him as a fox is hunted;—and yet she believed that she was being cruelly ill-used. For a time all that dependence on Lord Mistletoe and her uncle deserted her. What effect could they have on a man who would write such a letter as that? Had she known that the words were the words of his brother-in-law, even that would have given her some hope.

But what should she do? Whatever steps she took she must take at once. And she must tell her mother. Her mother's help would be necessary to her now in whatever direction she might turn her mind. She almost thought that she would abandon him without another word. She had been strong in her reliance on family aid till the time for invoking it had come; but now she believed that it would be useless. Could it be that such a man as this would be driven into marriage by the interference of Lord

Mistletoe! She would much like to bring down some
punishment on his head;—but in doing so she would cut
all other ground from under her own feet. There were
still open to her Patagonia and the Paragon.
She hated the Paragon, and she recoiled with shuddering from the idea of Patagonia. But as for hating,—she
hated Lord Rufford too. And what was there that she
loved? She tried to ask herself some questions even as to
that. There certainly was no man for whom she cared
a straw; nor had there been for the last six or eight years.
Even when he was kissing her she was thinking of her
built-up hair, of her pearl powder, her paint, and of
possible accidents and untoward revelations. The loan of
her lips had been for use only, and not for any pleasure
which she had even in pleasing him. In her very swoon
she had felt the need of being careful at all points. It was all
labour, and all care,—and, alas, alas, all disappointment!
But there was a future through which she must live.
How might she best avoid the misfortune of poverty for
the twenty, thirty, or forty years which might be accorded
to her? What did it matter whom or what she hated?
The housemaid probably did not like cleaning grates; nor
the butcher killing sheep; nor the sempstress stitching
silks. She must live. And if she could only get away from
her mother that in itself would be something. Most
people were distasteful to her, but no one so much as her
mother. Here in England she knew that she was despised
among the people with whom she lived. And now she
would be more despised than ever. Her uncle and aunt,
though she disliked them, had been much to her. It was
something,—that annual visit to Mistletoe, though she
never enjoyed it when she was there. But she could well
understand that after such a failure as this, after such
a game, played before their own eyes in their own house
her uncle and her aunt would drop her altogether. She
had played this game so boldly that there was no retreat.
Would it not, therefore, be better that she should fly
altogether?
There was a time on that morning in which she had
made up her mind that she would write a most affectionate

letter to Morton, telling him that her people had now
agreed to his propositions as to settlement, and assuring
him that from henceforward she would be all his own.
She did think that were she to do so she might still go with
him to Patagonia. But, if so, she must do it at once. The
delay had already been almost too long. In that case she
would not say a word in reply to Lord Rufford, and
would allow all that to be as though it had never been.
Then again there arose to her mind the remembrance of
Rufford Hall, of all the glories, of the triumph over everybody. Then again there was the idea of a 'forlorn hope.'
She thought that she could have brought herself to do it,
if only death would have been the alternative of success
when she had resolved to make the rush.

It was nearly one when she went to her mother, and
even then she was undecided. But the joint agony of the
solitude and the doubts had been too much for her and
she found herself constrained to seek a counsellor. 'He
has thrown you over,' said Lady Augustus as soon as the
door was closed.

'Of course he has,' said Arabella, walking up the room,
and again playing her part even before her mother.

'I knew it would be so.'

'You knew nothing of the kind, mamma, and your
saying so is simply an untruth. It was you who put me
up to it.'

'Arabella, that is false.'

'It wasn't you, I suppose, who made me throw over
Mr. Morton and Bragton?'

'Certainly not.'

'That is so like you, mamma. There isn't a single thing
that you do or say that you don't deny afterwards.' These
little compliments were so usual among them that at the
present moment they excited no great danger. 'There's
his letter. I suppose you had better read it.' And she
chucked the document to her mother.

'It is very decided,' said Lady Augustus.

'It is the falsest, the most impudent, and the most
scandalous letter that a man ever wrote to a woman. I
could horsewhip him for it myself if I could get near him.'

'Is it all over, Arabella?'

'All over! What questions you do ask, mamma! No. It is not all over. I'll stick to him like a leech. He proposed to me as plainly as any man ever did to any woman. I don't care what people may say or think. He hasn't heard the last of me; and so he'll find.' And thus in her passion she made up her mind that she would not yet abandon the hunt.

'What will you do, my dear?'

'What will I do? How am I to say what I will do? If I were standing near him with a knife in my hand I would stick it into his heart. I would! Mistaken him! Liar! They talk of girls lying; but what girl would lie like that?'

'But something must be done.'

'If papa were not such a fool as he is, he would manage it all for me,' said Arabella dutifully. 'I must see my father, and I must dictate a letter for him. Where is papa?'

'In London, I suppose.'

'You must come up to London with me to-morrow. We shall have to go to his club and get him out. It must be done immediately; and then I must see Lord Mistletoe, and I will write to the duke.'

'Would it not be better to write to your papa?' said Lady Augustus, not liking the idea of being dragged away so quickly from comfortable quarters.

'No; it wouldn't. If you won't go I shall, and you must give me some money. I shall write to Lord Rufford too.'

And so it was at last decided, the wretched old woman being dragged away up to London on some excuse which the Connop Greens were not very sorry to accept. But on that same afternoon Arabella wrote to Lord Rufford.

'Your letter has amazed me. I cannot understand it. It seems to be almost impossible that it should really have come from you. How can you say that I have mistaken you? There has been no mistake. Surely that letter cannot have been written by you.

'Of course I have been obliged to tell my father everything.

'ARABELLA.'

On the following day at about four in the afternoon the mother and daughter drove up to the door of Graham's Club in Bond Street, and there found Lord Augustus. With considerable difficulty he was induced to come down from the whist room, and was forced into the brougham. He was a handsome fat man, with a long grey beard, who passed his whole life in eating, drinking, and playing whist, and was troubled by no scruples and no principles. He would not cheat at cards because it was dangerous and ungentlemanlike, and if discovered would lead to his social annihilation; but as to paying money that he owed to tradesmen, it never occurred to him as being a desirable thing as long as he could get what he wanted without doing so. He had expended his own patrimony and his wife's fortune, and now lived on an allowance made to him by his brother. Whatever funds his wife might have, not a shilling of them ever came from him. When he began to understand something of the nature of the business on hand, he suggested that his brother, the duke, could do what was desirable infinitely better than he could. 'He won't think anything of me,' said Lord Augustus.

'We'll make him think something,' said Arabella sternly. 'You must do it, papa. They'd turn you out of the club if they knew that you had refused.' Then he looked up in the brougham and snarled at her. 'Papa, you must copy the letter and sign it.'

'How am I to know the truth of it all?' he asked.

'It is quite true,' said Lady Augustus. There was very much more of it, but at last he was carried away bodily, and in his daughter's presence he did write and sign the following letter:—

'MY LORD,
        'I have heard from my daughter a story which has surprised me very much. It appears that she has been staying with you at Rufford Hall, and again at Mistletoe, and that while at the latter place you proposed marriage to her. She tells me with heart-breaking concern that you have now repudiated your own proposition,—not only

once made but repeated. Her condition is most distressing. She is in all respects your lordship's equal. As her father, I am driven to ask you what excuse you have to make, or whether she has interpreted you aright.

'I have the honour to be,

'Your very humble servant,

'AUGUSTUS TREFOIL.'

CHAPTER L

'IN THESE DAYS ONE CAN'T MAKE A MAN MARRY'

THIS was going on while Lord Rufford was shooting in the neighbourhood of Dillsborough; and when the letter was being put into its envelope at the lodgings in Orchard Street, his lordship was just sitting down to dinner with his guests at the Bush. At the same time John Morton was lying ill at Bragton;—a fact of which Arabella was not aware.

The letter from Lord Augustus was put into the post on Saturday evening; but when that line of action was decided upon by Arabella, she was aware that she must not trust solely to her father. Various plans were fermenting in her brain; all, or any of which, if carried out at all, must be carried out at the same time and at once. There must be no delay, or that final chance of Patagonia would be gone. The leader of a forlorn hope, though he be ever so resolved to die in the breach, still makes some preparation for his escape. Among her plans, the first in order was a resolution to see Lord Mistletoe, whom she knew to be in town. Parliament was to meet in the course of the next week and he was to move the address. There had been much said about all this at Mistletoe, from which she knew that he was in London preparing himself among the gentlemen at the Treasury. Then she herself would write to the duke. She thought that she could concoct a letter that would move even his heart. She would tell him that she was a daughter of the house of Trefoil,—and 'all that sort of thing.' She had it distinctly laid down in her mind. And then there was another move which she would make before she altogether threw up the game. She would force herself into Lord Rufford's presence and throw herself into his arms,—at his feet if need be,—and force him into compliance. Should she fail then she, too, had an idea what a raging woman could do. But her first step now must be with her cousin Mistletoe. She would not write to the duke till she had seen her cousin.

Lord Mistletoe when in London lived at the family house in Piccadilly, and thither early on the Sunday morning she sent a note to say that she especially wished to see her cousin and would call at three o'clock on that day. The messenger brought back word that Lord Mistletoe would be at home, and exactly at that hour the hired brougham stopped at the door. Her mother had wished to accompany her, but she had declared that if she could not go alone she would not go at all. In that she was right; for whatever favour the young heir to the family honours might retain for his fair cousin, who was at any rate a Trefoil, he had none for his uncle's wife. She was shown into his own sitting-room on the ground floor, and then he immediately joined her. 'I wouldn't have you shown upstairs,' he said, 'because I understand from your note that you want to see me in particular.'

'That is so kind of you.'

Lord Mistletoe was a young man about thirty, less in stature than his father or uncle, but with the same handsome inexpressive face. Almost all men take to some line in life. His father was known as a manager of estates; his uncle as a whist-player; he was minded to follow the steps of his grandfather and be a statesman. He was eaten up by no high ambition, but lived in the hope that by perseverance he might live to become a useful Under Secretary, and perhaps, ultimately, a Privy Seal. As he was well educated and laborious, and had no objection to sitting for five hours together in the House of Commons with nothing to do and sometimes with very little to hear, it was thought by his friends that he would succeed. 'And what is it I can do?' he said with that affable smile to which he had already become accustomed as a Government politician.

'I am in great trouble,' said Arabella, leaving her hand for a moment in his as she spoke.

'I am sorry for that. What sort of trouble?' He knew that his uncle and his aunt's family were always short of money, and was already considering to what extent he would go in granting her petition.

'Do you know Lord Rufford?'

'Lord Rufford! Yes;—I know him; but very slightly. My father knows him very much better than I do.'

'I have just been at Mistletoe, and he was there. My story is so hard to tell. I had better out with it at once. Lord Rufford has asked me to be his wife.'

'The deuce he has! It's a very fine property and quite unembarrassed.'

'And now he repudiates his engagement.' Upon hearing this the young lord's face became very long. He also had heard something of the past life of his handsome cousin, though he had always felt kindly to her. 'It was not once only.'

'Dear me! I should have thought your father would be the proper person.'

'Papa has written;—but you know what papa is.'

'Does the duke know of it,—or my mother?'

'It partly went on at Mistletoe. I would tell you the whole story if I knew how.' Then she did tell him her story, during the telling of which he sat profoundly silent. She had gone to stay with Lady Penwether at Lord Rufford's house, and then he had first told her of his love. Then they had agreed to meet at Mistletoe, and she had begged her aunt to receive her. She had not told her aunt at once, and her aunt had been angry with her because they had walked together. Then she had told everything to the duchess and had begged the duchess to ask the duke to speak to Lord Rufford. At Mistletoe Lord Rufford had twice renewed his offer,—and she had then accepted him. But the duke had not spoken to him before he left the place. She owned that she thought the duchess had been a little hard to her. Of course she did not mean to complain, but the duchess had been angry with her because she had hunted. And now, in answer to the note from herself, had come a letter from Lord Rufford in which he repudiated the engagement. 'I only got it yesterday and I came at once to you. I do not think you will see your cousin treated in that way without raising your hand. You will remember that I have no brother?'

'But what can I do?' asked Lord Mistletoe.

She had taken great trouble with her face, so that she was able to burst out into tears. She had on a veil which partly concealed her. She did not believe in the effect of a pocket handkerchief, but sat with her face half averted. 'Tell him what you think about it,' she said.

'Such engagements, Arabella,' he said, 'should always be authenticated by a third party. It is for that reason that a girl generally refers her lover to her father before she allows herself to be considered as engaged.'

'Think what my position has been! I wanted to refer him to my uncle and asked the duchess.'

'My mother must have had some reason. I'm sure she must. There isn't a woman in London knows how such things should be done better than my mother. I can write to Lord Rufford and ask him for an explanation;— but I do not see what good it would do.'

'If you were in earnest about it he would be—afraid of you.'

'I don't think he would in the least. If I were to make a noise about it, it would only do you harm. You wouldn't wish all the world to know that he had——'

'Jilted me! I don't care what the world knows. Am I to put up with such treatment as that and do nothing? Do you like to see your cousin treated in that way?'

'I don't like it at all. Lord Rufford is a good sort of man in his way, and has a large property. I wish with all my heart that it had come off all right; but in these days one can't make a man marry. There used to be the alternative of going out and being shot at;—but that is over now.'

'And a man is to do just as he pleases?'

'I am afraid so. If a man is known to have behaved badly to a girl, public opinion will condemn him.'

'Can anything be worse than his treatment of me?'

Lord Mistletoe could not tell her that he had alluded to absolute knowledge and that at present he had no more than her version of the story;—or that the world would require more than that before the general condemnation of which he had spoken would come. So he sat in silence and shook his head. 'And you think that I should put up with it quietly!'

'I think that your father should see the man.' Arabella shook her head contemptuously. 'If you wish it I will write to my mother.'

'I would rather trust to my uncle.'

'I don't know what he could do;—but I will write to him if you please.'

'And you won't see Lord Rufford?'

He sat silent for a minute or two, during which she pressed him over and over again to have an interview with her recreant lover, bringing up all the arguments that she knew, reminding him of their former affection for each other, telling him that she had no brother of her own, and that her own father was worse than useless in such a matter. A word or two she said of the nature of the prize to be gained, and many words as to her absolute right to regard that prize as her own. But at last he refused. 'I am not the person to do it,' he said. 'Even if I were your brother I should not be so,—unless with the view of punishing him for his conduct;—in which place the punishment to you would be worse than any I could inflict on him. It cannot be good that any young lady should have her name in the mouths of all the lovers of gossip in the country.'

She was going to burst out at him in her anger, but before the words were out of her mouth she remembered herself. She could not afford to make enemies, and certainly not an enemy of him. 'Perhaps, then,' she said, 'you had better tell your mother all that I have told you. I will write to the duke myself.'

And so she left him, and as she returned to Orchard Street in the brougham, she applied to him every term of reproach she could bring to mind. He was selfish, and a coward, and utterly devoid of all feeling of family

honour. He was a prig, and unmanly, and false. A real
cousin would have burst out into a passion, and have
declared himself ready to seize Lord Rufford by the
throat and shake him into instant matrimony. But this
man, through whose veins water was running instead of
blood, had no feeling, no heart, no capability for anger!
Oh, what a vile world it was! A little help,—so very little,
—would have made everything straight for her! If her
aunt had only behaved at Mistletoe as aunts should
behave, there would have been no difficulty. In her
misery she thought that the world was more cruel to her
than to any other person in it.

On her arrival at home, she was astounded by a letter
that she found there,—a letter of such a nature that it
altogether drove out of her head the purpose which she
had of writing to the duke on that evening. The letter
was from Mr. John Morton, and now reached her
through the lawyer to whom it had been sent by private
hand for immediate delivery. It ran as follows:—

'DEAREST ARABELLA,
      'I am very ill,—so ill that Dr. Fanning, who has
come down from London, has, I think, but a poor
opinion of my case. He does not say that it is hopeless,—
and that is all. I think it right to tell you this, as my
affection for you is what it always has been. If you wish to
see me, you and your mother had better come to Bragton
at once. You can telegraph. I am too weak to write more.
                         'Yours most affectionately,
                                   'JOHN MORTON.
'There is nothing infectious.'

'John Morton is dying!' she almost screamed out to her
mother.
      'Dying!'
      'So he says. Oh, what an unfortunate wretch I am!
Everything that touches me comes to grief.' Then she
burst out into a flood of true unfeigned tears.
      'It won't matter so much,' said Lady Augustus, 'if you
mean to write to the duke, and go on with this other—
affair.'

'Oh, mamma, how can you talk in that way?'

'Well, my dear; you know——'

'I am heartless. I know that. But you are ten times worse. Think how I have treated him!'

'I don't want him to die, my dear; but what can I say? I can't do him any good. It is all in God's hands, and if he must die,—why it won't make so much difference to you. I have looked upon all that as over for a long time.'

'It is not over. After all, he has liked me better than any of them. He wants me to go to Bragton.'

'That of course is out of the question.'

'It is not out of the question at all. I shall go.'

'Arabella!'

'And you must go with me, mamma.'

'I will do no such thing,' said Lady Augustus, to whom the idea of Bragton was terrible.

'Indeed you must. He has asked me to go, and I shall do it. You can hardly let me go alone.'

'And what will you say to Lord Rufford?'

'I don't care for Lord Rufford. Is he to prevent my going where I please?'

'And your father,—and the duke,—and the duchess! How can you go there after all that you have been doing since you left?'

'What do I care for the duke and the duchess. It has come to that, that I care for no one. They are all throwing me over. That little wretch Mistletoe will do nothing. This man really loved me. He has never treated me badly. Whether he live or whether he die, he has been true to me.' Then she sat and thought of it all. What would Lord Rufford care for her father's letter? If her cousin Mistletoe would not stir in her behalf, what chance had she with her uncle? And, though she had thoroughly despised her cousin, she had understood and had unconsciously believed much that he had said to her. 'In these days one can't make a man marry!' What horrid days they were! But John Morton would marry her to-morrow if he were well,—in spite of all her ill usage! Of course, he would die, and so she would again be overwhelmed;—but yet she would go and see him. As she

determined to do so, there was something even in her
hard callous heart softer than the love of money, and
more human than the dream of an advantageous settlement in life.

CHAPTER LI

THE SENATOR'S SECOND LETTER

IN the meantime our friend the Senator, up in London,
was much distracted in his mind, finding no one to
sympathise with him in his efforts, conscious of his own
rectitude of purpose, always brave against others, and yet
with a sad doubt in his own mind whether it could be
possible that he should always be right and everybody
around him wrong.

Coming away from Mr. Mainwaring's dinner he had
almost quarrelled with John Morton, or rather John
Morton had altogether quarrelled with him. On their
way back from Dillsborough to Bragton the minister
elect to Patagonia had told him, in so many words, that
he had misbehaved himself at the clergyman's house.
'Did I say anything that was untrue?' asked the Senator.
'Was I inaccurate in my statements? If so, no man alive
will be more ready to recall what he has said and ask for
pardon.' Mr. Morton endeavoured to explain to him
that it was not his statements which were at fault so much
as the opinions based on them and the language in which
those opinions were given. But the Senator could not be
made to understand that a man had not a right to his
opinions, and a right also to the use of forcible language
as long as he abstained from personalities. 'It was
extremely personal,—all that you said about the purchase
of livings,' said Morton. 'How was I to know that?' rejoined the Senator. 'When in private society I inveigh
against pickpockets I cannot imagine, sir, that there
should be a pickpocket in the company.' As the Senator
said this he was grieving in his heart at the trouble he
had occasioned, and was almost repenting the duties he
had imposed on himself; but yet his voice was bellicose
and antagonistic. The conversation was carried on till
Morton found himself constrained to say that, though he

entertained great personal respect for his guest, he could not go with him again into society. He was ill at the time, though neither he himself knew it nor the Senator. On the next morning Mr. Gotobed returned to London without seeing his host, and before the day was over, Dr. Nupper was at Morton's bedside. He was already suffering from gastric fever.

The Senator was, in truth, unhappy as he returned to town. The intimacy between him and the late Secretary of Legation at his capital had arisen from a mutual understanding between them that each was to be allowed to see the faults and to admire the virtues of their two countries, and that conversation between them was to be based on the mutual system. But nobody can, in truth, endure to be told of shortcomings, either on his own part or on that of his country. He himself can abuse himself, or his country; but he cannot endure it from alien lips. Mr. Gotobed had hardly said a word about England which Morton himself might not have said; but such words coming from an American had been too much even for the guarded temper of an unprejudiced and phlegmatic Englishman. The Senator, as he returned alone to London, understood something of this; and when a few days later he heard that the friend who had quarrelled with him was ill, he was discontented with himself and sore at heart.

But he had his task to perform, and he meant to perform it to the best of his ability. In his own country he had heard vehement abuse of the old country from the lips of politicians, and had found at the same time almost on all sides great social admiration for the people so abused. He had observed that every Englishman of distinction was received in the States as a demigod, and that some who were not very great in their own land had been converted into heroes in his. English books were read there; English laws were obeyed there; English habits were cultivated, often at the expense of American comfort. And yet it was the fashion among orators to speak of the English as a wornout, stupid, and enslaved people. He was a thoughtful man, and all this had perplexed him;

so that he had obtained leave from his State and from Congress to be absent during a part of a short Session, and come over determined to learn as much as he could. Everything he heard, and almost everything he saw, offended him at some point. And yet, in the midst of it all, he was conscious that he was surrounded by people who claimed and made good their claims to superiority. What was a lord, let him be ever so rich and have ever so many titles? And yet, even with such a popinjay as Lord Rufford he himself felt the lordship. When that old farmer at the hunt breakfast had removed himself and his belongings to the other side of the table, the Senator, though aware of the justice of his cause, had been keenly alive to the rebuke. He had expressed himself very boldly at the rector's house at Dillsborough, and had been certain that not a word of real argument had been possible in answer to him. But yet he left the house with a feeling almost of shame, which had grown into real penitence before he reached Bragton. He knew that he had already been condemned by Englishmen as ill-mannered, ill-conditioned, and absurd. He was as much alive as any man to the inward distress of heart which such a conviction brings with it to all sensitive minds. And yet he had his purpose, and would follow it out. He was already hard at work on the lecture which he meant to deliver somewhere in London before he went back to his home duties, and had made it known to the world at large that he meant to say some sharp things of the country he was visiting.

Soon after his return to town, he was present at the opening of Parliament, Mr. Mounser Green of the Foreign Office having seen that he was properly accommodated with a seat. Then he went down to the election of a member of Parliament in the little borough of Quinborough. It was unfortunate for Great Britain, which was on its trial, and unpleasant also for the poor Senator, who had appointed himself judge, that such a seat should have fallen vacant at that moment. Quinborough was a little town of 3,000 inhabitants, clustering round the gates of a great Whig marquis, which had been spared—who

can say why?—at the first Reform Bill, and having but
one member, had come out scatheless from the second.
Quinborough still returned its one member with something less than 500 constituents, and in spite of household
suffrage and the ballot had always returned the member
favoured by the marquis. This nobleman, driven no
doubt by his conscience to make some return to the
country for the favour shown to his family, had always
sent to Parliament some useful and distinguished man,
who without such patronage might have been unable to
serve his country. On the present occasion, a friend of
the people,—so called,—an unlettered demagogue, such
as is in England in truth distasteful to all classes, had
taken himself down to Quinborough as a candidate in
opposition to the nobleman's nominee. He had been
backed by all the sympathies of the American Senator,
who knew nothing of him or his unfitness, and nothing
whatever of the patriotism of the marquis. But he did
know what was the population and what the constituency
of Liverpool, and also what were those of Quinborough.
He supposed that he knew what was the theory of representation in England, and he understood correctly that
hitherto the member for Quinborough had been the
nominee of that great lord. These things were horrid to
him. There was to his thinking a fiction,—more than
fiction, a falseness,—about all this, which not only would,
but ought to bring the country prostrate to the dust.
When the working-man's candidate, whose political programme consisted of a general disbelief in all religions,
received—by ballot!—only nine votes from those 500
voters, the Senator declared to himself that the country
must be rotten to the core. It was not only that Britons
were slaves,—but that 'they hugged their chains.' To the
gentleman who assured him that the Right Honble.
———— would make a much better member of Parliament than Tom Bobster the plasterer from Shoreditch, he
in vain tried to prove that the respective merits of the two
men had nothing to do with the question. It had been
the duty of those 500 voters to show to the world that in
the exercise of a privilege entrusted to them for the public

service, they had not been under the dictation of their rich neighbour. Instead of doing so, they had, almost unanimously, grovelled in the dust at their rich neighbour's feet. 'There are but one or two such places left in all England,' said the gentleman. 'But those one or two,' answered the Senator, 'were wilfully left there by the Parliament which represented the whole nation.'

Then, quite early in the session, immediately after the voting of the address, a motion had been made by the Government of the day for introducing household suffrage into the counties. No one knew the labour to which the Senator subjected himself in order that he might master all these peculiarities,—that he might learn how men became members of parliament, and how they ceased to be so, in what degree the House of Commons was made up of different elements, how it came to pass that, though there was a House of Lords, so many lords sat in the lower chamber. All those matters, which to ordinary educated Englishmen are almost as common as the breath of their nostrils, had been to him matter of long and serious study. And as the intent student, who has zealously buried himself for a week among commentaries and notes, feels himself qualified to question Porson and to Be-Bentley Bentley, so did our Senator believe, while still he was groping among the rudiments, that he had all our political intricacies at his fingers' ends. When he heard the arguments used for a difference of suffrage in the towns and counties, and found that even they who were proposing the change were not ready absolutely to assimilate the two, and still held that rural ascendancy,— feudalism as he called it,—should maintain itself by barring a fraction of the House of Commons from the votes of the majority, he pronounced the whole thing to be a sham. The intention was, he said, to delude the people. 'It is all coming,' said the gentleman who was accustomed to argue with him in those days. He spoke in a sad vein, which was in itself distressing to the Senator. 'Why should you be in such a hurry?' The Senator suggested that if the country delayed much longer this imperative task of putting its house in order, the roof would have

fallen in before the repairs were done. Then he found
that this gentleman, too, avoided his company, and declined to sit with him any more in the Gallery of the
House of Commons.

Added to all this was a private rankling sore in regard
to Goarly and Bearside. He had now learned nearly all
the truth about Goarly, and had learned also that Bearside had known the whole when he had last visited that
eminent lawyer's office. Goarly had deserted his sup-
porters, and had turned evidence against Scrobby, his
partner in iniquity. That Goarly was a rascal the Senator
had acknowledged. So far, the general opinion down in
Rufford had been correct. But he could get nobody to
see,—or at any rate, could get nobody to acknowledge,—
that the rascality of Goarly had had nothing to do with
the question as he had taken it up. The man's right to his
own land,—his right to be protected from pheasants and
foxes, from horses and hounds,—was not lessened by the
fact that he was a poor, ignorant, squalid, dishonest
wretch. Mr. Gotobed had now received a bill from
Bearside for £42 7s. 9d. for costs in the case, leaving, after
the deduction of £15 already paid, a sum of £27 7s. 9d.
stated to be still due. And this was accompanied by an
intimation that as he, Mr. Gotobed, was a foreigner soon
about to leave the country, Mr. Bearside must request
that his claim might be settled quite at once. No one
could be less likely than our Senator to leave a foreign
country without paying his bills. He had quarrelled with
Morton,—who also at this time was too ill to have given
him much assistance. Though he had become acquainted
with half Dillsborough, there was nobody there to whom
he could apply. Thus he was driven to employ a London
attorney, and the London attorney told him that he had
better pay Bearside; the Senator remembering at the time
that he would also have to pay the London attorney for
his advice. He gave this second lawyer authority to con-
clude the matter, and at last Bearside accepted £20.
When the London attorney refused to take anything for
his trouble, the Senator felt such conduct almost as an
additional grievance. In his existing frame of mind, he

would sooner have expended a few more dollars than be driven to think well of anything connected with English law.

It was immediately after he had handed over the money in liquidation of Bearside's claim that he sat down to write a further letter to his friend and correspondent Josiah Scroome. His letter was not written in the best of tempers; but still, through it all, there was a desire to be just, and an anxiety to abstain from the use of hard phrases. The letter was as follows:—

'Fenton's Hotel, St. James' Street, London,
'Feb. 12, 187—.

'MY DEAR SIR,

'Since I last wrote I have had much to trouble me and little perhaps to compensate me for my trouble. I told you, I think, in one of my former letters that wherever I went I found myself able to say what I pleased as to the peculiarities of this very peculiar people. I am not now going to contradict what I said then. Wherever I go I do speak out, and my eyes are still in my head and my head is on my shoulders. But I have to acknowledge to myself that I give offence. Mr. Morton, whom you knew at the British Embassy in Washington,—and who I fear is now very ill,—parted from me, when last I saw him, in anger because of certain opinions I had expressed in a clergyman's house, not as being ill-founded but as being antagonistic to the clergyman himself. This I feel to be unreasonable. And in the neighbourhood of Mr. Morton's house, I have encountered the ill-will of a great many,—not for having spoken untruth, for that I have never heard alleged,—but because I have not been reticent in describing the things which I have seen.

'I told you, I think, that I had returned to Mr. Morton's neighbourhood, with the view of defending an oppressed man against the power of the lord who was oppressing him. Unfortunately for me the lord, though a scapegrace, spends his money freely and is a hospitable, kindly-hearted, honest fellow; whereas the injured victim has turned out to be a wretched scoundrel. Scoundrel though

he is, he has still been ill used; and the lord, though good-
natured, has been a tyrant. But the poor wretch has
thrown me over and sold himself to the other side, and
I have been held up to ignominy by all the provincial
newspapers. I have also had to pay through the nose
$175 for my quixotism—a sum which I cannot very well
afford. This money I have lost solely with the view of
defending the weak, but nobody with whom I have discussed the matter seems to recognise the purity of my
object. I am only reminded that I have put myself into
the same boat with a rascal.

'I feel from day to day how thoroughly I could have
enjoyed a sojourn in this country if I had come here without any line of duty laid down for myself. Could I have
swum with the stream and have said yes or no as yes or no
was expected, I might have revelled in generous hospitality. Nothing can be pleasanter than the houses here if
you will only be as idle as the owners of them. But when
once you show them that you have an object, they become
afraid of you. And industry,—in such houses as I now
speak of,—is a crime. You are there to glide through the
day luxuriously in the house,—or to rush through it
impetuously on horseback or with a gun if you be a
sportsman. Sometimes when I have asked questions
about the most material institutions of the country, I have
felt that I was looked upon with absolute loathing. This
is disagreeable.

'And yet I find it more easy in this country to sympathise with the rich than with the poor. I do not here
describe my own actual sympathies, but only the easiness
with which they might be evoked. The rich are at any
rate pleasant. The poor are very much the reverse.
There is no backbone of mutiny in them against the
oppression to which they are subjected; but only the
whining of a dog that knows itself to be a slave and
pleads with his soft paw for tenderness from his master;—
or the futile growlings of the caged tiger who paces up
and down before his bars and has long ago forgotten to
attempt to break them. They are a long-suffering race,
who only now and then feel themselves stirred up to

contest a point against their masters on the basis of
starvation. 'We won't work but on such and such terms,
and if we cannot get them we will lie down and die.'
That I take it is the real argument of a strike. But they
never do lay down and die. If one in every parish, one in
every county, would do so, then the agricultural labourers
of the country might live almost as well as the farmers'
pigs.

'I was present the other day at the opening of Parliament. It was a very grand ceremony,—though the Queen
did not find herself well enough to do her duty in person.
But the grandeur was everything. A royal programme
was read from the foot of the throne, of which even I knew
all the details beforehand, having read them in the newspapers. Two opening speeches were then made by two
young lords,—not after all so very young,—which sounded
like lessons recited by schoolboys. There was no touch of
eloquence,—no attempt at it. It was clear that either of
them would have been afraid to attempt the idiosyncrasy
of passionate expression. But they were exquisitely
dressed and had learned their lessons to a marvel. The
flutter of the ladies' dresses, and the presence of the peers,
and the historic ornamentation of the house were all very
pleasant; but they reminded me of a last year's nut, of
which the outside appearance has been mellowed and
improved by time,—but the fruit inside has withered
away and become tasteless.

'Since that I have been much interested with an attempt,
—a further morsel of cobbling*—which is being done to
improve the representation of the people. Though it be
but cobbling, if it be in the right direction one is glad of
it. I do not know how far you may have studied the
theories and systems of the British House of Commons,
but, for myself, I must own that it was not till the other
day that I was aware that, though it acts together as one
whole, it is formed of two distinct parts. The one part is
sent thither from the towns by household suffrage; and,
this, which may be said to be the healthier of the two as
coming more directly from the people, is nevertheless
disfigured by a multitude of anomalies. Population

hardly bears upon the question. A town with 15,000 inhabitants has two members,—whereas another with 400,000 has only three, and another with 50,000 has one. But there is worse disorder than this. In the happy little village of Portarlington 200 constituents choose a member among them, or have one chosen for them by their careful lord;—whereas in the great city of London something like 25,000 registered electors only send four to Parliament. With this the country is presumed to be satisfied. But in the counties, which by a different system send up the other part of the House, there exists still a heavy property qualification for voting. There is, apparent to all, a necessity for change here;—but the change proposed is simply a reduction of the qualification, so that the rural labourer,—whose class is probably the largest, as it is the poorest, in the country,—is still disfranchised, and will remain so, unless it be his chance to live within the arbitrary line of some so-called borough. For these boroughs, you must know, are sometimes strictly confined to the aggregations of houses which constitute the town, but sometimes stretch out their arms so as to include rural districts. The divisions, I am assured, were made to suit the aspirations of political magnates when the first Reform Bill was passed!* What is to be expected of a country in which such absurdities are loved and sheltered?

'I am still determined to express my views on these matters before I leave the country, and am with great labour preparing a lecture on the subject. I am assured that I shall not be debarred from my utterances because that which I say is unpopular. I am told that as long as I do not touch Her Majesty or Her Majesty's family, or the Christian religion,—which is only the second Holy of Holies,—I may say anything. Good taste would save me from the former offence, and my own convictions from the latter. But my friend who so informs me doubts whether many will come to hear me. He tells me that the serious American is not popular here, whereas the joker is much run after. Of that I must take my chance. In all this I am endeavouring to do a duty, feeling every day more strongly my own inadequacy. Were I to follow my own wishes, I should return by the next steamer to my duties at home.

'Believe me to be,
'Dear Sir,

'The Honble. Josiah Scroome, 'With much sincerity,
'125, Q Street,   'Yours truly,
'Minnesota Avenue, 'ELIAS GOTOBED.'
'Washington.'

CHAPTER LII

PROVIDENCE INTERFERES

THE battle was carried on very fiercely in Mr. Masters' house in Dillsborough, to the misery of all within it; but the conviction gained ground with every one there that Mary was to be sent to Cheltenham for some indefinite time. Dolly and Kate seemed to think that she was to go, never to return. Six months, which had been vaguely mentioned as the proposed period of her sojourn, was to them almost as indefinite as eternity. The two girls had been intensely anxious for the marriage, wishing to have Larry for a brother, looking forward with delight to their share in the unrestricted plenteousness of Chowton Farm, longing to be allowed to consider themselves at home among the ricks*and barns and wide fields; but at this moment things had become so tragic that they were cowed and unhappy,—not that Mary should still refuse Larry Twentyman, but that she should be going away for so long a time. They could quarrel with their elder sister while the assurance was still with them that she would be there to forgive them; but now that she was going away, and that it had come to be believed by both of them that poor Lawrence had no chance, they were sad and downhearted. In all that misery the poor attorney had the worst of it. Mary was free from her stepmother's zeal and her stepmother's persecution, at any rate, at night; but the poor father was hardly allowed to sleep. For Mrs. Masters never gave up her game as altogether lost. Though she might be driven alternately into towering passion and prostrate hysterics, she would

still come again to the battle. A word of encouragement
would, she said, bring Larry Twentyman back to his
courtship, and that word might be spoken, if Mary's visit
to Cheltenham were forbidden. What did the letter
signify, or all the girl's protestations? Did not everybody
know how self-willed young women were; but how they
could be brought round by proper usage! Let Mary once
be made to understand that she would not be allowed to
be a fine lady, and then she would marry Mr. Twentyman quick enough. But this 'Ushanting,' this journeying
to Cheltenham, in order that nothing might be done, was
the very way to promote the disease! This Mrs. Masters
said in season and out of season, night and day, till the
poor husband longed for his daughter's departure, in
order that that point might, at any rate, be settled. In
all these disputes he never quite yielded. Though his
heart sank within him, he was still firm. He would turn
his back to his wife and let her run on with her arguments
without a word of answer, till at last he would bounce out
of bed and swear that, if she did not leave him alone, he
would go and lock himself into the office and sleep with
his head on the office desk.

Mrs. Masters was almost driven to despair; but at last
there came to her a gleam of hope, most unexpectedly.
It had been settled that Mary should make her journey
on Friday, the 12th of February, and that Reginald
Morton should again accompany her. This in itself was
to Mrs. Morton an aggravation of the evil which was
being done. She was not in the least afraid of Reginald
Morton; but this attendance on Mary was, in the eyes of
her stepmother, a cockering of her up, a making a fine
lady of her, which was in itself of all things the most
pernicious. If Mary must go to Cheltenham, why could
she not go by herself, second-class, like any other young
woman? 'Nobody would eat her,' Mrs. Masters declared.
But Reginald was firm in his purpose of accompanying
her. He had no objection whatever to the second class, if
Mrs. Masters preferred it. But as he meant to make the
journey on the same day, of course they would go together.
Mr. Masters said that he was very much obliged. Mrs.

Masters protested that it was all trash from beginning
to the end.

Then there came a sudden disruption to all these plans,
and a sudden renewal of her hopes to Mrs. Masters, which
for one half day nearly restored her to good humour.
Lady Ushant wrote to postpone the visit, because she herself had been summoned to Bragton. Her letter to Mary,
though affectionate, was very short. Her grandnephew
John, the head of the family, had expressed a desire to see
her, and with that wish she was bound to comply. Of
course, she said, she would see Mary at Bragton; or, if
that were not possible, she herself would come into Dillsborough. She did not know what might be the length of
her visit, but when it was over, she hoped that Mary
would return with her to Cheltenham. The old lady's
letter to Reginald was much longer, because in that she
had to speak of the state of John Morton's health, and of
her surprise that she should be summoned to his bedside.
Of course she would go, though she could not look forward with satisfaction to a meeting with the Honble. Mrs.
Morton. Then she could not refrain from alluding to the
fact that, 'if anything were to happen' to John Morton,
Reginald himself would be the squire of Bragton.
Reginald, when he received this, at once went over to the
attorney's house, but he did not succeed in seeing Mary.
He learned, however, that they were all aware that the
journey had been postponed.

To Mrs. Masters it seemed that all this had been a dis-
pensation of Providence. Lady Ushant's letter had been
received on the Thursday, and Mrs. Masters at once found
it expedient to communicate with Larry Twentyman.
She was not excellent herself at the writing of letters, and
therefore she got Dolly to be the scribe. Before the Thursday evening the following note was sent to Chowton Farm:

'DEAR LARRY,

'Pray come and go to the club with father on
Saturday. We haven't seen you for so long! Mother has
got something to tell you.

'Your affectionate friend,
'DOLLY.'

When this was received the poor man was smoking his moody pipe in silence as he roamed about his own farm-yard in the darkness of the night. He had not as yet known any comfort, and was still firm in his purpose of selling the farm. He had been out hunting once or twice, but fancied that people looked at him with peculiar eyes. He could not ride, though he made one or two forlorn attempts to break his neck. He did not care in the least whether they found or not; and when Captain Glomax was held to have disgraced himself thoroughly by wasting an hour in digging out and then killing a vixen, he had not a word to say about it. But, as he read Dolly's note, there came back something of life into his eyes. He had forsworn the club, but would certainly go when thus invited. He wrote a scrawl to Dolly,—'I'll come,' and, having sent it off by the messenger, tried to trust that there might yet be ground for hope. Mrs. Masters would not have allowed Dolly to send such a message without good reason.

On the Friday Mrs. Masters could not abstain from proposing that Mary's visit to Cheltenham should be regarded as altogether out of the question. She had no new argument to offer,—except this last interposition of Providence in her favour. Mr. Masters said that he did not see why Mary should not return with Lady Ushant. Various things, however, might happen. John Morton might die, and then who could tell whether Lady Ushant would ever return to live at Cheltenham? In this way the short-lived peace soon came to an end, especially as Mrs. Masters endeavoured to utilize for general family purposes certain articles which had been purchased with a view to Mary's prolonged residence away from home. This was resented by the attorney, and the peace was short-lived.

On the Saturday Larry came,—to the astonishment of Mr. Masters, who was still in his office at half-past seven. Mrs. Masters at once got hold of him and conveyed him away into the sacred drawing-room. 'Mary is not going,' she said.

'Not going to Cheltenham!'

'It has all been put off. She shan't go at all if I can help it.'

'But why has it been put off, Mrs. Masters?'

'Lady Ushant is coming to Bragton. I suppose that poor man is dying.'

'He is very ill, certainly.'

'And if anything happens there who can say what may happen anywhere else? Lady Ushant will have some-thing else except Mary to think of, if her own nephew comes into all the property.'

'I didn't know she was such friends with the Squire as that.'

'Well;—there it is. Lady Ushant is coming to Bragton and Mary is not going to Cheltenham.'

This she said as though the news must be of vital im-portance to Larry Twentyman. He stood for a while scratching his head as he thought of it. At last it appeared to him that Mary's continual residence in Dillsborough would of itself hardly assist him. 'I don't see, Mrs. Masters, that that will make her a bit kinder to me.'

'Larry, don't you be a coward,—nor yet soft.'

'As for coward, Mrs. Masters, I don't know——'

'I suppose you really do love the girl?'

'I do;—I think I've shown that.'

'And you haven't changed your mind?'

'Not a bit.'

'That's why I speak open to you. Don't you be afraid of her. What's the letter which a girl like that writes? When she gets tantrums into her head of course she'll write a letter.'

'But there's somebody else, Mrs. Masters.'

'Who says so? I say there ain't nobody;—nobody. If anybody tells you that it's only just to put you off. It's just poetry and books and rubbish. She wants to be a fine lady.'

'I'll make her a lady.'

'You make her Mrs. Twentyman, and don't you be made by any one to give it up. Go to the club with Mr. Masters now, and come here just the same as usual. Come to-morrow and have a gossip with the girls together and show that you can keep your pluck up. That's the way to win her.' Larry did go to the club and did think very much of it as he walked home. He had promised to come on the Sunday afternoon, but he could not bring himself to believe in that theory of books and poetry put forward by Mrs. Masters. Books and poetry would not teach a girl like Mary to reject her suitor if she really loved him.

CHAPTER LIII

LADY USHANT AT BRAGTON

ON the Sunday Larry came into Dillsborough and had 'his gossip with the girls' according to order;—but it was not very successful. Mrs. Masters, who opened the door for him, instructed him in a special whisper 'to talk away just as though he did not care a fig for Mary.' He made the attempt manfully,—but with slight effect. His love was too genuine, too absorbing, to leave with him the power which Mrs. Masters assumed him to have when she gave him such advice. A man cannot walk when he has broken his ankle-bone, let him be ever so brave in the attempt. Larry's heart was so weighted that he could not hide the weight. Dolly and Kate had also received hints, and struggled hard to be merry. In the afternoon a walk was suggested, and Mary complied; but when an attempt was made by the younger girls to leave the lover and Mary together, she resented it by clinging closely to Dolly; and then all Larry's courage deserted him. Very little good was done on the occasion by Mrs. Masters' manœuvres.

On the Monday morning, in compliance with a request made by Lady Ushant, Mary walked over to Bragton to see her old friend. Mrs. Masters had declared the request to be very unreasonable. 'Who is to walk five miles and back to see an old woman like that?' To this Mary had replied that the distance across the fields to Bragton was only four miles, and that she had often walked it with her sisters for the very pleasure of the walk. 'Not in weather like this,' said Mrs. Masters. But the day was well enough.

Roads in February are often a little wet, but there was no rain falling. 'I say it's unreasonable,' said Mrs. Masters. 'If she can't send a carriage she oughtn't to expect it.' This coming from Mrs. Masters, whose great doctrine it was that young women ought not to be afraid of work, was so clearly the effect of sheer opposition that Mary disdained to answer it. Then she was accused of treating her stepmother with contempt.

She did walk to Bragton, taking the path by the fields and over the bridge, and loitering for a few minutes as she leant upon the rail. It was there and there only that she had seen together the two men who between them seem to cloud all her life,—the man whom she loved and the man who loved her. She knew now,—she thought that she knew quite well,—that her feelings for Reginald Morton were of such a nature that she could not possibly become the wife of any one else. But had she not seen him for those few minutes on this spot, had he not fired her imagination by telling her of his desire to go back with her over the sites which they had seen together when she was a child, she would not, she thought, have been driven to make to herself so grievous a confession. In that case it might have been that she would have brought herself to give her hand to the suitor of whom all her friends approved.

And then with infinite tenderness she thought of all Larry's virtues,—and especially of that great virtue in a woman's eyes, the constancy of his devotion to herself. She did love him,—but with a varied love,—a love which was most earnest in wishing his happiness, which would have been desirous of the closest friendship, if only nothing more was required. She swore to herself a thousand times that she did not look down upon him because he was only a farmer, that she did not think herself in any way superior to him. But it was impossible that she should consent to be his wife. And then she thought of the other man,—with feelings much less kind. Why had he thrust himself upon her life and disturbed her? Why had he taught her to think herself unfit to mate with this lover who was her equal? Why had he assured her that were she to do so her old friends would be revolted? Why had he exacted from her a promise,—a promise which was sacred to her,—that she would not so give herself away? Yes;—the promise was certainly sacred; but he had been cold and cruel in forcing it from her lips. What business was it of his? Why should he have meddled with her? In the shallow streamlet of her lowly life the waters might have glided on, slow but smoothly, had he not taught them to be ambitious of a rapider, grander course. Now they were disturbed by mud, and there could be no pleasure in them.

She went on over the bridge, and round by the shrubbery to the hall door, which was opened to her by Mrs. Hopkins. Yes, Lady Ushant was there;—but the young squire was very ill, and his aunt was then with him. Mr. Reginald was in the library. Would Miss Masters be shown in there, or would she go up to Lady Ushant's own room? Of course she replied that she would go upstairs and there wait for Lady Ushant.

When she was found by her friend she was told at length the story of all the circumstances which had brought Lady Ushant to Bragton. When John Morton had first been taken ill,—before any fixed idea of danger had occurred to himself or to others,—his grandmother had come to him. Then, as he gradually became weaker, he made various propositions which were all of them terribly distasteful to the old woman. In the first place he had insisted on sending for Miss Trefoil. Up to this period Mary Masters had hardly heard the name of Miss Trefoil, and almost shuddered as she was at once immersed in all these family secrets. 'She is to be here to-morrow,' said Lady Ushant.

'Oh dear,—how sad!'

'He insists upon it, and she is coming. She was here before, and it now turns out that all the world knew that they were engaged. That was no secret, for everybody had heard it.'

'And where is Mrs. Morton now?' Then Lady Ushant went on with her story. The sick man had insisted on making his will, and had declared his purpose of leaving the property to his cousin Reginald. As Lady Ushant said, there was no one else to whom he could leave it with any propriety;—but this had become a matter for bitter contention between the old woman and her grandson.

'Who did she think should have it?' asked Mary.

'Ah;—that I don't know. That he has never told me. But she has had the wickedness to say,—oh,—such things of Reginald. I knew all that before;—but that she should repeat them now is terrible. I suppose she wanted it for some of her own people. But it is so horrible, you know, —when he was so ill! Then he said that he should send for me, so that what is left of the family might be together. After that she went away in anger. Mrs. Hopkins says that she did not even see him the morning she left Bragton.'

'She was always high-tempered,' said Mary.

'And dictatorial beyond measure. She nearly broke my poor dear father's heart. And then she left the house because he would not shut his doors against Reginald's mother. And now I hardly know what I am to do here; or what I may say to this young lady when she comes to-morrow.'

'Is she coming alone?'

'We don't know. She has a mother, Lady Augustus Trefoil,—but whether Lady Augustus will accompany her daughter we have not heard. Reginald says certainly not, or they would have told us so. You have seen Reginald?'

'No, Lady Ushant.'

'You must see him. He is here now. Think what a difference it will make to him.'

'But Lady Ushant,—is he so bad?'

'Dr. Fanning almost says that there is no hope. This poor young woman that is coming;—what am I to say to her? He has made his will. That was done before I came. I don't know why he shouldn't have sent for your father, but he had a gentleman down from town. I suppose he will leave her something; but it is a great thing that Bragton should remain in the family. Oh dear, oh dear, —if any one but a Morton were to be here it would break my heart. Reginald is the only one left now. He's getting

old and he ought to marry. It is so serious when there's
an old family property.'

'I suppose he will—only——'

'Yes; exactly. One can't even think about it while this
poor young man is lying so ill. Mrs. Morton has been
almost like his mother, and has lived upon the Bragton
property,—absolutely lived upon it,—and now she is
away from him because he chooses to do what he likes
with his own. Is it not awful? And she would not put her
foot in the house if she knew that Reginald was here. She
told Mrs. Hopkins as much, and she said that she wouldn't
so much as write a line to me. Poor fellow; he wrote it
himself. And now he thinks so much about it. When
Dr. Fanning went back to London yesterday I think he
took some message to her.'

Mary remained there till lunch was announced but
refused to go down into the parlour, urging that she was
expected home for dinner. 'And there is no chance for
Mr. Twentyman?' asked Lady Ushant. Mary shook her
head. 'Poor man! I do feel sorry for him, as everybody
speaks so well of him. Of course, my dear, I have nothing
to say about it. I don't think girls should ever be in a
hurry to marry, and if you can't love him——'

'Dear Lady Ushant, it is quite settled.'

'Poor young man! But you must go and see Reginald.'
Then she was taken into the library and did see Reginald.
Were she to avoid him,—specially,—she would tell her
tale almost as plainly as though she were to run after him.
He greeted her kindly, almost affectionately, expressing
his extreme regret that his visit to Cheltenham should
have been postponed and a hope that she would be much
at Bragton. 'The distance is so great, Reginald,' said
Lady Ushant.

'I can drive her over. It is a long walk, and I had made
up my mind to get Runciman's little phaeton. I shall
order it for to-morrow if Miss Masters will come.' But
Miss Masters would not agree to this. She would walk
over again some day as she liked the walk, but no doubt
she would only be in the way if she were to come often.

'I have told her about Miss Trefoil,' said Lady Ushant.

'You know, my dear, I look upon you almost as one of
ourselves because you lived here so long. But perhaps you
had better postpone coming again till she has gone.'

'Certainly, Lady Ushant.'

'It might be difficult to explain. I don't suppose she
will stay long. Perhaps she will go back the same day.
I am sure I shan't know what to say to her. But when
anything is fixed, I will send you in word by the postman.'

Reginald would have walked back with her across the
bridge, but that he had promised to go to his cousin immediately after lunch. As it was he offered to accompany
her a part of the way, but was stopped by his aunt, greatly
to Mary's comfort. He was now more beyond her reach
than ever,—more utterly removed from her. He would
probably become Squire of Bragton, and she, in her
earliest days, had heard the late Squire spoken of as
though he were one of the potentates of the earth. She
had never thought it possible; but now it was less possible
than ever. There was something in his manner to her
almost protective, almost fatherly,—as though he had
some authority over her. Lady Ushant had authority
once, but he had none. In every tone of his voice she felt
that she heard an expression of interest in her welfare,—
but it was the interest which a grown-up person takes in
a child, or a superior in an inferior. Of course he was her
superior, but yet the tone of his voice was distasteful to
her. As she walked back to Dillsborough she had told
herself that she would not go again to Bragton without
assuring herself that he was not there.

When she reached home many questions were asked of
her, but she told nothing of the secrets of the Morton
family which had been so openly confided to her. She
would only say that she was afraid that Mr. John Morton
was very ill.

CHAPTER LIV

ARABELLA AGAIN AT BRAGTON

ARABELLA TREFOIL had adhered without flinching
to the purpose she had expressed of going down to
Bragton to see the sick man. And yet at that very time

she was in the midst of her contest with Lord Rufford.
She was aware that a correspondence was going on
between her father and the young lord, and that her
father had demanded an interview. She was aware also
that the matter had been discussed at the family mansion
in Piccadilly, the duke having absolutely come up to
London for the purpose, and that the duke and his
brother, who hardly ever spoke to each other, had
actually had a conference. And this conference had had
results. The duke had not altogether consented to interfere, but had agreed to a compromise proposed by his son.
Lord Augustus should be authorised to ask Lord Rufford
to meet him in the library of the Piccadilly mansion,—so
that there should be some savour of the dukedom in what
might be done and said there. Lord Rufford would by
the surroundings be made to feel that in rejecting Arabella
he was rejecting the duke and all the Mayfair belongings,
and that in accepting her he would be entitled to regard
himself as accepting them all. But by allowing thus much
the duke would not compromise himself,—nor the
duchess, nor Lord Mistletoe. Lord Mistletoe, with that
prudence which will certainly in future years make him
a useful assistant to some minister of the day, had seen all
this, and so it had been arranged.

But, in spite of these doings, Arabella had insisted on
complying with John Morton's wish that she should go
down and visit him in his bed at Bragton. Her mother,
who in these days was driven almost to desperation by her
daughter's conduct, tried her best to prevent the useless
journey, but tried in vain. 'Then,' she said in wrath to
Arabella, 'I will tell your father, and I will tell the duke,
and I will tell Lord Rufford that they need not trouble
themselves any further.' 'You know, mamma, that you
will do nothing of the kind,' said Arabella. And the poor
woman did do nothing of the kind. 'What is it to them
whether I see the man or not?' the girl said. 'They are
not such fools as to suppose that because Lord Rufford
has engaged himself to me now, I was never engaged to
any one before. There isn't one of them doesn't know
that you had made up an engagement between us and

had afterwards tried to break it off.' When she heard
this the unfortunate mother raved, but she raved in vain.
She told her daughter that she would not supply her with
money for the expenses of her journey, but her daughter
replied that she would have no difficulty in finding her
way to a pawn shop. 'What is to be got by it?' asked the
unfortunate mother. In reply to this Arabella would say,
'Mamma, you have no heart;—absolutely none. You
ought to manœuvre better than you do, for your feelings
never stand in your way for a moment.' All this had to
be borne, and the old woman was forced at last not only
to yield but to promise that she would accompany her
daughter to Bragton. 'I know how all this will end,' she
said to Arabella. 'You will have to go your way and I
must go mine.' 'Just so,' replied the daughter. 'I do not
often agree with you, mamma; but I do there altogether.'

Lady Augustus was absolutely at a loss to understand
what were the motives and what the ideas which induced
her daughter to take the journey. If the man were to die,
no good could come of it. If he were to live, then surely
that love which had induced him to make so foolish a
petition would suffice to ensure the marriage, if the
marriage should then be thought desirable. But, at the
present moment, Arabella was still hot in pursuit of Lord
Rufford;—to whom this journey, as soon as it should be
known to him, would give the easiest mode of escape!
How would it be possible that they two should get out at
the Dillsborough Station and be taken to Bragton without
all Rufford knowing it. Of course there would be hymns
sung in praise of Arabella's love and constancy, but such
hymns would be absolutely ruinous to her. It was growing clear to Lady Augustus that her daughter was giving
up the game and becoming frantic as she thought of her
age, her failure, and her future. If so, it would be well
that they should separate.

On the day fixed a close carriage awaited them at the
Dillsborough Station. They arrived both dressed in
black and both veiled,—and with but one maid between
them. This arrangement had been made with some
vague idea of escaping scrutiny rather than from

economy. They had never hitherto been known to go
anywhere without one apiece. There were no airs on the
station now as on that former occasion,—no loud talking;
not even a word spoken. Lady Augustus was asking herself why,—why she should have been put into so lament-
able a position, and Arabella was endeavouring to think
what she would say to the dying man.

She did not think that he was dying. It was not the
purport of her present visit to strengthen her position by
making certain of the man's hand should he live. When
she said that she was not as yet quite so hard-hearted as
her mother, she spoke the truth. Something of regret,
something of penitence, had at times crept over her in
reference to her conduct to this man. He had been very
unlike others on whom she had played her arts. None of
her lovers, or mock lovers, had been serious and stern and
uncomfortable as he. There had been no other who had
ever attempted to earn his bread. To her the butterflies
of the world had been all in all, and the working bees had
been a tribe apart with which she was no more called
upon to mix than is my lady's spaniel with the kennel
hounds. But the chance had come. She had consented
to exhibit her allurements before a man of business and
the man of business had at once sat at her feet. She had
soon repented,—as the reader has seen. The alliance had
been distasteful to her. She had found that the man's
ways were in no wise like her ways,—and she had found
also that were she to become his wife, he certainly would
not change. She had looked about for a means of escape,
—but as she did so she had recognized the man's truth.
No doubt he had been different from the others, less gay
in his attire, less jocund in his words, less given to flattery
and sport and gems and all the little wickednesses which
she had loved. But they,—those others had, one and all
struggled to escape from her. Through all the gems and
mirth and flattery there had been the same purpose. They
liked the softness of her hand, they liked the flutter of her
silk, they liked to have whispered in their ears the bold
words of her practised raillery. Each liked for a month
or two to be her special friend. But then, after that, each

had deserted her as had done the one before; till in each
new alliance she felt that such was to be her destiny, and
that she was a rolling stone which would never settle
itself, straining for waters which would never come lip
high. But John Morton, after once saying that he loved
her, had never tired, had never wished to escape. He had
been so true to his love, so true to his word, that he had
borne from her usage which would have fully justified
escape had escape been to his taste. But to the last he had
really loved her, and now, on his death bed, he had sent
for her to come to him. She would not be coward enough
to refuse his request. 'Should he say anything to you about
his will don't refuse to hear him, because it may be of the
greatest importance,' Lady Augustus whispered to her
daughter as the carriage was driven up to the front door.

It was then four o'clock, and it was understood that the
two ladies were to stay that one night at Bragton, a letter
having been received by Lady Ushant that morning informing her that the mother as well as the daughter was
coming. Poor Lady Ushant was almost beside herself,—
not knowing what she should do with the two women,
and having no one in the house to help her. Something
she had heard of Lady Augustus, but chiefly from Mrs.
Hopkins, who certainly had not admired her master's
future mother-in-law. Nor had Arabella been popular;
but of her Mrs. Hopkins had only dared to say that she
was very handsome and 'a little upstartish.' How she was
to spend the evening with them Lady Ushant could not
conceive,—it having been decided, in accordance with
the doctor's orders, that the interview should not take
place till the next morning. When they were shown in,
Lady Ushant stood just within the drawing-room door
and muttered a few words as she gave her hand to each.
'How is he?' asked Arabella, throwing up her veil boldly,
as soon as the door was closed. Lady Ushant only shook
her head. 'I knew it would be so. It is always so with
anything I care for.'

'She is so distressed, Lady Ushant,' said the mother,
'that she hardly knows what she does.' Arabella shook
her head. 'It is so, Lady Ushant.'

'Am I to go to him now?' said Arabella. Then the old lady explained the doctor's orders, and offered to take them to their rooms. 'Perhaps I might say a word to you alone? I will stay here if you will go with mamma.' And she did stay till Lady Ushant came down to her. 'Do you mean to say it is certain,' she asked,—'certain that he must—die?'

'No;—I do not say that.'

'It is possible that he may recover?'

'Certainly it is possible. What is not possible with God?'

'Ah;—that means that he will die.' Then she sat herself down and almost unconsciously took off her bonnet and laid it aside. Lady Ushant, then looking into her face for the first time, was at a loss to understand what she had heard of her beauty. Could it be the same girl of whom Mrs. Hopkins had spoken and of whose brilliant beauty Reginald had repeated what he had heard? She was haggard, almost old, with black lines round her eyes. There was nothing soft or gracious in the tresses of her hair. When Lady Ushant had been young, men had liked hair such as was that of Mary Masters. Arabella's yellow locks,—whencesoever they might have come,—were rough and uncombed. But it was the look of age, and the almost masculine strength of the lower face, which astonished Lady Ushant the most. 'Has he spoken to you about me?' she asked.

'Not to me.' Then Lady Ushant went on to explain that though she was there now as the female representative of the family, she had never been so intimate with John Morton as to admit of such confidence as that suggested.

'I wonder whether he can love me,' said the girl.

'Assuredly he does, Miss Trefoil. Why else should he send for you?'

'Because he is an honest man. I hardly think that he can love me much. He was to have been my husband, but he will escape that. If I thought that he would live I would tell him that he was free.'

'He would not want to be—free.'

'He ought to want it. I am not fit for him. I have

come here, Lady Ushant, because I want to tell him the truth.'

'But you love him?' Arabella made no answer, but sat looking steadily into Lady Ushant's face. 'Surely you do love him.'

'I do not know. I don't think I did love him, though now I may. It is so horrible that he should die, and die while all this is going on. That softens one, you know. Have you ever heard of Lord Rufford?'

'Lord Rufford; the young man?'

'Yes; the young man.'

'Never, particularly. I knew his father.'

'But not this man? Mr. Morton never spoke to you of him?'

'Not a word.'

'I have been engaged to him since I became engaged to your nephew.'

'Engaged to Lord Rufford,—to marry him?'

'Yes, indeed.'

'And will you marry him?'

'I cannot say. I tell you this, Lady Ushant, because I must tell somebody in this house. I have behaved very badly to Mr. Morton, and Lord Rufford is behaving as badly to me.'

'Did John know of this?'

'No; but I meant to tell him. I determined that I would tell him had he lived. When he sent for me, I swore that I would tell him. If he is dying, how can I say it?' Lady Ushant sat bewildered, thinking over it, understanding nothing of the world in which this girl had lived, and not knowing now how things could have been as she described them. It was not as yet three months since, to her knowledge, this young woman had been staying at Bragton as the affianced bride of the owner of the house,—staying there with her own mother and his grandmother,—and now she declared that since that time she had become engaged to another man, and that that other man had already jilted her! And yet she was here that she might make a death-bed parting with the man who regarded himself as her affianced husband. 'If I were sure that he were dying, why should I trouble him?' she said again.

Lady Ushant found herself utterly unable to give any counsel to such a condition of circumstances. Why should she be asked? This young woman had her mother with her. Did her mother know all this, and nevertheless bring her daughter to the house of a man who had been so treated! 'I really do not know what to say,' she replied at last.

'But I was determined that I would tell some one. I thought that Mrs. Morton would have been here.' Lady Ushant shook her head. 'I am glad she is not, because she was not civil to me when I was here before. She would have said hard things to me, though not perhaps harder than I have deserved. I suppose I may still see him to-morrow?'

'Oh yes; he expects it.'

'I shall not tell him now. I could not tell him if I thought he were dying. If he gets better, you must tell him all.'

'I don't think I could do that, Miss Trefoil.'

'Pray do; pray do. I call upon you to tell him everything.'

'Tell him that you will be married to Lord Rufford?'

'No; not that. If Mr. Morton were well to-morrow, I would have him,—if he chose to take me after what I have told you.'

'You do love him, then?'

'At any rate, I like no one better.'

'Not the young lord?'

'No; why should I like him? He does not love me. I hate him! I would marry Mr. Morton to-morrow, and go with him to Patagonia, or anywhere else, if he would have me after hearing what I have done.' Then she rose from her chair; but before she left the room she said a word further. 'Do not speak a word to my mother about this. Mamma knows nothing of my purpose. Mamma only wants me to marry Lord Rufford, and to throw Mr. Morton over. Do not tell any one else, Lady Ushant; but if he is ever well enough, then you must tell him.' After that she went, leaving Lady Ushant in the room astounded by the story she had heard.

CHAPTER LV

'I HAVE TOLD HIM EVERYTHING'

THAT evening was very long and very sad to the three ladies assembled in the drawing-room at Bragton Park, but it was probably more so to Lady Augustus than the other two. She hardly spoke to either of them; nor did they to her; while a certain amount of conversation in a low tone was carried on between Lady Ushant and Miss Trefoil. When Arabella came down to dinner she received a message from the sick man. He sent his love, and would so willingly have seen her instantly,— only that the doctor would not allow it. But he was so glad,—so very glad that she had come! This Lady Ushant said to her in a whisper, and seemed to say it as though she had not heard a word of that frightful story which had been told to her not much more than an hour ago. Arabella did not utter a word in reply, but put out her hand, secretly as it were, and grasped that of the old lady to whom she had told the tale of her later intrigues. The dinner did not keep them long, but it was very grievous to them all. Lady Ushant might have made some effort to be at least a complaisant hostess to Lady Augustus had she not heard this story,—had she not been told that the woman, knowing her daughter to be engaged to John Morton, had wanted her to marry Lord Rufford. The story having come from the lips of the girl herself, had moved some pity in the old woman's breast in regard to her; but for Lady Augustus she could feel nothing but horror.

In the evening Lady Augustus sat alone, not even pretending to open a book or to employ her fingers. She seated herself on one side of the fire with a screen in her hand, turning over such thoughts in her mind as were perhaps customary to her. Would there ever come a period to her misery, an hour of release in which she might be in comfort ere she died? Hitherto from one year to another, from one decade to the following, it had all been struggle and misery, contumely and contempt.

She thought that she had done her duty by her child, and her child hated and despised her. It was but the other day that Arabella had openly declared that in the event of her marriage she would not have her mother as a guest in her own house. There could be no longer hope for triumph and glory;—but how might she find peace so that she might no longer be driven hither and thither by this ungrateful tyrant child? Oh,—how hard she had worked in the world, and how little the world had given her in return!

Lady Ushant and Arabella sat at the other side of the fire, at some distance from it, on a sofa, and carried on a fitful conversation in whispers, of which a word would now and then reach the ears of the wretched mother. It consisted chiefly of a description of the man's illness, and of the different sayings which had come from the doctors who had attended him. It was marvellous to Lady Augustus, as she sat there listening, that her daughter should condescend to take an interest in such details. What could it be to her now how the fever had taken him, or why or when? On the very next day,—the very morning on which she would go and sit,—ah so uselessly,—by the dying man's bedside her father was to meet Lord Rufford at the ducal mansion in Piccadilly, to see if anything could be done in that quarter! It was impossible that she should really care whether John Morton's lease of life was to be computed at a week's purchase or at that of a month! And yet Arabella sat there asking sick-room questions and listening to sick-room replies as though her very nature had been changed. Lady Augustus heard her daughter inquire what food the sick man took, and then Lady Ushant at great length gave the list of his nourishment. What sickening hypocrisy! thought Lady Augustus.

Lady Augustus must have known her daughter well; and yet it was not hypocrisy. The girl's nature, which had become thoroughly evil from the treachery it had received, was not altered. Such sudden changes do not occur more frequently than other miracles. But zealously as she had practised her arts she had not as yet practised them long enough not to be cowed by certain outward circumstances. There were moments when she still heard in her imagination the sound of that horse's foot as it struck the skull of the unfortunate fallen rider;—and now the purport of the death of this man whom she had known so intimately and who had behaved so well to her,—to whom her own conduct had been so foully false, —for a time brought her back to humanity. But Lady Augustus had got beyond that and could not at all understand it.

By nine they had all retired for the night. It was necessary that Lady Ushant should again visit her nephew, and the mother and daughter went to their own rooms. 'I cannot in the least make out what you are doing,' said Lady Augustus in her most severe voice.

'I dare say not, mamma.''

'I have been brought here, at a terrible sacrifice——'

'Sacrifice! What sacrifice? You are as well here as anywhere else.'

'I say I have been brought here at a terrible sacrifice for no purpose whatever. What use is it to be? And then you pretend to care what this poor man is eating and drinking and what physic he is taking when, the last time you were in his company, you wouldn't so much as look at him for fear you should make another man jealous.'

'He was not dying then.'

'Psha!'

'Oh yes. I know all that. I do feel a little ashamed of myself when I am almost crying for him.'

'As if you loved him!'

'Dear mamma, I do own that it is foolish. Having listened to you on these subjects for a dozen years at least I ought to have got rid of all that. I don't suppose I do love him. Two or three weeks ago I almost thought I loved Lord Rufford, and now I am quite sure that I hate him. But if I heard to-morrow that he had broken his neck out hunting, I ain't sure but what I should feel something. But he would not send for me as this man has done.'

'It was very impertinent.'

'Perhaps it was ill-bred, as he must have suspected something as to Lord Rufford. However, we are here now.'

'I will never allow you to drag me anywhere again.'

'It will be for yourself to judge of that. If I want to go anywhere, I shall go. What's the good of quarrelling? You know that I mean to have my way.'

The next morning neither Lady Augustus nor Miss Trefoil came down to breakfast, but at ten o'clock Arabella was ready, as appointed, to be taken into the sick man's bedroom. She was still dressed in black, but had taken some trouble with her face and hair. She followed Lady Ushant in, and silently standing by the bedside, put her hand upon that of John Morton, which was lying outside on the bed. 'I will leave you now, John,' said Lady Ushant, retiring, 'and come again in half an hour.'

'When I ring,' he said.

'You mustn't let him talk for more than that,' said the old lady to Arabella as she went.

It was more than an hour afterwards when Arabella crept into her mother's room, during which time Lady Ushant had twice knocked at her nephew's door, and had twice been sent away. 'It is all over, mamma!' she said.

Lady Augustus looked into her daughter's eyes and saw that she had really been weeping. 'All over!'

'I mean for me,—and you. We have only got to go away.'

'Will he—die?'

'It will make no matter though he should live for ever. I have told him everything. I did not mean to do it because I thought that he would be weak; but he has been strong enough for that.'

'What have you told him?'

'Just everything,—about you and Lord Rufford and myself,—and what an escape he had had not to marry me. He understands it all now.'

'It is a great deal more than I do.'

'He knows that Lord Rufford has been engaged to me.' She clung to this statement so vehemently that she had really taught herself to believe that it was so.

'Well!'

'And he knows also how his lordship is behaving to me.'

Of course he thinks that I have deserved it. Of course I have deserved it. We have nothing to do now but to go back to London.'

'You have brought me here all the way for that?'

'Only for that! As the man was dying, I thought that I would be honest just for once. Now that I have told him, I don't believe that he will die. He does not look to be so very ill.'

'And you have thrown away that chance?'

'Altogether. You didn't like Bragton, you know, and therefore it can't matter to you.'

'Like it!'

'To be sure you would have got rid of me had I gone to Patagonia. But he will not go to Patagonia now, even if he gets well; and so there was nothing to be gained. The carriage is to be here at two to take us to the station, and you may as well let Judith come and put the things up.'

Just before they took their departure Lady Ushant came to Arabella, saying that Mr. Morton wanted to speak one other word to her before she went. So she returned to the room, and was again left alone at the man's bedside. 'Arabella,' he said, 'I thought that I would tell you that I have forgiven everything.'

'How can you have forgiven me? There are things which a man cannot forgive.'

'Give me your hand,' he said,—and she gave him her hand. 'I do forgive it all. Even should I live, it would be impossible that we should be man and wife.'

'Oh yes.'

'But, nevertheless, I love you. Try,—try to be true to some one.'

'There is no truth left in me, Mr. Morton. I should not dishonour my husband if I had one, but still I should be a curse to him. I shall marry some day, I suppose, and I know it will be so. I wish I could change with you,— and die.'

'You are unhappy now?'

'Indeed I am. I am always unhappy. I do not think you can tell what it is to be so wretched. But I am glad that you have forgiven me.' Then she stooped down and kissed his hand. As she did so he touched her brow with his hot lips, and then she left him again. Lady Ushant was waiting outside the door. 'He knows it all,' said Arabella. 'You need not trouble yourself with the message I gave you. The carriage is at the door. Good-bye. You need not come down. Mamma will not expect it.' Lady Ushant, hardly knowing how she ought to behave, did not go down. Lady Augustus and her daughter got in Mr. Runciman's carriage without any farewells, and were driven back from the park to the Dillsborough Station. To poor Lady Ushant the whole thing had been very terrible. She sat silent and unoccupied the whole of that evening, wondering at the horror of such a history. This girl had absolutely dared to tell the dying man all her own disgrace, and had travelled down from London to Bragton with the purpose of doing so! When next she crept into the sick-room she almost expected that her nephew would speak to her on the subject; but he only asked whether that sound of wheels which he heard beneath his window had come from the carriage which had taken them away, and then did not say a further word of either Lady Augustus or her daughter.

'And what do you mean to do now?' said Lady Augustus, as the train approached the London terminus.

'Nothing.'

'You have given up Lord Rufford?'

'Indeed I have not.'

'Your journey to Bragton will hardly help you much with him.'

'I don't want it to help me at all. What have I done that Lord Rufford can complain of? I have not abandoned Lord Rufford for the sake of Mr. Morton. Lord Rufford ought only to be too proud, if he knew it all.'

'Of course he could make use of such an escapade as this?'

'Let him try. I have not done with Lord Rufford yet, and so I can tell him. I shall be at the duke's in Piccadilly to-morrow morning.'

'That will be impossible, Arabella.'

'They shall see whether it is impossible. I have got

beyond caring very much what people say now. I know
the kind of way papa would be thrown over if there is no
one there to back him. I shall be there, and I will ask
Lord Rufford to his face whether we did not become
engaged when we were at Mistletoe.'

'They won't let you in.'

'I'll find a way to make my way in. I shall never be his
wife. I don't know that I want it. After all what's the
good of living with a man if you hate each other,—or
living apart, like you and papa?'

'He has income enough for anything!' exclaimed Lady
Augustus, shocked at her daughter's apparent blindness.

'It isn't that I'm thinking of; but I'll have my revenge
on him. Liar! To write and say that I had made a mistake! He had not the courage to get out of it when we
were together; but when he had run away in the night,
like a thief, and got into his own house, then he could
write and say that I had made a mistake! I have sometimes pitied men when I have seen girls hunting them
down; but, upon my word, they deserve it.' This renewal
of spirit did something to comfort Lady Augustus. She
had begun to fear that her daughter, in her despair,
would abandon altogether the one pursuit of her life; but
it now seemed that there was still some courage left for
the battle.

That night nothing more was said, but Arabella
applied all her mind to the present condition of her
circumstances. Should she or should she not go to the
House in Piccadilly on the following morning? At last
she determined that she would not do so, believing that
should her father fail she might make a better opportunity
for herself afterwards. At her uncle's house she would
hardly have known where or how to wait for the proper
moment of her appearance. 'So you are not going to
Piccadilly?' said her mother on the following morning.

'It appears not,' said Arabella.

CHAPTER LVI

'NOW WHAT HAVE YOU GOT TO SAY?'

IT may be a question whether Lord Augustus Trefoil or Lord Rufford looked forward to the interview which was to take place at the duke's mansion with the greater dismay. The unfortunate father whose only principle in life had been that of avoiding trouble would have rather that his daughter should have been jilted a score of times than that he should have been called upon to interfere once. There was in this demand upon him a breach of a silent but well-understood compact. His wife and daughter had been allowed to do just what they pleased and to be free of his authority, upon an understanding that they were never to give him any trouble. She might have married Lord Rufford, or Mr. Morton, or any other man she might have succeeded in catching, and he would not have troubled her either before or after her marriage. But it was not fair that he should be called upon to interfere in her failures. And what was he to say to this young lord? Being fat and old and plethoric he could not be expected to use a stick and thrash the young lord. Pistols were gone,—a remembrance of which fact perhaps afforded some consolation. Nobody now need be afraid of anybody, and the young lord would not be afraid of him. Arabella declared that there had been an engagement. The young lord would of course declare that there had been none. Upon the whole he was inclined to believe it most probable that his daughter was lying. He did not think it likely that Lord Rufford should have been such a fool. As for taking Lord Rufford by the back of his neck and shaking him into matrimony, he knew that that would be altogether out of his power. And then the hour was so wretchedly early. It was that little fool Mistletoe who had named ten o'clock,—a fellow who took Parliamentary papers to bed with him, and had a blue book brought to him every morning at half-past seven with a cup of tea. By ten o'clock Lord Augustus would not have had time to take his first glass of soda and brandy preparatory to the labour of getting into his clothes. But he was afraid of his wife and daughter, and absolutely did get into a cab at the door of his lodgings in Duke Street, St. James', precisely at a quarter past ten. As the duke's house was close to the corner of Clarges Street the journey he had to make was not long.

Lord Rufford would not have agreed to the interview but that it was forced upon him by his brother-in-law. 'What good can it do?' Lord Rufford had asked. But his brother-in-law had held that that was a question to be answered by the other side. In such a position Sir George thought that he was bound to concede as much as this,— in fact to concede almost anything short of marriage. 'He can't do the girl any good by talking,' Lord Rufford had said. Sir George assented to this, but nevertheless thought that any friend deputed by her should be allowed to talk, at any rate once. 'I don't know what he'll say. Do you think he'll bring a big stick?' Sir George, who knew Lord Augustus, did not imagine that a stick would be brought. 'I couldn't hit him, you know. He's so fat that a blow would kill him.' Lord Rufford wanted his brother-in-law to go with him;—but Sir George assured him that this was impossible. It was a great bore. He had to go up to London all alone,—in February, when the weather was quite open and hunting was nearly coming to an end. And for what? Was it likely that such a man as Lord Augustus should succeed in talking him into marrying any girl? Nevertheless he went, prepared to be very civil, full of sorrow at the misunderstanding but strong in his determination not to yield an inch. He arrived at the mansion precisely at ten o'clock and was at once shown into a back room on the ground floor. He saw no one but a very demure old servant who seemed to look upon him as one who was sinning against the Trefoil family in general, and who shut the door upon him, leaving him as it were in prison. He was so accustomed to be the absolute master of his own minutes and hours that he chafed greatly as he walked up and down the room for what seemed to him the greater part of a day. He looked repeatedly at his watch, and at half-past ten

declared to himself that if that fat old fool did not come
within two minutes he would make his escape.

'The fat old fool' when he reached the house asked for
his nephew and endeavoured to persuade Lord Mistletoe
to go with him to the interview. But Lord Mistletoe was
as firm in refusing as had been Sir George Penwether.
'You are quite wrong,' said the young man, with well-
informed sententious gravity. 'I could do nothing to help
you. You are Arabella's father, and no one can plead her
cause but yourself.' Lord Augustus dropped his eyebrows over his eyes as this was said. They who knew him
well and had seen the same thing done when his partner
would not answer his call at whist or had led up to his
discard were aware that the motion was tantamount to
a very strong expression of disgust. He did not, however,
argue the matter any further, but allowed himself to be
led away slowly by the same solemn servant. Lord Rufford had taken up his hat preparatory to his departure,
when Lord Augustus was announced just five minutes
after the half hour.

When the elder man entered the room the younger one
put down his hat and bowed. Lord Augustus also bowed,
and then stood for a few moments silent with his fat hands
extended on the round table in the middle of the room.
'This is a very disagreeable kind of thing, my lord,' he said.

'Very disagreeable, and one that I lament above all
things,' answered Lord Rufford.

'That's all very well;—very well indeed;—but, damme,
what's the meaning of it all? That's what I want to ask.
What's the meaning of it all?' Then he paused as though
he had completed the first part of his business,—and
might now wait awhile till the necessary explanation had
been given. But Lord Rufford did not seem disposed to
give any immediate answer. He shrugged his shoulders,
and, taking up his hat, passed his hand once or twice
round the nap. Lord Augustus opened his eyes very wide
as he waited and looked at the other man; but it seemed
that the other man had nothing to say for himself. 'You
don't mean to tell me, I suppose, that what my daughter
says isn't true?'

'Some unfortunate mistake, Lord Augustus;—most unfortunate.'

'Mistake be ——.' He stopped himself before the sentence was completed, remembering that such an interview should be conducted on the part of him, as father, with something of dignity. 'I don't understand anything about mistakes. Ladies don't make mistakes of that kind. I won't hear of mistakes.' Lord Rufford again shrugged his shoulders. 'You have engaged my daughter's affections.'

'I have the greatest regard for Miss Trefoil.'

'Regard be ——.' Then again he remembered himself. 'Lord Rufford, you've got to marry her. That's the long and the short of it.'

'I am sure I ought to be proud.'

'So you ought.'

'But ——'

'I don't know the meaning of "but," my lord. I want to know what you mean to do.'

'Marriage isn't in my line at all.'

'Then what the d—— business have you to go about and talk to a girl like that? Marriage not in your line! Who cares for your line? I never heard such impudence in all my life. You get yourself engaged to a young lady of high rank and position and then you say that—— marriage isn't in your line.' Upon that he opened his eyes still wider, and glared upon the offender wrathfully.

'I can't admit that I was ever engaged to Miss Trefoil.'

'Didn't you make love to her?'

The poor victim paused a moment before he answered this question, thereby confessing his guilt before he denied it. 'No, my lord; I don't think I ever did.'

'You don't think! You don't know whether you asked my daughter to marry you or not! You don't think you made love to her!'

'I am sure I didn't ask her to marry me.'

'I am sure you did. And now what have you got to say?' Here there was another shrug of the shoulders. 'I suppose you think because you are a rich man that you may do whatever you please. But you'll have to learn the difference. You must be exposed, sir.'

'I hope for the lady's sake that as little as possible may be said of it.'

'D—— the ——!' Lord Augustus in his assumed wrath was about to be very severe on his daughter, but he checked himself again. 'I'm not going to stop here talking all day,' he said. 'I want to hear your explanation and then I shall know how to act.' Up to this time he had been standing, which was unusual with him. Now he flung himself into an armchair.

'Really, Lord Augustus, I don't know what I've got to say. I admire your daughter exceedingly. I was very much honoured when she and her mother came to my house at Rufford. I was delighted to be able to show her a little sport. It gave me the greatest satisfaction when I met her again at your brother's house. Coming home from hunting we happened to be thrown together. It's a kind of thing that will occur, you know. The duchess seemed to think a great deal of it; but what can one do? We could have had two postchaises, of course,—only one doesn't generally send a young lady alone. She was very tired, and fainted with the fatigue. That I think is about all.'

'But,—damme, sir, what did you say to her?' Lord Rufford again rubbed the nap of his hat. 'What did you say to her first of all, at your own house?'

'A poor fellow was killed out hunting, and everybody was talking about that. Your daughter saw it herself.'

'Excuse me, Lord Rufford, if I say that that's what we used to call shuffling* at school. Because a man broke his neck out hunting ——'

'It was a kick on the head, Lord Augustus.'

'I don't care where he was kicked. What has that to do with your asking my daughter to be your wife?'

'But I didn't.'

'I say you did,—over and over again.' Here Lord Augustus got out of his chair, and made a little attempt to reach the recreant lover;—but he failed, and fell back again into his armchair. 'It was first at Rufford, and then you made an appointment to meet her at Mistletoe. How do you explain that?'

'Miss Trefoil is very fond of hunting.'

'I don't believe she ever went out hunting in her life before she saw you. You mounted her,—and gave her a horse,—and took her out,—and brought her home. Everybody at Mistletoe knew all about it. My brother and the duchess were told of it. It was one of those things that are plain to everybody as the nose on your face. What did you say to her when you were coming home in that postchaise?'

'She was fainting.'

'What has that to do with it? I don't care whether she fainted or not. I don't believe she fainted at all. When she got into that carriage she was engaged to you, and when she got out of it she was engaged ever so much more. The duchess knew all about it. Now what have you got to say?' Lord Rufford felt that he had nothing to say. 'I insist upon having an answer.'

'It's one of the most unfortunate mistakes that ever were made.'

'By G——!' exclaimed Lord Augustus, turning his eyes up against the wall, and appealing to some dark ancestor who hung there. 'I never heard of such a thing in all my life; never!'

'I suppose I might as well go now,' said Lord Rufford after a pause.

'You may go to the d——, sir,—for the present.' Then Lord Rufford took his departure, leaving the injured parent panting with his exertions.

As Lord Rufford went away he felt that that difficulty had been overcome with much more ease than he had expected. He hardly knew what it was that he had dreaded, but he had feared something much worse than that. Had an appeal been made to his affections he would hardly have known how to answer. He remembered well that he had assured the lady that he loved her, and had a direct question been asked him on that subject he would not have lied. He must have confessed that such a declaration had been made by him. But he had escaped that. He was quite sure that he had never uttered a hint in regard to marriage, and he came away from the duke's house almost with an assurance that he had done nothing that was worthy of much blame.

Lord Augustus looked at his watch, rang the bell, and ordered a cab. He must now go and see his daughter, and then he would have done with the matter—for ever. But as he was passing through the hall, his nephew caught hold of him and took him back into the room. 'What does he say for himself?' asked Lord Mistletoe.

'I don't know what he says. Of course he swears that he never spoke a word to her.'

'My mother saw him paying her the closest attention.'

'How can I help that? What can I do? Why didn't your mother pin him then and there? Women can always do that kind of thing if they choose.'

'It is all over, then?'

'I can't make a man marry if he won't. He ought to be thrashed within an inch of his life. But if one does that kind of thing, the police are down upon one. All the same, I think the duchess might have managed it if she had chosen.' After that he went to the lodgings in Orchard Street, and there repeated his story. 'I have done all I can,' he said, 'and I don't mean to interfere any further. Arabella should know how to manage her own affairs.'

'And you don't mean to punish him?' asked the mother.

'Punish him! How am I to punish him? If I were to throw a decanter at his head, what good would that do?'

'And you mean to say that she must put up with it?' Arabella was sitting by as these questions were asked.

'He says that he never said a word to her. Who am I to believe?'

'You did believe him, papa?'

'Who said so, miss? But I don't see why his word isn't as good as yours. There was nobody to hear it, I suppose. Why didn't you get it in writing, or make your uncle fix him at once? If you mismanage your own affairs, I can't put them right for you.'

'Thank you, papa. I am so much obliged to you. You

come back and tell me that every word he says is to be taken for gospel, and that you don't believe a word I have spoken. That is so kind of you! I suppose he and you will be the best friends in the world now. But I don't mean to let him off in that way. As you won't help me, I must help myself.'

'What did you expect me to do?'

'Never to leave him till you had forced him to keep his word. I should have thought that you would have taken him by the throat in such a cause. Any other father would have done so.'

'You are an impudent, wicked girl, and I don't believe he was ever engaged to you at all,' said Lord Augustus, as he took his leave.

'Now you have made your father your enemy,' said the mother.

'Everybody is my enemy,' said Arabella. 'There are no such things as love and friendship. Papa pretends that he does not believe me, just because he wants to shirk the trouble. I suppose you'll say you don't believe me next.'

Chapter LVII

MRS. MORTON RETURNS

A FEW days after that on which Lady Augustus and her daughter left Bragton, old Mrs. Morton returned to that place. She had gone away in very bitterness of spirit against her grandson in the early days of his illness. For some period antecedent to that there had come up causes for quarrelling. John Morton had told her that he had been to Reginald's house, and she, in her wrath, replied that he had disgraced himself by doing so. When those harsh words had been forgotten, or at any rate forgiven, other causes of anger had sprung up. She had endeavoured to drive him to repudiate Arabella Trefoil, and in order that she might do so effectually had contrived to find out something of Arabella's doings at Rufford and at Mistletoe. Her efforts in this direction had had an effect directly contrary to that which she had

intended. There had· been moments in which Morton
had been willing enough to rid himself of that burden.
He had felt the lady's conduct in his own house, and had
seen it at Rufford. He, too, had heard something of
Mistletoe. But the spirit within him was aroused at the
idea of dictation, and he had been prompted to contradict
the old woman's accusation against his intended bride,
by the very fact that they were made by her. And then
she threatened him. If he did these things,—if he would
consort with an outcast from the family such as Reginald
Morton, and take to himself such a bride as Arabella
Trefoil, he could never more be to her as her child. This
of course was tantamount to saying that she would leave
her money to some one else,—money which, as he well
knew, had been collected from the Bragton property. He
had ever been to her as her son, and yet he was aware of
a propensity on her part to enrich her own noble relatives
with her hoards,—a desire from gratifying which she had
hitherto been restrained by conscience. Morton had been
anxious enough for his grandmother's money, but, even
in the hope of receiving it, would not bear indignity
beyond a certain point. He had therefore declared it to
be his purpose to marry Arabella Trefoil, and because he
had so declared almost had brought himself to forgive
that young lady's sins against him. Then, as his illness
became serious, there arose the question of disposing of
the property in the event of his death. Mrs. Morton was
herself very old, and was near her grave. She was apt to
speak of herself as one who had but a few days left to her
in this world. But, to her, property was more important
than life or death;—and rank probably more important
than either. .She was a brave, fierce, evil-minded, but
conscientious old woman,—one, we may say, with very
bad lights indeed, but who was steadfastly minded to
walk by those lights, such as they were. She did not
scruple to tell her grandson that it was his duty to leave
the property away from his cousin Reginald, nor to allege
as a reason for his doing so that in all probability Reginald
Morton was not the legitimate heir of his great-grandfather, Sir Reginald. For such an assertion John Morton

knew there was not a shadow of ground. No one but this old woman had ever suspected that the Canadian girl whom Reginald's father had brought with him to Bragton had been other than his honest wife;—and her suspicions had only come from vague assertions, made by herself in blind anger till at last she had learned to believe them. Then, when in addition to this, he asserted his purpose of asking Arabella Trefoil to come to him at Bragton, the cup of her wrath was overflowing, and she withdrew from the house altogether. It might be that he was dying. She did in truth believe that he was dying. But there were things more serious to her than life or death. Should she allow him to trample upon all her feelings because he was on his death-bed,—when perhaps in very truth he might not be on his death-bed at all? She, at any rate, was near her death,—and she would do her duty. So she packed up her things—to the last black skirt of an old gown, so that every one at Bragton might know that it was her purpose to come back no more. And she went away.

Then Lady Ushant came to take her place, and with Lady Ushant came Reginald Morton. The one lived in the house and the other visited it daily. And, as the reader knows, Lady Augustus came with her daughter. Mrs. Morton, though she had gone,—for ever,—took care to know of the comings and goings at Bragton. Mrs. Hopkins was enjoined to write to her and tell her everything; and though Mrs. Hopkins with all her heart took the side of Lady Ushant and Reginald, she had never been well inclined to Miss Trefoil. Presents too were given and promises were made; and Mrs. Hopkins, not without some little treachery, did from time to time send to the old lady a record of what took place at Bragton. Arabella came and went, and Mrs. Hopkins thought that her coming had not led to much. Lady Ushant was always with Mr. John,—such was the account given by Mrs. Hopkins;—and the general opinion was that the squire's days were numbered.

Then the old woman's jealousy was aroused, and, perhaps, her heart was softened. It was still hard black winter, and she was living alone in lodgings in London. The noble cousin, a man nearly as old as herself, whose children she was desirous to enrich, took but little notice of her, nor would she have been happy had she lived with him. Her life had been usually solitary, with little breaks to its loneliness occasioned by the visits to England of him whom she had called her child. That this child should die before her, should die in his youth, did not shock her much. Her husband had done so, and her own son, and sundry of her noble brothers and sisters. She was hardened against death. Life to her had never been joyous, though the trappings of life were so great in her eyes. But it broke her heart that her child should die in the arms of another old woman who had always been to her as an enemy. Lady Ushant, in days now long gone by, but still remembered as though they were yesterday, had counselled the reception of the Canadian female. And Lady Ushant, when the Canadian female and her husband were dead, had been a mother to the boy whom she, Mrs. Morton, would so fain have repudiated altogether. Lady Ushant had always been 'on the other side;' and now Lady Ushant was paramount at Bragton.

And doubtless there was some tenderness, though Mrs. Morton was unwilling to own even to herself that she was moved by any such feeling. If she had done her duty in counselling him to reject both Reginald Morton and Arabella Trefoil,—as to which she admitted no doubt in her own mind;—and if duty had required her to absent herself when her counsel was spurned, then would she be weak and unmindful of duty should she allow any softness of heart to lure her back again. It was so she reasoned. But still some softness was there; and when she heard that Miss Trefoil had gone, and that her visit had not, in Mrs. Hopkins's opinion, 'led to much,' she wrote to say that she would return. She made no request and clothed her suggestion in no words of tenderness; but simply told her grandson that she would come back—as the Trefoils had left him.

And she did come. When the news was first told to Lady Ushant by the sick man himself, that lady proposed

that she should at once go back to Cheltenham. But
when she was asked whether her animosity to Mrs.
Morton was so great that she could not consent to remain
under the same roof, she at once declared that she had no
animosity whatsoever. The idea of animosity running
over nearly half a century was horrible to her; and therefore, though she did in her heart of hearts dread the other
old woman, she consented to stay. 'And what shall
Reginald do?' she asked. John Morton had thought
about this too, and expressed a wish that Reginald should
come regularly,—as he had come during the last week
or two.

It was just a week from the day on which the Trefoils
had gone that Mrs. Morton was driven up to the door in
Mr. Runciman's fly. This was at four in the afternoon,
and had the old woman looked out of the fly window she
might have seen Reginald making his way by the little
path to the bridge which led back to Dillsborough. It was
at this hour that he went daily, and he had not now
thought it worth his while to remain to welcome Mrs.
Morton. And she might also have seen, had she looked
out, that with him was walking a young woman. She
would not have known Mary Masters; but had she seen
them both, and had she known the young woman, she
would have declared in her pride that they were fit
associates. But she saw nothing of this, sitting there
behind her veil, thinking whether she might still do anything, and if so, what she might do to avert the present
evil destination of the Bragton estate. There was an
honourable nephew of her own,—or rather a great-
nephew,—who might easily take the name, who would so
willingly take the name! or if this were impracticable,
there was a distant Morton, very distant, whom she had
never seen and certainly did not love, but who was clearly
a Morton, and who would certainly be preferable to that
young enemy of forty years' standing. Might there not
be some bargain made? Would not her dying grandson
be alive to the evident duty of enriching the property and
leaving behind him a wealthy heir? She could enrich the
property and make the heir wealthy by her money.

'How is he?' That of course was the first question when Mrs. Hopkins met her in the hall. Mrs. Hopkins only shook her head and said that perhaps he had taken his food that day a little better than on the last. Then there was a whisper, to which Mrs. Hopkins whispered back her answer. Yes,—Lady Ushant was in the house,—was at this moment in the sick man's room. Mr. Reginald was not staying there,—had never stayed here,—but came every day. He had only just left. 'And is he to come still?' asked Mrs. Morton with wrath in her eyes. Mrs. Hopkins did not know but was disposed to think that Mr. Reginald would come every day. Then Mrs. Morton went up to her own room,—and while she prepared herself for her visit to the sick room Lady Ushant retired. She had a cup of tea, refusing all other refreshment, and then, walking erect as though she had been forty instead of seventy-five, she entered her grandson's chamber and took her old place at his bedside.

Nothing was then said about Arabella, nor, indeed, at any future time was her name mentioned between them; nor was anything then said about the future fate of the estate. She did not dare to bring up the subject at once, though, on the journey down from London, she had determined that she would do so. But she was awed by his appearance and by the increased appanages of his sick bed. He spoke, indeed, of the property, and expressed his anxiety that Chowton Farm should be bought, if it came into the market. He thought that the old acres should be redeemed, if the opportunity arose—and if the money could be found. 'Chowton Farm!' exclaimed the old woman, who remembered well the agony which had attended the alienation of that portion of the Morton lands.

'It may be that it will be sold.'

'Lawrence Twentyman sell Chowton Farm! I thought he was well off.' Little as she had been at Bragton she knew all about Chowton Farm,—except that its owner was so wounded by vain love as to be like a hurt deer. Her grandson did not tell her all the story, but explained to her that Lawrence Twentyman, though not poor, had

other plans of life, and thought of leaving the neighbourhood. She, of course, had the money; and as she believed
that land was the one proper possession for an English
gentleman of ancient family, she doubtless would have
been willing to buy it, had she approved of the hands into
which it would fall. It seemed to him that it was her duty
to do as much for the estate with which all her fortune had
been concerned. 'Yes,' she said; 'it should be bought,—
if other things suited. We will talk of it to-morrow, John.'
Then he spoke of his mission to Patagonia, and of his
regret that it should be abandoned. Even were he ever
to be well again, his strength would return to him too late
for this purpose. He had already made known to the
Foreign Office his inability to undertake that service.
But she could perceive that he had not in truth abandoned
his hopes of living, for he spoke of much of his ambition
as to the public service. The more he thought of it, he
said, the more certain he became that it would suit him
better to go on with his profession than to live the life of
a country squire in England. And yet she could see the
change which had taken place since she was last there,
and was aware that he was fading away from day to
day.

It was not till they were summoned to dine together
that she saw Lady Ushant. Very many years had passed
since last they were together, and yet neither seemed to
the other to be much changed. Lady Ushant was still
soft, retiring, and almost timid; whereas Mrs. Morton
showed her inclination to domineer even in the way in
which she helped herself to salt. While the servant was
with them very little was said on either side. There was
a word or two from Mrs. Morton, to show that she considered herself the mistress there, and a word from the
other lady proclaiming that she had no pretensions of
that kind. But after dinner, in the little drawing-room,
they were more communicative. Something of course
was said as to the health of the invalid. Lady Ushant was
not the woman to give a pronounced opinion on such
a subject. She used doubtful, hesitating words, and
would in one minute almost contradict what she had said

in the former. But Mrs. Morton was clever enough to perceive that Lady Ushant was almost without hope. Then she made a little speech with a fixed purpose. 'It must be a great trouble to you, Lady Ushant, to be so long away from home.'

'Not at all,' said Lady Ushant, in perfect innocence. 'I have nothing to bind me anywhere.'

'I shall think it my duty to remain here now,—till the end.'

'I suppose so. He has always been almost the same to you as your own.'

'Quite so; quite the same. He is my own.' And yet, thought Lady Ushant, she left him in his illness! She, too, had heard something from Mrs. Hopkins of the temper in which Mrs. Morton had last left Bragton. 'But you are not bound to him in that way.'

'Not in that way, certainly.'

'In no way, I may say. It was very kind of you to come when business made it imperative on me to go to town; but I do not think we can call upon you for further sacrifice.'

'It is no sacrifice, Mrs. Morton.' Lady Ushant was as meek as a worm, but a worm will turn. And, though innocent, she was quick enough to perceive that at this, their first meeting, the other old woman was endeavouring to turn her out of the house.

'I mean that it can hardly be necessary to call upon you to give up your time.'

'What has an old woman to do with her time, Mrs. Morton?'

Hitherto Mrs. Morton had smiled. The smile, indeed, had been grim, but it had been intended to betoken outward civility. Now there came a frown upon her brow, which was more grim and by no means civil. 'The truth is, that at such a time one who is almost a stranger——'

'I am no stranger,' said Lady Ushant.

'You had not seen him since he was an infant.'

'My name was Morton as his is, and my dear father was the owner of this house. Your husband, Mrs. Morton, was his grandfather and my brother. I will allow no one to tell me that I am a stranger at Bragton. I have lived here many more years than you.'

'A stranger to him, I meant. And now that he is ill——'

'I shall stay with him—till he desires me to go away. He asked me to stay and that is quite enough.' Then she got up and left the room with more dignity,—as also she had spoken with more earnestness,—than Mrs. Morton had given her credit for possessing. After that the two ladies did not meet again till the next day.

CHAPTER LVIII

THE TWO OLD LADIES

ON the next morning Mrs. Morton did not come down to breakfast, but sat alone upstairs nursing her wrath. During the night she had made up her mind to one or two things. She would never enter her grandson's chambers when Lady Ushant was there. She would not speak to Reginald Morton, and should he come into her presence while she was at Bragton she would leave the room. She would do her best to make the house, in common parlance, 'too hot' to hold that other woman. And she would make use of those words which John had spoken concerning Chowton Farm as a peg on which she might hang her discourse in reference to his will. If in doing all this she should receive that dutiful assistance which she thought that he owed her,—then she should stand by his bedside, and be tender to him, and nurse him to the last as a mother would nurse a child. But if, as she feared, he were headstrong in disobeying, then she would remember that her duty to her family, if done with a firm purpose, would have lasting results, while his life might probably be an affair of a few weeks,—or even days.

At about eleven Lady Ushant was with her patient when a message was brought by Mrs. Hopkins. Mrs. Morton wished to see her grandson and desired to know whether it would suit him that she should come now. 'Why not?' said the sick man, who was sitting up in his bed. Then Lady Ushant collected her knitting and was

about to depart. 'Must you go because she is coming?'
Morton asked. Lady Ushant, shocked at the necessity of
explaining to him the ill feeling that existed, said that
perhaps it would be best. 'Why should it be best?' Lady
Ushant shook her head, and smiled, and put her hand
upon the counterpane,—and retired. As she passed the
door of her rival's room she could see the black silk dress
moving behind the partly open door, and as she entered
her own she heard Mrs. Morton's steps upon the corridor.
The place was almost 'too hot' for her. Anything would
be better than scenes like this in the house of a dying man.

'Need my aunt have gone away?' he asked after the
first greeting.

'I did not say so.'

'She seemed to think that she was not to stay.'

'Can I help what she thinks, John? Of course she feels
that she is——'

'Is what?'

'An interloper—if I must say it.'

'But I have sent for her, and I have begged her to stay.'

'Of course she can stay if she wishes. But, dear John,
there must be much to be said between you and me which,
—which cannot "interest her;" or which, at least, she
ought not to hear.' He did not contradict this in words,
feeling himself to be too weak for contest; but within his
own mind he declared that it was not so. The things
which interested him now were as likely to interest his
great-aunt as his grandmother, and to be as fit for the
cars of the one, as for those of the other.

An hour had passed after this, during which she
tended him, giving him food and medicine, and he had
slept, before she ventured to allude to the subject which
was nearest to her heart. 'John,' she said at last, 'I have
been thinking about Chowton Farm.'

'Well.'

'It certainly should be bought.'

'If the man resolves on selling it.'

'Of course; I mean that. How much would it be?'
Then he mentioned the sum which Twentyman had
named, saying that he had inquired and had been told

that the price was reasonable. 'It is a large sum of money, John.'

'There might be a mortgage for part of it.'

'I don't like mortgages. The property would not be yours at all if it were mortgaged as soon as bought. You would pay 5 per cent. for the money and only get 3 per cent. from the land.' The old lady understood all about it.

'I could pay it off in two years,' said the sick man.

'There need be no paying off, and no mortgage, if I did it. I almost believe I have got enough to do it.' He knew very well that she had much more than enough. 'I think more of this property than of anything in the world, my dear.'

'Chowton Farm could be yours, you know.'

'What should I do with Chowton Farm? I shall probably be in my grave before the slow lawyer would have executed the deeds.' And I in mine, thought he to himself, before the present owner has quite made up his mind to part with his land. 'What would a little place like that do for me? But in my father-in-law's time it was part of the Bragton property. He sold it to pay the debts of a younger son, forgetting, as I thought, what he owed to the estate;'—it had in truth been sold on behalf of the husband of this old woman who was now complaining— 'and if it can be recovered it is our duty to get it back again. A property like this should never be lessened. It is in that way that the country is given over to shop-keepers and speculators, and is made to be like France or Italy. I quite think that Chowton Farm should be bought. And though I might die before it was done, I would find the money.'

'I knew what your feeling would be.'

'Yes, John. You could not but know it well. But——' Then she paused a moment, looking into his face. 'But I should wish to know what would become of it— eventually.'

'If it were yours you could do what you pleased with it.'

'But it would be yours.'

'Then it would go with the rest of the property.'

'To whom would it go? We have all to die, my dear,

and who can say whom it may please the Almighty to take first?'

'In this house, ma'am, every one can give a shrewd guess. I know my own condition. If I die without children of my own every acre I possess will go to the proper heir. Thinking as you do, you ought to agree with me in that.'

'But who is the proper heir?'

'My cousin Reginald. Do not let us contest it, ma'am. As certainly as I lie here, he will have Bragton when I am gone.'

'Will you not listen to me, John?'

'Not about that. How could I die in peace were I to rob him?'

'It is all your own,—to do as you like with.'

'It is all my own, but not to do as I like with. With your feelings, with your ideas, how can you urge me to such an injustice?'

'Do I want it for myself? I do not even want it for any one belonging to me. There is your cousin Peter.'

'If he were the heir he should have it,—though I know nothing of him, and believe him to be but a poor creature and very unfit to have the custody of a family property.'

'But he is his father's son.'

'I will believe nothing of that,' said the sick man, raising himself in his bed. 'It is a slander;—it is based on no evidence whatsoever. No one even thought of it but you.'

'John, is that the way to speak to me?'

'It is the way to speak of an assertion so injurious.' Then he fell back again on his pillows, and she sat by his bedside for a full half-hour speechless, thinking of it all. At the end of that time she had resolved that she would not yet give it up. Should he regain his health and strength,—and she would pray fervently night and day that God would be so good to him,—then everything would be well. Then he would marry and have children, and Bragton would descend in the right line. But were it to be ordained otherwise,—should it be God's will that he must die,—then, as he grew weaker, he would become more plastic in her hands, and she might still prevail. At present he was stubborn with the old stubbornness, and would not see with her eyes. She would bide her time, and be careful to have a lawyer ready. She turned it all over in her mind, as she sat there watching him in his sleep. She knew of no one but Mr. Masters, whom she distrusted as being connected with the other side of the family,—whose father had made that will by which the property in Dillsborough had been dissevered from Bragton. But Mr. Masters would probably obey instructions, if they were given to him definitely.

She thought of it all, and then went down to lunch. She did not dare to refuse altogether to meet the other woman, lest such resolve on her part might teach those in the house to think that Lady Ushant was the mistress. She took her place at the head of the table, and interchanged a few words with her grandson's guest, which, of course, had reference to his health. Lady Ushant was very ill able to carry on a battle of any sort, and was willing to show her submission in everything,—unless she were desired to leave the house. While they were still sitting at table, Reginald Morton walked into the room. It had been his habit to do so regularly for the last week. A daily visitor does not wait to have himself announced. Reginald had considered the matter, and had determined that he would follow his practice just as though Mrs. Morton were not there. If she were civil to him, then would he be very courteous to her. It had never occurred to him to expect conduct such as that with which she greeted him. The old woman got up and looked at him sternly—'My nephew, Reginald,' said Lady Ushant, supposing that some introduction might be necessary. Mrs. Morton gathered the folds of her dress together and, without a word, stalked out of the room. And yet she believed,—she could not but believe,—that her grandson was on his deathbed in the room above!

'Oh, Reginald, what are we to do?' said Lady Ushant.

'Is she like that to you?'

'She told me last night that I was a stranger, and that I ought to leave the house.'

'And what did you say?'

'I told her I should stay while he wished me to stay. But it is all so terrible, that I think I had better go.'

'I would not stir a step—on her account.'

'But why should she be so bitter? I have done nothing to offend her. It is more than half even my long lifetime since I saw her. She is nothing; but I have to think of his comfort. I suppose she is good to him; and though he may bid me stay, such scenes as this in the house must be a trouble to him.' Nevertheless, Reginald was strong in opinion that Lady Ushant ought not to allow herself to be driven away, and declared his own purpose of coming daily, as had of late been his wont.

Soon after this, Reginald was summoned to go upstairs, and he again met the angry woman in the passage, passing her, of course, without a word. And then Mary came to see her friend, and she also encountered Mrs. Morton, who was determined that no one should come into that house without her knowledge. 'Who is that young woman?' said Mrs. Morton to the old housekeeper.

'That is Miss Masters, my lady.'

'And who is Miss Masters? and why does she come here at such a time as this?'

'She is the daughter of Attorney Masters, my lady. It was she as was brought up here by Lady Ushant.'

'Oh,—that young person.'

'She's come here generally of a day now to see her ladyship.'

'And is she taken up to my grandson?'

'Oh dear, no, my lady. She sits with Lady Ushant for an hour or so, and then goes back with Mr. Reginald.'

'Oh,—that is it, is it? The house is made use of for such purposes as that!'

'I don't think there is any purposes, my lady,' said Mrs. Hopkins, almost roused to indignation, although she was talking to the acknowledged mistress of the house, whom she always called 'my lady.'

Lady Ushant told the whole story to her young friend, bitterly bewailing her position. 'Reginald tells me not to go, but I do not think that I can stand it. I should not mind the quarrel so much, only that he is so ill.'

'She must be a very evil-minded person.'

'She was always arrogant and always hard. I can remember her just the same; but that was so many years ago. She left Bragton then because she could not banish his mother from the house. But to bear it all in her heart so long is not like a human being, let alone a woman. What did he say to you going home yesterday?'

'Nothing, Lady Ushant.'

'Does he know that it will all be his if that poor fellow should die? He never speaks to me as though he thought of it.'

'He would certainly not speak to me about it. I do not think he thinks of it. He is not like that.'

'Men do consider such things. And they are only cousins; and they have never known each other! Oh, Mary!'

'What are you thinking of, Lady Ushant?'

'Men ought not to care for money or position, but they do. If he comes here, all that I have will be yours.'

'Oh, Lady Ushant!'

'It is not much, but it will be enough.'

'I do not want to hear about such things now.'

'But you ought to be told. Ah, dear;—if it could be as I wish!' The imprudent, weak-minded, loving old woman longed to hear a tale of mutual love,—longed to do something which should cause such a tale to be true on both sides. And yet she could not quite bring herself to express her wish either to the man or to the woman.

Poor Mary almost understood it, but was not quite sure of her friend's meaning. She was, however, quite sure that if such were the wish of Lady Ushant's heart, Lady Ushant was wishing in vain. She had twice walked back to Dillsborough with Reginald Morton, and he had been more sedate, more middle-aged, less like a lover than ever. She knew now that she might safely walk with him, being sure that he was no more likely to talk of love than would have been old Dr. Nupper had she accepted the offer which he had made her of a cast in his gig.* And now that Reginald would probably become Squire of Bragton, it was more impossible than ever. As Squire of Bragton, he would seek some highly born bride, quite out of her way, whom she could never know. And then she would see neither him—nor Bragton any more. Would it not have been better that she should have married Larry Twenty-man, and put an end to so many troubles beside her own?

Again she walked back with him to Dillsborough, passing as they always did across the little bridge. He seemed to be very silent as he went, more so than usual,—and as was her wont with him, she only spoke to him when he addressed her. It was only when he got out on the road that he told her what was on his mind. 'Mary,' he said, 'how will it be with me if that poor fellow dies?'

'In what way, Mr. Morton?'

'All that place will be mine. He told me so just now.'

'But that would be of course.'

'Not at all. He might give it to you if he pleased. He could not have an heir who would care for it less. But it is right that it should be so. Whether it would suit my taste or not to live as Squire of Bragton,—and I do not think it would suit my taste well,—it ought to be so. I am the next, and it will be my duty.'

'I am sure you do not want him to die.'

'No, indeed. If I could save him by my right hand,—if I could save him by my life, I would do it.'

'But of all lives it must surely be the best.'

'Do you think so? What is such a one likely to do? But then what do I do, as it is? It is the sort of life you would like,—if you were a man.'

'Yes,—if I were a man,' said Mary. Then he again relapsed into silence, and hardly spoke again till he left her at her father's door.

<h2>Chapter LIX</h2>

<h2>THE LAST EFFORT</h2>

WHEN Mary reached her home she was at once met by her stepmother in the passage with tidings of importance. 'He is upstairs in the drawing-room,' said

Mrs. Masters. Mary, whose mind was laden with thoughts of Reginald Morton, asked who was the he. 'Lawrence Twentyman,' said Mrs. Masters. 'And now, my dear, do, do think of it before you go to him.' There was no anger now in her stepmother's face,—but entreaty and almost love. She had not called Mary 'my dear' for many weeks past,—not since that journey to Cheltenham. Now she grasped the girl's hand as she went on with her prayer. 'He is so good and so true! And what better can there be for you? With your advantages, and Lady Ushant, and all that, you would be quite the lady at Chowton. Think of your father and sisters;—what a good you could do them! and think of the respect they all have for him, dining with Lord Rufford, the other day, and all the other gentlemen. It isn't only that he has got plenty to live on, but he knows how to keep it as a man ought. He's sure to hold up his head and be as good a squire as any of 'em.' This was a very different tale;—a note altogether changed! It must not be said that the difference of the tale and the change of the note affected Mary's heart; but her stepmother's manner to her did soften her. And then why should she regard herself or her own feelings? Like others she had thought much of her own happiness, had made herself the centre of her own circle, had, in her imagination, built castles in the air and filled them according to her fancy. But her fancies had been all shattered into fragments; not a stone of her castles was standing; she had told herself unconsciously that there was no longer a circle and no need for a centre. The last half-hour which she had passed with Reginald Morton on the road home had made quite sure that which had been sure enough before. He was altogether out of her reach, thinking only of the new duties which were coming to him. She would never walk with him again; never put herself in the way of indulging some fragment of an illusory hope. She was nothing now,—nothing even to herself. Why should she not give herself and her services to this young man if the young man chose to take her as she was? It would be well that she should do something in the world. Why should she

not look after his house, and mend his shirts, and reign
over his poultry-yard? In this way she would be useful,
and respected by all,—unless, perhaps, by the man she
loved. 'Mary, say that you will think of it once more,'
pleaded Mrs. Masters.

'I may go upstairs,—to my own room?'

'Certainly: do;—go up and smooth your hair. I will
tell him that you are coming to him. He will wait. But
he is much in earnest now,—and so sad,—that I know he
will not come again.'

Then Mary went upstairs, determined to think of it.
She began at once, woman-like, to smooth her hair as her
stepmother had recommended, and to remove the dust
of the road from her face and dress. But not the less was
she thinking of it the while. Could she do it, how much
pain would be spared even to herself! How much that
was now bitter as gall in her mouth would become,—not
sweet,—but tasteless! There are times in one's life in
which the absence of all savour seems to be sufficient for
life in this world. Were she to do this thing she thought
that she would have strength to banish that other man
from her mind,—and at last from her heart. He would be
there, close to her, but of a different kind and leading
a different life. Mrs. Masters had told her that Larry
would be as good a squire as the best of them; but it
should be her care to keep him and herself in their
proper position, to teach him the vanity of such aspirations. And the real squire opposite, who would despise
her,—for had he not told her that she would be despicable
if she married this man,—would not trouble her then.
They might meet on the roads, and there would be a cold
question or two as to each other's welfare, and a vain
shaking of hands,—but they would know nothing and
care for nothing as to each other's thoughts. And there
would come some stately dame who, hearing how things
had been many years ago, would perhaps——. But no;—
the stately dame should be received with courtesy, but there
should be no patronising. Even in these few minutes upstairs she thought much of the stately dame, and was quite
sure that she would endure no patronage from Bragton.

She almost thought that she could do it. There were hideous ideas afflicting her soul dreadfully, but which she strove to banish. Of course she could not love him,—not at first. But all those who wished her to marry him, including himself, knew that;—and still they wished her to marry him. How could that be disgraceful which all her friends desired? Her father, to whom she was, as she knew well, the very apple of his eye, wished her to marry this man; and yet her father knew that her heart was elsewhere. Had not women done it by hundreds, by thousands, and had afterwards performed their duties well as mothers and wives. In other countries, as she had read, girls took the husbands found for them by their parents as a matter of course. As she left the room, and slowly crept downstairs, she almost thought she would do it. She almost thought;—but yet, when her hand was on the lock, she could not bring herself to say that it should be so.

He was not dressed as usual. In the first place, there was a round hat on the table, such as men wear in cities. She had never before seen such a hat with him except on a Sunday. And he wore a black cloth coat, and dark brown pantaloons, and a black silk handkerchief. She observed it all, and thought that he had not changed for the better. As she looked into his face, it seemed to her more common—meaner than before. No doubt he was good-looking,—but his good looks were almost repulsive to her. He had altogether lost his little swagger;—but he had borne that little swagger well, and in her presence it had never been offensive. Now he seemed as though he had thrown aside all the old habits of his life, and was pining to death from the loss of them. 'Mary,' he said, 'I have come to you,—for the last time. I thought I would give myself one more chance, and your father told me that I might have it.' He paused, as though expecting an answer. But she had not yet quite made up her mind. Had she known her mind, she would have answered him frankly. She was quite resolved as to that. If she could once bring herself to give him her hand, she would not coy it for a moment. 'I will be your wife, Larry.' That

was the form on which she had determined, should she
find herself able to yield. But she had not brought herself to it as yet. 'If you can take me, Mary, you will,—
well,—save me from life-long misery, and make the man
who loves you the best-contented and the happiest man
in England.'

'But, Larry, I do not love you.'

'I will make you love me. Good usage will make a wife
love her husband. Don't you think you can trust
me?'

'I do believe that I can trust you for everything good.'

'Is that nothing?'

'It is a great deal, Larry, but not enough;—not enough
to bring together a man and woman as husband and wife.
I would sooner marry a man I loved, though I knew he
would ill-use me.'

'Would you?'

'To marry either would be wrong.'

'I sometimes think, dearest, that if I could talk better
I should be better able to persuade you.'

'I sometimes think you talk so well that I ought to be
persuaded;—but I can't. It is not lack of talking.'

'What is it, then?'

'Just this;—my heart does not turn itself that way. It is
the same chance that has made you——partial to me.'

'Partial! Why I love the very air you breathe. When
I am near you, everything smells sweet. There isn't anything that belongs to you but I think I should know it,
though I found it a hundred miles away. To have you in
the room with me would be like heaven,—if I only knew
that you were thinking kindly of me.'

'I always think kindly of you, Larry.'

'Then say that you will be my wife.' She paused, and
became red up to the roots of her hair. She seated herself
on a chair, and then rose again—and again sat down.
The struggle was going on within her, and he perceived
something of the truth. 'Say the word once, Mary;—say
it but once.' And as he prayed to her he came forward
and went down upon his knees.

'I cannot do it,' she replied at last, speaking very

hoarsely, not looking at him, not even addressing herself to him.

'Mary!'

'Larry, I cannot do it. I have tried, but I cannot do it. Oh Larry, dear Larry, do not ask me again. Larry, I have no heart to give. Another man has it all.'

'Is it so?' She bowed her head in token of assent. 'Is it that young parson?' exclaimed Larry, in anger.

'It is not. But, Larry, you must ask no questions now. I have told you my secret that all this might be set at rest. But if you are generous, as I know you are, you will keep my secret, and will ask no questions. And Larry, if you are unhappy, so am I. If your heart is sore, so is mine. He knows nothing of my love, and cares nothing for me.'

'Then throw him aside.'

She smiled and shook her head. 'Do you think I would not if I could? Why do you not throw me aside?'

'Oh, Mary!'

'Can not I love as well as you? You are a man, and have the liberty to speak of it. Though I cannot return it, I can be proud of your love, and feel grateful to you. I cannot tell mine. I cannot think of it without blushing. But I can feel it, and know it, and be as sure that it has trodden me down and got the better of me as you can. But you can go out into the world and teach yourself to forget.'

'I must go away from here then.'

'You have your business and your pleasures, your horses and your fields and your friends. I have nothing— but to remain here and know that I have disobliged all those that love me. Do you think, Larry, I would not go and be your wife if I could? I have told you all, Larry, and now do not ask me again.'

'Is it so?'

'Yes;—it is so.'

'Then I shall cut it all. I shall sell Chowton and go away. You tell me I have my horses and my pleasures! What pleasures? I know nothing of my horses,—not whether they are lame or sound. I could not tell you of one of them whether he is fit to go to-morrow. Business!

The place may farm itself for me, for I can't stay there. Everything sickens me to look at it. Pleasures indeed!'

'Is that manly, Larry?'

'How can a man be manly when the manliness is knocked out of him? A man's courage lies in his heart;—but if his heart is broken where will his courage be then? I couldn't hold my head up here any more,—and I shall go.'

'You must not do that,' she said, getting up and laying hold of his arm.

'But I must do it.'

'For my sake you must stay here, Larry;—so that I may not have to think that I have injured you so deeply. Larry, though I cannot be your wife, I think I could die of sorrow if you were always unhappy. What is a poor girl that you should grieve for her in that way? I think if I were a man I would master my love better than that.' He shook his head and faintly strove to drag his arm from out of her grasp. 'Promise me that you will take a year to think of it before you go.'

'Will you take a year to think of me?' said he, rising again to sudden hope.

'No, Larry, no. I should deceive you were I to say so. I deceived you before when I put it off for two months. But you can promise me without deceit. For my sake, Larry?' And she almost embraced him as she begged for his promise. 'I know you would wish to spare me pain. Think what will be my sufferings if I hear that you have really gone from Chowton. You will promise me, Larry?'

'Promise what?'

'That the farm shall not be sold for twelve months.'

'Oh yes;—I'll promise. I don't care for the farm.'

'And stay there if you can. Don't leave the place to strangers. And go about your business,—and hunt,—and be a man. I shall always be thinking of what you do. I shall always watch you. I shall always love you,—always,—always,—always. I always have loved you;—because you are so good. But it is a different love. And now, Larry, good-bye.' So saying, she raised her face to look into his eyes. Then he suddenly put his arm round

her waist, kissed her forehead, and left the room without
another word.

Mrs. Masters saw him as he went, and must have known
from his gait what was the nature of the answer he had
received. But yet she went quickly upstairs to inquire.
The matter was one of too much consequence for a mere
inference. Mary had gone from the sitting-room, but her
stepmother followed her upstairs to her bed-chamber.
'Mamma,' she said, 'I couldn't do it;—I couldn't do it.
I did try. Pray do not scold me. I did try, but I could
not do it.' Then she threw herself into the arms of the
unsympathetic woman,—who, however, was now somewhat less unsympathetic than she had hitherto been.

Mrs. Masters did not understand it all; but she did perceive that there was something which she did not understand. What did the girl mean by saying that she had
tried and could not do it? Try to do it! If she tried why
could she not tell the man that she would have him?
There was surely some shame-facedness in this, some
over-strained modesty which she, Mrs. Masters, could not
comprehend. How could she have tried to accept a man
who was so anxious to marry her, and have failed in the
effort? 'Scolding I suppose will be no good now,' she
said.

'Oh no!'

'But——. Well; I suppose we must put up with it.
Everything on earth that a girl could possibly wish for!
He was that in love that it's my belief he'd have settled it
all on you if you'd only asked him.'

'Let it go, mamma.'

'Let it go! It's gone I suppose. Well;—I ain't going to
say any more about it. But as for not sorrowing, how is
a woman not to sorrow when so much has been lost? It's
your poor father I'm thinking of, Mary.' This was so
much better than she had expected that poor Mary
almost felt that her heart was lightened.

Chapter LX

AGAIN AT MISTLETOE

THE reader will have been aware that Arabella Trefoil
was not a favourite at Mistletoe. She was so much
disliked by the duchess that there had almost been words
about her between her grace and the duke since her
departure. The duchess always submitted, and it was the
rule of her life to submit with so good a grace that her
husband, never fearing rebellion, should never be driven
to assume the tyrant. But on this occasion the duke had
objected to the term 'thoroughly bad girl,' which had
been applied by his wife to his niece. He had said that
'thoroughly bad girl' was strong language, and when the
duchess defended the phrase he had expressed his opinion
that Arabella was only a bad girl and not a thoroughly
bad girl. The duchess had said that it was the same thing.
'Then,' said the duke, 'why use a redundant expletive
against your own relative?' The duchess, when she was
accused of strong language, had not minded it much; but
her feelings were hurt when a redundant expletive was
attributed to her. The effect of all this had been that the
duke in a mild way had taken up Arabella's part, and
that the duchess, following her husband at last, had been
brought round to own that Arabella, though bad, had
been badly treated. She had disbelieved, and then believed, and had again disbelieved Arabella's own statement as to the offer of marriage. But the girl had certainly
been in earnest when she had begged her aunt to ask her
uncle to speak to Lord Rufford. Surely when she did she
must have thought that an offer had been made to her.
Such offer, if made, had no doubt been produced by very
hard pressure;—but still an offer of marriage is an offer,
and a girl, if she can obtain it, has a right to use such an
offer as so much property. Then came Lord Mistletoe's
report after his meeting with Arabella up in London.
He had been unable to give his cousin any satisfaction,
but he was clearly of opinion that she had been ill-used.
He did not venture to suggest any steps, but did think

that Lord Rufford was bound as a gentleman to marry
the young lady. After that, Lord Augustus saw her
mother up in town and said that it was a d—— shame.
He in truth had believed nothing, and would have been
delighted to allow the matter to drop. But as this was not
permitted, he thought it easier to take his daughter's part
than to encounter family enmity by entering the lists
against her. So it came to pass that down at Mistletoe
there grew an opinion that Lord Rufford ought to marry
Arabella Trefoil.

But what should be done? The duke was alive to the
feeling that, as the girl was certainly his niece, and as she
was not to be regarded as a thoroughly bad girl, some
assistance was due to her from the family. Lord Mistletoe
volunteered to write to Lord Rufford; Lord Augustus
thought that his brother should have a personal interview
with his young brother peer, and bring his strawberry leaves
to bear. The duke himself suggested that the duchess
should see Lady Penwether,—a scheme to which her grace
objected strongly, knowing something of Lady Penwether
and being sure that her strawberry leaves would have no
effect whatever on the baronet's wife. At last it was
decided that a family meeting should be held, and Lord
Augustus was absolutely summoned to meet Lord Mistletoe at the paternal mansion.

It was now years since Lord Augustus had been at
Mistletoe. As he had never been separated,—that is,
formally separated,—from his wife, he and she had been
always invited there together. Year after year she had
accepted the invitation,—and it had been declined on his
behalf, because it did not suit him and his wife to meet
each other. But now he was obliged to go there,—just at
the time of the year when whist at his club was most
attractive. To meet the convenience of Lord Mistletoe—
and the House of Commons,—a Saturday afternoon was
named for the conference, which made it worse for Lord
Augustus, as he was one of a little party which had private
gatherings for whist on Sunday afternoons. But he went
to the conference, travelling down by the same train with
his nephew; but not in the same compartment, as he

solaced with tobacco the time which Lord Mistletoe
devoted to parliamentary erudition.

The four met in her grace's boudoir, and the duke
began by declaring that all this was very sad. Lord
Augustus shook his head and put his hands in his trousers
pockets,—which was as much as to say that his feelings
as a British parent were almost too strong for him. 'Your
mother and I think that something ought to be done,'
said the duke, turning to his son.

'Something ought to be done,' said Lord Mistletoe.

'They won't let a fellow go out with a fellow now,' said
Lord Augustus.

'Heaven forbid,' said the duchess, raising both her
hands.

'I was thinking, Mistletoe, that your mother might
have met Lady Penwether.'

'What could I do with Lady Penwether, duke? Or
what could she do with him? A man won't care for what
his sister says to him. And I don't suppose she'd undertake to speak to Lord Rufford on the subject.'

'Lady Penwether is an honourable and an accomplished
woman.'

'I dare say;—though she gives herself abominable airs.'

'Of course, if you don't like it, my dear, it shan't be
pressed.'

'I thought, perhaps, you'd see him yourself,' said Lord
Augustus, turning to his brother. 'You'd carry more
weight than anybody.'

'Of course I will if it be necessary; but it would be disagreeable,—very disagreeable. The appeal should be
made to his feelings, and that I think would better come
through female influence. As far as I know the world
a man is always more prone to be led in such matters by
a woman than by another man.'

'If you mean me,' said the duchess, 'I don't think I
could see him. Of course, Augustus, I don't wish to say
anything hard of Arabella. The fact that we have all met
here to take her part will prove that, I think. But I didn't
quite approve of all that was done here.'

Lord Augustus stroked his beard and looked out of the

window. 'I don't think, my dear, we need go into that just now,' said the duke.

'Not at all,' said the duchess, 'and I don't intend to say a word. Only if I were to meet Lord Rufford he might refer to things which,—which,—which—— In point of fact I had rather not.'

'I might see him,' suggested Lord Mistletoe.

'No doubt that might be done with advantage,' said the duke.

'Only that, as he is my senior in age, what I might say to him would lack that weight which any observations which might be made on such a matter should carry with them.'

'He didn't care a straw for me,' said Lord Augustus.

'And then,' continued Lord Mistletoe, 'I so completely agree with what my father says as to the advantage of female influence! With a man of Lord Rufford's temperament female influence is everything. If my aunt were to try it?' Lord Augustus blew the breath out of his mouth and raised his eyebrows. Knowing what he did of his wife, or thinking that he knew what he did, he did not conceive it possible that a worse messenger should be chosen. He had known himself to be a very bad one, but he did honestly believe her to be even less fitted for the task than he himself. But he said nothing,—simply wishing that he had not left his whist for such a purpose as this.

'Perhaps Lady Augustus had better see him,' said the duke. The duchess, who did not love hypocrisy, would not actually assent to this, but she said nothing. 'I suppose my sister-in-law would not object, Augustus?'

'G—— Almighty only knows,' said the younger brother. The duchess, grievously offended by the impropriety of this language, drew herself up haughtily.

'Perhaps you would not mind suggesting it to her, sir,' said Lord Mistletoe.

'I could do that by letter,' said the duke.

'And when she has assented, as of course she will, then perhaps you wouldn't mind writing a line to him to make an appointment. If you were to do so he could not refuse.' To this proposition the duke returned no immediate answer; but looked at it round and round carefully. At last, however, he acceded to this also, and so the matter was arranged. All these influential members of the ducal family met together at the ducal mansion on Arabella's behalf, and settled their difficulty by deputing the work of bearding the lion, of tying the bell on the cat, to an absent lady whom they all despised and disliked.

That afternoon the duke, with the assistance of his son, who was a great writer of letters, prepared an epistle to his sister-in-law and another to Lord Rufford, which was to be sent as soon as Lady Augustus had agreed to the arrangement. In the former letter a good deal was said as to a mother's solicitude for her daughter. It had been felt, the letter said, that no one could speak for a daughter so well as a mother;—that no other's words would so surely reach the heart of a man who was not all evil but who was tempted by the surroundings of the world to do evil in this particular case. The letter began 'My dear sister-in-law,' and ended 'Your affectionate brother-in-law, Mayfair,' and was in fact the first letter that the duke had ever written to his brother's wife. The other letter was more difficult, but it was accomplished at last, and confined itself to a request that Lord Rufford would meet Lady Augustus Trefoil at a place and at a time, both of which were for the present left blank.

On the Monday Lord Augustus and Lord Mistletoe were driven to the station in the same carriage, and on this occasion the uncle said a few strong words to his nephew on the subject. Lord Augustus, though perhaps a coward in the presence of his brother, was not so with other members of the family. 'It may be very well you know, but it's all d—— nonsense.'

'I'm sorry that you should think so, uncle.'

'What do you suppose her mother can do?—a thoroughly vulgar woman. I never could live with her. As far as I can see wherever she goes everybody hates her.'

'My dear uncle!'

'Rufford will only laugh at her. If Mayfair would have gone himself, it is just possible that he might have done something.'

' My father is so unwilling to mix himself up in these things.'

'Of course he is. Everybody knows that. What the deuce was the good then of our going down there? I couldn't do anything, and I knew he wouldn't. The truth is, Mistletoe, a man now-a-days may do just what he pleases. You ain't in that line and it won't do you any good knowing it, but since we did away with pistols everybody may do just what he likes.'

'I don't like brute force,' said Lord Mistletoe.

'You may call it what you please; but I don't know that it was so brutal, after all.' At the station they separated again, as Lord Augustus was panting for tobacco, and Lord Mistletoe for parliamentary erudition.

CHAPTER LXI

THE SUCCESS OF LADY AUGUSTUS

LADY AUGUSTUS was still staying with the Connop Greens in Hampshire when she received the duke's letter, and Arabella was with her. The story of Lord Rufford's infidelity had been told to Mrs. Connop Green, and, of course, through her to Mr. Connop Green. Both the mother and daughter affected to despise the Connop Greens; but it is so hard to restrain one's self from confidences when difficulties arise! Arabella had by this time quite persuaded herself that there had been an absolute engagement, and did in truth believe that she had been most cruelly ill-used. She was headstrong, fickle, and beyond measure insolent to her mother. She had, as we know, at one time gone down to the house of her former lover, thereby indicating that she had abandoned all hope of catching Lord Rufford. But still the Connop Greens either felt or pretended to feel great sympathy with her, and she would still declare from time to time that Lord Rufford had not heard the last of her. It was now more than a month since she had seen that perjured lord at Mistletoe, and more than a week since her father had brought him so uselessly up to London. Though determined that Lord Rufford should hear more of her, she hardly knew how to go to work, and on these days spent most of her time in idle denunciations of her false lover. Then came her uncle's letter, which was of course shown to her.

She was quite of opinion that they must do as the duke directed. It was so great a thing to have the duke interesting himself in the matter, that she would have assented to anything proposed by him. The suggestion even inspired some temporary respect, or at any rate observance, towards her mother. Hitherto her mother had been nobody to her in the matter,—a person belonging to her whom she had to regard simply as a burden. She could not at all understand how the duke had been guided in making such a choice of a new emissary; but there it was under his own hand, and she must now in some measure submit herself to her mother, unless she were prepared to repudiate altogether the duke's assistance. As to Lady Augustus herself, the suggestion gave to her quite a new life. She had no clear conception what she should say to Lord Rufford if the meeting were arranged, but it was gratifying to her to find herself brought back into authority over her daughter. She read the duke's letter to Mrs. Connop Green, with certain very slight additions, —or innuendos as to additions,—and was pleased to find that the letter was taken by Mrs. Connop Green as positive proof of the existence of the engagement. She wrote begging the duke to allow her to have the meeting at the family house in Piccadilly, and to this prayer the duke was obliged to assent. 'It would,' she said, 'give her so much assistance in speaking to Lord Rufford!' She named a day also, and then spent her time in preparing herself for the interview by counsel with Mrs. Green and by exacting explanations from her daughter.

This was a very bad time for Arabella,—so bad that, had she known to what she would be driven, she would probably have repudiated the duke and her mother altogether. 'Now, my dear,' she began, 'you must tell me everything that occurred, first at Rufford, and then at Mistletoe.'

'You know very well what occurred, mamma.'

'I know nothing about it, and unless everything is told me, I will not undertake this mission. Your uncle evidently thinks that by my interference the thing may be arranged. I have had the same idea all through myself, but as you have been so obstinate, I have not liked to say so. Now, Arabella, begin from the beginning. When was it that he first suggested to you the idea of marriage?'

'Good heavens, mamma!'

'I must have it from the beginning to the end. Did he speak of marriage at Rufford? I suppose he did, because you told me that you were engaged to him when you went to Mistletoe.'

'So I was.'

'What had he said?'

'What nonsense! How am I to remember what he said? As if a girl ever knows what a man says to her.'

'Did he kiss you?'

'Yes.'

'At Rufford?'

'I cannot stand this, mamma. If you like to go you may go. My uncle seems to think it is the best thing, and so I suppose it ought to be done. But I won't answer such questions as you are asking for Lord Rufford and all that he possesses.'

'What am I to say then? How am I to call back to his recollection the fact that he committed himself, unless you will tell me how and when he did so?'

'Ask him if he did not assure me of his love when we were in the carriage together.'

'What carriage?'

'Coming home from hunting.'

'Was that at Mistletoe or Rufford?'

'At Mistletoe, mamma,' replied Arabella, stamping her foot.

'But you must let me know how it was that you became engaged to him at Rufford.'

'Mamma, you mean to drive me mad,' exclaimed Arabella as she bounced out of the room.

There was very much more of this, till at last Arabella

found herself compelled to invent facts. Lord Rufford,
she said, had assured her of his everlasting affection in the
little room at Rufford, and had absolutely asked her to
be his wife coming home in the carriage with her to
Stamford. She told herself that though this was not
strictly true, it was as good as true,—as that which was
actually done and said by Lord Rufford on those occasions
could have had no other meaning. But before her mother
had completed her investigation, Arabella had become so
sick of the matter that she shut herself up in her room, and
declared that nothing on earth should induce her to open
her mouth on the subject again.

When Lord Rufford received the letter he was aghast
with new disgust. He had begun to flatter himself that
his interview with Lord Augustus would be the end of the
affair. Looking at it by degrees with coolness he had
allowed himself to think that nothing very terrible could
be done to him. Some few people, particularly interested
in the Mistletoe family, might give him a cold shoulder,
or perhaps cut him directly; but such people would not
belong to his own peculiar circle, and the annoyance
would not be great. But if all the family, one after
another, were to demand interviews with him up in
London, he did not see when the end of it would be.
There would be the duke himself, and the duchess, and
Mistletoe. And the affair would in this way become
gossip for the whole town. He was almost minded to
write to the duke saying that such an interview could do no
good; but at last he thought it best to submit the matter
to his mentor, Sir George Penwether. Sir George was
clearly of opinion that it was Lord Rufford's duty to see
Lady Augustus. 'Yes, you must have interviews with all
of them if they ask it,' said Sir George. 'You must show
that you are not afraid to hear what her friends have got
to say. When a man gets wrong he can't put himself right
without some little annoyance.'

'Since the world began,' said Lord Rufford, 'I don't
think that there was ever a man born so well adapted for
preaching sermons as you are.' Nevertheless he did as he
was bid, and consented to meet Lady Augustus in Picca-

dilly on the day named by her. On that very day the
hounds met at Impington, and Lord Rufford began to
feel his punishment. He assented to the proposal made
and went up to London, leaving the members of the
U.R.U. to have the run of the season from the Impington
coverts.

When Lady Augustus was sitting in the back room of
the mansion waiting for Lord Rufford she was very much
puzzled to think what she would say to him when he
came. With all her investigation she had received no
clear idea of the circumstances as they occurred. That
her daughter had told her a fib in saying that she was
engaged when she went to Mistletoe, she was all but
certain. That something had occurred in the carriage
which might be taken for an offer she thought possible.
She therefore determined to harp upon the carriage as
much as possible and to say as little as might be as to the
doings at Rufford. Then as she was trying to arrange her
countenance and her dress and her voice, so that they
might tell on his feelings, Lord Rufford was announced.
'Lady Augustus,' said he at once, beginning the lesson
which he had taught himself, 'I hope I see you quite well.
I have come here because you have asked me, but I really
don't know that I have anything to say.'

'Lord Rufford, you must hear me.'

'Oh yes; I will hear you certainly, only this kind of
thing is so painful to all parties, and I don't see the use
of it.'

'Are you aware that you have plunged me and my
daughter into a state of misery too deep to be fathomed?'

'I should be sorry to think that.'

'How can it be otherwise? When you assure a girl in
her position in life that you love her—a lady whose rank
is quite as high as your own——'

'Quite so,—quite so.'

'And when in return for that assurance you have
received vows of love from her,—what is she to think, and
what are her friends to think?' Lord Rufford had always
kept in his mind a clear remembrance of the transaction
in the carriage, and was well aware that the young lady's

mother had inverted the circumstances, or, as he expressed it to himself, had put the cart before the horse. He had assured the young lady that he loved her, and he had also been assured of her love; but her assurance had come first. He felt that this made all the difference in the world; so much difference that no one cognizant in such matters would hold that his assurance, obtained after such a fashion, meant anything at all. But how was he to explain this to the lady's mother? 'You will admit that such assurances were given?' continued Lady Augustus.

'Upon my word I don't know. There was a little foolish talk, but it meant nothing.'

'My lord!'

'What am I to say? I don't want to give offence, and I am heartily sorry that you and your daughter should be under any misapprehension. But, as I sit here, there was no engagement between us;—nor, if I must speak out, Lady Augustus, could your daughter have thought that there was an engagement.'

'Did you not——embrace her?'

'I did. That's the truth.'

'And after that you mean to say——'

'After that I mean to say that nothing more was intended.' There was a certain meanness of appearance about the mother which emboldened him.

'What a declaration to make the mother of a young lady, and that young lady the niece of the Duke of Mayfair!'

'It's not the first time such a thing has been done, Lady Augustus.'

'I know nothing about that,—nothing. I don't know whom you may have lived with. It never was done to her before.'

'If I understand right she was engaged to marry Mr. Morton when she came to Rufford.'

'It was all at an end before that.'

'At any rate you both came from his house.'

'Where he had been staying with Mrs. Morton.'

'And where she has been since,—without Mrs. Morton.'

'Lady Ushant was there, Lord Rufford.'

'But she has been staying at the house of this gentleman
to whom you admit that she was engaged a short time
before she came to us.'

'He is on his death-bed, and he thought that he had
behaved badly to her. She did go to Bragton the other
day, at his request,—merely that she might say that she
forgave him.'

'I only hope that she will forgive me too. There is
really nothing else to be said. If there were anything I
could do to atone to her for this——trouble.'

'If you only could know the brightness of the hopes you
have shattered,—and the purity of that girl's affection
for yourself!'

It was then that an idea—a low-minded idea—occurred
to Lord Rufford. While all this was going on he had of
course made various inquiries about this branch of the
Trefoil family and had learned that Arabella was
altogether portionless. He was told, too, that Lady
Augustus was much harassed by impecuniosity. Might it
be possible to offer a recompense? 'If I could do anything else, Lady Augustus;—but really I am not a marrying man.' Then Lady Augustus wept bitterly; but while
she was weeping, a low-minded idea occurred to her also.
It was clear to her that there could be no marriage. She
had never expected that there would be a marriage. But
if this man who was rolling in wealth should offer some
sum of money to her daughter,—something so considerable as to divest the transaction of the meanness which
would be attached to a small bribe,—something which
might be really useful throughout life, would it not be her
duty, on behalf of her dear child, to accept such an offer?
But the beginnings of such dealings are always difficult.
'Couldn't my lawyer see yours, Lady Augustus?' said
Lord Rufford.

'I don't want the family lawyer to know anything about
it,' said Lady Augustus. Then there was silence between
them for a few moments. 'You don't know what we have
to bear, Lord Rufford. My husband has spent all my
fortune,—which was considerable; and the duke does
nothing for us.' Then he took a bit of paper and, writing

on it the figures '£6,000,' pushed it across the table. She
gazed at the scrap for a minute, and then, borrowing his
pencil without a word, scratched out his lordship's figures,
and wrote '£8,000,' beneath them; and then added, 'No
one to know it.' After that, he held the scrap for two or
three minutes in his hands, and then wrote beneath the
figures, 'Very well. To be settled on your daughter. No
one shall know it.' She bowed her head, but kept the
scrap of paper in her possession. 'Shall I ring for your
carriage?' he asked. The bell was rung, and Lady
Augustus was taken back to the lodgings in Orchard
Street in the hired brougham. As she went she told herself that if everything else failed, £400 a year would
support her daughter, or that in the event of any further
matrimonial attempt such a fortune would be a great
assistance. She had been sure that there could be no
marriage, and was disposed to think that she had done
a good morning's work on behalf of her unnatural child.

Chapter LXII

'WE SHALL KILL EACH OTHER'

LADY AUGUSTUS, as she was driven back to Orchard
Street, and as she remained alone during the rest of
that day and the next in London, became a little afraid of
what she had done. She began to think how she should
communicate her tidings to her daughter, and thinking of
it grew to be nervous and ill at ease. How would it be
with her should Arabella still cling to the hope of marrying the lord? That any such hope would be altogether
illusory Lady Augustus was now sure. She had been
quite certain that there was no ground for such hope
when she had spoken to the man of her own poverty. She
was almost certain that there had never been an offer of
marriage made. In the first place, Lord Rufford's word
went further with her than Arabella's,—and then his story
had been consistent and probable, whereas hers had been
inconsistent and improbable. At any rate, ropes and horses
would not bring Lord Rufford to the hymeneal altar.

That being so, was it not natural that she should then have considered what result would be next best to a marriage? She was very poor, having saved only some few hundreds a year from the wreck of her own fortune. Independently of her, her daughter had nothing. And in spite of this poverty Arabella was very extravagant, running up bills for finery without remorse wherever credit could be found, and excusing herself by saying that on this or that occasion such an expenditure was justified by the matrimonial prospects which it opened out to her. And now, of late, Arabella had been talking of living separately from her mother. Lady Augustus, who was thoroughly tired of her daughter's company, was not at all averse to such a scheme;—but any such scheme was impracticable without money. By a happy accident the money would now be forthcoming. There would be £400 a year for ever, and nobody would know whence it came. She was confident that they might trust to the lord's honour for secrecy. As far as her own opinion went, the result of the transaction would be most happy. But still she feared Arabella. She felt that she would not know how to tell her story when she got back to Marygold Place. 'My dear, he won't marry you; but he is to give you £8,000.' That was what she would have to say, but she doubted her own courage to put her story into words so curt and explanatory. Even at thirty £400 a year has not the charms which accompany it to eyes which have seen sixty years. She remained in town that night and the next day, and went down by train to Basingstoke on the following morning with her heart not altogether free from trepidation.

Lord Rufford, the very moment that the interview was over, started off to his lawyer. Considering how very little had been given to him, the sum he was to pay was prodigious. In his desire to get rid of the bore of these appeals, he had allowed himself to be foolishly generous. He certainly would never kiss a young lady in a carriage again,—nor even lend a horse to a young lady till he was better acquainted with her ambition and character. But the word had gone from him and he must be as good as his word. The girl must have her £8,000, and must have it instantly. He would put the matter in such a position, that if any more interviews were suggested, he might with perfect safety refer the suggester back to Miss Trefoil. There was to be secrecy, and he would be secret as the grave. But in such matters one's lawyer is the grave. He had proposed that two lawyers should arrange it. Objection had been made to this, because Lady Augustus had no lawyer ready;—but on his side some one must be employed. So he went to his own solicitor and begged that the thing might be done quite at once. He was very definite in his instructions, and would listen to no doubts. Would the lawyer write to Miss Trefoil on that very day; —or rather not on that very day, but the next. As he suggested this, he thought it well that Lady Augustus should have an opportunity of explaining the transaction to her daughter before the lawyer's letter should be received. He had, he said, his own reason for such haste. Consequently, the lawyer did prepare the letter to Miss Trefoil at once, drafting it in his noble client's presence. In what way should the money be disposed so as best to suit her convenience? The letter was very short, with an intimation that Lady Augustus would no doubt have explained the details of the arrangement.

When Lady Augustus reached Marygold, the family were at lunch, and as strangers were present nothing was said as to the great mission. The mother had already bethought herself how she must tell this and that lie to the Connop Greens, explaining that Lord Rufford had confessed his iniquity, but had disclosed that, for certain mysterious reasons, he could not marry Arabella,— though he loved her better than all the world. Arabella asked some questions about her mothers's shopping and general business in town, and did not leave the room till she could do so without the slightest appearance of anxiety. Mrs. Connop Green marvelled at her coolness, knowing how much must depend on the answer which her mother had brought back from London, and knowing nothing of the contents of the letter which Arabella had received that morning from the lawyer. In a moment or two Lady Augustus followed her daughter upstairs, and on going into her own room found the damsel standing in the middle of it with an open paper in her hand. 'Mamma,' she said, 'shut the door.' Then the door was closed. 'What is the meaning of this?' and she held out the lawyer's letter.

'The meaning of what?' said Lady Augustus, trembling.

'I have no doubt you know, but you had better read it.'

Lady Augustus read the letter and attempted to smile. 'He has been very quick,' she said. 'I thought I should have been the first to tell you.'

'What is the meaning of it? Why is the man to give me all that money?'

'Is it not a good escape from so great a trouble? Think what £8,000 will do. It will enable you to live in comfort wherever you may please to go.'

'I am to understand then you have sold me,—sold all my hopes and my very name and character, for £8,000!'

'Your name and character will not be touched, my dear. As for his marrying you, I soon found that that was absolutely out of the question.'

'This is what has become of sending you to see him! Of course I shall tell my uncle everything.'

'You will do no such thing. Arabella, do not make a fool of yourself. Do you know what £8,000 will do for you? It is to be your own,—absolutely beyond my reach or your father's.'

'I would sooner go into the Thames off Waterloo Bridge than touch a farthing of his money,' said Arabella with a spirit which the other woman did not at all understand. Hitherto in all these little dirty ways they had run with equal steps. The pretences, the subterfuges, the lies of the one had always been open to the other. Arabella, earnest in supplying herself with gloves from the pockets of her male acquaintances, had endured her mother's tricks with complacency. She had condescended when living in humble lodgings to date her letters from a well-known hotel, and had not feared to declare that she had done so in their family conversations. Together they had fished in turbid waters for marital nibbles, and had told

mutual falsehoods to unbelieving tradesmen. And yet the
younger woman, when tempted with a bribe worth lies
and tricks as deep and as black as Acheron, now stood on
her dignity and her purity and stamped her foot with
honest indignation!

'I don't think you can understand it,' said Lady
Augustus.

'I can understand this,—that you have betrayed me;
and that I shall tell him so in the plainest words that I
can use. To get his lawyer to write and offer me money!'

'He should not have gone to his lawyer. I do think he
was wrong there.'

'But you settled it with him;—you, my mother;—a
price at which he should buy himself off! Would he have
offered me money if he did not know that he had bound
himself to me?'

'Nothing on earth would make him marry you. I
would not for a moment have allowed him to allude to
money if that had not been quite certain.'

'Who proposed the money first?'

Lady Augustus considered a moment before she
answered. 'Upon my word, my dear, I can't say. He
wrote the figures on a bit of paper; that was the way.'
Then she produced the scrap. 'He wrote the figures first
—and then I altered them, just as you see. The proposition came first from him, of course.'

'And you did not spit at him!' said Arabella, as she tore
the scrap into fragments.

'Arabella,' said the mother, 'it is clear that you do not
look into the future. How do you mean to live? You are
getting old.'

'Old!'

'Yes, my love,—old. Of course I am willing to do
everything for you, as I always have done,—for so many
years, but there isn't a man in London who does not
know how long you have been about it.'

'Hold your tongue, mamma,' said Arabella, jumping up.

'That is all very well, but the truth has to be spoken.
You and I cannot go on as we have been doing.'

'Certainly not. I would sooner be in a workhouse.'

'And here there is provided for you an income on which you can live. Not a soul will know anything about it. Even your own father need not be told. As for the lawyer, that is nothing. They never talk of things. It would make a man comparatively poor quite a fit match. Or, if you do not marry, it would enable you to live where you pleased independently of me. You had better think twice of it before you refuse it.'

'I will not think of it at all. As sure as I am living here I will write to Rufford this very evening and tell him in what light I regard both him and you.'

'And what will you do then?'

'Hang myself.'

'That is all very well, Arabella, but hanging yourself and jumping off Waterloo Bridge do not mean anything. You must live, and you must pay your debts. I can't pay them for you. You go into your own room, and think of it all, and be thankful for what Providence has sent you.'

'You may as well understand that I am in earnest,' the daughter said, as she left the room. 'I shall write to Lord Rufford to-day, and tell him what I think of him and his money. You need not trouble yourself as to what shall be done with it, for I certainly shall not take it.'

And she did write to Lord Rufford as follows:—

'MY LORD,
        'I have been much astonished by a letter I have received from a gentleman in London, Mr. Shaw, who I presume is your lawyer. When I received it I had not as yet seen mamma. I now understand that you and she between you have determined that I should be compensated by a sum of money for the injury you have done me! I scorn your money. I cannot think where you found the audacity to make such a proposal, or how you have taught yourself to imagine that I should listen to it. As to mamma, she was not commissioned to act for me, and I have nothing to do with anything she may have said. I can hardly believe that she should have agreed to such a proposal. It was very little like a gentleman in you to offer it.

'Why did you offer it? You would not have proposed to give me a large sum of money like that without some reason. I have been shocked to hear that you have denied that you ever engaged yourself to me. You know that you were engaged to me. It would have been more honest and more manly if you had declared at once that you repented of your engagement. But the truth is that till I see you myself and hear what you have to say out of your own mouth I cannot believe what other people tell me. I must ask you to name some place where we can meet. As for this offer of money, it goes for nothing. You must have known that I would not take it.

'ARABELLA.'

It was just the end of February, and the visit of the Trefoil ladies to the Connop Greens had to come to an end. They had already overstaid the time at first arranged, and Lady Augustus, when she hinted that another week at Marygold,—'just till this painful affair was finally settled,'—would be beneficial to her, was informed that the Connop Greens themselves were about to leave home. Lady Augustus had reported to Mrs. Connop Green that Lord Rufford was behaving very badly, but that the matter was still in a 'transition state.' Mrs. Connop Green was very sorry, but——. So Lady Augustus and Arabella betook themselves to Orchard Street, being at that moment unable to enter in upon better quarters.

What a home it was,—and what a journey up to town! Arabella had told her mother that the letter to Lord Rufford had been written and posted, and since that hardly a word had passed between them. When they left Marygold in the Connop Green carriage they smiled, and shook hands, and kissed their friends in unison, and then sank back into silence. At the station they walked up and down the platform together for the sake of appearance, but did not speak. In the train there were others with them and they both feigned to be asleep. Then they were driven to their lodgings in a cab, still speechless. It was the mother who first saw that the horror of this if continued would be too great to be endured. 'Arabella,' she said, in a hoarse voice, 'why don't you speak?'

'Because I've got nothing to say.'

'That's nonsense. There is always something to say.'

'You have ruined me, mamma; just ruined me.'

'I did for you the very best I could. If you would have been advised by me, instead of being ruined, you would have had a handsome fortune. I have slaved for you for the last twelve years. No mother ever sacrificed herself for her child more than I have done for you, and now see the return I get. I sometimes think that it will kill me.'

'That's nonsense.'

'Everything I say is nonsense,—while you tell me one day that you are going to hang yourself, and another day that you will drown yourself.'

'So I would if I dared. What is it that you have brought me to? Who will have me in their houses when they hear that you consented to take Lord Rufford's money?'

'Nobody will hear it unless you tell them.'

'I shall tell my uncle and my aunt and Mistletoe, in order that they may know how it is that Lord Rufford has been allowed to escape. I say that you have ruined me. If it had not been for your vulgar bargain with him, he must have been brought to keep his word at last. Oh, that he should have ever thought it was possible that I was to be bought off for a sum of money!'

Later on in the evening, the mother again implored her daughter to speak to her. 'What's the use, mamma, when you know what we think of each other? What's the good of pretending? There is nobody here to hear us.' Later on still she herself began. 'I don't know how much you've got, mamma; but whatever it is, we'd better divide it. After what you did in Piccadilly, we shall never get on together again.'

'There is not enough to divide,' said Lady Augustus.

'If I had not you to go about with me, I could get taken in pretty nearly all the year round.'

'Who'd take you?'

'Leave that to me. I would manage it, and you could join with some other old person. We shall kill each other if we stay like this,' said Arabella, as she took up her candle.

'You have pretty nearly killed me as it is,' said the old woman, as the other shut the door.

CHAPTER LXIII

CHANGES AT BRAGTON

DAY after day old Mrs. Morton urged her purpose with her grandson at Bragton, not quite directly as she had done at first, but by gradual approaches and little soft attempts made in the midst of all the tenderness which, as a nurse, she was able to display. It soon came to pass that the intruders were banished from the house, or almost banished. Mary's daily visits were discontinued immediately after that last walk home with Reginald Morton which has been described. Twice in the course of the next week she went over, but on both occasions she did so early in the day, and returned alone just as he was reaching the house. And then, before a week was over, early in March, Lady Ushant told the invalid that she would be better away. 'Mrs. Morton doesn't like me,' she said, 'and I had better go. But I shall stay for a while at Hoppet Hall, and come in and see you from time to time till you get better.' John Morton replied that he should never get better; but though he said so then, there was at times evidence that he did not yet quite despond as to himself. He could still talk to Mrs. Morton of buying Chowton Farm, and was very anxious that he should not be forgotten at the Foreign Office.

Lady Ushant had herself driven to Hoppet Hall, and there took up her residence with her nephew. Every other day Mr. Runciman's fly came for her, and carried her backwards and forwards to Bragton. On those occasions she would remain an hour with the invalid, and then would go back again, never even seeing Mrs. Morton, though always seen by her. And twice after this banishment Reginald walked over. But on the second occasion there was a scene. Mrs. Morton, to whom he had never spoken since he was a boy, met him in the hall and told him that his visits only disturbed his sick cousin. 'I certainly will not disturb him,' Reginald had said. 'In the condition in which he is now he should not see many people,' rejoined the lady. 'If you will ask Dr. Fanning, he will tell you the same.' Dr. Fanning was the London doctor, who came down once a week, whom it was improbable that Reginald should have an opportunity of consulting. But he remembered, or thought that he remembered, that his cousin had been fretful and ill-pleased during his last visit, and so turned himself round and went home without another word.

'I am afraid there may be—I don't know what,' said Lady Ushant to him in a whisper the next morning.

'What do you mean?'

'I don't know what I mean. Perhaps I ought not to say a word. Only so much does depend on it!'

'If you are thinking about the property, aunt, wipe it out of your mind. Let him do what he pleases, and don't think about it. No one should trouble their minds about such things. It is his to do what he pleases with it.'

'It is not him that I fear, Reginald.'

'If he chooses to be guided by her, who shall say that he is wrong? Get it out of your mind. The very thinking about such things is dirtiness!' The poor old lady submitted to the rebuke, and did not dare to say another word.

Daily Lady Ushant would send over for Mary Masters, thinking it cruel that her young friend should leave her alone, and yet understanding in part the reason why Mary did not come to her constantly at Hoppet Hall. Poor Mary was troubled much by these messages. Of course she went now and again. She had no alternative but to go, and yet, feeling that the house was his house, she was most unwilling to enter it. Then grew within her a feeling, which she could not analyse, that he had ill-used her. Of course she was not entitled to his love. She would acknowledge to herself over and over again that he had never spoken a word to her which could justify her in expecting his love. But why had he not let her alone?

Why had he striven by his words and his society to make
her other than she would have been had she been left to
the atmosphere of her stepmother's home? Why had he
spoken so strongly to her as to that young man's love?
And then she was almost angry with him because, by a
turn in the wheel of fortune, he was about to become, as
she thought, Squire of Bragton. Had he remained simply
Mr. Morton of Hoppet Hall it would still have been
impossible. But this exaltation of her idol altogether out
of her reach was an added injustice. She could remember
not the person, but all the recent memories of the old
Squire, the veneration with which he was named, the
masterdom which was attributed to him, the unequalled
nobility of his position in regard to Dillsborough. His
successor would be to her as some one crowned, and
removed by his crown altogether from her world. Then
she pictured to herself the stately dame who would
certainly come, and she made fresh resolutions with a sore
heart.

'I don't know why you should be so very little with
me,' said Lady Ushant, almost whining. 'When I was at
Cheltenham you wanted to come to me.'

'There are so many things to be done at home.'

'And yet you would have come to Cheltenham.'

'We were in great trouble then, Lady Ushant. Of
course, I would like to be with you. You ought not to
scold me, because you know how I love you.'

'Has the young man gone away altogether now, Mary?'

'Altogether.'

'And Mrs. Masters is satisfied?'

'She knows it can never be, and therefore she is quiet
about it.'

'I was sorry for that young man, because he was so
true.'

'You couldn't be more sorry than I was, Lady Ushant.
I love him as though he were a brother. But——'

'Mary, dear Mary, I fear you are in trouble.'

'I think it is all trouble,' said Mary, rushing forward
and hiding her face in her old friend's lap as she knelt on
the ground before her. Lady Ushant longed to ask a

question, but she did not dare. And Mary Masters longed to have one friend to whom she could confide her secret, —but neither did she dare.

On the next day, very early in the morning, there came a note from Mrs. Morton to Mr. Masters, the attorney. Could Mr. Masters come out on that day to Bragton and see Mrs. Morton? The note was very particular in saying that Mrs. Morton was to be the person seen. The messenger, who waited for an answer, brought back word that Mr. Masters would be there at noon. The circumstance was one which agitated him considerably, as he had not been inside the house at Bragton since the days immediately following the death of the old Squire. As it happened, Lady Ushant was going to Bragton on the same day, and at the suggestion of Mr. Runciman, whose horses in the hunting season barely sufficed for his trade, the old lady and the lawyer went together. Not a word was said between them as to the cause which took either of them on their journey, but they spoke much of the days in which they had known each other, when the old squire was alive, and Mr. Masters thanked Lady Ushant for her kindness to his daughter. 'I·love her almost as though she were my own,' said Lady Ushant. 'When I am dead she will have half of what I have got.'

'She will have no right to expect that,' said the gratified father.

'She will have half or the whole,—just as Reginald may be situated then. I don't know why I shouldn't tell her father what it is I mean to do.' The attorney knew to a shilling the amount of Lady Ushant's income, and thought that this was the best news he had heard for many a day.

While Lady Ushant was in the sick man's room, Mrs. Morton was closeted with the attorney. She had thought much of this step before she had dared to take it, and even now doubted whether it would avail her anything. As she entered the book-room in which Mr. Masters was seated she almost repented. But the man was there, and she was compelled to go on with her scheme. 'Mr.

Masters,' she said, 'it is, I think, a long time since you
have been employed by this family.'

'A very long time, madam,'

'And I have now sent for you under circumstances of
great difficulty,' she answered; but as he said nothing she
was forced to go on. 'My grandson made his will the other
day up in London, when he thought that he was going
out to Patagonia.' Mr. Masters bowed. 'It was done
when he was in sound health, and he is not now satisfied
with it.' Then there was another bow, but not a word was
spoken. 'Of course you know that he is very ill.'

'We have all been very much grieved to hear it.'

'I am sure you would be, for the sake of old days.
When Dr. Fanning was last here he thought that my
grandson was something better. He held out stronger
hopes than before. But still he is very ill. His mind has
never wavered for a moment, Mr. Masters.' Again Mr.
Masters bowed. 'And now he thinks that some changes
should be made;—indeed, that there should be a new
will.'

'Does he wish me to see him, Mrs. Morton?'

'Not to-day, I think. He is not quite prepared to-day.
But I wanted to ask whether you could come at a
moment's notice,—quite at a moment's notice. I thought
it better, so that you should know why we sent for you if
we did send,—so that you might be prepared. It could
be done here, I suppose?'

'It would be possible, Mrs. Morton.'

'And you could do it?'

Then there was a long pause. 'Altering a will is a very
serious thing, Mrs. Morton. And when it is done on what
perhaps may be a death-bed, it is a very serious thing
indeed. Mr. Morton, I believe, employs a London
solicitor. I know the firm, and more respectable gentlemen do not exist. A telegram would bring down one of
the firm from London by the next train.'

A frown, a very heavy frown, came across the old
woman's brow. She would have repressed it had it been
possible;—but she could not command herself, and
the frown was there. 'If that had been practicable,

Mr. Masters,' she said, 'we should not have sent for you.'

'I was only suggesting, madam, what might be the best course.'

'Exactly. And of course I am much obliged. But if we are driven to call upon you for your assistance, we shall find it?'

'Madam,' said the attorney very slowly, 'it is, of course, part of my business to make wills, and, when called upon to do so, I perform my business to the best of my ability. But in altering a will during illness great care is necessary. A codicil might be added——'

'A new will would be necessary.'

A new will, thought the attorney, could only be necessary for altering the disposition of the whole estate. He knew enough of the family circumstances to be aware that the property should go to Reginald Morton whether with or without a will,—and also enough to be aware that this old lady was Reginald's bitter enemy. He did not think that he could bring himself to take instructions from a dying man,—from the Squire of Bragton on his death-bed,—for an instrument which should alienate the property from the proper heir. He, too, had his strong feelings, perhaps his prejudices, about Bragton. 'I would wish that the task were in other hands, Mrs. Morton.'

'Why so?'

'It is hard to measure the capacity of an invalid.'

'His mind is as clear as yours.'

'It might be so,—and yet I might not be able to satisfy myself that it was so. I should have to ask long and tedious questions, which would be offensive. And I should find myself giving advice,—which would not be called for. For instance, were your grandson to wish to leave this estate away from the heir——'

'I am not discussing his wishes, Mr. Masters.'

'I beg your pardon, Mrs. Morton, for making the suggestion;—but, as I said before, I should prefer that he should employ—some one else.'

'You refuse then?'

'If Mr. Morton were to send for me, I should go to him

instantly. But I fear I might be slow in taking his instructions;—and it is possible that I might refuse to act on them.' Then she got up from her chair and, bowing to him with stately displeasure, left the room.

All this she had done without any authority from her grandson, simply encouraged in her object by his saying, in his weakness, that he would think of her proposition. So intent was she on her business that she was resolved to have everything ready if only he could once be brought to say that Peter Morton should be his heir. Having abandoned all hopes for her noble cousin, she could tell her conscience that she was instigated simply by an idea of justice. Peter Morton was, at any rate, the legitimate son of a well-born father and a well-born mother. What had she or any one belonging to her to gain by it? But forty years since a brat had been born at Bragton in opposition to her wishes,—by whose means she had been expelled from the place; and now it seemed to her to be simple justice that he should on this account be robbed of that which would otherwise be naturally his own. As Mr. Masters would not serve her turn she must write to the London lawyers. The thing would be more difficult; but, nevertheless, if the sick man could once be got to say that Peter should be his heir she thought that she could keep him to his word. Lady Ushant and Mr. Masters went back to Dillsborough in Runciman's fly, and it need hardly be said that the attorney said nothing of the business which had taken him to Bragton.

This happened on a Wednesday,—Wednesday the 3rd of March. On Friday morning, at four o'clock, during the darkness of the night, John Morton was lying dead on his bed, and the old woman was at his bedside. She had done her duty by him as far as she knew how in attending him,—had been assiduous with the diligence of much younger years; but now as she sat there, having had the fact absolutely announced to her by Dr. Nupper, her greatest agony arose from the feeling that the roof which covered her, probably the chair in which she sat, were the property of Reginald Morton—'Bastard!' she said to herself between her teeth; but she so said it that neither

Dr. Nupper, who was in the room, nor the woman who was with her should hear it.

Dr. Nupper took the news into Dillsborough, and as the folk sat down to breakfast they all heard that the Squire of Bragton was dead. The man had been too little known, had been too short a time in the neighbourhood, to give occasion for tears. There was certainly more of interest than of grief in the matter. Mr. Masters said to himself that the time had been too short for any change in the will, and therefore felt tolerably certain that Reginald would be the heir. But for some days this opinion was not general in Dillsborough. Mr. Mainwaring had heard that Reginald had been sent away from Bragton with a flea in his ear, and was pretty certain that when the will was read it would be found that the property was to go to Mrs. Morton's friends. Dr. Nupper was of the same opinion. There were many in Dillsborough with whom Reginald was not popular;—and who thought that some man of a different kind would do better as Squire of Bragton. 'He don't know a fox when he sees un,' said Tony Tuppet to Larry Twentyman, whom he had come across the county to call upon and to console.

CHAPTER LXIV

THE WILL

ON that Saturday the club met at Dillsborough,— even though the Squire of Bragton had died on Friday morning. Through the whole of that Saturday the town had been much exercised in its belief and expressions, as to the disposition of the property. The town knew very well that Mr. Masters, the attorney, had been sent for to Bragton on the previous Wednesday,—whence the deduction as to a new will, made of course under the auspices of Mrs. Morton,—would have been quite plain to the town, had not a portion of the town heard that the attorney had not been for a moment with the dying man during his visit. This latter piece of information had come through Lady Ushant, who had been in her nephew's bedroom the whole time;—but Lady Ushant had not much personal communication with the town generally, and would probably have said nothing on this subject had not Mr. Runciman walked up to Hoppet Hall behind the fly, after Mr. Masters had left it; and, while helping her ladyship out, made inquiry as to the condition of things at Bragton generally. 'I was sorry to hear of their sending for any lawyer,' said Mr. Runciman. Then Lady Ushant protested that the lawyer had not been sent for by her nephew, and that her nephew had not even seen him. 'Oh, indeed,' said Mr. Runciman, who immediately took a walk round his own paddock with the object of putting two and two together. Mr. Runciman was a discreet man, and did not allow this piece of information to spread itself generally. He told Dr. Nupper, and Mr. Hampton, and Lord Rufford,—for the hounds went out on Friday, though the Squire of Bragton was lying dead;—but he did not tell Mr. Mainwaring, whom he encountered in the street of the town as he was coming home early, and who was very keen to learn whatever news there was.

Reginald Morton on Friday did not go near Bragton. That of course was palpable to all, and was a great sign that he himself did not regard himself as the heir. He had for awhile been very intimate at the house, visiting it daily—and during a part of that time the grandmother had been altogether absent. Then she had come back, and he had discontinued his visits. And now he did not even go over to seal up the drawers, and to make arrangements as to the funeral. He did not at any rate go on the Friday,—nor on the Saturday. And on the Saturday, Mr. Wobytrade, the undertaker, had received orders from Mrs. Morton to go at once to Bragton. All this was felt to be strong against Reginald. But when it was discovered that on the Saturday afternoon Mrs. Morton herself had gone up to London, not waiting even for the coming of any one else to take possession of the house,— and that she had again carried all her personal luggage with her,—then opinion in Dillsborough again veered. Upon the whole the betting was a point or two in favour of Reginald, when the club met.

Mrs. Masters, who had been much quelled of late, had been urgent with her husband to go over to the Bush; but he was unwilling, he said, to be making jolly while the Squire of Bragton was lying unburied. 'He was nothing to you, Gregory,' said his wife, who had in vain endeavoured to learn from him why he had been summoned to Bragton. 'You will hear something over there, and it will relieve your spirits.' So instigated, he did go across, and found all the accustomed members of the club congregated in the room. Even Larry Twentyman was present, who of late had kept himself aloof from all such meetings. Both the Botseys were there, and Nupper, and Harry Stubbings, and Ribbs the butcher. Runciman himself, of course, was in the room, and he had introduced on this occasion Captain Glomax, the master of the hunt, who was staying at his house that night,—perhaps with a view to hunting duties on the Monday, perhaps in order that he might hear something as to the Bragton property. It had already been suggested to him that he might possibly hire the house for a year or two at little more than a nominal rent, that the old kennels might be resuscitated, and that such arrangements would be in all respects convenient. He was the master of the hunt, and, of course, there was no difficulty as to introducing him to the club.

Captain Glomax was speaking in a somewhat dictatorial voice,—as becomes a Master of Hounds, though perhaps it should be dropped afterwards,—when the attorney entered. There was a sudden rise of voices striving to interrupt the captain, as it was felt by them all that Mr. Masters must be in possession of information; but the captain himself went on. 'Of course it is the place for the hounds. Nobody can doubt that who knows the country and understands the working of it. The hunt ought to have subscribed and hired the kennels and stables permanently.'

'There would have wanted two to that bargain, captain,' said Mr. Runciman.

'Of course there would; but what would you think of a man who would refuse such a proposition when he didn't

want the place himself? Do you think, if I'd been there,
foxes would have been poisoned in Dillsborough Wood?
I'd have had that fellow Goarly under my thumb.'

'Then you'd have had an awful blackguard under your
thumb, Captain Glomax,' said Larry, who could not
restrain his wrath when Goarly's name was mentioned.

'What does that matter, if you get foxes?' continued
the Master. 'But the fact is, gentlemen in a county like
this always want to have everything done for them, and
never to do anything for themselves. I'm sick of it, I
know. Nobody is fonder of hunting a country than I am,
and I think I know what I'm about.'

'That you do,' said Fred Botsey, who, like most men,
was always ready to flatter the Master.

'And I don't care how hard I work. From the first of
August till the end of May I never have a day to myself,
what with cubbing and then the season, and entering the
young hounds, and buying and selling horses; by George
I'm at it the whole year!'

'A Master of Hounds looks for that, Captain,' said the
innkeeper.

'Looks for it! Yes; he must look for it. But I wouldn't
mind that, if I could get gentlemen to pull a little with
me. I can't stand being out of pocket as I have been, and
so I must let them know. If the country would get the
kennels and the stables, and lay out a few pounds so that
horses and hounds and men could go into them, I wouldn't
mind having a shot for the house. It's killing work where
I am now,—the other side of Rufford, you may say.'
Then he stopped; but no one would undertake to answer
him. The meaning of it was that Captain Glomax
wanted £500 a year more than he received, and every
one there knew that there was not £500 a year more to
be got out of the country,—unless Lord Rufford would
put his hand into his pocket. Now, the present stables
and the present kennels had been 'made comfortable' by
Lord Rufford, and it was not thought probable that he
would pay for the move to Bragton.

'When's the funeral to be, Mr. Masters?' asked Runciman, who knew very well the day fixed, but who thought

it well to get back to the subject of real interest in the town.

'Next Thursday, I'm told.'

'There's no hurry with weather like this,' said Nupper, professionally.

'They can't open the will till the late squire is buried,' continued the innkeeper, 'and there will be one or two very anxious to know what is in it.'

'I suppose it will all go to the man who lives up here at Hoppet Hall,' said the captain,—'a man that was never outside a horse in his life!'

'He's not a bad fellow,' said Runciman.

'He's a very good fellow,' said the attorney, 'and I trust he may have the property. If it be left away from him, I for one shall think that a great injustice has been done.' This was listened to with attention, as every one there thought that Mr. Masters must know.

'I can't understand,' said Glomax, 'how any man can be considered a good fellow as a country gentleman who does not care for sport. Just look at it all round. Suppose others were like him, what would become of us all?'

'Yes indeed, what would become of us?' asked the two Botseys in a breath.

'Ho'd 'ire our 'orses, Runciman?' suggested Harry Stubbings with a laugh.

'Think what England would be!' said the captain. 'When I hear of a country gentleman sticking to books and all that, I feel that the glory is departing from the land. Where are the sinews of war to come from? That's what I want to know.'

'Who will it be, Mr. Masters, if the gent don't get it?' asked Ribbs, from his corner on the sofa.

This was felt to be a pushing question. 'How am I to know, Mr. Ribbs?' said the attorney. 'I didn't make the late squire's will;—and if I did you don't suppose I should tell you.'

'I'm told that the next is Peter Morton,' said Fred Botsey. 'He's something in a public office up in London.'

'It won't go to him,' said Fred's brother. 'That old

lady has relations of her own who have had their mouths open for the last forty years.'

'Away from the Mortons altogether!' said Harry. 'That would be an awful shame.'

'I don't see what good the Mortons have done this last half century,' said the captain.

'You don't remember the old squire, captain,' said the innkeeper, 'and I don't remember him well. Indeed I was only a little chap when they buried him. But there's that feeling left behind him to this day, that not a poor man in the country wouldn't be sorry to think that there wasn't a Morton left among 'em. Of course a hunting gentlemen is a good thing.'

'About the best thing out,' said the captain.

'But a hunting gentleman isn't everything. I know nothing of the old lady's people,—only this that none of their money ever came into Dillsborough. I'm all for Reginald Morton. He's my landlord as it is, and he's a gentleman.'

'I hate foreigners coming,' said Ribbs.

"E ain't too old to take to it yet,' said Harry. Fred Botsey declared that he didn't believe in men hunting unless they began young. Whereupon Dr. Nupper declared that he had never ridden over a fence till he was forty-five, and that he was ready now to ride Fred across country for a new hat. Larry suggested that a man might be a good friend to sport though he didn't ride much himself;—and Runciman again asserted that hunting wasn't everything. Upon the whole Reginald was the favourite. But the occasion was so special that a little supper was ordered, and I fear the attorney did not get home till after twelve.

Till the news reached Hoppet Hall that Mrs. Morton had taken herself off to London, there was great doubt there as to what ought to be done, and even then the difficulty was not altogether over. Till she was gone neither Lady Ushant nor her nephew would go there, and he could only declare his purpose of attending the funeral whether he were asked or not. When his aunt again spoke of the will he desired her with much emphasis not to allude to the subject. 'If the property is to come to me,' he said, 'anything of good that may be in it cannot be much sweeter by anticipation. And if it is not I shall only encourage disappointment by thinking of it.'

'But it would be such a shame.'

'That I deny altogether. It was his own to do as he liked with it. Had he married I should not have expected it because I am the heir. But, if you please, aunt, do not say a word more about it.'

On the Sunday morning he heard that Mrs. Morton was gone to London, and then he walked over to Bragton. He found that she had locked and sealed up everything with so much precision that she must have worked hard at the task from the hour of his death almost to that of her departure. 'She never rested herself all day,' said Mrs. Hopkins, 'till I thought she would sink from very weariness.' She had gone into every room and opened every drawer, and had had every piece of plate through her fingers, and then Mrs. Hopkins told him that just as she was departing she had said that the keys would be given to the lawyer. After that he wandered about the place, thinking what his life would be should he find himself the owner of Bragton. At this moment he almost felt that he disliked the place, though there had been times in which he had thought that he loved it too well. Of one thing he was conscious,—that if Bragton should become his, it would be his duty to live there. He must move his books, his pipes, and other household gods from Hoppet Hall, and become an English squire. Would it be too late for him to learn to ride to hounds? Would it be possible that he should ever succeed in shooting a pheasant, if he were to study the art patiently? Could he interest himself as to the prevalence or decadence of ground game? And what must he do with his neighbours? Of course he would have to entertain Mr. Mainwaring and the other parsons, and perhaps once in the year to ask Lord Rufford to dine with him. If Lord Rufford came, what on earth would he say to him?

And then there arose another question. Would it not be his duty to marry,—and, if so, whom? He had been distinctly told that Mary Masters had given her heart to

some one, and he certainly was not the man to ask for the
hand of a girl who had not a heart to give. And yet he
thought that it would be impossible that she should marry
any other person. He spent hours in walking about the
grounds, looking at the garden and belongings which
would so probably be his own within a week, and thinking
whether it would be possible that he should bring a mistress to preside over them. Before he reached home he
had made up his mind that only one mistress would be
possible, and that she was beyond his reach.

On the Tuesday he received a scrawl from Mrs. Hopkins with a letter from the lawyer—addressed to her.
The lawyer wrote to say that he would be down on
Wednesday evening, would attend the funeral, and read
his client's will after they had performed the ceremony.
He went on to add that in obedience to Mrs. Morton's
directions he had invited Mr. Peter Morton to be present
on the occasion. On the Wednesday, Reginald again
went over, but left before the arrival of the two gentlemen.
On the Thursday he was there early, and of course took
upon himself the duty of chief mourner. Peter Morton
was there and showed, in a bewildered way, that he had
been summoned rather to the opening of the will than to
the funeral of a man he had never seen.

Then the will was read. There were only two names
mentioned in it. John Morton left £5,000 and his watch
and chain and rings to Arabella Trefoil, and everything
else of which he was possessed to his cousin Reginald
Morton.

'Upon my word I don't know why they sent for me,'
said the other cousin, Peter.

'Mrs. Morton seemed to think that you would like to
pay a tribute of respect,' said the lawyer. Peter looked at
him and went upstairs and packed his portmanteau. The
lawyer handed over the keys to the new squire, and then
everything was done.

Chapter LXV
THE NEW MINISTER

'POOR old Paragon!' exclaimed Archibald Currie, as he stood with his back to the fire among his colleagues at the Foreign Office on the day after John Morton's death.

'Poor young Paragon! that's the pity of it,' said Mounser Green. 'I don't suppose he was turned thirty, and he was a useful man,—a very useful man. That's the worst of it. He was just one of those men that the country can't afford to lose, and whom it is so very hard to replace.' Mounser Green was always eloquent as to the needs of the public service, and did really in his heart of hearts care about his office. 'Who is to go to Patagonia, I'm sure I don't know. Platitude was asking me about it, and I told him that I couldn't name a man.'

'Old Platitude always thinks that the world is coming to an end,' said Currie. 'There are as good fish in the sea as ever were caught.'

'Who is there? Monsoon won't go, even if they ask him. The Paragon was just the fellow for it. He had his heart in the work. An immense deal depends on what sort of a man we have in Patagonia at the present moment. If Paraguay gets the better of the Patagonese all Brazil will be in a ferment, and you know how that kind of thing spreads among half-caste Spaniards and Portuguese. Nobody can interfere but the British Minister. When I suggested Morton I knew I had the right man if he'd only take it.'

'And now he has gone and died!' said Hoffman.

'And now he has gone and died,' continued Mounser Green. ' "I never nursed a dear gazelle," and all the rest of it. Poor Paragon! I fear he was a little cut about Miss Trefoil.'

'She was down with him the day before he died,' said young Glossop. 'I happen to know that.'

'It was before he thought of going to Patagonia that she was at Bragton,' said Currie.

'That's all you know about it, old fellow,' said the

indignant young one. 'She was there a second time, just before his death. I had it from Lady Penwether, who was in the neighbourhood.'

'My dear little boy,' said Mounser Green, 'that was exactly what was likely to happen, and he yet may have broken his heart. I have seen a good deal of the lady lately, and under no circumstances would she have married him. When he accepted the mission that at any rate was all over.'

'The Rufford affair had begun before that,' said Hoffman.

'The Rufford affair as you call it,' said Glossop, 'was not an affair at all.'

'What do you mean by that?' asked Currie.

'I mean that Rufford was never engaged to her,—not for an instant,' said the lad, urgent in spreading the lesson which he had received from his cousin. 'It was all a dead take-in.'

'Who was taken in?' asked Mounser Green.

'Well;—nobody was taken in as it happened. But I suppose there can't be a doubt that she tried her best to catch him, and that the duke and duchess and Mistletoe, and old Trefoil, all backed her up. It was a regular plant. The only thing is it didn't come off.'

'Look here, young shaver;'—this was Mounser Green again:—'when you speak of a young lady do you be a little more discreet.'

'But didn't she do it, Green?'

'That's more than you or I can tell. If you want to know what I think, I believe he paid her a great deal of attention and then behaved very badly to her.'

'He didn't behave badly at all,' said young Glossop.

'My dear boy, when you are as old as I am, you will have learned how very hard it is to know everything. I only say what I believe, and perhaps I may have better ground for believing than you. He certainly paid her a great deal of attention, and then her friends,—especially the duchess,—went to work.'

'They've wanted to get her off their hands these six or eight years,' said Currie.

'That's nonsense again,' continued the new advocate, 'for there is no doubt she might have married Morton all the time had she pleased.'

'Yes;—but Rufford!—a fellow with sixty thousand a year!' said Glossop.

'About a third of that would be nearer the mark, Glossy. Take my word for it, you don't know everything yet, though you have so many advantages.' After that Mounser Green retreated to his own room with a look and tone as though he were angry.

'What makes him so ferocious about it?' asked Glossop when the door was shut.

'You are always putting your foot in it,' said Currie. 'I kept on winking to you but it was no good. He sees her almost every day now. She's staying with old Mrs. Green in Portugal Street. There has been some break up between her and her mother, and old Mrs. Green has taken her in. There's some sort of relationship. Mounser is the old woman's nephew, and she is aunt by marriage to the Connop Greens down in Hampshire, and Mrs. Connop Green is first cousin to Lady Augustus.'

'If Dick's sister married Tom's brother what relation would Dick be to Tom's mother? That's the kind of thing, isn't it?' suggested Hoffman.

'At any rate, there she is, and Mounser sees her every day.'

'It don't make any difference about Rufford,' said young Glossop stoutly.

All this happened before the will had been declared,—when Arabella did not dream that she was an heiress. A day or two afterwards she received a letter from the lawyer, telling her of her good fortune, and informing her that the trinkets would be given up to her and the money paid,—short of legacy duty,—whenever she would fix a time and place. The news almost stunned her. There was a moment in which she thought that she was bound to reject this money, as she had rejected that tendered to her by the other man. Poor as she was, greedy as she was, alive as she was to the necessity of doing something for herself,—still this legacy was to her at first bitter rather than sweet. She had never treated any man so ill as she had treated this man;—and it was thus that he punished her! She was alive to the feeling that he had always been true to her. In her intercourse with other men there had been generally a battle carried on with some fairness. Diamond had striven to cut diamond. But here the dishonesty had all been on one side, and she was aware that it had been so. In her later affair with Lord Rufford, she really did think that she had been ill-used; but she was quite alive to the fact that her treatment of John Morton had been abominable. The one man, in order that he might escape without further trouble, had in the grossest manner, sent to her the offer of a bribe. The other,—in regard to whose end her hard heart was touched, even her conscience seared,—had named her in his will as though his affection was unimpaired. Of course she took the money, but she took it with inward groans. She took the money and the trinkets, and the matter was all arranged for her by Mounser Green.

'So, after all, the Paragon left her whatever he could leave,' said Currie in the same room at the Foreign Office. A week had passed since the last conversation, and at this moment Mounser Green was not in the room.

'Oh dear no,' said young Glossy. 'She doesn't have Bragton. That goes to his cousin.'

'That was entailed, Glossy, my boy.'

'Not a bit of it. Everybody thought he would leave the place to another Morton, a fellow he'd never seen, in one of those Somerset House Offices. He and this fellow who is to have it, were enemies,—but he wouldn't put it out of the right line. It's all very well for Mounser to be down on me, but I do happen to know what goes on in that country. She gets a pot of money, and no end of family jewels; but he didn't leave her the estate as he might have done.'

At that moment Mounser Green came into the room. It was rather later than usual, being past one o'clock;—and he looked as though he were flurried. He didn't speak for a few minutes, but stood before the fire smoking a cigar. And there was a general silence,—there being now a feeling among them that Arabella Trefoil was not to be talked about in the old way before Mounser Green. At last he spoke himself. 'I suppose you haven't heard who is to go to Patagonia after all?'

'Is it settled?' asked Currie.

'Anybody we know?' asked Hoffman.

'I hope it's no d—— outsider,' said the too energetic Glossop.

'It is settled;—and it is somebody you know;—and it is not a d—— outsider; unless, indeed, he may be considered to be an outsider in reference to that branch of the service.'

'It's some consul,' said Currie. 'Backstairs from Panama, I'll bet a crown.'

'It isn't Backstairs, it isn't a consul. Gentlemen, get out your pocket-handkerchiefs. Mounser Green has consented to be expatriated for the good of his country.'

'You going to Patagonia!' said Currie. 'You're chaffing,' said Glossop. 'I never was so shot in my life,' said Hoffman.

'It's true, my dear boys.'

'I never was so sorry for anything in all my born days,' said Glossop, almost crying. 'Why on earth should you go to Patagonia?'

'Patagonia!' ejaculated Currie. 'What will you do in Patagonia?'

'It's an opening, my dear fellow,' said Mounser Green, leaning affectionately on Glossop's shoulder. 'What should I do by remaining here? When Drummond asked me, I saw he wanted me to go. They don't forget that kind of thing.' At that moment a messenger opened the door, and the Senator Gotobed, almost without being announced, entered the room. He had become so intimate of late at the Foreign Office, and his visits were so frequent, that he was almost able to dispense with the assistance of any messenger. Perhaps Mounser Green and his colleagues were a little tired of him;—but yet, after their fashion, they were always civil to him, and remembered, as they were bound to do, that he was one of the leading politicians of a great nation. 'I have secured the hall,' he said at once, as though aware that no news could be so important as the news he thus conveyed.

'Have you indeed?' said Currie.

'Secured it for the fifteenth. Now the question is——'

'What do you think,' said Glossop, interrupting him without the slightest hesitation. 'Mounser Green is going to Patagonia, in place of the poor Paragon.'

'I beg to congratulate Mr. Green with all my heart.'

'By George, I don't,' said the juvenile clerk. 'Fancy congratulating a fellow on going to Patagonia! It's what I call an awful sell*for everybody.'

'But as I was saying, I have the hall for the fifteenth.'

'You mean to lecture, then, after all?' said Green.

'Certainly I do; I am not going to be deterred from doing my duty because I am told there is a little danger. What I want to know is whether I can depend on having a staff of policemen.'

'Of course there will be police,' said Green.

'But I mean some extra strength. I don't mind for my-self, but I should be so unhappy if there were anything of a commotion.' Then he was assured that the officers of the police force would look to that, and was assured also that Mounser Green and the other gentlemen in the room would certainly attend the lecture. 'I don't suppose I shall be gone by that time,' said Mounser Green in a melancholy tone of voice.

CHAPTER LXVI
'I MUST GO'

'Rufford, March 5th.

'MY DEAR MISS TREFOIL,

'I am indeed sorry that I should have offended you by acceding to a suggestion which, I think I may say, originated with your mother. When she told me that her circumstances and yours were not in a pecuniary point of view so comfortable as they might be, I did feel that it was in my power to alleviate that trouble. The sum of money mentioned by my lawyer was certainly named by your mother. At any rate, pray believe that I meant to be of service.

'As to naming a place where we might meet, it really could be of no service. It would be painful to both of us, and could have no good result. Again apologizing for having inadvertently offended you by adopting the views which Lady Augustus entertained, I beg to assure you that I am,

'Yours faithfully,
'RUFFORD.'

This letter came from the peer himself, without assistance. After his interview with Lady Augustus, he simply told his mentor, Sir George, that he had steadfastly denied the existence of any engagement, not daring to acquaint him with the offer he had made. Neither, therefore, could he tell Sir George of the manner in which the young lady had repudiated the offer. That she should have repudiated it was no doubt to her credit. As he thought of it afterwards, he felt that, had she accepted it, she would have been base indeed. And yet, as he thought of what had taken place at the house in Piccadilly, he was confident that the proposition had in some way come from her mother. No doubt he had first written a sum of money on the fragment of paper which she had preserved; and the evidence would so far go against him. But Lady Augustus had spoken piteously of their joint property,—and had done so in lieu of insisting with a mother's indignation on her daughter's rights. Of course she had intended to ask for money. What other purpose could she have had? It was so he had argued at the moment, and so he had argued since. If it were so, he would not admit that he had behaved unlike a gentleman in offering the money. Yet he did not dare to tell Sir George, and, therefore, was obliged to answer Arabella's letter without assistance.

He was not altogether sorry to have his £8,000, being fully as much alive to the value of money as any brother peer in the kingdom, but he would sooner have paid the money than be subject to an additional interview. He

had been forced up to London to see, first the father, and
then the mother, and thought that he had paid penalty
enough for any offence that he might have committed.
An additional interview with the young lady herself
would distress him beyond anything,—would be worse
than any other interview. He would sooner leave Rufford
and go abroad than encounter it. He promised himself
that nothing should induce him to encounter it. Therefore, he wrote the above letter.

Arabella, when she received it, had ceased to care very
much about the insult of the offer. She had then
quarrelled with her mother, and had insisted on some
separation even without any arrangement as to funds.
Requiring some confidant, she had told a great deal,
though not quite all, to Mrs. Connop Green, and that
lady had passed her on for a while to her husband's aunt
in London. At this time she had heard nothing of John
Morton's will, and had perhaps thought with some
tender regret of the munificence of her other lover, which
she had scorned. But she was still intent on doing something. The fury of her despair was still on her, so that she
could not weigh the injury she might do herself against
some possible gratification to her wounded spirit. Up to
this moment she had formed no future hope. At this
epoch she had no string to her bow. John Morton was
dead;—and she had absolutely wept for him in solitude,
though she had certainly never loved him. Nor did she
love Lord Rufford. As far as she knew how to define her
feelings, she thought that she hated him. But she told
herself hourly that she had not done with him. She was
instigated by the true feminine Medea feeling*that she
would find some way to wring his heart,—even though in
the process she might suffer twice as much as he did. She
had convinced herself that in this instance he was the
offender. 'Painful to both of us!' No doubt! But because
it would be painful to him, it should be exacted. Though
he was a coward and would fain shirk such pain, she
could be brave enough. Even though she should be
driven to catch him by the arm in the open street, she
would have it out with him. He was a liar and a coward,

and she would, at any rate, have the satisfaction of telling him so.

She thought much about it before she could resolve on what she would do. She could not ask old Mrs. Green to help her. Mrs. Green was a kind old woman, who had lived much in the world, and would wish to see much of it still, had age allowed her. Arabella Trefoil was at any rate the niece of a duke, and the duke, in this affair with Lord Rufford, had taken his niece's part. She opened her house and as much of her heart as was left to Arabella, and was ready to mourn with her over the wicked lord. She could sympathize with her too, as to the iniquities of her mother, whom none of the Greens loved. But she would have been frightened by any proposition as to Medean vengeance.

In these days,—still winter days, and not open to much feminine gaiety in London, even if, in the present constitution of her circumstances, gaiety would have come in her way,—in these days the hours in her life which interested her most, were those in which Mr. Mounser Green was dutifully respectful to his aunt. Patagonia had not yet presented itself to him. Some four or five hundred a year, which the old lady had at her own disposal, had for years past contributed to Mounser's ideas of duty. And now Arabella's presence at the small house in Portugal Street certainly added a new zest to those ideas. The niece of the Duke of Mayfair, and the rejected of Lord Rufford, was at the present moment an interesting young woman in Mounser Green's world. There were many who thought that she had been ill-used. Had she succeeded, all the world would have pitied Lord Rufford; —but as he had escaped, there was a strong party for the lady. And gradually Mounser Green, who some weeks ago had not thought very much of her, became one of the party. She had brought her maid with her; and when she found that Mounser Green came to the house every evening, either before or after dinner, she had recourse to her accustomed lures. She would sit quiet, dejected, almost broken-hearted in the corner of a sofa; but when he spoke to her she would come to life and raise her eyes,

—not ignoring the recognised objection of her jilted
position, not pretending to this minor stag of six tines*
that she was a sprightly unwooed young fawn, fresh out
of the forest,—almost asking him to weep with her, and
playing her accustomed lures, though in a part which she
had not hitherto filled.

But still she was resolved that her Jason should not as
yet be quit of his Medea. So she made her plot. She
would herself go down to Rufford, and force her way into
her late lover's presence in spite of all obstacles. It was
possible that she should do this and get back to London
the same day,—but, to do so, she must leave London by
an early train at 7 a.m., stay seven or eight hours at
Rufford, and reach the London station at 10 p.m. For
such a journey there must be some valid excuse made to
Mrs. Green. There must be some necessity shown for
such a journey. She would declare that a meeting was
necessary with her mother, and that her mother was at
any town she chose to name at the requisite distance from
London. In this way she might start with her maid before
daylight, and get back after dark, and have the meeting
with her mother—or with Lord Rufford, as the case
might be. But Mounser Green knew very well that Lady
Augustus was in Orchard Street, and knew also that
Arabella was determined not to see her mother. And if
she declared her purpose, without a caution to Mounser
Green, the old woman would tell her nephew, and the
nephew would unwittingly expose the deceit. It was
necessary therefore that she should admit Mounser Green
to, at any rate, half a confidence. This she did. 'Don't
ask me any questions,' she said. 'I know I can trust you.
I must be out of town the whole day, and perhaps the
next. And your aunt must not know why I am going or
where. You will help me?' Of course he said that he
would help her; and the lie, with a vast accompaniment
of little lies, was told. There must be a meeting on business matters between her and her mother, and her mother
was now in the neighbourhood of Birmingham. This was
the lie told to Mrs. Green. She would go down, and, if
possible, be back on the same day. She would take her

maid with her. She thought that in such a matter as that she could trust her maid, and was in truth afraid to travel alone. 'I will come in the morning and take Miss Trefoil to the station,' said Mounser, 'and will meet her in the evening.' And so the matter was arranged.

The journey was not without its drawbacks and almost its perils. Summer or winter Arabella Trefoil was seldom out of bed before nine. It was incumbent on her now to get up on a cold March morning,—when the lion had not as yet made way for the lamb,—at half-past five. That itself seemed to be all but impossible to her. Nevertheless she was ready, and had tried to swallow half a cup of tea, when Mounser Green came to the door with a cab a little after six. She had endeavoured to dispense with this new friend's attendance, but he had insisted, assuring her that without some such aid no cab would be forthcoming. She had not told him and did not intend that he should know to what station she was going. 'You begged me to ask no questions,' he said when he was in the cab with her, the maid having been induced most unwillingly to seat herself with the cabman on the box,—'and I have obeyed you. But I wish I knew how I could help you.'

'You have helped me, and you are helping me. But do not ask anything more.'

'Will you be angry with me if I say that I fear you are intending something rash?'

'Of course I am. How could it be otherwise with me? Don't you think there are turns in a person's life when she must do something rash. Think of yourself. If everybody crushed you; if you were ill-treated beyond all belief; if the very people who ought to trust you doubted you, wouldn't you turn upon somebody and rend him?'

'Are you going to rend anybody?'

'I do not know as yet.'

'I wish you would let me go down with you.'

'No; that you certainly cannot. You must not come even into the station with me. You have been very good to me. You will not now turn against me.'

'I certainly will do nothing but what you tell me.'

'Then here we are,—and now you must go. Jane can

carry my hand-bag and cloak. If you chose to come in
the evening at ten it will be an additional favour.'

'I certainly will do so. But, Miss Trefoil, one word.'
They were now standing under cover of the portico in
front of the railway station, into which he was not to be
allowed to enter. 'What I fear is this,—that in your first
anger you may be tempted to do something which may
be injurious to—to your prospects in life.'

'I have no prospects in life, Mr. Green.'

'Ah; that is just it! There are for most of us moments
of unhappiness, in which we are tempted by our misery
to think that we are relieved, at any rate, from the burden
of caution, because nothing that can occur to us can
make us worse than we are.'

'Nothing can make me worse than I am.'

'But in a few months or weeks,' continued Mounser
Green, bringing up in his benevolence all the wisdom of
his experience, 'we have got a new footing amidst our
troubles, and then we may find how terrible is the injury
which our own indiscretion has brought on us. I do not
want to ask any questions, but—it might be so much
better that you should abandon your intention, and go
back with me.'

She seemed to be almost undecided for a moment as
she thought over his words. But she remembered her
pledge to herself that Lord Rufford should find that she
had not done with him yet. 'I must go,' she said in a
hoarse voice.

'If you must——'

'I must go. I have no way out of it. Good-bye, Mr.
Green; I cannot tell you how much obliged to you I am.'
Then he turned back, and she went into the station and
took two first-class tickets for Rufford. At that moment
Lord Rufford was turning himself comfortably in his bed.
How would he have sprung up, and how would he have
fled, had he known the evil that was coming upon him!
This happened on a Thursday, a day on which, as
Arabella knew, the U.R.U. did not go out;—the very
Thursday on which John Morton was buried and the will
was read at Bragton.

She was fully determined to speak her mind to the man, and to be checked by no feminine squeamishness. She would speak her mind to him, if she could force her way into his presence. And in doing this she would be debarred by no etiquette. It might be that she would fail, that he would lack the courage to see her, and would run away, even before all the servants, when he should hear who was standing in the hall. But, if he did so, she would try again, even though she should have to ride out into the hunting-field after him. Face to face she would tell him that he was a liar and a slanderer and no gentleman, though she should have to run round the world to catch him. When she reached Rufford, she went to the town and ordered breakfast and a carriage. As soon as she had eaten the meal, she desired the driver in a clear voice to take her to Rufford Hall. Was her maid to go with her? No. She would be back soon, and her maid would wait there till she had returned.

Chapter LXVII

IN THE PARK

THIS thing that she was doing required an infinite amount of pluck,—of that sort of hardihood which we may not quite call courage, but which in a world well provided with policemen is infinitely more useful than courage. Lord Rufford himself was endowed with all the ordinary bravery of an Englishman, but he could have flown as soon as run into a lion's den as Arabella was doing. She had learned that Lady Penwether and Miss Penge were both at Rufford Hall, and understood well the difficulty there would be in explaining her conduct should she find herself in their presence. And there were all the servants there to stare at her, and the probability that she might be shown to the door and told that no one there would speak to her. She saw it all before her, and knew how bitter it might be;—but her heart was big enough to carry her through it. She was dressed very simply, but still by no means dowdily, in a black silk dress, and though she wore a thick veil when she got out of the fly and rang the door bell, she had been at some pains with her hair before she left the inn. Her purpose was revenge; but still she had an eye to the possible chance,—the chance barely possible of bringing the man to submit.

When the door was opened she raised her veil and asked for Lord Rufford;—but as she did so she walked on through the broad passage which led from the front door into a wide central space which they called the billiard-room, but which really was the hall of the house. This she did as a manifesto that she did not mean to leave the house because she might be told that he was out or could not be seen, or that he was engaged. It was then nearly one o'clock, and no doubt he would be there for luncheon. Of course he might be, in truth, away from home, but she must do her best to judge of that by the servant's manner. The man knew her well, and not improbably had heard something of his master's danger. He was, however, very respectful and told her that his lordship was out in the grounds;—but that Lady Penwether was in the drawing-room. Then a sudden thought struck her, and she asked the man whether he would show her in what part of the grounds she might find Lord Rufford. Upon that he took her to the front door and pointing across the park to a belt of trees, showed her three or four men standing round some piece of work. He believed, he said, that one of those men was his lordship.

She bowed her thanks and was descending the steps on her way to join the group, when whom should she see but Lady Penwether coming into the house with her garden-hat and gloves. It was unfortunate; but she would not allow herself to be stopped by Lady Penwether. She bowed stiffly and would have passed on without a word but that was impossible. 'Miss Trefoil!' said Lady Penwether with astonishment.

'Your brother is just across the park. I think I see him and will go to him.'

'I had better send and tell him that you are here,' said her ladyship.

'I need not trouble you so far. I can be my own messenger. Perhaps you will allow the fly to be sent round to the yard for half-an-hour.' As she said this she was still passing down the steps.

But Lady Penwether knew that it behoved her to prevent this if it might be possible. Of late she had had little or no conversation with her brother about Miss Trefoil, but she had heard much from her husband. She would be justified, she thought, in saying or in doing almost anything which would save him from such an encounter. 'I really think,' she said, 'that he had better be told that you are here,' and as she spoke she strove to put herself in the visitor's way. 'You had better come in, Miss Trefoil, and he shall be informed at once.'

'By no means, Lady Penwether. I would not for worlds give him or you so much trouble. I see him and I will go to him.' Then Lady Penwether absolutely put out her hand to detain her; but Arabella shook it off angrily and looked into the other woman's face with fierce eyes. 'Allow me,' she said, 'to conduct myself at this moment as I may think best. I shall do so, at any rate.' Then she stalked on, and Lady Penwether saw that any contest was hopeless. Had she sent the servant on with all his speed, so as to gain three or four moments, her brother could hardly have fled through the trees in face of the enemy.

Lord Rufford, who was busy planning the prolongation of a ha-ha fence, saw nothing of all this; but after a while he was aware that a woman was coming to him, and then gradually he saw who that woman was. Arabella when she had found herself advancing closer went slowly enough. She was sure of her prey now, and was wisely mindful that it might be well that she should husband her breath. The nearer she drew to him the slower became her pace, and more majestic. Her veil was thrown back, and her head was raised in the air. She knew these little tricks of deportment and could carry herself like a queen. He had taken a moment or two to consider. Should he fly? It was possible. He might vault over a railed fence in among the trees at a spot not ten yards from her, and then it would be impossible that she should run him down. He might have done it had not the men been there to see it. As it was he left them in the other direction and came forward to meet her. He tried to smile pleasantly as he spoke to her. 'So I see that you would not take my advice,' he said.

'Neither your advice nor your money, my lord.'

'Ah, I was so sorry about that. But indeed, indeed, the fault was not mine.'

'They were your figures that I saw upon the paper, and by your orders, no doubt, that the lawyer acted. But I have not come to say much of that. You meant, I suppose, to be gracious.'

'I meant to be good-natured.'

'I dare say. You were willing enough to give away what you did not want. But there must be more between us than any question of money. Lord Rufford, you have treated me most shamefully.'

'I hope not. I think not.'

'And you yourself must be well aware of it,—quite as well aware of it as I am. You have thrown me over and absolutely destroyed me; and why?' He shrugged his shoulders. 'Because you have been afraid of others; because your sister has told you that you were mistaken in your choice. The women around you have been too many for you, and have not allowed you to dispose of your hand, and your name, and your property as you pleased. I defy you to say that this was not your sister's doing.' He was too much astounded to contradict her rapidly, and she passed on, not choosing to give him time for contradiction. 'Will you have the hardihood to say that you did not love me?' Then she paused, thinking that he would not dare to contradict her then, feeling that she was on strong ground. 'Were you lying when you told me that you did? What did you mean when I was in your arms up in the house there? What did you intend me to think that you meant?' Then she stopped, standing well in front of him, and looking fixedly into his face.

This was the very thing that he had feared. Lord

Augustus had been a trouble. The duke's letter had been a trouble. Lady Augustus had been a trouble; and Sir George's sermons had been troublesome. But what were they all when compared to this? How is it possible that a man should tell a girl that he has not loved her when he has embraced her again and again? He may know it, and she may know it, and each may know that the other knows it; but to say that he does not and did not then love her is beyond the scope of his audacity, unless he be a heartless Nero. 'No one can grieve about this so much as I do,' he said, weakly.

'Cannot I grieve more, do you think,—I who told all my relatives that I was to become your wife, and was justified in so telling them? Was I not justified?'

'I think not.'

'You think not!. What did you mean, then? What were you thinking of when we were coming back in the carriage from Stamford,—when with your arms round me you swore that you loved me better than all the world? Is that true? Did you so swear?' What a question for a man to have to answer! It was becoming clear to him that there was nothing for him but to endure and be silent. Even to this interview the gods would, at last, give an end. The hour would pass, though, alas! so slowly, and she could not expect that he should stand there to be rated much after the accustomed time for feeding. 'You acknowledge that, and do you dare to say that I had no right to tell my friends?'

There was a moment in which he thought it was almost a pity that he had not married her. She was very beautiful in her present form,—more beautiful, he thought, than ever. She was the niece of a duke, and certainly a very clever woman. He had not wanted money, and why shouldn't he have married her? As for hunting him, that was a matter of course. He was as much born and bred to be hunted as a fox. He could not do it now, as he had put too much power into the hands of the Penwethers, but he almost wished that he had. 'I never intended it,' he said.

'What. did you intend? After what has occurred, I

suppose I have a right to ask such a question. I have made
a somewhat unpleasant journey to-day, all alone, on purpose to ask that question. What did you intend?' In his
great annoyance he struck his shovel angrily against the
ground. 'And I will not leave you till I get an answer to
the question. What did you intend, Lord Rufford?' There
was nothing for him but silence and a gradual progress
back towards the house.

But from the latter resource she cut him off for a time.
'You will do me the favour to remain with me here till
this conversation is ended. You cannot refuse me so slight
a request as that, seeing the trouble to which you have
put me. I never saw a man so forgetful of words. You
cannot speak. Have you no excuse to offer,—not a word
to say in explanation of conduct so black that I don't
think here in England I ever heard a case to equal it?
If your sister had been treated so!'

'It would have been impossible.'

'I believe it. Her cautious nature would have trusted
no man as I trusted you. Her lips, doubtless, were never
unfrozen till the settlements had been signed. With her
it was a matter of bargain, not of love. I can well believe
that.'

'I will not talk about my sister.'

'It seems to me, Lord Rufford, that you object to talk
about anything. You certainly have been very uncommunicative with reference to yourself. Were you lying
when you told me that you loved me?'

'No.'

'Did I lie when I told the duchess that you had
promised me your love? Did I lie when I told my mother
that in these days a man does not always mention marriage when he asks a girl to be his wife? You said you
loved me, and I believed you, and the rest was a thing
of course. And you meant it. You know you meant it.
When you held me in your arms in the carriage you know
you meant me to suppose that it would always be so.
Then the fear of your sister came upon you, and of your
sister's husband,—and you ran away! I wonder whether
you think yourself a man!' And yet she felt that she had

not hit him yet. He was wretched enough; and she could see that he was wretched;—but the wretchedness would pass away as soon as she was gone. How could she stab him so that the wound would remain? With what virus could she poison her arrow, so that the agony might be prolonged. 'And such a coward too! I began to suspect it when you started that night from Mistletoe,—though I did not think then that you could be all mean, all cowardly. From that day to this, you have not dared to speak a word of truth. Every word has been a falsehood.'

'By heavens, no.'

'Every word a falsehood! and I, a lady,—a lady whom you have so deeply injured, whose cruel injury even you have not the face to deny,—am forced by your cowardice to come to you here, because you have not dared to come out to meet me. Is that true!'

'What good can it do?'

'None to me, God knows. You are such a thing that I would not have you now I know you, though you were twice Lord Rufford. But I have chosen to speak my mind to you and to tell you what I think. Did you suppose that when I said that I would meet you face to face I was to be deterred by such girl's excuses as you made? I chose to tell you to your face that you are false, a coward, and no gentleman, and though you had hidden yourself under the very earth I would have found you.' Then she turned round and saw Sir George Penwether standing close to them.

Lord Rufford had seen him approaching for some time, and had made one or two futile attempts to meet him. Arabella's back had been turned to the house, and she had not heard the steps or observed the direction of her companion's eyes. He came so near before he was seen that he heard her concluding words. Then Lord Rufford with a ghastly attempt at pleasantry introduced them. 'George,' he said, 'I do not think you know Miss Trefoil. Sir George Penwether;—Miss Trefoil.'

The interview had been watched from the house, and the husband had been sent down by his wife to mitigate

the purgatory which she knew that her brother must be
enduring. 'My wife,' said Sir George, 'has sent me to ask
Miss Trefoil whether she will not come in to lunch.'

'I believe it is Lord Rufford's house,' said Arabella.

'If Miss Trefoil's frame of mind will allow her to sit
at table with me I shall be proud to see her,' said Lord
Rufford.

'Miss Trefoil's frame of mind will not allow her to eat
or to drink with such a dastard,' said she, turning away
in the direction of the park gates. 'Perhaps, Sir George,
you will be kind enough to direct the man who brought
me here to pick me up at the lodge.' And so she walked
away,—a mile across the park,—neither of them caring
to follow her.

It seemed to her as she stood at the lodge gate, having
obstinately refused to enter the house, to be an eternity
before the fly came to her. When it did come she felt
as though her strength would barely enable her to climb
into it. And when she was there she wept, with bitter
throbbing woe, all the way to Rufford. It was over now,
at any rate. Now there was not a possible chance on
which a gleam of hope might be made to settle. And how
handsome he was, and how beautiful the place, and how
perfect would have been the triumph could she have
achieved it! One more word, one other pressure of the
hand in the postchaise, might have done it! Had he
really promised her marriage she did not even now think
that he would have gone back from his word. If that
heavy stupid duke would have spoken to him that night
at Mistletoe, all would have been well! But now,—
now there was nothing for her but weeping and gnashing
of teeth. He was gone, and poor Morton was gone; and
all those others, whose memories rose like ghosts before
her;—they were all gone. And she wept as she thought
that she might perhaps have made a better use of the gifts
which Providence had put in her way.

When Mounser Green met her at the station she was
beyond measure weary. Through the whole journey she
had been struggling to restrain her sobs so that her maid
should neither hear nor see them. 'Don't mind me, Mr.

Green; I am only tired,—so tired,' she said as she got into the carriage which he had brought.

He had with him a long, formal-looking letter addressed to herself. But she was too weary to open it that night. It was the letter conveying the tidings of the legacy which Mr. Morton had made in her favour.

CHAPTER LXVIII

LORD RUFFORD'S MODEL FARM

AT this time Senator Gotobed was paying a second visit to Rufford Hall. In the matter of Goarly and Scrobby he had never given way an inch. He was still strongly of opinion that a gentleman's pheasants had no right to eat his neighbour's corn, and that if damage were admitted, the person committing the injury should not take upon himself to assess the damage. He also thought, —and very often declared his thoughts,—that Goarly was justified in shooting not only foxes, but hounds also when they came upon his property, and in moments of excitement had gone so far as to say that not even horses should be held sacred. He had, however, lately been driven to admit that Goarly himself was not all that a man should be, and that Mrs. Goarly's goose was an impostor. It was the theory,—the principle for which he combated, declaring that the evil condition of the man himself was due to the evil institutions among which he had been reared. By degrees evidence had been obtained of Scrobby's guilt in the matter of red herrings, and he was to be tried for the offence of putting down poison. Goarly was to be the principal witness against his brother conspirator. Lord Rufford, instigated by his brother-in-law, and liking the spirit of the man, had invited the Senator to stay at the Hall while the case was being tried at the Rufford Quarter Sessions. I am afraid the invitation was given in a spirit of triumph over the Senator rather than with genuine hospitality. It was thought well that the American should be made to see in public the degradation of the abject creature with whom he had sympathized.

Perhaps there were some who thought that in this way they would get the Senator's neck under their heels. If there were such they were likely to be mistaken, as the Senator was not a man prone to submit himself to such treatment.

He was seated at table with Lady Penwether and Miss Penge when Lord Rufford and his brother-in-law came into the room, after parting with Miss Trefoil in the manner described in the last chapter. Lady Penwether had watched their unwelcome visitor as she took her way across the park, and had whispered something to Miss Penge. Miss Penge understood the matter thoroughly, and would not herself have made the slightest allusion to the other young lady. Had the Senator not been there the two gentlemen would have been allowed to take their places without a word on the subject. But the Senator had a marvellous gift of saying awkward things, and would never be reticent. He stood for a while at the window in the drawing-room before he went across the hall, and even took up a pair of field-glasses to scrutinise the lady; and when they were all present, he asked whether that was not Miss Trefoil whom he had seen down by the new fence. Lady Penwether, without seeming to look about her, did look about her for a few seconds to see whether the question might be allowed to die away unanswered. She perceived, from the Senator's face, that he intended to have an answer.

'Yes,' she said, 'that was Miss Trefoil. I am very glad that she is not coming in to disturb us.'

'A great blessing,' said Miss Penge.

'Where is she staying?' asked the Senator.

'I think she drove over from Rufford,' said the elder lady.

'Poor young lady! She was engaged to marry my friend, Mr. John Morton. She must have felt his death very bitterly. He was an excellent young man;—rather opinionated, and perhaps too much wedded to the traditions of his own country; but, nevertheless, a painstaking, excellent young man. I had hoped to welcome her as Mrs. Morton in America.'

'He was to have gone to Patagonia,' said Lord Rufford, endeavouring to come to himself after the sufferings of the morning.

'We should have seen him back in Washington, sir. Whenever you have anything good in diplomacy, you generally send him to us. Poor young lady! Was she talking about him?'

'Not particularly,' said his lordship.

'She must have remembered that when she was last here he was of the party, and it was but a few weeks ago, —only a little before Christmas. He struck me as being cold in his manner as an affianced lover. Was not that your idea, Lady Penwether?'

'I don't think I observed him especially.'

'I have reason to believe that he was much attached to her. She could be sprightly enough; but at times there seemed to come a cold melancholy upon her too. It is, I fancy, so with most of your English ladies. Miss Trefoil always gave me the idea of being a good type of the English aristocracy.' Lady Penwether and Miss Penge drew themselves up very stiffly. 'You admired her, I think, my lord.'

'Very much indeed,' said Lord Rufford, filling his mouth with pigeon-pie as he spoke, and not lifting his eyes from his plate.

'Will she be back to dinner?'

'Oh dear no,' said Lady Penwether. There was something in her tone which at last startled the Senator into perceiving that Miss Trefoil was not popular at Rufford Hall.

'She only came for a morning call,' said Lord Rufford.

'Poor young woman! She has lost her husband, and I am afraid, now has lost her friends also. I am told that she is not well off;—and, from what I see and hear, I fancy that here in England a young lady without a dowry cannot easily replace a lover. I suppose, too, Miss Trefoil is not quite in her first youth.'

'If you have done, Caroline,' said Lady Penwether to Miss Penge, 'I think we'll go into the other room.'

That afternoon Sir George asked the Senator to accom-

pany him for a walk. Sir George was held to be responsible for the Senator's presence, and was told by the ladies
that he must do something with him. The next day,
which was Friday, would be occupied by the affairs of
Scrobby and Goarly, and on the Saturday he was to
return to town. The two started about three with the
object of walking round the park and the home farm,
—the Senator intent on his duty of examining the ways of
English life to the very bottom. 'I hope I did not say anything amiss about Miss Trefoil,' he remarked, as they
passed through a shrubbery gate into the park.

'No; I think not.'

'I thought your good lady looked as though she did not
like the subject.'

'I am not sure that Miss Trefoil is very popular with
the ladies up there.'

'She's a handsome young woman, and clever, though,
as I said before, given to melancholy, and sometimes
fastidious. When we were all here I thought that Lord
Rufford admired her, and that poor Mr. Morton was a
little jealous.'

'I wasn't at Rufford then. Here we get out of the park
on to the home farm. Rufford does it very well,—very
well indeed.'

'Looks after it altogether himself?'

'I cannot quite say that. He has a land-bailiff, who
lives in the house there.'

'With a salary?'

'Oh yes; £120 a year I think the man has.'

'And that house?' asked the Senator. 'Why, the house
and garden are worth £50 a year.'

'I dare say they are. Of course it costs money. It's
near the park, and had to be made ornamental.'

'And does it pay?'

'Well, no; I should think not. In point of fact, I know
it does not. He loses about the value of the ground.'

The Senator asked a great many more questions, and
then began his lecture. 'A man who goes into trade, and
loses by it, cannot be doing good to himself or to others.
You say, Sir George, that it is a model farm; but it's a

model of ruin. If you want to teach a man any other business, you don't specially select an example in which the proprietors are spending all their capital without any return. And if you would not do this in shoemaking, why in farming?'

'The neighbours are able to see how work should be done.'

'Excuse me, Sir George, but it seems to me that they are enabled to see how work should not be done. If his lordship would stick up over his gate a notice to the effect that everything seen there was to be avoided, he might do some service. If he would publish his accounts half-yearly in the village newspaper——'

'There isn't a village newspaper.'

'In the *Rufford Gazette*. There is a *Rufford Gazette*, and Rufford isn't much more than a village. If he would publish his accounts half-yearly in the *Rufford Gazette*, honestly showing how much he had lost by his system, how much capital had been misapplied and how much labour wasted, he might serve as an example, like the pictures of "The Idle Apprentice". I don't see that he can do any other good,—unless it be to the estimable gentleman who is allowed to occupy the pretty house. I don't think you'd see anything like that model farm in our country, sir.'

'Your views, Mr. Gotobed, are utilitarian rather than picturesque.'

'Oh! if you say that it is done for the picturesque, that is another thing. Lord Rufford is a wealthy lord, and can afford to be picturesque. A green sward I should have thought handsomer, as well as less expensive, than a ploughed field; but that is a matter of taste. Only why call a pretty toy a model farm? You might mislead the British rustics.'

They had by this time passed through a couple of fields which formed part of the model farm, and had come to a stile leading into a large meadow. 'This, I take it,' said the Senator, looking about him, 'is beyond the limits of my lord's plaything.'

'This is Shugborough,' said Sir George, 'and there is

John Runce, the occupier, on his pony. He, at any rate,
is a model farmer.' As he spoke Mr. Runce slowly trotted
up to them, touching his hat, and Mr. Gotobed recognized
the man who had declined to sit next to him at the hunting breakfast. Runce also thought that he knew the
gentleman. 'Do you hunt to-morrow, Mr. Runce?' asked
Sir George.

'Well, Sir George, no; I think not. I b'lieve I must go
to Rufford and hear that fellow Scrobby get it hot and
heavy.'

'We seem all to be going that way. You think he'll be
convicted, sir?'

'If there's a juryman left in the country worth his salt,
he'll be convicted,' said Mr. Runce, almost enraged at
the doubt. 'But that other fellow—he's to get off. That's
what kills me, Sir George.'

'You're alluding to Mr. Goarly, sir?' said the Senator.

'That's about it, certainly,' said Runce, still looking
very suspiciously at his companion.

'I almost think he is the bigger rogue of the two,' said
the Senator.

'Well,' said Runce; 'well, I don't know as he ain't. Six
of one and half a dozen of the other! That's about it.'
But he was evidently pacified by the opinion.

'Goarly is certainly a rascal all round,' continued the
Senator. Runce looked at him to make sure whether he
was the man who had uttered such fearful blasphemies at
the breakfast-table. 'I think we had a little discussion
about this before, Mr. Runce.'

'I am very glad to see you have changed your principles, sir.'

'Not a bit of it. I am too old to change my principles,
Mr. Runce. And much as I admire this country I don't
think it's the place in which I should be induced to do so.'
Runce looked at him again with a scowl on his face and
with a falling mouth. 'Mr. Goarly is certainly a blackguard.'

'Well;—I rather think he is.'

'But a blackguard may have a good cause. Put it in
your own case, Mr. Runce. If his lordship's pheasants
ate up your wheat——'

'They're welcome;—they're welcome! The more the merrier. But they don't. Pheasants know when they're well off.'

'Or if a crowd of horsemen rode over your fences, don't you think——'

'My fences! They'd be welcome in my wife's bedroom if the fox took that way. My fences! It's what I has fences for,—to be ridden over.'

'You didn't exactly hear what I have to say, Mr. Runce.'

'And I don't want. No offence, sir, if you be a friend of my lord's;—but if his lordship was to say hisself that Goarly was right, I wouldn't listen to him. A good cause, and he going about at dead o'night with his pocket's full of p'ison! Hounds and foxes all one!—or little childer either for the matter o' that if they happened on the herrings!'

'I have not said his cause was good, Mr. Runce.'

'I'll wish you good-evening, Sir George,' said the farmer, reining his pony round. 'Good-evening to you, sir,' and Mr. Runce trotted or rather ambled off, unable to endure another word.

'An honest man, I dare say,' said the Senator.

'Certainly;—and not a bad specimen of a British farmer.'

'Not a bad specimen of a Briton generally;—but still, perhaps, a little unreasonable.' After that Sir George said as little as he could, till he had brought the Senator back to the hall.

'I think it's all over now,' said Lady Penwether to Miss Penge, when the gentlemen had left them alone in the afternoon.

'I'm sure I hope so,—for his sake. What a woman to come here by herself in that way!'

'I don't think he ever cared for her in the least.'

'I can't say that I have troubled myself much about that,' replied Miss Penge. 'For the sake of the family generally, and the property, and all that, I should be very very sorry to think that he was going to make her Lady Rufford. I dare say he has amused himself with her.'

'There was very little of that, as far as I can learn;—
very little encouragement indeed! What we saw here was
the worst of it. He was hardly with her at all at Mistletoe.'

'I hope it will make him more cautious;—that's all,'
said Miss Penge. Miss Penge was now a great heiress,
having had her lawsuit respecting certain shares in a
Welsh coal mine settled since we last saw her. As all the
world knows, she came from one of the oldest Com-
moner's families in the West of England, and is, moreover
a handsome young woman, only 27 years of age. Lady
Penwether thinks that she is the very woman to be mistress of Rufford, and I do not know that Miss Penge
herself is averse to the idea. Lord Rufford has been too
lately wounded to rise at the bait quite immediately; but
his sister knows that her brother is impressionable and
that a little patience will go a long way. They have,
however, all agreed at the hall that Arabella's name shall
not again be mentioned.

CHAPTER LXIX

SCROBBY'S TRIAL

RUFFORD was a good deal moved as to the trial of
Mr. Scrobby. Mr. Scrobby was a man who not long
since had held his head up in Rufford and had the reputation of a well-to-do tradesman. Enemies had perhaps
doubted his probity; but he had gone on and prospered,
and, two or three years before the events which are now
chronicled, had retired on a competence. He had then
taken a house with a few acres of land, lying between
Rufford and Rufford Hall,—the property of Lord
Rufford, and had commenced genteel life. Many in the
neighbourhood had been astonished that such a man
should have been accepted as a tenant in such a house;
and it was generally understood that Lord Rufford himself had been very angry with his agent. Mr. Scrobby did
not prosper greatly in his new career. He became a
guardian of the poor and quarrelled with all the Board.
He tried to become a municipal councillor in the borough,
but failed. Then he quarrelled with his landlord, insisted

on making changes in the grounds which were not authorized by the terms of his holding, would not pay his rent, and was at last ejected,—having caused some considerable amount of trouble. Then he occupied a portion of his leisure with spreading calumnies as to his lordship, and was generally understood to have made up his mind to be disagreeable. As Lord Rufford was a sportsman rather than anything else, Scrobby studied how he might best give annoyance in that direction, and some time before the Goarly affair, had succeeded in creating considerable disturbance. When a man will do this pertinaciously, and when his selected enemy is wealthy and of high standing, he will generally succeed in getting a party round him. In Rufford there were not a few who thought that Lord Rufford's pheasants and foxes were a nuisance,—though probably these persons had never suffered in any way themselves. It was a grand thing to fight a lord,—and so Scrobby had a party.

When the action against his lordship was first threatened by Goarly and when it was understood that Scrobby had backed him with money, there was a feeling that Scrobby was doing rather a fine thing. He had not, indeed, used his money openly, as the Senator had afterwards done; but that was not Scrobby's way. If Goarly had been ill-used any help was legitimate, and the party as a party was proud of their man. But when it came to pass that poison had been laid down, 'wholesale' as the hunting-men said, in Dillsborough Wood, in the close vicinity of Goarly's house, then the party hesitated. Such strategy as that was disgusting;—but was there reason to think that Scrobby had been concerned in the matter? Scrobby still had an income, and ate roast meat or boiled every day for his dinner. Was it likely that such a man should deal in herrings and strychnine?

Nickem had been at work for the last three months, backed up by the funds which had latterly been provided by the lord's agent, and had in truth run the matter down. Nickem had found out all about it, and in his pride had resigned his stool in Mr. Masters' office. But the Scrobby party in Rufford could not bring itself to

believe that Nickem was correct. That Goarly's hands
had actually placed the herrings no man either at Rufford
or Dillsborough had doubted. Such was now Nickem's
story. But of what avail would be the evidence of such a
man as Goarly against such a man as Scrobby? It would
be utterly worthless unless corroborated, and the Scrobby
party was not yet aware how clever Nickem had been.
Thus all Rufford was interested in the case.

Lord Rufford, Sir George Penwether, his lordship's
agent, and Mr. Gotobed, had been summoned as witnesses,
—the expenditure of money by the Senator having by
this time become notorious; and on the morning of the
trial they all went into the town in his lordship's drag.
The Senator, as the guest, was on the box-seat with his
lordship, and as they passed old Runce trotting into
Rufford on his nag, Mr. Gotobed began to tell the story
of yesterday's meeting, complaining of the absurdity of
the old farmer's anger.

'Penwether told me about it,' said the lord.

'I suppose your tenant is a little crazy?'

'By no means. I thought he was right in what he said,
if I understood Penwether.'

'He couldn't have been right. He turned from me in
disgust simply because I tried to explain to him that a
rogue has as much right to be defended by the law as an
honest man.'

'Runce looks upon these men as vermin which ought
to be hunted down.'

'But they are not vermin. They are men;—and till they
have been found guilty they are innocent men.'

'If a man had murdered your child, would he be
innocent in your eyes till he was convicted?'

'I hope so;—but I should be very anxious to bring
home the crime against him. And should he be found
guilty even then he should not be made subject to other
punishment than that the law awards. Mr. Runce is
angry with me because I do not think that Goarly should
be crushed under the heels of all his neighbours. Take
care, my lord. Didn't we come round that corner rather
sharp?'

Then Lord Rufford emphatically declared that such men as Scrobby and Goarly should be crushed, and the Senator, with an inward sigh, declared that between landlord and tenant, between peer and farmer, between legislator and rustic, there was, in capacity for logical inference, no difference whatever. The British heart might be all right; but the British head was,—ah,—hopelessly wooden! It would be his duty to say so in his lecture, and perhaps some good might be done to so gracious but so stolid a people, if only they could be got to listen.

Scrobby had got down a barrister from London, and therefore the case was allowed to drag itself out through the whole day. Lord Rufford, as a magistrate, went on to the bench himself,—though he explained that he only took his seat there as a spectator. Sir George and Mr. Gotobed were also allowed to sit in the high place,—though the Senator complained even of this. Goarly and Scrobby were not allowed to be there, and Lord Rufford, in his opinion, should also have been debarred from such a privilege. A long time was occupied before even a jury could be sworn, the barrister earning his money by browbeating the provincial bench and putting various obstacles in the way of the trial. As he was used to practice at the assizes of course he was able to domineer. This juror would not do, nor that. The chairman was all wrong in his law. The officers of the Court knew nothing about it. At first there was quite a triumph for the Scrobbyites, and even Nickem himself was frightened. But at last the real case was allowed to begin, and Goarly was soon in the witness-box. Goarly did not seem to enjoy the day, and was with difficulty got to tell his own story even on his own side. But the story when it was told was simple enough. He had met Mr. Scrobby accidentally in Rufford and they two had together discussed the affairs of the young lord. They came to an agreement that the young lord was a tyrant and ought to be put down, and Scrobby showed how it was to be done. Scrobby instigated the action about the pheasants, and undertook to pay the expenses if Goarly would act in the other little matter. But, when he found that the Senator's money was forthcoming, he had been anything but as good as his word. Goarly swore that in hard cash he had never seen more than four shillings of Scrobby's money. As to the poison, Goarly declared that he knew nothing about it; but he certainly had received a parcel of herrings from Scrobby's own hands, and in obedience to Scrobby's directions, had laid them down in Dillsborough Wood the very morning on which the hounds had come there. He owned that he supposed that there might be something in the herrings, something that would probably be deleterious to hounds as well as foxes,—or to children should the herrings happen to fall into children's hands; but he assured the Court that he had no knowledge of poison,—none whatever. Then he was made by the other side to give a complete and a somewhat prolonged account of his own life up to the present time,—this information being of course required by the learned barrister on the other side; in listening to which the Senator did become thoroughly ashamed of the Briton whom he had assisted with his generosity.

But all this would have been nothing had not Nickem secured the old woman who had sold the herrings,—and also the chemist, from whom the strychnine had been purchased as much as three years previously. This latter feat was Nickem's great triumph,—the feeling of the glory of which induced him to throw up his employment in Mr. Masters' office, and thus brought him and his family to absolute ruin within a few months in spite of the liberal answers which were made by Lord Rufford to many of his numerous appeals. Away in Norrington the poison had been purchased as much as three years ago, and yet Nickem had had the luck to find it out. When the Scrobbyites heard that Scrobby had gone all the way to Norrington to buy strychnine to kill rats, they were Scrobbyites no longer. 'I hope they'll hang 'un. I do hope they'll hang 'un,' said Mr. Runce quite out loud from his crowded seat just behind the attorney's bench.

The barrister of course struggled hard to earn his money. Though he could not save his client, he might annoy the other side. He insisted, therefore, on bringing the whole affair of the pheasants before the court, and examined the Senator at great length. He asked the Senator whether he had not found himself compelled to sympathize with the wrongs he had witnessed. The Senator declared that he had witnessed no wrongs. Why then had he interfered? Because he had thought that there might be wrong, and because he wished to see what power a poor man in this country would have against a rich one. He was induced still to think that Goarly had been ill-treated about the pheasants;—but he could not take upon himself to say that he had witnessed any wrong done. But he was quite sure that the system on which such things were managed in England was at variance with that even justice which prevailed in his own country! Yes;—by his own country he did mean Mikewa. He could tell that learned gentleman, in spite of his sneers, and in spite of his evident ignorance of geography, that nowhere on the earth's surface was justice more purely administered than in the great Western State of Mikewa. It was felt by everybody that the Senator had the best of it.

Mr. Scrobby was sent into durance*for twelve months with hard labour, and Goarly was conveyed away in the custody of the police, lest he should be torn to pieces by the rough lovers of hunting who were congregated outside. When the sentence had reached Mr. Runce's ears, and had been twice explained to him, first by one neighbour and then by another, his face assumed the very look which it had worn when he carried away his victuals from the Senator's side at Rufford Hall, and when he had turned his pony round on his own land on the previous evening. The man had killed a fox and might have killed a dozen hounds, and was to be locked up only for twelve months! He indignantly asked his neighbour what had come of Van Dieman's Land* and what was the use of Botany Bay.*

On their way back to Rufford Hall, Lord Rufford would have been triumphant, had not the Senator checked him. 'It's a bad state of things altogether,' he said. 'Of course, the promiscuous use of strychnine is objectionable.'

'Rather,' said his lordship.

'But is it odd that an utterly uneducated man, one whom his country has left to grow up in the ignorance of a brute, should have recourse to any measure, however objectionable, when the law will absolutely give him no redress against the trespass made by a couple of hundred horsemen?' Lord Rufford gave it up, feeling the Senator to be a man with whom he could not argue.

CHAPTER LXX

AT LAST

WHEN once Mrs. Morton had taken her departure for London, on the day after her grandson's death, nothing further was heard of her at Bragton. She locked up everything and took all the keys away, as though still hoping,—against hope,—that the will might turn out to be other than she expected. But when the lawyer came down to read the document, he brought the keys back with him, and no further tidings reached Dillsborough respecting the old woman. She still drew her income as she had done for half a century, but never even came to look at the stone which Reginald put up on the walls of Bragton church to perpetuate the memory of his cousin. What moans she made she made in silent obscurity, and devoted the remainder of her years to putting together money for members of her own family who took no notice of her.

After the funeral, Lady Ushant returned to the house at the request of her nephew, who declared his purpose of remaining at Hoppet Hall for the present. She expostulated with him and received from him an assurance that he would take up his residence as squire at Bragton as soon as he married a wife,—should he ever do so. In the meantime he could, he thought, perform his duties from Hoppet Hall as well as on the spot. As a residence for a bachelor he preferred, he said, Hoppet Hall to the park. Lady Ushant yielded and returned once again to her old home,—the house in which she had been born,—and gave up her lodgings at Cheltenham. The word that he said about his possible marriage set her mind at work, and induced her to put sundry questions to him. 'Of course you will marry?' she said.

'Men who have property to leave behind them usually do marry, and as I am not wiser than others, I probably may do so. But I will not admit that it is a matter of course. I may escape yet.'

'I do hope you will marry. I hope it may be before I die, so that I may see her.'

'And disapprove of her, ten to one.'

'Certainly I shall not if you tell me that you love her.'

'Then I will tell you so,—to prevent disagreeable results.'

'I am quite sure there must be somebody that you like, Reginald,' she said after a pause.

'Are you? I don't know that I have shown any very strong preference. I am not disposed to praise myself for many things, but I really do think that I have been as undemonstrative as most men of my age.'

'Still I did hope——'

'What did you hope?'

'I won't mention any name. I don't think it is right. I have observed that more harm than good comes of such talking, and I have determined always to avoid it. But——.' Then there was another pause. 'Remember how old I am, Reginald, and when it is to be done give me at any rate the pleasure of knowing it.' Of course he knew to whom she alluded, and of course he laughed at her feeble caution. But he would not say a word to encourage her to mention the name of Mary Masters. He thought that he was sure that were the girl free he would now ask her to be his wife. If he loved any one it was her. If he had ever known a woman with whom he thought it would be pleasant to share the joy and labours of life, it was Mary Masters. If he could imagine that any one constant companion would be a joy to him she would be that person. But he had been distinctly informed that she was in love with some one, and not for worlds would he ask for that which had been given to another. And not for worlds would he hazard the chance of a refusal. He

thought that he could understand the delight, that he
could thoroughly enjoy the rapture, of hearing her
whisper with downcast eyes, that she could love him. He
had imagination enough to build castles in the air in
which she reigned as princess, in which she would lie
with her head upon his bosom and tell him that he was
her chosen prince. But he would hardly know how to
bear himself should he ask in vain. He believed he could
love as well as Lawrence Twentyman, but he was sure
that he could not continue his quest as that young man
had done.

When Lady Ushant had been a day or two at the house
she asked him whether she might invite Mary there as her
guest,—as her perpetual guest.—'I have no objection in
life,' he said;—'but take care that you don't interfere with
her happiness.'

'Because of her father and sisters?' suggested the innocent old lady.

    ' "Has she a father, has she a mother;
      Or has she a dearer one still than all other?" '*

said Reginald laughing.

'Perhaps she has.'

'Then don't interfere with her happiness in that direction. How is she to have a lover come to see her out
here?'

'Why not? I don't see why she shouldn't have a lover
here as well as in Dillsborough. I don't object to lovers,
if they are of the proper sort;—and I am sure Mary
wouldn't have anything else.' Reginald told her she
might do as she pleased, and made no further inquiry as
to Mary's lovers.

A few days afterwards Mary went with her boxes to
Bragton,—Mrs. Masters repeating her objections but repeating them with but little energy. Just at this time a
stroke of good fortune befell the Masters family generally
which greatly reduced her power over her husband.
Reginald Morton had spent an hour in the attorney's
office, and had declared his purpose of restoring Mr.

Masters to his old family position in regard to the Bragton estate. When she heard it she felt at once that her dominion was gone. She had based everything on the growing inferiority of her husband's position, and now he was about to have all his glory back again! She had inveighed against gentlemen from the day of her marriage,—and here he was, again to be immersed up to his eyes in the affairs of a gentleman. And then she had been so wrong about Goarly, and Lord Rufford had been so much better a client! And ready money had been so much more plentiful of late, owing to poor John Morton's ready-handed honesty! She had very little to say about it when Mary packed her boxes and was taken in Mr. Runciman's fly to Bragton.

Since the old days, the old days of all, since the days to which Reginald had referred when he asked her to pass over the bridge with him, she had never yet walked about the Bragton grounds. She had often been to the house, visiting Lady Ushant; but she had simply gone thither and returned. And indeed, when the house had been empty, the walk from Dillsborough to the bridge and back had been sufficient exercise for herself and her sisters. But now she could go whither she listed, and bring her memory to all the old spots. With the tenacity as to household matters, which characterised the ladies of the country some years since, Lady Ushant employed all her mornings and those of her young friend in making inventories of everything that was found in the house; but her afternoons were her own, and she wandered about with a freedom she had never known before. At this time Reginald Morton was up in London, and had been away nearly a week. He had gone intending to be absent for some undefined time, so that Lady Ushant and Mrs. Hopkins were free from all interruption. It was as yet only the middle of March, and the lion had not altogether disappeared; but still Mary could get out. She did not care much for the wind; and she roamed about among the leafless shrubberies, thinking,—probably not of many things,—meaning always to think of the past, but unable to keep her mind from the future, the future which should so soon be present. How long would it be before the coming of that stately dame? Was he in quest of her now? Had he perhaps postponed his demand upon her till fortune had made him rich? Of course, she had no right to be sorry that he had inherited the property which had been his almost of right;—but yet, had it been otherwise, might she not have had some chance? But, oh, if he had said a word to her, only a word more than he had spoken already,—a word that might have sounded like encouragement to others beside herself, and then have been obliged to draw back because of the duty which he owed to the property,—how much worse would that have been? She did own to herself that the squire of Bragton should not look for his wife in the house of a Dillsborough attorney. As she thought of this, a tear ran down her cheek and trickled down unto the wooden rail of the little bridge.

'There's no one to give you an excuse now, and you must come and walk round with me,' said a voice, close to her ear.

'Oh, Mr. Morton, how you have startled me!'

'Is there anything the matter, Mary?' said he, looking up into her face.

'Only you have startled me so.'

'Has that brought tears into your eyes?'

'Well,—I suppose so,' she said, trying to smile. 'You were so very quiet, and I thought you were in London.'

'So I was this morning, and now I am here. But something else has made you unhappy.'

'No; nothing.'

'I wish we could be friends, Mary. I wish I could know your secret. You have a secret.'

'No,' she said, boldly.

'Is there nothing?'

'What should there be, Mr. Morton?'

'Tell me why you were crying.'

'I was not crying. Just a tear is not crying. Sometimes one does get melancholy. One can't cry when there is any one to look, and so one does it alone. I'd have been laughing if I knew that you were coming.'

'Come round by the kennels. You can get over the wall;—can't you?'

'Oh yes.'

'And we'll go down the old orchard, and get out by the corner of the park fence.' Then he walked and she followed him, hardly keeping close by his side, and thinking as she went how foolish she had been not to have avoided the perils and fresh troubles of such a walk. When he was helping her over the wall he held her hands for a moment, and she was aware of unusual pressure. It was the pressure of love,—or of that pretence of love which young men, and perhaps old men, sometimes permit themselves to affect. In an ordinary way, Mary would have thought as little of it as another girl. She might feel dislike to the man, but the affair would be too light for resentment. With this man it was different. He certainly was not justified in making the slightest expression of factitious affection. He at any rate should have felt himself bound to abstain from any touch of peculiar tenderness. She would not say a word. She would not even look at him with angry eyes. But she twitched both her hands away from him as she sprang to the ground. Then there was a passage across the orchard,—not more than a hundred yards, and after that a stile. At the stile she insisted on using her own hand for the custody of her dress. She would not even touch his outstretched arm. 'You are very independent,' he said.

'I have to be so.'

'I cannot make you out, Mary. I wonder whether there is still anything rankling in your bosom against me.'

'Oh dear no. What should rankle with me?'

'What indeed;—unless you resent my—regard.'

'I am not so rich in friends as to do that, Mr. Morton.'

'I don't suppose there can be many people who have the same sort of feeling for you that I have.'

'There are not many who have known me so long, certainly.'

'You have some friend, I know,' he said.

'More than one, I hope.'

'Some special friend. Who is he, Mary?'

'I don't know what you mean, Mr. Morton.' She then thought that he was still alluding to Lawrence Twentyman.

'Tell me, Mary.'

'What am I to tell you?'

'Your father says that there is some one.'

'Papa!'

'Yes;—your father.'

Then she remembered it all;—how she had been driven into a half confession to her father. She could not say there was nobody. She certainly could not say who that some one was. She could not be silent, for by silence she would be confessing a passion for some other man,—a passion which certainly had no existence. 'I don't know why papa should talk about me,' she said, 'and I certainly don't know why you should repeat what he said.'

'But there is some one?' She clenched her fist, and hit out at the air with her parasol, and knit her brows as she looked up at him with a glance of fire in her eye which he had never seen there before. 'Believe me, Mary,' he said, 'if ever a girl had a sincere friend, you have one in me. I would not tease you by impertinence in such a matter. I will be as faithful to you as the sun. Do you love any one?'

'Yes,' she said, turning round at him with ferocity, and shouting out her answer as she pressed on.

'Who is he, Mary?'

'What right have you to ask me? What right can any one have? Even your aunt would not press me as you are doing.'

'My aunt could not have the same interest. Who is he, Mary?'

'I will not tell you.'

He paused a few moments, and walked on a step or two before he spoke again. 'I would it were I,' he said.

'What!' she ejaculated.

'I would it were I,' he repeated.

One glance of her eye stole itself round into his face, and then her face was turned quickly to the ground. Her parasol, which had been raised, drooped listless from her hand. All unconsciously she hastened her steps, and became aware that the tears were streaming from her eyes. For a moment or two it seemed to her that all was still hopeless. If he had no more to say than that, certainly she had not a word. He had made her no tender of his love. He had not told her that in very truth she was his chosen one. After all, she was not sure that she understood the meaning of those words, 'I would it were I.' But the tears were coming so quick that she could see nothing of the things around her, and she did not dare even to put her hand up to her eyes. If he wanted her love,—if it was possible that he really wished for it,—why did he not ask for it? She felt his footsteps close to hers, and she was tempted to walk on quicker even than before. Then there came the fingers of a hand round her waist, stealing gradually on till she felt the pressure of his body on her shoulders. She put her hand up weakly, to push back the intruding fingers,—only to leave it tight in his grasp. Then,—then was the first moment in which she realised the truth. After all, he did love her. Surely he would not hold her there unless he meant her to know that he loved her. 'Mary,' he said. To speak was impossible, but she turned round and looked at him with imploring eyes. 'Mary,—say that you will be my wife.'

CHAPTER LXXI

'MY OWN, OWN HUSBAND'

YES;—it had come at last. As one may imagine to be the certainty of Paradise to the doubting, fearful, all but despairing soul when it has passed through the gates of death, and found in new worlds a reality of assured bliss, so was the assurance to her, conveyed by that simple request, 'Mary, say that you will be my wife.' It did not seem to her that any answer was necessary. Will it be required that the spirit shall assent to its entrance into Elysium? Was there room for doubt? He would never go back from his word now. He would not have spoken the word had he not been quite, quite certain. And he had loved her all that time,—when she was so hard to him!

It must have been so. He had loved her, this bright one, even when he thought that she was to be given to that clay-bound rustic lover! Perhaps that was the sweetest of it all, though in draining the sweet draught she had to accuse herself of hardness, blindness, and injustice. Could it be real? Was it true that she had her foot firmly placed in Paradise? He was there, close to her, with his arm still round her, and her fingers grasped within his. The word wife was still in her ears,—surely the sweetest word in all the language! What protestation of love could have been so eloquent as that question? 'Will you be my wife?' No true man, she thought, ever ought to ask the question in any other form. But her eyes were still full of tears, and as she went she knew not where she was going. She had forgotten all her surroundings, being only aware that he was with her, and that no other eyes were on them.

Then there was another stile on reaching which he withdrew his arm and stood facing her with his back leaning against it. 'Why do you weep?' he said;—'and, Mary, why do you not answer my question? If there be anybody else you must tell me now.'

'There is nobody else,' said she almost angrily. 'There never was. There never could be.'

'And yet there was somebody!' She pouted her lips at him, glancing up into his face for half a second, and then again hung her head down. 'Mary, do not grudge me my delight.'

'No;—no;—no!'

'But you do.'

'No. If there can be delight to you in so poor a thing, have it all.'

'Then you must kiss me, dear,' She gently came to him,—oh so gently,—and with her head still hanging, creeping towards his shoulder, thinking, perhaps, that the motion should have been his, but still obeying him, and then, leaning against him, seemed as though she would stoop with her lips to his hand. But this he did not endure. Seizing her quickly in his arms he drew her up, till her not unwilling face was close to his, and there he kept her till she was almost frightened by his violence. 'And now, Mary, what do you say to my question? It has to be answered.'

'You know.'

'But that will not do. I will have it in words. I will not be shorn of my delight.'

That it should be a delight to him, was the very essence of her heaven. 'Tell me what to say,' she answered. 'How may I say it best?'

'Reginald Morton,' he began.

'Reginald,' she repeated it after him, but went no farther in naming him.

'Because I love you better than any other being in the world—'

'I do.'

'Ah, but say it.'

'Because I love you, oh, so much better than all the world besides.'

'Therefore, my own, own husband——'

'Therefore, my own, own——' Then she paused.

'Say the word.'

'My own, own husband.'

'I will be your true wife.'

'I will be your own true loving wife.' Then he kissed her again.

'That,' he said, 'is our little marriage ceremony under God's sky, and no other can be more binding. As soon as you, in the plenitude of your maiden power, will fix a day for the other one, and when we can get that over, then we will begin our little journey together.'

'But, Reginald!'

'Well, dear!'

'You haven't said anything.'

'Haven't I? I thought I had said it all.'

'But you haven't said it for yourself!'

'You say what you want,—and I'll repeat it quite as well as you did.'

'I can't do that. Say it yourself.'

'I will be your true husband for the rest of the journey; —by which I mean it to be understood that I take you into partnership on equal terms, but that I am to be allowed to manage the business just as I please.'

'Yes;—that you shall,' she said, quite in earnest.

'Only as you are practical and I am vague, I don't doubt that everything will fall into your hands before five years are over, and that I shall have to be told whether I can afford to buy a new book, and when I am to ask all the gentry to dinner.'

'Now you are laughing at me because I shall know so little about anything.'

'Come, dear; let us get over the stile and go on for another field, or we shall never get round the park.' Then she jumped over after him, just touching his hand. 'I was not laughing at you at all. I don't in the least doubt that in a very little time you will know everything about everything.'

'I am so much afraid.'

'You needn't be. I know you well enough for that. But suppose I had taken such a one as that young woman who was here with my poor cousin. Oh, heavens!'

'Perhaps you ought to have done so.'

'I thank the Lord that hath delivered me.'

'You ought,—you ought to have chosen some lady of high standing,' said Mary, thinking with ineffable joy of the stately dame who was not to come to Bragton. 'Do you know what I was thinking only the other day about it?—that you had gone up to London to look for some proper sort of person.'

'And how did you mean to receive her?'

'I shouldn't have received her at all. I should have gone away. You can't do it now.'

'Can't I?'

'What were you thanking the Lord for so heartily?'

'For you.'

'Were you? This is the sweetest thing you have said yet. My own;—my darling;—my dearest! If only I can so live that you may be able to thank the Lord for me in years to come!'

I will not trouble the reader with all that was said at every stile. No doubt very much of what has been told was repeated again and again so that the walk round the park was abnormally long. At last, however, they reached the house, and as they entered the hall, Mary whispered to him, 'Who is to tell your aunt?' she said.

'Come along,' he replied, striding upstairs to his aunt's bedroom, where he knew she would be at this time. He opened the door without any notice and, having waited till Mary had joined him, led her forcibly into the middle of the room. 'Here she is,' he said;—'my wife elect.'

'Oh, Reginald!'

'We have managed it all, and there needn't be any more said about it except to settle the day. Mary has been looking about the house and learning her duty already. She'll be able to have every bedstead and every chair by heart, which is an advantage ladies seldom possess.' Then Mary rushed forward and was received into the old woman's arms.

When Reginald left them, which he did very soon after the announcement was made, Lady Ushant had a great deal to say. 'I have been thinking of it, my dear,—oh,—for years;—ever since he came to Hoppet Hall. But I am quite sure the best way is never to say anything. If I had interfered there is no knowing how it might have been.'

'Then, dear Lady Ushant, I am so glad you didn't,' said Mary,—being tolerably sure at the same time within her own bosom that her loving old friend could have done no harm in that direction.

'I wouldn't say a word though I was always thinking of it. But then he is so odd, and no one can know what he means sometimes. That's what made me think when Mr. Twentyman was so very pressing——'

'That couldn't—couldn't have been possible.'

'Poor young man!'

'But I always told him it was impossible.'

'I wonder whether you cared about Reginald all that time.' In answer to this Mary only hid her face in the old woman's lap. 'Dear me! I suppose you did all along. But I am sure it was better not to say anything, and now what will your papa and mamma say?'

'They'll hardly believe it at first.'

'I hope they'll be glad.'

'Glad! Why, what do you suppose they would want me to do? Dear papa! And dear mamma too, because she has really been good to me. I wonder when it must be?' Then that question was discussed at great length, and Lady Ushant had a great deal of very good advice to bestow. She didn't like long engagements, and it was very essential for Reginald's welfare that he should settle himself at Bragton as soon as possible. Mary's pleas for a long day were not very urgent.

That evening at Bragton was rather long and rather dull. It was almost the first that she had ever passed in company with Reginald, and there now seemed to be a necessity of doing something peculiar, whereas there was nothing peculiar to be done. It was his custom to betake himself to his books after dinner; but he could hardly do so with ease in company with the girl who had just promised him to be his wife. Lady Ushant too wished to show her extreme joy, and made flattering but vain attempts to be ecstatic. Mary, to tell the truth, was longing for solitude, feeling that she could not yet realize her happiness.

Nor even when she was in bed could she reduce her mind to order. It would have been all but impossible even had he remained the comparatively humble lord of Hoppet Hall;—but that the squire of Bragton should be her promised husband was a marvel so great that from every short slumber she waked with fear of treacherous dreams. A minute's sleep might rob her of her joy and declare to her in the moment of waking that it was all an hallucination. It was not that he was dearer to her, or that her condition was the happier, because of his position and wealth;—but that the chance of his inheritance had lifted him so infinitely above her! She thought of the little room at home which she generally shared with one of her sisters, of her all too scanty wardrobe, of her daily tasks about the house, of her stepmother's late severity, and of her father's cares. Surely he would not hinder her from being good to them; surely he would let the young girls come to her from time to time! What an added happiness it would be if he would allow her to pass on to them some sparks of the prosperity which he was bestowing on her! And then her thoughts travelled on to poor Larry. Would he not be more contented now;—now, when he would be certain that no further frantic efforts could avail him anything. Poor Larry! Would Reginald permit her to regard him as a friend? And would he submit to friendly treatment? She could look forward and see him happy with his wife, the best loved of their neighbours;—for who was there in the world better than Larry? But she did not know how two men who had both been her lovers, would allow themselves to be brought together. But, oh, what peril had been there! It was but the other day she had striven so hard to give the lie to her love and to become Larry's wife. She shuddered beneath the bedclothes as she thought of the danger she had run. One word would have changed all her Paradise into a perpetual wail of tears and waste of desolation. When she woke in the morning from her long sleep an effort was wanting to tell her that it was all true. Oh, if it had slipped from her then;—if she had waked after such a dream to find herself loving in despair with a sore bosom and angry heart!

She met him downstairs, early, in the study, having her first request to make to him. Might she go in at once after breakfast and tell them all? 'I suppose I ought to go to your father,' he said. 'Let me go first,' she pleaded hanging on his arm. 'I would not think that I was not mindful of them from the very beginning.' So she was driven into Dillsborough in the pony carriage which had been provided for old Mrs. Morton's use, and told her own story. 'Papa,' she said, going to the office door. 'Come into the house;—come at once.' And then, within her father's arms, while her step-mother listened, she told them of her triumph. 'Mr. Reginald Morton wants me to be his wife, and he is coming here to ask you.'

'The Lord in heaven be good to us,' said Mrs. Masters holding up both her hands, 'Is it true, child?'

'The squire!' ejaculated the father.

'It is true, papa,—and,—and,——'

'And what, my love?'

'When he comes to you, you must say I will be.'

There was not much danger on that score. 'Was it he that you told me of?' said the attorney. To this she only nodded her assent. 'It was Reginald Morton all the time? Well!'

'Why shouldn't it be he?'

'Oh no, my dear! You are a most fortunate girl,— most fortunate! But somehow I never thought of it, that a child of mine should come to live at Bragton and have it, one may say, partly as her own! It is odd after all that has come and gone. God bless you, my dear, and make you happy! You are a very fortunate child.'

Mrs. Masters was quite overpowered. She had thrown herself on to the old family sofa and was fanning herself with her handkerchief. She had been wrong throughout and was now completely humiliated by the family success; and yet she was delighted, though she did not dare to be triumphant. She had so often asked both father and daughter what good gentlemen would do to either of them; and now the girl was engaged to marry the richest gentleman in the neighbourhood! In any expression of joy she would be driven to confess how wrong she had always been. How often had she asked what would come of Ushanting! This it was that had come of Ushanting. The girl had been made fit to be the companion of such a one as Reginald Morton, and had now fallen into the position which was suited to her. 'Of course we shall see nothing of you now,' she said in a whimpering voice. It was not a gracious speech, but it was almost justified by disappointments.

'Mamma, you know that I shall never separate myself from you and the girls.'

'Poor Larry!' said the woman sobbing. 'Of course it is all for the best; but I don't know what he'll do now.'

'You must tell him, papa,' said Mary; 'and give him my love and bid him be a man.'

Chapter LXXII

'BID HIM BE A MAN'

THE little phaeton remained in Dillsborough to take Mary back to Bragton. As soon as she was gone the attorney went over to the Bush with the purpose of borrowing Runciman's pony so that he might ride over to Chowton Farm and at once execute his daughter's last request. In the yard of the inn he saw Runciman himself and was quite unable to keep his good news to himself. 'My girl has just been with me,' he said, 'and what do you think she tells me?'

'That she is going to take poor Larry after all. She might do worse, Mr. Masters.'

'Poor Larry! I am sorry for him. I have always liked Larry Twentyman. But that is all over now.'

'She's not going to have that tweedledum young parson, surely?'

'Reginald Morton has made her a set offer.'

'The squire!' Mr. Masters nodded his head three times. 'You don't say so. Well, Mr. Masters, I don't begrudge it you. He might do worse. She has taken her pigs well to market at last.'

'He's to come to me at four this afternoon.'

'Well done, Miss Mary! I suppose it's been going on ever so long?'

'We fathers and mothers,' said the attorney, 'never really know what the young ones are after. Don't mention it just at present, Runciman. You are such an old friend that I couldn't help telling you.'

'Poor Larry!'

'I can have the pony, Runciman?'

'Certainly you can, Mr. Masters. Tell him to come in and talk it all over with me. If we don't look to it he'll be taking to drink regular.' At that last meeting of the club, when the late squire's will was discussed, at which, as the reader may perhaps remember, a little supper was also discussed in honour of the occasion, poor Larry had not only been present but had drank so pottle deep, that the

landlord had been obliged to put him to bed at the inn,
and he had not been at all as he ought to have been after
Lord Rufford's dinner. Such delinquencies were quite
outside the young man's accustomed way of life. It had
been one of his recognised virtues that, living as he did
a good deal among sporting men, and with a full command of means, he had never drank. But now he had
twice sinned before the eyes of all Dillsborough, and
Runciman thought that he knew how it would be with
a young man in his own house who got drunk in public to
drown his sorrow. 'I wouldn't see Larry go astray and
spoil himself with liquor,' said the good-natured publican,
'for more than I should like to name.' Mr. Masters
promised to take the hint and rode off on his mission.

The entrance to Chowton Farm and Bragton gate were
nearly opposite, the latter being perhaps a furlong nearer
to Dillsborough. The attorney when he got to the gate
stopped a moment and looked up the avenue with pardon-
able pride. The great calamity of his life, the stunning
blow which had almost unmanned him when he was young
and from which he had never quite been able to rouse
himself, had been the loss of the management of the Bragton property. His grandfather and his father had been
powerful at Bragton, and he had been brought up in the
hope of walking in their paths. Then strangers had come
in, and he had been dispossessed. But how was it with
him now? It had almost made a young man of him again
when Reginald Morton, stepping into his office, asked
him as a favour to resume his old task. But what was that
in comparison with this later triumph? His own child
was to be made queen of the place! His grandson, should
she be fortunate enough to be the mother of a son, would
be the squire himself! His visits to the place for the last
twenty years had been very rare indeed. He had been
sent for lately by old Mrs. Morton,—for a purpose which
if carried out would have robbed him of all his good fortune,—but he could not remember when, before that, he
had even passed through the gateway. Now it would
all become familiar to him again. That pony of Runciman's was pleasant in his paces, and he began to calculate

whether the innkeeper would part with the animal. He stood thus gazing at the place for some minutes till he saw Reginald Morton in the distance turning a corner of the road with Mary at his side. He had taken her from the phaeton and had then insisted on her coming out with him before she took off her hat. Mr. Masters as soon as he saw them trotted off to Chowton Farm.

Finding Larry lounging at the little garden gate Mr. Masters got off the pony and taking the young man's arm, walked off with him towards Dillsborough Wood. He told all his news at once, almost annihilating poor Larry by the suddenness of the blow. 'Larry, Mr. Reginald Morton has asked my girl to marry him, and she has accepted him.'

'The new squire!' said Larry, stopping himself on the path, and looking as though a gentle wind would suffice to blow him over.

'I suppose it has been that way all along, Larry, though we have not known it.'

'It was Mr. Morton then that she told me of?'

'She did tell you?'

'Of course there was no chance for me if I wanted her. But why didn't they speak out, so that I could have gone away? Oh, Mr. Masters!'

'It was only yesterday she knew it herself.'

'She must have guessed it.'

'No;—she knew nothing till he declared himself. And to-day, this very morning, she has bade me come to you and let you know it. And she sent you her love.'

'Her love!' said Larry, chucking the stick which he held in his hands down to the ground and then stooping to pick it up again.

'Yes;—her love. Those were her words, and I am to tell you from her—to be a man.'

'Did she say that?'

'Yes;—I was to come out to you at once, and bring you that as a message from her.'

'Be a man! I could have been a man right enough if she would have made me one;—as good a man as Reginald Morton, though he is squire of Bragton. But of course

I couldn't have given her a house like that, nor a carriage, nor made her one of the county people. If it was to go in that way, what could I hope for?'

'Don't be unjust to her, Larry.'

'Unjust to her! If giving her every blessed thing I had in the world at a moment's notice was unjust, I was ready to be unjust any day of the week or any hour of the day.'

'What I mean is that her heart was fixed that way before Reginald Morton was Squire of Bragton. What shall I say in answer to her message? You will wish her happiness;—will you not?'

'Wish her happiness! Oh, heavens!' He could not explain what was in his mind. Wish her happiness! yes;— the happiness of the angels. But not him,—nor yet with him! And as there could be no arranging of this, he must leave his wishes unsettled. And yet there was a certain relief to him in the tidings he had heard. There was now no more doubt. He need not now remain at Chowton thinking it possible that the girl might even yet change her mind.

'And you will bear in mind that she wishes you to be a man.'

'Why did she not make me one? But that is all, all over. You tell her from me that I am not the man to whimper because I am hurt. What ought a man to do that I can't do?'

'Let her know that you are going about your old pursuits. And, Larry, would you wish her to know how it was with you at the club last Saturday?'

'Did she hear of that?'

'I am sure she has not heard of it. But if that kind of thing becomes a habit, of course she will hear of it. All Dillsborough would hear of it, if that became common. At any rate it is not manly to drown it in drink.'

'Who says I do that? Nothing will drown it.'

'I wouldn't speak if I had not known you so long, and loved you so well. What she means is that you should work.'

'I do work.'

'And hunt. Go out to-morrow and show yourself to everybody.'

'If I could break my neck I would.'

'Don't let every farmer's son in the county say that Lawrence Twentyman was so mastered by a girl that he couldn't ride on horseback when she said him nay.'

'Everybody knows it, Mr. Masters.'

'Go among them as if nobody knew it. I'll warrant that nobody will speak of it.'

'I don't think any one of 'em would dare to do that,' said Larry brandishing his stick.

'Where is it that the hounds are to-morrow, Larry?'

'Here; at the old kennels.'

'Go out and let her see that you have taken her advice. She is there, at the house, and she will recognize you in the park. Remember that she sends her love to you, and bids you be a man. And Larry, come in and see us sometimes. The time will come, I don't doubt, when you and the squire will be fast friends.'

'Never!'

'You do not know what time can do. I'll just go back now because he is to come to me this afternoon. Try and bear up, and remember that it is she who bids you be a man.' The attorney got upon his pony and rode back to Dillsborough.

Larry, who had come back to the yard to see his friend off, returned by the road into the fields, and went wandering about for a while in Dillsborough Wood. 'Bid him be a man!' Wasn't he a man? Was it disgraceful to him as a man to be broken-hearted, because a woman would not love him? If he were provoked he would fight,—perhaps better than ever, because he would be reckless. Would he not be willing to fight Reginald Morton with any weapon which could be thought of for the possession of Mary Masters! If she were in danger would he not go down into the deep, or through fire to save her? Were not his old instincts of honesty and truth as strong in him as ever? Did manliness require that his heart should be invulnerable? If so, he doubted whether he could ever be a man.

But what if she meant that manliness required him to hide the wound? Then there did come upon him a feeling of shame as he remembered how often he had spoken of

his love to those who were little better than strangers to
him, and a thought that perhaps such loquacity was
opposed to the manliness which she recommended. And
his conscience smote him as it brought to his recollection
the condition of his mind as he woke in Runciman's bed
at the Bush on last Sunday morning. That, at any rate,
had not been manly. How would it be with him if he
made up his mind never to speak again to her, and
certainly not to him, and to take care that that should be
the only sign left of his suffering? He would hunt and be
keener than ever;—he would work upon the land with
increased diligence; he would give himself not a moment
to think of anything. She should see and hear what he
could do;—but he would never speak to her again. The
hounds would be at the old kennels to-morrow. He would
be there. The place no doubt was Morton's property,
but on hunting mornings all the lands of the county,—
and of the next counties if they can be reached,—are the
property of the hunt. Yes; he would be there; and she
should see him in his scarlet coat, and smartest cravat,
with his boots and breeches neat as those of Lord Rufford;
—and she should know that he was doing as she bade
him. But he would never speak to her again!

As he was returning round the wood, whom should he
see skulking round the corner of it but Goarly?

'What business have you in here?' he said, feeling half
inclined to take the man by the neck and drag him out of
the copse.

'I saw you, Mr. Twentyman, and I wanted to have a
word with you.'

'You are the biggest rascal in all Rufford,' said Larry.
'I wonder the lads have left you with a whole bone in
your skin.'

'What have I done worse than any other poor man,
Mr. Twentyman? When I took them herrings I didn't
know there was p'ison; and if I hadn't took 'em, another
would. I am going to cut it out of this, Mr. Twentyman.'

'May the——go along with you!' said Larry, wishing
his neighbour a very pleasant companion.

'And of course I must sell the place. Think what it

would be to you! I shouldn't like it to go into his lordship's hands. It's all through Bean, I know, but his
lordship has had a down on me ever since he came to the
property. It's as true as true about my old woman's
geese. There's forty acres of it. What would you say to
£40 an acre?'

The idea of having the two extra fields made Larry's
mouth water, in spite of his misfortunes. The desire for
land among such as Larry Twentyman is almost a disease
in England. With these two fields he would be able to
walk almost round Dillsborough Wood without quitting
his own property. He had been talking of selling Chowton
within the last week or two. He had been thinking of
selling it at the moment when Mr. Masters rode up to
him. And yet now he was almost tempted to a new
purchase by this man. But the man was too utterly a
blackguard,—was too odious to him.

'If it comes into the market, I may bid for it as well as
another,' he said, 'but I wouldn't let myself down to have
any dealings with you.'

'Then, Mr. Larry, you shall never have a sod of it,'
said Goarly, dropping himself over the fence on to his
own field.

A few minutes afterwards Larry met Bean, and told
him that Goarly had been in the wood. 'If I catch him,
Mr. Twentyman, I'll give him sore bones,' said Bean.
'I wonder how he ever got back to his own place alive
that day.' Then Bean asked Larry whether he meant to
be at the meet to-morrow, and Larry said that he thought
he should. 'Tony's almost afraid to bring them in even
yet,' said Bean; 'but if there's a herring left in this wood,
I'll eat it myself—strychnine and all.'

After that, Larry went and looked at his horses, and
absolutely gave his mare 'Bicycle' a gallop round the big
grass field himself. Then those who were about the place
knew that something had happened, and that he was in
a way to be cured. 'You'll hunt to-morrow, won't you,
Larry?' said his mother, affectionately.

'Who told you?'

'Nobody told me;—but you will, Larry; won't you?'

'May be I will.' Then, as he was leaving the room, when he was in the door-way, so that she should not see his face, he told her the news. 'She 's going to marry the squire, yonder.'

'Mary Masters!'

'I always hated him from the first moment I saw him. What do you expect from a fellow who never gets a-top of a horse?' Then he turned away, and was not seen again till long after tea-time.

CHAPTER LXXIII

'IS IT TANTI?'

REGINALD MORTON entertained serious thoughts of cleansing himself from the reproach which Larry cast upon him when describing his character to his mother. 'I think I shall take to hunting,' he said to Mary.

'But you'll tumble off, dear.'

'No doubt I shall, and I must try to begin in soft places. I don't see why I shouldn't do it gradually in a small way. I shouldn't ever become a Nimrod, like Lord Rufford or your particular friend Mr. Twentyman.'

'He is my particular friend.'

'So I perceive. I couldn't shine as he shines, but I might gradually learn to ride after him at a respectful distance. A man at Rome ought to do as the Romans do.'

'Why wasn't Hoppet Hall Rome as much as Bragton?'

'Well;—it wasn't. While fortune enabled me to be happy at Hoppet Hall——'

'That is unkind, Reg.'

'While fortune oppressed me with celibate misery at Hoppet Hall, nobody hated me for not hunting;—and as I could not very well afford it, I was not considered to be entering a protest against the amusement. As it is now, I find that unless I consent to risk my neck at any rate five or six times every winter, I shall be regarded in that light.'

'I wouldn't be frightened into doing anything I didn't like,' said Mary.

'How do you know that I shan't like it? The truth is, I have had a letter this morning from a benevolent philosopher which has almost settled the question for me. He wants me to join a society for the suppression of British sports as being barbarous and anti-pathetic to the intellectual pursuits of an educated man. I would immediately shoot, fish, hunt, and go out ratting,* if I could hope for the least success. I know I should never shoot anything but the dog and the gamekeepers, and that I should catch every weed in the river; but I think that in the process of seasons I might jump over a hedge.'

'Kate will show you the way to do that.'

'With Kate and Mr. Twentyman to help me, and a judicious system of liberal tips to Tony Tuppett, I could make my way about on a quiet old nag, and live respected by my neighbours. The fact is, I hate with my whole heart the trash of the philanimalists.'*

'What is a—a—I didn't quite catch the thing you hate?'

'The thing is a small knot of self-anxious people who think that they possess among them all the bowels of the world.'

'Possess all the what, Reginald?'

'I said bowels,—using an ordinary but very ill-expressed metaphor. The ladies and gentlemen to whom I allude, not looking very clearly into the system of pains and pleasures in accordance with which we have to live, put their splay feet down now upon this ordinary operation and now upon that, and call upon the world to curse the cruelty of those who will not agree with them. A lady whose tippet*is made from the skins of twenty animals who have been wired in the snow and then left to die of starvation——'

'Oh, Reginald!'

'That is the way of it. I am not now saying whether it is right or wrong. The lady with the tippet will justify the wires and the starvation because, as she will say, she uses the fur. An honest blanket would keep her just as warm. But the fox, who suffers perhaps ten minutes of agony, should he not succeed as he usually does in getting away,—is hunted only for amusement! It is true

that the one fox gives amusement for hours to perhaps
some hundred;—but it is only for amusement. What riles
me most is that these would-be philosophers do not or
will not see that recreation is as necessary to the world as
clothes or food, and the providing of the one is as legitimate a business as the purveying of the other.'

'People must eat and wear clothes.'

'And practically they must be amused. They ignore the
great doctrine of "tanti".'*

'I never heard of it.'

'You shall, dear, some day. It is the doctrine by which
you should regulate everything you do, and every word
you utter. Now do you and Kate put on your hats and
we'll walk to the bridge.'

This preaching of a sermon took place after breakfast at
Bragton on the morning of Saturday, and the last order
had reference to a scheme they had on foot to see the
meet at the old kennels. On the previous afternoon
Reginald Morton had come into Dillsborough and had
very quietly settled everything with the attorney. Having
made up his mind to do the thing he was very quick in
the doing of it. He hated the idea of secrecy in such an
affair, and when Mrs. Masters asked him whether he had
any objection to have the marriage talked about, expressed his willingness that she should employ the town
crier to make it public if she thought it expedient. 'Oh,
Mr. Morton, how very funny you are!' said the lady.
'Quite in earnest, Mrs. Morton,' he replied. Then he
kissed the two girls who were to be his sisters, and
finished the visit by carrying off the younger to spend a
day or two with her sister at Bragton. 'I know,' he said,
whispering to Mary as he left the front door, 'that I ought
not to go out hunting so soon after my poor cousin's
death; but as he was a cousin once removed, I believe I
may walk as far as the bridge without giving offence.'

When they were there they saw all the arrivals just as
they were seen on the same spot a few months earlier
by a very different party. Mary and Kate stood on the
bridge together, while he remained a little behind leaning
on the stile. She, poor girl, had felt some shame in

showing herself, knowing that some who were present would have heard of her engagement, and that others would be told of it as soon as she was seen. 'Are you ashamed of what you are going to do?' he asked.

'Ashamed! I don't suppose that there is a girl in England so proud as I am at this minute.'

'I don't know that there is anything to be proud of, but if you are not ashamed, why shouldn't you show yourself? Marriage is an honourable state!' She could only pinch his arm, and do as he bade her.

Glomax in his tandem,* and Lord Rufford in his drag,* were rather late. First there came one or two hunting men out of the town, Runciman, Dr. Nupper, and the hunting saddler. Then there arrived Henry Stubbings with a string of horses, mounted by little boys, ready for his customers, and full of wailing to his friend Runciman. Here was nearly the end of March and the money he had seen since Christmas was little more, as he declared, than what he could put into his eye and see none the worse. 'Charge 'em ten per cent. interest,' said Runciman. 'Then they thinks they can carry on for another year,' said Stubbings despondingly. While this was going on, Larry walked his favourite mare 'Bicycle' on to the ground, dressed with the utmost care, but looking very moody, almost fierce, as though he did not wish anybody to speak to him. Tony Tuppett, who had known him since a boy, nodded at him affectionately and said how glad he was to see him; but even this was displeasing to Larry. He did not see the girls on the bridge, but took up his place near them. He was thinking so much of his own unhappiness and of what he believed others would say of him, that he saw almost nothing. There he sat on his mare, carrying out the purpose to which he had been led by Mary's message, but wishing with all his heart that he was back again, hidden within his own house at the other side of the wood.

Mary, as soon as she saw him, blushed up to her eyes, then turning round looked with wistful eyes into the face of the man she was engaged to marry, and with rapid step walked across the bridge up to the side of Larry's horse and spoke to him with her sweet low voice. 'Larry,' she said. He turned round to her very quickly, showing how much he was startled. Then she put up her hand to him, and of course he took it. 'Larry, I am so glad to see you. Did papa give you a message?'

'Yes, Miss Masters. He told me, I know it all.'

'Say a kind word to me, Larry.'

'I—I—I—You know very well what 's in my mind. Though it were to kill me, I should wish you well.'

'I hope you'll have a good hunt, Larry.' Then she retired back to the bridge and again looked to her lover to know whether he would approve. There were so few there, and Larry had been so far apart from the others, that she was sure no one had heard the few words which had passed between them; nor could any one have observed what she had done, unless it were old Nupper, or Mr. Runciman, or Tony Tuppett. But yet she thought that it perhaps was bold, and that he would be angry. But he came up to her, and placing himself between her and Kate, whispered into her ear, 'Bravely done, my girl. After a little I will try to be as brave, but I could never do it as well.' Larry in the meantime had moved his mare away, and before the Master had arrived, was walking slowly up his own road to Chowton Farm.

The captain was soon there, and Lord Rufford with his friends, and Harry Stubbings' string and Tony were set in motion. But, before they stirred, there was a consultation,—to which Bean, the gamekeeper, was called,—as to the safety of Dillsborough Wood. Dillsborough Wood had not been drawn yet since Scrobby's poison had taken effect on the old fox, and there were some few who affected to think that there still might be danger. Among these was the Master himself, who asked Fred Botsey with a sneer whether he thought that such hounds as those were to be picked up at every corner. But Bean again offered to eat any herring that might be there, poison included, and Lord Rufford laughed at the danger. 'It 's no use my having foxes, Glomax, if you won't draw the cover.' This the lord said with a touch of anger, and the lord's anger, if really roused, might be injurious. It was therefore decided that the hounds should again be put through the Bragton shrubberies,—just for compliment to the new squire,—and that then they should go off to Dillsborough Wood as rapidly as might be.

Larry walked his beast all the way up home very slowly, and, getting off her, put her into the stable and went into the house.

'Is anything wrong?' asked the mother.

'Everything is wrong.' Then he stood with his back to the kitchen fire for nearly half an hour without speaking a word. He was trying to force himself to follow out her idea of manliness, and telling himself that it was impossible. The first tone of her voice, the first glance at her face, had driven him home. Why had she called him Larry again and again, so tenderly, in that short moment, and looked at him with those loving eyes? Then he declared to himself, without uttering a word, that she did not understand anything about it; she did not comprehend the fashion of his love when she thought, as she did think, that a soft word would be compensation. He looked round to see if his mother or the servant were there, and when he found that the coast was clear, he dashed his hand to his eyes and knocked away the tears. He threw up both his arms and groaned, and then he remembered her message—'Bid him be a man.'

At that moment he heard the sound of horses, and going near the window, so as to be hidden from curious eyes as they passed, he saw the first whip trot on, with the hounds after him, and Tony Tuppett among them. Then there was a long string of horsemen, all moving up to the wood, and a carriage or two, and after them the stragglers of the field. He let them all go by, and then he repeated the words again, 'Bid him be a man.' He took up his hat, jammed it on to his head, and went out into the yard. As he crossed to the stables, Runciman came up alone. 'Why, Larry, you'll be late,' he said.

'Go on, Mr. Runciman; I'll follow.'

'I'll wait till you are mounted. You'll be better for somebody with you. You've got the mare, have you? You'll show some of them your heels if they get away from here. Is she as fast as she was last year, do you think?'

'Upon my word, I don't know,' said Larry, as he dragged himself into the saddle.

'Shake yourself, old fellow, and don't carry on like that. What is she, after all, but a girl?' The poor fellow looked at his intending comforter, but could not speak a word. 'A man shouldn't let hisself be put upon by circumstances so as to be only half his self. Hang it, man, cheer up, and don't let 'em see you going about like that! It ain't what a fellow of your kidney ought to be. If they haven't found I'm a nigger,—and, by the holy, he's away! Come along, Larry, and forget the petticoats for half an hour.' So saying, Runciman broke into a gallop, and Larry's mare doing the same, he soon passed the inn-keeper, and was up at the covert side just as Tony Tuppett, with half a score of hounds round him, was forcing his way through the bushes out of the coverts into the open field. 'There ain't no poison this time, Mr. Twentyman,' said the huntsman, as, settling his eye on a gap in the further fence, he made his way across the field.

The fox headed away for a couple of miles towards Impington, as was the custom with the Dillsborough foxes, and then turning to the left, was soon over the county borders into Ufford. The pace from the first starting was very good. Larry, under such provocation as that, of course, would ride, and he did ride. Up as far as the county brook many were well up. The land was no longer deep; and, as the field had not been scattered at the starting, all the men who usually rode were fairly well placed as they came to the brook; but it was acknowledged afterwards that Larry was over it the first. Glomax got into it,—as he always does into brooks,—and young Runce hurt his horse's shoulder at the opposite bank. Lord Rufford's horse balked it, to the lord's disgust; but took it afterwards, not losing very much ground. Tony went in and out, the crafty old dog knowing the one bit of hard ground. Then they crossed Purbeck Field, as it is still called, which, twenty years since, was a wide waste of land, but is now divided by new fences, very grievous to half-blown horses. Sir John Purefoy got a nasty fall over some stiff timber, and here many a half-hearted rider turned to the right into the lane. Hampton and his lordship, and Battersby, with Fred Botsey and Larry, took it all as it came, but through it all not one of them could give Larry a lead. Then there was manœuvring into a wood and out of it again, and that saddest of all sights to the riding man, a cloud of horsemen on the road as well placed as though they had ridden the line through-out. In getting out of the road Hampton's horse slipped up with him, and, though he saw it all, he was never able again to compete for a place. The fox went through the Hampton Wick coverts without hanging a moment, just throwing the hounds for two minutes off their scent at the gravel pits. The check was very useful to Tony, who had got his second horse, and came up sputtering, begging the field, for G——'s sake, to be,—in short, to be anywhere but where they were. Then they were off again down the hill to the left, through Mappy Springs, and along the top of Ilveston Copse, every yard of which is grass, till the number began to be select. At last, in a turnip field, three yards from the fence, they turned him over, and Tony, as he jumped off his horse among the hounds, acknowledged to himself that Larry might have had his hand first upon the animal had he cared to do so.

'Twentyman, I'll give you two hundred for your mare,' said Lord Rufford.

'Ah, my lord, there are two things that would about kill me.'

'What are they, Larry?' asked Harry Stubbings.

'To offend his lordship, or to part with the mare.'

'You shall do neither,' said Lord Rufford; 'but, upon my word, I think she's the fastest thing in this county.' All of which did not cure poor Larry, but it helped to enable him to be a man.

The fox had been killed close to Norrington, and the run was remembered with intense gratification for many a long day after. 'It's that kind of thing that makes hunt-ing beat everything else,' said Lord Rufford, as he went

home. That day's sport certainly had been 'tanti,'*and
Glomax and the two counties boasted of it for the next
three years.

Chapter LXXIV

BENEDICT

LADY PENWETHER declared to her husband that she
had never seen her brother so much cowed as he had
been by Miss Trefoil's visit to Rufford. It was not only
that he was unable to assert his usual powers immediately
after the attack made upon him, but that on the following day, at Scrobby's trial, on the Saturday when he
started to the meet, and on the Sunday following when he
allowed himself to be easily persuaded to go to church,
he was silent, sheepish, and evidently afraid of himself.
'It is a great pity that we shouldn't take the ball at the
hop,'*she said to Sir George.
'What ball;—and what hop?'
'Get him to settle himself. There ought to be an end to
this kind of thing now. He has got out of this mess,
but every time it becomes worse and worse, and he'll be
taken in horribly by some harpy*if we don't get him to
marry decently. I fancy he was very nearly going in this
last affair.' Sir George, in this matter, did not quite agree
with his wife. It was in his opinion right to avoid Miss
Trefoil, but he did not see why his brother-in-law should
be precipitated into matrimony with Miss Penge.
According to his ideas in such matters a man should be
left alone. Therefore, as was customary with him when
he opposed his wife, he held his tongue. 'You have been
called in three or four times when he has been just on the
edge of the cliff.'
'I don't know that that is any reason why he should be
pushed over.'
'There is not a word to be said against Caroline. She
has a fine fortune of her own, and some of the best blood
in the kingdom.'
'But if your brother does not care for her——'
'That's nonsense, George. As for liking, it's all the

same to him. Rufford is good-natured, and easily pleased, and can like any woman. Caroline is very good-looking,—a great deal handsomer than that horrid creature ever was,—and with manners fit for any position. I've no reason to wish to force a wife on him; but of course he'll marry, and unless he's guided, he'll certainly marry badly.'

'Is Miss Penge in love with him?' asked Sir George, in a tone of voice that was intended to be provoking. His wife looked at him, asking him plainly by her countenance whether he was such a fool as that! Was it likely that any untitled young lady of eight-and-twenty should be wanting in the capacity of being in love with a young lord, handsome and possessed of forty thousand a year without encumbrances? Sir George, though he did not approve, was not eager enough in his disapproval to lay any serious embargo on his wife's proceedings.

The first steps taken were in the direction of the hero's personal comfort. He was flattered and petted, as his sister knew how to flatter and pet him;—and Miss Penge, in a quiet way, assisted Lady Penwether in the operation. For a day or two he had not much to say for himself;—but every word he did say was an oracle. His horses were spoken of as demigods, and his projected fishing operations for June and July became matters of most intense interest. Evil things were said of Arabella Trefoil, but in all the evil things said no hint was given that Lord Rufford had behaved badly or had been in danger. Lady Penwether, not quite knowing the state of his mind, thought that there might still be some lurking affection for the young lady. 'Did you ever see anybody look so vulgar and hideous as she did when she marched across the park?' asked Lady Penwether.

'Thank goodness I did not see her,' said Miss Penge.

'I never saw her look so handsome as when she came up to me,' said Lord Rufford.

'But such a thing to do!'

'Awful!' said Miss Penge.

'She's the pluckiest girl I ever came across in my life,' said Lord Rufford. He knew very well what they were at,

and was already almost inclined to think that they might
as well be allowed to have their way. Miss Penge was
ladylike, quiet, and good, and was like a cool salad in
a man's mouth after spiced meat. And the money would
enable him to buy the Purefoy property, which would
probably be soon in the market. But he felt that he
might as well give them a little trouble before he allowed
himself to be hooked. It certainly was not by any arrangement of his own that he found himself walking alone with
Miss Penge that Sunday afternoon in the park; nor did it
seem to be by hers. He thought of that other Sunday at
Mistletoe, when he had been compelled to wander with
Arabella, when he met the duchess, and when, as he often
told himself, a little more good-nature or a little more
courage on her grace's part would have completed the
work entirely. Certainly, had the duke come to him that
night, after the journey from Stamford, he would have
capitulated. As he walked along, and allowed himself to
be talked to by Miss Penge, he did tell himself that she
would be the better angel of the two. She could not hunt
with him, as Arabella would have done; but then a man
does not want his wife to gallop across the country after
him. She might perhaps object to cigars and soda water
after eleven o'clock, but then what assurance had he that
Arabella would not have objected still more loudly. She
had sworn that she would never be opposed to his little
pleasures; but he knew what such oaths were worth.
Marriage altogether was a bore; but having a name and
a large fortune, it was incumbent on him to transmit them
to an immediate descendant. And perhaps it was a worse
bore to grow old without having specially bound any
other human being to his interests. 'How well I recollect
that spot!' said Miss Penge. 'It was there that Major
Caneback took the fence.'

'That was not where he fell.'

'Oh no; I did not see that. It would have haunted me
for ever had I done so. But it was there that I thought he
must kill himself. That was a terrible time, Lord Rufford.'

'Terrible to poor Caneback, certainly.'

'Yes, and to all of us. Do you remember that fearful

ball? We were all so unhappy,—because you suffered so much.'

'It was bad.'

'And that woman who persecuted you! We all knew that you felt it.'

'I felt that poor man's death.'

'Yes; and you felt the other nuisance too.'

'I remember that you told me that you would cling on to my legs.'

'Eleanor said so; and when it was explained to me, what clinging on to your legs meant, I remember saying that I wished to be understood as being one to help. I love your sister so well that anything which would break her heart would make me unhappy.'

'You did not care for my own welfare in the matter?'

'What ought I to say, Lord Rufford, in answer to that? Of course I did care. But I knew it was impossible that you should really set your affections on such a person as Miss Trefoil. I told Eleanor that it could come to nothing. I was sure of it.'

'Why should it have come to nothing, as you call it?'

'Because you are a gentleman, and because she—is not a lady. I don't know that we women can quite understand how it is that you men amuse yourselves with such persons.'

'I did not amuse myself.'

'I never thought you did very much. There was something, I suppose, in her riding, something in her audacity, something, perhaps, in her vivacity; but through it all I did not think that you were enjoying yourself. You may be sure of this, Lord Rufford, that when a woman is not specially liked by any other woman, she ought not to be specially liked by any man. I have never heard that Miss Trefoil had a female friend.'

From day to day there were little meetings and conversations of this kind, till Lord Rufford found himself accustomed to Miss Penge's solicitude for his welfare. In all that passed between them the lady affected a status that was altogether removed from that of making or receiving love. There had come to be a peculiar friendship,—because of Eleanor. A week of this kind of thing had not gone by before Miss Penge found herself able to talk of, and absolutely to describe, this peculiar feeling, and could almost say how pleasant was such friendship, divested of the burden of all amatory possibilities. But, through it all, Lord Rufford knew that he would have to marry Miss Penge.

It was not long before he yielded in pure weariness. Who has not felt, as he stood by a stream into which he knew that it was his fate to plunge, the folly of delaying the shock? In his present condition he had no ease. His sister threatened him with a return of Arabella. Miss Penge required from him sensational conversation. His brother-in-law was laughing at him in his sleeve. His very hunting friends treated him as though the time were come. In all that he did the young lady took an interest which bored him excessively,—to put an end to which he only saw one certain way. He therefore asked her to be Lady Rufford before he got on his drag to go out hunting on the last Saturday in March. 'Rufford,' she said, looking up into his face with her lustrous eyes, and speaking with a sweet, low, silvery voice, 'are you sure of yourself?'

'Oh yes.'

'Quite sure of yourself?'

'Never was so sure in my life.'

'Then, dearest, dearest Rufford, I will not scruple to say that I also am sure.' And so the thing was settled, very much to his comfort. He could hardly have done better had he sought through all England for a bride. She will be true to him, and never give him cause for a moment's jealousy. She will like his title, his house, and his property. She will never spend a shilling more than she ought to do. She will look very sharply after him, but will not altogether debar him from his accustomed pleasures. She will grace his table, nurse his children, and never for a moment give him cause to be ashamed of her. He will think that he loves her, and, after a lapse of ten or fifteen years, will probably really be fond of her. From the moment that she is Lady Rufford she will love him,— as she loves everything that is her own.

In spite of all his antecedents, no one doubted his faith

in this engagement;—no one wished to hurry him very much. When the proposition had been made and accepted, and when the hero of it had gone off on his drag, Miss Penge communicated the tidings to her friend. 'I think he has behaved very wisely,' said Lady Penwether.

'Well;—feeling as I do of course I think he has. I hope he thinks the same of me. I had many doubts about it, but I do believe that I can make him a good wife.' Lady Penwether thought that her friend was hardly sufficiently thankful, and strove to tell her so in her own gentle, friendly way. But Miss Penge held her head up and was very stout, and would not acknowledge any cause for gratitude. Lady Penwether, when she saw how it was to be, gave way a little. Close friendship with her future sister-in-law would be very necessary to her comfort, and Miss Penge, since the law-suit was settled, had never been given to yielding.

'My dear Rufford,' said the sister affectionately, 'I congratulate you with all my heart; I do indeed. I am quite sure that you could not have done better.'

'I don't know that I could.'

'She is a gem of inestimable price, and most warmly attached to you. And if this property is to be bought, of course the money will be a great thing.'

'Money is always comfortable.'

'Of course it is, and then there is nothing to be desired. If I had named the girl that I would have wished you to love, it would have been Caroline Penge.' She need hardly have said this as she had in fact been naming the girl for the last three or four months. The news was soon spread about the country and the fashionable world; and everybody was pleased,—except the Trefoil family.

Chapter LXXV

ARABELLA'S SUCCESS

WHEN Arabella Trefoil got back to Portugal Street after her visit to Rufford, she was ill. The effort she had made, the unaccustomed labour, and the necessity of holding herself aloft before the man who had rejected her,

were together more than her strength could bear, and she
was taken up to bed in a fainting condition. It was not
till the next morning that she was able even to open the
letter which contained the news of John Morton's legacy.
When she had read the letter and realized the contents,
she took to weeping in a fashion very unlike her usual
habits. She was still in bed, and there she remained for
two or three days, during which she had time to think of
her past life,—and to think also a little of the future. Old
Mrs. Green came to her once or twice a day, but she was
necessarily left to the nursing of her own maid. Every
evening Mounser Green called and sent up tender
enquiries; but in all this there was very little to comfort
her. There she lay with the letter in her hand, thinking
that the only man who had endeavoured to be of service
to her was he whom she had treated with unexampled
perfidy. Other men had petted her, had amused themselves with her, and then thrown her over, had lied to her
and laughed at her, till she had been taught to think that
a man was a heartless, cruel, slippery animal, made
indeed to be caught occasionally, but in the catching of
which infinite skill was wanted, and in which infinite
skill might be thrown away. But this man had been true
to her to the last in spite of her treachery!

She knew that she was heartless herself, and that she
belonged to a heartless world;—but she knew also that
there was a world of women who were not heartless. Such
women had looked down upon her as from a great height,
but she in return had been able to ridicule them. They
had chosen their part, and she had chosen hers,—and had
thought that she might climb to the glory of wealth and
rank, while they would have to marry hard-working
clergymen and briefless barristers. She had often been
called upon to vindicate to herself the part she had
chosen, and had always done so by magnifying in her
own mind the sin of the men with whom she had to deal.
At this moment she thought that Lord Rufford had
treated her villainously, whereas her conduct to him had
been only that which the necessity of the case required.
To Lord Rufford she had simply behaved after the

manner of her class, heartless of course, but only in the
way which the 'custom of the trade' justified. Each had
tried to circumvent the other, and she as the weaker had
gone to the wall. But John Morton had believed in her
and loved her. Oh, how she wished that she had deserted
her class, and clung to him,—even though she should now
have been his widow! The legacy was a burden to her.
Even she had conscience enough to be sorry for a day or
two that he had named her in his will.

And what should she do with herself for the future?
Her quarrel with her mother had been very serious, each
swearing that under no circumstances would she again
consent to live with the other. The daughter of course
knew that the mother would receive her again should she
ask to be received. But in such case she must go back
with shortened pinions*and blunted beak. Her sojourn
with Mrs. Green was to last for one month, and at the
end of that time she must seek for a home. If she put
John Morton's legacy out to interest, she would now be
mistress of a small income;—but she understood money
well enough to know to what obduracy of poverty she
would thus be subjected. As she looked the matter closer
in the face the horrors became more startling and more
manifest. Who would have her in their houses? Where
should she find society,—where the possibility of lovers?
What would be her life, and what her prospects? Must
she give up for ever the game for which she had lived, and
own that she had been conquered in the fight and beaten
even to death? Then she thought over the long list of her
past lovers, trying to see whether there might be one of
the least desirable at whom she might again cast her
javelins. But there was not one.

The tender messages from Mounser Green came to her
day by day. Mounser Green, as the nephew of her
hostess, had been very kind to her; but hitherto he had
never appeared to her in the light of a possible lover. He
was a clerk in the Foreign Office, waiting for his aunt's
money;—a man whom she had met in society and whom
she knew to be well thought of by those above him in
wealth and rank; but she had never regarded him as prey,

—or as a man whom any girl would want to marry. He
was one of those of the other sex who would most probably look out for prey,—who, if he married at all, would
marry an heiress. She, in her time, had been on good
terms with many such a one,—had counted them among
her intimate friends, had made use of them and had been
useful to them,—but she had never dreamed of marrying
any one of them. They were there in society for altogether
a different purpose. She had not hesitated to talk to
Mounser Green about Lord Rufford,—and though she
had pretended to make a secret of the place to which she
was going when he had taken her to the railway, she had
not at all objected to his understanding her purpose. Up
to that moment there had certainly been no thought on
her part of transferring what she was wont to call her
affections to Mounser Green as a suitor.

But as she lay in bed, thinking of her future life, tidings
were brought to her by Mrs. Green that Mounser had
accepted the mission to Patagonia. Could it be that her
destiny intended her to go out to Patagonia as the wife, if
not of one Minister, then of another? There would be
a career,—a way of living, if not exactly that which she
would have chosen. Of Patagonia, as a place of residence,
she had already formed ideas. In some of those moments
in which she had foreseen that Lord Rufford would be
lost to her, she had told herself that it would be better to
reign in Hell than serve in Heaven* Among Patagonian
women she would probably be the first. Among English
ladies it did not seem that at present she had any prospect
of a high place. It would be long before Lord Rufford
would be forgotten,—and she had not space enough
before her for forgettings which would require time for
their accomplishment. Mounser Green had declared
with energy that Lord Rufford had behaved very badly.
There are men who feel it to be their mission to come in
for the relief of ladies who have been badly treated. If
Mounser Green wished to be one of them on her behalf,
and to take her out with him to his very far-away employment, might not this be the best possible solution of her
present difficulties?

On the evening of the third day after her return she was able to come downstairs, and the line of thought which has been suggested for her induced her to undertake some trouble with the white and pink robe, or dressing-gown, in which she appeared. 'Well, my dear, you are smart,' the old lady said.

> ' "Odious in woollen;—'twould a saint provoke,
>   Were the last words which poor Narcissa spoke," ⁂

said Arabella, who had long since provided herself with this quotation for such occasions. 'I hope I am not exactly dying, Mrs. Green; but I don't see why I should not object to be "frightful," as well as the young lady who was.'

'I suppose it's all done for Mounser's benefit?'

'Partly for you, partly for Mounser, and a good deal for myself. What a very odd name. Why did they call him Mounser? I used to think it was because he was in the Foreign Office,—a kind of chaff, as being half a Frenchman.'

'My mother's maiden name was Mounser, and it isn't French at all. I don't see why it should not be as good a Christian name as Willoughby or Howard.'

'Quite as good, and much more distinctive. There can't be another Mounser Green in the world.'

'And very few other young men like him. At my time of life I find it very hard his going away. And what will he do in such a place as that,—all alone and without a wife?'

'Why don't you make him take a wife?'

'There isn't time now. He'll have to start in May.'

'Plenty of time. Trousseaux are now got up by steam, and girls are kept ready to marry at the shortest notice. If I were you I should certainly advise him to take out some healthy young woman, capable of bearing the inclemencies of the Patagonian climate.'

'As for that the climate is delicious,' said Mrs. Green, who certainly was not led by her guest's manner to suspect the nature of her guest's more recent intentions.

Mounser Green on this afternoon came to Portugal

Street before he himself went out to dinner, choosing the hour at which his aunt was wont to adorn herself. 'And so you are to be the hero of Patagonia?' said Arabella as she put out her hand to congratulate him on his appointment.

'I don't know about heroism, but it seems that I am to go there,' said Mounser with much melancholy in his voice.

'I should have thought you were the last man to leave London willingly.'

'Well, yes; I should have said so myself. And I do flatter myself I shall be missed. But what had I before me here? This may lead to something.'

'Indeed you will be missed, Mr. Green.'

'It's very kind of you to say so.'

'Patagonia! It is such a long way off!' Then she began to consider whether he had ever heard of her engagement with the last Minister-elect to that country. That he should know all about Lord Rufford was a matter of course; but what chance could there be for her if he also knew that other affair? 'We were intimately acquainted with Mr. Morton in Washington, and were surprised that he should have accepted it.'

'Poor Morton! He was a friend of mine. We used to call him the Paragon because he never made mistakes. I had heard that you and Lady Augustus were a good deal with him in Washington.'

'We were, indeed. You do not know my good news as yet, I suppose? Your Paragon, as you call him, has left me five thousand pounds.' Of course, it would be necessary that he should know it some day if this new plan of hers were to be carried out;—and if the plan should fail, his knowing it could do no harm.

'How very nice for you! Poor Morton!'

'It is well that somebody should behave well, when others treat one so badly, Mr. Green. Yes; he has left me five thousand pounds.' Then she showed him the lawyer's letter. 'Perhaps, as I am so separated at present from all my own people by this affair with Lord Rufford, you would not mind seeing the man for me?' Of course, he promised to see the lawyer and to do everything that was necessary. 'The truth is, Mr. Green, Mr. Morton was very warmly attached to me. I was a foolish girl, and could not return it. I thought of it long, and was then obliged to tell him that I could not entertain just that sort of feeling for him. You cannot think how bitter is my regret;—that I should have allowed myself to trust a man so false and treacherous as Lord Rufford, and that I should have perhaps added a pang to the deathbed of one so good as Mr. Morton.' And so she told her little story; —not caring very much whether it were believed or not, but finding it to be absolutely essential that some story should be told.

During the next day or two, Mounser Green thought a great deal about it. That the story was not exactly true, he knew very well. But it is not to be expected that a girl, before her marriage, should be exactly true about her old loves. That she had been engaged to Lord Rufford, and had been cruelly jilted by him he did believe. That she had at one time been engaged to the Paragon he was almost sure. The fact that the Paragon had left her money was a strong argument that she had not behaved badly to him. But there was much that was quite certain. The five thousand pounds were quite certain; and the money, though it could not be called a large fortune for a young lady, would pay his debts and send him out a free man to Patagonia. And the family honours were certainly true. She was the undoubted niece of the Duke of Mayfair, and such a connection might in his career be of service to him. Lord Mistletoe was a prig, but would probably be a member of the Government. Mounser Green liked dukes, and loved a duchess in his heart of hearts. If he could only be assured that this niece would not be repudiated, he thought that the speculation might answer in spite of any ambiguity in the lady's antecedents.

'Have you heard about Arabella's good fortune?' young Glossop asked the next morning at the office.

'You forget, my boy,' said Mounser Green, 'that the young lady of whom you speak is a friend of mine.'

'Oh Lord! So I did. I beg your pardon, old fellow.'

There was no one else in the room at the moment, and Glossop in asking the question had, in truth, forgotten what he had heard of this new intimacy.

'Don't you learn to be ill-natured, Glossop. And remember that there is no form so bad as that of calling young ladies by their Christian names. I do know that poor Morton has left Miss Trefoil a sum of money which is, at any rate, evidence that he thought well of her to the last.'

'Of course it is. I didn't mean to offend you. I wouldn't do it for worlds,—as you are going away.' That afternoon, when Green's back was turned, Glossop gave it as his opinion that something particular would turn up between Mounser and Miss Trefoil, an opinion which brought down much ridicule upon him from both Hoffman and Archibald Currie. But before that week was over,—in the early days of April,—they were forced to retract their opinion, and to do honour to young Glossop's sagacity. Mounser Green was engaged to Miss Trefoil, and for a day or two the Foreign Office could talk of nothing else.

'A very handsome girl,' said Lord Drummond to one of his subordinates. 'I met her at Mistletoe. As to that affair with Lord Rufford, he treated her abominably.' And when Mounser showed himself at the office, which he did boldly, immediately after the engagement was made known, they all received him with open arms and congratulated him sincerely on his happy fortune. He himself was quite contented with what he had done, and thought that he was taking out for himself the very wife for Patagonia.

CHAPTER LXXVI

THE WEDDING

NO sooner did the two new lovers, Mounser Green and Arabella Trefoil, understand each other than they set their wits to work to make the best of their natural advantages. The latter communicated the fact, in a very dry manner, to her father and mother. Nothing

was to be got from them, and it was only just necessary
that they should know what she intended to do with herself. 'My dear mamma, I am to be married, some time
early in May, to Mr. Mounser Green, of the Foreign
Office. I don't think you know him, but I dare say you
have heard of him. He goes to Patagonia immediately
after the wedding, and I shall go with him. Your
affectionate daughter, Arabella Trefoil.' That was all
she said, and the letter to her father was word for word
the same. But how to make use of those friends who were
more happily circumstanced was matter for frequent
counsel between her and Mr. Green. In these days I do
not think that she concealed very much from him. To
tell him all the little details of her adventures with Lord
Rufford would have been neither useful nor pleasant;
but, as to the chief facts, reticence would have been
foolish. To the statement that Lord Rufford had
absolutely proposed to her she clung fast, and really did
believe it herself. That she had been engaged to John
Morton she did not deny; but she threw the blame of that
matter on her mother, and explained to him that she had
broken off the engagement down at Bragton, because she
could not bring herself to regard the man with sufficient
personal favour. Mounser was satisfied, but was very
strong in urging her to seek, yet once again, the favour of
her magnificent uncle and her magnificent aunt.

'What good can they do us?' said Arabella, who was
almost afraid to make the appeal.

'It would be everything for you to be married from
Mistletoe,' he said. 'People would know then that you
were not blamed about Lord Rufford. And it might
serve me very much in my profession. These things do
help very much. It would cost us nothing, and the proper
kind of notice would then get into the newspapers. If you
will write direct to the duchess, I will get at the duke
through Lord Drummond. They know where we are
going, and that we are not likely to want anything else
for a long time.'

'I don't think the duchess would have mamma if it
were ever so.'

'Then we must drop your mother for the time,—that's all. When my aunt hears that you are to be married from the duke's she will be quite willing that you should remain with her till you go down to Mistletoe.'

Arabella, who perhaps knew a little more than her lover, could not bring herself to believe that the appeal would be successful, but she made it. It was a very difficult letter to write, as she could not but allude to the rapid transference of her affections. 'I will not conceal from you,' she said, 'that I have suffered very much from Lord Rufford's heartless conduct. My misery has been aggravated by the feeling that you and my uncle will hardly believe him to be so false, and will attribute part of the blame to me. I had to undergo an agonizing revulsion of feeling, during which Mr. Green's behaviour to me was at first so considerate and then so kind that it has gone far to cure the wound from which I have been suffering. He is so well known in reference to foreign affairs, that I think my uncle cannot but have heard of him; my cousin Mistletoe is certainly acquainted with him; and I think you cannot but approve of the match. You know what is the position of my father and my mother, and how little able they are to give us any assistance. If you would be kind enough to let us be married from Mistletoe, you will confer on both of us a very, very great favour.' There was more of it, but that was the first of the prayer; and most of the words given above came from the dictation of Mounser himself. She had pleaded against making the direct request, but he had assured her that in the world, as at present arranged, the best way to get a thing is to ask for it. 'You make yourself, at any rate, understood,' he said; 'and you may be sure that people who receive petitions do not feel the hardihood of them so much as they who make them.' Arabella, comforting herself by declaring that the duchess at any rate, could not eat her, wrote the letter and sent it.

The duchess at first was most serious in her intention to refuse. She was indeed made very angry by the request. Though it had been agreed at Mistletoe that Lord Rufford had behaved badly the duchess was thoroughly well aware that Arabella's conduct had been abominable. Lord Rufford probably had made an offer, but it had been extracted from him by the vilest of manœuvres. The girl had been personally insolent to herself. And this rapid change,—this third engagement within a few weeks, —was disgusting to her as a woman. But, unluckily for herself, she would not answer the letter till she had consulted her husband. As it happened, the duke was in town, and while he was there Lord Drummond got hold of him. Lord Drummond had spoken very highly of Mounser Green, and the duke, who was never dead to the feeling that, as the head of the family, he should always do what he could for the junior branches, had almost made a promise. 'I never take such things upon myself,' he said, 'But if the duchess has no objection, we will have them down to Mistletoe.'

'Of course if you wish it,' said the duchess, with more acerbity in her tone than the duke had often heard there.

'Wish it? What do you mean by wishing it? It will be a great bore.'

'Terrible!'

'But she is the only one there is, and then we shall have done with it.'

'Done with it! They will be back from Patagonia before you can turn yourself, and then of course we must have them here.'

'Drummond tells me that Mr. Green is one of the most useful men they have at the Foreign Office;—just the man that one ought to give a lift to.' Of course the duke had his way. The duchess could not bring herself to write the letter, but the duke wrote to his dear niece saying that 'they' would be very glad to see her, and that if she would name the day proposed for the wedding, one should be fixed for her visit to Mistletoe.

'You had better tell your mother and your father,' Mounser said to her.

'What's the use? The duchess hates my mother, and my father never goes near the place.'

'Nevertheless tell them. People care a great deal for appearances.' She did as she was bid, and the result was that Lord Augustus and his wife on the occasion of their daughter's marriage met each other at Mistletoe,—for the first time for the last dozen years.

Before the day came round Arabella was quite astonished to find how popular and fashionable her wedding was likely to be, and how the world at large approved of what she was doing. The newspapers had paragraphs about alliances and noble families, and all the relatives sent tribute. There was a gold candlestick from the duke, a gilt dish from the duchess,—which came, however, without a word of personal congratulation,— and a gorgeous set of scent-bottles from cousin Mistletoe. The Connop Greens were lavish with sapphires, the De Brownes with pearls, and the Smijths with opal. Mrs. Gore sent a huge carbuncle which Arabella strongly suspected to be glass. From her paternal parent there came a pair of silver nut-crackers, and from the maternal a second-hand dressing-case newly done up. Old Mrs. Green gave her a couple of ornamental butter-boats, and salt-cellars innumerable came from distant Greens. But there was a diamond ring—with a single stone,—from a friend, without a name, which she believed to be worth all the rest in money value. Should she send it back to Lord Rufford or make a gulp and swallow it? How invincible must be the good-nature of the man when he could send her such a present after such a rating as she had given him in the park at Rufford! 'Do as you like,' Mounser Green said to her when she consulted him.

She very much wished to keep it. 'But what am I to say; and to whom?'

'Write a note to the jewellers saying that you have got it.' She did write to the jeweller saying that she had got the ring,—'from a friend;' and the ring with the other tribute went to Patagonia. He had certainly behaved very badly to her, but she was quite sure that he would never tell the story of the ring to any one. Perhaps she thought that as she had spared him in the great matter of eight thousand pounds, she was entitled to take this smaller contribution.

It was late in April when she went down to Mistletoe,

the marriage having been fixed for the 3rd of May. After that they were to spend a fortnight in Paris, and leave England for Patagonia at the end of the month. The only thing which Arabella dreaded was the meeting with the duchess. When that was once over she thought that she could bear with equanimity all that could come after. The week before her marriage could not be a pleasant week, but then she had been accustomed to endure evil hours. Her uncle would be blandly good-natured. Mistletoe, should he be there, would make civil speeches to compensate for his indifference when called upon to attack Lord Rufford. Other guests would tender to her the caressing observance always shown to a bride. But as she got out of the ducal carriage at the front door, her heart was uneasy at the coming meeting.

The duchess herself almost went to bed when the time came, so much did she dread the same thing. She was quite alone, having felt that she could not bring herself to give the affectionate embrace which the presence of others would require. She stood in the middle of the room, and then came forward three steps to meet the bride. 'Arabella,' she said, 'I am very glad that everything has been settled so comfortably for you.'

'That is so kind of you, aunt,' said Arabella, who was watching the duchess closely,—ready to jump into her aunt's arms if required to do so, or to stand quite aloof.

Then the duchess signified her pleasure that her cheek should be touched,—and it was touched. 'Mrs. Pepper will show you your room. It is the same you had when you were here before. Perhaps you know that Mr. Green comes down to Stamford on the first, and that he will dine here on that day and on Sunday.'

'That will be very nice. He had told me how it was arranged.'

'It seems that he knows one of the clergymen in Stamford, and will stay at his house. Perhaps you will like to go upstairs now.'

That was all there was, and that had not been very bad. During the entire week the duchess hardly spoke to her another word, and certainly did not speak to her a word in private. Arabella now could go where she pleased without any danger of meeting her aunt on her walks. When Sunday came nobody asked her to go to church. She did go twice, Mounser Green accompanying her to the morning service;—but there was no restraint. The duchess only thought of her as a disagreeable ill-conducted incubus, who luckily was about to be taken away to Patagonia.

It had been settled on all sides that the marriage was to be very quiet. The bride was, of course, consulted about her bridesmaids, as to whom there was a little difficulty. But a distant Trefoil was found willing to act, in payment for the unaccustomed invitation to Mistletoe, and one Connop Green young lady, with one De Browne young lady, and one Smijth young lady came on the same terms. Arabella herself was surprised at the ease with which it was all done. On the Saturday Lady Augustus came, and on the Sunday Lord Augustus. The parents, of course, kissed their child, but there was very little said in the way either of congratulation or farewell. Lord Augustus did have some conversation with Mounser Green, but it all turned on the probability of there being whist in Patagonia. On the Monday morning they were married, and then Arabella was taken off by the happy bridegroom.

When the ceremony was over it was expected that Lady Augustus should take herself away as quickly as possible —not perhaps on that very afternoon, but at any rate, on the next morning. As soon as the carriage was gone, she went to her own room and wept bitterly. It was all done now. Everything was over. Though she had quarrelled daily with her daughter for the last twelve years,—to such an extent lately that no decently civil word ever passed between them,—still there had been something to interest her. There had been something to fear and something to hope. The girl had always had some prospect before her, more or less brilliant. Her life had had its occupation, and future triumph was possible. Now it was all over. The link by which she had been bound to the world was broken. The Connop Greens and the Smijths would no longer have her,—unless it might be on short and special occasions, as a great favour. She knew that she was an old woman, without money, without blood, and without attraction, whom nobody would ever again desire to see. She had her things packed up, and herself taken off to London, almost without a word of farewell to the duchess, telling herself as she went that the world had produced no other people so heartless as the family of the Trefoils.

'I wonder what you will think of Patagonia?' said Mounser Green, as he took his bride away.

'I don't suppose I shall think much. As far as I can see one place is always like another.'

'But then you will have duties.'

'Not very heavy I hope.'

Then he preached her a sermon, expressing a hope, as he went on, that as she was leaving the pleasures of life behind her, she would learn to like the work of life. 'I have found the pleasures very hard,' she said. He spoke to her of the companion he hoped to find, of the possible children who might be dependent on their mother, of the position which she would hold, and in the manner which she should fill it. She, as she listened to him, was almost stunned by the change in the world around her. She need never again seem to be gay in order that men might be attracted. She made her promises and made them with an intention of keeping them; but it may, we fear, be doubted whether he was justified in expecting that he could get a wife fit for his purpose out of the school in which Arabella Trefoil had been educated. The two, however, will pass out of our sight, and we can only hope that he may not be disappointed.

Chapter LXXVII

THE SENATOR'S LECTURE.—NO. I

WEDNESDAY, April 14th, was the day at last fixed for the Senator's lecture. His little proposal to set England right on all those matters in which she had hitherto gone astray had created a considerable amount of attention. The Goarly affair, with the subsequent trial of Scrobby, had been much talked about, and the Senator's doings in reference to it had been made matter of comment in the newspapers. Some had praised him for courage, benevolence, and a steadfast purpose. Others had ridiculed his inability to understand manners different from those of his own country. He had seen a good deal of society both in London and in the country, and had never hesitated to express his opinions with an audacity which some had called insolence. When he had trodden with his whole weight hard down on individual corns, of course he had given offence,—as on the memorable occasion of the dinner at the parson's house in Dillsborough. But, on the whole, he had produced for himself a general respect among educated men which was not diminished by the fact that he seemed to count quite as little on that as on the ill-will and abuse of others. For some days previous to the delivery of the lecture the hoardings in London were crowded with sesquipedalian * notices of the entertainment, so that Senator Gotobed's great oration on 'The Irrationality of Englishmen' was looked forward to with considerable interest.

When an intelligent Japanese travels in Great Britain or an intelligent Briton in Japan, he is struck with no wonder at national differences. He is on the other hand rather startled to find how like his strange brother is to him in many things. Crime is persecuted, wickedness is condoned, and goodness treated with indifference in both countries. Men care more for what they eat than anything else, and combine a closely defined idea of meum * with a lax perception as to tuum? Barring a little difference of complexion and feature the Englishman would make a good Japanese, or the Japanese a first-class Englishman. But when an American comes to us, or a Briton goes to the States, each speaking the same language, using the same cookery, governed by the same laws, and wearing the same costume, the differences which present themselves are so striking that neither can live six months in the country of the other without a holding up of the hands and a torrent of exclamations. And in nineteen cases out of twenty the surprise and the ejaculations take the place of censure. The intelligence of the American, displayed through the nose, worries the Englishman. The unconscious self-assurance of the Englishman, not always unaccompanied by a sneer, irritates the American. They meet as might a lad from Harrow · and another from Mr. Brumby's successful mechanical cramming establishment. The Harrow boy cannot answer a question, but is sure that he is the proper thing, and is ready to face the world on that assurance. Mr. Brumby's paragon is shocked at the other's inaptitude for examination, but is at the same time tortured by envy of he knows not what. In this spirit we Americans and Englishmen go on writing books about each other, sometimes with bitterness enough, but generally with good final results. But in the meantime there has sprung up a jealousy which makes each inclined to hate the other at first sight. Hate is difficult and expensive, and between individuals soon gives place to love. 'I cannot bear Americans as a rule, though I have been very lucky myself with a few friends.' Who in England has not heard that form of speech, over and over again? And what Englishman has travelled in the States without hearing abuse of all English institutions uttered amidst the pauses of a free-handed hospitality which has left him nothing to desire?

Mr. Senator Gotobed had expressed his mind openly wheresoever he went, but, being a man of immense energy, was not content with such private utterances. He could not liberate his soul without doing something in public to convince his cousins that in their general practices of life they were not guided by reason. He had no object of making money. To give him his due we must own that he had no object of making fame. He was impelled by that intense desire to express himself which often amounts to passion with us, and sometimes to fury with Americans, and he hardly considered much what reception his words might receive. It was only when he was told by others that his lecture might give offence which possibly would turn to violence, that he made enquiry as to the attendance of the police. But though they should tear him to pieces he would say what he had to say. It should not be his fault if the absurdities of a people whom he really loved were not exposed to light, so that they might be acknowledged and abandoned.

He had found time to travel to Birmingham, to Manchester, to Liverpool, to Glasgow and to other places, and really thought that he had mastered his great subject. He had worked very hard, but was probably premature in thinking that he knew England thoroughly. He had, however, undoubtedly dipped into a great many matters, and could probably have told many Englishmen much that they didn't know about their own affairs. He had poked his nose everywhere, and had scrupled to ask no question. He had seen the miseries of a casual ward, the despair of an expiring strike, the amenities of a city slum, and the stolid apathy of a rural labourer's home. He had measured the animal food consumed by the working classes, and knew the exact amount of alcohol swallowed by the average Briton. He had seen also the luxury of baronial halls, the pearl-drinking extravagance of commercial palaces, the unending labours of our pleasure-seekers—as with Lord Rufford, and the dullness of ordinary country life—as experienced by himself at Bragton. And now he was going to tell the English people at large what he thought about it all.

The great room at St. James's Hall had been secured for the occasion, and Lord Drummond, the Minister of State for Foreign Affairs, had been induced to take the chair. In these days our governments are very anxious to be civil to foreigners, and there is nothing that a robust Secretary of State will not do for them. On the platform there were many members of both Houses of Parliament, and almost everybody connected with the Foreign Office. Every ticket had been taken for weeks since. The front benches were filled with the wives and daughters of those on the platform, and back, behind, into the distant spaces in which seeing was difficult and hearing impossible, the crowd was gathered at 2s. 6d. a head, all of which was going to some great British charity. From half-past seven to eight Piccadilly and Regent Street were crammed, and when the Senator came himself with his chairman he could hardly make his way in at the doors. A great treat was expected, but there were among the officers of police some who thought that a portion of the audience would not bear quietly the hard things that would be said, and that there was an uncanny gathering of roughs about the street who were not prepared to be on their best behaviour when they should be told that Old England was being abused.

Lord Drummond opened the proceedings by telling the audience in a voice clearly audible to the reporters and the first half dozen benches, that they had come there to hear what a well-informed and distinguished foreigner thought of their country. They would not, he was sure, expect to be flattered. Than flattery nothing was more useless or ignoble. This gentleman, coming from a new country in which tradition was of no avail and on which the customs of former centuries had had no opportunities to engraft themselves, had seen many things here which, in his eyes, could not justify themselves by reason. Lord Drummond was a little too prolix for a chairman, and at last concluded by expressing 'his conviction that his countrymen would listen to the distinguished Senator with that courtesy which was due to a foreigner and due also to the great and brotherly nation from which he had come.'

Then the Senator rose, and the clapping of hands and kicking of heels was most satisfactory. There was, at any rate, no prejudice at the onset. 'English ladies and gentlemen,' he said, 'I am in the unenviable position of having to say hard things to you for about an hour and a half together, if I do not drive you from your seats before my lecture is done. And this is the more the pity because I could talk to you for three hours about your country and not say an unpleasant word. His lordship has told you that flattery is not my purpose. Neither is praise, which would not be flattery. Why should I collect three or four thousand people here to tell them of virtues the consciousness of which is the inheritance of each of them? You are brave and generous,—and you are lovely

to look at, with sweetly polished manners; but you know
all that quite well enough without my telling you. But it
strikes me that you do not know how little prone you are
to admit the light of reason into either your public or
private life, and how generally you allow yourselves to be
guided by traditions, prejudices, and customs which should
be obsolete. If you will consent to listen to what one
foreigner thinks,—though he himself be a man of no
account,—you may perchance gather from his words
something of the opinion of bystanders in general, and so
be able, perhaps a little, to rectify your gait and your
costume and the tones of your voice, as we are all apt to
do when we come from our private homes, out among
the eyes of the public.'

This was received very well. The Senator spoke with
a clear sonorous voice, no doubt with a twang, but so
audibly as to satisfy the room in general. 'I shall not,' he
said, 'dwell much on your form of government. Were
I to praise a republic I might seem to belittle your throne
and the lady who sits on it,—an offence which would not
be endured for a moment by English ears. I will take the
monarchy as it is, simply remarking that its recondite
forms are very hard to be understood by foreigners, and
that they seem to me to be for the most part equally dark
to natives. I have hardly as yet met two Englishmen who
were agreed as to the political power of the Sovereign;
and most of those of whom I have enquired have assured
me that the matter is one as to which they have not found
it worth their while to make enquiry.' Here a voice from
the end of the hall made some protestation, but the nature
of the protest did not reach the platform.

'But,' continued the Senator, now rising into energy,
'though I will not meddle with your form of government,
I may, I hope, be allowed to allude to the political agents
by which it is conducted. You are proud of your Parliament.'

'We are,' said a voice.

'I wonder of which House. I do not ask the question
that it may be answered, because it is advisable at the
present moment that there should be only one speaker.

That labour is, unfortunately for me, at present in my hands, and I am sure you will agree with me that it should not be divided. You mean probably that you are proud of your House of Commons,—and that you are so because it speaks with the voice of the people. The voice of the people, in order that it may be heard without unjust preponderance on this side or on that, requires much manipulation. That manipulation has in latter years been effected by your Reform Bills, of which during the last half century there have in fact been four or five,— the latter in favour of the ballot having been perhaps the greatest. There have been bills for purity of elections,— very necessary; bills for creating constituencies, bills for abolishing them, bills for dividing them, bills for extending the suffrage, and bills, if I am not mistaken, for curtailing it. And what has been the result? How many men are there in this room who know the respective nature of their votes? And is there a single woman who knows the political worth of her husband's vote? Passing the other day from the Bank of this great metropolis to its suburb called Brentford, journeying as I did the whole way through continuous rows of houses, I found myself at first in a very ancient borough returning four members,— double the usual number,—not because of its population but because it has always been so. Here I was informed that the residents had little or nothing to do with it. I was told, though I did not quite believe what I heard, that there were no residents. The voters, however, at any rate, the influential voters, never pass a night there, and combine their city franchise with franchises elsewhere. I then went through two enormous boroughs, one so old as to have a great political history of its own, and the other so new as to have none. It did strike me as odd that there should be a new borough, with new voters, and new franchises, not yet ten years old, in the midst of this city of London. But when I came to Brentford, everything was changed. I was not in a town at all, though I was surrounded on all sides by houses. Everything around me was grim and dirty enough, but I am supposed to have reached, politically, the rustic beauties of the country.

Those around me, who had votes, voted for the county of
Middlesex. On the other side of the invisible border, I
had just passed the poor wretch with 3s. a day who lived
in a grimy lodging or a half-built hut, but who at any
rate possessed the political privilege. Now I had suddenly
emerged among the aristocrats, and quite another state
of things prevailed. Is that a reasonable manipulation of
the votes of the people? Does that arrangement give to
any man an equal share in his country? And yet I fancy
the thing is so little thought of that few among you are
aware that in this way the largest class of British labour is
excluded from the franchise in a country which boasts
of equal representation.

'The chief object of your first Reform Bill*was that of
realizing the very fact of representation. Up to that time
your members of the House of Commons were, in truth,
deputies of the Lords or of other rich men. Lord A., or
Mr. B., or perhaps Lady C., sent whom she pleased to
Parliament to represent this or that town, or occasionally
this or that county. That absurdity is supposed to be past,
and on evils that have been cured no one should dwell.
But how is it now? I have a list,—in my memory, for
I would not care to make out so black a catalogue in
legible letters,—of forty members who have been returned
to the present House of Commons by the single voices of
influential persons. What will not forty voices do even in
your Parliament? And if I can count forty, how many
more must there be of which I have not heard?' Then
there was a voice calling upon the Senator to name those
men, and other voices denying the fact. 'I will name no
one,' said the Senator. 'How could I tell what noble
friend I might put on a stool of repentance by doing so?'
And he looked round on the gentlemen on the platform
behind him. 'But I defy any member of Parliament here
present to get up and say that it is not so.' Then he
paused a moment. 'And if it be so, is that rational? Is
that in accordance with the theory of representation as to
which you have all been so ardent, and which you
profess to be so dear to you? Is the country not over-
ridden by the aristocracy when Lord Lambswool not

only possesses his own hereditary seat in the House of Lords, but also has a seat for his eldest son in the House of Commons?'

Then a voice from the back called out, 'What the deuce is all that to you?'

CHAPTER LXXVIII

THE SENATOR'S LECTURE.—NO. II

'IF I see a man hungry in the street,' said the Senator, instigated by the question asked him at the end of the last chapter, 'and give him a bit of bread, I don't do it for my own sake but for his.' Up to this time the Britishers around him on the platform and those in the benches near to him had received what he had said with a good grace. The allusion to Lord Lambswool had not been pleasant to them, but it had not been worse than they had expected. But now they were displeased. They did not like being told that they were taking a bit of bread from him in their own political destitution. They did not like that he, an individual, should presume that he had bread to offer to them as a nation. And yet, had they argued it out in their own minds, they would have seen that the Senator's metaphor was appropriate. His purpose of being there was to give advice, and theirs in coming to listen to it. But it was unfortunate. 'When I ventured to come before you here I made all this my business,' continued the Senator. Then he paused and glanced round the hall with a defiant look. 'And now about your House of Lords,' he went on. 'I have not much to say about the House of Lords, because if I understand rightly the feeling of this country, it is already condemned.' 'No such thing.' 'Who told you that?' 'You know nothing about it.' These and other words of curt denial came from the distant corners, and a slight murmur of disapprobation was heard even from the seats on the platform. Then Lord Drummond got up and begged that there might be silence. Mr. Gotobed had come there to tell them his views, and as they had come there expressly to listen to him, they could not without impropriety interrupt him.

'That such will be the feeling of the country before long,'
continued the Senator, 'I think no one can doubt who has
learned how to look to the signs of the times in such
matters. Is it possible that the theory of an hereditary
legislature can be defended with reason? For a legislature
you want the best and wisest of your people.' 'You don't
get them in America,' said a voice which was beginning
to be recognized. 'We try, at any rate,' said the Senator.
'Now, is it possible that an accident of birth should give
you excellence and wisdom? What is the result? Not
a tenth of your hereditary legislators assemble in the
beautiful hall that you have built for them. And of that
tenth the greater half consists of counsellors of state, who
have been placed there in order that the business of the
country may not be brought to a standstill. Your
hereditary chamber is a fiction supplemented by the
element of election,—the election resting generally in the
very bosom of the House of Commons.' On this subject,
although he had promised to be short, he said much more,
which was received for the most part in silence. But when
he ended by telling them that they could have no right
to call themselves a free people till every legislator in the
country was elected by the votes of the people, another
murmur was heard through the hall.

'I told you,' said he, waxing more and more energetic,
as he felt the opposition which he was bound to overcome,
'that what I had to say to you would not be pleasant. If
you cannot endure to hear me, let us break up and go
away. In that case I must tell my friends at home that the
tender ears of a British audience cannot bear rough words
from American lips. And yet if you think of it we have
borne rough words from you and have borne them with
good humour.' Again he paused, but as none rose from
their seats he went on, 'Proceeding from hereditary
legislature I come to hereditary property. It is natural
that a man should wish to give to his children after his
death the property which he has enjoyed, during their
life. But let me ask any man here who has not been born
an eldest son himself, whether it is natural that he should
wish to give it all to one son. Would any man think of

doing so, by the light of his own reason,—out of his own head, as we say? Would any man be so unjust to those who are equal in his love, were he not constrained by law, and by custom more iron-handed even than the law?' The Senator had here made a mistake very common with Americans, and a great many voices were on him at once. 'What law?' 'There is no law.' 'You know nothing about it.' 'Go back and learn.'

'What!' cried the Senator, coming forward to the extreme verge of the platform and putting down his foot as though there were strength enough in his leg to crush them all; 'Will any one have the hardihood to tell me that property in this country is not affected by primogeniture? "Go back and learn the law." I know the law perhaps better than most of you. Do you mean to assert that my Lord Lambswool can leave his land to whom he pleases? I tell you that he has no more than a life-interest in it, and that his son will only have the same.' Then an eager Briton on the platform got up and whispered to the Senator for a few minutes, during which the murmuring was continued. 'My friend reminds me,' said the Senator, 'that the matter is one of custom rather than law; and I am obliged to him. But the custom which is damnable and cruel, is backed by law which is equally so. If I have land I can not only give it all to my eldest son, but I can assure the right of primogeniture to his son, though he be not yet born. No one I think will deny that there must be a special law to enable me to commit an injustice so unnatural as that.

'Hence it comes that you still suffer under an aristocracy almost as dominant, and in its essence as irrational, as that which created feudalism.' The gentlemen collected on the platform looked at each other and smiled, perhaps failing to catch the exact meaning of the Senator's words. 'A lord here has a power, as a lord, which he cannot himself fathom and of which he daily makes an unconscious but most deleterious use. He is brought up to think it natural that he should be a tyrant. The proclivities of his order are generous and as a rule he gives more than he takes. But he is as injurious in the one process as in the

other. Your ordinary Briton in his dealing with a lord
expects payment in some shape for every repetition of the
absurd title;—and payment is made. The titled aristocrat
pays dearer for his horse, dearer for his coat, dearer for
his servant than other people. But in return he exacts
much which no other person can get. Knowing his own
magnanimity he expects that his word shall not be
questioned. If I may be allowed I will tell you a little
story as to one of the most generous gentlemen I have had
the happiness of meeting in this country, which will
explain my meaning.'

Then without mentioning names he told the story of
Lord Rufford, Goarly, and Scrobby, in such a way as
partly to redeem himself with his audience. He acknowledged how absolutely he had been himself befooled, and
how he had been done out of his money by misplaced
sympathy. He made Mrs. Goarly's goose immortal, and
in imitating the indignation of Runce the farmer and
Bean the gamekeeper showed that he was master of considerable humour. But he brought it all round at last to
his own purpose, and ended this episode of his lecture by
his view of the absurdity and illegality of British hunting.
'I can talk about it to you,' he said, 'and you will know
whether I am speaking the truth. But when I get home
among my own people, and repeat my lecture there, as
I shall do,—with some little additions as to the good
things I have found here from which your ears may be
spared,—I shall omit this story as I know it will be impossible to make my countrymen believe that a hundred
harum-scarum tomboys may ride at their pleasure over
every man's land, destroying crops and trampling down
fences, going, if their vermin leads them there, with
reckless violence into the sweet domestic gardens of
your country residences;—and that no one can either
stop them or punish them. An American will believe
much about the wonderful ways of his British cousin,
but no American will be got to believe that till he
sees it.'

'I find,' said he, 'that this irrationality, as I have
ventured to call it, runs through all your professions. We

will take the Church as being the highest at any rate in its objects.' Then he recapitulated all those arguments against our mode of dispensing Church patronage with which the reader is already familiar if he has attended to the Senator's earlier words as given in this chronicle. 'In other lines of business there is, even here in England, some attempt made to get the man best suited for the work he has to do. If any one wants a domestic servant he sets about the work of getting a proper person in a very determined manner indeed. But for the care,—or, as you call it, the cure,—of his soul, he has to put up with the man who has bought the right to minister to his wants; or with him whose father wants a means of living for his younger son,—the elder being destined to swallow all the family property;—or with him who has become sick of drinking his wine in an Oxford college;—or with him again, who has pleaded his cause successfully with a bishop's daughter.' It is not often that the British public is angered by abuse of the Church, and this part of the lecture was allowed to pass without strong marks of disapprobation.

'I have been at some trouble,' he continued, 'to learn the very complex rules by which your army is now regulated, and those by which it was regulated a very short time since. Unhappily for me I have found it in a state of transition, and nothing is so difficult to a stranger's comprehension as a transition state of affairs. But this I can see plainly—that every improvement which is made is received by those whom it most concerns with a horror which amounts almost to madness. So lovely to the ancient British, well-born, feudal instinct is a state of unreason, that the very absence of any principle endears to it institutions which no one can attempt to support by argument. Had such a thing not existed as the right to purchase military promotion, would any satirist have been listened to who had suggested it was a possible outcome of British irrationality? Think what it carries with it! The man who has proved himself fit to serve his country by serving it in twenty foughten fields, who has bled for his country and perhaps preserved his country,

shall rot in obscurity because he has no money to buy
promotion, whereas the young dandy who has done no
more than glitter along the pavements with his sword and
spurs shall have the command of men:—because he has
so many thousand dollars in his pocket.'

'*Buncombe*,' shouted the inimical voice.

'But is it *Buncombe*?' asked the intrepid Senator. 'Will
any one who knows what he is talking about say that I
am describing a state of things which did not exist yesterday? I will acknowledge that this has been rectified,
though I see symptoms of relapse. A fault that has been
mended is a fault no longer. But what I speak of now is the
disruption of all concord in your army caused by the
reform which has forced itself upon you. All loyalty has
gone;—all that love of his profession which should be the
breath of a soldier's nostrils. A fine body of fighting
heroes is broken-hearted, not because injury has been
done to them or to any of them, but because the system
had become peculiarly British by reason of its special
absurdity, and therefore peculiarly dear.'

'Buncombe,' again said the voice, and the word was
now repeated by a dozen voices.

'Let any one shew me that it is. Buncombe. If I say
what is untrue, do with me what you please. If I am
ignorant, set me right and laugh at me. But if what I say
is true, then your interruption is surely a sign of imbecility.
I say that the change was forced upon you by the feeling
of the people, but that its very expediency has demoralized
the army, because the army was irrational. And how is it
with the navy? What am I to believe when I hear so
many conflicting statements among yourselves?' During
this last appeal, however, the noise at the back of the hall
had become so violent, that the Senator was hardly able
to make his voice heard by those immediately around
him. He himself did not quail for a moment, going on
with his gestures, and setting down his foot as though he
were still confident in his purpose of overcoming all
opposition. He had not much above half done yet.
There were the lawyers before him, and the Civil Service,
and the railways, and the commerce of the country, and

the labouring classes. But Lord Drummond and others near him were becoming terrified, thinking that something worse might occur unless an end were put to the proceedings. Then a superintendent of police came in and whispered to his lordship. A crowd was collecting itself in Piccadilly and St. James's Street, and perhaps the Senator had better be withdrawn. The officer did not think that he could safely answer for the consequences if this were carried on for a quarter of an hour longer. Then Lord Drummond having meditated for a moment, touched the Senator's arm and suggested a withdrawal into a side room for a minute. 'Mr. Gotobed,' he said, 'a little feeling has been excited and we had better put an end to this for the present.'

'Put an end to it?'

'I am afraid we must. The police are becoming alarmed.'

'Oh, of course; you know best. In our country a man is allowed to express himself unless he utters either blasphemy or calumny. But I am in your hands and of course you must do as you please.' Then he sat down in a corner, and wiped his brow. Lord Drummond returned to the hall, and there endeavoured to explain that the lecture was over for that night. The row was so great that it did not matter much what he said, but the people soon understood that the American Senator was not to appear before them again.

It was not much after nine o'clock when the Senator reached his hotel, Lord Drummond having accompanied him thither in a cab. 'Good night, Mr. Gotobed,' said his lordship. 'I cannot tell you how much I respect both your purpose and your courage;—but I don't know how far it is wise for a man to tell any other man, much less a nation, of all his faults.'

'You English tell us of ours pretty often,' said the Senator.

When he found himself alone he thought of it all, giving himself no special credit for what he had done, acknowledging to himself that he had often chosen his words badly, and expressed himself imperfectly, but declaring to himself through it all that the want of reason among Britishers was so great, that no one ought to treat them as wholly responsible beings.

CHAPTER LXXIX

THE LAST DAYS OF MARY MASTERS

THE triumph of Mary Masters was something more than a nine days' wonder to the people of Dills-borough. They had all known Larry Twentyman's intentions and aspirations, and had generally condemned the young lady's obduracy, thinking, and not being slow to say, that she would live to repent her perversity. Runciman, who had a thoroughly warm-hearted friendship for both the attorney and Larry, had sometimes been very severe on Mary. 'She wants a touch of hardship,' he would say, 'to bring her to. If Larry would just give her a cold shoulder for six months, she'd be ready to jump into his arms.' And Dr. Nupper had been heard to remark that she might go further and fare worse. 'If it were my girl I'd let her know all about it,' Ribbs the butcher had said in the bosom of his own family. When it was found that Mr. Surtees the curate was not to be the fortunate man, the matter was more inexplicable than ever. Had it then been declared that the owner of Hoppet Hall had proposed to her, all these tongues would have been silenced, and the refusal even of Larry Twenty-man would have been justified. But what was to be said and what was to be thought when it was known that she was to be the mistress of Bragton? For a day or two the prosperity of the attorney was hardly to be endured by his neighbours. When it was first known that the steward-ship of the property was to go back into his hands, his rise in the world was for a time slightly prejudicial to his popularity; but this greater stroke of luck, this latter promotion which would place him so much higher in Dillsborough than even his father or his grandfather had ever been, was a great trial of friendship.

Mrs. Masters felt it all very keenly. All possibility for reproach against either her husband or her step-daughter was of course at an end. Even she did not pretend to say that Mary ought to refuse the squire. Nor, as far as Mary was concerned, could she have further recourse to the evils of Ushanting, and the perils of social intercourse with ladies and gentlemen. It was manifest that Mary was to be a lady with a big house and many servants, and no doubt, a carriage and horses. But still Mrs. Masters was not quite silenced. She had daughters of her own, and would solace herself by declaring to them, to her husband, and to her specially intimate friends, that of course they would see no more of Mary. It wasn't for them to expect to be asked to Bragton, and as for herself she would much rather not. She knew her own place and what she was born to, and wasn't going to let her own children spoil themselves and ruin their chances by dining at seven o'clock, and being waited upon by servants at every turn. Thank God her girls could make their own beds, and she hoped they might continue to do so at any rate till they had houses of their own.

And there seemed to Dillsborough to be some justification for all this in the fact that Mary was now living at Bragton, and that she did not apparently intend to return to her father's house. At this time Reginald Morton himself was still at Hoppet Hall, and had declared that he would remain there till after his marriage. Lady Ushant was living at the big house which was henceforth to be her home. Mary was her visitor, and was to be married from Bragton as though Bragton were her residence rather than the squire's. The plan had originated with Reginald, and when it had been hinted to him that Mary would in this way seem to slight her father's home, he had proposed that all the Masters should come and stay at Bragton previous to the ceremony. Mrs. Masters yielded as to Mary's residence, saying with mock humility that of course she had no room fit to give a marriage feast to the squire of Bragton, but she was steadfast in saying to her husband, who made the proposition to her, that she would stay at home. Of course she would be present at

the wedding; but she would not trouble the like of Lady
Ushant by any prolonged visiting.

The wedding was to take place about the beginning of
May, and all these things were being considered early in
April. At this time one of the girls was always at Bragton,
and Mary had done her best, but hitherto in vain, to
induce her step-mother to come to her. When she heard
that there was a doubt as to the accomplishment of the
plan for the coming of the whole family, she drove herself
into Dillsborough in the old phaeton and then pleaded
her cause for herself. 'Mamma,' she said, 'won't you
come with the girls and papa on the 29th?'

'I think not, my dear. The girls can go,—if they like it.
But it will be more fitting for papa and me to come to the
church on the morning.'

'Why more fitting, mamma?'

'Well, my dear; it will.'

'Dear mamma;—why,—why?'

'Of course, my dear, I am very glad that you are going
to get such a lift.'

'My lift is marrying the man I love.'

'That of course is all right. I have nothing on earth to
say against it. And I will say that through it all you have
behaved as a young woman should. I don't think you
meant to throw yourself at him.'

'Mamma!'

'But as it has turned up, you have to go one way and
me another.'

'No!'

'But it must be so. The Squire of Bragton is the Squire,
and his wife must act accordingly. Of course you'll be
visiting at Rufford and Hampton Wick, and all the places.
I know very well who I am, and what I came from. I'm
not a bit ashamed of myself, but I'm not going to stick
myself up with my betters.'

'Then, mamma, I shall come and be married from
here.'

'It's too late for that now, my dear.'

'No;—it is not.' And then a couple of tears began to
roll down from her eyes. 'I won't be married without

your coming in to see me the night before, and being with me in the morning when I dress. Haven't I been a good child to you, mamma?' Then the step-mother began to cry also. 'Haven't I, mamma?'

'Yes, my dear,' whimpered the poor woman.

'And won't you be my mamma to the last;—won't you?' And she threw her arms round her step-mother's neck and kissed her. 'I won't go one way, and you another. He doesn't wish it. It is quite different from that. I don't care a straw for Hampton Wick and Rufford; but I will never be separated from you and the girls and papa. Say you will come, mamma. I will not let you go till you say you will come.' Of course she had her own way, and Mrs. Masters had to feel with a sore heart that she also must go out Ushanting. She knew, that in spite of her domestic powers, she would be stricken dumb in the drawing-room at Bragton and was unhappy.

Mary had another scheme in which she was less fortunate. She took it into her head that Larry Twentyman might possibly be induced to come to her wedding. She had heard how he had ridden and gained honour for himself on the day that the hounds killed their fox at Norrington, and thought that perhaps her own message to him had induced him so far to return to his old habits. And now she longed to ask him, for her sake, to be happy once again. If any girl ever loved the man she was going to marry with all her heart, this girl loved Reginald Morton. He had been to her, when her love was hopeless, so completely the master of her heart that she could not realise the possibility of affection for another. But yet she was pervaded by a tenderness of feeling in regard to Larry which was love also,—though love altogether of another kind. She thought of him daily. His future well-being was one of the cares of her life. That her husband might be able to call him a friend was among her prayers. Had anybody spoken ill of him in her presence she would have resented it hotly. Had she been told that another girl had consented to be his wife, she would have thought that girl to be happy in her destiny. When she heard that he was leading a wretched, moping, aimless life for her sake, her heart was sad within her. It was necessary to the completion of her happiness that Larry should recover his tone of mind and be her friend. 'Reg,' she said, leaning on his arm out in the park, 'I want you to do me a favour.'

'Watch and chain?'

'Don't be an idiot. You know I've got a watch and chain.'

'Some girls like two. To have the wooden bridge pulled down and a stone one built?'

'If any one touched a morsel of that sacred timber he should be banished from Bragton for ever. I want you to ask Mr. Twentyman to come to our wedding.'

'Who's to do it? Who's to bell the cat?'

'You.'

'I would sooner fight a Saracen, or ride such a horse as killed that poor major. Joking apart, I don't see how it is to be done. Why do you wish it?'

'Because I am so fond of him.'

'Oh;—indeed!'

'If you're a goose, I'll hit you. I am fond of him. Next to you and my own people, and Lady Ushant, I like him best in all the world.'

'What a pity you couldn't have put him up a little higher.'

'I used to think so too;—only I couldn't. If anybody loved you as he did me, offering you everything he had in the world,—thought that you were the best in the world, —would have given his life for you, would not you be grateful?'

'I don't know that I need wish to ask such a person to my wedding.'

'Yes, you would, if in that way you could build a bridge to bring him back to happiness. And, Reg, though you used to despise him——'

'I never despised him.'

'A little I think,—before you knew him. But he is not despicable.'

'Not at all, my dear.'

'He is honest and good, and has a real heart of his own.'

'I am afraid he has parted with that.'

'You know what I mean, and if you won't be serious I shall think there is no seriousness in you. I want you to tell me how it can be done.'

Then he was serious, and tried to explain to her that he could not very well do what she wanted. 'He is your friend you know rather than mine;—but if you like to write to him you can do so.'

This seemed to her to be very difficult, and, as she thought more of it, almost impossible. A written letter remains, and may be taken as evidence of so much more than it means. But a word sometimes may be spoken which, if it be well spoken,—if assurance of its truth be given by the tone and by the eye of the speaker,—shall do so much more than any letter, and shall yet only remain with the hearer as the remembrance of the scent of a flower remains! Nevertheless she did at last write the letter, and brought it to her husband. 'Is it necessary that I should see it?' he asked.

'Not absolutely necessary.'

'Then send it without.'

'But I should like you to see what I have said. You know about things, and if it is too much or too little, you can tell me.' Then he read the letter,—which ran as follows:—

'Dear Mr. Twentyman,

'Perhaps you have heard that we are to be married on Thursday, May 6th. I do so wish that you would come. It would make me so much happier on that day. We shall be very quiet; and if you would come to the house at eleven you could go across the park with them all to the church. I am to be taken in a carriage because of my finery. Then there will be a little breakfast. Papa and mamma and Dolly and Kate would be so glad;—and so would Mr. Morton. But none of them will be half so glad as your old, old, affectionate friend,

'MARY MASTERS.'

'If that don't fetch him,' said Reginald, 'he is a poorer creature than I take him to be.'

'But I may send it?'

'Certainly you may send it.' And so the letter was sent across to Chowton Farm.

But the letter did not 'fetch' him; nor am I prepared to agree with Mr. Morton that he was a poor creature for not being 'fetched.' There are things which the heart of a man should bear without whimpering, but which it cannot bear in public with that appearance of stoical indifference which the manliness of a man is supposed to require. Were he to go, should he be jovial before the wedding party or should he be sober and saturnine? Should he appear to have forgotten his love, or should he go about lovelorn among the wedding guests? It was impossible,—at any rate impossible as yet,—that he should fall into that state of almost brotherly regard which it was so natural that she should desire. But as he had determined to forgive her, he went across that afternoon to the house and was the bearer of his own answer. He asked Mrs. Hopkins who came to the door whether she were alone, and was then shown into an empty room where he waited for her. She came to him as quickly as she could, leaving Lady Ushant in the middle of the page she was reading, and feeling as she tripped downstairs that the colour was rushing to her face. 'You will come, Larry?' she said.

'No, Miss Masters.'

'Let me be Mary till I am Mrs. Morton,' she said, trying to smile. 'I was always Mary.' And then she burst into tears. 'Why,—why won't you come?'

'I should only stalk about like a ghost. I couldn't be merry as a man should be at a wedding. I don't see how a man is to do such a thing.' She looked up into his face imploring him,—not to come, for that she felt now to be impossible,—but imploring him to express in some way forgiveness of the sin she had committed against him. 'But I shall think of you and wish you well.'

'And after that we shall be friends?'

'By and bye,—if he pleases.'

'He will please;—he does please. Of course he saw what I wrote to you. And now, Larry, if I have ever treated you badly, say that you pardon me.'

'If I had known it——' he said.

'How could I tell you, till he had spoken? And yet I knew it myself! It has been so,—oh,—ever so long! What could I do? You will say that you will forgive me.'

'Yes;—I will say that.'

'And you will not go away from Chowton?'

'Oh, no! They tell me I ought to stay here, and I suppose I shall stay. I thought I'd just come over and say a word. I'm going away to-morrow for a month. There is a fellow has got some fishing in Ireland. Good-bye.'

'Good-bye, Larry.'

'And I thought perhaps you'd take this now.' Then he brought out from his pocket a little ruby ring which he had carried often in his pocket to the attorney's house, thinking that perhaps then might come the happy hour in which he could get her to accept it. But the hour had never come as yet, and the ring had remained in the little drawer beneath his looking-glass. It need hardly be said that she now accepted the gift.

CHAPTER LXXX

CONCLUSION

THE Senator for Mikewa,—whose name we have taken for a book which might perhaps have been better called 'The Chronicle of a Winter at Dillsborough' —did not stay long in London after the unfortunate close of his lecture. He was a man not very pervious to criticism, nor afraid of it, but he did not like the treatment he had received at St. James's Hall, nor the remarks which his lecture produced in the newspapers. He was angry because people were unreasonable with him, which was surely unreasonable in him who accused Englishmen generally of want of reason. One ought to take it as a matter of course that a bull should use his horns, and a wolf his teeth. The Senator read everything that was said of him, and then wrote numerous letters to the different journals which had condemned him. Had any one accused him of an untruth? Or had his inaccuracies been glaring? Had he not always expressed his readiness to acknowledge his own mistake if convicted of ignorance? But when he was told that he had persistently trodden upon all the corns of his English cousins, he declared that corns were evil things which should be abolished, and that with corns such as these there was no mode of abolition so efficacious as treading on them.

'I am sorry that you should have encountered anything so unpleasant,' Lord Drummond said to him when he went to bid adieu to his friend at the Foreign Office.

'And I am sorry too, my lord,—for your sake rather than my own. A man is in a bad case who cannot endure to hear of his faults.'

'Perhaps you take our national sins a little too much for granted.'

'I don't think so, my lord. If you knew me to be wrong, you would not be so sore with me. Nevertheless, I am under deep obligation for kind-hearted hospitality. If an American can make up his mind to crack up everything he sees here, there is no part of the world in which he can get along better.' He had already written a long letter home to his friend Mr. Josiah Scroome, and had impartially sent to that gentleman, not only his own lecture, but also a large collection of the criticisms made on it. A few weeks afterwards he took his departure, and when we last heard of him was thundering in the Senate against certain practices on the part of his own country which he thought to be unjust to other nations. Don Quixote was not more just than the Senator or more philanthropic, nor perhaps more apt to wage war against the windmills.

Having in this our last chapter given the place of honour to the Senator, we must now say a parting word as to those countrymen of our own who have figured in our pages. Lord Rufford married Miss Penge, of course, and used the lady's fortune in buying the property of Sir John Purefoy. We may probably be safe in saying that the acquisition added very little to his happiness.

What difference can it make to a man whether he has
forty or fifty thousand pounds a year,—or, at any rate,
to such a man? Perhaps Miss Penge herself was an
acquisition. He did not hunt so often or shoot so much,
and was seen in church once at least on every Sunday.
In a very short time his friends perceived that a very
great change had come over him. He was growing fat,
and soon disliked the trouble of getting up early to go to
a distant meet; and, before a year or two had passed away,
it had become an understood thing that in country houses
he was not one of the men who went down at night into
the smoking-room in a short dressing-coat and a picturesque cap. Miss Penge had done all this. He had had
his period of pleasure, and no doubt the change was
desirable; but he sometimes thought with regret of the
promise Arabella Trefoil had made him, that she would
never interfere with his gratification.

At Dillsborough everything during the summer after
the squire's marriage fell back into its usual routine. The
greatest change made there was in the residence of the
attorney, who with his family went over to live at Hoppet
Hall, giving up his old house to a young man from
Norrington who had become his partner, but keeping the
old office for his business. Mrs. Masters did, I think, like
the honour and glory of the big house, but she would
never admit that she did. And when she was constrained
once or twice in the year to give a dinner to her step-
daughter's husband and Lady Ushant that, I think, was
really a period of discomfort to her. When at Bragton she
could, at any rate, be quiet, and Mary's caressing care
almost made the place pleasant to her.

Mr. Runciman prospers at the Bush, though he has
entirely lost his best customer, Lord Rufford. But the
U.R.U. is still strong, in spite of the philosophers, and in
the hunting season the boxes of the Bush Inn are full of
horses. The club goes on without much change, Mr.
Masters being very regular in his attendance, undeterred
by the grandeur of his new household. And Larry is
always there, with increased spirit, for he has dined two
or three times lately at Hampton Wick, having met young

Hampton at the squire's house at Bragton. On this point Fred Botsey was for a time very jealous; but he found that Larry's popularity was not to be shaken, and now is very keen in pushing an intimacy with the owner of Chowton Farm. Perhaps the most stirring event in the neighbourhood has been the retirement of Captain Glomax from the post of Master. When the season was over he made an application to Lord Rufford respecting certain stable and kennel expenses, which that nobleman snubbed very bluntly. Thereupon the captain intimated to the committee that unless some advances were made he should go. The committee refused, and thereupon the captain went; not altogether to the dissatisfaction of the farmers, with whom an itinerant Master is seldom altogether popular. Then for a time there was great gloom in the U.R.U. What hunting man or woman does not know the gloom which comes over a hunting county when one Master goes before another is ready to step into his shoes? There had been a hope, a still growing hope, that Lord Rufford would come forward at any such pinch; but since Miss Penge had come to the front that hope had altogether vanished. There was a word said at Rufford on the subject, but Miss Penge,—or Lady Rufford as she was then,—at once put her foot on the project and extinguished it. Then, when despair was imminent, old Mr. Hampton gave way, and young Hampton came forward, acknowledged on all sides as the man for the place. A Master always does appear at last; though for a time it appears that the kingdom must come to an end because no one will consent to sit on the throne.

Perhaps the most loudly triumphant man in Dillsborough was Mr. Mainwaring, the parson, when he heard of the discomfiture of Senator Gotobed. He could hardly restrain his joy, and confided first to Dr. Nupper and then to Mr. Runciman his opinion, that of all the blackguards that had ever put their foot in Dillsborough, that vile Yankee was the worst. Mr. Gotobed was no more a Yankee* than was the parson himself;—but of any distinction among the citizens of the United States, Mr. Mainwaring knew very little.

A word or two more must be said of our dear friend
Larry Twentyman; for in finishing this little story we
must own that he has in truth been our hero. He went
away on his fishing expedition, and when he came back
the girl of his heart had become Mrs. Morton. Hunting
had long been over then, but the great hunting difficulty
was in course of solution, and Larry took his part in the
matter. When there was a suggestion as to a committee
of three,—than which nothing for hunting purposes can
be much worse,—there was a question whether he should
not be one of them. This nearly killed both the Botseys.
The evil thing was prevented by the timely pressure put
on old Mr. Hampton; but the excitement did our friend
Larry much good. 'Bicycle' and the other mare were at
once summered with the greatest care, and it is generally
understood that young Hampton means to depend upon
Larry very much in regard to the Rufford side of the
country. Larry has bought Goarly's two fields, Goarly
having altogether vanished from those parts, and is
supposed to have Dillsborough Wood altogether in his
charge. He is frequently to be seen at Hoppet Hall, calling there every Saturday to take down the attorney to the
Dillsborough club,—as was his habit of old; but it would
perhaps be premature to say that there are very valid
grounds for the hopes which Mrs. Masters already enter-
tains in reference to Kate. Kate is still too young and
childish to justify any prediction in that quarter.

What further need be said as to Reginald and his happy
bride? Very little;—except that in the course of her
bridal tour she did gradually find words to give him a
true and accurate account of all her own feelings from
the time at which he first asked her to walk with him
across the bridge over the Dill and look at the old place.
They had both passed their childish years there, but
could have but little thought that they were destined then
to love and grow old together. 'I was longing, longing,
longing to come,' she said.

'And why didn't you come?'

'How little you know about girls! Of course I had to
go with the one I—I—I—; well, with the one I did not

love down to the very soles of his feet. And then there was the journey with the parrot. I rather liked the bird. I don't know that you said very much, but I think you would have said less if there had been no bird.'

'In fact I have been a fool all along.'

'You weren't a fool when you took me out through the orchard and caught me when I jumped over the wall. Do you remember when you asked me, all of a sudden, whether I should like to be your wife? You weren't a fool then.'

'But you knew what was coming.'

'Not a bit of it. I knew it wasn't coming. I had quite made up my mind about that. I was as sure of it;—oh, as sure of it as I am that I've got you now. And then it came;—like a great thunderclap.'

'A thunderclap, Mary!'

'Well;—yes. I wasn't quite sure at first. You might have been laughing at me;—mightn't you?'

'Just the kind of joke for me!'

'How was I to understand it all in a moment? And you made me repeat all those words. I believed it then, or I shouldn't have said them. I knew that must be serious.' And so she deified him, and sat at his feet looking up into his eyes, and fooled him for a while into the most perfect happiness that a man ever knows in this world. But she was not altogether happy herself till she had got Larry to come to her at the house at Bragton and swear to her that he would be her friend.

EXPLANATORY NOTES

1 *prebendaries:* honorary canons—or for that matter any clergyman receiving an honorarium for serving in the church.

graziers: ranchers; cattle-grazers.

those modern improvements which have of late become common throughout England: probably a reference to the Victorian gothic effort to restore and at the same time modernize ancient ecclesiastical fabrics—a widespread fad during the latter half of the nineteenth century. Thomas Hardy (1840–1928) was engaged in this sort of work as a young man. It was part of the aftermath of the Oxford Movement as well as of the gothic revival; a number of eighteenth-century churches were 'improved' in an attempt to make them look gothic. Many architectural historians have deplored this late Victorian mania for 'modernizing'—nor does Trollope, who apparently uses the phrase 'modern improvements' ironically here, seem enthusiastic about them. In *The Mayor of Casterbridge* (1886), however, Hardy refers to eighteenth-century architecture as 'a compilation rather than a design' (ch. 21).

3 *posting inns:* inns where horses were changed for fast carriages, especially those transporting the mail.

farmers' ordinary: a tavern or eating house serving meals to all at a fixed price.

to beat up wine: to mix by stirring, or whip up.

chancel: that part of a church lying east of the nave, including choir and sanctuary.

4 *Ribston pippins:* apples especially popular in the nineteenth century, grown from seedlings rather than cuttings.

5 *coverts:* hiding places affording cover for game.

Hurlingham: an exclusive social and sports club (still extant) in Fulham, London.

those who go out with the hounds: that is, those who hunt foxes.

8 *Brasenose:* Brasenose College, Oxford.

Quieta non movere: the Latin equivalent of Sir Robert

Walpole's famous motto, 'Let sleeping dogs lie.' Literally translated, the phrase means 'Don't move quiet things.'

9   *bye:* day off.

10   *sold out:* that is, sold his commission to another.

    the Honourable Mrs. Morton: a courtesy title, informing us that Mrs Morton is descended from nobility; in fact she is the daughter of a viscount. In his novels Trollope often uses the title ironically, giving it to distinctly dishonourable characters; the Honourable Mrs Stantiloup in *Dr. Wortle's School* (1880) would be another example of this.

11   *éclat:* conspicuous success.

14   *palmy:* flourishing, prosperous.

    a ha-ha fence: sunk fence.

21   *knocked to Jericho:* destroyed.

23   *hunters:* horses for hunting.

25   *Elysium:* paradise.

38   *billicock hat:* a round, low-crowned, wide-brimmed, hard felt hat—an antecedent of the bowler hat.

41   *ekkery:* that is, equerry—a household officer charged with care of horses.

57   *tandem:* a two-wheeled cart having seats back to back, usually with the front one somewhat elevated.

58   *breeches:* short trousers covering the hips and thighs and fitting snugly at the lower edges at or just below the knee.

59   *spinnies:* small woods or copses with undergrowth.

60   *gammon:* talk.

61   *stubble field:* a field with a low, rough surface—one, for example, reaped but not ploughed.

62   *'vulpecide':* the murdering of foxes.

70   *'Regularly mulled':* in this context, thoroughly searched or examined.

74   *tom-tit:* a small bird.

75   *skurry:* that is, scurry, or run.

78   *tithes:* a voluntary tax, usually one-tenth of income, levied by the Church for the support of its establishments and clergymen.

82   *phaeton:* a light, four-wheeled, horse-drawn vehicle.

88   *par:* level.

94   *young hobbledehoys:* awkward, gawky youths; Trollope
      describes his younger self as one in his *Autobiography*
      (1883).

96   *turkey poult:* a young turkey.

132 *'to run a mucker':* to fall, or come to grief.

133 *Ulster:* a long, loose, heavy overcoat, of Irish origin;
      Arabella is not averse to gambling.

136 *convenances:* conventional proprieties.

140 *Aut Cæsar aut nihil:* the Latin phrase is ambiguous here. It
      means 'Either Caesar or nothing', and would have been
      the sort of cheer the soldiers of Julius Caesar (reigned
      48–44 BC) shouted out during rallies. But 'Aut Caesar aut
      nihil' was also the motto of Cesare Borgia (1476–1507),
      son of Pope Alexander VI. Cesare Borgia, among other
      things, was an accomplished soldier, one of whose
      ambitions was to rule over a unified Italy; he was
      probably the unscrupulous model for Machiavelli's *The
      Prince* (1513). Certainly there is something Machiavellian
      about Arabella—and this might help resolve the apparent
      ambiguity—but then Machiavelli's prince is much more
      successful than she is in getting what he wants. She is,
      perhaps, a would-be Machiavellianist. On the other
      hand, Trollope may simply be misquoting; 'Aut Caesar
      aut nullus'—slightly different from the phrase given here,
      and meaning 'Either Caesar or no one'—is associated by
      Seutonius with slogans of the soldiers of Caligula (reigned
      AD 37–41), who of course was also one of the twelve
      Caesars. In any case, Arabella means that she will be
      Lady Rufford—or no one.

154 *transtygian:* across the frontier of the lower world; that is,
      hellish.

167 *tarradiddle:* fib.

180 *maundering:* slow and idle.

189 *Minister Plenipotentiary:* ambassador.

191 *Mens conscia recti:* Latin, meaning 'a mind conscious of
      what is right'. Quoted from Virgil's *Aeneid*, I, 604: 'et mens
      sibi conscia recti'.

204 *make such ducks and drakes of:* squander.

208 *in the Blues:* that is, Major Caneback had been an officer in

the Royal Horse Guards, one of the household cavalry regiments which traditionally guards the British sovereign.

212 *duennas:* Spanish for chaperons.

219 *hipped:* obsessed.

226 *'Coventry':* here meaning ostracism, exclusion.

227 *cocker her up:* indulge or pamper her.

fandangled: foolish or trifling.

240 *Job:* the Old Testament hero who endures afflictions and deprivations with faith and fortitude.

244 *cat's cradle:* a game in which a string looped into a pattern like a cradle on the fingers of one person's hand is transferred to the hands of another so as to form a different figure.

248 *the Fitzwilliam:* a real, as opposed to a fictional, hunt; Trollope often rode to hounds with it.

postchaise: a carriage, usually having a closed body, on four wheels and seating two to four persons.

249 *the Pytchley:* see *Fitzwilliam;* p. 248 above.

266 *trivet:* tripod; an emblem of stability.

291 *rhodomontade:* vain boasting, bragging, bluster.

292 *pleuro:* pneumonia.

299 *Cæsar still clinging to his Commentaries as he struggled in the waves:* while in Alexandria, Julius Caesar (see p. 140, above) found himself caught between two enemy forces on a mole, and had to swim for it. This he did, holding the manuscript of his *Commentaries on the Gallic Wars* safely out of the water. The episode is recounted in Plutarch's *Caesar* (49). Trollope published an edition of Caesar's *Commentaries* in 1870; the volume was criticized by some reviewers for deficient classical scholarship.

313 *St. Anthony:* there are numerous saints named Anthony. The most famous are St. Anthony of Egypt (250–356), sometimes called St. Anthony of the Desert, one of the most renowned of the early desert fathers, who was a close associate of the Greek St. Athanasius (293?–373) in the fight against Arianism—Athanasius' *Life of St. Anthony* is a kind of textbook of the ascetic life; and St. Anthony of Padua (1195–1231), a follower of St. Francis of Assisi

(d. 1226) and the patron saint of those hunting for lost objects. The context suggests that Lord Rufford may be referring to St. Anthony of Egypt, remembered chiefly for his asceticism. He retreated to the desert for greater solitude and became very holy; disciples flocked to him, and he tried to escape into greater solitude. Because of his extraordinary holiness, the forces of evil sent him tempting apparitions in the shape of beautiful women, but he withstood them. He is the hero of Flaubert's *Le Tentation de Sainte-Antoine* (1874), published in the year before Trollope began to write *The American Senator*.

322 *cock his beaver too high:* look down his nose at others— become conceited or vain as a result of an exaggerated idea of his own position.

333 *whose own withers at this moment were by no means unwrung:* who was not untouched, or undiminished; who had not entirely escaped either. Trollope is paraphrasing a passage from the play-within-the-play scene in *Hamlet*, Act III.

340 *brougham:* a light, closed carriage with seats inside for two or four.

356 *cobbling:* rough or careless patching up; today we might say 'papering over'.

357 *when the first Reform Bill was passed!:* the reference is to the great Reform Act of 1832.

358 *ricks:* haystacks.

387 *shuffling:* equivocation; evasion or jumbling of the issue.

404 *gig:* a light, two-wheeled, one-horse carriage.

408 *coy it:* act coyly.

425 *£6,000 ... £8,000:* in terms of today's buying power (1986), Rufford offers about £100,000 ($140,000), and Lady Augustus pushes him up to £130,000 ($180,000).

  £400 a year would support her daughter: that is, five per cent annual interest on £8,000. Such an income now would have the buying power of about £6,000 ($8,000); but interest rates were much lower in Trollope's day.

429 *Acheron:* a river in Hades; or, alternatively, Hell itself.

448 *'I never nursed a dear gazelle':* quoted from 'The Fire Worshippers' section of the famous poem by Thomas Moore (1779–1852), *Lalla Rookh* (1817), i, 279–86.

> Oh! ever thus, from childhood's hour
> I've seen my fondest hopes decay;
> I never lov'd a tree or flow'r
> But 'twas the first to fade away.
> I never nurs'd a dear gazelle,
> To glad me with its soft black eye,
> But when it came to know me well,
> And love me, it was sure to die.

The mawkish, self-pitying tone of the poem was often parodied in the nineteenth century, which knew *Lalla Rookh* well—e.g., Dick Swiveller in Dickens's *The Old Curiosity Shop* (1840–1): 'I never nursed a dear gazelle, to glad me with its soft black eye, but when it came to know me well, it was sure to marry a market-gardener.'

453 *sell:* betrayal, deception, hoax.

455 *the true feminine Medea feeling:* Medea was an enchantress noted in Greek legend and drama for helping the heroic Jason to win the Golden Fleece—and for killing her children, setting fire to the palace, and fleeing when he deserted her. Trollope means that Arabella, if frustrated in her attempt to win Lord Rufford, might retaliate by doing something desperate, violent, or vengeful.

456 *Medean vengeance:* see p. 455, above.

457 *tines:* antlers.

she was resolved that her Jason should not as yet be quit of his Medea: see p. 455, above.

472 *green sward:* a turf green with grass growing on it.

477 *drag:* conveyance.

480 *sent into durance:* imprisoned.

Van Dieman's Land and . . . Botany Bay: Australian sites to which prisoners convicted of serious offences were often transported in the nineteenth century.

483 *'Has she a father, has she a mother;*
Or has she a dearer one still than all other?': quoted from the sixth stanza of 'The Bridge of Sighs', by Thomas Hood (1799–1845)—a poem well known to Trollope's audience, about a young lady who, after giving up her virtue, jumps off the Bridge of Sighs in Venice and drowns herself.

496 *so pottle deep:* so much; actually, about half a gallon.

503 *Nimrod:* used here in the sense of a mighty hunter; Nimrod was the great-grandson of Noah.

504   *ratting:* catching or hunting rats.

      philanimalists: lovers of animals; the movement to protect animals from hunters and others grew up in the latter years of the nineteenth century. Trollope, an avid hunter, opposed the movement vehemently; Reginald Morton speaks for him here.

      tippet: cape made of fur.

505   *'tanti':* Latin, meaning 'enough'.

506   *tandem:* see p. 57, above.

      drag: see p. 477, above.

510   *half-blown:* breathless.

511   *'tanti':* see p. 505, above.

      take the ball at the hop: take advantage of the present situation.

      harpy: leech, or shrew; at any rate, a predatory woman.

512   *oracle:* in this sense, an authoritative or wise expression.

518   *pinions:* wings; that is, with her wings clipped.

519   *it would be better to reign in Hell than serve in Heaven:* Lucifer's famous declaration in Milton's *Paradise Lost* (first printed 1667), I, 263.

520   *'Odious in wollen;—'twould a saint provoke,*
      Were the last words which poor Narcissa spoke.': quoted from the first of the *Moral Essays* (1731–5) of Alexander Pope (1688–1744), the Epistle to Cobham ('Of the Knowledge and Characters of Men'), 242–3. Narcissa, who prides herself on her couture, is annoyed because an old English law, intended to protect the woollen industry, decrees that everyone who dies in England must be buried in woollen clothing.

531   *sesquipedalian:* long—at least a foot and a half in size.

      meum . . . tuum: Trollope says that people are more concerned about themselves ('meum') and their own possessions than they are about other people ('tuum') and *their* possessions; in other words, most of us have a hard time keeping our hands off other people's property.

537   *your first Reform Bill:* see p. 357, above.

549   *Saracen:* Arab.

553   *Don Quixote . . . wage war against the windmills:* Don Quixote

is the dreamy, idealistic, impractical hero of the famous
picaresque novel (1605–15) by the Spanish writer Miguel
de Cervantes (1547–1616). A satirical romance, one
section (I, viii) of *Don Quixote* burlesques the chivalric
romance by depicting the hero, whose wits have been
disordered by inordinate devotion to tales of chivalry,
tilting against windmills, imagining them to be giants.
Don Quixote was translated into English in the year of
Cervantes' death; it profoundly influenced Henry Field-
ing (1707–54), and thus the development of the English
novel.

555   *Yankee:* as the rest of the sentence makes clear, the parson
uses the word in its most general sense—he means
'American'. Most Americans employ the word specifical-
ly to designate inhabitants of the northern United States,
and especially the New England states; southerners, on
the other hand, use it to describe anyone who is not a
native of the southern United States.

The Oxford World's Classics Website

www.worldsclassics.co.uk

- Browse the full range of Oxford World's Classics online

- Sign up for our monthly e-alert to receive information on new titles

- Read extracts from the Introductions

- Listen to our editors and translators talk about the world's greatest literature with our Oxford World's Classics audio guides

- Join the conversation, follow us on Twitter at OWC_Oxford

- Teachers and lecturers can order inspection copies quickly and simply via our website

www.worldsclassics.co.uk

American Literature

British and Irish Literature

Children's Literature

Classics and Ancient Literature

Colonial Literature

Eastern Literature

European Literature

Gothic Literature

History

Medieval Literature

Oxford English Drama

Poetry

Philosophy

Politics

Religion

The Oxford Shakespeare

A complete list of Oxford World's Classics, including Authors in Context, Oxford English Drama, and the Oxford Shakespeare, is available in the UK from the Marketing Services Department, Oxford University Press, Great Clarendon Street, Oxford OX2 6DP, or visit the website at www.oup.com/uk/worldsclassics.

In the USA, visit www.oup.com/us/owc for a complete title list.

Oxford World's Classics are available from all good bookshops. In case of difficulty, customers in the UK should contact Oxford University Press Bookshop, 116 High Street, Oxford OX1 4BR.

ANTHONY TROLLOPE   **An Autobiography**
The American Senator
Barchester Towers
Can You Forgive Her?
The Claverings
Cousin Henry
Doctor Thorne
The Duke's Children
The Eustace Diamonds
Framley Parsonage
He Knew He Was Right
Lady Anna
The Last Chronicle of Barset
Orley Farm
Phineas Finn
Phineas Redux
The Prime Minister
Rachel Ray
The Small House at Allington
The Warden
The Way We Live Now

JANE AUSTEN	**Emma**
	Mansfield Park
	Persuasion
	Pride and Prejudice
	Sense and Sensibility
MRS BEETON	**Book of Household Management**
LADY ELIZABETH BRADDON	**Lady Audley's Secret**
ANNE BRONTË	**The Tenant of Wildfell Hall**
CHARLOTTE BRONTË	**Jane Eyre**
	Shirley
	Villette
EMILY BRONTË	**Wuthering Heights**
SAMUEL TAYLOR COLERIDGE	**The Major Works**
WILKIE COLLINS	**The Moonstone**
	No Name
	The Woman in White
CHARLES DARWIN	**The Origin of Species**
CHARLES DICKENS	**The Adventures of Oliver Twist**
	Bleak House
	David Copperfield
	Great Expectations
	Nicholas Nickleby
	The Old Curiosity Shop
	Our Mutual Friend
	The Pickwick Papers
	A Tale of Two Cities
GEORGE DU MAURIER	**Trilby**
MARIA EDGEWORTH	**Castle Rackrent**

	Women's Writing 1778–1838
WILLIAM BECKFORD	**Vathek**
JAMES BOSWELL	**Life of Johnson**
FRANCES BURNEY	**Camilla**
	Cecilia
	Evelina
	The Wanderer
LORD CHESTERFIELD	**Lord Chesterfield's Letters**
JOHN CLELAND	**Memoirs of a Woman of Pleasure**
DANIEL DEFOE	**A Journal of the Plague Year**
	Moll Flanders
	Robinson Crusoe
	Roxana
HENRY FIELDING	**Joseph Andrews and Shamela**
	A Journey from This World to the Next and
	The Journal of a Voyage to Lisbon
	Tom Jones
WILLIAM GODWIN	**Caleb Williams**
OLIVER GOLDSMITH	**The Vicar of Wakefield**
MARY HAYS	**Memoirs of Emma Courtney**
ELIZABETH HAYWOOD	**The History of Miss Betsy Thoughtless**
ELIZABETH INCHBALD	**A Simple Story**
SAMUEL JOHNSON	**The History of Rasselas**
	The Major Works
CHARLOTTE LENNOX	**The Female Quixote**
MATTHEW LEWIS	**Journal of a West India Proprietor**
	The Monk
HENRY MACKENZIE	**The Man of Feeling**
ALEXANDER POPE	**Selected Poetry**

GUY DE MAUPASSANT	A Day in the Country and Other Stories A Life Bel-Ami Mademoiselle Fifi and Other Stories Pierre et Jean
PROSPER MÉRIMÉE	Carmen and Other Stories
MOLIÈRE	Don Juan and Other Plays The Misanthrope, Tartuffe, and Other Plays
BLAISE PASCAL	Pensées and Other Writings
JEAN RACINE	Britannicus, Phaedra, and Athaliah
ARTHUR RIMBAUD	Collected Poems
EDMOND ROSTAND	Cyrano de Bergerac
MARQUIS DE SADE	The Misfortunes of Virtue and Other Early Tales
GEORGE SAND	Indiana
MME DE STAËL	Corinne
STENDHAL	The Red and the Black The Charterhouse of Parma
PAUL VERLAINE	Selected Poems
JULES VERNE	Around the World in Eighty Days Journey to the Centre of the Earth Twenty Thousand Leagues under the Seas
VOLTAIRE	Candide and Other Stories Letters concerning the English Nation

ÉMILE ZOLA

L'Assommoir
The Attack on the Mill
La Bête humaine
La Débâcle
Germinal
The Ladies' Paradise
The Masterpiece
Nana
Pot Luck
Thérèse Raquin